"ENTRANCING, ECCENTRIC, HILARIOUS, pierced by fantasy the way a storm is pierced by lightning . . ."

—*People*

"A DAZZLING MODERN FAIRY TALE BY A STORYTELLER OF SEEMINGLY EFFORTLESS AND ARTLESS GRACE."

—*Joyce Carol Oates*

"MIRACULOUS . . . EXCELLENT . . . BOOK OF WONDERS . . ."

—*Vanity Fair*

"LARGE, EXTRAVAGANTLY WRITTEN . . . THIS BOOK IS SEDUCTIVE."

—*Philadelphia Inquirer*

"HELPRIN'S BOOK IS BREATHTAKING . . . HELPRIN IS SPLENDID, A MAJOR TALENT . . . funnier and shrewder than Thomas Wolfe and much more accurate in his poetic exuberance . . ."

—*Los Angeles Times Book Review*

"A WILD, ABUNDANT, GENEROUS BOOK, part dream, part mad invention, and all of it worth the trip."

—*Anne Tyler*

More . . .

WINTER'S TALE

MARK HELPRIN

PUBLISHED BY POCKET BOOKS NEW YORK

Portions of this novel originally appeared in slightly different form in The New Yorker *and in* Forthcoming.

POCKET BOOKS, a division of Simon & Schuster, Inc.
1230 Avenue of the Americas, New York, N.Y. 10020

Published by arrangement with Harcourt Brace Jovanovich, Inc.
Library of Congress Catalog Card Number: 83-273

ISBN: 0-671-50987-X

First Pocket Books printing August, 1984

10 9 8 7 6 5 4 3 2 1

POCKET and colophon are registered trademarks
of Simon & Schuster, Inc.

Printed in the U.S.A.

FOR MY FATHER
No One Knows the City Better

CONTENTS

*"I have been to another world,
and come back. Listen to me."*

PROLOGUE

A GREAT city is nothing more
than a portrait of itself, and yet when all is said and done, its arse-
nals of scenes and images are part of a deeply moving plan. As a
book in which to read this plan, New York is unsurpassed. For the
whole world has poured its heart into the city by the Palisades, and
made it far better than it ever had any right to be.

But the city is now obscured, as it often is, by the whitened mass
in which it rests—rushing by us at unfathomable speed, crackling
like wind in the mist, cold to the touch, glistening and unfolding,
tumbling over itself like the steam of an engine or cotton spilling
from a bale. Though the blinding white web of ceaseless sounds
flows past mercilessly, the curtain is breaking . . . it reveals amid
the clouds a lake of air as smooth and clear as a mirror, the deep
round eye of a white hurricane.

At the bottom of this lake lies the city. From our great height it seems small and distant, but the activity within it is apparent, for even when the city appears to be no bigger than a beetle, it is alive. We are falling now, and our swift unobserved descent will bring us to life that is blooming in the quiet of another time. As we float down in utter silence, into a frame again unfreezing, we are confronted by a tableau of winter colors. These are very strong, and they call us in.

·I·

THE CITY

A WHITE HORSE ESCAPES

THERE was a white horse, on a quiet winter morning when snow covered the streets gently and was not deep, and the sky was swept with vibrant stars, except in the east, where dawn was beginning in a light blue flood. The air was motionless, but would soon start to move as the sun came up and winds from Canada came charging down the Hudson.

The horse had escaped from his master's small clapboard stable in Brooklyn. He trotted alone over the carriage road of the Williamsburg Bridge, before the light, while the toll keeper was sleeping by his stove and many stars were still blazing above the city. Fresh snow on the bridge muffled his hoofbeats, and he sometimes turned his head and looked behind him to see if he was being followed. He was warm from his own effort and he breathed steadily, having loped four or five miles through the dead of Brooklyn past silent churches and shuttered stores. Far to the south, in the black, ice-choked waters of the Narrows, a sparkling light marked the ferry on its way to Manhattan, where only market men were up, waiting for the fishing boats to glide down through Hell Gate and the night.

The horse was crazy, but, still, he was able to worry about what he had done. He knew that shortly his master and mistress would arise and light the fire. Utterly humiliated, the cat would be tossed out the kitchen door, to fly backward into a snow-covered sawdust pile. The scent of blueberries and hot batter would mix with the sweet smell of a pine fire, and not too long afterward his master would stride across the yard to the stable to feed him and hitch him up to the milk wagon. But he would not be there.

This was a good joke, this defiance which made his heart beat in terror, for he was sure his master would soon be after him. Though he realized that he might be subject to a painful beating, he sensed that the master was amused, pleased, and touched by rebellion as often as not—if it were in the proper form and done well, courageously. A shapeless, coarse revolt (such as kicking down the stable door) would occasion the whip. But not even then would the master always use it, because he prized a spirited animal, and he knew of and was grateful for the mysterious intelligence of this white horse, an intelligence that even he could not ignore except at his peril and to his sadness. Besides, he loved the horse and did not really mind the chase through Manhattan (where the horse always went), since it afforded him the chance to enlist old friends in the search, and the opportunity of visiting a great number of saloons where he would inquire, over a beer or two, if anyone had seen his enormous and beautiful white stallion rambling about in the nude, without bit, bridle, or blanket.

The horse could not do without Manhattan. It drew him like a magnet, like a vacuum, like oats, or a mare, or an open, never-ending, tree-lined road. He came off the bridge ramp and stopped short. A thousand streets lay before him, silent but for the sound of the gemlike wind. Driven with snow, white, and empty, they were a maze for his delight as the newly arisen wind whistled across still untouched drifts and rills. He passed empty theaters, countinghouses, and forested wharves where the snow-lined spars looked like long black groves of pine. He passed dark factories and deserted parks, and rows of little houses where wood just fired filled the air with sweet reassurance. He passed the frightening common cellars full of ragpickers and men without limbs. The door of a market bar was flung open momentarily for a torrent of boiling water that splashed all over the street in a cloud of steam. He passed (and shied from) dead men lying in the round ragged coffins of their own frozen bodies. Sleds and wagons began to radiate from the markets, alive with the pull of their stocky dray horses, racing up the main streets, ringing bells. But he kept away from the markets, because there it was noontime even at dawn, and he followed the silent tributaries of the main streets, passing the exposed steelwork of buildings in the intermission of feverish construction. And he was seldom out of sight of the new bridges, which had married beautiful womanly Brooklyn to her rich uncle, Manhattan; had put the city's hand out to the country; and were the end of the past because they spanned not only distance and deep water but dreams and time.

The tail of the white horse swished back and forth as he trotted briskly down empty avenues and boulevards. He moved like a dancer, which is not surprising: a horse is a beautiful animal, but it is perhaps most remarkable because it moves as if it always hears music. With a certainty that perplexed him, the white horse moved south toward the Battery, which was visible down a long narrow street as a whitened field that was crossed by the long shadows of tall trees. By the Battery itself, the harbor took color with the new light, rocking in layers of green, silver, and blue. At the end of this polar rainbow, on the horizon, was a mass of white—the foil into which the entire city had been set—that was beginning to turn gold with the rising sun. The pale gold agitated in ascending waves of heat and refraction until it seemed to be a place of a thousand cities, or the border of heaven. The horse stopped to stare, his eyes filled with golden light. Steam issued from his nostrils as he stood in contemplation of the impossible and alluring distance. He stayed in the street as if he were a statue, while the gold strengthened and boiled

5

before him in a bed of blue. It seemed to be a perfect place, and he determined to go there.

He started forward but soon found that the street was blocked by a massy iron gate that closed off the Battery. He doubled back and went another way, only to find another gate of exactly the same design. Trying many streets, he came to many heavy gates, none of which was open. While he was stuck in this labyrinth, the gold grew in intensity and seemed to cover half the world. The empty white field was surely a way to that other, perfect world, and, though he had no idea of how he would cross the water, the horse wanted the Battery as if he had been born for it. He galloped desperately along the approachways, through the alleys, and over the snow-covered greens, always with an eye to the deepening gold.

At the end of what seemed to be the last street leading to the open, he found yet another gate, locked with a simple latch. He was breathing hard, and the condensed breath rose around his face as he stared through the bars. That was it: he would never step onto the Battery, there somehow to launch himself over the blue and green ribbons of water, toward the golden clouds. He was just about to turn and retrace his steps through the city, perhaps to find the bridge again and the way back to Brooklyn, when, in the silence that made his own breathing seem like the breaking of distant surf, he heard a great many footsteps.

At first they were faint, but they continued until they began to pound harder and harder and he could feel a slight trembling in the ground, as if another horse were going by. But this was no horse, these were men, who suddenly exploded into view. Through the black iron gate, he saw them running across the Battery. They took long high steps, because the wind had drifted the snow almost up to their knees. Though they ran with all their strength, they ran in slow motion. It took them a long time to get to the center of the field, and when they did the horse could see that one man was in front and that the others, perhaps a dozen, chased him. The man being chased breathed heavily, and would sometimes drive ahead in deliberate bursts of speed. Sometimes he fell and bolted right back up, casting himself forward. They, too, fell at times, and got up more slowly. Soon this spread them out in a ragged line. They waved their arms and shouted. He, on the other hand, was perfectly silent, and he seemed almost stiff in his running, except when he leapt snowbanks or low rails and spread his arms like wings.

As the man got closer, the horse took a liking to him. He moved well, though not like a horse or a dancer or someone who always hears music, but with spirit. What was happening appeared to be, solely because of the way that this man moved, more profound than a simple chase across the snow. Nonetheless, they gained on him. It was difficult to understand how, since they were dressed in heavy coats and bowler hats, and he was hatless in a scarf and winter jacket. He had winter boots, and they had low street shoes which had undoubtedly filled with numbing snow. But they were just as fast or faster than he was, they were good at it, and they seemed to have had much practice.

One of them stopped, spread his feet in the snow, raised a pistol in both hands, and fired at the fleeing man. The pistol crack echoed among the buildings facing the park and sent pigeons hurtling upward from the icy walks. The man in the lead looked back for a moment and then changed direction to cut in toward the streets, where the horse was standing mesmerized. They too changed course, and gained on him even more as they ran the hypotenuse of a triangle and he ran its second leg. They were not more than two hundred feet from him when another dropped behind to fire. The sound was so close that the horse came alive and jumped back.

The man who was trying to escape approached the gate. The horse backed up behind a woodshed. He wanted no part of this. But, being too curious, he was unable to keep himself hidden for long, and he soon stuck his head around the corner of the shed to see what would happen. The fleeing man opened the gate with a violent uppercut, moved to the other side of it, and slammed it shut. He took a heavy steel dirk from his belt and breathlessly pounded the latch into an unmovable position. Then, with an agonized look, he turned and started up the street.

His pursuers were already at the fence when he slipped on a pool of ice. He went down hard, striking his head on the ground and tumbling over himself until he came to rest. The horse's heart was thundering as he saw the dozen men throw themselves at the fence, like a squad of soldiers. They were perfectly criminal in appearance, with strange bent faces, clifflike brows, tiny chins, noses and ears that looked sewn-back-on, and hairlines that descended preposterously far (no glacier had ever ventured farther south). Their cruelty projected from them like sparks jumping a gap. One raised his pistol, but another—obviously their leader—said, "No! Not that way. We have him now. We'll do it slowly, with a knife." They started up the fence.

Had it not been for the horse peering at him from behind the woodshed, the downed man might have stayed down. His name was Peter Lake, and he said to himself out loud, "You're in bad shape when a horse takes pity on you, you stupid bastard," which got him moving. He rose to his feet and addressed the horse. The twelve men, who couldn't see the horse standing behind the shed, thought that Peter Lake had gone mad or was playing a trick.

"Horse!" he called. The horse pulled back his head. "Horse!" shouted Peter Lake. "Please!" and he opened his arms. The other men began to drop to the near side of the fence. They were taking their time because they were only a few feet away, the street was deserted, he was not moving, and they were sure that they had him.

Peter Lake's heart beat so hard that it made his body jerk. He felt ridiculous and out of control, like an engine breaking itself apart. "Oh Jesus," he said, vibrating like a mechanical toy, "Oh Jesus, Mary, and Joseph, send me an armored steamroller." Everything depended on the horse.

The horse bolted over the pool of ice toward Peter Lake, and lowered his wide white neck. Peter Lake took possession of himself and, throwing his arms around what seemed like a swan, sprang to the horse's back. He was up again, exulting even as the pistol shots rang out in the cold air. Having become his accomplice in one graceful motion, the horse turned and skittered, leaning back slightly on his haunches to get breath and power for an explosive start. In that moment, Peter Lake faced his stunned pursuers, and laughed at them. His entire being was one light perfect laugh. He felt the horse pitch forward, and then they raced up the street, leaving Pearly Soames and some of the Short Tail Gang backed

8

against the iron rails, firing their pistols and cursing—all twelve of them save Pearly himself, who bit his lower lip, squinted, and began to think of new ways to trap his quarry. The noise from their many pistols was deafening.

Already out of range, Peter Lake rode at a gallop. Pounding the soft snow, passing the shuttered stores, they headed north through the awakening city in a cloud of speed.

THE FERRY BURNS IN
MORNING COLD

LEAVING the Short Tails behind
would be easy, because not one of them (including Pearly, raised
in the Five Points just like the rest) knew how to ride. They were
masters of the waterfront and could do anything with a small boat,
but on land they walked, took the trolley, and jumped the gates of
the subway or the El. They had been chasing Peter Lake for three
years. They hunted him from one season to the next, driving him
back down into what he called "the tunnel"—the condition of continuous struggle from which he always expected to emerge and
never did.

Except when he found shelter with the clamdiggers of the Bayonne Marsh, Peter Lake had to be in Manhattan, where it was

never long before the Short Tails got wind of him and took up the chase. It was necessary for him to be in Manhattan because he was a burglar, and for a burglar to work anyplace else was a shattering admission of mediocrity. During those frenetic three years, he had often contemplated moving to Boston, but had always concluded that there was nothing in the place interesting enough to steal, it was laid out badly for burglars, it was too small, and he would probably run afoul there of the Simian Cantarellos (the leading gang, which wasn't much) in the same way that he had run afoul of the Short Tails, though undoubtedly for different reasons. In Boston, he had heard, when it got dark at night, it really got dark, and you could hardly move without bumping into men of the cloth. So he stayed on, hoping that the Short Tails might grow tired of the chase. They didn't, however, and his life in those years (except for peaceful interludes on the marsh) had been one of pursuit at close quarters.

He was not unused to being awakened just before dawn by the stampedelike pounding of the Short Tails' boots as they rushed up the rickety stairs of whatever temporary lodging he had procured. He had been diverted from the pleasures of hundreds of meals, scores of women, and dozens of rich unguarded houses by the sudden appearance of the Short Tails. Sometimes they materialized around him, by means that he could not fathom, not four feet away. Things were too close, the field of maneuver too tight, the stakes too high.

But now, with a horse, it would be different. Why hadn't he thought of a horse before? He could stretch his margin of safety almost immeasurably, and put not yards but miles between himself and Pearly Soames each time Pearly tried to close the gap. In summer, the horse could swim the rivers, and in winter, take him over the ice. He could make a refuge not only of Brooklyn (at risk, of course, of being lost in its infinity of confusing roads) but of the pine barrens, the Watchung Mountains, the endless beaches of Montauk, and the Hudson Highlands—all places difficult to reach by subway and discouraging to the citified Short Tails, who, despite their comfort with killing and corruption, were afraid of light-

11

ning, thunder, wild animals, forests, and the sound of tree frogs in the night.

Peter Lake spurred the horse. But the horse did not need encouragement, because he was scared, he loved to run, and the sun was high enough to sit on the roofs of buildings like a great open fire warming everything and limbering up his already limber muscles. He loved to run. He was like a big white bullet, his head up and out, his tail down and back, his ears streamlined with the wind as he vaulted forward. He took such long strides that he reminded Peter Lake of a kangaroo, and sometimes it seemed as if he were about to leave the ground and fly.

There was no sense in going to the Five Points. Though Peter Lake had many friends there and could hide in the thousands of underground chambers in which they danced and gamed, his arrival on an enormous white horse would electrify all the stool pigeons until they glowed with song. Besides, the Five Points wasn't that distant. He had the horse. He would take a tour, and go far.

They raced along the Bowery and were soon at Washington Square, where they flew through the arch like a circus animal slipping through a hoop. By this time, many pedestrians were on the streets, and these people frowned upon the recklessness of a horse and rider darting in and out of traffic. A policeman on an enclosed pedestal in Madison Square saw them coming up Fifth Avenue. Sensing that they wouldn't stop, he began to redirect traffic, for he had seen the horrifying results of a speeding horse in collision with a fragile automobile, and did not want to see it again. He had just managed to halt the various streams of automobiles, electric trucks, and horse-drawn wagons weaving past his stunted minaret, when he turned to see Peter Lake and his mount approaching at great velocity. The horse looked like a war monument sprung to life, and it sailed toward him like a missile. He blew his whistle. He waved his white gloved hands. This was unprecedented. They were charging the minaret, and must have been going thirty miles an hour. Nannies crossed themselves and clutched their children. Drovers stood up in their wagons. Old women averted their eyes. And the policeman froze stiffly in his golden booth.

Peter Lake spurred the horse again, and extended his right arm like a lance, pointing it at the motionless officer. As they went by in a blur of white, he lifted the man's cap from his head, saying, "Allow me to take your hat." The enraged policeman pivoted, took out his notebook, and furiously wrote a description of the horse's buttocks.

Peter Lake shot left into the Tenderloin, where the streets were so tied up that he found himself stopped dead, trapped by a water tanker and several entangled carriages. The teamsters were screaming; the horses whinnied to show their impatience; and a group of street arabs took the opportunity to start an artillery barrage of snow and ice balls. As he dodged these, he looked behind him and saw half a dozen blue dots running up the street from the east. They were far away, they were closing, they were slipping, they were sliding, they were police. Having neither saddle nor stirrups, he stood on the horse's back to see over the tanker and the carriages. The street was mortally choked and would need half an hour to revive. He dropped down and turned the horse around, intending to charge through the approaching phalanx and bump the blues. But the horse's courage was of a different sort, and he would have no part in it. He shuddered and shook his head as Peter Lake tried unsuccessfully to spur him on. The horse could not go forward and would not go back, and found himself moving sideways toward a lighted marquee which, even in morning, shone out with the words, "Saul Turkish Presents: Caradelba, the Spanish Gypsy."

Half full for the morning show, the theater was dark and overbrimming with dazzling blues and greens, except for center stage, where Caradelba danced half nude in a flash of white and cream-colored silk. At first Peter Lake and the horse stood at the top of the middle aisle, watching Caradelba and hoping that they had entered unobserved. But when the police came charging through the lobby, Peter Lake kicked the horse again and they galloped through the theater toward the orchestra pit. The musicians kept on playing, though they did slur as they saw the

13

tremendous head and body of the horse speeding at them from the darkness, like a white jack-o'-lantern mounted on the front of a locomotive.

The horse picked up speed. Peter Lake said, "Not likely that you're a jumper, too," and closed his eyes. The horse did more than jump. To his own surprise, he soared over the orchestra and landed almost soundlessly onstage next to the Spanish Gypsy—twenty feet across and eight feet up. Peter Lake was amazed that the horse had jumped so far and landed so gently. Caradelba was speechless. She was no more than a child, covered with pounds of makeup, slight of build, and confused in demeanor except when she was dancing. She took the instant appearance (as if from the air) of a horse and man upon it, suddenly sharing the stage, as a grave insult. It was as if by materializing full-blown on his enormous stallion, Peter Lake was making fun of her. She seemed about to cry. And the horse himself was not entirely self-possessed. He had never been in a theater before, let alone onstage. The lights beaming from darkness, the music, the soft subtle smell of Caradelba's makeup, and the vast molten blue velvet curtain, entranced him. He threw out his chest like a parade horse.

Peter Lake could not bring himself to leave until he had comforted Caradelba. Trading blows with resentful musicians, the police were forcing their way through the orchestra pit. Beguiled by the magic of the footlights, the horse discovered the glories of the theater and wanted some time to try out various facial expressions. Peter Lake, who had always been cool under fire, gathered his wits about him, dismounted, and even as the police began to struggle up the velvet ropes that hung from the apron, walked over to Caradelba, police cap in hand. In the Irish English in which he spoke, he said, "My dear Miss Candelabra. I would like to present to you, as a token of my affection and the admiration of the people of this great city, a souvenir police hat, which I just took from the tiny little head of the tiny little policeman who stands in the tiny little booth in Madison Square. As you can see," he said, motioning to the half-dozen police wading back through the musicians because they had been unable to scale the apron, "this is a real police hat,

14

and I've got to go." She took it from him and put it on her head. Its sober blue puffiness made her bare arms and shoulders seem even more voluptuous than they were, and she began to move once more in her arabesque fandango, as much for her own pleasure as for that of the audience. Peter Lake edged the horse from the blinding footlights. Then he jumped on his back and they exited stage right through a maze of ropes and flats to the winter street, which had cleared now, and they followed it back to Fifth Avenue, resuming the gallop uptown.

The law had recently been distracted from pursuit of Peter Lake by the fervor of the gang wars, which left a pile of corpses each morning in the Five Points, on the waterfront, and in unusual places such as church towers, girls' boarding schools, and spice warehouses. They had little time now for independent burglars like Peter Lake, but he imagined that if in galloping helter-skelter through fashionable thoroughfares he disturbed the "gentiles" (to his credit, he suspected that this was the wrong word), the police would have to come after him again, and that if they did, the Short Tails would back off. The trouble was that once the Short Tails had marked a man they never gave up on him—ever.

But he had many strategies to see him through the deadly traps of the wintry city, and schemes bloomed in front of him like rising storm clouds, opening their arms, willing to be embraced. There were as many ways to survive and as many ways to die as the city had in it streets, lines, and views. But the Short Tails were themselves so capable and knowing that they used the angles and lines of the maze, and the fluid roads and rivers, with a ratlike expertise of runs and burrows. The Short Tails had a terrible air of inevitability and speed—like insatiable time, the flow of water to its own level, or the spread of fire. Evading them even for just a week was a marvelous feat. He had been their prime target for three years.

With the police and the Short Tails after him, Peter Lake decided to leave Manhattan and let the two arms of the pincers pince themselves. Were both organizations to come up face to face in search of their vanished prey, the shock of collision might provide Peter Lake with three or four months of freedom. But such a convergence would come only if he removed himself. He decided to join the clamdiggers on the Bayonne Marsh, knowing that they would give him shelter and a place on dry land for the horse, since they had found Peter Lake and raised him (for a time) much in the style of benevolent wolves. They were fiercer than the Short Tails, who now dared not dip an oar or push a pole within miles of their spacious domain for fear of being instantly beheaded. No one had been able to subdue them, for not only were they extraordinary fighters and impossible to find, but their realm was only half-real, and anyone entering it without their approval was likely to vanish forever into the roaring clouds which swept over the mirrorlike waters. New Jersey had decided once to bring them to the mainstream of life, law, and taxes. Thirty marshals, state police, and Pinkerton agents disappeared permanently in the blinding white banks of speeding cloud. The lieutenant governor was cut in half in his sleep at his Princeton mansion. One of the Weehawken ferries was blown out of the water, rising twenty stories in a ball of flame with a report so deep that it shook every window for fifty miles around.

Peter Lake knew that though he might find refuge on the marsh he would always be drawn by the lights of Manhattan back across the river, no matter what the danger. The Baymen lived too close to the rushing infinity of the cloud wall. They were silent, intent, and hard to fathom, for time sped by them as fast as the sides of a railroad tunnel. A typical Bayman was too much the feverish aborigine, a professional oracle forever examining fish livers and talking in high-speed inexplicable runicisms. For Peter Lake, who had grown used to ringing pianos and pretty girls who played hard to get, a stay on the marsh was difficult. But he was capable of expedient reversion, and was always willing to bend and test his soul.

Perhaps he would spend a week or ten days there ice fishing, going to bed before the moon rose, eating endless rounds of roasted oysters, poling through the salty unfrozen estuaries, and exhilarating in the naked embrace of several women who found with him a certain breathless beauty in wild trancelike bouts of lovemaking while the unruly white wall shook their little houses in the reeds and the gales of winter piled snow on all the paths across the ice. He thought of Anarinda, the dark-haired, the peach-breasted, the star-eyed . . . and he headed for the North Ferry.

"Damn!" he said as they crested the rise before the docks facing the southernmost palisade. The ferry was burning in the middle of the ice-choked river, unable to move, unreachable at first, a blaze of orange bursting forth swollen bundles of disentangling black smoke. Ferries were always burning, and their boilers exploding, especially in winter when they were attacked by rushing islands of sharp heavy ice. The wonderful new bridges were the only remedy, but who could build a bridge across the Hudson?

It was a perfectly blue day. On the opposite shore, bands of color, individual trees, small white frame houses, and veins of red and purple in the high brown rock were all searingly visible. A strong cold wind brought the ice crashing down from upriver. Amid its bell-like shattering, black-coated firemen in whaleboats and on steam tugs struggled to pick up survivors and to pour icy water on the flames. Hundreds of spectators had arrived in spite of the morning cold: girls with hoops and skates, plumbers and joiners on their way to work, servants, dockmen, draymen, river men, and railroad workers. There were also vendors, anticipating the thousands who would arrive only after the ferry was a sulking trap of drifting charcoal, and then feed their curiosity on chestnuts, roasted corn, hot pretzels, and meat-on-the-spit. Peter Lake bought a bag of chestnuts from a wily man whose hands were inured to the heat of his fire. He picked the steaming chestnuts from amid the blinking red coals in the round fire pan. They were too hot to eat, so (after glancing left and right to see if any ladies were present) he put the steaming sack into his pants. Next to his stomach, they warmed his whole body. As he watched the ferry burn, the wind grew stronger, and long rows of willows bent south and shook off their white ice.

One of the spectators was staring not at the burning ferry but at Peter Lake, who dismissed this affront with contempt, because the man looking at him was a telegraph messenger. Peter Lake hated telegraph messengers. Perhaps it was because they should have been sleek matches for winged Mercury, and were invariably rotund, elephantine, molasses-blooded monsters who walked at a mile an hour and could not climb stairs. He surely would not take his attention from a burning ferry for fear of a chubby nitwit in a baglike uniform, a boxy hat with a little nameplate that read "Messenger Beals." And so what if Messenger Beals backed off into the crowd and disappeared? What if he did alert the Short Tails? All Peter Lake had to do if they showed up would be to leap on the horse and leave them far behind.

Several fireboat men were trying to board the burning ferry. They had no apparent reason to do so, for all the passengers were either dead or saved and the firemen could not hope to extinguish the flames simply by being closer to them. Why then were they working their way hand over hand on an alternately slack and taut rope that had started to burn, and dipped them now and then into the freezing river as the crowd took in its breath all at once? Peter Lake knew. They took power from the fire. The closer they fought it, the stronger they became. The firemen knew that though it sometimes killed them, the fire gave them priceless gifts.

Peter Lake applauded with everyone else as the firemen crossed on the burning line and dropped to the deck. As he watched, he peeled the chestnuts and shared them with the horse. After half an hour the ferry was just about to upend and a tug was charging intervening shelves of ice, trying to retrieve the exhausted firefighters, who, with their rope burnt away, stood alone and likely to go under if the ferry were to sink fast in midchannel.

With the corner of his eye (an area most highly developed in thieves) Peter Lake saw two automobiles coming down the road. There were a lot of these things, nothing strange about them, but this particular pair was coming at him full speed, one after the other, stuffed with Short Tails. As Peter Lake swung himself up onto the horse he saw Messenger Beals jumping up and down (very slowly) with excitement. The Short Tails would probably reward him with a huge dinner and a ticket to a music hall.

Peter Lake galloped south, abandoning the burning ferry for the open avenues that would take him past factories, milk plants, breweries, and railroad yards. He and the horse were quickly lost in the precincts of barrels, rails, and cubic mountains of lumber, among the gasworks, tanneries, rope walks, tenements, vaudeville houses, and the high gray spires of the iron bridges.

The Short Tails were once again not too far behind him, swift though embarrassed in their automobiles. But Peter Lake stayed ahead and pounded southward as the horse took strides so powerful that he almost flew.

PEARLY SOAMES

Iɴ all the universe there was only one photograph of Pearly Soames, and it showed Pearly with five police officers around him, one apiece for each of his legs and arms, and one for his head. They held him spread-eagled on a chair to which his waist and chest were firmly strapped. His face was clenched around tightly shut eyes, and it was possible to hear, even in black and white, the bellow that emerged from his throat. The enormous officer behind him had obvious trouble keeping the subject's face toward the camera, and he grasped Pearly's hair and beard as if he were holding an agitated poisonous snake. When the powder flashed in the pan, a coatrack toppled off to the left as a casualty of the struggle and was caught for all time, like the hand of an ornate clock, pointing toward two. Pearly Soames had not desired to be photographed.

His eyes were like razors and white diamonds. They were impossibly pale, lucid, and silver. People said, "When Pearly Soames opens his eyes, it's electric lights." He had a scar that went from the corner of his mouth to his ear. To look at it made the beholder feel a knife on his own skin, cutting deep and sharp, because Pearly Soames' scar was like a white trough reticulated with painful filaments of cold ivory. It had been with him since the age of four, a gift from his father, who had tried and failed to cut his son's throat.

Of course, it's bad to be a criminal. Everyone knows that, and can swear that it's true. Criminals mess up the world. But they are, as well, retainers of fluidity. In fact, one might make the case that New York would not have shone without its legions of contrary devils polishing the lights of goodness with their inexplicable opposition and resistance. It might even be said that criminals are a necessary component of the balanced equation which steadily and beautifully eats up all the time that is thrown upon its steely back. They are the sugar and alcohol of a city, a red flash in the mosaic, lightning on a hot night. So was Pearly.

So was Pearly all of these things, knowing at every instant exactly what he was and that everything he did was wrong, possessed with an agonizing account of himself, his mind quick to grasp the meaning of his merciless acts. Though he cared not at all for the mechanisms of equilibrium, if he had stopped, the life of the city would have fallen apart. For it required (among other things) balanced, opposing, and random forces, and he was set in the role of all three. Imagine the magic required to make a man cringe at the sight of a baby, and want to kill it. Pearly had that magic: he hated babies and wanted to kill them. They cried like cats on a fence, they had enormous round mouths, and they couldn't even hold up their own goddamned heads. They drove him crazy with their needs, their assumptions, and their innocence. He wanted to smash their assumptions and confound their innocence. He wanted to debate them despite the fact that they couldn't talk. He also hated small children too young to steal. What a tragic paradox. When they were small and could fit between bars, they didn't know what to do and couldn't carry anything. As soon as they got old enough

21

to understand what they were supposed to bring back from the other side, they were unable to get through. And it wasn't just children that he disliked for their vulnerability. He felt his chest heave with waves of uncontrollable violence at the sight of any cripple. He gnashed his teeth and wanted to kill them, to crush them into pulp, to silence their horrible self-pity, and bend the wheels of their chairs. He was a bomb-thrower, a lunatic, a master criminal, a devil, the golden dog of the streets.

Pearly Soames wanted gold and silver, but not, in the way of common thieves, for wealth. He wanted them because they shone and were pure. Strange, afflicted, and deformed, he sought a cure in the abstract relation of colors. But though he was drawn to fine and intense color, he was no connoisseur. Connoisseurs of paintings were curiously indifferent about color itself, and were seldom possessed by it. Rather, they possessed it. And they seemed to be easily sated. They were like the gourmets, who had to build castles of their food before they could eat it. They confused beauty and knowledge, passion and expertise. Not Pearly. Pearly's attraction to color was like an infection, or religion, and he came to it each time a starving man. Sometimes, on the street or sailing along the waterfront in a fast skiff, he would witness the sun's illumination of a flat plane of color that was given (like almost everything else in New York) a short and promiscuous embrace. Pearly always stopped, and if he froze in the middle of the street, traffic was forced to weave around him. Or if he were in a boat, he turned it to the wind and stayed with the color for as long as it lasted. House painters were subject to interludes of terror when Pearly would burst upon them and stand close, staring with his electric eyes at the rich glistening color flowing thickly from their wet brushes. It was bad enough if he were alone (they all knew him, and were well aware of his reputation), but he was not infrequently accompanied by a bunch of Short Tails. In that case, the painters trembled because they would be punished afterward for the time that the Short Tails were obliged to stand in silence with their hands in their pockets, observing the inexplicable mystery of Pearly's "color gravity," as he called it. Unable to complain to Pearly, they would leave a few of their number to beat up the painters.

Once, on their way to a gang war, Pearly and sixty of the Short Tails went marching through the streets like a Florentine army. They carried not only their customary concealed armament, but rifles, grenades, and swords as well. Ready for a fight, they were excited beyond measure. Their hearts smashed from inside their chests. Their eyes darted. Halfway to the site of battle, Pearly spied two painters slapping a fresh coat of enamel against the doorposts of a saloon. The little army came to a halt. Pearly approached the trembling painters. He put his eyes near the green and stood there, smelling it, lost in it. Refreshed, moved, and amazed, he stepped back, enwrapped in the color gravity. . . . "Put more on," he said. "I like to see it when it goes on, when it's wet. There's an instant of glory." They started another coat. (The saloonkeeper was delighted.) Pearly watched contentedly. "A nice landscape," he offered, "a fine landscape. It reminds me of certain parts of rich men's estates, where they don't let the sheep onto the green, and the green stays unfouled. You fellows keep it up. I'll be back in a day or two to see how it looks when it dries." And then they went off to the battle, with Pearly at the front fighting as no man could, having drawn from the wells of color.

This color gravity made him steal paintings. At first he had gone himself to art stores or sent his men, but they found nothing there except easels and paints. Then they caught on and began to raid the secure vaults of prestigious dealers, and the best-watched palaces on upper Fifth Avenue, where they found the most coveted of all paintings, the ones that sold for tens of thousands of dollars, that attracted the harried young hounds of the press, and about which critics dared not say a bad word. These were the paintings that were brought over from Europe in yachts, riding in their own private cabins with three Pinkerton guards. Pearly knew to steal them because he read the papers and received auction catalogs.

One night, his best burglars returned with five rolled canvases from Knoedler's. Pearly couldn't wait until morning. He ordered the paintings to be restretched and called for two-dozen storm lanterns and mirrors to light an enormous loft down near the bridges, the headquarters of the moment, for the Short Tails continually shifted from place to place in imitation of the Spanish Guerrillas. Pearly had the paintings put up on stands and covered with a velvet curtain. The lamps were lit, blazing clear light against the soft cloth. He stood back and prepared for a feast. With a nod of his head, he signaled his men to drop the velvet. "What!" he yelled, instinctively putting his hands on his pistol. "Did you steal what I told you to steal?" The burglars frantically rustled through the auction catalogs, comparing the titles Pearly had circled in red to those on the plaques they had stolen along with the canvases. They matched. Pearly was shown that they matched.

"I don't understand," he said, peering at his collection of great and famous names. "They're mud, black and brown. No light in them, and hardly any color. Who would paint a picture in black and brown?"

"I don't know, Pearly," answered Blacky Womble, his most trusted lieutenant.

"Why? Why would they do that? And why do all the rich people and the experts like these things? Don't they know? They're rich, they must know."

"I told you, Pearly, I can't figure it," said Blacky Womble.

"Shut up! Take 'em back. I don't want them here. Put them back in their frames."

"But we cut them out," protested the burglars, "and besides, in an hour it'll be light. There isn't enough time."

"Then put them back tomorrow night. Damn them! What a waste."

The next day saw a great stir when Knoedler's discovered that half a million dollars' worth of paintings had been stolen. And the day after that, the papers went wild reporting that the paintings had been replaced. They published on their front pages the contents of a note found pinned to one of the frames.

I don't want these. They're mud and they've got no color. Or at least the color is different from what I'm used to. Take any American city, in autumn, or in winter, when the light makes the colors dance and flow, and look at it from a distant hill or from a boat in the bay or on the river, and you will see in any section of the view far better paintings than in this lentil soup that you people have to pedigree in order to love. I may be a thief, but I know color when I see it in the flash of heaven or in the Devil's opposing tricks, and I know mud. Mr. Knoedler, you needn't worry about your paintings anymore. I'm not going to steal them. I don't like them.

Sincerely yours,
P. Soames

To comfort his wounded color gravity, Pearly's men went out to get him emeralds, gold, and silver. He didn't speak for days, until the warmth of the gold and the visual clatter of the fine silver healed him. Occasionally they would bring back the work of an American artist, or a Renaissance miniaturist, or any of the lively and unappreciated experimentalists, or some ancient whose work had not been boiled in linseed oil, and Pearly would have his feast—under a pier, upstairs at a stale-beer house, or amid the vats of a commandeered brewery. But the wonderful sights and scenes, the subtleties of true sacrificial color, the holiness of its coincidence in integral planes and intermingling currents, were not enough for Pearly. He wanted actually to live inside the dream that captured his eye, to spend his days and nights in a fume of burnished gold.

"I want a room of gold," he said, "solid, polished all the time with chamois, pure gold: the walls, ceiling, and floor of gold plate." Even the Short Tails were stunned. The city was theirs, but they had never thought to be like Inca kings, or to build a heavenly palace, or even to have a fixed address.

Blacky Womble risked contradicting his chief. "Pearly, no one in New York has a golden room, not even the richest banker. It's a waste of time. To steal that much gold would take a hundred years."

"That's where you're wrong," Pearly said. "We'll do it in a day."

"A day?"

"Like stealing poultry. And you think there's no golden room?

You're wrong. There are many millions of rooms and enclosed spaces in this city that stretches limitlessly down below the ground, up into the air, and into an infinite maze of streets. There might be more golden rooms in the city than there are stars in the heavens.''

"How could that be?" asked Blacky Womble.

"Have you ever heard of Sarganda Street, or Diamond Row, or the Avenues of the Nines and Twenties?"

"In New York?"

"Indeed—thoroughfares hundreds, thousands of miles long, that twist and coil and have branching from them innumerable intertwining streets each grander than the one before it.''

"Are they in Brooklyn? I don't know Brooklyn. No one does really. People always go there and never come back. Lotsa streets in Brooklyn nobody ever heard of, like Funyew-Ogstein-Crypt Boulevard.''

"That's some sort of Hebrew thing. But yes, they are in Brooklyn, and in Manhattan too. They run through each other, and are overlaid." Pearly's eyes were electric lights. Blacky Womble didn't always understand Pearly (especially when Pearly would send him out late at night to fetch a gallon of fresh paint), but he knew that Pearly got results, and he loved to watch him bristle and sweat, going at things like a wrestler or a boxer, unearthing treasures from the empty air, possessed and directed like an oracle. "The Avenues of the Nines and Twenties are coiled around one another like two copulating snakes. They run for thousands of miles.''

"In which direction, Pearly?"

"Up! Straight up!" answered Pearly, pointing at the dark ceiling, his eyes disappearing only to leave behind blank white eggs. Blacky Womble, too, stared at the darkness, and saw gray coilings and blue flashes. It was like being held over an infinitely deep pit. He forgot about gravity. He flew. His eyes were swallowed up by the loom of streets that Pearly had opened to him for just that instant. When he returned, he found Pearly gazing into his face, all set for business, as calm and sober as a laundry clerk on the day after Christmas.

"Even if Sarganda Street and the Avenues of the Nines and Twenties . . ."

"And Diamond Row."

"And Diamond Row, do exist, how are we going to steal enough gold to make a golden room? Don't get me wrong, I like the idea. But how will we work it?"

"The only way to do it is to steal it from one of the gold carriers that come through the Narrows."

Blacky Womble was taken aback. The Short Tails were the best of the gangs, the most powerful, the most daring. But they had never even robbed a major bank, except once, and that was one of those temporary branches that could be broken into with a can opener. The gold carriers were out of the question. First, no one really knew when they made port, because they set their courses on random generators (wire cages inside of which tumbled surplus Mah-Jongg blocks engraved with longitudes and latitudes). These ships zigged and zagged over the seas in incredible patterns. For example, to go from Peru to New York, one of the fast carriers might call at Yokohama six times—though a nondelivery port call for a gold carrier consisted of saluting from fifty miles at sea with a blue flare, and then vanishing into the night and distance. There was no way to know where one would be and when; they abhorred the sea-lanes; their arrivals were swift and unexpected. In fact, most people in New York did not know of them. Bakers baked their endless rows of cookies; mechanics worked at oily engines that smelled of flint and steel; and bank clerks worked their lines, piecing out and taking in tiny sums through the organizational baleen of their graceful human hands, never knowing that the wealth of great kingdoms was all around them, filtering through the streets of lower Manhattan like a tide in the reeds.

Of the many millions, perhaps ten thousand had seen a gold carrier in the harbor or tied up at its fortified pier for half an hour of off-loading, and of these no more than a thousand or so had known what they had seen. Of this thousand, nine hundred were honest, and did not think of larceny. Of the hundred who did, fifty were broken-down wrecks, not even criminal enough to steal from themselves. Of the rest, twenty might have been able, but had turned their talents to other things (such as opera, publishing, and the military); twenty were qualified criminals but lacked organizational skills, followings, and resources; five came up with inept and laughable schemes; and four might have tried it but for fatal accidents, coincidental distractions, and sudden dyspepsia—which is not to say that they would have succeeded. The one left was Pearly Soames, but even for him it was almost an impossible task, as these ships were the fastest and most agile in the world. They were well armed and armored. Deep in their hulls were stupendous vaults that could be opened only when the ship docked at one of the fortified piers, and special extraction mechanisms had pulled from the hull a series of alloy steel rods which tightly caged time-locked doors behind which were ten high-security stalls where the gold was locked in explosive strongboxes. An army guarded each removal.

Though Blacky Womble was a Caucasian, he was blacker than cobalt, and unlike the rest of the Short Tails, he wore a shiny black leather jacket. His hair was meshed about his ears in frightening whorls much like the path of Sarganda Street. His teeth were the closest match there was to Pearly's eyes. They were pointed like spires, serrated like long mountain ranges or institutional bread knives, crescent-shaped like scimitars, as sharp as finely honed scalpels, as strong as bayonets. And yet, somehow, he had a gentle, pacifying smile that could have rocked a baby to sleep. Despite the teeth, he was a nice man (for a Short Tail). He knew that Pearly's color gravity was all-consuming, that Pearly walked a thin line between madness and capability, always upping the stakes in service of his lust for color, and thereby retaining the loyalty of the Short Tails in never failing to amaze them. But it had to crash sometime, and they were waiting for Pearly to lose his touch. Blacky thought the time had come.

"Pearly, I fear for you," he said directly.

Pearly laughed. "You think I've gone around the bend."

"I won't tell anyone about this. I won't say anything. That way, you can think it o—"

"It's decided already. I'm going to tell the others. At the meeting."

They held their meetings underground or far above it, for the se-

28

cret deliberations of thieves could not take place in healthy locations such as common rooms or town squares, where they might
have become democratic and open, aired-out, unfestering, and
cool. They were held in deathly chambers or on the highest towers,
confronting either the grave or an open abyss. Pearly used these
sites to cook up his plots and galvanize the Short Tails. They felt
privileged to convene on the piers of the Brooklyn Bridge, waist-
deep in not entirely empty water tanks, nestled in terror between
the spars of the Statue of Liberty's crown, in the cellar beneath an
opium den on Doyer Street, or at the edge of the central sewer fall,
sitting like picnickers in the dark by the side of Niagara.

"Spread the word," Pearly said to Blacky Womble. "The meeting will be at midnight, Tuesday next, in the cemetery of the honored dead."

Blacky Womble choked and his eyes collapsed into his face. He
might have understood a gathering in high wind atop the city's
tallest tower, or one of those plucky convocations they had in the
rafters of Central Police Headquarters. But the cemetery of the
honored dead! Words of protest gushed out of his mouth, shredding themselves through the ivory sluice.

"Shut up, Blacky! Do as I told you."

"But lemme . . ."

Pearly Soames locked his eyes onto Blacky's. For Blacky, it was
like looking through the peephole of a Bessemer furnace. Any
more resistance from him, as well he knew, and out would pour
rivers of orange flame flaring into hot golden tongues to lash at the
newly burning world.

Meekly, Blacky asked how many were to be at the meeting.

Pearly had cooled somewhat, and answered straight. "Our full
complement, the hundred."

Loyal Blacky Womble collapsed in fear.

It was indeed an honor to be buried in the cemetery of the honored dead. Pearly had decided that a dead Short Tail deserved to be
interred as close to hell as possible, and that the burial should entail
as much risk to life and limb as could be imagined (the ultimate

29

honor to the fallen). Thus, all Short Tails killed in service were transported to crypts at the bottom of the Harlem River siphon.

To get Croton water into Manhattan, the city had built a monumental siphon. On both sides of the Harlem River, two shafts led straight down for a thousand feet to a quarter-mile pressure tunnel hewn through the rock. Halfway between the shafts was a silt chamber twenty-five feet square and twenty-five feet high. Here, one summer when a drought had rendered the siphon inoperable from July to September, the Short Tails had placed one hundred watertight crypts. It had been difficult enough at that time to ride on a tiny platform for ten minutes, holding your elbows at your sides so that they would not scrape the rock walls of the narrow shaft, and then to crawl at a mossy slitherous pace through 650 feet of tunnel so narrow that you felt as if you were being ramrodded into the barrel of a gun, until you broke out into the pitch-dark silt chamber, lit the candle, and listened to the rats scream in fright. It was bad to be a quarter of a mile and an hour away from the surface, from air, from the open; and straight up there was nothing but six hundred feet of solid rock and a hundred feet of mud, rubble, and filthy water. The two round openings in the silt chamber were exactly the size of the tunnel, smaller than a manhole. The sandhogs who worked on the crypts did so only because, had they not, Pearly would have killed their families. They finished quickly, and were grateful to be done, for it was frightening to go there even in a drought.

But when the water was flowing, and could be released at any time whatsoever from the Jerome Park Storage Reservoir to charge through the tunnels faster than a horse could run, then it was considerably worse, and a great honor for the deceased to have two Short Tails pull his corpse through the tunnel, hurriedly slam it into a crypt while they listened breathlessly for the rush of approaching water, and then lope prone through the tube of green moss, mad for breaking into the air, speeding along like wild jittery whipcords.

When E. E. Henry (for a time Peter Lake's partner, and one of the Short Tails' best woola boys) had been ground into small smithereens by a speeding engine on the El during an unsuccessful attempt at urbanizing train robbery, two Short Tails—Romeo Tan and Bat Charney—had volunteered to take what was left down into the crypt. Brave they were, for E. E. Henry had departed from this world one crystal-clear day in October after two solid weeks of rain. Upstate dams were overflowing as steadily as power looms vomiting out silver brocade, and the pressure tunnel was much in use as Jerome Park periodically disgorged inflowing lakes of freezing water.

Entering in bright moonlight late one night, they struggled through the shafts, carrying E. E. Henry in small sacks that they dragged after them with cords held between their teeth. Several inches of cold water lay on the bottom of the horizontal tunnel. As they sloshed through they could smell oxygen, which meant that the water was fresh. Were the Jerome Park sluices to be drawn open as Romeo Tan and Bat Charney crawled toward the silt chamber, they would die a horrible backward death, because the tunnel was too narrow for turning around. They stopped every now and then to listen, and heard nothing. Finally, Romeo Tan broke through to the silt chamber. Working in four feet of ice water, they lit the candle, pried open a crypt, threw in the sacks of E. E. Henry, slammed the door, said a two-word prayer ("Jesus Christ!"), dropped their hammer and crow, and made for the exit, hearts racing. Bat Charney made a step of his hands. As Romeo Tan's head reached the level of the tunnel he was about to enter, he heard a strange sound. It was like wind whistling over the peaks of high mountains, or the sound of a geyser minutes before it erupts. It was the water, which had just begun to pass through the gates at Jerome Park.

"Water!" he said to Bat Charney. At first they nearly collapsed, but soon they were snake-dancing through the tunnel, going faster than they would have thought possible. They dug so hard into the moss to pull themselves ahead that after a hundred feet they had no nails left, and their hands looked like newt paws. Still, they kept on, but it was too late. They heard the water explode into the silt chamber, and felt the displaced air rushing past them like a hurricane. Then came the torrent. Its icy mass, frothing and dark, banged into Bat Charney's feet, knocked out his false teeth, and jolted him forward into a fetal position. He drowned that way, but he saved Romeo Tan, since Bat's compacted body became a plug in the line shooting rapidly forward at the head of the water column. Romeo Tan lay on his back, sliding across the wet moss at the bottom of the tunnel as fast as a bullet. At the shaft, they curved upward and rose so fast that the flesh on Romeo Tan's face was pulled down until he looked like a bloodhound. He wondered what would happen when they hit the top, but he didn't wonder long, for they were shot from the mouth of the shaft (which they had left open) like cannonballs, or, rather, like a long cannonball and a trailing bunched-up wad. Romeo Tan felt his head break a splintering hole through the shingle roof over the entry. Suddenly he was flying free in the night, toward the stars and a bright moon which almost blinded him. The city on an autumn night, exciting and full of charms, was spread all around him. He could see lights, smoking chimneys, and fires at the edge of the windy parks. The Harlem River was covered with the glistening white paint of the moon. He wondered if he would fly into space. But he rose only two hundred feet above Morris Heights before he started down, and landed in an apple tree. His fall was broken as every single apple, perhaps five hundred of them, left the tree and thudded to the ground. Romeo Tan watched the apples roll down the hill and pile up against a farmer's shack. Then, for the rest of the night, he sat in the tree, under the moon, trying to reconstruct what had happened, wondering if everyone had to experience this kind of thing sooner or later, or if in fact it was a relatively isolated occurrence.

Pearly Soames wanted to take a hundred men down there and stay for an hour to explain his plan. As word spread throughout the city, one Short Tail after another felt his heart swim to his feet and cower like a dog. Their anxiety was infectious. Everyone in Manhattan was nervous. Even the music halls were gloomy. But at nine in the evening on Tuesday, the Short Tails assembled one hundred strong in the apple orchard around the siphon entrance, waiting to descend. There was much nervous talk and forced pleasantries about stealing, the conditions in various jails, and the state of the con. Romeo Tan, now a basket case, was allowed to be last in and first out. Pearly, as usual, was first in and would be last out. After three hours, all the Short Tails were stuffed into the silt chamber.

There they stood, pressed against the crypts, every ear cocked in the direction of Jerome Park. They seemed not to breathe, while Pearly paced back and forth in the light of a dozen flickering candles. All the burglars were there in black masks (some, out of habit, had even hauled sacks through the tunnel); the agile woola boys with their strong and springy legs; the well-tailored con men; the pickpockets; the guns (marksmen in the gang wars, who were held in low regard because they could pick neither pockets nor locks); even the chef, who was uncomfortable unless he could cook with hot provisions. Romeo Tan stood with his hand on the lip of the exit pipe, listening intently for a faint white roar. Pearly stopped pacing and looked at his men. For five minutes they didn't move a millimeter, and stood in terror of the deluge that might race through the Bronx tunnel into the chamber that was echoing with their heartbeats.

"Do I hear water?" asked Pearly, cocking his head. He watched all hundred Short Tails turn white, as if he had drawn a Venetian blind. "It took three hours to get in," he said, "so it will take three hours to get out. What's that!" They started, and then sighed as one, like inmates of hell. "I thought I heard something. I guess it was nothing. Would anyone like a glass of . . . water!" They moaned.

He pranced about as if his legs were stilts. "I have a proposition for you," he said.

But a horrified shudder passed through the crowd as a masked burglar shouted "Look!" and held up a pair of false teeth. Everyone remembered Bat Charney's shame about what he called his "elephant's castanets." All that was left of Bat rested aloft in the burglar's hand. They gazed at it meekly until Pearly cut short their devotions.

"Shall we proceed, gentlemen, or do you wish to increase the chance of being trapped forever in this underground tea bag (where we would flavor the city's drinking water for twenty years), by irrelevant stupidities such as a silent prayer over a pair of dentures?" Pearly's cheek was twitching, signifying one of the many species of his cool anger. "Imagine, if you will," he said, "that we are not in a dank and mossy crypt, but in a room of gold; that upon each

33

solid brick is stamped a fine and florid eagle, crown, or fleur-de-lys; that warm rays make the air softer and yellower than butter; that you breathe not this base, black, wet mist, but a sparkling bronze infusion that has been mellowed by its constant reverberation within walls of pure gold." He sucked in his breath. "The light of this room would be just that shade that we are told arises sometimes against the clouds beyond the bay, making the world gold the way it is said happens once in a . . . every . . . well . . . sometimes. My plan, you see," he said in pain, writhing internally, "is to build a golden room in a high place, and post watchmen to watch the clouds. When they turn gold, and the light sprays upon the city, the room will open. The light will stuff the chamber. Then the doors will seal shut. And the goldenness will be trapped forever." The thieves' mouths hung open. "You can come there, all of you! You can bathe in the light, drink in the air, run your hands along the smooth walls. Even in the pit and trough of night, the golden room will be brightly boiling. And it will be ours." Tranquilized with longing, he looked dreamily at the ceiling. "In the center, I will put a simple bed, and there I will repose in warmth and gold . . . for eternity."

For a moment, they forgot where they were, and bombarded Pearly with questions. When he told them what he intended, the cynics replied that he had lost his mind. No one could rob a gold carrier. But Pearly countered with a scheme. A lookout at Sandy Hook would scan the sea day and night from a tower that they would build in the guise of charitable works. Another lookout atop the Manhattan pier of the Brooklyn Bridge would keep an eye on Sandy Hook. The Short Tails would cut their work rate by two-thirds, for the specific purpose of keeping a force of fifty men always at the ready, poised to break out into the harbor fully armed in their swift fleet of winabouts—the fastest small sailing craft in the city, of which they had ten. When the Sandy Hook lookout saw the ship, he would launch a flare. Upon seeing the flare, the man on the bridge tower would, via a special line, telephone the alert Short Tails waiting in their boats under the docks at Korlaer's Hook. The Short Tails would immediately sally forth into the harbor. There, they would set up two buoys, and sail to and fro between them on a line perpendicular to the channel through which the carrier made its way to the fortified pier. The Short Tails would be dressed, one and all, as ladies, and, one and all, they would make sure that the winabouts in the fake regatta would be rammed and sunk by the very ship they planned to rob. It would take some precise boat handling, and the patience to sit in a dress under the docks for a month or two, but it would be worth it, for no captain would abandon fifty yachtswomen to drown in New York Harbor, and they would undoubtedly be taken up on deck, where they would remove from under their dresses the bristling arsenal for which they were famous, and proceed to take over the ship.

"So what," someone said. "The escorts would capture us soon after that. The Navy."

"No escort," answered Pearly, "is as fast or as well armed as a gold carrier."

"But it doesn't matter even so, Pearly. You can't get the gold out of those ships unless you have special machinery, and it all has to be done in a large dry dock."

"We'll build our own dry dock."

"That's preposterous," yelled a woola boy. "How are we going to build a dry dock? Even if we could, everyone in the world would notice. And when we took the ship there, they would just follow and catch us."

"That shows what a woola boy is good for," said Pearly. "Stick to Woola Woola until I promote you, my fancy young rabbit. We won't build the dry dock until we've taken the ship. We'll have all the time we want to do that, and all the time necessary to extract the gold by drilling a hole in the vault (one hole—we should be able to do that!) and building a big fire under the ship to melt the gold so it can run like lava right into our waiting pigs.

"The reason we'll have all the time in the world, and I mean time in profusion, is that when we take over the ship we'll head her west to the Bayonne Marsh and ram her through the barrier of white clouds."

An even colder chill spread throughout the chamber. "When you go beyond those clouds," said a sheepish pickpocket, "that's it. You don't come back. That's dying, Pearly."

"How do we know?" asked Pearly. "I've never known anyone to tell what's on the other side. Maybe they come back and keep their traps shut. Maybe it's great over there—lots of naked women, fruit on the trees, hula dancers with bare breasts, food for the taking, silk, motorcars, racetracks where you always win . . . and we might be able to make our way back. If and when we did, we'd be the richest men on earth. It sure beats holding up tobacco stores for cigar bands, doesn't it? Think of E. E. Henry. Think of Rascal T. Otis. They died for peanuts. I myself prefer to risk my all for something on a larger scale."

This latter appeal swung the company of thieves. They were willing to charge the cloud barrier. But a man with vast experience of the harbor (his specialty was looting pleasure yachts) pointed out that the reedy channels running mazelike to the white wall were not deep enough for an oceangoing vessel. Furthermore, he said, he had seen the cloud wall from less than a mile away while standing upon a harbor bar that had appeared suddenly after a storm. The cloud wall, he said, did not remain in the same place. It went around the city "like one a them Moibus belts," and oscillated along the ground. Sometimes it disappeared, bringing into view the rest of the country beyond (it was then that transcontinental railroad trains proceeded through the gap, rolling over blinding silver tracks that had been scoured to a gleam by the agitated base of the cloud wall), and sometimes it lifted like a stage curtain, disappearing wholly or partially into heaven. Sometimes it sank into the ground, leaving only silence and a sunny landscape. But when it was up, the base moved rapidly over a changing space of several miles. There were no certain limits to its traverse. It had been known even to cross the river and sweep through Manhattan, taking with it as it left those whose time had come.

Pearly supposed that they would have to dredge a channel as close to it as they could get, and trust to luck that the wall would sweep over them at the right moment. It was a risky business. The harbor man spoke up again, saying that dredging a channel would be nearly impossible. It would have to cut across the Bayonne Marsh, where the Baymen lived.

"It's come to it, then," said Pearly. "We'll have to make war on them, which means killing every single one. The sooner the better, before word gets out. They're wicked fierce. I fought one once and nearly died, and it was nowhere near the cloud wall or the marsh but on dry land in Manhattan, where he had landed in a gale and I mistook him for a simple fisherman. Their swords fly so fast you can't even see them. We'll have to take them by surprise. We'll go over there in canoes when the men are at work, kill the women and children, and wait in the huts. When the men come back, we'll catch them unprepared, and shoot them from behind cover. There's no sense in an open battle.''

When all the Short Tails finally filed out into the light of the declining moon—just ahead of a torrent of freezing black water that filled the siphon soon after they left—their spirits were high. Perhaps it was because of the beauty of the night, the felt-dark woods soft and cold, the orchard high on the hill, the view of the sparkling and serene city. They melted into the fields and trees as only they could, contemplating victory over the Baymen, willing even to dress as ladies and plunge into the harbor, apprehensive of penetrating the clouds, eager to build a fire under the ship so that the gold would pour out, and delighted to think that they could be the richest men on earth if only they could hold their courage.

Peter Lake, too, had been in the tea bag, pressed in a corner with a bunch of apprentice woola boys of whom he was one. At first he had been entranced by the venture. Pearly's description of the golden room made Peter Lake think of the deep dreams he had had in which golden animals with soft golden pelts nudged him in tender affection, and he stroked and kissed the smooth faces of marvelous flying horses, tame leopards, and good-natured seals. How canny, immoral, and thievish, to think of trapping the rare light (which he himself had never seen), and yet how admirable a rebellion. Peter Lake thought that in wanting the golden light in his peculiar way Pearly Soames had shown certain of the attributes of innocence. The thieves were in rebellion to capture the light of heaven—though they thought it was for the loot, or for Pearly's color gravity. For half an hour, Peter Lake had listened to the scheme, wanting it to succeed. He had even come to ignore the surroundings, devoid as they were of congeniality, and imagined that the chamber of gray granite was in fact a magical room of inner sunlit shining. But because of the plan against the Baymen, Peter Lake had become forever alienated from the Short Tails, and would have to betray them. He, and only he, knew that Pearly would never have his golden chamber.

PETER LAKE HANGS
FROM A STAR

Much has been written and said about Castle Garden, entryway for immigrants, inlet to a new life, bursting star. But seldom have those beyond its solemn silent spaces been ready to confess that once, in a different time, it loomed for them or for their parents like the gates of St. Peter. Its servants in deep ornate dress turned away those who were unsound and unfit, in a process of judgment that was both the work of bureaucrats and a dream. Many had crossed the ocean seeking light, and were suddenly hurled backward, tumbling through white waves and green oceans until the light receded into the point of a star in total darkness. Turned away, they died.

Off Castle Garden, a mile to the southeast, near the western edge of Governors Island, a ship lay resting through a foggy spring night before the long and arduous trip back to the old world—whether Riga, Naples, or Constantinople is not certain. But it was probably Constantinople, for the collection of people on deck and in the silent common spaces that once were echoing and jammed, was colorful enough still to represent the great mélange of races that, fleeing wounds and fire, drained from Asia, Asiatic Russia, and the Balkans. The ships that arrived also left. And they took with them, without fanfare, those who were forced to make two trips. Many of these people were nearly dead to begin with, and would have to be buried at sea on the voyage home. Others were well enough to return to hostile or empty villages, where they would live out their days in amazement that they had been to another world, and come back.

About a hundred people stayed awake that night on the neat little steamship off Governors Island, staring at the shining palisade of buildings and bridges across the water. It was late spring; the air was warm; the fog kept low and made the city beyond look even more dreamlike than it might have looked on a clearer night. Unable to see the land, they thought that America was a glowing island reaching infinitely high from the middle of a gentle sea.

They were quiet because they had been stunned. Their hearts had almost run out of their bodies when the line of people on deck finally started to move forward, and, with a great cheer, a thousand souls began to descend from the gangway into the new land. That morning, Brooklyn had spoken off to the right with its church bells, klaxons, and boat horns. The streets that ran up its sloping hills glittered and waved in the sun; they were the scene of constant traffic, as were the harbor, the piers, and the river lanes. Even the air was crowded with clouds and birds, fleeing together in the wind with unbent white energy. After so long in places so difficult, the immigrants could almost hear music as the buildings rose up ahead and sparkled. Here was a place that was infinitely variable and rich. Its gates were like the gates of heaven; and if there were some on the other side who said that this was not true, all one had to say was, "After what I have been through, the power of my dream makes it true. Even if this place is not the great beauty that I think it is, I'll make it so, one way or another." As they moved in the packed line, they looked over the rails and saw people beyond the barriers smiling at them as if to say, "Just wait! You have hard and good times ahead, as I did." The signals were from everywhere and very strong. The world they faced was terrifying and beautiful.

After they had stepped onto solid ground the line divided at the base of the gangway, and they walked quickly into an enormous room full of people. The windows were open, and sometimes spring air entered gently in warm breezes that smelled of flowers and trees. A family of three moved step by step to the head of the line. The man was sturdy and blond, with a carefully tended mustache, and eyes as blue as the wet blue cups in a palette of watercolors. His wife had a weak and lovely mouth that suggested vulnerability, sensitivity, and compassion, but, unlike the dark waddling pumpkins that stood around her, she was tall and strong. She carried their son, an infant. The father took the baby when she left him for the examining room. The people next to him thought that he was crazy, for he stroked the child almost mechanically, muttering something to it in a tight and desperate fashion, though he could not take his eyes off the door where she would come out. When finally she emerged, she shrugged her shoulders as if to say that she didn't know what the doctors had determined. Without a word, she took the baby, glad to get him back, and her husband left for another room. As he walked away, he saw that she had a symbol chalked on her back. Then, they examined him. They made him spit into a vial; they took some blood; and they scanned him rapidly while a clerk wrote down what they said. After he put on his clothes, they put a chalk mark on his back, too.

By early evening the meaning of the chalk marks was apparent. Most of the hall was empty, but about a hundred people remained. She was already crying by the time an official came and told them in their own language that they would be going back. "Why?" they asked, in fear and anger. To answer them, he made them turn around so he could tell them the one word that had kept them out. For this young peasant and his wife, that word had been "consumption."

41

"What about the child?" she asked. "Is there a place for him? If we have to go back, we'll leave him."

"No," answered the official. "The child stays with you." His expression implied that there was something wrong with a mother who wanted to leave her child.

"You don't understand," she said, shaking. "You don't understand what we left." But the official continued down the line of those he had to condemn, and disappeared in silence. They were left with their child in the rays of a very clear and harsh electric light.

The ship pulled into the harbor to lie at anchor, mainly, they thought, so that they would not try to jump off it. Even for those who knew how to swim, the water was far too cold, the distance to land too great, the currents too swift. Chunks of ice flowed past, hissing as they melted, sometimes knocking against the ship's steel plates like wooden mallets.

He tried to bribe the captain to take the baby ashore, but he didn't have enough, and, thus, the captain was not amenable. Perhaps if they had been turned back for other reasons it would not have been unthinkable to return to the place that they had been so glad to leave. But they knew that they would die, and they were determined to leave the child in America no matter how difficult it would be for them to part with him. It would be as difficult as dying.

They stood at the rail or they sat within the dark spaces, silently, just as the others did. Had they been on the open sea it would have been a time of fear. But they were at the base of a palatial city which glowed at them and filled their eyes with gold light. They were amazed by the bridges, which arched in strings of glowing pearls. Never having seen anything like them before, they did not understand their scale, and imagined them to be many miles high. They ached with envy and regret as they took in the spring night, unable to sleep.

He began to wander the halls. Why am I not man enough to accept this? Why am I so greedy? The picture of his wife leapt before his eyes. At first he started to cry, but then he became enraged. He slammed his fist against the bulkhead. A framed print jumped off the wall, its glass shattering about the corridor. "Greedy!" he shouted, fighting nothing and everything that ever was, at one and the same instant. Right in front of him was a wooden door of slatted panels, that begged to be kicked. He gave it one tremendous boot and knocked it off its hinges. It smashed down so hard and loud on the floor inside that several things happened. He jumped back in shock. The lights in the room went on. And a companion-way door swung closed.

For a moment, he froze, fearful that one of the crew had heard. But then he remembered that nearly everyone had taken a boat to shore. A few officers remained behind, sitting on chairs with their feet up on the rails of the bridge, smoking and talking as they, too, watched the lights of the city. They were too far away to hear.

He stepped inside to turn off the light. He was in a meeting room of some sort. Green leather chairs surrounded a dark wooden table. He looked about, shut off the light, and started back to the open deck.

Halfway down the hall, he stopped. A chill came over him, and he shuddered. Then he ran back to the room, found the light, and saw what he had come to see. In the corner, under a porthole, was a big glass case. In the glass case was a wooden model of the ship, the *City of Justice,* a replica about four feet long. It had a weighted keel, masts, smokestacks. It was detailed so finely that he pictured within it a little room in which a man stood staring at a model ship, inside of which was another room and another model, until the last one was not small, but larger than the universe, having reversed the cycles and rhythm of size in an inevitable buckling cusp.

He was an orderly man who never would have smashed down a door or hit walls with his fist. But that afternoon he and his young wife had received what they thought to be a death sentence. He took one of the heavy green chairs, lifted it, and brought it down upon the case. Another crash, and more shattered glass fell to the floor. It was, in its way, exhilarating.

On the dark and deserted fantail, he and his wife tied lines to the little ship and lowered it into the water. Not only did it float, it trimmed itself to the wind, and it refused to capsize even when an enormous swell from a passing tug hit the real ship and exploded over the replica like a tidal wave. Despite its remarkable stability, it rode high in the water, maintaining about half a foot of freeboard. After they retrieved it, he went off to find a box of tools. That was easy enough, on a half-deserted ship, for a man who had learned how to kick in doors. When he returned, he used a chisel to open a space aft of the rear funnel. Putting his hand inside, he discovered that the hollow hull was spacious and dry. It took until morning to construct a little bed in the interior, and a hinged vent that, if a wave swept over it, would close tightly and then reopen.

When a rapidly strengthening sun promised the first hot day of spring, they put their infant in the ship and lowered the ship over the side. They watched it ride swiftly out into the green and sunny open water until they could see it no longer. She cried, because everything that she loved was soon to be lost.

"You leave your children," he said, "and they make their way. It would have been almost the same. . . ." Unable to continue, he looked at her face, at the weak mouth that was like a thin crooked line. No longer was he her protector. They had become terribly equal, and when they took one another in their arms it was unlike anything they had ever done before, for it was the end. The ship sailed that afternoon. The whistle thundered. Steam issued from its stacks and raced up in doubling whitened plumes.

The miniature *City of Justice* darted on the waves like a pony as it drifted in and out of whirling eddies in the tidal race between Brooklyn and Manhattan. No one saw it as it sailed amid the full-sized harbor traffic, on several occasions escaping being crushed like an egg beneath the bows of huge barges and steamships, or rammed by the ferryboats in their monotonous sleepwalks from one shore to another. With the fall of evening, it was pointed toward the Jersey shore and the Bayonne Marsh.

This was a mysterious place of unchartable tangled channels and capacious bays that exploded into sight after issuing from narrow water tunnels—a topography that had a life of its own, and was constantly altered by the busy engraving of the cloud wall. The *City of Justice* worked its way gently up the channels and through the reeds. In a wide bay that was more fresh than salt, due to the six rivers that poured through it to the sea, the *City of Justice* bumped up against a long white sandbar and came to rest. It stayed there throughout a warm night of a hundred million stars, without a peep from the child—who was rocked to sleep by the small waves on the lake.

The Baymen had a cryptic saying: "Truth is no rounder than a horse's eye." Whatever it meant, they passed it on from generation to generation as they hunted and fished. They poled through the reeds so swiftly that even kingfishers could move no faster. They were united so with the air and water of the marsh, moving through them like privileged natural forces, that they could outrun the cloud wall. Though few from the land had ever seen it, the sight of a group of ragged Baymen howling and shrieking as they raced ahead of the galloping cloud wall was extraordinary. For the cloud wall was quick enough to envelop eagles. But the Baymen could beat it even in canoes, their paddles pounding the water like great engines, grimaces upon their hairy ragged faces, the canoe bows planing dangerously, crashing through white water and broken reeds. They surged ahead of the cloud wall, and, when the case was over, threw themselves into the water to cool off, the way a blacksmith plunges his hot iron into a bulbous tub to hiss and puff.

Thus, the unkempt and cockeyed Baymen were not afraid of fishing or digging clams in the beautiful deserted lakes and channels near the great white wall. In fact, most of the time they wanted the cloud wall to act up, to sweep and scour the yellow bars and golden reeds, and light out over the water after them. They liked to race it in their thin canoes, and were the only people in the world who could outwit it: if it caught them, they knew some things to say that might make it change its mind about snatching them up. There was much about them that was remarkable and good. However, they were primitive, ignorant, violent, and dirty. Though this was perhaps a steep price to pay for access to the fecund shallow lakes at the foot of the cloud wall, it was the way they were.

In the last hours of the clear night when the *City of Justice* grounded itself in a bar on the lake, Humpstone John, Abysmillard, and Auriga Bootes, all Baymen, set out to fish for the fat red snappers that had run a maze of channels from the Hudson and found the lakes. The three Baymen took note that the cloud wall agitated about two miles in the distance. It thundered, churned, flowed, boiled, crackled, screamed, and sang—a rapids set perfectly on edge. They cast out their nets. The water was fresh, and the reeds had begun to sprout green shoots.

As the sun emerged, the wind fled before it, whistling in the reeds and over the sand and water. The light glistened and turned in front of their eyes; now gold, now red, now white or yellow; and tones arose from the water—tones like bells or oboes or the singing of choirs from unimagined worlds. When the wave of light broke into white foam at the base of the wall and fell back to fill the crucible of city and bay with its brightness and warmth, the Baymen felt the presence of something powerful and benevolent, as if the sound and light presaged a tidal wave of strong gold that someday would sweep over everything and collide with the wall. They had heard of it. They had heard of the omnipotent glow that would spread about the bays and the city, of the light that would make stone and steel translucent. They hoped someday to see it, but did not dream that they would. In the mornings, though, they watched its tailings and remnants sweep up against the shore.

The nets had been cast and pulled in several times when the fishermen stopped to rest and to partake of dried fish wafers, radishes, hard bread, and clam beer. The most stimulating of all alcoholic beverages, the Baymen's clam beer changed color with age and temperature, and was perfect when it was purple. That meant that it was cold, thick, and dry—an indescribable ambrosia that made mead taste like horse piss. They sat in their long canoe, eating silently. Auriga Bootes, whose eyes always combed the horizon and shifted about from sea to sky, stood up straight, and pointed. "A ship in the lake," he said, with great surprise, for the lake was far too shallow for ships. Humpstone John, an elder of the Baymen, looked up and saw nothing. Since he knew the dimensions of the estuary, he had adjusted his gaze for sighting a real ship and passed over the *City of Justice* by ten or twenty degrees.

"Where, Auriga Bootes?" he asked. Abysmillard glanced about, still chewing loudly, seeing nothing that might have passed for a ship.

"There, John, there, John," answered Auriga Bootes, still pointing in the same direction. Then Humpstone John saw it, too.

"It seems very far away," he said, "but it seems close as well. It isn't moving. Perhaps it has been spit out from the cloud wall and left aground. There may be a good cargo on board—guns, tools, implements, molasses—" at this, Abysmillard perked up, because, for him, molasses was a magnificent delicacy—"and there may be confused souls." They put down their food and began to paddle in the direction of the *City of Justice*. Faster than they thought, they glided up to the ship, and were looming over it.

Like an ape, Abysmillard touched his own body, feeling ribs, nose, and knees. He could not understand what was happening, and thought that he had grown to be a giant. The other two knew what it was, but the illusion remained because the ship had been skillfully crafted. The wood of spars and decks was browner than an oiled nut. The hull's simulated black steel was as dull and dark as the side of a bull. And the brass fittings were as tarnished as if they had been years at sea, not in a glass case.

"You see that," said Humpstone John, indicating the ship's name in white. "That's writing."

"What's writing?" asked Auriga Bootes, staring at the funnel, which he thought might be what Humpstone John called writing.

"That," said Humpstone John, pointing directly at the bow. Auriga Bootes leaned over and jiggled an anchor in his fingers.

"This?" he asked.

"No! The white stuff, there."

"Oh, that. That's writing, huh. What does it do?"

"It's like talking, but it makes no sound."

"It's like talking, but it makes no sound," Auriga Bootes repeated. Then he and Abysmillard laughed deep, fat, snorting laughs. Sometimes, they thought, Humpstone John, despite his wisdom, was truly a fool.

The miniature ship was not much of a prize, but they decided to take it home anyway, and attached a line to the bow so that they could tow it behind their canoe. Halfway across the lake the baby awoke and began to cry. The three Baymen halted in the middle of their strokes. Stock-still as their paddles dripped water, they tilted their heads to find the sound. Humpstone John rustled through a pile of burlap rags in front of him, thinking that one of the Baymen had left a baby in the rags by mistake, or put it there as a joke. He found no baby, but the baby's cries continued. Still gliding, he pulled on the rope, and the *City of Justice* came near. The noise was from inside. Humpstone John pulled a broadsword from his belt and cracked open the ship the way one cracks an egg with a knife. A wizard with the sword, like all Baymen, he judged the thickness and strength of the wood in the stroke of the steel, and penetrated no farther than was necessary to split the shell. The sword was back in his belt before it had had a chance to gleam in the sun, and the baby hung in midair as the two halves of the now-dead replica parted and upended. Auriga Bootes snatched the child before it hit the water, and tossed it onto the burlap rags. Then, without the slightest acknowledgment of what had happened, they continued paddling. There was no point in talking about it. Abysmillard could not have talked about it even had he wished to do so. For him, thick tongue-tied stump that he was, it was as if nothing had happened. And as far as the other two were concerned, there was now another mouth to feed, another child who would laugh and giggle in the huts.

He was one of them until he reached the age of twelve. They had called him Peter, and then, to tell him apart from the several other boys of the same name, had chosen for him a last name that fit the way they thought of him—as the child pulled from the lake. He quickly learned most of what they had to teach, and was good at the things they did. There was no formal training, and the children just picked up the skills of the Baymen as they grew. For example, the ability they had with swords was unequaled, demanding extraordinary strength and coordination. But, more than that, it required a free path to the deed of the blade itself, as if it had already been done and needed only to be confirmed. Peter Lake learned the sword at a stroke, when he was eleven.

He had been in the back of a canoe, paddling for Humpstone John as the old man threw out his weighted circle net. They saw a figure walking toward them along the flats that led to the cloud wall, which that day was turbulent and gray. When it was upset, it often did strange things. The man who approached seemed to have come from the barrier itself. He was dazed but pugnacious, either some sort of ancient Japanese warrior or an escapee from an asylum on Cape May. He came directly at them, hand on his sword, shouting in the strangest language that Humpstone John or Peter Lake had ever heard. It wasn't English, and it wasn't Bay. Surmising that the newcomer thought he was in another time or another country, Humpstone John said, "This is the marsh. You probably want Manhattan. If you stop shouting, we'll take you there, where you'll probably find others like yourself, and even if not, it's not the kind of place where anyone will notice your outlandish modes. And will you please stop your jabbering and speak English."

The warrior responded by stepping forward knee-deep in the water in a rapid pivoting stance that indicated the onset of combat. Humpstone John suspected that no matter how conciliatory he might be, there was going to be a fight. He sighed as the samurai, or whatever he was, drew a long silver sword and rushed the boat, screaming like someone who has been pushed off a cliff. Humpstone John threw his round net in the air, withdrew the broadsword from its scabbard, and handed it to Peter Lake. "You try it," he said. "It's a good way to learn."

The samurai charged toward them with deafening screams.

"Where do I hold it?" Peter Lake asked.

"Where do you hold what?"

"The sword."

"By the handle, of course. Hurry, now. . . ."

The warrior stood two feet from the canoe. His long heavy blade stretched from the back of his head to his ankles, held executioner's style before an impending stroke. His face was grimaced so that he looked like a blowfish. The sword began to travel.

"You'd better block that blow," Humpstone John said calmly. Peter Lake held his broadsword perpendicular to that of his opponent—just in time for a chilling clash of metal against metal.

"Now what, John?" Peter Lake said, as the warrior's sword slid off his own and cut deep into the gunwales of the canoe.

"Try an upward stroke under his sword arm. Quickly."

"He uses both arms, John," Peter Lake answered, ducking his head as a whining blow passed almost invisibly where his neck had been.

"That's true, I warrant." Humpstone John thought for a moment. "Try either one."

The opposing swordsman uttered a terrifying cry as he thrust his blade in a two-handed lunge straight at Peter Lake's heart. Peter Lake parried it, and it cut off a large part of Humpstone John's beard.

"Crap!" said Humpstone John. "Get to it already. I love my beard."

"All right," said the young Peter Lake, and moved the razor-sharp broadsword in a quick stroke up, cutting deep into his opponent's left arm. That seemed to awaken something in him, for he made several other moves, so fast that they were nearly invisible, so graceful that they seemed to be one motion, and came very close to disemboweling the attacker, who dropped his sword into the shallows and stumbled toward the cloud wall—which then obliged him as either ambulance or undertaker (no one ever knew).

"Shall I fish up his sword, John?" Peter Lake asked, still shaking, but enormously proud that he had survived his first combat.

"Whose sword?" Humpstone John, who had returned to fishing, wanted to know.

"The man I just fought."

"Oh, him. What, his sword? Crap, it's tin. Leave it where it lies."

Peter Lake could, just barely, outrace the cloud wall when it oscillated across the sand flats, and he knew that he would never go without food or shelter as long as there were reeds standing upright in the water, and fish, clams, and crabs swimming, scuttling, and lying at rest among them. He could recite tolerably well in Bay, while the elders stared into the dying fire, satisfied with his skill. He had just begun, like all the Bay children of that age, to sleep with his sister. The Baymen practiced this (which was why Abysmillard was what he was) without thinking for a minute that it might not be a good idea. Peter Lake was set upon his sister, Anarinda, very early on. He was not really her brother, and, anyway, she did not conceive—no one would have at first. Anarinda was very beautiful, and Peter Lake was delighted. He asked Abysmillard and Auriga Bootes how long one could keep on doing what he had just learned. Abysmillard did not know of such things, and Auriga Bootes referred Peter Lake to Humpstone John, who replied, "Oh, four or five hundred years, I guess, depending upon your virility, and upon what it is that you call a year."

Caring little for definitions, Peter Lake thought that he was in a really fine position, since whatever a year was, it seemed like eternity, and Anarinda's nakedness and the way things went when they rolled about together in the warmth of the hut were greatly diverting. If this would last for another four or five hundred years . . . well, what more could anyone ask? That spring he grew quite smug, and thinking that this state would span half a dozen centuries, he sang, danced, and walked about humming to himself little ditties that he made up about Anarinda, such as:

> Oh, Anarinda, breasts as round as clams,
> Thighs as smooth as flounder's soul,
> Hair as gold as hay.
> In you my bell shall toll,
> Anarinda, Anarinda, darling of the bay.

But this happiness lasted nowhere near five hundred years. In fact, it lasted not even a week, for Humpstone John informed him that he had to leave. He would not be able to stay with the Baymen, because he had not been born a Bayman. They had taken good care of him for twelve years. Now he was on his own.

A year or two later and he would have been dying to go across the bay, as were all the boys of that age. But he was still young enough to feel that the marsh was everything there was of the world, and to be happy that there seemed to be little more, which is exactly why they sent him packing. They knew that to survive in Manhattan he would have to know something of bitterness before he arrived. And bitter he would always be at the thought of how they decked him out before he paddled across. They gave him a shell crown and a feather necklace (their symbols of manhood), a good broadsword, a new net, a bag of fish wafers, and a jug of clam beer. They told him that with these things he would be well prepared for the city. He had never given Manhattan much thought, for it had seemed only like a lot of high gray mountains that shone at night. He was sad to leave, but imagined that there he would find fine inlets teeming with fish, comfortable huts full of anarindas, and a life not unlike the life he had known. He crossed over early one evening in late spring.

Manhattan, a high narrow kingdom as hopeful as any that ever was, burst upon him full force, a great and imperfect steel-tressed palace of a hundred million chambers, many-tiered gardens, pools, passages, and ramparts above its rivers. Built upon an island from which bridges stretched to other islands and to the mainland, the palace of a thousand tall towers was undefended. It took in nearly all who wished to enter, being so much larger than anything else that it could not ever be conquered but only visited by force. Newcomers, invaders, and the inhabitants themselves were so confused by its multiplicity, variety, vanity, size, brutality, and grace, that they lost sight of what it was. It was, for sure, one simple structure, busily divided, lovely and pleasing, an extraordinary hive of the imagination, the greatest house ever built. Peter Lake knew this even as he stood on the Bowery in his homespun, shell crown, and feather necklace, at five o'clock in the evening, on a Friday in May.

He held the jug of purple clam beer in one hand, and the oily raccoon-skin bag of fish wafers in the other. He was dumbfounded, but learning fast. The first thing to happen was the theft of his canoe the minute he stepped out of it onto a pier at South Street. Hardly had he turned his back when shadowy forms emerged from the mossy pilings and sucked it in with them as if into hell. Within five minutes he saw boys carrying its splintered pieces to be sold for firewood. By the time he reached the Bowery, the wood was burning underneath the crackling flesh of fowl, pigs, and cows roasting for sale to passersby. As soon as the flames had died and yet another pig or lamb been positioned for a new burn, the sidewalk cooks had sold the ashes to gray-colored human wrecks who lugged huge bags of cinder and ash for sale to chemical companies and greenhouses. Peter Lake approached one of them and pointed at the enormous sack which almost hid its porter but for his tiny wizened head and two bloodshot popped eyes. "That's my canoe," he said.

"What's your canoe?" inquired the bulky miserable.

"That," answered Peter Lake, still pointing to the sack.

"That's your canoe, huh," said the ashman, regarding Peter Lake up and down from his shell crown to his muskrat booties. "Well then, you won't mind if old Jake Salween uses it to sail to China, will you? Good day to you, m'boy! They'll soon be taking you to Overweary's."

"Overweary's?"

"As if you didn't know! Outta my way, you crazy midget."

It seemed to Peter Lake that the city, or as much as he had seen of it, was similar to the cloud wall. Its motion, the sounds erupting from all directions, the great vitality, struck him as a cloud wall laid flat, like a boiling carpet. But, whereas the wall was white, the city was a palette of upwelling colors. Its forms and geometry entranced him—the orange blaze in clear upper windows; a gas lamp's green and white bell-like glare; leaping tongues of fire; red-hot booming chambers in the charcoal; shoe-black horses trotting airily at the head of varnished carriages; peaked and triangular roofs; the ballet of the crowds as they took stairs, turned corners, and forged across streets; the guttural noises of machinery (he heard in the distance a deep sound like that of the cloud wall, but it was the sound of steam engines, flywheels, and presses); sails that filled the ends of streets with billows of white or sharp angular planes, and then collapsed into the bordering buildings or made of themselves a guillotine; the shouts of costumed sellers; buildings (he had never seen buildings) deep inside of which were rows of sparkling lamps (he had never seen lamps), small trees and tables, and acres of beautiful upright women who, unlike the Baywomen, wore clothes that made them look like silky-skinned jungle birds, though more bosomy and at times more aloof. He had never seen uniforms, trolleys, glass windows, trains, and crowds. The city exploded upon him, bursting through the ring of white shells that crowned his head. He staggered about the fire and tumult of Broadway and the Bowery, not understanding everything he saw. For instance, a man turned a handle on a box, and music came out, while a small being, half-animal and half-man, danced about on the street and collected things in his hat. Peter Lake tried to talk to him. The man turning the handle said it would be wise to give the creature money.

"What's money?" asked Peter Lake.

"Money is what you give the monkey, or the monkey pee on you," replied the organ-grinder.

" 'Money is what you give the monkey . . . or the monkey pee on you,' " repeated Peter Lake, trying to understand. When he realized that the little man in the red suit was "the monkey," he realized as well that the monkey was peeing on him. He jumped back, determined (among other things) to get some money.

In an hour he was more tired than he had ever been; his feet ached and his muscles were tight; his head felt like a copper caldron that had been thrown down the stairs. The city was like war— battles raged all around, and desperate men were on the street in crawling legions. He had heard the Baymen tell of war, but they had never said it could be harnessed, its head held down, and made to run in place. On several score thousand miles of streets were many cataclysmic armies interacting without formation—ten thousand prostitutes on Broadway alone; half a million abandoned children; half a million of the lame and blind; scores of thousands of active criminals locked in perpetual combat with as many police; and the vast number of good citizens, who in their normal lives were as fierce and rapacious as other cities' wild dogs. They did not buy and sell, they made killings and beat each other out. They did not walk on the streets, they forged ahead like pikemen, teeth clenched and hearts pounding. The divisions between all the different stripes of desperado and the regular run-of-the-mill inhabitants were so fine and subtle that it was nearly impossible to identify a decent man. A judge who passed sentence on a criminal might deserve ten times more severe a condemnation, and might someday receive it from a colleague four times again as corrupt. The entire city was a far more complicated wheel of fortune than had ever been devised. It was a close model of the absolute processes of fate, as the innocent and the guilty alike were tumbled in its vast overstuffed drum, pushed along through trap-laden mazes, caught dying in airless cellars, or elevated to platforms of royal view.

Peter Lake had no more idea why he felt and sensed what he did than a patient in surgery has of what exactly is happening to him as he is sawed and cut. He was overcome by feeling. The city was a box of fire, and he was inside, burning and shaking, pierced continually by sights too sharp to catalog. He dragged himself about the maze of streets, lugging his purple beer and his fish wafers. There were no bays, no huts, no soft sandy places in which to lie down.

But there were anarindas. There were so many anarindas that he wondered if he were sane. They passed everywhere, to the side, above, below, deep within the glass-fronted boxes, like fish swimming enticingly in schools, gravityless and laughing. The supply was unending; it flowed like a river. Their voices were as fine as bells, crystal, birds, and song. He decided that he would do best if he picked an anarinda who would take him home with her. They could eat the fish wafers, drink the clam beer, shed their clothes, and roll about in whatever soft places these anarindas slept. He would choose the best one he could find. What anarinda, after all, could resist him in his shells, feathers, and furs, with an entire jug of clam beer at his side? Many anarindas passed, all fine. But the one he chose was special indeed. She was almost twice as tall as he was. Her broad face was so perfectly beautiful above a high gray collar (upon which was pinned an emerald) that she seemed like a goddess. She carried a sable wrap, and she had other jewels besides the emerald. It was wonderful, especially since she was about to step into a shiny black box pulled by two muscular horses.

Peter Lake approached her, indicated by a snap of the wrist first the bag of fish wafers and then the jug, and then held his chin up and stamped his feet in the insolent mating gesture of the Baymen. The shell crown jiggled and his feathers flew. At first, he thought that he had succeeded, because her eyes were wide with amazement. But then he saw an expression of fear move across her lovely

55

features like a cloud across the moon. The door slammed in his face, and the box moved away.

He repeated this seduction a number of times, but even the most ragged of anarindas disdained him. Exhausted as he was, and dejected, he wandered still, searching for a place to stay, for night had already fallen. Although he did not know where he was going, the streets were so tangled and numerous that he was never in the same place twice, and everywhere he went he found arresting scenes (a dog turning somersaults, a man wrapped in a white sheet cursing the crowd, the crash of two hearses). After three hours (it was only eight o'clock) the Bayonne Marsh seemed as faint and distant as another world, and he knew that he was now lost in a long and magnificent dream. Scenes and colors mounted, driven like the waves of a storm, until he reeled with confusion.

Then he came to a small park, a square surrounded by stone buildings. It was quiet, dark green, and as peaceful and promising as the emerald on its field of gray angora. There were trees, soft grass, and dark spaces. In the center was a fountain. All around the perimeter, gas lamps shone through the trees as they moved in the wind, casting patterns of light and dark. And an anarinda was dancing there with another anarinda. One was small and had red hair and a green shirt. The other was much larger and far more sensual (even though she was not much more than Peter Lake's age) and she had flying blond hair, red cheeks, and a hot cream-colored shirt. They were dancing around the fountain, arm in arm, in an old Dutch dance, their cheeks touching, their hands entwined. They had no music; they hummed. And there was no reason for them to be dancing that Peter Lake could see, except that it was an exceptionally beautiful night.

They wore loose-fitting brown shoes which clapped the macadam with a hollow jolly sound, and they dipped and turned with such fun that Peter Lake wanted to join in. So he did, resting jug, bag, and sword in a pile before he jumped out into the open space to dance. He danced somewhat like the Indians, from whom the Baymen had long before learned clam dances and strange roundelays in imitation of wind-blown reeds. Because the two girls were so happy, Peter Lake did a moon dance. He jumped and tucked, and played games from one fur-wrapped foot to another. They twirled about him as soon as his clinking shells came to their attention. The picture they made together was pleasing to passersby, who threw pieces of silver on the ground at their feet. This stuff, Peter Lake knew, was money. But though he had come to know what it was, he did not understand it for a long time after that, being puzzled by several of its mysterious rules. The first was that it was almost impossible to get. The second, that, once you had it, it was almost impossible to keep. The third, that these laws applied only to each individual but not to anyone else. In other words, though money was impossible to get and impossible to keep, for everyone else it flowed in by the bucketful and stayed forever. The fourth rule was that money liked to live in clean, shiny, colorful places of fine texture and alluring shadows. A lot of it seemed to reside at the edge of the park in tall houses of deep reddish-brown stone. On the other side of these houses' clear windows, warm lights were shining and wide clear panels of maroon, red, green, and white appeared, as did the sparkle of silver and the glow of flame. He could see this even while dancing. And he could feel that he was excluded from such places, even though the people who lived there threw coins at him for doing the moon dance. That was a further mystery. They threw coins at him for doing something he loved, something that was easy, something that he would have done anyway. When Peter Lake danced by the night fountain in the dark green square, and was given coins for his dancing, he became a thief. Though it would take a long time for him to understand the principle, it was that to be paid for one's joy is to steal. Having learned this lesson even if he did not understand it, he felt a bond with thieves, which was good, for the two girls were spielers.

"What are spielers?" he asked them as they splashed their reddened sweaty faces with cold water from the fountain.

"Where are you from," said the big one, "that you don't know what are spielers?"

"I'm from the marsh."

They didn't know what he was talking about. As they distributed the money they told him about spieling. "We dance, like in a crowd, and we get their attention. They throw money . . ."

"Money is what you give the monkey, or the monkey pee on you," said Peter Lake. The two girls looked at one another.

"They throw money, and Little Liza Jane picks their pockets. That's spieling."

"Why were you dancing now, after they stopped throwing money?"

"Dunno," said the big one. "Why not?"

The big one was Little Liza Jane, and the little one was Dolly. There had been a third, a dark girl named Bosca, but she had died not long before.

"What did she die of?" asked Peter Lake.

"The washtub," answered Little Liza Jane, without explaining further.

They took him in as a replacement for Bosca. He would dance with Dolly while Little Liza Jane picked pockets. He asked them if they had a soft place to sleep, and they said they did. It took them three hours to get there. They crossed several small rivers and five streams. They wound down a hundred crooked alleys that looked like opera sets. They passed over great bridges, through commercial squares where men ate fire and meat was roasted on swords, and by half a dozen wide doors that led far into smoky factories that pounded like hearts. As they walked, Peter Lake sang the sounds that he heard coming from within the iron workplaces—"Boom, atcha atcha rapumbella, boom, bok, atcha atcha, zeeeeeee-ah! bahlaka bahlaka bahlaka, ooooh-tak! chik chik chik chik! beema! um baba um baba, dilla dilla dilla, mash! um baba um baba, dilla dilla dilla okk!" He noticed that in the city people walked not only like chargers but in strange rhythmic dances—their bodies moving up and down, their arms going in and out, their hips tattooing in womanly zeal (if they were women, and, sometimes, even if not). He asked the two spielers if there were a war, or if something terrible had happened, because he could not understand the leaping fires, the homeless armies, the rubble, the commotion. They looked around, and said that nothing seemed to be out of the ordinary. He was ready to faint from exhaustion.

They reached a street of symmetrical tenements. The spielers lived not in the tenements themselves but within the hidden square they formed. They went through a dark whitewashed tunnel and discovered a vast concealed court surrounded by perhaps a hundred buildings. In the center was a broken garden not yet revived by spring, except for a dense growth of weeds. At its edge, dwarfed by the tenements, was a little shack. The spielers lived not in the shack but in its basement. They descended through a cellar door and found a small dark room with a tiny window near the ceiling. Some leftover coals glowed in the belly of an oil-drum stove. Dried vegetables hung on the wall, as did a pot and a few utensils. The one piece of furniture was an enormous bed with uneven legs that gave it a list, and upon it were half a dozen tired pillows, sheets, and blankets. Surprisingly, they were not too dirty. This was the soft place in which the spielers slept.

"Little Liza Jane lit a tallow lamp, and Dolly threw some wood in the stove," said Dolly after it was done. She often spoke of herself in the third person. "It will take an hour for the water to boil and the vegetables to cook." Peter Lake showed them the fish wafers and explained how to make a stew by shredding them and tying them in knots before tossing them in the boiling water, to improve the flavor.

They thought they would rest before they ate, but instead they drank most of the clam beer. Little Liza Jane pulled off her shirt in the crossing of her arms, and Dolly followed. Then they took off their skirts. Peter Lake was already in quite a float because of the clam beer, and this appealed to him rather strongly. Little Liza Jane was sixteen, and fully developed. Dolly was still pubescent, but what she lacked in volume she made up for in freshness, and, anyway, Little Liza Jane had volume enough for two. Her dancing bosom filled Peter Lake's eyes. He thought that what was now bound to occur would be the same as it had been with Anarinda, but with two anarindas. Moaning with pleasure, he removed his own clothes. This was as difficult as pulling a sidesaddle through a lobster trap. When finally he was free, he opened his eyes to feast upon the many breasts and legs in the bed. But they were all tangled up in one another already, and the two girls were breathing in slow lascivious hisses. He heard a small trickle of sucking. What was going on here? He checked to see if both were, as he had thought, anarindas. Both were anarindas—there was no doubt about that. This was something new, but since everything about the city was new, he was not surprised. He took note. They were not interested in him, although they let him enter and satisfy himself several times, after which he was not interested in them. Then, hours later, no one was interested in anyone anymore but only in the stew. They ate in silence, and went to sleep just before the sun came up.

As if they were smokers of opium, the three of them half heard the voice of Little Liza Jane. She said, "Tomorrow we'll go to Madison Square. There are a lot of suckers in Madison Square." And the gray smoke of sleep filled their little chamber and pressed them down pleasantly upon their soft, tilted bed.

The next morning, Peter Lake saw the city through different eyes, as he would from then on whenever he awoke. It was never the same from one day to the next. Dark, close, smoky afternoons; oceans of rain; autumn days clearer than crystal paperweights; sunshine and shadow—no one city existed.

He arose early. The two girls were caught up in the blankets. Peter Lake dressed and was quickly outside, the first to see the sun light the highest chimney top of the surrounding tenements. Standing in the garden, waist-deep in weeds, he wondered what the insides of these structures were like. He had never been in a building. For all he knew, when he opened the door he would see a new city within, as vast and entertaining as the one he had just discovered. On that late spring morning, almost summer, he went to the nearest tenement door and swung it open, expecting to see as if from a high hill a great city in winter laid out before him in a cold dawn. Someday, perhaps, he would. But now there was only darkness and a sickening smell. He cautiously negotiated a flight of stairs (having been raised on the marsh, he knew nothing of height) and came to a landing. Cord and twine had been tied all about the banisters. Children playing, he thought. He saw in the blackness that the dark walls were scratched and gouged. This was a horrible place, far from water, sky, or sand. He would have left and forgotten it had he not for some reason been impelled to go up one more flight of stairs. He was in the heart of the building now, as far away from the light as if he had been deep in the grave. He was just about to turn around when suddenly he became motionless with the graceful and quick self-restraint of a hunter who has stumbled upon his prey. A child stood before him, not an ordinary child, or so he hoped. It could not have been more than three or four, and was dressed in a filthy black smock. Its head was enormous, shaven, distorted. The brows and crown protruded as if to burst. In back, it was the same. Peter Lake winced. This creature, standing in the rubble, had its hand in its mouth, and was leaning against the wall, staring blankly ahead. Its jaws trembled, and the hideous swollen skull rocked back and forth in convulsive movements. Peter Lake's instincts told him that there was not much life left for it to live. He wanted to help, but he had no experience or memory to guide him. He could neither leave nor stay. He watched it shake and bob in the near-darkness until, somehow, he fell reeling back into the light.

Such a thing as the child left alone to die in the hallway was unknown on the marsh. But here, in the dawn, was mortality itself. In the city were places to fall from which one could never emerge— dark dreams and slow death, the death of children, suffering without grace or redemption, ultimate and eternal loss. The memory of the child stayed with him. But that was not to be the end of it, for reality went around in a twisting ring. Even the irredeemable would be redeemed, and there was a balance for everything. There had to be.

He went back to the spielers.

"Leave your sword," the girls had said, "or the leatherheads will take after you."

A Bayman never parted from his sword except to swim or roll. "I wouldn't leave my sword here," Peter Lake said, thinking that he had come up with a wonderful new phrase, "for a lot of money."

"That's a good one," said Dolly. "I hope you spiel better than that."

Madison Square was just as far as the park where he had met them. After a ferry, two bridges, a train, and half a dozen tunnels, they had to weave for several hours through a labyrinth of streets, passages, alleys, and arcades, all exploding with life. Peter Lake was exhausted even before he got to work. But then, in the middle of the wonderful park surrounded by high buildings interconnected by a web of aerial bridges, he began a series of moon dances, clam dances, and reed sways. Dolly danced around him, while Little Liza Jane walked to and fro in the crowd, picking pockets.

Little Liza Jane (a beauty, really) had a perfect venal sense, and when she saw a fat man in a plaid suit waltz out of the Bank of Turkey, she went for him like a bee. She discovered in his overcrowded wallet exactly $30,000. Trembling, she made Peter Lake stop a wild clam dance and accompany her and Dolly to a corner of the park. There they divided up equally, with Peter Lake's share of the morning's take amounting to $10,004.28. Little Liza Jane said that the police would be after them if the fat man complained, so it would be wise to break up and meet again that night. "Right here," she said. "Meanwhile, put the money in a bank."

"What's that?" asked Peter Lake. She taught him to read the word "bank" and told him that if he put money in the building where the word was written, the money would be safe. Peter Lake readily accepted this advice, and they parted. He found a bank, walked inside, tucked his pile of new bills neatly against a wall, and left, assured that he now had money, so that no monkeys would pee on him. With that out of the way, he wandered into the glass palace at Madison Square, intending to pass some time until work resumed in the evening.

Machines. Everywhere there were machines, and more machines. At first, Peter Lake thought they were animals that had learned how to dance in one place. For him, the metallic underworld, or overworld, was immediately glorious and irresistibly hypnotic. Never before had he seen such stuff. Light flooded in the windows and cut through high squadrons of palms. A suspended orchestra played swaybacked music attuned to the strange mechanical dances. From the center of an overfattened block of steel shapes, a green piston struggled to rise, gasping. Wheels of all colors everywhere trembled and reversed, and then set to rolling as if chased by a dog. Balls on rods rose and fell; gears ticked and tocked; slammer blocks crashed together repetitiously like angered elk. Little plumes of steam riffled through the palms, and surprise squirts of water and oil were spat out sideways from monstrous prestidigitating engines as large as a city square. Peter Lake loved these things. And there were two thousand of them on the floor, each and every one laboring and puffing. For the first time, he was glad to have been turned away from the marsh. In the movement of the machines, he saw beyond everything he had yet known. Like waves, wind, and water, they moved. They were, in themselves, power and elation.

Wandering among the machines—two thousand machines!—he grew dizzy and ecstatic. He didn't know what a single one of them was for, so he decided to ask. Standing next to each sputtering behemoth was a guardian of sorts, actually a salesman. Peter Lake had never met a salesman, and it is strange to imagine that a man with a fifty-ton $200,000 machine to hawk would spend any time at all with a twelve-year-old boy dressed in muskrat booties, skins, feathers, and shells. But all Peter Lake had to do was walk up to one of the giant engines and say to its guardian, "This, what is this?"

"What is this? What is this! This! my dear sir, is the Barkington-Payson Semi-Automatic Level-Seeking Underwater Caisson Drill and Dynamite Spacer! You will not find, in all this exhibition or in all the world, another SALSUCDADS that even compares with it. Let's start with the design. Come over here to the finely crafted pumble shoe fabricated in Düsseldorf. Notice the solid turkey piece, the gleaming yodelagnia, and the pure steel bellows spring. Now, the turkey piece is directly linked to a superbly calibrated meltonian rod, at the base of which you will find an unusual feature common only to top-of-the-line SALSUCDADS—a blue oscar chuck! This is the best quality you can get. I use it myself. I don't normally tell people this, but I'll tell you. I wouldn't go near any other SALSUCDADS. I swear, I'd trade my wife for it. Look at those intake blades. Have you ever seen such intake blades? The crust drill alone is worth the entire price of the machine. Pure salinium! A doubly protected fen wheel! Shielded from the pacer by a rock-solid tandy piece! Open it and feel the smooth calabrian underglide. Now, let's get to the point. You have half a million dollars of undercracking to budge across. Do you use a cheap piece of cat crap? Of course not, not someone like you. I know an expert when I look him in the eye. You can't fool me. You, my friend, are one of God's own mechanics! A craftsman like you wants to budge across with something solid and fine, something dependable and well constructed, the Barkington-Payson. Come over here and inspect the whistle pip. Pure volpinium! Now, let me let you in on a little secret about the price. . . ."

Peter Lake listened to him for two and a half hours. The boy's mouth hung open as he strained to understand every word. He thought that this, along with picking pockets and red-robed monkeys, was one of the cornerstones of the civilization into which he had tumbled. But he was interrupted by two police officers and a priest, who seized him, tied his hands behind his back, took him from the sparkling exhibition hall, put him in a prison wagon full of children, and drove him off to Reverend Overweary's Home for Lunatic Boys.

All over the city, children without parents could be found huddled together like rabbits, sleeping in the warmth of daylight, in barrels and cellars and wherever there was a little quiet and stillness. At night, the cold set them in motion and flung them into the arms of adventures and depredations for which children have never been suited and never will be. There were more than half a million of them, and they succumbed as fast or faster than did their elders to diseases and to violence, so that as often as not the coffins in potter's field were of diminutive and touching proportions: gravediggers could sometimes handle two or three at a time. No one knew the children's names (in some cases they had not even had names), and no one ever would. Sometimes people of good conscience would ask, "What happens to these children?" meaning all the children on the streets, summer and winter. The answer was that some grew up to work or steal; some passed from institution to institution, or cellar to cellar; and the rest were buried—out in the fields beyond the city, where it was quiet and flat and full of scrub.

Children sometimes lost their senses and wandered about, insane. And so there was the Overweary Home, set up to provide shelter and training for boys of the street who had gone mad. In one of their sweeps, Reverend Overweary's associates had noticed Peter Lake because of his costume.

He discovered rather quickly that the home was ruled by three men. Reverend Overweary himself was a tragic figure, always incapacitated by his deeply felt compassion for the boys. He was frequently in tears, and suffered greatly because of the sufferings of others. Because of this, he had neither the time nor the energy to supervise properly his second in command, Deacon Bacon, and Deacon Bacon was sure to find in each new batch a few boys who responded with vigor to his direct and enthusiastic attentions during the first delousing. The moment of truth came when Deacon Bacon joined the happy boys in the steaming baths, ready to apply the patubic acid. Peter Lake refused to have the patubic acid applied by the deacon, insisting upon doing it himself. Some of the new internees simply did not know. Some were eager for the approach of the kindly looking six-footer with horn-rimmed glasses and a nose like the beak of a bird. Things soon sorted themselves out (as they always do), and Reverend Overweary looked the other way as Deacon Bacon retired with his entourage for days at a time to a cottage which was furnished and decorated like a sultan's front parlor on an isle in the Sea of Marmara.

But who was Reverend Overweary to chastise his deacon? His house stood like a palace, dwarfing even the cell blocks of gray stone in which more than two thousand boys lived at any one time. Reverend Overweary threw extravagant balls to which he invited the rich, the intelligentsia, and visiting royalty. They came because the food was good and because they thought that he was a man of means who had channeled a personal fortune of millions into sheltering his charges. Quite the opposite. The boys supported him, for in the guise of training and education he leased them out in gangs to anyone who needed them. The going rate for unskilled labor was four to six dollars a day, twelve hours, no nonsense. Overweary had his boys out every day at five dollars a head. He spent a dollar on their upkeep, and thus realized a profit of about $8,000 a day; less, actually, for the totals were constantly eroded by sickness, death, and escape (the three of which often combined in a unified process). The compassionate reverend got the boys off the street, taught them how to work, saved them from potter's field, and took in several million dollars a year. When the boys left, they left without a cent.

Peter Lake stayed until he was almost fully grown. Though he was a slave, he was in paradise, this because of the third force in the equilibrium of the Overweary Home—Reverend Mootfowl.

The day that Peter Lake was seized in the machinery hall, Reverend Mootfowl had been in charge of the sweep. To the irritation of the police who accompanied him, he had insisted upon visiting the exhibition because he was unable to resist any display of technology, engineering, or machinery. He had been among the very first to staff the home, when things had not been so well organized, and prior to his "ordination" Overweary had sent him through a bunch of technical colleges. Mootfowl seemed to have no emotions, desires, or concerns, except those of metalworking, smithing, machine building, pump design, beam raising, cable spinning, and structural engineering. He was forever at the forge or workbench, crafting, cutting, designing. He lived steel, iron, and timber. He could fabricate anything. He was a mad craftsman, a genius of tools.

Peter Lake soon became one of the elite half-hundred that worked day and night in the glare of the forge. Brought to the subject early and hard, they became master mechanics, and they and Mootfowl were the right people in the right time, for the city had just begun to mechanize. Engines had come alive, and lighted every corner, crowning themselves in plumes of smoke and steam. Once they had been started, slowly, surely, there would never be an end to their rhythmic splendor. They added to the body of the city not just muscle and speed, but a new life for the tireless ride to the future. A staggering number of disparate things had to be strung together. Electricity was being introduced throughout—a savage, speedy, sparkling gleam. Steam in a honeycomb of tunnels, great engines to drive the dynamos, trains underneath the streets, and buildings built higher and higher, were a new world of and for mechanics. As the machines began their ascension, when the city itself became a machine, millions worked day and night in a fury to attend the birth, to make sure that the right things were done, to provide the steel and stone and hard tools with which the pulsing heart would be sustained.

Builders and machinists came from everywhere to layer the city in new steel. They were able to use materials as fast as the materials could be produced. Pennsylvania, an entire wilderness, became their smoking hearth. They stripped the forests just for frames to help the ironwork. They mined, logged, and blasted, and brought everything to the city to be put in order. Not surprisingly, they had a never-ending need for skillfully crafted small pieces. These were the things of steel that Peter Lake learned to mill and forge—gaskets, bolts, rocker arms, seals, platens, spokes—parts that had to be drawn from seething fires or machined straight and true. He had to learn as well how to tend the engines that powered the machines, to master the construction of the turbines that kept his fires white-hot, the intricate cam action of the automatic stokers, electrical systems, gears and transmissions, gasoline engines, pressure boilers, metallurgy, stress engineering—in short, the vast traditional physics of those who called themselves mechanics.

They worked in a huge shed that roared and glowed with dozens of fires and was littered with oily blackened tools of heavy steel. As the machines and flames sang together, they sounded like a percussion orchestra gone wild. The boys wore black leather aprons and heavy gloves. They had their own society among the fires and anvils, and they stayed on the job sixteen hours a day. Mootfowl himself worked twenty hours or more. The income from their skilled industry was substantial, but they cared only for the work. They traveled about the city on jobs and were known by their black aprons, their uncanny skills, and their insane devotion to their crafts—at which they became better and better, fulfilling the demands of the age.

He, Mootfowl, wore a Chinese hat to protect his hair from being singed by the forge when he knelt down on the oily floor to inspect the readiness of an excited piece of steel. The way he handled hot metal was a marvel of tenderness and dispatch. He could strike the

67

precise and necessary blow needed to create a strong thing from a seething moltenness. Mootfowl was quite tall. Even when Peter Lake was fully grown, he felt half Mootfowl's size. And Mootfowl had a rugged face of many handsome planes, sooty and shining, in which rested two sparkling owl's eyes. Each time he saw those eyes, Peter Lake was reminded of his days with the Baymen, when he would sometimes have for breakfast a hot roasted owl, buttered and sizzling. But those days were long over. Under Mootfowl's tutelage, he learned to read and write, to use mathematics, to bargain skillfully in the matter of jobs and commissions, and to know the city well enough to find his way about. Since half the boys were Irish, Peter Lake learned to speak in a flexible and true Irish dialect. He liked it well enough—it was like riding the waves—and he found after a few years that he could speak in no other way, except to recall slowly articulated phrases from lays in Bay. Still, he was often saddened by the loss of his original self, whatever that had been. He was not really a Bayman, not really Irish, and only partly one of Mootfowl's boys, since, unlike the gamy five-year-olds who were to be seen in a corner of the shed, learning to work with miniature tools, he had been apprenticed relatively late. He was not sure to what he had to be loyal. But he assumed that this uncertainty, like the other torments suffered by his fellow "lunatics," would someday vanish.

Meanwhile, Mootfowl and his group were ever at work as the city's structures took their places one upon the other, faster than reef-building corals. Each tower had a minute of free view, after which it would spend the rest of eternity contemplating the shins of its competitors. Not so the great bridges. They flowed out over the rivers, and would have airy views and be alone forever. Mootfowl worshiped bridges. He had worked on several, and when he heard that another was to be flung over a wide bend of the East River, toward Brooklyn, he was all feathers and wine for days, since he knew that a bridge of that length would require specially forged components and expert repairs. One of his more holy moments was when he told his boys about the time that he mended some broken ferris joints for Colonel Roebling after the four main cables of the Brooklyn Bridge had been spun across the river. Mootfowl had hung high above the water, as dizzy as a bird in a storm, with a forge hanging by his side. There he did the work, to the delight of thousands crossing below on the Fulton ferry.

"Jackson Mead," Mootfowl said with reverence and admiration, "has come from beyond the Ohio with a hundred good men and tons of money and steel from God knows where, to start another bridge. They arrived after a storm. The white wall had imprisoned the countryside for days and days. Just as it was lifting, out charged their train, parting the mist on the Erie Lackawanna tracks. It was a great surprise to the farmers, who said that the train hit the bottom of the curtain. They say, boys, that the top of the train was scraped and torn, that it shone from contact with the underside of the wall.

"Be that as it may, Jackson Mead is here, and the bridge will be going up. We should say prayers for it."

"Why?" asked one of the forge boys, a small adenoidal fellow who was always very skeptical.

Mootfowl glared at him. "A bridge," he proclaimed, "is a very special thing. Haven't you seen how delicate they are in relation to their size? They soar like birds; they extend and embody our finest efforts; and they utilize the curve of heaven. When a catenary of steel a mile long is hung in the clear over a river, believe me, God knows. Being a churchman, I would go as far as to say that the catenary, this marvelous graceful thing, this joy of physics, this perfect balance between rebellion and obedience, is God's own signature on earth. I think it pleases Him to see them raised. I think that is why the city is so rich in events. The whole island, you see, is becoming a cathedral."

"Does that leave out the Bronx?" someone asked.

"Yes," Mootfowl replied.

They put down their tools and bent their heads, and with the fires singing behind them, they prayed for the new bridge. As soon as they finished, Mootfowl sprang up like a steel spring. "Work," he commanded. "Work through the night. Tomorrow we'll apply for employment on the new bridge."

Not much was known about Jackson Mead except that he had placed many fine suspension bridges over the great rivers of the

West, some of which had taken years to complete and had been built to span nearly bottomless canyons and gorges. He was quoted in the newspapers as having said that a city could be truly great only if it were a city of high bridges. "The map image of London," he had lectured during a press conference in the offices of the bridge company, "and of Paris, too, compared to that of San Francisco or New York, is boring. To be magnificent, a city cannot resemble a round cradled organ, a heart-or-kidney-shaped thing suffocated by a vast green body. It must project, extend, fling itself in all inviting directions—over the water, in peninsulas, hills, soaring towers, and islands linked by bridges." The press had wondered why he included San Francisco in his examples, since there were no bridges there; and he had said, with a smile, "My mistake."

The papers, and the ladies, made much of his physical appearance. He was six feet and eight inches tall, but not skinny. He had snowy white hair and a mustache to match, and he wore white vested suits with a platinum chain to tether his watch, which was almost as big as a clock, but which, in his large hand, did not seem so. His excellent health and physique made it difficult to reckon his age. People said that he was so tremendous and robust, and that his eyes were so blue, because he ate raw buffalo meat, bathed in mineral water, and drank eagle urine. When publicly confronted with this, he said, "Yes, of course it's true," and then burst out laughing.

There were those who loved him, and those who did not. Peter Lake was awed when he, Mootfowl, and the forty-nine others were trooped into a sparsely furnished office, and there was Jackson Mead, like an oversized painting. Next to him, Mootfowl seemed like just a statuette. The image that came to Peter Lake was of Jackson Mead as bridegroom, and Mootfowl the representation of him soon to stand upon a cake. The young apprentice had to close his mouth, for he found it hanging open in wonder. And he made a conscious effort to narrow his eyes, which, as if to match his mouth, had become the size of half-dollars.

He couldn't see how anyone could hate this man, or report that he was hard and cruel. After all, there he was in white, his hair and mustache as fluffy as down, a soothing, balanced countenance, a satisfied man, a study in calm. Precisely this, Peter Lake discovered, was why people hated him. He got things done, and there was no hesitation about him. Others, weighted by ambivalence and uncertainty, envied someone who knew what he was meant to do and why—as if he had had a few centuries to solve the normal problems of existence and had then turned his attention to bridge building.

After Mootfowl explained their reason for being there, Jackson Mead said that it seemed like an attractive proposition, that he needed skilled smiths, mechanics, and machinists. But, he said, he was not convinced that these boys, eager as they were, were equal to the task.

"In anticipation of that, sir," replied Mootfowl, "I have designed a test. Choose, if you will, any of my boys, and assign them as difficult an operation as might be encountered. We are willing to be evaluated in such a manner." He stepped back, nervous and proud.

Jackson Mead said that he would hire them all if the boy that he chose could forge a heptagonal ferris piece without appreciable distortion. When he stood up to survey the applicants, it was as if he had climbed into a tower. They, in turn, felt a collective adolescent chill that turned to ice when the snowy-haired bridge builder pointed directly at a little fat boy huddled in the back, and said, "Him. A chain is only as strong as its weakest link, and that looks to me like the weak link."

He had chosen young Cecil Mature—five foot one, two hundred pounds, a face packed with untenable fat, and two black smiling slits where his eyes were supposed to have been. He was a squash cook at the home, who had begged to be made a mechanic. He wore a crenellated beanie that fit in perfect roundness over his waxed crew cut. His arms were like sausages, and when he waddled around quickly in his black apron he looked like a cannonball come alive. He had arrived fairly recently at Overweary's, his origins a mystery, though he claimed to have vague memories of life on an English herring boat. He was fourteen, and seemed not to know much of the world.

When made to understand that he had been chosen for the test, he broke into a joyous smile and ran out to the forge. Everyone followed, wondering what would happen. They liked him, it was true, but in the way that you like an awkward dog that loses its footing and skis down the stairs. Mootfowl had yet to draw out the fine strands of Cecil Mature's intelligence. The boy was eager, but seldom did things right. So, when he heated up a ferris piece and took it to the anvil, they winced. Each blow was more damaging than the one before. After five minutes, the ferris piece was badly mangled, but still capable of salvation. Cecil Mature put down his hammer and took a step backward. He adjusted his hat and peered through his slitlike eyes at the half-dead ferris piece. Then he stepped back to the anvil and really began to do it in. The ferris piece had been at one time a complicated jointure that looked like a cross between a carriage wheel and an arch. After being pounded for fifteen minutes by Cecil Mature, it was once again a rocky ore, something that looked, in fact, just like a newly fallen meteorite. When he was finished, Cecil Mature delicately stepped back into the group of boys and was quickly hidden among them. Jackson Mead thanked a whitened and speechless Mootfowl (who had not known that Cecil was along), and departed in his carriage to inspect a new shipment of steel braces.

Their single-file walk back to the workshop was taken by many to have been a funeral procession without a corpse. Mootfowl dismissed them, and they remained idle for a week. During this time, Mootfowl became deeply despondent, and lay all day, dejected, on top of his enormous tool trolley, staring at the skylight ablaze with the sun. Then he summoned Peter Lake.

Overjoyed, because he knew an active Mootfowl was indomitable, Peter Lake rushed to find his mentor furiously working on a framelike contraption which he had built in the middle of the workshop. Peter Lake thought that it was a new machine that they would show to Jackson Mead, and so redeem themselves.

He helped Mootfowl with some adjustments, but still did not understand what he was building, or why Mootfowl seemed crazed with excitement. "That's it," said Mootfowl, "only one last thing left. When I give the word, hit this bar with a sledgehammer, as hard as you can. I have to make one last measurement, one last fastening, and it is a matter of precision.'' Mootfowl disappeared behind a wooden shield through which ran the steel rod, and said, ''With all your strength, Peter Lake, strike now!'' Peter Lake struck an enormous blow, and waited for further instructions. He waited and waited—and when finally he looked behind the shield, he saw Mootfowl, smiling alertly, unusually still, serene, pinned through his heart to an oaken log.

''Oh Lord,'' Peter Lake said, too shocked to feel any grief even for a man he had loved so much. He had stuck Mootfowl like a butterfly.

You could not drive an iron stake through the heart of a man of the cloth, and expect to go unpunished. So Peter Lake went over the wall (there was no wall, actually), and those years were ended. He left his apron, but he took his sword.

Coursing the streets, swifting up and down the avenues, feeling the fire of his own strength, Peter Lake reflected upon his position. He was just short of twenty, and had recently affected a modest but thick blond mustache tinged with red and silver. His hair was beginning to thin over his forehead, which made him look older, and elevated his brow—a pleasant circumstance for a pleasant face. He was disarming, friendly, kind, and full of good humor. He looked a lot like every good man, and he saw sharply and in minute detail. Had he been an aristocrat, he would have gone far. As it was, he had the world before him, and he moved confidently through the city, well aware that he was an excellent mechanic, a strong young man with a trade. True, the police would be after him. But, unencumbered as he was, that would be no problem.

That is, he thought he was unencumbered, until he turned around and saw Cecil Mature. Cecil broke into a face-filling smile, which he now and then twitched off to unslit his eyes so he could see. ''Damn it, Cecil, did I say you could come?''

''No, but I did.''

''You have to go back. The police will be after me.''

''I don't care.''

''I care. Go home!''

"I wanna come with you!"

"You can't come with me. Now get out of here. Go home, Cecil."

"I can go anywhere I want."

"Do you realize that if you come after me they'll find me in half a day? When I go into the business of towing wide loads, I'll let you know."

"It's a free country. I can go anywhere I want. That's the law. A judge said that."

"I'll cut off your head."

"No you won't."

"I'll just lose you, that's all."

"No you won't. I can move fast. Besides, I can help. I can get vegetables, like in the school. They taught me to be a squash cook. I can cook squash good."

"That's exactly what I need, isn't it, while I flee on a murder charge—a squash cook." They were walking very fast through the Bowery. In fact, Cecil was trotting to keep up. "Jessie James had a squash cook; everyone knows that. Butch Cassidy had a squash cook. It's de rigueur."

"I can cook other things, do laundry, stand guard at night. I'm a good smith—not the best—but good."

They broke through the gabardine waves of people and patrons dashing and dancing on the Bowery. The sun was setting, writhing and gesticulating in the imperfect black glass of uncountable windows. Meat roasters and singers were flooded with the onslaught of new evening, and the music halls began to boom in strokes of purple, green, and orange. The music could be heard even from steamers churning down the East River into the dark, leaving the Manhattan jewel box for warm sweet nights of mockingbird and the moon in the countryside and on the shore.

"I can tattoo."

Peter Lake stopped dead. He turned to young Cecil. "You can what?"

"I can tattoo."

"How's that?"

"Before they put me in the wagon, I was an apprentice in a tattoo parlor."

"I thought you lived on a herring boat."

"After that. I became a tattooist."

"Where?"

"In China."

"Sure."

"I mean in that place where the Chinese are. What's it called? Chinatown!"

"All right, so what if you can tattoo."

"I can make money for food. I used to tattoo rich women, in their mansions, secretly."

"You?"

Cecil Mature shrugged his shoulders. "I would tattoo things all over their bodies. They would lie naked on their beds and I would tattoo them. I was ten."

Peter Lake began to see Cecil in a new light. "What did you tattoo on them?"

"Maps, Sanskrit, the Bill of Rights (I copied from books). I tattooed the bue-tox of the mayor's wife. Wa Fung told me what to do, while he and the mayor watched from behind a curtain. On one bue-tox, I put a map of Manhattan. On the other bue-tox, I put a map of Brooklyn. She did it for his birthday. They paid Wa Fung five hundred dollars, but I did all the work."

Impressed by this versatility, Peter Lake allowed Cecil Mature to come with him, but only on the understanding that they might part ways at any time, and that Cecil would have to abandon his scalloped cap. They went into a dry-goods store to buy a Chinese hat, because Mootfowl had worn a Chinese hat and so had Wa Fung, of whom Cecil had affectionate memories. Peter Lake's discourse in public was heavily Irish, like that of an hypnotic platform speaker. The sounds of the language were exquisite as he said to the proprietor, with courtly irony, "My squash cook and tattooist, Mr. Cecil Mature, would like to purchase a Chinese hat." The proprietor got one for him. Cecil put it on. It looked rakish.

They lived on roofs and under water towers, existing at first almost entirely on Cecil's tattoo jobs. But then, when things quieted down and the Mootfowl affair receded into the past, Peter Lake took blacksmith's work under false names, or no name at all, and life for them began to look more promising. Late one night when they were ravenously hungry from having worked hard all day, they went to a saloon to drink beer and eat roast beef, freshly baked bread, and greens. The saloon was bright and noisy. There were at least two hundred people inside, and a hot fire, and talk rose to the ceiling and then crashed back over the heads of the saloon-goers in a general rush of breaking murmurs. A captivating roast, full of sizzling juices, was placed between Peter Lake and Cecil Mature. They were about to begin, but the place suddenly became silent. There had been such a great babble, and now all that could be heard was the ice melting in the icebox.

Pearly Soames had walked in, searching for something to do. He looked like a great big bristling cat. His silver mustache, silver beard, and the feline sideburns that projected from his rosy cheeks gave him a mesmerizing power that would have awed a cobra. Confidence, energy, and rascality radiated from him as if he had a marching band in his heart. He loved to quiet saloons just for the fun of it. He had recently become chieftain of the Short Tails, after the cruel and calculated slaughter of Mayhew Rottinel, their cruel and calculating founder. And he moved over to the bar, surrounded by a disgusting retinue of Short Tails, like a lord mayor. He looked around and noticed Peter Lake and Cecil Mature poised above their roast. His gaze went straight to the short sword hanging on Peter Lake's belt.

"Can you use that sword?" he asked from halfway across the room.

Because it was as much a threat as it was a question, Peter Lake stood. A path opened between him and Pearly Soames. "Yes sir," he answered.

"Can you really use it?"

Peter Lake nodded.

"Then use it!" cried Pearly Soames, pitching an apple fast and hard toward Peter Lake.

When the apple disappeared, Peter Lake was holding the same position that he had held before. It seemed to all that he had not been quick enough to draw his sword. Pearly Soames sneered. But then pieces of the apple were produced from the crowd behind Peter Lake, and brought to Pearly. It had been cleanly quartered, so Pearly declared that it must have shattered against Peter Lake's chest. Peter Lake laughed, and said, no, he had sliced it up.

"Show me your sword."

The sword was clean.

"Of course," Peter Lake declared. "I cleaned it before I put it away."

"You did?"

"Yes, here." He showed Pearly Soames the streaks on his thigh where he had cleaned the sword. Even though Pearly bought them their roast, and plenty of beer, they knew that they were in trouble. But they were at an age when trouble was something they would have been hard pressed to do without.

He wanted them in the Short Tails. They protested that it was too dangerous. "Certainly not for you!" said Pearly, in a rare compliment. "Though, since I'm the one who's asking you to join us, it might be dangerous not to."

Unmoved, the two young men continued to devour the roast. Then Pearly's eyes sparkled. "I know you," he said. "Yes, I know you. You're the two fellas that drove a spike through the heart of that religious duck." They stopped chewing, and stared into Pearly's diamond eyes. "What was his name? Moocock? Barn Owl? Blue Bird? Ah yes . . . Mootfowl! A nifty job, a very nifty little act. Every leatherhead in the city is looking for you. And you, fat boy, have a rather conspicuous silhouette. Wouldn't you say? So! What shall it be?"

Peter Lake and Cecil Mature joined the Short Tails that evening.

More than ten years in the Short Tails taught Peter Lake a number of unorthodox trades. And he grew to know the city better and better, though he knew that it was too vast and mercurial to be comprehended. It changed continually—as he did, shifting from job to job in the Short Tails, who were a living encyclopedia of crime. Being with them, half-desperate all the time, was good training. He was able to see the city from many angles, as if he were stepping around a prism and peering in at the light. At the time of the meeting in the "tea bag" under the Harlem River, Peter Lake was working as a woola boy. He had been burglar, fancy bunco man, card sharp, art thief, dispatcher, engineer, bag man, envoy to the police, harbor thief, vault blaster. Being a woola boy was a relatively new possibility, since it was a rather narrow subspecialty that had come into being only recently.

It was called "Woola Woola," and was a complicated technique for looting trucks and wagons. The chief woola boy was Dorado Canes, under whom were a dozen men in the Woola Woola team. Two or three of the men in the team hid in a doorway or an alley and waited for a wagon to pass. As it did, the woola boy would come from nowhere and run up to the driver, jumping up and down and screaming "Woola woola woola! Woola woola woola! Woola woola woola!" as loudly as he could. The drivers were shocked and distracted, and the watchers in the shadows then emerged to loot the wagon. A good woola boy could jump five feet in the air from a standing position. He would cross his eyes and say things in addition to "Woola woola woola," and emit sharp birdlike honks. The teamsters stared open-mouthed and amazed, and did not notice until long afterward that their wagons were suddenly half empty.

As with all professions, Woola Woola had its refinements. Forever condemned to it (he had called Pearly the son of a whore, something which might have been forgiven had it not been the truth), Dorado Canes was hot for innovative improvements. First, he was determined to jump higher, so he loaded himself with weights and practiced jumping, or, as he called it, the "up and down stuff." Eventually he carried two hundred pounds of lead on special belts and shoulder harnesses. To compensate for this, his leg muscles developed until he was transformed into a living spring. From a standing position, he could fly ten feet in the air—a breathtaking sight. Then Peter Lake made a pair of alloy spring boots, which increased Dorado Canes' flight ceiling by five feet. Just the fact of a man jumping fifteen feet in the air while excitedly screaming "Woola woola woola!" was enough to hypnotize the wagon masters, but Dorado Canes didn't stop there. He made a pair of folding canvas wings, so that, when he spread his long arms, the wings extended and he could glide. By jumping out as well as up, he could land thirty feet from his starting place. He soon discovered that the drag of the wings, the spring boots, and the great strength and flexibility of his legs allowed him to jump from the third story of a building. With a little practice, he made it four, and then five, stories. Much impressed, Cecil Mature pointed out that since wagons were about one-story tall, Dorado Canes could jump from six floors up and land on top of them, or, in other words, he could operate at will from the roofs of tenements and commercial buildings. Dorado Canes stitched himself a one-piece suit of shiny black silk that covered his neck and head in a tight cowl, leaving only his face exposed. He made up before every job, painting his face and hands orange, with the eyes in white cockpits and the lips purple. The undersides of his wings were yellow. After his breathtaking work, Dorado Canes would always approach the benumbed drivers and say, "I'm Vinic Totmule. On behalf of the clergy, the mayor, and the chief of police, welcome to our city. Don't take any wooden nickels, don't fool about with wicked women, and if there is no commode in your hotel room, don't pee in the sink."

Peter Lake loved the Woola Woola, and was pleasantly resigned to a life of varied criminal practice. There was much to learn, lots of work, and always the chance of a big haul. By the time he reached his early thirties, he was familiar with the rules of mechanics, the arts of a thief, and the strange skills of the Baymen, and he was just becoming free enough of the many happy anxieties of early life to notice the great beauty of the city and enjoy it. He was calm, content, and resigned to his thinning hair. He wanted only to witness the tranquillity of the seasons, turn his eye to pretty women, and take in the great and ever-pleasing opera of the city.

All changed in the tea bag deep in the mud of the Harlem River's dense and mottled bed, when Pearly Soames alluded to the necessity of wiping out the Baymen, starting with the women and children. Peter Lake knew that if he attempted to dissuade Pearly, he would be killed. The only thing to do was to warn Humpstone John directly before the attack, and thus ensure that the Short Tails would be so badly hurt that they would never again even look in the direction of the Bayonne Marsh and the Newark Meadows.

This he did. When the one hundred Short Tails came drifting quietly on the mist, affixed by gravity to the floors of their slim brown canoes, the Bay villages were quiet. The Short Tails clutched their weapons, sure of an easy kill. But then the Baymen appeared as if from nowhere. Up they sprang from the water, blue with cold, after breathing patiently through reeds. Out they came from tunnels in the sand. They emerged from brakes of cattails, and dozens of them on Percherons and quarter horses came galloping down a spit of sand. They charged the Short Tails and dispatched them in great powerful strokes that made the air quiver. The enormous horses trampled the canoes, breaking them into pulp and staining the bloody water brown. Women and children with pikes harried the ablebodied among the enemy, chased stragglers, and dispatched the wounded. Terrified Short Tails tried to escape in the thigh-deep water and were struck dead by Baymen who overtook them in their swift canoes or on the horses that galloped in the shallows like trained prancers, churning a trail of foam and blood.

Romeo Tan, Blacky Womble, Dorado Canes, and ninety-four other Short Tails were killed. Poor Cecil Mature, just a boy in his twenties, ran like mad despite Peter Lake's urgings for him to stay close. A mounted swordsman was about to kill him when Peter Lake gave the thrilling and inimitable whistle that the Baymen used, and the swordsman turned back. But Cecil Mature continued running, and he vanished into the cloud wall, clutching his Chinese hat. He seemed to have been swallowed up completely and forever.

Cool even in a losing battle, Pearly Soames took time from dispatching not a few Baymen (he, too, had special ties, and a destiny, and was not about to die at the hands of clamdiggers and minnow fishermen, no matter how good they were at war) to note the effects of Peter Lake's whistle. Had it not been for that shrill call, he might have remained unaware that Peter Lake was neither fighting nor attacked. Now the last Short Tail, Pearly Soames fought his way to fast water, and escaped by submerging himself in the rapid current that flows out the Kill van Kull.

Heartsick, Peter Lake went back to the city (the cliffs of brown buildings were a warm and comforting attraction even for those in despair) and there watched from a distance as Pearly Soames rebuilt and reordered the Short Tails. Soon they were once again a hundred strong—faceless energetic soldiers, as wicked, obsessed, and steely as the age that bred them.

With the two automobiles a long way behind, the white horse flew in great sinuous bounds, sailing through the air in a breathtaking flash of muscle. Peter Lake was used to Bay horses that took big leaps to move efficiently through shallow water. But this horse was not just a strong bounder, he was a champion in self-discovery. Before he had escaped for good and thrown in his lot with Peter Lake, he hadn't been able to run as he was now running, or at least he did not remember it. There was a fire in his knobby white knees and in his dovelike breast. With precision that might have put an arrow to shame, he went south faster than any racehorse could have run. He could cover half a block in one stride, and his capacity steadily increased. At intersections packed with crooked lines of wagons, he jumped over whatever was in his way without knowing what lay beyond the obstructions. He had enough control and time to take such chances, for midway in flight he could spot empty runs upon which to land, and sail to them faultlessly to resume the gallop. He did something in the crowded streets way downtown, which made Peter Lake wonder. An entire block was full and waiting just north of Canal Street as heavy crosstown traffic tied everything up. With a muted and almost frightened whinny, the horse charged a crush of horses and trucks, and burst out above an amazed crowd, clearing the full block and Canal Street as well, landing almost on the corner of Lispenard. Though he had nearly lost his footing, by the time they reached the lean frozen trees at the Battery's edge he had become accustomed to very long leaps, and from then on could accomplish them with ease.

Peter Lake dismounted and walked in front of the white horse, who was shy and would not look directly at him. He had never seen such a lovely animal: gentle black eyes set far apart on a wide white face, a soft velvety nose of pink and beige, an expression that looked like a sad smile, and a noble neck and chest finer than the best of any bronze monuments. The ears were tall, animated, sharp, alert, upright, and pointed. They had bent back in the gallop and moved like ailerons to help deal with the onrush of air. His arrogant tail strutted back and forth over flanks that were like big white apples.

"What are you?" Peter Lake asked quietly. The horse then turned to look at him, and, he saw, with a chill, that the eyes were infinitely deep, opening like a tunnel to another universe. The horse's silence suggested that the beauty of his gentle black eyes had something of all that ever was or would ever be. And, like every horse, he was incorruptibly innocent. Peter Lake touched the soft nose and took the big face into his arms. "Good horse," he said. But, somehow, the animal's equanimity made Peter Lake very sad.

The people Peter Lake had known while on the run were on the run as well, tumbling through greed and fire, hardly able to breathe as the city overwhelmed them, winter and summer, laying waste to their powers merely with its unprecedented scale. What Peter Lake had not had the opportunity to learn in his more than thirty orphaned years was that these tumbling souls, the ones he hardly knew, often managed to find one another for a short time and to silence the din. In a rank of trees through which a cold wind was blowing, he looked into the eyes of a horse. And as if they were all alone on some vast and snowy field upstate, the city stilled. He hoped not to be forever like the many millions on the run, always in the pitch of events, robbed even of their own inner tenderness. Something in the horse's eyes told him that he was about to change. He had seen something in those black wells that took hold of him—a very tiny burst of gold which he had followed until he was overcome. He suspected that, in the gentle face and deep black eyes, he had seen everything.

Exhausted and cold, they left the Battery and returned to the streets. He intended to make his way uptown by way of the East

Side, and to bed the horse and find a place to hide. That he knew precisely where to go and how to get there was a benefit of his iron-working days. The best refuge was above the barrel of the sky, atop the glowing constellations. To get there, they went miles and miles through snow-covered streets, until the violet evening made sleep dance in their eyes.

A forest of silver struts and perforated metallic arches surrounded Peter Lake, who reclined comfortably in a bent and fruitless grove, where riveted limbs were lit here and there by the backwash of small electric lights on the floor. The floor itself was a great half-barrel, the ceiling a grid of steel. All this was warmed by nearly visible streams of air rising above the lights, which were the stars of the constellations in the great vaulted roof of Grand Central Station—recently built with the notion of installing the sky indoors to shine permanently and in green. Peter Lake was one of the few who knew that beyond the visible universe were beams and artifice, a homely support for that which seemed to float. And he had returned by craft and force to the back of the sky, where once in another life he had helped to forge the connections between the beams, to rest now amid the props of the designer's splendid intentions. He had provided himself with a plank platform of solid oak; a soft feather bed; a makeshift kitchen neatly tucked into a corner (canned goods and biscuits were stacked among the beams); a pile of technical books for late-night reading; a little lamp that had once been a star and had then disappeared without being missed from below; and a long rope on a drum, part of an elaborate escape system worthy of Mootfowl's best and brightest pupil.

He had spent an hour currying the horse and bedding him down in Royal Wind's stable for upper-class carriage horses. Royal Wind was the son of a Virginia plantation owner whose property had been confiscated during the Civil War. He was bitter, pompous, and clean, and could be trusted not to divulge that Peter Lake was about. The stallion himself, never having seen such elegance in Brooklyn, was sleeping in the stable after a meal of fresh oats and sweet water. He was covered with a thick blanket of pure cashmere, and the bulb in his stall was shaded so that it would not shine in his eyes.

Chases and struggles tire the heart and require long bouts of deep sleep. Peter Lake looked forward to a day or two of immobility on the vaulting. He would sleep well in the eternal twilight behind the sky, since all sound was reduced to the faint rush of faraway surf, there was plenty of fresh air, and privacy was assured. After running in bitter cold for the better part of a week, he slept in leaden stillness through the night, the following day, and the following night. He awoke in the morning, thirty-six hours later, breathing slowly and calmly, completely rested. With his strength renewed, he realized that he was ravenously hungry, and proceeded to cook an excellent bouillabaisse culled from cans of varied fish, tomatoes, wine, oil, and an enormous bottle of Saratoga spring water. After this, he bathed, shaved, and changed his clothes. There he was, like God in heaven or Emerson in his study, and he began to think and plan.

I have this fine horse, he thought to himself, and have come to love him for his eyes and gentle face. He can jump the length of a city block, and he could no doubt take me deep into the pine barrens, or up to the Highlands, or out to Montauk, where Pearly doesn't set foot. I could rest. But it would start all over when I came back again. And I'm rested. So I stay. But staying is much the same as running, because I always have to flee to the marsh or hide in lofts and cellars. What's the difference? It's the same as the Highlands or the pine barrens, but in miniature. There's no way out unless I become someone else. Perhaps I can change enough—not so they won't recognize me (they'll always recognize me sooner or later), but so that they won't care. If I became a nun, for example. They'd figure me for gone. Or if I were an ashman, or if I lost my legs, or if I found a devotion, a thing to get lost in even larger than the pine barrens. . . .

They say that in his devotion St. Stephen changed form before the eyes of those who watched, that he could rise in the air, and be many things, that he knew the past and future, that he traveled from one time to another, though he was a simple man. All this (he

84

thought, upraising his eyes and clearing his throat) is why they burned him.

Now, I'm no St. Stephen, but if I can concentrate hard enough on something apart from me, perhaps I can be changed. Mootfowl said that those who built the bridge were changed. Did he mean what I think he meant? He said that the city changed, too, and, strike me, Mootfowl was not one to care about little things. What if I become a monk? They would be smashed with wonder! Then they would kill me. What if I became an alderman, or something like that? They would kill me sure, since otherwise they'd have to pay me. What if I became a sweet-tooth and danced in a theater? Oh Jesus, I could never do that. What if I lived underground . . . a hermit, no, blind? I couldn't see them, but they could see me. Can I change into an animal? Never been done. Invisible! The scientists must have some sort of liquid. . . .

Suddenly he froze, like a stag in the bush who hears a faraway breaking of branches. The years of being chased had sharpened his senses, and he had heard running footsteps, barely audible, far below. They had the greedy rhythm of the hunt. He peered through a star at the shiny marble floor a hundred feet beneath him, and watched a line of men divide as if they were horses in a military tattoo. They went for the two sets of stairs that led to the constellations.

"Dead Rabbits!" he said. "That's who they are, but why them?" He opened a hatch that was to have been used once in several decades to lower a cable for the scaffolding upon which a painter would stand to freshen the signs of the zodiac. He grabbed the end of the rope, and let himself fall. As the rope slowly played off the drum, Peter Lake descended silently through the cavernous space under the stars. He was afraid, though, that he had not left in time, and he was right, for as he glided smoothly past the halfway point the rope began to slow. Then it stopped. He dangled listlessly far above the floor. Though thousands moved below, none saw him.

He couldn't drop. It was too high for that: he would hit the marble floor like an egg. He thought of swinging to and fro to catch a ledge on one of the walls. But then the Dead Rabbits found the crank for the escape drum, and Peter Lake started upward. "Dead Rabbits," he said. "Dead Rabbits. What a name."

Just before he reached the hatch (from which half a dozen Dead Rabbits were peering at him), he put his hand in the opening of a star, and swung apelike from it to another. Though it was almost impossible to hold on, he went hand over hand up the horn of Taurus, thinking to kick open another hatch and escape. With only three fingers in the last star, he started to raise himself for a kick. But the hatch opened and a bunch of Dead Rabbits appeared.

His leg dropped. He looked down at the floor so very far away. The three fingers began to weaken. His grip failed, he slipped, and cried out as he felt himself beginning to fall. But a Dead Rabbit had pushed his arm through the hatch, and he grasped Peter Lake's wrist as it flew past. The Dead Rabbit was strong. He pulled Peter Lake inside in one motion.

Peter Lake thought that they would do him in immediately. Though he could hardly breathe, he asked, "Why didn't you just let me fall? Does Pearly want me alive? Why Dead Rabbits?"

One of the Dead Rabbits spoke up. "We don't want to hurt you," he said. "We just want to talk."

Peter Lake closed his eyes in relief and disgust. "Tell me then, Dead Rabbit, what is it that you want to talk about?"

"We heard that you got this horse, and they said that it could fly."

"Did they."

"Yes. They swear it flew. It's all over the place now. We wanna buy the horse from you—for a good price—and put it in the circus."

"You stupid bastards. The horse can't fly."

"Everyone says he can."

"He can jump, that's all."

"How far?"

"A block or so. Maybe two."

"Two blocks!"

"Maybe."

"We'll buy him, Peter Lake, and enter him at Belmont."

"No," said Peter Lake. "You don't understand. He wouldn't

jump for money. He does it 'cause he likes it, or for some reason or other, but he wouldn't do it for money, if you know what I mean. That is, he won't do it without me, and I won't . . . and besides, he's not for sale.''

''We'll give you ten thousand dollars.''

''No.''

''Twenty thousand.''

''No.''

The Dead Rabbits looked at their chief, who had been hanging back amid the beams. ''Fifty thousand,'' he said.

''Didn't I tell you? He's not for sale.''

''Seventy-five, and that's it!''

''No.''

''Eighty.''

''Not selling.''

''Okay, one hundred. But that's all we can offer.''

''Chicory,'' Peter Lake said, ''you could have a million, and it still wouldn't do you any good.''

When the Dead Rabbits had finally been convinced that Peter Lake was not going to part with the horse, they filed morosely down the stone steps that followed the hump of the vault. At that moment Peter Lake decided that he had been chased as much as he could be chased. ''I'm getting out,'' he said to himself, his lips taut with determination. ''I'll do anything to do it, but I'm getting out.

''I'll chew nails!'' he screamed, and then added, very quietly, ''if necessary.''

Rather than chew nails, he decided to steal enough money so that he could set himself up and try to become something other, and perhaps better, than what he was. He felt strongly that it could be done. Not only was there the lesson of St. Stephen, but there was the example of Mootfowl, who had worked all his life in a fury to transform and exceed himself. He had failed. But, on the way, he had seen, perhaps, in the curling and rolling of a molten red block of steel, what Peter Lake had seen in the eyes of the white horse.

Peter Lake climbed an iron ladder to the outside roof. It was covered with knee-deep snow. The real stars blazed like faraway white flares and put to shame the imitations in the station ceiling: there were pinwheels of fire, round phosphorescent spirals of light. Peter Lake leaned into the wind while all around him the snow swirled in sparkling chains, their motion suspended and stilled, as in the stars. Deep within the high blazing tunnels, motion and stillness met and fused. The wind shrieking across the drifts on the station roof turned the snow to white vapor that flattened into spinning vortexes. Seen from afar, the city's pulsating lights were like stars, and the distant avenues and high plumes of steam that curled and twisted were like the star roads themselves.

"With all that I've seen," Peter Lake said to himself, "I've seen nothing. The city is like an engine, an engine just beginning to fire itself up." He could hear it. Its surflike roar matched the lights. Its ceaseless thunder was not for nothing.

BEVERLY

Isaac Penn, publisher of *The Sun*, built his house in the middle of lots and fields on the Upper West Side, so that it stood alone overlooking the reservoir in Central Park. "I have no desire," he had said, "to live with a bunch of dumbbells on Fifth Avenue. I was born in a little house in Hudson, not far from the wharves. There was noise twenty-four hours a day even before they put in the railroad, and loose pigs snorted around everywhere. Come to think of it, they do that in New York, too, but they wear waistcoats. That's where we lived. We were poor. I remember that all the proper people lived in the same place, like a bunch of cigars in a pack. They were mostly dumbbells who had never thought a decent thought in their lives, so they banded together to hide it.

"I like my house. It stands alone in the fresh air. My children like the house. They stand alone in the fresh air. I listen to them, not to Mrs. Astor—and she knows it."

Because Isaac Penn was so abrasive, outspoken, powerful, rich, wise, and old, the optometrist was very frightened when the master of the house himself met him at the door and escorted him in. He felt like a child who imagines that he is soon to be eaten by a huge unfriendly animal that lives in the dark. And, further, he could not understand why he had been summoned to appear with all his equipment at the Penns' house. He had the real carriage trade, and his celebrated customers always came to the shop. He was puzzled as well to see that Isaac Penn wore no spectacles, which he thought most unusual for an old man whose business flowed before his eyes in small print.

"Then we are not for you, I take it," the optometrist said to Isaac Penn, who had gone to sit in an enormous leather chair. He could hardly make himself heard over the piano that was being played in an adjoining room.

"What?" asked Isaac Penn.

"We are not for you, then, I take it."

"Who's we?" asked Isaac Penn, looking around the room.

"You don't need glasses yourself, sir, do you?"

"No," said Isaac Penn, still wondering if the optometrist had brought an assistant. "Never needed glasses. Grew up looking for whales. Glasses wouldn't have been the thing."

"Is it your wife that needs spectacles, Mr. Penn?"

"Dead," said Isaac Penn. The optometrist was silent, unable even to begin a forced condolence. In fact, he almost panicked, because he felt that for some reason Isaac Penn thought of him as an undertaker.

"I'm an optometrist," he blurted out defensively.

"I know," answered Isaac Penn. "Don't worry, I have some work for you. I want you to make a pair of spectacles for my daughter. That is she," he said, pointing to the sound of the music, "playing the piano. She'll be finished soon—half an hour, maybe an hour. It's nice, isn't it. Mozart."

The optometrist thought of his horse standing hitched to the wagon, in the snow. He thought of his dinner gone cold. He thought of his shattered dignity (he was, after all, a professional man), and he said, "Don't you think, Mr. Penn, that we should inform her that I have come to make her some spectacles? Wouldn't it be wise?"

"I don't think so," said Isaac Penn. "What's the point of interruptions? Let her play. When she's finished, you'll fashion her a pair of glasses. Do you have your stuff? I hope you do. She needs them tonight. This morning her brother sat on her spectacles, and they were the only pair she had. She has long eyelashes, unprecedented eyelashes. They bat the insides of her lenses. I think it's uncomfortable for her. Can you put the lenses far enough away so that she won't bat the glass with her lashes?" The optometrist nodded. "Good," said Isaac Penn, and leaned back to listen to the smooth tumult of the sonata. She was a superb pianist, almost flawless, at least as far as her father was concerned.

As the music continued, the optometrist set up his instruments and eye charts. Then he sat down and listened, barely breathing, wondering why such a man as Isaac Penn was so indulgent with his daughter. Actually, for reasons that he did not understand, the optometrist was afraid of her. His palms sweated. He began to dread the moment when she would finish and enter the room, royal princess that she was, to confront a simple grinder of lenses.

The front door burst open. Two adolescent boys pounded up the stairs and were gone sooner than the glass in the windows could stop vibrating from their entrance. Isaac Penn acknowledged this with a brief smile, and walked over to a corner desk upon which were many fresh *Suns*. Clattering noises and the smell of roasting chickens came from a nearby kitchen. A dozen fires burned, and the sweet winter woods scented the house with resin and cherry. The piano played. Darkness grew stronger. Finally, night and evening were solidly entrenched outside the house and inside wherever bright lamplight fought deep shadow.

When the piano stopped, the optometrist swallowed. He heard the cover close over the keyboard. And then a young woman appeared in the doorway, apparently blushing, with cheerful eyes that stared in the direction of the ice-clad windows. She breathed as if she had a fever, and the expression on her lovely face suggested a pleasant delirium. Her golden hair was lit so brilliantly in a crosslight that it appeared to be burning like the sun. She gripped the doorpost with her hands one on top of another, for steadiness and to indicate that she did not wish to interrupt the two men in the reception parlor. Though she was outwardly deferential, it was easy to see that she had no need to defer to anyone. The optometrist thought that her dress was too fetching and sensual for a girl who was hardly a woman, who was a daughter in a parlor, a piano player, a girl with fever standing in the presence of her father. The lace, without which the dress would have been scandalous, breathed rapidly up and down above her chest. It was hypnotic, too fast, unsettling. She had steady blue eyes, but she was so tired from playing the paino that she trembled, and held the doorpost now to try to stop herself from shaking.

Courtly and quick, Isaac Penn escorted her to a chair. "Beverly," he said, "this man has come to make you some new glasses."

Outside, the wind picked up in a sudden clear gale that had come unflinchingly from the north, descending quite easily from the pole, because all the ground between it and New York was white and windblown. On nights of arch cold and blazing stars, when the moon was in league with the snow, Beverly sometimes wondered why white bears did not arrive on the river ice, prowling silently in the silver light. The trees bent despite their winter stiffness, and some, in desperation, knocked and scratched against the windows. If a channel had been kept open in the frozen Hudson, any little bravely lighted boats would now be flying south, nearly airborne with sudden winter speed. Beverly had thought how strange and wonderful it would be if the earth were hurled far from its orbit, into the cold extremes of black space where the sun was a faint cool disc, not even a quartermoon, and night was everlasting. Imagine the industry, she thought, as every tree, every piece of coal, and every scrap of wood were burned for heat and light. Though the sea would freeze, men would go out in the darkness and pierce its glassy ice to find the stilled fish. But finally all the animals would be eaten and their hides and wool stitched and woven, all the coal would be burned, and not a tree would be left standing. Silence would rule the earth, for the wind would stop and the sea would be heavy glass. People would die quietly, buried in their furs and down.

"Your horse," she said to the optometrist, "will freeze to death if you leave him outside."

"Yes, I'm glad you reminded me. I must do something about that."

"We have a stable," Beverly said rather coolly.

"Why didn't you tell me you came in your own rig," scolded Isaac Penn, leaving to bring the horse into the stable. Beverly and the optometrist were alone.

She had no desire to intimidate him, and was unhappy that he was afraid of her. "Come, measure my eyes," she said. "I'm tired."

"I'll wait until your father returns." The optometrist was reluctant to be near her. It was not that he feared her illness but rather that he thought it improper to come close to the young woman while she was burning with fever, to feel the heat from her bare arms and neck, to feel her breath, to smell the sweetness that would undoubtedly arise, fever-stirred, from her lace and linen.

"It's all right," she said, closing her eyes momentarily. "You can start now. If you think it improper, then I don't know what to tell you. But do what you came to do."

Since all his instruments were set up, he began immediately, breathing through his nose when he was close to her, as tense and silent as a hunted insect. She, on the other hand, breathed through her mouth, rapidly, because of the fever. Her breath was sweet. He moved laboriously and carefully as he manipulated ivory rules, ebony flags, and lenses in a case, lined up by the dozen, waiting for their great moment—which was to be flipped back and forth while he intoned his chant, "Better this way, or this way. This way, or this way. This way, or this way."

How many thousands of times in a day, she thought, does he say, "this way, or this way." They are *his* words. He owns them. They must make him dizzy.

He thought she was beautiful. She was. Though she looked like a fully grown woman and carried herself like one, she had all the great and obvious attributes of youth. He desired, feared, and envied her. She was perfectly formed, rich, and young. And because he had to struggle for his living despite his many physical imperfections, she seemed to him to be gifted and blessed beyond measure, despite the fact that he knew that she had consumption and was full of the wisdom of those who are slowly dying. The fever and the delirium made for a relentless elevation. Opium could have done no better. Long bouts of fever, over months and years, were a dignified way to die, if only because death would have to take so much time to wrestle her down.

The room was full of motion that spread from her in a dancing half-circle. The fire leapt and bent, running in place like a frantic wheel, the windows rattled as the house breathed, and the trees scratched the glass now and then like dogs who scratch at doors. Beverly could see winter as it ran about the room on the light, darting from the white lances, rays, and silver crosses in the optical glass, to the fire, to the reflective windows, to the blue sphere of her own eye. The room, as she saw it, was a web of motion, a symphony of mischievous dancing particles quite like the smooth and placid notes of a fine concerto. If she could see all this while a nervous man flipped his lenses in examining her eyes, what would she see when the fever grew too great to bear? It didn't matter. Now there were only inexplicable shards of busy light seeking her out as if they were courtiers.

"The horse is in the stable," announced Isaac Penn as he returned. "Is there anything you want from your wagon? I can have it brought . . ."

"Just a moment, Mr. Penn," said the optometrist. "This way, or this way. This way, or this way. This way, or this way." He sat back, relieved and disappointed, and declared that Beverly had perfect vision. She did not need spectacles at all.

"She's worn glasses since she was a little girl," said Isaac Penn.

"What can I tell you? She doesn't need them now."

"Good. Send me the bill."

"For what? I made no spectacles."

"For coming here on such a night."

"I don't know what to charge."

"She can see well, can't she?"

"She can see perfectly."

"Then charge me for one pair of perfect spectacles."

When a dinner bell rang, everyone in the house began to assemble in the dining room, and, half bowing, the optometrist backed out the door, into the cold December night.

Dinner at the Penns was unusual in that they and their servants sat at the same table. Isaac Penn was no aristocrat. Having grown up, at first, on the wrong end of a whaling ship, he did not like the idea of separate messes for officers and men. And then, the Penn children (Beverly, before she grew up and got sick, Harry, Jack, and Willa, who was a child of three) were encouraged to bring their friends. "This is our society," stated Isaac. "Otherwise, we work. But here, all are equal, all are welcome, and all must wash their hands before eating."

So, that evening as the cold wind ripped up scrub in the park, as the stars ground into the sky their famous and inevitable tracks, and as a player piano in an adjoining room played popular waltzes, much to Beverly's chagrin (she liked popular waltzes, but was jealous of player pianos), the Penns (meaning Isaac, Beverly, Harry, Jack, and Willa), the Penns' friends (meaning blond Bridgett Lavelle, Jamie Absonord, and Chester Satin), and the Penns' servants (meaning Jayga, Jim, Leonora, Denura, and Lionel), gathered in the big dining room to eat. A fire burned in each of two fireplaces at either end of an informal table set with glimmering china and crystal and laden with an array of symmetrical chickens roasted and trussed, bowls of fresh salad, tureens of Nantucket potatoes in broth, and accessories such as condiments, seltzer, hardtack, and wine.

Chester Satin had slicked-down hair. He and Harry Penn were scared and guilty, and they looked it. They had skipped school that afternoon, gone downtown, and paid to see Caradelba dancing seminude like a Spanish Gypsy. And since Chester Satin had always been bold in a wicked way, he had purchased a stack of pornographic postcards. These now resided under a floorboard in Harry Penn's room, right above the dining room. Both Harry Penn and Chester Satin felt that the pictures were sure to come sizzling through the plaster and shame them forever. And they could not take their minds off the stack of lascivious women photographed in various states of undress. Their bustles and hoops were jauntily dropped, and you could see their legs below the knee, arms below the elbow, faces, necks, and (in one instance) "bosoms." These dishonored women had gone far beyond what decency allowed, and though clad in enough underwear to keep a polar explorer sweating at ninety below, they were ready to mortify the two boys simply by falling through the ceiling and floating into Isaac Penn's hands. Thus, throughout dinner, Harry and Chester behaved like condemned criminals.

Jack did his homework (it was allowed; any child could read at table), blond Bridgett Lavelle stared at Jack (who wanted to be an engineer), Jamie Absonord stuffed herself with chicken as though her assignment was to eat all the chickens in the world, and Beverly ate like a bear. She was slim, but she burned up all her food faster than the fireplaces swallowed up logs. The other children were growing, and had spent the day in the cold. With amazing speed, the chickens became white snowy bones, the potatoes vanished forever, and the wine disappeared from its bottles as if a magician were at the table. Then the fruit fled from around its pits, and the cakes rapidly became invisible. All the while, the player piano sped through light waltzes. During one of them the roll got stuck and Beverly got up to fix it. When she returned she found Isaac Penn staring sternly at a handful of pictures. The two boys were bent over the table, groaning, and there was a big hole in the ceiling.

"Lovely women," said Isaac Penn to Beverly, "but not a one holds a candle to your mother."

Before Beverly went to bed that night, she undressed and stared at herself in a full-length mirror. She was more beautiful than any of the women in Harry's photographs, far more beautiful. She wished that she could go dancing at Mouquin's and glide about the floor, using her beautiful body to its greatest effect, flowing with the music. She wished that a man would undress her and embrace her. The music circled about in her head as she took deepening swirls upon an imagined marble floor, and for lack of a man she embraced herself. Then she began to dress for bed: a far more practical matter, for Beverly Penn slept upon a platform on the roof, and it was unforgivingly cold up there. But despite the cold and perhaps because of it, the sights she saw were what other people would have called dreams, desires, miracles.

To Beverly, fires and tight rooms were like a death sentence. If the open air were not blowing past her face she felt as if she couldn't breathe. Her regimen, inclination, and promised salvation were one and the same—to stay outdoors, and this she did for all but three or four hours a day, hours in which she bathed, played the piano, and ate with the family. At all other times she could be found in her tent upon a special platform that Isaac Penn had commissioned to be built astride the peaks of the roof. Here she slept. Here she spent the day reading, or just watching the city, the clouds, birds, boats upon the river, and the wagons and cars on the streets below.

In winter she spent most of her time alone, for few people could sit very long in the bitter cold while the north wind came awash over them like a fall of icy water. Beverly was not only used to it but could not live without it. Her face and hands were usually sunburned, even in January. And despite her frailty and sickness she was as much inured to rough weather as a Grand Banks fisherman, a point of irony apparent when healthy visitors became insensate blocks of ice while she carried on as if she were in a blooming garden late in spring. The visitors were not as seasoned as she. Nor had they the elaborate exquisitely tailored wraps, coats, and hoods, not to mention the gloves, quilts, and sleeping sacks that she had, all of wool, down, or soft black sable. She had an Eskimo parka of down-lined sable that was probably the best piece of winter clothing in the world. It was light and comfortable, flexible, dry, and perfectly warm at all times. The fur hood drawn about her face was like a black sun. Her teeth were so white in contrast that when she broke into a sudden smile it was not unlike turning on a light.

Winter and summer, she climbed several flights, resting at each landing, until she came to a special staircase leading to a small door. From this door, a catwalk of steel and wood led to her platform, a deck on a steel truss that spanned two roof ridges. The platform was twenty by twelve, and upon it a little tent was anchored more securely than a circus trapeze, and with at least as many wires: the virtuoso rigger who had tied it down had engineered a catenary between pole and pole so the wind could pass over naturally. Three deck chairs faced in three directions to afford varied views, different positions in the wind, and constant attention from a weak winter sun. She had hinged windbreaks of heavy glass, mounted in an ingenious system of pulleys and tracks. She could raise the glass on all four sides up to five feet high. And she had a row of weatherproof cabinets. In the first were enough blankets, pillows, and wraps to have kept Napoleon's army warm in Russia. In the second was space for about thirty books, a stack of magazines, a pair of binoculars, a lap desk, and some games (Willa was allowed to come in the warmest part of the day to play checkers or war). In the third was a rack of vacuum bottles and canisters in which she could keep hot drinks and whatever food might strike her fancy. The fourth held a weather station. She was an expert at predicting the weather and hardly needed the barometer, thermometer, and wind gauges, but they were useful because she kept carefully penned records—as well as a running commentary on the birds and their behavior, the flowering of the trees, fires in the city (their bearing and duration; the height, density, and color of the smoke; etc., etc.), the passage of balloons and the appearance of kites, the way the sky looked and the kind of boats that went up and down the Hudson. Every now and then a great old schooner would pass, as silent as it was tall, and often the city was so busy that she was the only one to notice it.

At night as she lay on her bed in the open, or in the tent with some of the canvas rolled back so that she could see the sky, she watched the stars, not for ten minutes or a quarter-hour as most people did, but for hour after hour after hour. Even astronomers did not take in the sky with such devotion, for they were constantly occupied with charting, measurements, the fallibilities of their earthbound instruments, and concentration upon one or another celestial problem. Beverly had the whole of it; she could see it all;

and, unlike shepherds or drovers, and the rough and privileged woodsmen who work and sleep outdoors, she was not often tired. The abandoned stars were hers for the many rich hours of sparkling winter nights, and, unattended, she took them in like lovers. She felt that she looked out, not up, into the spacious universe, she knew the names of every bright star and all the constellations, and (although she could not see them) she was familiar with the vast billowing nebulae in which one filament of a wild and shaken mane carried in its trail a hundred million worlds. In a delirium of comets, suns, and pulsating stars, she let her eyes fill with the humming, crackling, hissing light of the galaxy's edge, a perpetual twilight, a gray dawn in one of heaven's many galleries.

With her face open to the bitter cold of the clear sky, she could track across the Milky Way, ticking off stars and constellations like a child naming the states. She hesitated only when a column of wavy air came streaming from a nearby chimney and shuffled the heavenly artifacts. Otherwise, she said their names in an almost hypnotic chant, as if she were calling to the high stars in the shifting black air of the December sky. "Columba, Lepus, Canis Major, Canis Minor, Procyon, Betelgeuse, Rigel, Orion, Taurus, Aldebaran, Gemini, Pollux, Castor, Auriga, Capella, the Pleiades, Perseus, Cassiopeia, Ursa Major, Ursa Minor, Polaris, Draco, Cepheus, Vega, the Northern Cross, Cygnus, Deneb, Delphinus, Andromeda, Triangulum, Aries, Cetus, Pisces, Aquarius, Pegasus, Fomalhaut." Her eye returned to Rigel and Betelgeuse, and then slipped back and forth from Rigel to Aldebaran, and to the Pleiades. In the smallest part of a second, she traveled from one to another, spanning light-years. Velocity and time, it seemed, were a matter of perspective.

She felt as if she knew the stars, and had been among them, or would be. Why was it that in planetarium lectures the telescopic photographs flashed upon the interior of the dome were so familiar—not just to her, but to everyone. Farmers and children, and, once, Paumanuk Indians pausing in their sad race to extinction, had all understood the sharp abstract images, immediately and from the heart. The nebulae, the sweep of galaxies, the centrifugal clusters—nothing more, really, than projected electric light on a plaster ceiling—carried them away in a trance, and the planetarium lecturer need not have said a word. And why was it that certain sounds, frequencies, and repetitious rhythmic patterns suggested stars, floating galaxies, and even the colorful opaque planets orbiting in subdued ellipses? Why were certain pieces of music (pre-Galilean, post-Galilean, it did not matter) harmonically and rhythmically linked to the stars and suggestive of the parallel light that rained upon the earth in illusory radiants bursting apart?

She had no explanation for these or a hundred other questions about the same matters. Since she had had to leave school, and had learned little of science when she had been there (girls did not take physics or chemistry), she was amazed to awaken one morning and find in her notebook long equations penned in her own hand. She thought that perhaps Harry was playing tricks. But the handwriting, without question, was her own. The notations went on for pages.

She took them to the planetarium lecturer, who didn't know what they were. She watched him for an hour as he sat in a pale flood of northern light that came in his window, bent over a rolltop desk, copying. He said that though he could make no sense whatsoever out of any of them, he found them intriguing. In his handwriting, they looked more authoritative.

"What do they mean?" she asked.

"I don't know," he answered. "But they look sensible. I'm going to keep them, if you don't object. Where did you get them?"

"I told you," she said.

"But really."

"Yes."

He stared at her. Who was she, this lovely blushing girl dressed in silk and sable. "What do they mean to you?" he asked, leaning back into the portable thicket of his gray vested suit.

Beverly took back her pages and studied them. After a while, she looked up. "They mean to me that the universe . . . growls, and sings. No, shouts."

The learned astronomer was shocked. In dealing with the public he was often confronted by lunatics and visionaries, some of whose theories were elegant, some absurd, and some, perhaps, right on the mark. But those were usually old bearded men who lived in lofts crowded with books and tools, eccentrics who walked around the city, pushing carts full of their belongings, madmen from state institutions that could not hold them. There was always something arresting and true about their thoughts, as if their lunacy were as much a gift as an affliction, though the heavy weight of the truth they sensed so strongly had clouded their reason, and all the wonder in what they said was shattered and disguised.

He would have been more comfortable had he been speaking with a disabled veteran of the Civil War, or a recluse inventor from some archaic Hudson River town: those were the people that normally came in with sheets of equations. That she was a pretty young girl still in her teens, privileged and well cared for, contrasted so sharply with her obsession that he was deeply saddened and even somewhat frightened.

"Growls?" he asked, gently.

"Yes."

"How, exactly?"

"Like a dog, but low, low. And then it shouts, mixed voices, tones, a white and silver sound."

The astronomer's eyes were already wide, but she made his heart thud when she said, "The light is silent, but then it clashes like cymbals, and arches out like a fountain, to travel and yet be still. It crosses space, without moving, on a fixed beam, as cleanly and silently as a pillar of ruby or diamond."

On the roof, she turned her eye again to Rigel, and then to Orion. The Pleiades were, as always, perfectly balanced in confounding asymmetry. Aldebaran winked. "You're flashing tonight," she said into the wind, and Aldebaran burst into a sparkling dance, deaf and dumb, but pleasing nonetheless to her heart. Rigel, Betelgeuse, and Orion, too, spoke to her. There was no finer church, no finer choir, than the stars speaking in silence to the many consumptives silently condemned, a legion upon the dark and hidden rooftops.

The legion of consumptives lay upon the rooftops that night in bitter cold as the wind came down from the north like a runner in lacrosse, violent and hard, to batter every living thing. They were there, out of sight in the square forest of tenements and across the bridges that dipped and shone better than diamond necklaces. They were there, each one alone—as all will someday be—in conversation with the stars, mining ephemeral love from cold and distant light. Ice was everywhere. The river was frozen very deep, the walks and trees brittle, the crust of the snow hard enough for horses. And yet the sleepers on the rooftops blazed on in their quilted coverlets like little furnaces, and when Beverly had had enough love that night from her lovers the stars, she turned quietly and contentedly, and fell asleep buried in her furs and down.

A GODDESS IN THE BATH

IN December, all the Penns except Beverly were to leave for the country house at the Lake of the Coheeries, which was so far upstate that no one could find it. Beverly was to join them for the holidays, by which time they were to have seen to the provision of the special sleeping-loggia that she required, and have opened the house to be ready to receive her after the long and harrowing journey from the city. She had in mind writing a telegram, begging to be excused from the winter gathering at the lake, for she was fitful and disturbed, and wanted to be alone. But, as it was, she would go by sleigh, river steamer, a second sleigh, and iceboat to a big house that stood on a small island in a crescent of the lakeshore, there to celebrate Christmas.

Isaac, Harry, Jack, and Willa (in her snowsuit, Willa looked like a cherub with the body of a pillow) were soon to go. Of the servants, only Jayga would remain. But, as soon as the family departed, Beverly would tell her to go home to her people in the Four Points. Beverly knew that Jayga's father was slowly dying, and she had made Isaac send the Posposils enough money to support them many times over. "But we have a charitable trust," Isaac had said. "We don't give away our money. That's what the trust is for, and it's entirely independent."

"Daddy," Beverly replied, "soon enough Harry will be on his own, and so will Jack. Willa has her own trust, and I'll be long buried. Tell me, what will you use the money for?" Isaac then gave with a vengeance, although he knew that all his money and all the money in the world could not influence what was pursuing Mr. Posposil, and Beverly, at such terribly close quarters.

So Jayga would leave and for several days the house would be empty but for Beverly, who, for no reason that she could understand, was convinced that something special was about to happen—that she would, perhaps, get well, or run a great and sudden fever that would finally kill her. But nothing seemed to happen. Two nights before they left, it snowed, and the stars were buried. The next night, a driven lace of white cloud hid even the moon. But Beverly had faith and patience. She waited. And then, on the day of departure, it cleared.

Peter Lake had been thinking so hard about St. Stephen that he became temporarily religious and actually set foot inside a church. It scared him half to death. He had never been in one before, for Reverend Overweary had not let the boys enter the gleaming silver sanctum that he had made them build near Bacon's Turkish bungalow. And a day could not pass when Peter Lake and his kind would not be denounced from half a thousand pulpits throughout the city. It was the enemy camp, and he was extremely uncomfortable as he padded down the great center aisle, assaulted by a multitude of unfamiliar colored rays wheeling in through the stained-glass windows. He had chosen the Maritime Cathedral, the city's most beautiful. It was to St. Patrick's and St. John's what Sainte-Chapelle was to Notre Dame. Its windows rose upright like fields of mountain wild flowers, illustrating scenes from ships and the sea. Isaac Penn had endowed the cathedral, insisting that the story of Jonah be splayed across its lighted windows. He had killed many whales.

There was Jonah, his mouth open in astonishment as he was swallowed by the whale. And the whale! This was no silly symbolic emblematic whale, with a man's mouth and the eyes of a hypnotized vaudevillian, but one filled with the beauty of real whales. He was long, black, and heavy, with a monstrous creased jaw. His baleen was yellowed and corrupt, honeycombed like a Chinese puzzle. The huge blue bastard was covered with old wounds and deep gashes. A steel harpoon claw still stuck in him, and he was blind in one eye. He planed water not like a little silver fish in a Renaissance miniature, but like a real whale that can smash and bruise the sea.

Peter Lake was quite surprised to find in this cathedral a hundred beautiful models of ships, sailing through nave and transept as if they were at sea on the major routes of trade. If this was what one found in a cathedral, then this was what one found in a cathedral. He had wanted to see what religion was, so that he might become like St. Stephen, and so that he might pray for Mootfowl. Although Mootfowl's death had long been forgotten, anyone who did remember it thought that Peter Lake had killed him. And he had, but not really. Mootfowl had killed himself—in a strange and peculiar fashion that tied Peter Lake to him forever. Why had Mootfowl been so dejected? Jackson Mead had remained for a few years, half-celebrated, half-obscure, while he built a great gray bridge across the East River. It was high, graceful, and mathematically perfect. Mootfowl would have loved it. But there were other bridges to be built, and Jackson Mead had vanished as inexplicably as he had arrived, disappearing with his train of reclusive mechanics, not even bothering to be present at the dedication. It was said that he was putting up bridges on the frontier—in Manitoba, Oregon, and California. These were, however, only rumors.

Peter Lake wondered how to pray. Mootfowl had often made them pray, but they had just knelt and faced the fire, staring at the suns and worlds that danced within it. That had been enough. There was no fire in the Maritime Cathedral, just the pure cold light that washed the great weeping colors from the windows. Peter Lake knelt. "Mootfowl," he whispered, "dear Mootfowl. . . ." He did not know what to say, but his lips moved in silence as he thought of the forge reflecting in Mootfowl's eyes, of his Chinese hat, the strong thin hands, and the absolute devotion to the mysterious things that he believed he could find in the conjunction of fire, motion, and steel. His lips moved, saying something other than what he thought. He had wanted to say that he had loved Mootfowl, but that had proved too difficult and inappropriate. So he backed out of the cathedral feeling as irresolute and frustrated as when he had entered. Who were those who found it so easy to pray? Did they really talk to God as if they were ordering in a restaurant? When he himself knelt down, he was tongue-tied.

Peter Lake sat on the horse, high above the sidewalk. He often felt that the horse was a heroic statue, a huge bronze whose job was to guard some public field without moving. But then the horse warmed to motion, and they cantered in slow and easy strides until they reached the park. Peter Lake had wanted to case some mansions on upper Fifth Avenue, but the horse leapt the lake at its narrow waist near the Bethesda Fountain, and took him to the West Side, to Isaac Penn's house, which he had never seen. Standing in the snow, he saw Isaac, Harry, Jack, Willa, and all the servants except Jayga, mounting three large sleighs, one of which was piled high with luggage. They pulled away in a ringing of bells and snapping of whips. The horses were harnessed in troikas. Peter Lake stood next to the white horse, and watched the house until nightfall.

The white horse sat down on his haunches, like a dog, and watched too. Within an hour, darkness closed over the city as if someone had slammed shut the door of an icehouse, and powerful winds began to move through the park like big trains long overdue from Canada. Peter Lake was hopping from foot to foot. He turned up his collar, acutely aware that his tweed jacket was whistling as the wind coursed through it. He turned to the horse, but the horse was still on his haunches, staring contentedly at the house. Peter Lake began to mumble complaints. "I'm not a horse," he said. "I get cold a lot faster, and I don't sleep standing up."

But the possibility of slowly freezing to death did not compromise his professionalism. He noticed that, of the seven chimneys, five had been smoking when the family got itself and all the luggage on the sleighs. Now only three were bending stars and sky with their viscous ribbons of heat. He suspected that they would soon shut down. But they didn't, and at about six o'clock a fourth began operation, and then a fifth. "Maybe it's oil," he said out loud. "An automatic system. But no, not even a house like that would have five furnaces. Maybe two, and two hot-water boilers, at the most. Those are fireplaces. Ah, I can smell 'em. Someone's in there."

At six-thirty, a light went on in one of the windows. After all the darkness he had been in, Peter Lake was blinded. He felt vulnerable, and stepped behind a tree. It was extremely cold, but he was right to have waited. The light was in the kitchen. A girl came briefly to the window. "They left a servant. It figures." But he waited still, for he was of that class himself (lower, in fact), and knew very well that when the master was away all kinds of things could happen. "It's a girl," he said to the horse. "I'll bet she has a lover. I'll bet he comes and they go on a six-day drunk. That would be fine with me. While they're sleeping naked in the master's silken bed, I'll go in and requisition the downstairs valuables. Now all we have to do . . . is wait for the lad to show."

At seven, there was a flash against the sky. Peter Lake thought it was a shooting star, or a rocket summoning a river pilot. It was neither, but, rather, Beverly opening the door to the spiral stairs which led down from the roof. Some other lights went on. She's turning down the covers, thought Peter Lake. Soon he'll arrive at the door, cast a few glances, and be whisked in like the milk.

Beverly descended to the kitchen. There, she ate with Jayga, who was already dressed for the street. They said few words. Both were women in love with men who did not exist, and they shared the resigned sadness that comes from too much dreaming and longing. They were used to imagining that when they were alone they were observed in their graces and beauties (in Jayga's case, these were to be found in the eye of the beholder) by a man who stood somewhere, perhaps on a platform in the air, invisibly. And when they did whatever they did, sewing, or playing the piano, or fixing their hair in front of a mirror, they did so with tender reference to his invisible presence, which they loved almost as if it were real.

As Jayga cleaned up, Beverly got ready for bed. No piano playing, no chess or backgammon, no games with Willa and her dolls. She missed Willa already. The child looked just like Isaac. She was not really pretty yet. But she was loved by all who saw her for her fine quality of face. Such a sweet little girl. And a shrieker! And a giggler! It was the first time that she would be able to remember a Christmas at the Lake of the Coheeries, and, because of that, Beverly thought not to send a telegram after all. She turned the white handle of the faucet to shut off a thick stream of hot water. In the morning, when no one was in the house, she would spend an hour in her father's wonderful bathing pool. But now she was tired. She said goodnight to Jayga, told her that she would expect to see her in a few days, and went back upstairs.

Peter Lake did not notice the second flash, when the roof door opened, because he was watching lights in different rooms as they went out one by one during Jayga's processional through the house. And then the kitchen light was extinguished. Jayga stepped out the front door and put a suitcase on the steps. She doublelocked the door and shook the handle to see if it were tight. Peter Lake was overjoyed to see a servant girl in her heavy coat and scarf, carrying a suitcase. After Jayga scurried down the street, he looked up to see that only three chimneys were now ribboning out heat, and even these were failing.

That's that, he thought. At four in the morning, the five cops on duty in Manhattan will be sitting around a wood stove in a whorehouse somewhere, looking out for the sergeant (who will be upstairs, unconscious, snoring into a pink feather boa, his knees curled up into the buttocks of a poor young girl from Cleveland). I'll hit the place at four and be out by five-thirty with the silverware, the cash, and half a dozen rolled-up Rembrandts.

He wondered, though, how such a prize could be left unprotected. Certainly they had intended to have the servant girl stand guard. That was it. She was ducking out. Of course they might have electrical alarms and other gadgets, but that only made it more fun.

He shivered. He had to have some roasted oysters and hot buttered rum or he would die. The horse had to have some oats and some hot alfalfa horse tea. They dashed through the night toward the music and fire of the Bowery, gliding swiftly over the park's snow-covered trails.

You could hear people eating in the roast oyster place from five blocks away. There is something about a roast oyster, a clean stinging taste of the blue sea, hotter than boiling oil, neatly packaged in its own bone-dry kiln, that makes even the most refined diners snort, sniffle, and hum as they eat. Peter Lake got the horse his due and then sailed into the oyster place at the peak of the dinner hour. It was a vast underground cave between the Bowery and Rochambeau. The walls of stone were gray and white throughout half a dozen grand galleries. Arches like those of a Roman aqueduct touched the floor and then bounced away. At seven-thirty on a Friday night, no less than five thousand people dined within this subterranean oyster bin. Four hundred oyster boys labored and cried as if they were edging a great ship into port, or rolling Napoleon's cannon through Russia. Candles, gas lanterns, and, here and there, clear electric lights illuminated paths between rumbling little fires. The background noise was not unlike the famous record that Thomas Alva Edison had made of Niagara Falls, and the trajectories of the flying oyster shells reminded some old veterans of the night air above Vicksburg.

A poor harried oyster boy appeared before Peter Lake, knitted his brows, and asked, "How many are you going to have?"

"Four dozen," said Peter Lake. "From the thyme-hickory fire."

"To drink?" asked the oyster boy.

"No," said Peter Lake. "To eat, boy. To drink, I'll have a knocker of buttered rum."

"Rum's out," said the boy. "We have hard cider."

"That's fine. And, oh yes, have you got a nice roasted owl?"

"A roast owl?" asked the oyster boy. "Don't got no roast

owls." Then he disappeared, but was back in less than a minute with four-dozen roasted oysters hotter than the finest open hearth in all of Pittsburgh, and a flaming quart of hard cider. Peter Lake reacted to all of this like a Bayman, and for an hour his eyes saw straight without a blink while he grunted and hummed, alongside those with pink skulls and dangling powdered wigs, in disgusting disarray amid a thousand loose and distended oyster bellies hanging by cords of white sinew.

"I like to relax myself before a burglary," Peter Lake said to a nearby barrister as they both stared over the horizons of their swollen stomachs, picked their teeth, danced with the orange tongues of fire, and partook of steaming hot tea in pewter mugs with hinged lids. "It makes sense to be slack before great exertion, to lose control in advance of a big job, don't you think?"

"I certainly do," said the barrister. "I always get drunk or go whoring the night before a big trial. I find that wildness of that kind clears my mind and makes of it a tabula rasa, so to speak, able indeed to accept the imprint of pytacorian energy."

"Well," answered Peter Lake, "I don't know what all that means, but I suppose that you must be a good lawyer, talking like that. Mootfowl said that a lawyer's job was to hypnotize people with intricate words, and then walk away with their property."

"An attorney, this Mootfowl?"

"A mechanic. A master of the forge. I loved him. He was my teacher. He could do anything with metal. He would beat it up into a darling frenzy, charm it into motionless white windings and red helixes of flame, and then strike it into just the shape willed by his mighty eye."

"Lovely," said the barrister.

Peter Lake floated up into one of the many clean white rooms and there slept a refreshing sleep until three in the morning, when he arose with an unusual sense of well-being and a great deal of energy. He washed, shaved, drank some ice water, and went into the cold. Moving through the deserted streets as if it were early summer, he was warm inside, wound up like a spring, happy, full of affection, and strong. And what a nice surprise it was to arrive at the stable and find that the horse, too, was awake and bright-eyed, bursting with energy, eager to set out.

Almost at four sharp, Beverly's eyes opened upon a spring scene in the stars. So pleasant, peaceful, clear, and calm were they, with human attention at the nadir, that even the winter air above her seemed warm and gentle. She saw no spirits, no open roads, but, instead, a summer sparkling of winking little stars that might have been the backdrop of a deliriously happy musical play.

Beverly smiled, delighted at how the universe suddenly seemed to have become an artifact of the Belle Époque—navy blue, dazzling, light, full of grace and joy, and as wonderful as the lucid moments before a rainstorm. She couldn't sleep, so she sat up, and then she rose to her feet without the customary effort. The stars were now all around her, and she hardly dared to move or breathe, for the air was still fresh and warm and she felt no fever. Could it be? Yes. There was no overheatedness upon rising, no deep labored breathing, no trembling. She pulled off the glistening sable hood and felt the benevolent air. Could it be, really? Yes, but she would have to be careful. She would go inside, bathe, take her temperature, and then see if, after a few hours, she still did not send the silver column soaring like a gull gliding on a summer thermal.

Peter Lake had arrived downstairs and begun to stalk around in the moonlight. All the nonacrobatic entry points were heavily barred. But that was hardly a problem: in his bag he had a portable acetylene torch that could slice through iron rods as if they were sausages. He was about to spark the torch, when he had a second thought. He rummaged in his knapsack and pulled out a voltmeter. There was a current running through them. They were so thick that, to bypass them electrically, he would have needed conductors of similar diameter to mimic their low resistance. He thought for a minute to get some—the Amsterdam Machine Works were not too distant, and he often went there at night, because they didn't keep a careful inventory and he had a key to the front door—but he saw that the bars were of varying thicknesses. When he examined them carefully he was astounded to find different strips of metal incorporated into them in complex helical patterns and inlaid crosshatchings. It would take a day at the blackboard just to figure out the theory of this alarm system. He had no hope of controverting it in the dark at six degrees above zero. Impressed and even delighted, Peter Lake went around the side of the house and climbed onto the broad ledge of a window.

He was now on the level of the parlor floor, having seen from the ground that the rectangular silver bands often traced in Egyptian fashion around the edges of grandiose parlor windows, were absent—though it was never much of a chore to foil them, as long as one insisted upon remaining delicate. The window in front of him was locked and alarmed, but all he had to do was cut a nice big hole in the glass and step through gingerly onto the piano.

The moon saved him, for it cleared the eaves and shone down upon the glass, illuminating ten thousand hair-thin channels etched on the inner surface like orderly rime. He took out his loupe and examined them. By some sophisticated technique that even he did not know, the fine lines had been filled with hardly visible strips of metal. Obviously, every opening in the place was rigged. Peter Lake did not know that Isaac Penn was obsessed by burglars, and had taken heroic steps to bar their entry.

"That's all right," said Peter Lake. "They can jam up the windows and doors. That's fine. But they can't wire every square foot of the walls and roof. And since there's no one here, I'll cut myself a hatch."

At the very instant that Beverly opened the door to the iron stairs and the flash appeared in the sky, Peter Lake's steel grappling hook was thrown in a perfect arc, and traveled smoothly up to the roof. It took hold with a sound like that of an ax lodging in a piece of timber. But Beverly didn't hear it, for the hook landed and the door slammed at the same time. With his tool-laden knapsack on his back, Peter Lake climbed hand over hand up the knotted rope, like an alpinist, talking to the hook all the while, begging it not to pull out. Beverly made circles around the pole of the spiral staircase, as if she were dancing down the steps of a palace filled with music. Four o'clock in the morning.

Still, the city did not stir. A few thin willows of smoke rose straight and undisturbed, and on the river some pilot lights could be seen on vessels moored fast to buoys or stranded in the ice. Light-headed and obsessed, both Beverly and Peter Lake were furiously engaged. She whirled about the second floor, tossing off her clothes as she went, waiting for enough water to fill the bathing pool so that she could take shelter in it away from the cold air that would be playing in invisible eddies above it. She was not used to such exertion, and probably should have refrained, but she danced the way people often do when they are unobserved—as unfettered and unselfconscious as a child, skipping like a lamb. Peter Lake was hard at work on the roof, panting like a bicyclist, turning a heavy auger.

"This goddamned roof's three feet thick," he said to himself as the drill went deeper and deeper and did not break through. He thought that he had hit a sleeper, so he started a new hole. After a few minutes, the brace came to rest against the top of the roof, and the bit still had not broken through. "What's going on here?" asked Peter Lake, with tremendous irritation. Usually, he would already have been knocking at the fence's door. He did not know that Isaac Penn (being an eccentric and heinously wealthy old whaler) had had the house built by New England's finest ship-wrights, specifying that the roof be crafted like the hull of a polar whaler built to survive pack ice. For some reason, Isaac Penn was afraid of meteorites, and because of that the attic of his house was, more or less, a solid block of wood. The timbers were so thick and tight that Peter Lake could not have sawed open an entrance for himself had he had until June to accomplish the task. He grew more and more apprehensive as he realized that he might have to go down a chimney. It was bad enough doing that in summer, but in winter it usually entailed difficult complications.

As Peter Lake climbed along the roof, Beverly prepared to enter the bath. Isaac Penn's bathing pool was a tank of black slate and beige marble ten feet long, eight feet wide, and five feet deep. Water flowed into it over a smooth stone ledge along its entire length, came upwelling in an explosion of bubbles from jets at the bottom, and played over the surface after spewing from the yawning mouths of golden whales. All the Penn children, most lately Willa, had learned to swim there. And despite his deserved reputation for being a pillar of virtue, Isaac Penn did not object to men and women bathing together in the nude, as long as it was not done coyly. He had learned the custom in Japan, and maintained that it was highly civilized. Had the public known, he would have been pilloried.

The pool was half full, a churning sea of warm white bubbles. Peter Lake found the roof door and the lighted spiral staircase. He thought it might have been a trap, but he also thought that it might have been good luck. It was a heavy steel door: someone had mistakenly left it unlocked after leaving the solarium. Deciding to try it, he took out his pistol. Beverly raised her arms. No fever, it seemed. She caught a glimpse of herself in the mirror. She was beautiful; and how wonderful to be beautiful and not wasting away. Peter Lake peered in through the roof door, allowing his eyes to adjust to the light. Then he took a step, and Beverly tossed herself, feet first, with a whoop, into the whirlpool. He turned dizzily down the steps. She spread her arms and revolved easily in the current. Just as he reached the main floor, pistol in hand, eyes darting to and fro, she took hold of a golden whale and stretched out her feet to kick in place, singing to herself. She had plaited her hair in a loose braid, and it lay suspended in the clear shallows that washed across her back. Her limbs, smoother and more perfect than ivory, beautiful in themselves as examples of form, beautiful in their motion balanced one against the other, were stretched out and lean, and her arms made a lute shape as she clutched the golden whale in front of her. If the fever were to come back, it would do so after the bath, and make her once again redder than a field of hot roses. But she didn't think about it, and she kicked and sang as the water flooded over the fall.

No longer fearful of entrapment, Peter Lake reached Isaac Penn's study. It was sumptuous indeed, something a burglar might pray for—ten thousand leather-bound books (some in glass cases); a glimmering collection of ancient navigational instruments, chronometers, and brass-sheathed telescopes; and half a dozen oil paintings. Peter Lake looked at a book in one of the glass cases. A printed card next to it read "Gutenberg Bible." Worthless, thought Peter Lake, since it could not have been very old, having come

114

from Guttenberg, a town in New Jersey just south of North Bergen and north of West New York. Someone there was printing up tremendous unreadable Bibles.

Right over a dark mahogany desk as spacious as a room in servants' quarters was a painting of a racehorse standing in a meadow. Behind such a painting, Peter Lake knew, one could always find a vault. He swung the painting out from the wall. "It's as big as a vault in a bank," he said out loud. And it was, but it was in Isaac Penn's study, and that meant something.

Isaac Penn was in many ways a genius. But he was also peculiar and eccentric. Enamored of the sciences, he had wanted to name his last child Oxygen, but everyone had prevailed in getting him to choose a more conventional appellation, which was lucky for little Willa. Years before, however, he had managed to saddle Harry with the rather uncommon middle name of Brazil. And he had prevailed entirely in the design of his house. One of its more unusual features was the vault that Peter Lake was so happy to find. Though the house itself was a fortress, still, Isaac Penn had thought to make sure that anyone who did manage to break in would be kept busy. Thus the vault was not a vault but rather a solid plug of molybdenum steel which extended into the wall for five feet. Peter Lake began to drill.

Half an hour later, the brace for the two-inch bit began to grind steel. He pulled away the drill and inserted a probe. He hadn't broken through. Must have been machined imprecisely, he thought, or maybe my bit's worn down. He took a set of calipers from his bag and measured the tool—exactly two inches. One of those foil deals, he said to himself, and placed an awl in the boring. He struck it hard with the steel mallet, and the mallet went shooting back over his shoulder and bounced off the wall. A three-inch door? Impossible: it couldn't be opened. Let me check this. After careful measuring and calculation, he determined that the radius of the opening and the design of the hinge did not permit of a three-inch-thick door. He would try three inches anyway. He put in a longer bit, and resumed drilling.

Upstairs, Beverly did not know if the fever had returned or if the heat she felt was only because of the bath. She sweated as if she had 105, and feared that, though the fever might have gone away, her flirtation with steam and hot water had invited it back. Perhaps she should have been totally silent and held her breath, hoping that the fever would run blindly throughout the house unable to find her and then crash out a window to dissipate in the snow. But she was not sure that her indiscretion would not, in the end, serve her well, for she remembered what her father had said about those who bide too much of their time and keep too much counsel. He had told her, "God is not fooled by silence." He had told her always to have courage, and sometimes to step into the breach—though he need not have told her, for it seemed to have been her temperament from the very start. So she cleared the steam from the mirror with a bold sweep of her hand and revealed a gorgeous sweating girl with a gleam of water covering her reddened face and chest. Fight the fever. Fight it, and, if necessary, go down fighting. The courage would not go unrewarded, would it? That is to be seen, she thought. But, meanwhile, there was no question—she would fight. She wrapped herself in a blanket-sized towel and fastened it near her shoulder with a silver clasp. With the fever, even standing upright was taxing. When she went into the hall on her way downstairs to play the piano, the cool air was like a breeze in the mountains.

Peter Lake, too, was sweating. When the brace ground to a halt, he pulled out the drill and blew away the tailings. In went the probe. Solid. In went the awl. He struck it a stupendous blow, and was nearly killed by the ricocheting hammer, which, this time, lodged in the wall behind him. His wrist and fingers stinging, Peter Lake forgot what he had broken in to do, and changed to a ten-inch bit. "I'm going to break through this bastard," he said, angrily and with a trace of insanity, "even if it kills me." Then he rolled up his shirt sleeves, and began to drill yet again. Sweat poured down his face, stinging his eyes, dripping onto the crimson carpet.

Beverly glided past the door of the study. Peter Lake saw a diffuse white reflection in the wet steel of the auger, and turned, half expecting to see a ghost. But she was already in the kitchen. He went back to his task, gripping the slippery beet-colored handle of the brace with all his strength as he worked it.

While she stared into the hell of the toaster, Beverly heard the squeaking and mincing of the drill. Muffled within the walls, it sounded like a very large rat. Her eyes shot about suspiciously. Since when were there rats in the Penn house? She imagined him and shuddered, visualizing rats in the honeycombed tunnels that passed through the dead in their graves, among the horrible tangle of roots that embraced the ground as pale and blind as maggots. But the rat would undoubtedly be satisfied with whatever was deep in the walls. Besides, gnawing sounds from inside a house always went away, and then seemed as if they had never been there. Up popped two scones, and she deftly caught them in midair.

Peter Lake hit ten inches. His muscles ached. He was thirsty. Just before Beverly passed by the study door on her way to the conservatory (and this time, looking to her left, she would have seen him), he threw himself on a leather couch and closed his eyes in exhaustion.

She placed the little china plate that held the scones, and a bone-white cup of hot tea, on the piano. When she was a girl her father had scolded her for doing that. The piano did have some heat rings on it, but it had always sounded the same. She opened the keyboard cover and out flashed a smiling monster of soft ivory. What would she play? Perhaps "Les Adieux." It was one of her favorite pieces, and with it she might say goodbye to the fever. But no, the beauty of "Les Adieux" was also an invitation to return, strong enough to call back a galloping horse and its rider. Remembering what her father had said about those who were unduly silent, she decided upon a piece of music that was pure courage, the allegro of the Brahms "Violin Concerto," which she had in a piano transcription. She got it out and spread it open. The steam from the tea rose past the notes; their pattern was like what an eagle might see as he wheeled over a range of steep mountains. The opening was so bold and true that she feared to start, for its drawn-out melody was no less than a cry from a human heart. She shuddered, and then she began. The beauty of the music exploded through the house as its first phrases were sustained, echoed, and elevated by those that followed.

Peter Lake had been lying back on the couch, slack. His tools were strewn about the room. Neither crouching nor alert, nor packed-up and ready, as his profession dictated, he was, to the contrary, uncharacteristically vulnerable. And when the music erupted furiously, it caught him completely off guard. He flew into the air, his heart stopped, and then he sank down with the expression of a dog kicked from sleep by a screen door. However, he recovered very quickly—another part of his profession—and by the time he was on his feet he was no longer a burglar attacked by a violin concerto, but a man. He left his tools and jacket where they had been, and walked toward the sound.

This was not the ringing piano of the music hall, sweet and sad, but something far higher. It moved him not as a succession of abstract sounds, but as if it were, rather, as simple and evident as the great strings of greenish-white pearls that glistened along the bridge catenaries at night. When early evening came, they were there, shining out, the symbol of something that he loved very much but did not really know. What would he have done if the lights of the bridges did not light in early evening? They were his center calm, his reassurance, and much more than that. This music sounded to Peter Lake like the sparkling signal that the lights tapped out in the mist.

He arrived at the door of the conservatory, defenseless, as the echo and timbre of Beverly's grand piano rang through him in a resonance as solid and direct as one of the physical laws. Running that fierce black engine was a girl in a towel. She was sweating, working hard, lost in powering the wide end of the speeding piano. Her hair was half wet, still plaited, delirious. She sang and spoke to the piano, cajoling it, tempting it, encouraging it. She spoke under her breath, and her lips moved to emphasize and verify. "Yes," she said. "Now!" She hummed notes, or sang them, she closed her eyes, and sometimes she struck down very hard, or withdrew with a smile. But she was working all the time; her hands were moving; the tendons and muscles in her neck and shoulders shifted and flowed like those of an athlete. Peter Lake could not see that she was almost crying. He didn't know what was happening to him, and was resentful of the deep emotions that he tried to control and could not, so that, though he wanted to, he was unable to back away. He stood there, rooted, until Beverly, breathing hard, finished the piece and slammed down the keyboard cover. Her breathing was most peculiar. It was the breathing of someone deep in the lucid darkness of a fever.

She put her hands on the piano and leaned against it so she wouldn't fall. Peter Lake neither moved nor took his eyes off her. He was deeply ashamed, mortified. He had come to steal, he had broken in, he was streaked with sweat and dirt from his work at the drill, and he was staring at Beverly without her knowledge.

He had unspeakable admiration for the way she had risen from obvious weakness to court with such passion the elusive and demanding notes that he had heard. She had done what Mootfowl had always argued. She had risen above herself, right before his eyes. She had risen, and then fallen back, weakened, vulnerable, alone. He wanted to follow her in this. And, then, she was beautiful, half naked, glowing as if she had just stepped from a bath. Her fatigue seemed almost like drunkenness or abandon. Her bare shoulders alone might have absorbed his attention for many weeks. He was overwhelmed.

But how in the world would he, could he, approach her? It seemed to him as if the new dawn took an hour to fill the room, and all the while they were frozen in position. He finally concluded that she was, simply, unapproachable, and that he dared not try. As the dawn wind gently shook the windows, he took a step backward, hoping to leave unobserved while she was immobile at the piano.

When he did, the floor gave a wonderful, tortured, wooden squeak which told unmistakably of live weight. He froze, hoping that it would go unnoticed. She lifted and turned her head. And then she saw him. Half in delirium, she fixed her open gaze upon his face. Though her reaction built steadily within her, she gave no clue to what it was. He, on the other hand, felt shame flooding his cheeks like a hot geyser.

He could say nothing. He had no right to be there, he had already been profoundly changed, he was not good at small talk, she was half naked, it was dawn, and he loved her.

He moved his foot up and down on the loose plank that had given him away. It sounded like a child's toy being pressed. He kept on moving his foot up and down, and he looked as if he were about to burst into tears. "It squeaks," he said, with such emotion that he thought the whole world had gone mad. "It squeaks."

Beverly looked at the piano, and then back at Peter Lake. "What?" she asked, her voice rising gently. "What did you say?"

"Nothing," replied Peter Lake. "It's not important."

She began to laugh. It was very loud at first, and reminded them that (except for the music) the house had long been silent. He, too, laughed, rather politely, and cautiously. She put her hand to her face, closed her eyes, and sighed. Then she was quiet, with her hand to her face still, until another short burst of laughter. Then she pressed her forehead very hard, and she cried. The tears came terribly fast. Now she, too, was salty and streaked. It was horribly bitter crying, but it was soon over, and when she looked up again, she was drained, or so it seemed.

Morning sun now made the room as white as sugar, and the drafts and breezes made it cold. "If you're what I've got," she said, "then you're what I'll take." He might have been offended, but she did not sound in the least sorry for herself. It was as if she knew about him more even than he did. He nodded to say that he understood. Whatever it was, it did not appear to be a marriage made in heaven. For the first time in his life, he felt exactly what he was, and he was not impressed. Still, he wanted to embrace her. But that seemed out of the question, and the room grew whiter and whiter.

Underneath them, in the basement, the automatic furnace switched on, and the entire shiplike frame of the Penn house shuddered. They could hear the rhythmic beating of the oil burner and the bright yellow pounding of the flame. He wanted more than anything in the world to embrace her. But it seemed out of the question.

Then she turned to him and stretched out her arms. And he went to her as if he had been born for it.

ON THE MARSH

THAT the river had frozen solid was cause for festivity and alarm. People immediately pitched colorful tents and built dangerous bonfires upon the ice, which, in one short day, became the site of a medieval fair for those who had been drawn out onto the river to see their city, now silent, in heart-filling perspective. Because the ferries had been trapped, the wagoners and produce men were the first out, taking mule trains, horse caravans, and even motor trucks across the new white roads. There were many who said that an ice age approached. They huddled like rats, around their fires and in their flannel beds, despairing, forgetful of the power of spring.

Traveling one night in a heavy snow, Peter Lake used the ice as a road to the Bayonne Marsh. Though he could see nothing but blinding flashes cascading before him in a void of pulsating blue, he made his way faultlessly by listening to the distant roar of the cloud wall. It was a pure sound, like that of the cutting torch, or of a mysterious choir singing all sounds. It hinted that, beyond the furious barrier, a deep past and a bright and beautiful future were somehow combined.

In navigating, he used the fully laden sound like a light, and thought that if the sound were alive—a chorus of spirits, somehow animate, perhaps a god—it would not be displeased that he made it a beacon, keeping it always to his left by ten degrees. And he found not only the right path, but a safe one, by listening to the ice, muffled by newly fallen snow, as it resounded under the slow steps of the white horse.

Most horses, sensing the water underneath, would have been afraid. A fall through splintered ice would have meant drowning in cold black water, itself suffocated under an unyielding white plate and thousands of feet of vibrating blue air choked with cotton. But the white horse was unafraid, and moved as steadily as if he had been on a track. He kept his head up, and followed the sound of the clouds with what seemed to be affection. Peter Lake could hardly see the animal beneath him as white as the thickly falling snow, but he could sense that the horse was on his own ride, relearning what he had known long before. And it was not unpleasant, plodding slowly over the ice, to discover that of all the means to the tranquillity he now sought, a quiet snowfall was the most elegant and the most generous.

Hours out, when he knew he was on the marsh because the ice rose in long whalish humps over the dunes, and brittle cattails jingled as they were shaken by his horse's hooves, he sensed that he was being watched. Well he understood how careful the Baymen became when the marsh froze and roving bands could cross over and lay waste their villages. The Baymen remembered the Hessians, and the Indians, and others even before them. Certain that they were watching him, he advanced into the pressure of their eyes as if to the beat of a drum. The horse was alert, trying for silence in his steps.

Then they closed with breathless speed, a full circle of them in cowled white robes of thick rabbit fur, their winter dress. The ring they made of their spear points was a mechanical expression of the ineluctable, an absolute zero of escape. How silently they had come, how perfectly they had appeared from the blinding mist, as if they had been part of it. Peter Lake spoke to them in the ceremonial language. They recognized him and brought him in.

He always took good care of the horse. After all, he loved him. And while he was clearing a space between two enormous dappled Percherons, so that the white horse, who was even bigger than they were, would be warm and comfortable in the thickly reeded quonset stable, Humpstone John pushed his way through the door of felt panels. As Humpstone John grew accustomed to the light that streamed from a brass candle-lantern, he appeared stunned. This was not unusual, for he was a man who was often in the presence of great things. He looked at the horse with tremendous satisfaction. Peter Lake saw in John's eyes the delight at seeing an old friend, and he saw as well that it was not on account of him.

The horse snorted. He didn't know John, that was clear. John addressed Peter Lake in English. "Where did you get him?" he asked.

"I got him . . . uh, I got him. . . ."

"Well, where did you get him?"

"I didn't really get him. He was just there."

"Where?"

"On the Battery. I had almost had it—the Short Tails. I fell. When I got up I couldn't run anymore. I thought it was the bucket. And then he came from . . ."

"From your left."

"From my left." Peter Lake nodded. "How did you know?"

"Have you named him?" asked John.

"No."

"You don't know his name, do you?"

"No. There wasn't any way to know." He thought for a minute. "He can jump. Jesus, can he jump. The Dead Rabbits wanted to buy him and put him in the circus." Then his voice lowered. "John, he can jump four blocks."

"Not surprised."

"You know about him. Why is that?"

"Peter Lake, I thought that you might come to no good (and you may yet). And when we sent you across the river, all alone, I had little hope that you would make out decently in that place." When he said "that place," he said it with the dread and revulsion that the Baymen had for the city. "I thought that you were gone from us, and would become one of them. . . ."

"I have," said Peter Lake.

"Maybe you have. But that's not the end of it."

"Why?"

"You remember that there are ten songs."

"Yes."

"That one learns them, beginning at age thirteen, one each decade."

"Yes. I never learned them."

"I know, Peter Lake. We sent you away. The first, the song of thirteen, has to do with the just shape of the world. It is nature's song, and is about water, air, fire, and things like that. I cannot ever sing you any of these, not anymore. But I can say that the second one, the song of twenty-three, is the song of women; and the third one, the third song, Peter Lake, is the song of Athansor."

"Athansor?"

"Yes," said Humpstone John, "Athansor . . . the white horse."

The next morning, when the snow stopped and the sky became cold crystal, every Bayman from everywhere arrived to view Athansor—that is, every Bayman who knew the song of the white horse. Refusing Peter Lake any information about what the song said, they just gazed in amazement at Athansor, who had had no idea that this was his name, but came to recognize it by noon. Peter Lake was irritated because, as he put it, he wanted to know what he was driving around. It didn't take him long to stop wondering, since he thought he would never find out—it was harder to pry a secret from a Bayman than it was to open a sick clam. He went to the white horse and comforted him, and was comforted in turn to realize that the horse's sudden renown and new name meant nothing. It just doesn't matter, he thought; he's the white horse; his nose is still soft and warm; nothing has changed.

But something had changed, or was changing. Everything always did, no matter how much he loved what he had. The only redemption would be if all the tumbling and rearrangement were to mean something. But he was aware of no pattern. If there were one great equality, one fine universal balance that he could understand, then he would know that there were others, and that someday the curtain of the world would lift onto a sunny springlike stillness and reveal that nothing—nothing—had been for nought, neither the suffering of all the children that he had seen suffering, nor the agony of the child in the hallway, nor love that ends in death: nothing. He doubted that he would have a hint of any greater purpose, and did not ever expect to see the one instant of unambiguous justice that legend said would make the cloud wall gold.

Covered with furs, he lay in his hut, staring out an open door at Manhattan far across the white and frozen bay. He had spent two decades in the city that sat on the horizon like something floating in the clouds, and now he knew what the gray and red palisade was; he knew its scale, its music, its interior, the sound of its engines, the plan of its streets. Great as they were, the bridges were fathomable. He understood how the new skyscrapers were built. Mechanics built them, and he was a mechanic. For twenty years, he had been on the streets of that city, and he loved it. He was a guide, an intimate. And yet, from a distance, catching the sun in the clear, it looked like nothing he had ever known. Following its brown spine as far as his eye could see, he lifted his head to pass over the spires of tall buildings. A hundred plumes of smoke and steam curled about this sleeping thing, which would not have surprised him had it immediately come alive. Its growing animation was catapulted across the ice, and though it was sleeping in dark chains, he had no doubt that someday it would rise and brighten, like a whale bursting from the sea into light and air.

It was easy to become lost in vivid memories of such a city, and they assaulted him with the energy and disorder of the streets themselves. Within the traffic of many forms and colors, serene images spoke quietly, but they were as bright as enameled miniatures, and as lovely to recall.

A family of South American grandees had toured the park one summer day, in a line of four carriages pulled by horses as gray as November. It seemed that they were used to another life in a place that was vast, wild, and full of sun and animals, and as they rode in the lacquered carriages, they carried themselves like knights. The women were more alluring than Spanish dancers at the core of their frenzy: sex gleamed all about them like metal. There were a silent patriarch and matriarch, each of whom had wise old eyes, and hair whiter than the unprinted edge of a postage stamp. Peter Lake had envied them as they approached: though they did not know the city, they were obviously masters of some foreign ground. As they came closer he saw that sitting with the driver in the front carriage was a cretin or idiot—a son, brother, or grandson of those within the scallop of the carriage itself. He was dressed like them, but his eyes bulged, and he drooled from a smile that was far too easy. His hair seemed like fur, and his limbs were loose and dangling. Every now and then the grandmother would stand up in the carriage, steady herself with one hand, and pat him like a dog, while the others talked to him affectionately. For him, it must have been a great thing to ride with the driver. They were not in the least embarrassed by this stroke of fortune. On the contrary, they seemed to benefit from it, as sails flying through bright air benefit from a suffocated keel ploughing blindly through dark water. He was one of them, and always would be. They loved him. The carriages had long passed, but Peter Lake never would forget the boy's pale moonish face bobbing up and down at the head of the procession.

Now and then, from the windswept platforms of the Brooklyn crossing, he saw the ranks of soldierly skyscrapers in their tight stone lines. Once, late in spring, he watched them stop a continental sea of cloud and mist, damming it up like the water in a millpond, until it sifted through their fingers and made them individual islands. At night they were a palisade of flickering light. Long after everyone was asleep, they conspired in wind tones and vibrations. They held through the blinding weather, speaking in their strange static, trying to touch across great heights, striving to effect the

126

marriage of heaven and hell to which they were pledged. Watching in a storm, Peter Lake had seen lightning dance across their granite needles in sheets of solid white.

But no memory, no matter how fine, sharp, or powerful, could match his memory of Beverly. It was electrifying and perfect— except that he could not remember the color of her eyes. They were round, bright, and beautiful, that was sure, but were they green, brown, or blue? Why remember the color of her eyes, when she was dying? But blue-eyed (was she blue-eyed?) Beverly, in a claret scarf, drew him back to her when he least expected and wanted it.

He tried to distract himself. Remembering a string of fortunate summers, he summoned from his bed on the windswept ice a picture of Manhattan reverberating with heat. There he was, bobbing and floating on rafts of color high above the streets: silvered canyons and warm red brick, the lisp of a huge broken clock, trees like bells shuddering sound in green, silent streets as dark and elegant as mirrors in dim light, a thousand paintings left and right—islands in the stream cascading from above, the heat of pale stone, merchants forever frozen who never ceased to move, cooing purple pigeons shaped like shells, an arsenal of roses in the park, streets that crossed in forks and chimes, leopard shadows, dappled lines. But what was it without green-eyed (was she green-eyed?) Beverly in her claret scarf.

He might hide deep in the city, and lose himself in the blurring colors, the violent action, the wavering summer furnaces of air at the end of every street. But then, enjoying the pleasure of being lost, he would turn to find that he had been followed, and changed. Brown-eyed Beverly (was she brown-eyed?), in her claret scarf, could easily pull him from his contemplations. A young girl, a frailty, simple and true, who had been unable to stand up from the piano and had had to be carried; a girl half his age; a girl who could not shoot a gun, had never been in an oyster house, atop a tower, or under the wharves; a girl hotter always than noon in August; a girl who knew nothing; had thrown him so hard that he would be out of breath forever.

The city took lives in an instant, by the hundred, without a blink. She would be quickly overwhelmed amid the tenements, she would

127

vanish and disappear, she would melt on the barriers, she would be lost, exhausted, unable to follow as he made his way through the bladed maze. And yet, those green, blue, brown eyes followed him down all streets, on all paths, everywhere, effortlessly.

The best thing to do was to stop it while he still could, since it was something that would lead nowhere, painfully. There was no shortage of women for him in that sea of architecture that lay across the ice. The women there, in seemingly infinite number, were as startling and beautiful as a quiet green square at the exit of a wildly busy street. They could clasp him tight in their speech, keeping him like a pearl in a stiff silver mount, because it had always been easy for him to fall in love with just a voice—a source of endless trouble when he used the telephone. One woman had been so consumed with jealousy that she tried to shoot him as he was standing at the bar of an oyster house. A bullet lodged in mahogany, another killed a clam, and yet another drilled a hole in the blade of a slicing machine. Peter Lake turned to her, and asked, "What does this have to do with romance?" She and all the others were quickly fading as Beverly took hold. Beverly. This one young girl colored his mind and memory as if he had been dragged through a trench of dye.

How could he explain this to Mootfowl, who was always present, in the air, as if Peter Lake lived in a painting and Mootfowl were a figure in a painting within the painting. Sitting high up in an arched window in the sunlight, staring into the chapel of Peter Lake's life, Mootfowl was always willing to forgive, but he had to hear the truth. And the truth, as Peter Lake saw it, was that the girl was consumptive—not just consumptive, but near death. He knew of such things from a lifetime among the dark or glowing souls ready to depart the plain of tenement rooftops and sail through the air. The child in the hallway was by no means the only one he had seen about to cross worlds. They were as numerous as flowers in spring and could be found by the row in lofts full of iron beds, or overflowing into the neglected gardens of hospitals for the poor. As they drifted upward, ghosts, they could not even cry out.

She would soon join the disappearing souls, faintly glowing, gossamer. How could he trust that he loved her? She was rich, and there was much to gain. The rich died, too, disappointing all those who thought that somehow they didn't. Peter Lake had no illusions about mortality. He knew that it made everyone perfectly equal, and that the treasures of the earth were movement, courage, laughter, and love. The wealthy could not buy these things. On the contrary, they were for the taking. Though Peter Lake was, by his account, a fortunate man, he was not wealthy. That was something else entirely, which depended solely upon things like gold, silver, and commercial paper (he had stolen a lot of commercial paper from banks: it was hard to fence). Beverly was an heiress to the kind of fortune that altered one's character in contemplating it, the kind of fortune that was like an injection of stimulants directly into the bloodstream. His heart pounded when he thought of the millions, the scores of millions, the hundreds of millions.

How could he explain to the airborne Mootfowl that what had overtaken him was love and not greed. She was soon to die, and he would love other women who had, as Mootfowl used to say, a faster grip on the world. And how would he explain to a clerical spirit in a lighted window that his lust and love had finally converged, undiminished.

He had carried her from the piano, not to the reception room nor to her father's study, but to a bedroom. There, he put her down on cotton sheets as fresh and cool as silk, and watched in amazement as she removed the clasp from the towel that was wrapped about her, and, while leaning back on the pillows as if she were about to suffer a medical examination, undraped herself. She breathed heavily—the feverish breathing—and stared straight ahead. Then she forced herself to look at him, and saw that he was more frightened than she.

She took a deep breath and moistened her lips. Then she exhaled, and said to the man standing by her bedside, ''I've never done this before.''

''Done what?'' answered Peter Lake.

''Made love,'' she said.

''That's crazy. You're burning up. It's too rough,'' Peter Lake said almost all at once.

''Go to hell!'' she screamed.

"But, miss," he said, "it's not that you're not beautiful, it's that I . . ."

"You what," she asked, half imploringly and half in disgust.

"I broke into the house." He shook his head. "I came to steal."

"If you don't make love to me," she said, "I don't think anyone ever will. I'm eighteen. I've never been kissed on the mouth. I don't know anyone, you see. I'm sorry. But I have a year." She closed her eyes. "Maybe, according to the doctor who came from Baltimore, a year and a half. In Boston they said six months—and that was eight months ago. So I'm two months dead," she whispered, "and you can do with me whatever you want."

Peter Lake, who was both decisive and brave, thought for a moment. "That is exactly what I will do," he said as he sat down on the bed to gather her in his arms. He pulled her in and swung her over and began to kiss her forehead and her hair. At first she was as limp and shocked as someone who has begun to fall from a great height. It was as if her heart had stopped.

She had not counted on affection. It startled her. He kissed her temples, her cheeks, and her hair, and stroked her shoulders as tenderly as if she had been a cat. She closed her eyes and cried, much satisfied by the tears as they forced their way past a dark curtain and rolled down her face.

Beverly Penn, who had the courage of someone who is often confronted by that which is gravely important, had not expected that someone else would be that way too. Peter Lake seemed to love her in exactly the way that she loved everything that she knew she would lose. He kissed her, and stroked her, and spoke to her. How surprised she was at what he said. He told her about the city, as if it were a live creature, pale and pink, that had a groin and blood and lips. He told her about spring in Prince Street, about the narrow alleys full of flowers, protected by trees, quiet and dark. He told her about the colors in coats and clothes and on the stage and in all kinds of lights, and that their random movement made them come alive. "Prince Street," he said, "is *alive*. The buildings are as ruddy as flesh. I've seen them breathe. I swear it." He surprised even himself.

He talked to her for hours. He talked himself dry. She leaned back on the pillows, pleased to be naked in front of him, relaxed, calm, smiling. He talked hills. He talked gardens. What he said was so gentle, strong, and full of counterpoint and rhyme, that he was not even sure that it was not singing. And long before he was all talked out and exhausted, she had fallen in love with him.

Her fever had subsided enough so that she could feel the coolness of the room. After a comfortable moment of silence and ringing in the ears, he bent over, and, in kissing her breasts, was overcome by a graceful, mobile desire. She was cool to the touch, and though she had imagined with stunning accuracy everything that they did in their rush to find one another out, she had not had the slightest idea of the power and abandon with which they united. It was as if they had been kept from one another for a thousand years and would not come together for yet another thousand. But now, chest against chest, arm cradled in arm, hallucinatory and light, they felt as if they were whirling in a cloud.

How would he explain to the airborne Mootfowl that, when her fever returned and she grew delirious and begged Peter Lake to marry her, he thought to do it quickly, so that she could not change her mind. She wouldn't live too long, and he was thinking of the money. Then he had wept. Half asleep, she hadn't even known. The next morning, when he left, she stood at the back of the stairs, shorn of all her powers, which he carried away in complete indifference as if, in the large white bed, they had traded substance and spirit. He knew that she had given him everything she had, and as he left her he was thinking about lathes and machines and complicated measurements, and things that were precision-milled with surfaces as smooth as glass or polished brass.

He was in love with her, he was not unmoved because she was Isaac Penn's daughter, and the two factions were much at war. In the painting's bright corner, Mootfowl seemed amused, which surprised Peter Lake, who had thought he was guilty of a great transgression. But the laughter and color in the bright window at the periphery of his vision suggested that this was not so.

And then he saw a strange white cloud moving across the now golden face of the city's cliffs in the sunset. It changed shape and form as it flew about the towers like a whimsical ghost. He realized what it was—pigeons, millions of pigeons, in a cloud electrified by reflection. They wheeled across the skyline like particles of smoke in Brownian motion, caught brilliantly in a dark chamber by a clear stroke of light reverberating between a sky and floor of yellow brass. Next to the bodies of the buildings they were like mites, or snow, or confetti, or dust . . . and yet they were one single flight, rising like a plume in the wind. Peter Lake knew from this that the city would take care, for it was a magical gate through which those who entered passed in innocent longing, taking every hope, showing touching courage—and for good reason. The city would take care. There was no choice but to trust the architect's dream that was spread before him as compact as an engine, solid and sure, shimmering over the glinting ice. He lay back, resigned until he saw her again not to know the color of her eyes.

And then he was suddenly overwhelmed. It was as if a thousand bolts of lightning had converged to lift him. All he could see was blue, electric blue, wet shining warm blue, blue with no end, everywhere, blue that glowed and made him cry out, blue, blue, her eyes were blue.

LAKE OF THE COHEERIES

IN winter, the Lake of the Coheeries was the scene of a siege. No Renaissance engine belching fire or hurling stone could keep pace with even one white clap of a New York winter, and winter there clapped as endlessly as a paddlewheel on one of the big white boats slapping across the lake in seasons gone by. Battalions of arctic clouds droned down from the north to bomb the state with snow, to bleach it as white as young ivory, to mortar it with frost that would last from September to May. Lost in this white siege was the town of Lake of the Coheeries, which in comparison to the infinite, dazzling, never-ending lake that terminated, some people said, in China, was about the size of a shoebox.

The lake itself ate up all the snow until mid-December. Then, after it froze over, the snow swept across it in drifts and made a maze of corridors wide enough for cargo iceboats, with walls of snow higher than canal banks. Iceboat masts could be seen running along the tops. Sometimes a brave soul would go aloft in a balloon to direct a snow-shoveling crew in cutting the walls of the maze so that the iceboats would have a straighter path from one side of the lake to the other. But within a week or less, the maze would be restored by shifting winds and drift-filled cuts, and the iceboat men once again had to guess, call out to one another, and sometimes halt to climb a bank and peer around. And then when winter really came, in January, the snow completely covered the lake, and transportation across it required horses and sleds.

That December the ice was empty and unmarred, as perfect as a mirror, and iceboats were able to wing about like martins and kingfishers. They tracked their ways across the flawless glass like glaziers' cutting wheels. The Penns had crossed the lake at eighty miles per hour. Willa was dumbfounded. As he had held her on his lap, in the wind, Isaac Penn explained. This was Dutch—as if saying so could account for the speed, the sliding, the great knives on the slick ice. But Willa accepted it without question. It was Dutch. That explained it. No need to wonder anymore. The idea was within its warm wool sock. Giddiness, speed, sea horizons, and azure ice were Dutch, and the child held tight to the magic of the word.

Not so the telegraph man who climbed aboard his flyer with a message for Isaac Penn and shot across the ice in the dark, heading for the eastern shore, where a cluster of lights marked the Penn summer house ablaze with the festivities of Christmas. The telegraph man held his lines tightly in gloves of fur and leather. His hands were cramped with exertion, his arms near to falling off, his face knotted up to trace the shortest path across the black ice. At first the lights appeared not to get closer. Then they gradually got bigger until, at the end, he seemed to be speeding toward them faster than light itself. He had to whoa his iceboat like a horse— slackening the sail, dragging the brake, then lifting the brake, and coming about. He made the flyer creep and crawl the last half-mile to the Penns' dock, and every now and then he patted the telegram to summon in its yellow crunch the assurance that it had not been blown out of his vest.

Isaac Penn was known for lugubrious depressions, deep melancholia, moments of heavenly equilibrium, and mad flights of happiness and joy. His moods infected everyone around him. When Isaac Penn was down, the world was grayer than London's rain-laden trees. When Isaac Penn was up, it was every room bursting forth with tympanums and brass; a medieval street fair of the heart; the Midwest in May; flights of soaring birds; it was Willa's laugh rolling about, as capricious and dependable as the surf. That night in the Lake of the Coheeries the summer house was as bright as a candle in a paper cup. It was the evening before Christmas Eve, and Isaac Penn pranced about like a mad goat. He danced with Willa, stooping way down; he boxed with Harry; they did reels in front of the fire, with the rug rolled back—the servants, too, and the closest neighbors, the Gamelys. Knees flew into the air, followed by dancing hose and puppetlike legs. Dresses twisted in light yellow overjoyed with torque and pitch. Rum, champagne, cakes, and roasts were everywhere. (Well, not everywhere: they weren't in the fireplace, or on top of the harp, or pasted on the ceiling.) The house was warm and bright. Even the cats danced.

The telegraph man knocked at the door. When they opened it, there he was, covered with snow and ice, a bush in winter. When he entered, he shielded his eyes against the light, which came at him throbbing like a drum, and he walked around as if he were a cinch bug, making little circles, stopping short stubbornly. They gave him a cup of daffodil punch, and as his mustache icicles melted into it and the great big standy-up circus organ played "Turkey in the Straw," he said, "Telegram."

My, but he was surprised—even scared—by their reaction. They danced and applauded like a bunch of lunatics. "All I said was 'telegram,' " he protested, "not 'the second coming.' "

"God bless you!" they screamed, and applauded once more, stunning the man who had just spent a dark hour fleeing like a spirit over the floor of ice. "A telegram! A telegram!"

Lunatics, he thought to himself, typical downstate lunatics. Then he gave them the telegram.

135

Harry read it: " 'Cannot come Lake of the Coheeries Christmas. Will spend Christmas dancing at Mouquin's with Peter Lake. I love you all. My life is ablaze. Kiss Willa especially. Beverly.' "

As Isaac Penn stood in the middle of the floor, puzzled, the dance music played on. Mouquin's? How could Beverly dance at Mouquin's? It was hot and crowded. What was she going to do to herself? And who the hell was Peter Lake?

Peter Lake was all fear, when, shortly before Christmas, he took himself and the white horse (or, as he now called him, Athansor) up to the Penn house high on the cloudy park's northwest flank. He remembered Beverly best not for the dazed moments in love, and not for the way she had changed him when he saw her at the piano, but for the way she had looked when he left. She was standing at the back of the stairs, in a harsh northern light that softened in the golden mist of her disarrayed hair. She looked at him with unmatchable simplicity. Her expression said nothing, reflected nothing; in it was no ambition for him, no snare, no plan. Not even affection. Perhaps she was too tired to do anything but gaze at him without a thought. There were no barriers between them then, and he would always remember her standing alone at the foot of the stairs, about to ascend into the cold crest of light which broke like surf against her hair. That was Beverly.

The house she lived in was unsuited to such ravishing simplicity, for it was an essay in whimsy, ingenuity, and laughter. It was stronger than the upturned hull of an ark, bristling with impediments, and as inviting as the round green wreath that hung on the front door. The front door itself was pale blue, almost gray. Had Pearly passed by, he would have stopped. "I know how these things work," Peter Lake said under his breath, addressing the wreath. "It was too fast, too fast. Such a rapid conversion is bound to have a middling end. She'll be embarrassed to death just to see me. She won't be able to look at me. Then she'll get mad. Four minutes after that, I'll be back on the street."

The door swung out at him, which was quite a surprise, for front doors usually opened in. The surprise was evident on his face, so Jayga said, "Mr. Penn says that doors should open out, like the breach on a parrot or something. He says that he likes to pack people into the house as if he was loading a doll glenn. I don't know what he means by it, but the doors swing out. What's your business?" She gave him a quick up and down. "We don't have no trade entrance."

"Beverly."

Jayga looked this way and that, and then said, "Oh Lord!" Thinking that she could turn back the clock, she asked, "What's your business? We don't got no trade entrance."

"Beverly," Peter Lake answered calmly.

"Beverly who?"

"Beverly Penn."

"Miss Beverly Penn? The Miss?"

"Miss Beverly Penn," Peter Lake echoed, "the Miss."

"You?" Jayga asked in astonishment. "You don't look like no Harberd boy."

"Me. I'm not a Harberd boy. I'm just like you, ya folla?"

Tremendously disturbed, Jayga took him up to the roof, where Beverly lay on a deck chair, her face to the clouds. It was almost warm in the protected enclosure, and she seemed more rested, and stronger, than she had been when he had met her. In fact, she was a study in equanimity, as tranquil as the steady subdued gray of the low roof of clouds. How beautiful she was. She suggested to him the qualities of strength and sureness which he, a man always on the run, longed for most. She made him feel as if his battles were behind him, and she excited in him, for the first time, the desire to be married. He enjoyed the thought of the handsome couple he imagined they might be. This, and more, followed from just a glance.

Jayga went downstairs, all stirred up, as servants often are on behalf of their masters. Peter Lake sat down on an uncushioned deck chair opposite Beverly's. His charcoal-colored coat made eaves and dormers about his knees. If he had had a hat (he didn't wear a hat), he would have taken it off. The city was preparing for Christmas. Though they both could feel the oncoming tension, there was peace.

Then occurred a rare thing about which men and women sometimes dream. They carried on a full conversation in complete silence, discerning feelings, plans, exclamations, jokes, opinions, laughter, and dreams—rapidly, silently, inexplicably. Their eyes and faces were as mobile as changing light upon a mottled sandbar when clear water agitates above it. Peter Lake sometimes stole big horse-choker diamonds; white, yellow, or rose. And during the lovely hours before his rendezvous with the fence, he spent much time entranced by the light dancing through them. They, like Beverly and Peter Lake, seemed to be able to speak in silence.

Much that was strange, not for its substance, but for the way in which it was communicated, passed between them without resistance. Yes, they were delighted by one another's image in daylight, outside. He was handsome and she beautiful, and it was a pleasant surprise to receive a gift greater than even memory could give. They confided in one another that they were in love. Marriage seemed to be an excellent idea, for what had they to worry about in the way of unseen hurdles when it was likely that she would not last another year?

"Mouquin's?" Peter Lake asked, breaking the silence. "I can't go to Mouquin's."

"But I want to," said Beverly, with complete disregard for Peter Lake's objection, chattering away selfishly as they descended the stairs. "I can wear my mother's gown. The clothes that she had are now at the peak of fashion. I have her blue-and-white silk dress."

"That's fine," said Peter Lake. "That's just fine. But . . ."

"And Mouquin's, they say, is a yellow wooden building that, on the outside, seems to be an ordinary boardinghouse, but is like a French dancing hall inside, with balustrades of marble, banks of ferns, an orchestra, and people coming, and going, and dancing. They dance as if no one else is there—the people who are in love. And everyone is dressed to the nines, my father said. He said that what makes the place so wonderful, so happy, is that it has a sad edge."

"A sad edge indeed," said Peter Lake, settling back into a brown velvet couch in the library. "A sad edge indeed, especially for me. I can't go to Mouquin's. Mouquin's is where Pearly Soames practically lives." Then he told her of how Pearly had vowed to drive a sword into him, and that, despite Pearly's clumsiness and banality (Pearly often hit his head on things, tripped, and closed doors on his fingers), he honored his promises and was capable of achieving the most extraordinary ends. "I've been to Mouquin's, you see, and it isn't that great. At least it doesn't seem to be worth dying for."

Beverly lay back against the brown velvet and closed her eyes. The heat was beginning to make her tired in a lovely and contentious fashion. Jayga tried to busy herself in the kitchen, but could not resist spying on them, and went every minute or so to the opening over the hunt board to peer down the long dark hall toward the library and its red walls and bright lamps. Mouquin's moved before Beverly's eyes in a vision suggesting nothing less than a new world, a mute and snowy Russian Easter compressed within the translucent chamber of an alabaster viewing egg, a sort of miniature paradise which, if entered, might be the scene of miracles. She thought, recklessly, that dancing at Mouquin's could drive out the disease, flood it with devastating light, and provide a curtain of time and beauty through which she might pass to another side where there was no such thing as fever, and where those who loved one another lived forever. Peter Lake's difficulties with Pearly seemed slight.

"I can't imagine," she said, "that Pearly would harm you while you danced with me."

"Is that so!"

"Yes. I feel very strongly, though I don't know why, that you are safe with me, anywhere—Mouquin's included, Pearly's bedchamber included, the darkest hole in the tombs included."

Peter Lake was amazed—not only at the presumption that she was capable of protecting him, but because he, for some reason, believed her. "I'd rather not test your powers, if it's all right with you," he said, anyway, for safety's sake.

"I want to go to Mouquin's!" she screamed so loudly that Jayga jumped up and banged her head on a caldron that was hanging above her. Unable to cry out in pain, she did a long and silent Morris Dance.

"I tell you that no harm will come to you there. It's more of a

139

risk for me—to go in a carriage in a mountain of stiff clothes, to dance, to drink, to sit in a hot, tense, happy room. Pearly won't touch you."

He believed her. When she was tired she was stranger than an oracle, talking in certainties and pronouncements, insistent, selfish, delirious. She leaned back again, exhausted. He could hear only the sound of her breathing, a clock pendulum, and something thumping around in the kitchen. To dance with Beverly at Mouquin's might very well stand Pearly on his head. And if it didn't, so what. It would be a fine finish. He would drink plenty of champagne, and all the haut monde, the beau monde, and the low monde freely intermixing at Mouquin's would see his demise. What the hell, he thought, it's the quick turns that mean you're alive.

"All right," he said. "I'll go with you to Mouquin's. But let's wait until New Year's Eve, when they'll be going full blast."

"Good," she replied. "That way, we'll have time to go to the Lake of the Coheeries, where my family is. I want to see my father, and Willa. I want you to meet them."

She sounded weak, drifting off. He wondered what he would be drawn into by this pretty young girl who often spoke in the manner of a will. He had no idea of where it might lead, but he did know that he loved her.

"To the Lake of the Coheeries?" he asked. "Well then, to the Lake of the Coheeries."

"I'm glad," she said, so softly that he could hardly hear her.

A little pine was lashed to the tall black stack of the Albany boat. Its branches were bent back from steady combat with the wind. But no matter, it was still a Christmas tree. Peter Lake and Beverly drove into a dark hold where Athansor would stay in a comfortable stable with two or three other horses, and where the sleigh was then bolted to the deck. Clear electric lights suddenly came up full as the generator was coupled to newly idling engines. Peter Lake and Beverly, he in his gray coat and she in a smooth fortune of sable, suddenly became brightly visible to one another. He satisfied himself that Athansor was well set, and then took Beverly's arm to lead her upstairs to their cabin—not that he knew where he was going, although she did. She had occupied that cabin a hundred times.

As they were about to go inside, Peter Lake looked over the rail at the dock below. Vendors were selling hot loaves of bread, chestnuts, tea, and coffee. "I ought to get some bread and tea for the passage. No, tea will cool; beer, I suppose, would be better!"

"It isn't necessary," she answered.

"Why? We have to eat."

"There's a restaurant on board, and if you want you can summon a steward at four o'clock in the morning and order roast oysters, hot rum, ribs of beef, and everything that goes with anything that strikes your fancy."

"In that case," Peter Lake replied, "to hell with chestnuts."

The cabin was on two decks. Downstairs were a large dining table over which hung a gimballed oil lamp (left, after electrification, at Isaac Penn's request), captain's beds, bunk beds, a desk, a settee, and a complete bathroom. Upstairs were another sea bed, and a few leather chairs facing a plate-glass window that looked out to starboard. Since the boat left at noon to go upriver, the starboard view showed all the intricacies the sun could illumine.

"This is our cabin," Beverly said. "The *Brayton Ives* carries newsprint for *The Sun* down from Glens Falls. The line does well on account of the paper, so they keep this cabin for us whenever we want to use it. We have to pay, but at the rate for a regular cabin. They're small, but they're all right. Once, when we were children, Harry and I stayed in one, because there were so many Penns going to the lake that all the beds were taken."

The boat cast off and moved into the ice-free channel. Without removing their coats, they fell back on one of the beds and kissed all the way to Riverdale. Even above the throb of the engines they could hear brass bands on the Upper West Side, and faint choirs from within the smaller churches. But they didn't get up until Riverdale, when they went out on deck and saw a wilderness. Whitened palisades, rolling hills, glimmering iced trees, and the Tappan Zee miles ahead broadening like a route to the poles were their Christmas, and the hot drumlike sounds of the engine their Christmas music.

At Tarrytown, the setting sun made steeples, towers, and brick buildings on the hill as red and orange as tropical fruit. By the time they passed Ossining, dusk had fallen and the snow-covered fields were blue and violet. All the houses of Ossining, ranged upward on the hills, glowed like fireflies from light within as happy families and unhappy families, and those that were neither and both, gathered around pre-Christmas dinners in the Dutch style. And, undoubtedly, there were a few boys still on the ponds, racing in near-darkness down the narrow cleared lanes which ran like cold canyons through walls of oak and cattail. The river at Ossining was so wide, beautiful, and still, the shelf of ice on Croton Bay so endless and arctic, the mountains to the north so mountainly, the woods on the east bank so lovely, the fields and orchards so beckoning with the lights of fine houses at their edges or in the hollows of hills, that Peter Lake and Beverly stayed on deck though the wind made their faces frozen and numb.

Haverstraw Bay was mainly open, but the channel was littered with enormous blocks of ice against which the iron-sheathed prow of the *Brayton Ives* smashed on the downstroke. Each time this happened, it was as if ten thousand bells had been rolled down a great staircase. This combined well with the great pressure of the wind, the straining of the engine, and the miscellaneous blasts of the steam whistle. Peter Lake and Beverly, faces stoked to fire by the north wind, watched the ship charge one white slab after another and crush it into floating confetti or simply crack it in half.

The mountains into which the river wound, now whitened by winter, were, in summer, green and rolling hills, or high brown ridges covered with lightning-killed trees in which armies of eagles had their enormous nests. Not even half a day out of New York, were shadowy valleys so dark and deserted that they might have been on the frontier. No lights could be seen north of Haverstraw, and Verplanck, where iceboats reigned, was all in bed or by the fire, with lamps extinguished. The hills were barren, the water black, the ice thickening with each sally of the *Brayton Ives*. But she kept on smashing into it; and the rougher it got, the more she fought.

They slept through a night of charging and pitching, and dreamt

142

of circling the earth like angels, with hands outspread to guide their flight. Smoke sometimes curled in the open window and burnt their sleeping eyes, but it soon curled out again, and they found themselves high above the sea, or whistling over some dark range of mountains deep in central Asia. Then, feeling as if their lives had been spent charging the ice, they awoke to a subzero dawn and a great commotion on deck.

"What have we got to burn?" the captain screamed from his wheelhouse.

"Oak and pitch pine, sir," answered a deckhand from the ice-cluttered forecastle. "And a shipment of mahogany," he added as an afterthought.

"Start with the pitch pine. Cover that with oak. If we don't have full steam, throw in the goddamned mahogany. We'll pay for it."

The *Brayton Ives* had come to Conn Hook, where the river was so narrow that the ice seemed like a straight marble road. They had to drive themselves up on the brittle shelf (as if the ship were a mechanical duck flippering out of a pond) and break it with the sidewheeler's enormous weight. This was no mere river navigation; it was winter war.

The ship backed a quarter of a mile through the shattered plates it had just broken, and rested as the wood moved on a chain of hands into the mouth of the boiler. The furnaces screamed with summer, and could be heard throughout the fields. Pressure mounted. The chief engineer squinted at his gauges, watching them climb. Three columns of colored water passed warning bands of red. He held his breath—1,750—1,800—1,850—1,900—1,950—1,975—2,000! He shifted the boat into full speed, wondering if the machinery would tolerate the strain or provide yet another fatal explosion on the river.

Gears and decoupled governors spun into invisibility. Viscous oil thinned. Shafts began to smoke, even though cabin boys doused them with buckets of cold water. The paddles began to spin, digging a trench in the river water and vaporizing it like a saw. The *Brayton Ives* ran its quarter-mile as fast as a cannon shell, and hit the ice. In slow but unstoppable motion it climbed the shelf and

143

keeled its way for a thousand feet. Centered in the channel as before, paddlewheels chipping the ice like milling machines gone mad, the *Brayton Ives* had skidded so far out of the water that crew members and captain, and Peter Lake and Beverly now standing on the listing third deck, weren't sure what had happened or where they were.

"Explode!" said the chief engineer as he pulled the safety valve and a rush of steam shot high over the Hudson with a whistle that could be heard at the northern end of Lake Champlain. As the whistle grew weaker, they found themselves listing high and dry on the ice. The wheels had stopped turning. The open water from which they had sprung was so far back that they couldn't see it. The *Brayton Ives* looked like a toy ship in a winter window dressing.

A man near the bow started to move, but the captain gestured for him to stop. Like everyone else, the captain was listening. Eyes darted from the white river to the ship's master standing with raised hands. A minute passed, two minutes, three, and four. After five minutes, the nonbelievers were sure that the captain had put the ship out of service until a caisson of dynamite could be brought from West Point. But the captain remained on the open bridge, his hands still in the same position, listening.

"Look," said Beverly, "he's smiling." He had broken into a satisfied smile, and his arms had dropped to his side. The deck crew thought that he was taking the defeat with humor, and they began to laugh. He shook his finger at them, and looked over their heads.

Every eye on the ship turned to the north, from which a noise like the sustained crack of a whip echoed down the valley. A black line dividing the ice spread toward them. The captain had known what was going to happen long before anyone else (which was why he was the captain). Then the world seemed to collapse as the solidified river split in two for miles and the ship fell with a roar into a chasm of liberated water. A way was open before them as clear as a slip between piers. They got up steam and proceeded calmly to the north—where there seemed to be no people, but only mountains, lakes, reedy snow-filled steppes, and winter gods who played with storms and stars.

Jayga had watched as Peter Lake and Beverly packed the sleigh, hitched up Athansor, and drove off, bundled in furs. Then, a minute later, she had run to the police station to deafen the desk sergeant with a tale from one of the pieces of Shakespearean tragedy that she had seen declaimed in the beer halls. It was a loose cross between *Othello*, *Lear*, *Hamlet*, and *When We Were Young In Killarney, Molly*, delivered with a combination of speed and thunder which came too thickly to admit of much grammar.

"The young miss and her swan done canteloped," said Jayga to the desk sergeant. "I knew he weren't no quality. Bezooks, he hangs around all night, he does. Lend me your ears! Fourscore and twenty-nine years ago, I did remember from the prick of tails what when he was loft to give and crovet with sateen robes and silken duvets. Hath thee no grime?"

"What was that?" the sergeant wanted to know. "Are you here to report a crime?"

"Bezooks I am! Damn your face, piebald strumpet!"

She thought that if she were to talk to the police on behalf of the Penns, this was the way to do it. And so it went, as Jayga manufactured details that drew the sergeant toward her until his stomach smothered the police blotter like a small hippo reclining upon a pocket Bible. Peter Lake had strange red eyes. Lightning danced from his whip. The horse could fly (she had seen it in the air, circling the house while its master was inside). Begging her mistress to stay, she had clutched at her heels and thrown herself in front of the sleigh, but to no avail. After half an hour of shrieking, when the tale was told, Jayga exclaimed, "Oh! I left my biscuits in the oven!" and disappeared from the station house so quickly that the police thought they had dreamed her.

Telegrams sparked to and fro between *The Sun* and the Lake of the Coheeries. The telegraph man worked harder that Christmas than ever before, and made an iceboat track across the lake straighter than the barrel of a Sharps rifle.

BEVERLY MISSING STOP JAYGA SAYS ELOPED WITH SEER STOP
ADVISE STOP

WHAT QUESTION MARK EXCLAMATION POINT FIND HER STOP
CHECK THE ROOF STOP LOOK EVERYWHERE STOP

EVERYONE LOOKING EVERYWHERE STOP CANNOT FIND HER
STOP ADVISE STOP

LOOK HARDER STOP

STILL CANNOT FIND BEVERLY STOP

LOOK EVERYWHERE STOP

WHERE IS EVERYWHERE QUESTION MARK STOP

DO YOU WANT SPECIFICS QUESTION MARK STOP

YES STOP

HOSPITALS HOTELS WAREHOUSES RESTAURANTS BAKERIES
ROPEWALKS STABLES CARGO VESSELS DAIRY BARNS PRODUCE
TERMINALS BREWERIES GREENHOUSES ABATTOIRS BATHS
POULTRY MARKETS GOVERNMENT OFFICES RETAIL ESTABLISH-
MENTS WELDING LOFTS INDUSTRIAL GARAGES GYMNASIUMS
FORGES SCHOOLS ART STUDIOS HIRING HALLS DANCE PALACES
LIBRARIES THEATERS OYSTER BARS POTTERY BARNS SQUASH
COURTS PRINTING HOUSES AUCTION PLACES LABORATORIES
TELEPHONE EXCHANGES RAILROAD STATIONS BEAUTY PAR-
LORS MORGUES PIERS ARMORIES COFFEE SHOPS CLUBS KILNS
MUSEUMS POLICE STATIONS BICYCLE TRACKS TANNERIES
JAILS BARBERSHOPS REHEARSAL ROOMS BANKS BARS CON-
VENTS MONASTERIES SALAD KITCHENS STEAMSHIP TERMINALS
CHURCHES GALLERIES CONFERENCE CENTERS WHOREHOUSES

146

MUSIC SCHOOLS AEROPLANE HANGARS AND OBSERVATION
TOWERS STOP

DID YOU LOOK IN THE BASEMENT STOP

YES STOP

The *Brayton Ives* halted at the foot of high mountains along the
river's west bank, and a ramp was put down onto the ice. All was
serene as engines idled and hissed, and no movement could be
sensed. And then Athansor came bursting out of the side of the
ship, his hooves thundering on the ramp, pulling behind him the
sleigh with Peter Lake and Beverly. Before the sailors could haul in
the planks, Athansor was galloping on the white roads that led into
and over the mountains. There were no railings at the thousand-
foot drops, but only ice-clad trees and evergreen bushes long
encased in thick sarcophagi of snow. They went up and up, ricocheting left and right in terrifying skids, crossing the frozen
mountains under a cloudless polar sky. Finally they halted in a
small notch and looked west at the greatest plain Peter Lake had
ever seen. It stretched for hundreds of miles in three directions, and
was covered with forests, fields, rivers, towns, and the Lake of the
Coheeries—twenty miles distant, silent, snow-covered, wider than
the call of a French horn, shimmering on its horizon with white
illusory waves, a separate kingdom of the unrecorded frontier.
They almost flew down the mountain, and then Athansor ran at ferocious speed along a wide, straight, and snowy road that led to the
lake.

He was galloping like a fire horse, on the sleigh path that paral-
leled the iceboat road, when Beverly stood up and said, "That's
my family!" indicating an iceboat zipping toward them in the
trench. Isaac Penn recognized his own sleigh, and released the sail
as he pushed the brake into the ice, sending up a rooster tail of glit-
ter. In the sound of the horse's deep breathing and the luffing of the
sail, the Penns stared at Beverly and Peter Lake, and they stared
back. Though no one could think of anything to say, Willa leaned
over and reached for Beverly—her favorite, her darling. Peter Lake

147

jumped from the sleigh and lifted the child into Beverly's arms. Willa seemed like a little bear frisking with its mother, because both she and her sister were clothed in shiny black fur, and Beverly held her as if she would never let go.

Willa closed her eyes and slept contentedly; the iceboat was pivoted around; Peter Lake cracked the whip; and they raced to the house on the lakeshore under a sky of solid delft azure. "Drive hard, Peter Lake, drive hard," said Beverly, holding the child.

He had never had a family. But there he was, suddenly, almost a husband and father. Small scenes can be so beautiful that they change a man forever. He would never forget that noontime on a lake of ice, nor would he ever forget her words.

"Drive hard," she had said. He would. Things were different. All he wanted now was love.

They slept until evening, Beverly in a specially constructed loggia outside, and Peter Lake in an upstairs bedroom. He awoke in complete darkness and struggled through halls and passageways until he found himself in a huge room, staring at two fires and the Penns, all of whom were wide-awake, including Beverly, who had come in from the cold. Peter Lake announced that he had to go to see his horse, and backed out the front door. The air was a mountain of crystal through which a bright moon shone. He followed the sled tracks to the stable, where he peeked in at Athansor dreaming contentedly under a thick scarlet blanket. Clearheaded, Peter Lake returned to the house, and found that everyone except Isaac Penn was busy in the kitchen cooking up a feast to feed the Huns, the Mongols, and the Eskimos. Isaac Penn was enthroned in a leather chair, staring at the fire, tapping his thin fingers on the heavy arm.

Peter Lake sat down on a wooden bench next to the fireplace and looked Isaac Penn squarely in the eyes. He expected yet another staring contest, as with Pearly. Peter Lake knew that powerful men could cut people down to size with their eyes, and often did. Jackson Mead and Mootfowl had done it benevolently, but they had done it. Thus, Peter Lake expected to be raked, combed, and shaken down, because Isaac Penn was much more than Pearly's match. Indeed, to Isaac Penn, Pearly was just a sharp-toothed puppy. This was because Isaac Penn was the man behind the city's mirror. He had almost supreme power over the city's conception of itself, and, by small adjustments, could hypnotize and entrance it. If he wished, he could have it flail its limbs in an alarming fit. He could scare it to death, empty its streets, or make it want to hide in a hole. Because Isaac Penn could move New York in such a way that its strength would shame the giants of the earth, or lift the city's hand to have it flick the dust from a baby's eye, Peter Lake expected one of those meetings where he was made to feel like an aspiring young gnat.

What a surprise, then, when Isaac Penn looked him in the eye and said quite sheepishly (he even looked slightly like a sheep, which was probably what accounted for the wonderful expression that so distinguished Willa from other children—Beverly did not look like a sheep), "Um, ah, do you take wine with your meals?"

"Sometimes," answered Peter Lake.

"Good, we'll have wine tonight. Would claret be all right with you? Château Moules du Lac, ninety-eight?"

"Oh yes, anything," replied Peter Lake. "But isn't it pronounced 'claray'?"

"No. Claret. You say the 't,' just as in 'filet.' "

"Filet? I thought it was 'filay.' "

"No. Filet, just as in wallet. You don't say 'wallay,' do you? You say wallet. Same with filet and claret." Isaac Penn leaned back in his chair. Peter Lake was beginning to feel at ease. Why, he thought, did I expect anything other than this rather timid old fellow?

"You know what?" said Isaac Penn.

"Sir?"

"You look like a crook. Who are you, what do you do, what is your relationship to Beverly, are you aware of her special condition, and what are your motivations, intentions, and desires? Tell the absolute truth, don't elaborate, stop if a child or servant comes in, and be brief."

"How can I be brief? These are complicated questions."

"You can be brief. If you were one of my journalists, you'd be finished by now. God created the world in six days. Ape him."

149

"I'll try."

"Unnecessary."

"All right."

"Unnecessary."

"My name is Peter Lake. You're right. I'm a crook. I'm a burglar, but I'm really a mechanic—and a good one. I love Beverly. Our relationship goes by no name. I have no intentions; I am aware of her special condition; I desire her; I am moved . . . by love. When we drove across the lake this afternoon and Beverly held the little girl in her arms, I felt a responsibility far more satisfying than any pleasure I have ever known.

"I realize that the child is yours. I realize that Beverly may die. And I am more than aware of my own shortcomings as a father, a provider, and a protector. And though I know about machines, I'm ignorant. I know that I'm ignorant. And I know . . . I know that the strange little family on the sleigh must soon break up. But Willa loves Beverly. Beverly is virtually her mother. And I think that we should help to take care of her for a while, not so much for her sake, as for Beverly's. Do you understand?"

"How do I know," asked Isaac Penn, "that you are not moved merely by vanity or curiosity. How do I know that you aren't here for the sake of the money in this family?"

Peter Lake was in full possession of himself. "I was an orphan," he said. "Orphans don't have vanity. I'm not sure why, but one needs parents to be vain. No matter what my faults, I tend to approach things with a certain gratitude, and those who are vain have little ability to feel grateful. As for curiosity, well, I've seen a lot, too much in fact. Curiosity has no bearing on the matter. I don't know why you brought it up."

"And money? Do you know why I brought that up?"

"Yes, I thought of the money. It excited me." He smiled. "It really did. I had escalating dreams—of being your right-hand man; of doing all the things that men of power and wealth have occasion to do; of wearing a different suit every day, and clean linen. I became a senator, President. Beverly lived. Our children were great in their turn. The articles on us in the encyclopedia were so long that they took up most of the volume 'L.' All around the country there were monuments to me, of marble as white as snow. In the end, I confess, I was flying about the universe. Beverly and I touched the moon, and flew off to the stars. But, mind you, after a few hours of this, there was no place else to go. After just a few hours of walking with kings, I was very glad to be Peter Lake, of whom no one has ever heard, completely anonymous, free.

"Mr. Penn, the only people who want that kind of stuff are those who are too stupid to imagine it and then be done with it. Now, this may sound strange to you, sir, and it's new to me (within the last few days, as I see it), but I want responsibility. That, to me, is the highest glory. I want to give, not take. And I love Beverly."

"Do you realize—what shall I call you?"

"Everyone always calls me by both my names."

"Do you realize, Peter Lake, that the money, the presence of the money, can erode and corrupt those feelings?"

"I do, sir. I've seen it myself. I feel it within me, too."

"So, then, what do you intend to do to prevent this—assuming that you will have that privilege?"

"I know just what to do. I'm not educated, but I'm not a fool. After . . . if . . . Beverly dies, I'll disappear. I don't want any of this." He indicated with a sweep of his arm the room in which they sat, but he meant, actually, everything in the world.

"You think I would let you do that? The man that my daughter loves? And she does. She told me so—and she didn't have to."

"It isn't up to you."

"Well, I'll tell you, Peter Lake, I would let you do that. My impulse would be to provide for you for the rest of your life, to bring you into the family, to make you one of us. But I won't. It's for Beverly. Do you see?"

"Yes. I see. Of course I see. And, further, Mr. Penn, I was not meant, evidently, to have a family in the sense in which you refer to it. I was not born to be protected, but, I warrant, to protect."

"Then we are in agreement. I assume that you will stop being a burglar, and revert to being a mechanic."

Peter Lake nodded. "There is one thing, one thing which I will ask. I need your help for it alone."

"And what is that?"

"A child. There was once a child that I saw in a hallway, in a tenement, a long time ago. Of all the things I have ever seen, this I remember best. It has been with me ever since . . ."

But then Peter Lake was interrupted by the whole troupe exiting from the kitchen, their cheeks red from the heat of the oven, platters of food and bottles of wine in their hands. Before they sat at the table to eat, Beverly sent them all to wash up, not because they needed to (their hands were very clean), but because she wanted to embrace her father and thank him for accepting Peter Lake, as she knew he had, from his expression and that of Peter Lake—and because she had been listening at the door.

Late that night, refreshed and strengthened by a good dinner and much free laughter, Isaac Penn and Peter Lake sat in the small study, staring at the fire. The heat ran around half a dozen logs that had become red cylinders of flame, changing their colors until they looked like six suns in a black universe of firebrick. Their glow was an invisible wind that irradiated the room and froze the two men in place—like deer in a forest which is burning all around them, who lift their heads to the highest and brightest flames and look into a tunnel of white light.

"The doctors told me," said Isaac Penn, as if he were talking to himself, "that she would be dead in a few months. That was almost a year ago." He glanced at an ice-covered window in which the moon had gone all astray, and listened to the wind coming off the Lake of the Coheeries as it could only there, on a midwinter night, like the roaring jet winds of Mars or Saturn. "It's a mystery to me that she can sleep outside, in that. She wasn't supposed to. In winter, she's supposed to come in. But she refuses, even up here. I can never get used to thinking that my daughter is out there in that caldron of ice. And yet, in the mornings, she comes to breakfast revived after twelve hours in cold that would kill a strong healthy man. The wind and snow cover her, attack her. At first, I used to beg her to come in; but then I realized that doing what she does is what keeps her alive."

"How?"

"I don't know."

"I wonder," said Peter Lake, aware that he was in a warm comfortable place in a vast sea of snow and ice which maneuvered beyond the walls like a wild unopposed army. "I wonder about the others."

"What others?"

"The thousands, the hundreds of thousands, like Beverly."

"We're all like Beverly. She's early, that's all."

"But it doesn't have to be that way."

"What way? Be clear."

"The poor should not have to suffer, as they do, in their millions, and die young."

"The poor? Do you mean everyone? Certainly you mean everyone in New York, for in New York even the rich are poor. But is Beverly poor according to your definition? No. And yet, what's the difference?"

"The difference," said Peter Lake, "is that small children, their mothers, and their fathers, live and die like beasts. They don't have special sleeping porches, a hundred pounds of down and sable, marble baths as big as pools, ranks of doctors from Harvard and Johns Hopkins, salvers of roast meat, hot drinks in silver vacuum bottles, and cheerful happy families. I want Beverly to have these things, and would die rather than see her go without them. But there is a difference. The child I once saw in a hallway was barefoot, bareheaded, dressed in filthy rags, starving, blind, abandoned. He had no feather bed. He was near death. And he was standing, because he didn't have a place to lie down and die."

"I know this," Isaac Penn asserted. "I've seen such things far more often than you have. You forget that I was a poorer man than you have ever been, for a longer time than you have yet lived. I had a father and a mother, and brothers and sisters, and they all died young, too soon. I know all these things. Do you think I'm a fool? In *The Sun* we bring injustices to the attention of the public, and suggest sensible means to correct inequities where they serve no purpose. I realize that there is too much needless and cruel suffering. But you, you don't seem to understand that these people whom you profess to champion have, in their struggles, compensations."

"What compensations?"

"Their movements, passions, emotions; their captured bodies and captured senses are directed with no less certainty than the microscopic details of the seasons, or the infinitesimal components of the city's great and single motion. They are, in their seemingly random actions, part of a plan. Don't you know that?"

"I see no justice in that plan."

"Who said," lashed out Isaac Penn, "that you, a man, can always perceive justice? Who said that justice is what you imagine? Can you be sure that you know it when you see it, that you will live long enough to recognize the decisive thunder of its occurrence, that it can be manifest within a generation, within ten generations, within the entire span of human existence? What you are talking about is common sense, not justice. Justice is higher and not as easy to understand—until it presents itself in unmistakable splendor. The design of which I speak is far above our understanding. But we can sometimes feel its presence.

"No choreographer, no architect, engineer, or painter could plan more thoroughly and subtly. Every action and every scene has its purpose. And the less power one has, the closer he is to the great waves that sweep through all things, patiently preparing them for the approach of a future signified not by simple human equity (a child could think of that), but by luminous and surprising connections that we have not imagined, by illustrations terrifying and benevolent—a golden age that will show not what we wish, but some bare awkward truth upon which rests everything that ever was and everything that ever will be. There is justice in the world, Peter Lake, but it cannot be had without mystery. We try to bring it about without knowing exactly what it is, and only touch upon it. No matter, for all the flames and sparks of justice throughout all time reach to invigorate unseen epochs—like engines whose power glides on hidden lines to upwell against the dark in distant cities unaware."

"I don't know," said Peter Lake, confused. "I think of Beverly, and I'm not sure about the golden age of which you speak, which is beyond our lives, and which we will never see. Think of Beverly. How could it be?''

Isaac Penn got up from his chair to leave the room. At the door, he turned to Peter Lake, who felt cold and alone. Isaac Penn was an old man, and sometimes he became dreadfully grave, as if he were in the presence of a thousand tormenting spirits. His eyes reflected the fire. They seemed unnatural, like tunnels of flame into a soul grown so deep that it must soon leave life. ''Have you not yet realized that Beverly has seen the golden age—not one that was, nor one that will be, but one that is here? Though I am an old man, I have not yet seen it. And she has. That is what has broken my heart.''

The approach of Christmas had turned the children into excited little dynamos of greed, and Christmas morning saw an impressive trading of loot, in which nothing was notable save Willa's present for her father, the first gift she had given in her life. She had taken a day and a half to decide, and then Peter Lake had driven across the lake and over to the town of Lake of the Coheeries, where he bought it. Isaac Penn opened his presents last, and, in one big box that had had holes cut into it, he found a fat white rabbit with a tag around its neck that read ''From Willa.''

On the afternoon of Christmas Day, Beverly and Peter Lake went for a ride and took more than half a dozen children with them—Willa; Jack; Harry; Jamie Absonord (who had recently arrived by train and iceboat, and whose heart still throbbed for Jack, though, now, neither would look at the other for any reason whatsoever); and the two Gamely children and Sarah Shingles, plump and whimsical Coheeries youth with perfectly balanced Yankee sharpness, Indian magic, English competence, and Dutch madness. The stocky, cold-proof Gamelys and young Sarah sat in the high back seat of the sleigh, looking like a row of Bavarian wood carvings, ready for anything.

Since the lake was covered with perfectly flat hard-packed snow, Athansor had at last an endless place in which to run. When Peter Lake slackened the reins to give him his head, he pointed himself straight down the length of the lake and bolted for the horizon. They picked up speed. Everyone settled in his seat and closed his coat. The horse went faster and faster. He soon exceeded the peak velocity of the fastest horse-drawn sleighs, and he was just loping. Then he really began to run. The wind hit them so hard that they had to bend into it and squint. They drew up even to an iceboat speeding along a cleared track and passed it so fast that it looked as if it were rushing the other way. Next, Athansor lifted his head and took a series of long shallow leaps. The sleigh left the surface and flew through the air. It touched lightly every now and then, but the runners seldom met the snow, and when they did there was a short hiss as it was vaporized to steam. The children were amazed, but not frightened. As they raced west into the setting sun, they saw it stop still, reverse itself, and start to climb. "Dear God," said Peter Lake, swallowing hard, "the sun is rising in the west!" But no one heard him, for the wind was attacking them with such strength that the world seemed to have turned into a siren. They were moving so fast they couldn't see anything of the shore except a smooth white streak like an enamel band on a china bowl. Even the Gamelys had to hunker down in the wind and hope for the best. Then Athansor slowed. The runners returned to the ground, the wind grew weaker, the sun had stopped and once again begun to sink, and they could see the shore. When Athansor fell into trotting like any other horse, Peter Lake directed him to the soft early lights of a settlement ahead.

It was a tiny town somewhere so deep in New York's western sprint that the local Iroquois were still awaiting Pierre de la Tranche. The village was covered by thirty feet of snow, which made its houses look like the creations of mad architects who built in holes in the ground. But the tavern was in the clear, and its lights shone out upon the lake from a windblown knoll. Smoke exited the chimneys in remarkably thin and solid lines. The children took note of this for their future drawing.

Athansor trotted up to the tavern barn and turned to Peter Lake as though to ask if he should bring the sleigh inside. Beverly said no, she would wait where they were while Peter Lake took the children for some hot Antwerp Flinders. Peter Lake protested. She should come in too. Why not? It was not Mouquin's; they wouldn't be dancing; she wouldn't be in a corseted gown; and they might spend all of a quarter of an hour there before the trip back.

"No," said Beverly, "I feel especially hot." He put his hand on her cheek, and then on her forehead. She was thermal equilibrium itself. But she did seem agitated.

"Beverly," said Peter Lake, "tell me why you don't want to go in there."

"I told you," she answered. "I feel feverish."

He thought for a moment. "Is it because of me?" he asked. "Because I'm not a gentleman with a sleigh driver and the right clothes?" He gestured toward the inside of the barn, where two dozen rigs and two dozen horses were packed in stalls and wooden ways, and two dozen coachmen were having a party of their own around a forge that had been pressed into social service. This village was a popular destination for many young people who regularly drove into the country to have dinner and drink at a favored tavern. The very rich always went the farthest out.

"You know it's not that," answered Beverly. "I'd much rather have the man who drives the sleigh than the man who is driven in it. I'll be all right. We'll go to Mouquin's. Here," she said, passing him bright-eyed Willa, who was excited by the unfamiliar blackness of a winter night. "Willa needs a hot drink." By this time the older children were tumbling over one another in the snow. Peter Lake put Willa on his shoulder and jumped down to join them. He turned to Beverly for a moment, and then walked toward the tavern.

He and the six children attracted much attention inside. Lovely women came over to talk to Willa, Jamie Absonord, and the delicious-looking and beady-eyed but beautiful little Shingles girl, Sarah. Their escorts smiled approvingly. Peter Lake wanted Beverly to be with him. It didn't seem right without her, and he was embarrassed by the stares that, with Beverly present, would have made him proud.

The room was full of the fire, excitement, and ease that come

157

from dancing. It made Peter Lake's heart spring back in memory of the nineteenth—his—century, when he had grown up, and when things had been quieter, wilder, and more beautiful—although, surrounded by children and dancers at an out-of-the-way inn on the Lake of the Coheeries, he felt that he was in a time when beauty mattered, and he had only to think of Beverly, outside, beyond the tar-black windows, to confirm it.

"Nine Antwerp Flinders," he said to the barmaid. "Seven without the gin. Wait a minute. Make that nine Antwerp Flinders—one with an eighth of gin, for this little girl; six with half gin (Jamie Absonord squealed in anticipation of being slightly drunk); one with triple; and one in a closed container to take when we go, double gin. Heavy on the cinnamon, heavy on the lemon, heavy on the cream, lots of minced plum."

The Antwerp Flinders arrived boiling hot. Peter Lake and the children drank them as they watched an impassioned quadrille of two-dozen elegant dancers. The seasoned floor planks shook and the fires across the room blinked at them through a snapping gate of silk and taffeta gowns, and swallowtail coats of English gem wool. Not fully appreciative of a dance between the sexes (except for Harry, who was suffering some inexplicable adolescent madness that made him recline against the wall and sleep like a narcoleptic), the children got into a hot and tipsy game of Duck Thumb.

Peter Lake was still sad that Beverly remained outside. He missed her so much that he became absolutely saturated with love, which made him breathe slowly in painful pleasure and feel a glow throughout his body, which traveled from here to there as it overflowed the containers that contained it. So he nearly vaulted the table, and rushed outside. He made his way to the side of the barn, where Athansor was eating some hay. No Beverly there. He peeked inside. Not there, either. Then he saw some tracks that led around back. He followed them into the darkness, between pines heavily laden with snow, and there he found Beverly standing on the hillside, hands clasped, staring into the tavern. Before she knew that he was there, he saw what she was looking at. It was a nearly silent miniature; a little lighted cube; like a paper house with a candle in it. Distance and darkness converted an ebullient scene full of motion and glare into something sad and whole, and of another time. He saw that Beverly had taken it and clasped it to her, as if it were a jewel in its intricate foil. She had by distance converted it into a painting, or an accidental photograph, that touched her to the quick. She had remained outside because she had never had the opportunity for society, and she was afraid. Innocent things, such as a dance in a tavern, terrified her. He realized that Mouquin's would be a test of courage more for her than for him.

He thought at first that it might be easy to lead her inside to the music and dancing. There was, truly, nothing to fear. But she did fear, and it had brought her outside, to a position in which she could embrace the scene and know its spirit. This was not unlike Peter Lake's far views of the city, from which he always learned a great deal more than he would have from within. No, he wouldn't try to coax her in—even though she might be adored there. He would not bring her in, he would join her on the intense periphery.

He closed upon her in the snow. She was almost ashamed at being discovered alone amid the pines. But she saw from his expression that he had understood, and she knew that now he was really with her.

They peered through the windows for a while and watched the children at their table, completely absorbed in Duck Thumb. Harry, sleeping against the wall, looked like an overworked medieval cookboy. Then Peter Lake raided the place and kidnapped the children, and they were all in the sleigh once again, speeding eastward into the ferocious dark. Beverly drank her Antwerp Flinder. They were content to wrap themselves in blankets and furs and lean back as Athansor pulled the sleigh, not as fast as before, but at least as fast as the pleasing clip of a prestigious through-train.

Above them, in the cold, was a confused hiss of clouds and stars racing past in islands and lakes. It was such a hypnotic sound that they tilted their heads to stare at the chirping, crackling, rhythmically beating sea of starlight and fast-flowing cloud. On they traveled, on and on, smooth as the wind, gliding selflessly over ice and snow on the strong steel runners.

Athansor, the white horse, moved in time with the diffuse static from above. Though he had the power and joy of a fast horse heading for his stable, they could sense in his happiness much more than that. They could sense that the hypnotic rhythm in which he moved was that of an unimaginably long journey. He was running in a way that they had never seen. His strides became lighter and lighter, harder and harder, and more and more perfect. He seemed to be readying himself to shed the world.

THE HOSPITAL IN
PRINTING HOUSE SQUARE

IN the same way that certain sections of the city were mortal battlegrounds, some parts of the calendar were always more warlike than others, and during the days between Christmas and the new year all elements seemed to conspire to subdue the soul. Fire, rain, sickness, cold, and death were everywhere spread through the dark as in a painting of hell. People struggled until exhaustion, giving everything they had, and the days were packed with trials and mysteries.

When the Penns and Peter Lake returned from Lake of the Coheeries they found snow locked in combat with warm humid winds that had come on a raid from the Gulf of Mexico. The atmosphere was full of the tangled gray trails that would mark future battles in the air;

and the city's children, released from school and trapped inside all day by sleet, were at wit's end. Then events began to speed up, as if an engine were determined to pull the year from its trough and was running as fast and hard as the stokers could lay on more coal.

The mayor, his wife, and a train of favored flunkies descended upon the Penns one afternoon, all so drunk that their breathing made the house into a vapor-bomb more dangerous than a silo in late summer. Included in the party was the commissioner of police. Needless to say, this made Peter Lake skittish, especially because the commissioner repeatedly looked at him and then screwed up his face as if saying to himself, "Who is that?" Several years before, in one of the fits of late adolescence that had followed Peter Lake well into his thirties, he had written the very police commissioner who now puzzled after his identity a series of insulting, burn-the-bridges, flirt-with-self-destruction, challenge-the-devil, vitriolic letters that began with lines such as, "My dear incompetent buffoon of a Police Commissioner . . . ," or, "To the pathetic fungus who calls himself Commissioner of Police . . . ," or, simply, "Flea."

As Jayga and Leonora served hot lemon tea and steaming scones, Peter Lake hung in the corner, swallowing a lot but not eating. Every now and then, the police commissioner glanced in his direction. Peter Lake's portrait was in the Rogues' Gallery. At the time he had posed for the police photographer, he had been something of a dandy, and was pictured as two black marbles staring from a mass of sealskin lapels, a sealskin hat, and mustaches from which artisans might have taken inspiration for their work in wrought iron. He was then known as "Grand Central Pete, Bunco and Confidence," which was how he had signed his letters—title and all. Not daring to upstage the mayor, the police commissioner was quiet and had much opportunity for reflection. As he sobered up, he began to recognize Peter Lake, who excused himself and went up to the roof. There, sheltered from a cold gray rain, Beverly was sitting in her tent, reading a *National Geographic* article entitled, "The Gentle Hottentots."

"Think of something!" commanded Peter Lake after apprising her of the danger.

"At the moment, all I can think about is Hottentots," she said, but then knitted her blond eyebrows and concentrated. Peter Lake did not know why he had come to her for a way out, when he was the one so well practiced in schemes and escapes. He thought that it might be that, more than wanting to elude the police commissioner, he wanted to watch Beverly engaged in a problem.

"He knows by now, doesn't he?"

"No, but he's at the brink."

"Then we've got to drive him from it. I know. We'll show them the painting. My father said he wanted the mayor to see it anyway."

"What painting?"

"There's a painting in the basement. You don't know about it."

As they entered the reception room, Isaac Penn was saying, "The oddest thing about the elite—of which, I suppose, I am now one—is that they rule so . . . daintily. The great mass of people, in which one finds brave soldiers, firebrands, geniuses, and inspired mechanics, is paralyzed in the face of these human delicacies with their garden parties, their unprotected estates, their inebriated stumbles, their pastel clothing, and their disempowering obsessions with disempowering things. When a workingman moves among them, he is most amazed: amazed at how small they make him feel, amazed at their frailty, amazed that they are yet invincible, amazed that he, a bull, is ruled by a butterfly."

"Yes," said the mayor, too drunk to get the point. "Isn't it funny the way poor people dress like clowns? The poorer they are, the more ridiculous they look. It's as if the circus is their Brooks Brothers. And they're so ugly."

"Oh, I don't know," interjected Peter Lake from the doorway, where he was standing arm in arm with Beverly. "It's not just the poor who make themselves look like clowns. The rich do it, too. After all, look at their fragile and preposterous formal clothing: they might as well wear feathers. In fact, they do. And then there's the fashion, among the high elite, of tattooing things across their bue-tox. I've heard," continued Peter Lake, staring directly at the mayor, "that certain socially prominent women of this city actually have maps tattooed across their bue-tox."

Everyone except the mayor and his wife laughed into his tea, and the flunkies said things like, "Nonsense!" or "Fiddle-de-diddle!"

"Oh no, not fiddle-de-diddle," lectured Peter Lake, gliding with Beverly into the center of the room, like two ships of the Great White Fleet. "Not nonsense either. Mr. Mayor," he asked, giving the mayor a start, "surely you, in your position, have heard of such things?"

"What things?" the mayor replied, nervously.

"Maps on the bue-tox. Maps of Manhattan on one bue-tox. Maps of Brooklyn on the other bue-tox. Etcetera, etcetera, etcetera."

"Well . . ." said the mayor. "Actually . . . I sort of . . . yes, yes . . . I have!"

Peter Lake bowed, and then dazzled all the drunks by introducing them to Beverly. They had heard that she was beautiful, and an invalid of some sort, and they had assumed that she would waste away until her wedding night and then quickly recover the way so many young women did when they found out that they had taken pleasure for peril. They did not know and could not apprehend by appearances that she had tuberculosis of lung and bone.

"Didn't you want to show the mayor the painting?" she asked her father.

"Yes, I did," he answered.

"Oh, a new painting?" the mayor asked, glad to change the subject.

"Relatively new."

"Who did it?"

"The man who painted it doesn't want to be known. He only wants to know."

"Come now!" someone said.

"It's quite true," replied Isaac Penn.

"Let's guess from his initials!" offered a woman who spent

most of her time drinking liqueurs that were too sweet and playing card games that were too simple.

"M.C.," said Isaac Penn. "Guess all you want. You'll never know."

As they wound down a long spiral of bronze stairs, deeper into the rock than some of the ladies cared to go, the mayor spoke up. "Why do you keep it down here?"

"This is the biggest room we have," answered Isaac Penn, "and the painting is rather large."

"When you want to exhibit it, you'll have to roll it up to get it out of here."

"No," said Isaac Penn. "It doesn't roll up."

"Really," said the mayor, somewhat nervous himself about the great number of stairs, "I hope this isn't solely on my account."

"Mr. Mayor," answered his host, "in this infinite universe, whole worlds have been created for the instruction and elevation of a few simple souls. Believe me, it's no trouble for me to show you this painting, which, as far as I am concerned . . ." Here Isaac Penn was drowned out by a sound that rose from beneath them as if it were a thick misty cloud. Peter Lake immediately recognized it as the crackling static of the stars and the white wall. It grew louder and louder, until, finally, they came to the bottom of the stairs, and faced the painting, from which the sound was coming.

They stood motionlessly, clutching their sides, struggling to keep their balance; that is, everyone but Isaac Penn and Beverly—and Peter Lake, who was not afraid of heights. They were in a room of astounding proportions where the only illumination came from the painting itself, which was easily thirty feet high and sixty feet long, and unlike any painting they had ever seen, for it moved. It sent changing images, moving light, and the static of clouds and stars speeding in a tidal wave toward its viewers, who felt as if they had discovered a hidden underground sea.

"What technique is this? What colors?" asked half of them at once.

Isaac Penn replied, "A new technique. New colors."

The painting was of a city at night, as seen from above, and though they recognized some things they knew, most of it was unfamiliar, because there were lights by the billions, actually sparkling, moving along distant roads in thick concentrations the likes of which the viewers had never imagined, moving along the rivers, and through the air. The city they saw looked real, of inconceivable scale, and frighteningly like their own.

"Move closer," urged Isaac Penn, and they were able to see more and more as they did. The liqueur-and-cards woman nearly fainted when, upon close examination, she saw a tiny pair of legs scurrying along under an open umbrella. They were able to see in perfect detail. The bridges, of which there were hundreds, had lighted and glowing buildings suspended from their catenaries and stacked upon the roadways as on the Ponte Vecchio. The view changed, as if they were flying past it, and they felt like birds gliding above quiet streets and deep canyons that were mysteriously three-dimensional. They experienced a pleasurable vertigo like that of walking on a country road in fall as torrents of leaves float in a rush of wind, flooding the air with new depth, putting the scene under water, and banishing gravity.

This city enabled anyone who looked at it from afar to soar above it, to rise effortlessly, to know that despite its labyrinthine divisions it was an appeal to heaven simpler in the end than the blink of an eye. It was, like New York (and certainly it must have been New York—after the tribulations of the present had long been forgotten), a city of random beauty. Anything within it that was beautiful was beautiful in spite of itself, and would come to light surprisingly, apart from all expectations. Everything that moved was seen to move with a slow and unworldly grace. Flying machines moved across the sky like lucid planets in ascension, but they did not rocket away, they rose slowly—without shock, in full confidence.

"What city is this great city?" the mayor asked, clearly moved. "Is it New York?"

"Of course it's New York," Isaac Penn replied. "Look at it. What other city could it be?"

"But can it be?"

"What do you mean?" said Isaac Penn. "It's right in front of you."

Peter Lake was convinced that Beverly was the key to these scenes. She was so marvelous that, when he tried to think of her, her description rolled away from him like a dropped coin, and all that was left was a feeling of joy. Nevertheless, he noticed that she was acting like a bored caretaker, behaving as if she were a dutiful daughter hearing for the ten-thousandth time her father's description of his collected art, and dreaming what young girls dream in the presence of their parents' aged friends. She climbed a little fixed ladder onto the raised platform over which the painting was hung, and sat with her head in her hands, facing the guests. Nearly inside the living view, almost as if she were on a windy precipice high in the air, she looked toward the back of the room and now and then glanced at Peter Lake.

Peter Lake could hardly decide what to watch—the living painting, or the girl who sat in front of it. He noted, however, that this indecision was pleasing in itself.

If the child in the hallway had lived, which he most probably had not, he would have grown to manhood, and would need no one's help. If he had died, Peter Lake would never find him, for he would have been buried in one of the potter's fields, in an unmarked mass grave. Many of these last resting places had been built over, and were now smothered forever under boiler rooms and basements. The child, male or female (he did not even know), might have been thirty feet under a packed coal bin in the cellar of a boardinghouse full of clerks and shop girls.

Nonetheless, several days before the new year, Peter Lake left early in the morning and rode Athansor to Korlaer's Hook, where he had landed in his canoe long before, and from which he intended to retrace his path. This was not only a nearly impossible feat of memory (the city had changed), but the Short Tails were now so thick around Korlaer's Hook, driven there by new laws and a new economy, that he was certain to be spotted. The morning was sunny and clear as he trotted Athansor along the fenced mall of

Chrystie Street. Its row trees were varnished with ice in thin wafers of painstaking exactitude, and when the wind blew, they jangled like crystal chandeliers.

Down by the bridges, he passed the hotel Kleinwaage—not a big hotel, but, on balance, a good one, famous for its charcoal-grilled steaks, fluffy white beds, and green public rooms choked with fresh flowers. As he rode past, he scanned the façade.

Walking with incredible pomposity down the bleached marble staircase was a fat figure in an ermine coat. He carried a cane, strutted like a millionaire, and was studded here and there with big diamonds. He had all the makings of a rich spice merchant—which is what Peter Lake would have taken him to be, were it not for the dark slit eyes in a massive fat face, the single eyebrow, the heavy breathing, and the Chinese hat.

"Cecil," said Peter Lake.

Cecil Mature turned in alarm, unslit his eyes to see who was calling, and then, in an attempt to run down the street, made his little sausagelike legs into an invisible windmill. Needless to say, he could not outrun Athansor.

"Cecil, why are you running?"

Cecil stopped. His face began to bend and quiver the way it always did when he spoke. "You're not supposed to see me."

"What are you talking about? I thought you were dead. What happened?"

"I'm not supposed to tell."

"Who said you're not supposed to tell?"

"They did," answered Cecil, pointing at the hotel.

"Who's they?"

"Jackson Mead."

"He's back? You're with him? I don't understand. What happened?"

"I can't say."

"C'mon, Cecil Mature, you're talking to me."

"First of all, my name isn't Cecil Mature."

"What, then?"

"*Mr.* Cecil Wooley."

Peter Lake stared at his old friend, hardly knowing what to say.

"My name is Mr. Cecil Wooley, and I work for Jackson Mead."

"Are you the squash cook?"

"Nope."

"Potato chef?"

"Nope."

"What?"

"Chief . . . structural . . . *engineer*," said Cecil, a lighthouse of pride. "And I bet you can't guess who's the overall engineer-in-chief and first assistant to Jackson Mead."

"Who?"

"The Reverend Doctor Mootfowl, that's who!"

"It can't be."

"It is."

Just at that moment, Jackson Mead came out of the hotel, with a hundred retainers. It was a pleasure and a shock to see him. "I gotta go," said Cecil. "It's against the rules. I'm not supposed to talk to anyone."

"I want to see Mootfowl."

"You can't. He's already on the ship. We're leaving today at noon for the Gulf Coast and South America, where we're going to build bridges—fourteen of them."

"When will you be back?"

"I don't know," said Cecil, swept away by Jackson Mead and the mass of tall men who followed.

"The ferris piece!" screamed out Peter Lake.

"He forgave me," cried Cecil, and then was lost to view as the entourage turned onto Park Place and headed for the great white ship that would take them to the Gulf.

It did not take Peter Lake long to gallop after them. But a line of trolleys cut him off from the route to the wharves. "Jump!" he commanded. Athansor had not jumped in a while, because he had been concentrating on pure speed and sustained flight. Thus, he was unable to clear the trolleys, and landed on top. Mortified, he stayed there despite everything that Peter Lake said to get him off, and they rode backward into Chinatown, where the inhabitants looked in wonder at the man mounted upon a pure white horse on top of a streetcar. They thought it was some sort of American joke, or perhaps an advertisement that (like most others) they did not understand. One of them started screaming that it was the President, and they all started screaming that it was the President, because they thought it was Theodore Roosevelt (who was not President then, but who had been not long before). Then Athansor galloped down the length of the cars and jumped, soaring over a group of tenements and leaving Chinatown and its astonished population Republicans forever.

When he reached the wharf, he saw the white ship under a steep slope of billowing sail heading out into a harbor full of whitecaps and windy blue. He had expected as much, and he was beginning to sense a pattern in such things. According to Cecil, Mootfowl was once again alive. Peter Lake wondered what would be the fate of the many others who lived amid the city's complicated machinery and hearthlike engines.

Looking up at a row of high bridges, he recognized the one on which he had crossed with the spielers, and he realized that the house must have been on one of the islands of Diamond Reef. He spurred Athansor with a word, they ascended the white ramps that led to the bridge, and were soon so high over the river that they felt as if they were sailing within the cloud archipelagoes and winter stars above the Lake of the Coheeries.

After several transits of the islands via the tremendous steel bridges that connected them, Peter Lake came to the proper place, and he sensed his way through miles of streets and squares until he found the old Dutch façades behind which had been the spielers' little house. But the tenements were empty, and in the space that had been their courtyard was an industrial building with soot-black walls and chimneys. The factory, or whatever it was, took up the whole block and pressed from inside against the old fronts, showing through glassless windows like a whale bulging from within a house.

Peter Lake tried the doors. Had they opened, they would have given onto solid walls. He bent his head back to see the height of the chimneys. Seven in a row reached hundreds of feet in the air, and each one was busy inventing plumes to drift and unravel.

He went around the other side and found an industrial door that was half as big as the building. At its base was an opening which, though twice the height of a man on horseback, seemed like a tiny missing tooth at the foot of a tower of baleen. From it came a river of light and air, and a sound of whirling contentment—whether dynamos, or motors, he did not know. Athansor carried him in at a slow gentle walk.

A vast room stretched before him, disappearing in its own dimness both ahead and above. The roof was not visible, but high overhead were acres of catwalks, grids, and traveling cranes. Some of the cranes proceeded slowly into the distance, with an extremely smooth and dampened movement that struck Peter Lake as unusual. It appeared that the beam hoists were directed from lighted house-sized boxes attached to their ends. Though they seemed to flow to and fro with a good deal of deliberation, no one could be seen inside. They were too far away, and the buttery yellow light that came out in straight rays from their big windows was white and blinding at its source. Though Athansor perked up his ears when he raised his head to follow them (as if they were mysteriously slow insects), neither he nor Peter Lake could hear anything except the white sound from the machinery on the floor.

The machines themselves were as big as office buildings, olive green, gray, and blue, and lacquered to a shine. Stairs traveled up their sides to steel ledges and landings which led to avenues and ways within. Lights of all colors sparkled in banks of blinking wildflowers; arched piping as thick as mine shafts bent from one massive block to another; and though everything about these engines was still, a steady sound like that of a dozen muted Niagaras gave the unfailing impression of speed, motion, and enveloping progression.

They walked along the line of machinery until they were discovered by a workman who was emerging from one of the long passages inside. He said nothing as he approached. But in his expressionless face and jewel-like eyes he was expression itself held down and stilled. Peter Lake had heard Beverly say that the greater the stillness, the farther you could travel, until, in absolute immobility, you achieved absolute speed. If you could hold your breath, batten yourself down, and stop every atom from its agitation within you, she had said, you could vault past infinity. All this was beyond his comprehension. He took note, however, that, within this building, Athansor, his quiet and affectionate horse, had the air of a horse who enters the yard of a familiar smith. He wondered with what Athansor had once been shod, and would perhaps someday be shod again.

"Can't you see the sign?" asked the workman.

"What sign?"

"That sign," he said, pointing to an enormous luminous panel which read "Entry Forbidden."

"In fact, I didn't see it," responded Peter Lake. "What is this place?"

"A power station," the worker answered. "I thought that was obvious."

"What kind of power station?" was the next question from Peter Lake—skilled mechanic, builder and repairer of electric motors, dynamos, steam turbines, and internal combustion engines.

"A relay station."

"For what?"

"For the power that comes in here."

"From where?"

"I don't know. It's just a relay station. I'm not an engineer."

"I've seen every kind of power station there is."

"Then you should know, shouldn't you."

"Yes. But I don't. I've never seen or heard of anything like this."

The workman made a gesture of contempt. "It's been here for so many years," he said, "that I couldn't even count 'em."

"It hasn't been here for that long. Twenty years ago, people lived in the tenements. In the courtyard there was a little house with a dirt floor. The spielers lived in there: they were pickpockets . . ."

172

"I know," the workman cut in. "Little Liza Jane, Dolly, and Bosca, the dark girl."

"How did you know that?"

"I was here then, too. I lived over there, right about where that block of machinery is, see?"

"In a tenement?"

"That's right. Everyone's dead now, or moved away."

"Do you remember a little child who lived in that building there," asked Peter Lake, pointing at the empty space above a bank of lights, "and who was very sick—about so high, could hardly see, and had a horribly large head, a swollen skull?"

"I told you, they're all gone. But if he was like that, they might have taken him to the hospital."

"Which hospital?"

"The hospital that serves the islands, and served them then—the hospital in Printing House Square."

"But that's in Manhattan."

"The ambulances just go over the bridge."

The morgue of the hospital in Printing House Square was a windowless room in a subbasement with not even an airshaft. Fifty autopsy tables stood under glaring spotlights, and on every single one a body was in repose. On some, as many as ten infants were turned sideways and lined up from one end of the table to the other like a row of disabled pistons. The corpses were of all ages and colors—men, women, children, derelicts as big as horses and as loose as a bundle of rags, muscular workers in rigor mortis, slight girls with hardly any flesh on them, criminals whose last accomplishment had been to collect a bullet hole the size of a dime, a decapitated East Indian whose head stared at its body from across the room, young children with puzzled and painful expressions, men and women who never thought it would end this way, luckless people whose last expression was surprise.

A doctor in a bloodstained coat moved from table to table dictating notes into a speaking tube that he pulled after him on an overhead track, and sometimes bending over a corpse to examine or open it. Peter Lake was immobilized in the doorway. He could neither go in nor pull himself away. The eyes of the dead were focused at random everywhere, and one could not help but be in their field of view.

"Searching for someone, no doubt," the doctor said to Peter Lake without looking up. "Chances are that you won't find him here. If you don't know why, I'll tell you." He spoke as if he were still dictating, and the appearance of Peter Lake were only another condition to be noted and examined. "These people don't ever have anyone who comes after them. They're the ones who fall through the cracks. Where are their parents, their children, brothers, sisters, friends? They're here, or they were here, or they will be soon. Do you think that the ones who are still breathing want to get near this place before they have to? You couldn't drag them down here with a windlass."

When Peter Lake said nothing, it seemed only to spur the doctor on. "Maybe you're from some reform group, and you've come to gather evidence." He glanced at Peter Lake and concluded from his expression and appearance that he was not. "They come down here to snap pictures. They get a thrill here—that's why they come. They take stupendous joy in the indignation and compassion they feel on account of these mangled stiffs; it's their roller coaster. I know this," he said, making a tragic incision across the abdomen of an adolescent girl, "and I'll tell you why. Since I'm here all the time and take apart fifty of these things a day, I can't feel for each and every one of them. I'm not God. I don't have that much in me. The ladies' aides and the social critics sense immediately that I couldn't give a goddamn about all this inedible meat, and that's just what they want. They know they're better than the miserable bastards they try to help, but they really enjoy thinking that they're better than the rest of us, who aren't as 'compassionate' as they are." He turned to Peter Lake again, and said, "You notice how often that very word escapes their lips? They use it like a cudgel. Beware."

What he did next, as a matter of routine, made Peter Lake close his eyes in horror. But the doctor continued, his hands glistening, as if nothing had happened. "They come down here for their own benefit. It's as clear as day that they love it. The great irony and

174

perfect joke is that the wretches on the bottom of the barrel get these self-serving scum as champions. Some champions! They feed off the poor—first materially, and then in spirit. But they deserve each other in a way, because vice and stupidity were made to go together.

"I know that, you see, because I was poor. But I rose like a rocket, and I know how the whole thing works. The ones who are always on your side, or so they think, are the ones who keep you down. Everything they do keeps you down. They'll forgive you for anything. Rob, rape, pillage, and kill, and they'll defend you to yourself. They understand all outrages, and all your failings and faults, too. Perfect! You can go on that way forever. What do they care? Excuse me: they do care. They want it that way."

He bent over to make a short cut, as thin as a hair, across the chest of the emaciated blond girl that he had just eviscerated. "How would they make a living, these servants of the poor, if there were no poor?

"What enabled me to rise above all the people who don't know enough to come in out of the rain is that one day I looked face to face at a man who hated half of everything I was and had the courage to tell me so. I remember his very words. He said, 'What you're doing is hideous—a perfect way to die young. Unless you want to live sweetly only in the hereafter, you ought to learn how to do the right thing.' " The doctor stopped what he was doing, dropped his hands to his sides, and looked directly at Peter Lake. "I hate the poor. Look what they do to themselves. How could you not hate them, unless you thought that they should be like this."

Putting down his scalpel, he reflected for a moment. "Forgive me," he asked. "Sometimes I talk to the living in the same way that I talk to the dead. And maybe they do get to me more than I think. You are looking for someone, though. Why else would you be here?"

Peter Lake nodded.

"Age?"

"A child."

"Sex?"

"I don't know. It seemed like a boy, perhaps."

"Race?"

"Irish or Italian, I think."

"Those are not races. Where from?"

"From the islands."

"We don't get so many of those anymore, not since they industrialized. The population was decimated."

"This was before that."

"Twenty years ago?"

"That's right."

"Maybe, maybe . . . I could help you find someone who passed through this place twenty hours ago—maybe. But not twenty days ago, and not twenty weeks, and never under any circumstances twenty months. Twenty years? That's almost funny. You might as well go to a wheat field in Kansas and try to trace an individual grain that fell off the stalk two decades before you got there. Whole generations spring up and die without being remembered. Everyone is forgotten. If the parents are alive, which I doubt, I guarantee you that they, too, have forgotten.

"Look, there you find child prostitutes, not one or two, but dozens. They live, if you can call it that, until about age nineteen. Then it's too much cocaine, or syphilis, or a knife. Shall I take you to the room where we keep only the pieces that we find, and the cadavers that have been two months in the river—or for years in some hovel, undiscovered? Shall I show you the half-dozen other rooms in this hospital where these scenes are repeated? And what of the other hospitals? Printing House Square is small and tame. Even in the private institutions uptown you can see a show just like this: there is nothing as disgusting as an obese cadaver in which all the futile pleasures of many years finally arise to fill it full-blown with stinking rotten gases. The city is burning and under siege. And we are in a war in which everyone is killed and no one is remembered."

"What am I supposed to do, then," Peter Lake asked, "if it's like you say?"

"Is there someone you love?"

"Yes."

"A woman?"

"Yes."

"Then go home to her."

"And who will remember *her?*"

"No one. That's just the point. You must take care of all that now."

ACELDAMA

P ETER Lake rode Athansor at a lope over snow-covered streets with the north wind against him. It was very cold, and the wind put icicles in his mustache. Though the doctor hadn't known that the woman Peter Lake loved was in the midst of dying, his advice could not have been more appropriate or more painful to hear, especially because it echoed what Beverly had said not long before in the second (though by far not the last) delirium in which he was to see her. "I'm just like you," she had told him. "I come from another age. But there are many things we must take care of now."

Because he was confounded so by the strength of his love for Beverly, its suddenness, and its onrushing end, and perhaps because he had no way of helping her, he joined her in what she believed. Far-fetched as it was, he accepted it simply because he

178

loved her and would share any mortification or pathetic confusion just to be with her. And only after he had come to half-believe what she said did he give it any thought—only after he had been to the hospital in Printing House Square.

If she were correct, it would explain why the world sometimes seemed to be a stage behind which was a strangely benevolent, superior, and indifferent power. The suffering of the innocent would be accounted for, if, in ages to come or ages that had been, the reasons for everything were revealed and balances were evened. It would explain destiny, and coincidence, and his image of the city as if he had been looking from high above at a living creature with a pelt of dusky light. It would explain the things that called to Beverly from a far distance and a far time. It would suggest that Athansor, who could leap high into the air, was leaping toward something he already knew. It would explain the strong feeling Peter Lake had that every action in the world had eventual consequences and would never be forgotten, as if it were entered in a magnificent ledger of unimaginable complexity. He thought that it might explain freedom, memory, transfiguration, and justice—though he did not know how.

Peter Lake remembered when, once, for no apparent reason, Pearly had leapt back, drawn his pistols, and fired ten .45-caliber rounds at a dark window behind which had been nothing but a winter night. Pearly had shaken for an hour afterward, saying that, leering at him from the outside window, with its teeth bared, was a giant dog twenty feet high, the White Dog of Afghanistan, come to get him from another time. Peter Lake thought he was mad—too much bumping of the head on doorposts and tabletops. When Pearly had finally stopped quivering, he slept for forty-eight hours and had nightmares every single minute.

The Baymen were waiting, Peter Lake knew, for a great window in the cloud wall to open and reveal a burning city that was not consumed, a city that thrashed like an animal and yet did not move, a city suspended in the air. Sharp on detail and alert to small signs, they insisted that such a thing would appear, and that, after it did, the world would light up in gold.

All these things were shaken about within Peter Lake like pots and pans banging against the side of a peddler's swaybacked horse. It was hard to bear the weight of partial revelations which refused to venture past the tip of his tongue. He was no Mootfowl or Isaac Penn, not a deep thinker at all, but just a man. He was only Peter Lake, and he rode to the Penns' with the uncomplicated expectation of taking a bath in the slate bathing pool and then watching Beverly as she dressed to go to Mouquin's. He rode fast through the lights of early winter traffic, weaving among panting horses, clouds of steam, lacquered carriages with brass lamps, and showers of dry cold snow. Athansor's gait was so smooth that riding him was like riding a noiseless whip, or gliding down the slope of a mid-ocean swell. Peter Lake and Beverly would go to Mouquin's oblivious of all dangers. The new year was rolling at them as wide and full as a tide racing up the bay, sweeping over old water in an endless coil of ermine cuff.

With Athansor bedded down on a pallet of hay in the Penns' stable, forelegs stretched before him and head bowed in a restful dream, Peter Lake ran up to the second floor of the house and spun the hot-water valves. After the bitter cold, the water was an unparalleled joy. As he floated and turned, buoyed by great volumes of foaming bubbles, the door opened and Beverly came in.

"They're all at *The Sun*," she announced, pulling her blouse over her head in a movement as quick as a good fly-fisherman's cast. "The New Year's party won't be over until seven or eight."

"What about Jayga?" Peter Lake asked, wary of Jayga's compulsive peeping and eavesdropping.

"Jayga at this moment is under my father's desk in the city room, a tray of smoked salmon on her knees, a magnum of French champagne at her side. They find her on the third of January, after an exhaustive search of the entire building. She will have eaten enough salmon, caviar, chopped liver, and shrimp to carry her through a much longer hibernation. But only she, Harry, and I know that. We are her confidants."

"We're alone then."

"Yes!" Beverly shouted, and threw herself into the pool.

They embraced as they floated, they circled, they were turned by flowing water and dashed under the falls. Beverly's unplaited hair spread around her, soft and humid; her breasts had their own way in the water; she kicked her long graceful legs in a rose-and-white scissors; the heat added a fine patina to her skin; and her penetrating eyes were softened and cheered. They glided over to a ledge, where they talked, their words half hidden in the white fall.

Numb with desire, Peter Lake managed to tell her what had happened with Cecil Mature, Mootfowl, Jackson Mead, and the doctor in the hospital in Printing House Square. She had no answers for him. Though she was reassuring, her method was inexplicable. She made no reference to his implied questions, and continued to speak in calm certainties.

"There are animals in the stars," she declared, "like the animal that you describe, with a pelt of light, and deep endless eyes. Astronomers think that the constellations were imagined. They were not imagined at all. There are animals, far distant, that move and thrash smoothly, and yet are entirely still. They aren't made up of the few stars in the constellations that represent them—they're too vast—but these point in the directions in which they lie."

"How can they be bigger than the distance between stars?" he asked.

"All the stars that you can see in the sky don't even make up the tip of a horn, or the lash of an eye. Their shaggy coats and rearing heads are formed of a curtain of stars, a haze, a cloud. The stars are a mist, like shining cloth, and can't be seen individually. The eyes of these creatures are wider than a thousand of the universes that we think we know. And the celestial animals move about, they frisk, they nuzzle, they paw and roll—all in infinite time, and the crackling of their coats is what makes the static and hissing which bathes an infinity of worlds."

Peter Lake stared at the water as it came over the fall. "I'm as crazy as you are," he said, "maybe crazier. I believe you. I do believe you."

"That's only love," Beverly answered. "You don't have to believe me. It's all right if you don't. The beauty of the truth is that it need not be proclaimed or believed. It skips from soul to soul, changing form each time it touches, but it is what it is, I have seen it, and someday you will, too."

He lifted her in the water and set her gently on a slightly higher step. "How do you know all this?"

She smiled. "I see it. I dream it."

"But if they're just dreams, then why do you speak as if they're facts?"

"They're not just dreams. Not anymore. I dream more than I wake now, and, at times, I have crossed over. Can't you see? I've been there."

Contradictions, paradoxes, and strong waves of feeling were things that Peter Lake had long before learned to call his own, so he was not surprised to be surprised by the gentleness of Mouquin's usually boisterous New Year's Eve. He remembered that it had been the same when the century had turned, when the celebrants had been unable to celebrate and could only stand in awe of history as it moved its massive weight (as Peter Lake saw it) like the vault door of a central bank. On the night of December 31, 1899, despite a thousand bottles of champagne and a hundred years of anticipation, Mouquin's had been as quiet as a church on the Fourth of July. Women had wept, and men had found it hard to hold back the tears. As the clockwork of the millennia moved a notch in front of their eyes, it had taken their thoughts from small things and reminded them of how vulnerable they were to time.

But this odd-numbered frozen year far outdid the turn of the century in solemnity and emotion. Then, the quiet had set in an hour or so before midnight. Now, when Peter Lake and Beverly arrived at nine, they and the well-dressed people who had come for an evening of drunken dancing found themselves bathed in clear light, aware of every detail, tranquil, and contemplative. There was no customary ring of people around the fire soaking up its heat and screaming at each other, with drinks in their hands and an eye always cocked to see who had come in out of the cold. Nor did the women magnetize the scene as they could and often did, setting the pace for their men. There was no tension as in richer places, and none of the usual dances like the Barn Rush, the Rumbling Buffalo, the Grapesy Dandy, or the Birdwalla Shuffle. When the orchestra finally did begin to play, the incomparably beautiful "Chantpleure and Winterglad" of A. P. Clarissa was offered for stillwater quadrilles and other dances of counterpoint and restraint in which mainly the eyes moved, and the heart pounded as if in the breast of a hunted stag.

This was no place for Pearly, but he and a dozen Short Tails were there anyway with what they called women—high-toned madams, corrupted country girls sick of working all day in hairdressing salons and oyster houses, lady pickpockets, and professional gun-bearing molls with, as Pearly said, "teats so sharp they could cut cheese." When Pearly saw Peter Lake come in, he rose in anger and his eyes began to electrify. But when Beverly joined Peter Lake, it was as if her presence sent darts into Pearly's flesh, pacifying him with antivenom. Glazed and paralyzed, he and the other Short Tails could do nothing but stare fixedly toward the kitchen, in the manner of a Five Points cretin with a tin cup. Astounded molls tugged at the Short Tails' sleeves and turned to one another in amazement. The Short Tails were dreaded ambassadors of the underworld, whose active presence was feared and tolerated. Had Mouquin's not accepted them, they would have immediately burned it to the ground. Despite the fact that Pearly usually hit his head when he came through the doorway, he and his underlings ruled the place. But now they were entombed in a nerve dream. A dentist could have worked his wily and expensive arts on them without eliciting the slightest protest.

Peter Lake glanced at Pearly, a giant white cat all suited-up in clothes half a century out of date, and wondered how long his enemy would be immobilized. Beverly seemed able to push Pearly deeper and deeper into a condition in which he was cemented in a body that was trapped absolutely stilled in time.

Peter Lake and Beverly took a table and ordered a bottle of champagne, which was brought to them in a silver bucket full of hysterical ice.

"The only time I ever saw this place this dull was the night before nineteen hundred," Peter Lake said. "Maybe, purely by coincidence, all the people here have just lost dear relatives."

"Liven it up," Beverly commanded. "I want to dance—the way they were dancing at the inn that night."

"Who, me?" Peter Lake wanted to know. "How can I liven it up? I suppose I could shoot or stab Pearly now that he's stuck on the flypaper of time. But then everyone would run out. We'll have a quiet evening, and wait for the new year."

"No," she said. "It's my last damned New Year. I'd like to see some fire in it."

She turned about in her seat and faced a set of French doors against which the cold wind was pushing a shower of winter stars. Without warning, they burst open. Then, inexplicably, the next set of doors flew open, too, and so on and so forth right down the line, until the twenty-one sets of doors at Mouquin's had all opened in a machine-gunlike percussion that stopped the orchestra and the dancers. The fresh air stoked the fire and turned it from a softly purring cat into an enraged Bessemer furnace, and the icicle-covered trees outside began to ring like a thousand sleigh bells. Then the hands of the clock started to race like the tortoise and the hare, and both reached midnight at the same time. The clock struck along with every clock in New York, and church bells, fireworks, and ship whistles sounded all at once, turning the entire city into a giant hurdy-gurdy.

It soon got so cold that the men rushed to close the doors. When they had shut them and the room was again silent, they saw that several women had begun to cry. The women said it was because of the numbing air that had washed over their bare shoulders, but even strangers embraced sadly as they coasted into the new year and felt its strength commencing. They cried because of the magic and the contradictions; because time had passed and time was left; because they saw themselves as if they were in a photograph that had winked fast enough to contradict their mortality; because the city around them had conspired to break a hundred thousand hearts; and because they and everyone else had to float upon this sea of troubles, watertight. Sometimes there were islands, and when they found them they held fast, but never could they hold fast enough not to be moved and once again overwhelmed.

"Country dances!" shouted a man as he jumped to his feet, and he was echoed by the fashionable crowd. In lightness and relief they began even before the music caught up to them. Now the floor of Mouquin's pounded under the pure white reels of the winter countryside, and the magic of the Lake of the Coheeries swirled almost visibly about them. Beverly, in a blue silk dress, danced with Peter Lake. There was much talk among the crowd as Pearly and the Short Tails began to thaw. Glasses sparkled until they broke. The room grew hot. Beverly was dancing. In the oyster houses, in the stove-lit salons of the ferryboats out on the bay, in the ballrooms uptown so gilt and argent that in the daytime they thought they were banks, in the common rooms of hospitals, and in the miserable dark cellars, they danced—even if only for a moment.

Peter Lake sensed that some stupendous inner machinery of the world had turned, rendering its decision, and that much would follow. But soon he stopped thinking and was quickly lost in the sight of Beverly, a young blond and blue-eyed schoolgirl who twirled and kicked with the rest. Her hair flew. The music seemed to be in her, and she stomped the floor at just the right times, a precise and joyous part of the dance. She had always conserved her motions, gathering them to her and storing their power. Now she unleashed them. He had never seen her this way: she had never been this way. Though he feared for her, he sensed that this scene would not be lost, and that by some mechanism of translation or preservation it would last and be free sometime to start up again. Her motions flowed in a hundred thousand pictures, each of searing beauty, each on its way through the black cold of archless accommodating space. They would land somewhere, he thought, bravely. Everything always comes to rest, and flourishes. That, anyway, was his hope.

They lost themselves in dancing, staking everything upon the images that billowed out from Mouquin's and expanded effortlessly in all directions.

"I was terrified," Beverly said as they were riding home in a motorized taxi.

"Terrified? How do you figure that? You were the queen of the world. First you put Pearly to sleep. Then you seemed to have opened the doors, stoked the fire, and made the clock spin. You led the dances like a prima ballerina. The evening revolved around you. When we left, the party collapsed like a wet tent."

"I was so afraid," she said. "I was trembling the whole time."

Peter Lake lifted a skeptical eyebrow. She ignored him.

"I'm so glad it's over. I hate crowds of people. I wanted to do it once," she pronounced with measured deliberation, "and I've done it."

"I didn't see that you were at all nervous."

"But I was."

"There wasn't the slightest sign of it."

"That's because it was so deep."

No one was home when they arrived. New Year's had scattered the Penns all around New York. Even Willa was sleeping over at the house of Melissa Bees, the daughter of Crawford Bees, yet another master-builder, a lord of stone and steel. Peter Lake and Beverly threw themselves down on a couch in Beverly's second-floor bedroom. He noticed that she was hot and sweating, but she seemed so happy and light that he believed her when she told him that it was just the normal evening elevation in temperature. After a bath, and some cold hours on the roof in the dry winter air, she said, she would be fine. She felt as if she were getting better, and claimed that she was stronger than she had ever been. In fact, she wanted to try cycling or skating the next day, for she was sure that she could breathe more easily now. Something had happened. Despite her optimism, Peter Lake was scared, and despite his fear, they made love.

They were at once so desperate and so determined that they kept their clothes on, and, to get to her, Peter Lake had to go through a stage set of silk and cotton. And once he had found his way and entered her, they stared at one another as if across a dinner table. His carnation was still pinned to his jacket. Her velvet ribbons still hung correctly. They might have been at a formal party, and yet they arose from the same base, and they were pinioned together underneath all the clothes tighter, hotter, and wetter than they had ever been. As if they were dancing, they put their hands on the small of one another's backs, and moved their fingers slowly up and down the slick surfaces of their clothing. Beverly's delicate features seemed to rise from a fountain of blue, and the skirts spread over the bed were like the water that had fallen back from the plume.

They weren't watchful, and wouldn't have cared if anyone had come into the house. Isaac Penn knew very well what was going on. In other circumstances, it would have been scandalous that the young, fragile, and refined Beverly should be allowed, during her sickness, to know the bittersweet pleasures of a worldly woman. But Isaac Penn recognized that she had fallen in love with Peter Lake, and, despite the risk, wanted her to be free in whatever time she had left to compress the passions that are allowed to us in this life.

She had indeed discovered grace, or madness, in her visions of the starlight. Whichever it was, it frightened her father when she hinted at it or tried to tell him about it, for he knew that young people gifted with long, sharp, and noble vision often paid for it in an early death.

Sometimes, when visiting her on the roof, in the deepest part of the night, he expected to find her asleep, but would instead find her in a breathless trance, possessed, her eyes forced open and fixed on the constellations. "What do you see?" he would ask, frightened for her sanity. "What is it that you see?"

And once, only once, when he found her in the slack and weakened state of someone who had just been seized, broken, and released, she had tried to tell him. He barely understood her when she spoke about a sky full of animals whose pelts were made of an infinite number of stars. They moved slowly and smoothly, for, really, they were motionless. Though their faces could not be seen, they were smiling. There were horses in dark celestial meadows, and other animals that flew, fought, or played—all without moving—in swirling ruby-colored places of complete silence. "Places," she said, "where we have been."

"I cannot comprehend this," answered her father. "The gods of my understanding have been always hidden in clouds and very far away."

"Oh no, Daddy," she had said. "They are here."

"What do you mean?"

"I mean, they are here."

By spring, Beverly's soul had ascended. She died on a windy gray day in March when the sky was full of darting crows and the world lay prostrate and defeated after winter. Peter Lake was at her side, and it ruined him forever. It broke him as he had not ever imagined he could have been broken. He would never again be young, or able to remember what it was like to be young. What he had once taken to be pleasures would appear to him in his defeat as hideous and deserved punishments for reckless vanity. He would never drive from his mind the things she said before she died— ravings about scarves that were songs, torrents of silver sparks, stags with voices like horns, and feasts in fields of black light where the dandelions were suns. And for the rest of his days he would be oppressed by the image of her whitened emaciated body eternally motionless in a dark root-pierced grave—*or so he thought*.

Shortly after Beverly's death, Isaac Penn followed. One night he called Harry into his bedroom, and said, "I'm dying right now. I feel tremendous speed. I'm frightened. Falling." And then he died, as if he had been snatched away by some great thing that had been passing at unimaginable speed.

Willa and Jack were farmed out to relatives in the country, the servants were given annuities and dismissed, and the house was sold and soon demolished to make way for a new school. Harry left for Harvard, from which he would then go to the war in France. *The Sun* stayed much the same, ready for Harry to survive Château-Thierry and the Marne if he could, and return to take charge. Suddenly and sadly, the Penns disappeared from the city. In several strokes, a thriving family was silenced. For Peter Lake, who had never before known loneliness, the city was now empty. But even defeated soldiers sometimes survive. If they make the right motions, they are brought from battle. Peter Lake was left alive.

When there was no one remaining to care for, and nothing more to do, he took Athansor and rode into the Five Points, reckless and angry, trying as best he could to run into Pearly. He wanted to die. But all that summer, as if by magic, he stayed out of Pearly's way and remained (to his disgust) a free man. He wandered about on Athansor, who, for lack of exercise and sympathy, began to seem more and more like an ordinary white horse that used to drive a milk wagon in Brooklyn. Where Peter Lake went is anyone's guess, for at times his whereabouts were hidden even from him. The deep maze of the city, its winding streets, tumultuous avenues, and remote squares, circles, and courts with their teeming thousands, swallowed him up easily, and he became one of the great army of the unknown, the ragmen, the wanderers, the ones who cried on the street.

Though he always managed to feed Athansor, and sometimes managed to feed himself, he was never aware of how he did it, except that he could walk down a crowded street and emerge with a hundred dollars that seemed to come from the air but which came, really, from people's pockets. He hated the idea of this, and fought not to do it. But his hands were more loyal to his stomach than to his head. He had grown ragged, and his clothes were old—but not as old as his face. One day, a wet-eyed young dandy in a sealskin coat approached him and put a bunch of silver coins in his hand, saying, "For you, Father."

"I'm not your father, you stupid son of a bitch," was Peter Lake's reply, but he kept the money.

As uncomfortable as a penitent who has sworn some stupendous oath, Peter Lake wanted to part with the silver. He and Athansor wandered a few miles, and then stopped while a convoy of military trucks crossed their path. It took so long that he dismounted and looked around. He was standing in front of a movie theater, something of which he had recently heard, and he decided to see what was inside.

He was not expecting the darkness to be shattered by a stunning explosion of light. But the perfect square of even white fire upon the wall seemed to have a heart and depth. The light was measured in pulses much more rapid than those of a furnace. He heard the even gait of electrically driven gears, and the flutelike pitch of a high-speed cooling fan that was undoubtedly beneath them. Dust was trapped in the slanted beam of arc-light like a herd of buffalo embarrassed by the intruding lamp of a locomotive, and the particles scattered about the huge hall, transforming it into a universe of mobile stars. How strange it was when the physics and mystery combined to depict people in ordinary rooms, on the street, or tied to railroad tracks. For half an hour, Peter Lake watched a world of gray in which everything moved too fast and actors spoke in silence. White light filled the room again, and then deferred to a small sketch entitled, "A Winter Scene in Brooklyn—How We Were."

A village appeared, snow-covered and motionless. Then a horse drawing a sled galloped across the wall and vanished into the curtains. Doors opened, half a dozen women came out, and as if life proceeded in this fashion, they began to churn butter. All at once, they went back in, and the same scene was repeated with men chopping wood, then milkmen delivering milk, boys delivering papers, and a long parade of police chasing a long parade of crooks. All the police were in one group, as were all the crooks.

"What's 'were' about that?" asked Peter Lake indignantly and aloud.

"Shhh!" hissed a woman who had not removed her hat.

Then another white flash struck Peter Lake and pushed him back in his chair. They were to witness a film portrait—"The City in the Third Millennium." When it came on the screen, Peter Lake almost jumped up to shout in anger: this was a film of the painting that had been done for the Penns. Titles announced each moving tableau. "Flight" was a wonder of floating lights traversing the night sky over the city. There were hundreds of these lights, as graceful as schooners but as fast as express trains, tracing lines in the darkness with a remarkable purposefulness. The city had grown upward into cliffs of silver boxes that flashed and glowed and shone out over the water in a rippled musical pattern. Remarkably, most of what was visible in it was light itself. Cold wind raced along the narrow boulevards, jingling the frozen trees. Winter clouds, small and tight, filtered through the ramparts like a river threading through a weir. The clouds moved at a height only about a quarter that of the buildings, and yet they were not low clouds or fog but those high riders that come with strong dry winds. How could this be?

Another title appeared: "As the City of the Future Burns." Flames could not be seen, only vast banks of illuminated smoke that coiled over the city in braids or swelled like mountains. Then the film broke, and Peter Lake was caught up in blinding white almost as if he were trapped in the backwash of a waterfall crashing into its thundering pool.

Athansor was waiting like a dog tied up outside a store. His silent dispirited master slowly walked him to the east. Athansor's coat was streaked with soot and dust, and he didn't look much like a statue anymore. Peter Lake was tired and worn out, and had no place to go. But it was one of those nights in mid-September when, like a cannonade in the distance, Canada threatens winter, and because they had to find shelter they ended up in a cellar, not far from the great bridge. A tallow candle lit a small room in which were a few piles of straw. Athansor stood near one wall, and Peter Lake sat down and rested his back against another. After a while, a man came in and put a bucket of oats and a bucket of water in front of the horse. He left, and returned carrying an iron skillet of grilled fish and vegetables in one hand and two bottles of cold beer in the other. These he put down in front of his guest. "You want hot water in the morning?" he asked.

"Sure," said Peter Lake. "I haven't had hot water in a while."

"Then the lodging for you and the horse, the oats, the hot water, the food, beer, and the candle will be two dollars altogether—two and a half if you don't want anyone else in here with you. You can pay in the morning. Checkout time is eleven A.M."

"Checkout time?"

"I used to work in a hotel."

The fish and vegetables were fresh, the beer ice-cold, and the straw warm and comfortable. Peter Lake was reminded of his first night in the city, with the spielers, when he and they had fallen asleep by the light of a flickering tallow candle. But now there were no women. He thought that he might never touch, love, or be with a woman again. Everything had come apart, and the world was gray rain. With even a harder road ahead than he thought, he fell asleep clutching straw between his fingers, content to be alone in a warm and dirty cellar.

Athansor, on the other hand, stood straight and lifted his head. He was restless, his ears slewed about continuously as if he were keeping track of a mosquito, and his eyes shot back and forth. Had Peter Lake not been lost in sleep, he would have seen that his white horse was tensed like a war-horse who senses a distant battle. There was something in the air, and as the white horse grew more and more alert, astonishing memories began to flood his heart.

Many hours later, Peter Lake had a dream in which he saw himself lying on the straw, with his back against the wooden wall for warmth. Athansor, a white blur in the darkness, was fretting and ill at ease. Peter Lake knew that he was dreaming, and was not surprised when, long before morning, silver light began to flood through the cracks where the cellar walls neared ground level, and the one high window began to frost over as if it were plated with ice and taking the full blast of a beaming December moon. This light grew stronger, like the dawn, but it was much faster, and it had no warm halftones, blood colors, yellows, or oven-whites. Instead, it was all whited silver and blue that grew thicker and brighter as it approached. Had it had the weight of ordinary sunlight, it would have shattered the dream, but being the kind of illumination that seems to make everything float, it only made the dream more profound.

The strengthening silver-blue light was accompanied by a collection of restless sounds. Tones and static battled, entwined in a war that led them upward. Wind and voices were woven into an impenetrable shield. It was the incandescent cloud wall in full agitation, moving toward Manhattan and pushing before it the lost and broken sound and light that would be swept along the island's edge like amber and sparkling shells driven onto a beach in a necklace-making storm.

But this hurricane had a solid eye, a calm center that would pass over the city in pressureless tranquillity, a shaft of silence with no upward limit. Its approach awakened Peter Lake in his dream, and he sat up with silver flooding his eyes. Athansor could hardly control himself. He was trembling and stomping as if his time had finally come. Frozen motionless, with his eyes at the roof of his soul, Peter Lake could feel Athansor's inner powers as if they were huge engines and whining turbines.

The wind began to rage from the south. Trees bent and their leaves shuddered in prolonged rushes. Peter Lake heard garbage-can lids pop off and rocket away like artillery shells. The garbage cans themselves were rolling at high velocity along the streets and smashing through store windows, like solid iron projectiles. The timbers of the house rocked and groaned as wind and light raced one another for dominance. Neither won, but the earth trembled as it was swept entirely clean. Then the howling wind stopped, and an all-encompassing calm surrounded the city and shut it down. Nothing moved, neither man nor animal. The waters were still, and all objects seemed rooted in place.

Now the light began truly to flood. It was frightening. It burst upon the harbor in a blinding beam, and tracked toward the city. "It's a dream, it's a dream," Peter Lake told himself over and over even as he trembled. "It's a dream." The door to the cellar was lifted gently from its hinges and it flew up, disappearing silently. The silver beam washed down the steps into the straw-filled room and flooded it with cool light.

Suddenly, the light went out, and it was night. Still in the dream, Peter Lake sank back against the wall, able to breathe again. The short time he had to get his wits did him little good, for now he saw. Could it be, even in a dream? Glowing in white, silver, and blue, Beverly was standing at the entrance to the cellar, in a sphere of reverberating beams as round as the moon. She glided down the ramp of light that had brought her. In her hand was a horse's bridle of what appeared to be chains of stars or sharp diamonds. She was the source of her own illumination, and, next to her, Athansor seemed like a small Shetland. Though he was calmed by her presence, as if he had been expecting it, Peter Lake of the dream fainted dead away. But Peter Lake the dreamer watched as Beverly, her hair plaited in the old fashion, curried Athansor and spoke to him unintelligibly. Her motions and expressions were not unlike those of a girl attending to her pony, but she radiated light.

Peter Lake the dreamer saw Peter Lake of the dream wake, and watch as Beverly finished with Athansor. Then she turned, looked at him directly, and moved toward him. When she was near, he closed his hand around the celestial bridle. Though she smiled and though her eyes danced, she withdrew the bridle. He gripped it so hard that it cut into his hands, but he was unable to hold it, and he felt himself awakening in the dark. He wanted to stay with Beverly in the strangely lighted room full of mysterious curling static and woolly amber tones, but the dream faded, the light was withdrawn, and the last he could remember was a feeling of unutterable pain and loss, and anger at his sentence of darkness.

An hour before the natural light, a strange operation began outside the stable where Peter Lake had dreamed of Beverly. Almost in panic, the Short Tails, their allies, and the allies of their allies, arrayed themselves, their weapons, and their machines in military formations throughout the streets and on the squares. Pearly charged from place to place on a spotted gray horse, directing the order of battle. In Brooklyn, one of his lieutenants began to march a body of troops toward the Great Bridge. This was the last mobilization of the gangs before the war swept them away like dust in the wind.

It was a swan song, and the swan that sang it was all bent out of shape. In their decline, the gangs had become repositories for a strange set of criminals. Most of the two thousand soldiers busily assembling were under five feet tall. They did not dash from place to place with the grace of men born to arms, they waddled. Many of the fat ones had Cecil Mature's slitlike eyes but not his redeeming sweetness. A third of their number was seriously lame, and hobbled about. Another third, or more, made strange "ticky-tacky" sounds. When they talked they sounded like corks popping from champagne bottles, chickens, garglers, and groaning dogs. The ones who were most ordinary were the ferocious-looking cutthroats who in the old days had been called "wild dogs," because they would recognize no friend, and turned upon one another more easily than could be tolerated by even the most anarchic gangs. Now they were the troops.

Pearly had assembled the remnants of the Short Tails, the Dead Rabbits, the Plug Uglies, the Happy Jacks, the Rock Gang, the Rag Gang, the Stable Gang, the Wounded Ribs, the White Switch Gang, the Corlears Hook Rats, the Five Points Steel Bar Gang, the Alonzo Truffos, the Dog Harps, the Moon Bayers, the Snake Hoops, the Bowery Devils, and many others. There were more than two thousand of them, including every independent dirk man, goon, and rougher-upper in the city.

The police had been bribed to evacuate the area south of Chambers Street. Pearly assured them that he was after only one man, and that no property would be damaged. He marshaled his armies of deformed waddlers and bristling mad dogs, like a real general—riding here and there, jumping his dappled gray over lines of his own men, and testing the deployments. He spoke to the Brooklyn side by telephone. It was ready. "Is Manhattan ready?" they asked. Pearly answered in the affirmative. Sixteen hundred soldiers in Manhattan were fully armed and properly positioned. Though the cloud wall was unsettled, and had moved up the bay, it often did so in late September as the seasons changed, and Pearly was willing to bet that when the sun came up and stabilized the day, the cloud wall would recede. The sun did come up, and illuminated a massive army of squat criminal beings, who could not resist talking loudly to each other, because they hoped for blood. They had real weapons, and they liked to use them.

Pearly waited for Peter Lake to emerge from the cellar where the innkeeper had sworn that he was hiding. Sparks flew from him as if from a big gray cat in a dry winter storm. He could hardly stay still, his head nodded up and down as if it were keeping time, and his razor eyes fixed on the open ramp of the basement stable.

Peter Lake awoke with a start. "Christ!" he said, and fell back against the straw. It was already half-light, and when he was either very happy or very unhappy he could never fall asleep again after awakening. He sat up, and saw Athansor, who looked as if he wanted to race. Peter Lake had seen other horses with the same ur-

195

gent need to run, but it had always been at Belmont just before post time, when a syringe full of atropine was working its dangerous wonders. Athansor looked as if he could outrun ten of that kind of horse, one after another.

Peter Lake himself felt astoundingly strong and energetic. He was wide-awake, and he wanted only to ride Athansor. "I'll take him up to the country," he said out loud. "We'll run like hell across the whole goddamned state." He got to his feet and walked toward what he hoped would be the bucket of hot water that he had asked for, delivered early. It was only the water from the previous evening. When he looked down at it to see if it was steaming, he saw that his palms and fingers were badly cut, as if he had held onto a chain of sharp diamonds that was pulled through his hands.

He hadn't time to reflect, and guessed that he would do well to hurry, for Athansor's energy was now so intense that the walls of the stable vibrated like a station shed into which six locomotives had come in train.

Then Peter Lake heard the sound of the sixteen hundred men, now in their places, ready, and no longer required to mute their unusual voices. "What the hell is that?" Peter Lake asked himself, and then dashed up the ramp to face a phalanx of about eight hundred of them arranged in a crescent across an empty square, not more than fifty yards away. Pearly was mounted on his gray, smiling as confidently as a knife-thrower. Peter Lake smiled in recognition. "You've done well, Pearly," he shouted across the gap. "But it's not over yet."

"No, Peter Lake," Pearly shouted back. "It's not over yet."

"What do you think you'll accomplish," Peter Lake asked after seeing Pearly's army, "with these idiots and buffoons?" He didn't wait for an answer, but went back inside and leapt upon Athansor, who shot away with tremendous force. Peter Lake intended simply to jump the ranks and be off. How could Pearly have been so stupid? Athansor emerged from the stable like an express train. The chubby little trolls had to catch their breath.

But he quickly wheeled to a stop. Peter Lake felt his blood beating. There would be no jumping, for this strange and pathetic army had raised a forest of sharp pikes thirty and forty feet long. They

196

were too close for Athansor to clear their blades: he could not simply rise straight up in the air.

With the way blocked except for a small opening on the left, Peter Lake spurred Athansor and made for the breach. Closing behind him, Pearly's army came alive with a shout. It had been carefully planned. As soon as Peter Lake was clear, a hundred little men appeared in the opening of a side street and blocked the way with pikes. Nets had been hung from booms and spars mounted on buildings, and a dozen vicious dogs were unleashed to harry Athansor. He trampled them easily, or sailed over them, but they slowed him down. Not a single shot had been fired. Pearly's soldiers were too busy funneling Peter Lake onto the bridge ramp. Peter Lake could see what they were trying to do, but he had no escape. The closer he got to the bridge, the more nets there were, the more pikes, the louder the cries of his pursuers.

Finally, with nowhere else to go, and a hundred sharp pike heads jabbing at him, Athansor sidled reluctantly onto the ramp. His mouth frothed. He showed his teeth. He looked for an opportunity either to fight or to soar over his enemies, and found none. They had hung heavy nets along the suspension cables all the way out to the towers. He had no choice but to try for Brooklyn.

As Peter Lake expected, the Brooklyn side, too, was all netted up, its cables choked with heavy hawsers and trawler nets. The walkway was filled with pikemen marching toward him. Athansor could have cleared the pikes, but the cathedral-like arches were blocked with weighted nets that reached down to within a few feet of the pike-heads.

Peter Lake galloped east and west, trying to find a way out. He knew that many horses in many battles had been wheeled around and spurred in just the way he was directing Athansor, made to imitate pacing tigers, while their riders were breathless with fear. They had nowhere to go, so they went back and forth. The city shone in a bed of autumn blue to the north and west. Brooklyn was still asleep. The river had black wind lines penned across its face. And to the south was the open harbor, across which stretched the cloud wall, furious and close, buckling in the middle of the bay, sucking at the water and creating a line of breakers that rolled from its base.

High above the river, hundreds of feet above the water, all they could do was rush to and fro as the enemy closed. The only way out that Peter Lake could see was in the conjunction of the two forces. During the fighting, he might be able to get to the rear and escape. He had no weapons. Athansor breathed hard.

Both lines stopped. Pearly was too smart to create the confusion for which Peter Lake hoped. They halted in place, fixed their pikes close to the nets, and stood their ground. Only then did groups of fighters pass through the two main bodies. There were about a hundred. They had shorter pikes, swords, and pistols. Pearly knew that a mob could not be a tight enough seal, so he set them still and had the best men step forward to kill Peter Lake and his horse.

"We have no choice," Peter Lake said to Athansor. "This time, we fight."

The first group closed. They were timid, as well they should have been. Athansor reared and pushed the pikes aside. He charged into the soldiers and knocked them over. He bit and trampled them. But he was in a forest of pikes, and they cut him on the flanks and chest. When a second group saw his blood, they joined the fight and fired their pistols. A swordsman lunged for Peter Lake and slashed him across the back. Peter Lake felt no pain. He took the sword. Now he had a weapon, and he flailed angrily and hard.

Athansor reared and placed his hooves deep into the chests of the attackers. The sound was of underbrush breaking. As sword struck sword it became clear to Peter Lake that he was going to die. They fired into Athansor's face, and their bullets smashed into his bones and tattered his ears like flags above a fortress. Lead pierced his muscles, and lodged in his gut. Peter Lake, too, was cut and bleeding everywhere. He felt cold. Then Pearly commanded his fighters to fall back. Peter Lake was left with the dead scattered all around him. He and Athansor were shaking from their wounds. They moved about meaninglessly. Then Peter Lake saw that Pearly had a second and yet a third wave ready to do battle. This could not be borne.

He looked at the river below. It was very far, too far. But it was a lovely blue, and a much better way to die, if he had to, than upon the bloodstained boards of the Great Bridge. There was nothing to lose. They would jump.

The wind whistled through nets and cable. Peter Lake gave one last glance to the city, and turned south to the marshes. As the second wave started to close, Athansor began the tiger pacing, but this time it was north-south, across the narrow walkway of the bridge. They thought he was crazed. Trying for the kill, they fired their pistols. But he ignored them. When he was ready, he leaned back on his haunches. Pearly's men stopped, for they had never seen such a sight. Athansor arched on visible waves of power. He compressed himself into something almost round. Then, with a roar, he unfolded in a long white silken movement, and flew into the air, parting a thick steel cable that had been in his way, and clearing the nets with ease.

Momentarily suspended over the bay, Peter Lake expected to fall, and would have been satisfied with what he expected. But there was no fall. Athansor rose, and sped outward, stretching his wounded forelegs before him as the air whistled past. The horse and rider were headed for the white wall. Peter Lake looked back and saw that the city was small and silent, and seemed no larger than a beetle. As they broke into the cloud wall the world became a storm of rushing white mist that screamed and shrieked like a choir of shrill and tormented voices.

They flew for hours; it got harder and harder to breathe and more and more difficult for Peter Lake to hold on. As Athansor's speed increased, the clouds rushing by whited out in a blur. Peter Lake thought of the city. A shelter from the absolute and the lordly, it now seemed like such a loving place, even though it had been so hard. Bright images came before his eyes now that he was snowblind, and he ached for the color, the softness, and the sheen of the city that was an island in time.

Finally Athansor tore through the roof of the clouds. They found themselves in a black and airless ether. What Peter Lake saw was what Beverly had described, and he was awed beyond his capacity for awe. He couldn't breathe, and he knew that if he stayed on the horse he would die. So he touched Athansor gently, and threw himself off to fall back upon the field of clouds. That was the last he saw of the high clear world, for his fall became clouded and tumbling and timeless. There were lakes in the clouds that simply gave upon the sea, and there were deeper, longer columns that curved through whitened air. He fell, and he fell, and he had no will. His arms and legs flailed. His neck was like the soft neck of a baby.

Peter Lake tumbled through the world of white. And then, entirely forgotten, he vanished deep into its infinite fury.

·II·

FOUR GATES
TO THE CITY

FOUR GATES TO THE CITY

Every city has its gates, which need not be of stone. Nor need soldiers be upon them or watchers before them. At first, when cities were jewels in a dark and mysterious world, they tended to be round and they had protective walls. To enter, one had to pass through gates, the reward for which was shelter from the overwhelming forests and seas, the merciless and taxing expanse of greens, whites, and blues—wild and free—that stopped at the city walls.

In time the ramparts became higher and the gates more massive, until they simply disappeared and were replaced by barriers, subtler than stone, that girded every city like a crown and held in its spirit. Some claim that the barriers do not exist, and disparage them. Although they themselves can penetrate the new walls with no effort, their spirits (which, also, they claim do not exist) cannot, and are left like orphans around the periphery.

To enter a city intact it is necessary to pass through one of the new gates. They are far more difficult to find than their solid predecessors, for they are tests, mechanisms, devices, and implementations of justice. There once was a map, now long gone, one of the ancient charts upon which colorful animals sleep or rage. Those who saw it said that in its illuminations were figures and symbols of the gates. The east gate was that of acceptance of responsibility, the south gate that of the desire to explore, the west gate that of devotion to beauty, and the north gate that of selfless love. But they were not believed. It was said that a city with entryways like these could not exist, because it would be too wonderful. Those who decide such things decided that whoever had seen the map had only imagined it, and the entire matter was forgotten, treated as if it were a dream, and ignored. This, of course, freed it to live forever.

LAKE OF THE COHEERIES

THE upper Hudson was as different from New York and its expansive baylands as China was different from Italy, and it would have taken a Marco Polo to introduce one to the other. If the Hudson were likened to a serpent, then the city was the head, in which were found the senses, expressions, brain, and fangs. The upper river was milder, stronger, the muscular neck and smoothly elongated body. There was no rattle to this snake. Albany sometimes tried to rattle, but failed to emit an audible sound.

First of all, the Hudson landscape was a landscape of love. To reach it by sea, one had to have a series of glorious weddings, crossing the sparkling bands that were the high bridges. Then one sailed into tranquil, capacious, womanly bays, the banks of which were spread as wide and trusting as any pair of long legs that ever were. Then began an infinity of pleasant convolutions. There were whole valleys on tributaries, each with many thousand well-tended gardens. Towns along the banks were entirely subsumed in their devotion to one great view, or in the memory of one portion of one century in which they enjoyed a seemingly endless spell of clear weather. There were old opera houses, great estates, hidden root cellars and spring enclosures, gray churches built by the Dutch, wharves that stretched a mile into the river and were hung on some days with dozens of sturgeon each of four hundred pounds or more and bursting with roe. The skating was unparalleled, except perhaps in Holland, for the early Dutch had built several hundred miles of canals through wilderness, swamp, field, and village, upon which a skater could glide all alone under the moonlight for a long winter's night, and hardly know that he had been out ten minutes. Often boys or girls would come home in the blare of early morning, after a night of racing the moon, having fallen deeply in love.

On the Hudson, infatuation was a great and complicated phenomenon. It was sometimes ridiculous and endearing: that is, to see adolescents caught painfully in the pleasant traps into which they eagerly jump. They would go about town sighing and talking to themselves. "I love you," they would say to the imagined beloved, though it might have appeared to someone else that they were speaking to a snow shovel or an egg crate. The valley seemed to have run on love. But, luckily, commerce and farming were richly endowed, and the seasons were intense and fruitful (ice and maple sugar in the winter; shellfish and flowers in the spring; vegetables, grain, and berries in summer; everything at fall harvest; and lumber, minerals, whale products, beef, mutton, wool, and manufactures all year-round), for if they were not, there would have been chaos.

On the Hudson, there was always the opportunity to be educated deeply in the heart. The beauty of the landscape did the rest, along with the magic of the moon, the river's hot and reedy bays, the glittering silver ice, days of summer or days of snow submerged in an ocean of clear blue air, fields never-ending, the wind from Canada, and the great city to the south.

* * *

The water of the Lake of the Coheeries was as lush and blue as the water of a round and opalescent glacial pool. Its plentiful fish were full of silvery fight (rising above the lake like flashing swords), and they fled from place to place in a spectral bath of intense and unvarying fidelity. It could be angry and brutal in storms, and drinking from it was an awakening and a blessing. And sometime not too deep in winter, each year, the Lake of the Coheeries would surprise everyone by freezing over during the night. In the second week of December at the latest, the inhabitants of Lake of the Coheeries Town sat by their fires after dinner and stared into the darkness around their rafters as Canadian winds rode in hordes and attacked their settlement from the north. These winds had been born and raised in the arctic, and had learned their manners on the way down, in Montreal—or so it was said, since the people of Lake of the Coheeries hadn't much respect for the manners or mores of Montreal. The winds ripped off tiles, broke branches, and toppled unwired chimneys. When they came up, everyone knew that winter had begun, and that a long time would pass before the spring made the lake light yellow with melting streams that fled from newly breathing fields.

But one winter the winds were harder and colder than they had ever been. The night they started had seen birds smashed against cliffs and trees, children crying, and candles flickering. Mrs. Gamely, her daughter Virginia, and Virginia's infant, Martin, stayed in their tiny house and imagined pure hell on the lake. They could hear huge waves breaking against the soft wiglike tufts where the fields met the water. In the middle of the lake, said Mrs. Gamely, the water was being blown into giant foamy castles, and all the great monsters from the deep, including the Donamoula, were being ploughed up and turned over like roots in a new field. "Listen," she said. "You can hear them shrieking as they tumble about. Poor creatures! Even though they are a cross between seaborne spiders, writhing serpents, and the sharpest knives; even though their eyes are big and open and have no eyelashes, and they stare at you like cockeyed beggars; and even though their teeth are a forest of bony razors, still, it's a shame to hear them crying like that."

Virginia fastened onto the darkness, listening for the shrieks of sea creatures being tossed like a salad in the middle of the lake. All she heard was the wind. Mrs. Gamely rolled her tiny eyes and held up one finger. "Shh," she said, and listened. "There! Hear them?"

"No!" answered Virginia. "I hear only the wind."

"But don't you hear the creatures, too, Virginia?"

"No, Mother, only the wind."

"I'll bet the little warmkin hears them," Mrs. Gamely said, referring to the baby sleeping soundly in its fat flannels. "There *are* creatures, you know," she continued. "I've seen them. When I was a little girl on the north side of the lake (way before I married Theodore), we used to see them all the time. Of course, that was long ago. They ran in schools, and came to the shore near the house, just like tame dogs. Sometimes they would leap over the dock, and sink a rowboat. My sister and I used to stand on the pier and feed them pies. They loved pies. The Donamoula, who was about two hundred feet long and fifty feet around, loved cherry pies. We would throw the cherry pie into the air, and he would catch it with his forty-foot tongue. One day, my father decided that this was too dangerous, and he made us stop. The Donamoula never came by after that." She knitted her brows. "I wonder if he would remember me."

Ever challenged by her mother's unorthodox views, Virginia thought of a means to answer the question that had just been posed. She looked at her mother and was pleased and amazed by the sly, robust intelligence in the old woman's face, by her massive form which was neither fat nor tall nor thick, by the large strong hands, the shapeless velvet and muslin dress with a green yoke, the two sweet little eyes set close together in a glowing cheeky face topped with a haystack of soft white hair, and the purring white rooster (his comb was mandarin red) that she held in her arms and occasionally stroked.

"If Jack went away for fifty years"—Jack was the rooster, Quebec-born, originally Jacques—"and then came back, would he recognize *me?*" Virginia asked.

"Roosters don't live for fifty years, Virginia. And besides, he

208

would go back to Canada and probably never return. They speak French there, you know, and can never do anything right. They would probably turn him into a cocoa van, or use him as a mold for a weather vane."

"Well, let's just say he could go away for fifty years and then come back."

"Okay. But where would he go?"

"To Peru."

"Why Peru?"

Conversations like these, touching on every subject known to man, would often usurp a good part of the night. Mrs. Gamely had never learned to read or write, and used her daughter as a scribe, and as a researcher among encyclopedias, questioning her at length about everything she found. The old woman's sense of organization was a miracle of randomness as illogical and rich as the branches of a blossoming fruit tree. She could easily discuss 150 subjects in an hour and a half, and Virginia would still finish awed and enlightened by what seemed to be a relentless and perfect plan.

Though Mrs. Gamely was by all measures prescientific and illiterate, she did know words. Where she got them was anyone's guess, but she certainly had them. Virginia speculated that the people on the north side of the lake, steeped in variations of English both tender and precise, had made with their language a tool with which to garden a perfect landscape. Those who are isolated in small settlements may not know of the complexities common to great cities, but their hearts are rich, and so words are generated and retained. Mrs. Gamely's vocabulary was enormous. She knew words no one had ever heard of, and she used words every day that had been mainly dead or sleeping for hundreds of years. Virginia checked them in the Oxford dictionary, and found that (almost without exception) Mrs. Gamely's usage was flawlessly accurate. For instance, she spoke of certain kinds of dogs as Leviners. She called the areas near Quebec march-lands. She referred to diclesiums, liripoops, rapparees, dagswains, bronstrops, caroteels, opuntias, and soughs. She might describe something as patibulary, fremescent, pharisaic, Roxburghe, or glockamoid, and words like mormal, jeropigia, endosmic, mage, palmerin, thos, vituline, Turonian, galingale, comprodor, nox, gaskin, secotine, ogdoad, and pintulary fled from her lips in Pierian saltarellos. Their dictionary looked like a sow's ear, because Virginia spent inordinate proportions of her days racing through it, though when Mrs. Gamely was angry a staff of ten could not have kept pace with her, and half a dozen linguaphologists would have collapsed from hypercardia.

"Where did you learn all those words, Mother?" Virginia might ask.

Mrs. Gamely would shrug her shoulders. "We were raised with them, I suppose." She didn't always speak incomprehensibly. In fact, she sometimes went for months at a time strapped down firmly to a strong and worthy matrix of Anglo-Saxon derivatives. Then, Virginia breathed easy, and the rooster was so happy that had he been a chicken he would have laid three eggs a day. Or was he a chicken? Who knows? The point is, he thought he was a cat.

The wind rose even more, leveling haystacks, collapsing barns, driving the lake onto the fields. Mrs. Gamely and Virginia could hear a ferocious jingling as billions of ice fragments shuffled together on the swells, sounding like the lost souls of all the insects that had ever lived. The house groaned and swayed, but it had been built to weather storms, and was the work of Theodore Gamely, who, before he had been killed, had intended it to shelter his wife and daughter no matter what might happen to him. Now his youthful wife was an old woman, the daughter in her thirties; and they had been in the house alone for all that time, except when Virginia went off to marry a French-Canadian named Boissy d'Anglas, and came back three years later with a newborn son.

"Do you think the house will fall down?" asked Mrs. Gamely.

"No, I don't think so," Virginia answered.

"I've never known the wind to blow like this. The coming winter is going to be very difficult."

"It's always difficult."

"But this time," said the mother, "I think the cold is going to break the back of the land. Animals will die. Food will run out. People will get sick."

In combination with the wind, such pronouncements sounded accurate. In fact, whenever Mrs. Gamely spoke solemnly, she was

210

usually right. Whether or not what she predicted would come true, that night the wind reached almost two hundred miles an hour, and the temperature of the still air was minus five degrees Fahrenheit.

After an unusually bone-shaking blast, Mrs. Gamely got up and paced in circles about the center of the room. Wood burned in the stove, hot and bright. She circled the kitchen table, face upturned to the ceiling. Up there, it was a swirling purple, while the walls and floors were the color of warm rose, cream, and yellow. The roof rattled. Jack jumped into Mrs. Gamely's arms, and she held him like a cat. "Is there snow, Mother?" Virginia asked, almost as if she were still a child.

"Not in this wind," replied Mrs. Gamely. She threw some more wood into the stove, and went to the corner to get her double-barreled shotgun. She said that, on a night of great cold, bonds break, prisons open, lunatics are pushed over the brink, animals go berserk, and the monsters in the lake might try to come into the house.

They sat there all night, not bothering to go to bed. Although Christmas was some weeks off, it felt like Christmas Eve, and Virginia swayed slightly back and forth with her baby in her arms, dreaming and remembering. Their house was stocked with enough dry wood for two winters, and the pantry was packed up to the ceiling with smoked meats, fowl, and cheeses; dried beef and vegetables; sacks of rice, flour, and potatoes; canned goods; preserves; local wine; and things that the two women needed for their prodigious skills in cooking and baking. The shelf was filled with books that were hard to read, that could devastate and remake one's soul, and that, when they were finished, had a kick like a mule. On the beds, unused that night, were goosedown quilts as light as whipped cream and three feet thick. Virginia had had some difficult times, and there would undoubtedly be more hard times ahead. But now she was home, in a bay of tranquillity, and it was pleasant just to dream.

Canada: the name itself was as flat and cool as a snow-covered field. It took Virginia and Boissy d'Anglas two days on his sleigh to get to the Laurentians, and what pleasure to watch the moon swell up from the horizon amid the gaps between snow-bound trees. Her years in Canada were difficult to recall, but the memory of the journey there was clear, and all she really needed.

211

They started out one afternoon, when the sun was low and gold. The snow that day had been warmer than the air, and had shone with a yellowish glow like that of evening light against a brick wall. Two horses, one brown and one nearly red, had pulled north into the wilderness at an even canter which they might have sustained forever, and did sustain deep into the night—through which they traveled as if in daylight, thanks to a blinding moon reflected by the snow.

The horses loved the fresh track before them, and ran across open fields and between stands of pine as if they were racing. Boissy d'Anglas and the young woman that he had nearly abducted were possessed. Their faces were on fire and their eyes were alight. Minute by minute, shadows were transformed into mountains or groves as they closed upon them and could see the winter-etching in ledges and leaves. Lakes and leaping streams appeared and disappeared on both sides of the road, and as they took the hills and curves the landscape seemed to roll as if it were the ocean. The perfectly round and frozen moon was as bright as ice. The horses were so happy to be running under the aurora that they probably could have gone all the way to Canada without stopping.

But they were made to halt when they arrived at the edge of a frozen lake that stretched north like a highway between lines of hills and jagged mountains done in bristling silver. "I don't know if we should camp here and start out tomorrow, or drive until the horses drop. This is the road we follow for two hundred miles. If I set them off within the hour, they'll die sooner than not finish."

"Can you sleep?" Virginia asked, implying that she could not. "Do you think the horses could sleep?"

"No," he said, snapping the reins, and, as the sleigh thudded onto the snow-covered surface of the lake, they were off.

They crossed rivers, railroads, and roads; they passed lighted settlements and whining mills; they penetrated high cold forests, lighting their way with lanterns when the moon was obscured by the trees. Virginia did not know if she were on the sleigh, racing through a freezing and dark pine forest and dreaming of home, or at home by the fire, dreaming of how she had once been taken up completely by the muffled pounding of horses' hooves on the snow.

Morning came to Mrs. Gamely and Virginia the way it comes to a sick and feverish child—slowly, overheated, and stale. Mrs. Gamely threw open the door and looked out. As a cold river of blue air came to redeem the hot room, she said, "Not one flake of snow fell in all that wind. What good was it? All it did was steal away the heat and make us burn a lot of wood."

"What about the lake?" Virginia asked.

"The lake?"

"Did the lake freeze?"

Mrs. Gamely shrugged her shoulders. Virginia got up and put on a quilted jacket. The baby was placed gently into a cocoon of the same stuff, and they went down to the lake. Even before they rounded the corner of the house, they knew that the lake had frozen, for they heard no lapping or breaking waves, and the wind was even and shrill instead of being divided into a hundred different sounds, like birdsong, as it hit the whitecaps.

The lake had frozen in one night, which meant that a harsh winter was due. Just how difficult it would get could be forecast by the smoothness of the ice. The finer it was, the harder would be the succeeding months, although—in the days before it snowed—ice-boating would be unlike anything on earth. Mrs. Gamely had seen the lake in its smooth state before, but never like this.

It lay there almost laughing at its own perfection. There was not a ripple, streak, or bubble to be seen. The terrible wind and the incessant castellations of foam had been banished and leveled by the fast freeze of heavy blue water. Not a flake of snow skidded across the endless glass, which was as perfect as an astronomer's mirror.

"The monsters must be sealed in tight," Mrs. Gamely said. Then she grew silent in contemplation of the winter to come. The ice was airless, smooth, and dark.

For two weeks the sun rose and set on Lake of the Coheeries Town, low and burnished, spinning out a mane of golden brass threads. A steady and gentle breeze moved from west to east on the lake, sweeping the flawless black ice clean in a continuous procession of chattering icicles and twigs that fled from wind and sun like ranks of opera singers who run from their scenes gaily and full of

213

energy in a stage direction stolen from streams, surf, and the storms which fleece autumnal forests.

Even though the air temperature never went above ten degrees, the weather was mild because the wind was light and the sky cloudless. With their wells freezing up and their world nearly still, the inhabitants of the town took to the ice in a barrage of Dutch pursuits that saw the sun rise and set, and gave the village the busy and peculiar appearance of a Flemish winter scene. Perhaps they had inherited it; perhaps the historical memory deep within them, like the intense colors with which the landscape was painted, was renewable. A Dutch village arose along the lake. Iceboats raced from west to east and tacked back again, their voluminous sails like a hundred flowers gliding noiselessly across the ice. Up close, there was only a slight sound as gleaming steel runners made their magical cut. A little way in the distance, they sounded like a barely audible steam engine. Miniature villages sprang up on the lake, comprised of fishing booths ranged in circles, with flapping doors and curling pigtails of smoke from stovepipe chimneys. Firelight from these shelters reflected across the ice at night in orange and yellow lines that each came to a daggerlike point. Boys and girls disappeared together, on skates, pulled into the limitless distance by a ballooning sail attached to their thighs and shoulders. When they had traveled so far on the empty mirror that they could see no shore, they folded the sail, put it on the ice, and lay on its tame billows to fondle and kiss, keeping a sharp eye on the horizon for the faraway bloom of an iceboat sail, lest they be discovered and admired to death by the younger children who sailed boats into the empty sections just to see such things.

Blazing fires on shore ringed inward bays and harbors like necklaces. At each one, there was steaming chocolate, or rum and cider, and venison roasting on a spit. Skating on the lake in darkness, firing a pistol to keep in touch with a friend, was like traveling in space, for there were painfully bright stars above and all the way down to a horizon that rested on the lake like a bell jar. The stars were reflected perfectly, though dimly, in the ice, frozen until they could not sparkle. Long before, someone had had the idea of laying down wide runners, setting the light-as-a-white-wedding-cake village bandstand on them, and hitching up a half-dozen plough horses with ice shoes to tow the whole thing around at night. With lights shining from the shell, an entire enchanted village skated behind it as the Coheeries orchestra played a lovely, lucid, magical piece such as "Rhythm of Winter," by A. P. Clarissa. When the farmers all along the undulating lakeshore saw a chain of tiny orange flames, and the shining white castle moving dreamlike through the dark (like a dancer making quick steps under concealing skirts), they strapped on their skates and pogoed through their fields to leap onto the ice and race to the magic that glided across the horizon. As they approached, they were astonished by the music, and by the ghostly legions of men, women, and children skating in the darkness behind the bandshell. They looked like the unlit tail of a comet. Young girls twirled and pirouetted to the music: others were content just to follow.

This carnival used up much of the stored reserves of firewood, food, supplies, and feed. It was a foolish thing to do, but the people of Lake of the Coheeries were not able to ignore the perfect weather, which got them rolling at fever pitch. They were careless and crazy. Squandering their gains in the relaxation of their souls, they danced, they sang, and they damned the hard winter to come, affirming their trust in nature by following to the letter its paradoxical orchestrations. Even Mrs. Gamely, a paragon of conservation, gave freely of her stores and participated in the ruthless cooking of a dozen feasts and the fearless baking of a hundred pies. She and Virginia skated behind the bandshell. They danced on the shore in marvelous, civilized, humorous reels in which the old contributed wit when they could not contribute grace, and the young listened to their elders, who told them in their dancing to hold on, to love, to be patient, and, most of all, to trust. No one could be blind to this lesson after seeing Mrs. Gamely, a widow upon whom the years had come down hard, dancing and laughing on the soft shore, or even on the ice.

By the middle of January, no one had enough food. They were stretching it out, hoping that it might last until summer (which was impossible), and everyone was disastrously fat and unhealthy from the wild eating in December. ''The icicles have come home to roost,'' declared Mrs. Gamely, slightly subdued, but not yet melancholy. ''The way I figure it,'' she said, sweeping the pantry with her motile and patibulary eyes, ''we have enough food to last until about March. So what. March is cold. Lamston Tarko and his dog froze to death on the last day of March, thirty seven. How are we going to eat? That's the question.''

''Don't the other villages have food that they can give us?'' asked Virginia.

''No. Their harvests were ruined by hail. Ours weren't, and we did so well that we gave them enough to survive on. We didn't even sell it, we gave it. But now we're all on the same goat. The way the wind blows in winter, no one will come to help. Besides, we've always done for ourselves. I wish Antoine Bonticue were here. He could think of something, and so might have Theodore.''

''Who was Antoine Bonticue?''

''He died before you were born. He used to live between Coheeries and the march-lands. He was Swiss, and he went around in a spider cart.''

''He was Swiss and he went around in a spider cart?'' repeated Virginia.

''Yes,'' said Mrs. Gamely. ''Spider carts are wonderful. They're very quiet, and you can't drive them on busy roads, because the spiders tend to get crushed. They're also somewhat slow, but they're quite economical, especially for light loads. As you might be able to tell from his name, Antoine Bonticue weighed less than a hundred pounds. He was some sort of engineer, and he used to stretch cables and pulleys from one place to another. Evidently, rigging cables is therapy for the Swiss: or part of their theology. What was it that he used to say? 'A balanced arc between mountain rows/as servant to his master shows/the power of besieged belief/in something something something, something something something—something to do with ducks, or rainbows.'

''Theodore would know what to do. We will, too. After all, we have until March.''

Then they made dinner by slicing off a chunk of smoked beef, spilling upon the table half a pound of dried corn, and grating some hard cheese into a small pile of dairy sawdust. A purée of these three things went to feed the baby. The rest became a kind of land-locked bouillabaisse into which dill brought its springlike scent and red pepper was shaken until the dish that they cooked had enough life to attack them as they devoured it. The sting was satisfying, but the two women were left hungry. What will we do in March? they wondered.

That night, perhaps because it was already the fifth night that they had gone to bed hungry, the answer came to Virginia in a dream that was served up as richly and elegantly as hotel food that lives deep inside booming silver domes and rides from place to place on noiseless carts.

She dreamed of spring in a great city of fuming gray squares and whited sepulchers, of bending willows, and rivers that turned up their spring bellies in wind-flaked sapphire, a city that coiled around its own churches and squares in a weave of streets like a basket of nested snakes, a city of smooth silk hats and cool gray coats, of silent music played on flashing cloud light, of delirious green trees, of stores that led to secret tunnels, of clear days, and crystal palaces, and endless portraits ever arising. This city became alive, and was her lover. She took it without inhibition, grappling with it breathlessly and nude. She sweated, rolled her closed eyes, and sawed back and forth from thigh to thigh, as it overwhelmed her with its surging colors.

The dream taught her that cities are not unlike huge animals which eat, sleep, work, and love. It taught her what it was like for something as massy and giant as a whale to make love unbraced in the gravityless blue ocean. And it taught her that her future (she had always known that her future was in her, waiting to be shaken out) was in the city, and that she would spend her life in the place that she had seen in the dream.

When she awakened she was still half dreaming and still wet from her extraordinary labor, but she calculated immediately that, if she were to go away with the baby, Mrs. Gamely would have more than enough upon which to survive, and might even help someone else.

Mrs. Gamely's initial opposition was silenced by the beauties

217

and accuracies of the recounted dream. "Though I haven't ever been there," Virginia said, "I seem to have known it all well enough to have created it." To Virginia's surprise, Mrs. Gamely did not bring up the misfire with Boissy d'Anglas. Instead, she grew as excited as a follower of a lost cause who sees in her old age the possibility that the cause may revive and succeed.

They embraced a thousand times before Virginia left, and it made them cry each time. The last thing Mrs. Gamely said to her daughter was, "Remember, what we are trying to do in this life is to shatter time and bring back the dead. Rise, Virginia. Rise and see the whole world."

Virginia did not know exactly what her mother had meant.

The lake was covered with snow by the time Virginia and her baby rode along its length in a huge troika pulled by horses heavy enough to shake even the thick ice of the Lake of the Coheeries as they pounded down the snow road. By afternoon, they were in the mountains, ascending steadily, turning on hairpin terraces from which they could see a world of white and blue. Now and then a snowy hawk rose from the background camouflage of glistening bone-white fields, and navigated the ocean of air, slipping sideways on the wing more gracefully than a skater.

As they neared the top of the range, they watched the effects of high winds upon the accumulated drifts. Powerful continental gusts burst upon cornices and sculptured ridges, sending up vertical jets of loosed snow. Behind these white silk curtains were glowing rims of gold where the sun shone through their crests. There was so much screaming and whistling that the bells of the troika could hardly be heard. The sleigh driver halted on a round cakelike knob, the summit. Resting there, they saw a landscape of ice and snow crossed and covered by hills and ridges from which white powder rocketed into the air. The horses dipped their heads and shook their ice-encrusted manes. "From here on," said the sleigh driver, shouting with difficulty through his muffler and the blasts of mountain air, "you can't see the lake, but only the east and, soon, the Hudson. Take one last look, for we are now on our way to a different place."

The road led not through fields and past overlooks, but deeper and deeper within an untouched forest, between rock cliffs a thousand feet high, near ice-covered gorges where falls and flumes pounded like jackhammers and covered hundred-foot oaks in freezing spray. They glided over dimly lit roads, springing upon shocked families of deer that had an air of offended innocence, and which they sent white-tailed into the forest, carrying their solid six-foot horns like little battleaxes with which they smashed down waxy bushes bloody with red berries. They drove through vaulted mahogany-colored courses made by trees and snow, and the horses leapt ahead, swallowing the space in front of them and effortlessly compressing the air of the cool snow tunnels. Virginia held her baby to her, inside her coat. His name, for the moment anyway, was Martin d'Anglas, which seemed very apt for a swordsman who swung on ropes, or a legionnaire, and much less apt for a little newt all wrapped up in blue. His mouth and nose stuck out of a navy cashmere balaclava, and he took the cold air like a puppy. Virginia threw back her head to look for hawks and eagles, and was surprised at the many she saw perched in gothic nests high in the trees. They watched, unconcerned, as the troika slipped past. "Look at all those dignified eagles up there," she said to the driver. "If they didn't look like they were made of porcelain and gold, I would swear that they were justices of the Supreme Court, in retirement."

A long gradual slope led to the riverbank, and they came down it just at dusk, to an inn by the Hudson. Pigs huddled together in the yard, singing for the innkeeper to let them into the pig quarters for the night. Muffins of pure white smoke emerged from the chimney. Virginia and Martin (she had already begun to pronounce the name in English) would stay until early morning, when a giant iceboat that could hold half a dozen passengers and their luggage would take them downriver as far as the open channel, where they would get a boat south. In the middle of the night, the innkeeper's wife—a woman with cheeks redder than the rash that sometimes appeared on Martin's two tiny hams—knocked on the door. Virginia switched on the light. She was uncomfortable from a lush and tremendous dinner of lambchops, cornbread, and dandelion salad. The light glared at her, and, in response to its rays, Martin began to punch with his springy little arms and legs. Virginia held her robe closed. "What is it?" she asked.

"Sorry to wake you, dear," said the innkeeper's wife with a voice that had lived many years in a crock of mint jelly, "but Mr. Fteley just got a telephone call from Oscawana. The iceboat's not running, something about the drifts of snow, so you'll have to skate down there tomorrow, first thing. The cutter will wait until noon. If you leave at eight, you should make it in plenty of time. Mr. Fteley will pull a sled with the luggage."

"I see," said Virginia. "How many miles is it from here to Oscawana?"

"Just twenty," answered Mrs. Fteley, "and the wind will be at your back."

"Oh," said Virginia, as Mrs. Fteley disappeared. She turned off the light, and then fell asleep within five seconds. She dreamed of skating, and (as so often happened) the next morning she found herself replicating exactly what she had imagined.

For hours and hours, she skated nearly in a trance, centered between the mountain banks, on a road of white ice. She was one of those women whose legs seem to come up to everyone else's shoulders. It would have been impossible to keep her in jail, since, no matter how far across the room the jailer hung his key she would have been able to hook the ring around a toe and bring it to her with one sinuous fold of thigh and calf. So she was a natural speed skater. One long push was good for fifty yards: and she could push for hours. She was only five eleven, but her figure was perfect. Her hair was blue-black, as glistening as the thick pelt of a healthy seal. She had a perfectly formed white smile that was soft, inviting, and full of power. She was not quite as arresting in photographs as she was in the flesh, for her beauty was sprung directly from her soul, and proved that physical features count little unless they are illumined from within. Nor was she beautiful in a coy sense, either. When she was severe, she looked severe. When she was angry, she looked angry.

With Martin bundled up and riding on her back, she skated downriver, rounding its curling bends and keeping her eyes upon the converging shorelines and ice. She would stop every now and then and put Martin in front of her, kneeling to check on him. He was so well wrapped that he slept as if he were at home in a cradle. Then she would hoist him up and begin again, more and more powerfully. Though the wind was at her back, she was going fast enough so that her hair was pushed from her face.

Behind her at a distance of a mile or so came Mr. Fteley, the innkeeper, pulling a light sled. They traveled silently past sleeping settlements of red brick and slattern wood. At a bend in the river, near Constitution Island, Virginia saw an icehouse in which she decided to rest and escape the wind. Skating at full speed, she turned to stop just before the dock, the silver blades of her skates sending up an abrupt shower of fresh-milled crystals that hung in the air and sparkled. Around the side of the building was an entrance bay for boats and sleds, through which she glided into the dark interior, expelling half a dozen frightened sparrows. It was full of hay and templed blocks of ice in glassy walls that reached up to the roof beams. She was much warmer away from the wind, and she glowed from her exercise. She swung Martin around and unwrapped him. He was awake and smiling, as if he were in on a wonderful joke. Perhaps he was happy because his mother was radiant in the darkness, her cold reddened face central to the scheme of symmetrical light that came through the cracks in the walls. As the blood coursed through her, it brought with it lucidity, equanimity, and a light pounding rhythm that set the baby up and had probably made him smile. While she fed him she listened to her own blood beating, and tilted her head back to stare into the darkness, where the birds lived, beyond the ice blocks.

Long before, in the most severe winter the Coheeries had ever known (until the one they were in) the farmers had cut ice from the Lake of the Coheeries and filled an icehouse on the lakeshore not far from where the Gamelys lived. There was so much of it that it remained, underneath fresh ice cut in subsequent years, for half a century. Then the icehouse was sold to a man who wanted it for a printing shop, and no one put any more ice in it. Soon the old ice was reached, and one summer, when Virginia was six or seven, she was playing near the blocks that had been recently uncovered after half a hundred years. The unrelenting heat that had driven her inside the icehouse was melting these veteran glass bricks and creating little rivers of fresh water. Virginia thought that she was alone. She pressed her palms up against a melting slab full of stilled bubbles, and licked it. Mrs. Gamely had warned her to stay out of the icehouse, because it was full of terrible dangers. "The Donamoula comes into the icehouse at night," Mrs. Gamely had said, "to chew on blocks of ice and slap his tongue against the salt. If he sees you there," she told the rapt little girl, "he might think that you are an hors d'oeuvre. Stay out of the icehouse!"

Though afraid of the Donamoula, Virginia had wanted nonetheless to see him, and maybe even to ride him across the lake, like a torpedo. The way Mrs. Gamely described him, it was a safe bet to warrant that even if he did eat little girls, it was only by mistake. Anyway, she moved about with the stiffness peculiar to children who imagine that they are being observed by sea monsters or things that live under the bed at night, and every once in a while she would glance toward the lake door to see if the Donamoula had arrived.

Just when she had completely forgotten the Donamoula, she heard a percussive, wet, sudden, fishy slap. She would not have moved, could not have moved, for all the blueberries in the Adirondacks. Again, the same fishy slap, met this time in the cold mysterious air by yet another, of lower pitch. Dizzy with fear, Virginia moved her head a quarter-turn. No Donamoula. She looked around, convinced that she was about to be encoiled by the swift forty-foot tongue that could catch a cherry pie the way a darter newt catches a bloime bug. No Donamoula, and yet the sounds kept coming—slap slap, quasha, flaship, swipa, spatch!

As her fear subsided she realized that the noise was coming from atop the pyramid of ice. She climbed up, numbing her hands and knees. At the summit, near the hottest space under the eaves, not far from a summer sunray that had broken through a rotted shake and shot down in a tight yellow beam, was a little blue lake of newly melted fifty-year-old ice. Splashing about in this lake were two enormous shad that, years before she was born, had been frozen still, and had now come to life and were smashing their flippant tails in protest and joy. They were silver and gold, and their eyes looked like wise old rainbows.

Virginia remembered the intense unmatchable pleasure of taking the two shad by their twitching scaly tails and carrying them down the pyramid so that she could toss them, in the most beautiful, airborne, moment of their lives, into the lake, where they vanished in the dark water—perhaps to tell their tale to the other fish and refresh the population with the intricate mystery of youth in age, and age in youth. Magic, she knew, was all about time, and could stop it and hold it for the inquisitive eye to look through as if through cold and splendid ice.

She shifted her gaze from the darkness to the white glare flooding through the doorway. For a fraction of a second, Mr. Fteley appeared in the opening, panting along in front of the sled, and then disappeared. Martin was quickly rewrapped. Up he went onto her back, and out she flew from the icehouse, like a racehorse from the start, chasing after Mr. Fteley.

She was in a fine mood when, in a confusion of wind that whipped their scarves in all directions, she caught him. Shouting now over the anarchic wind—they were in a widening bay—she said, "Mr. Fteley, why can't the iceboat make it upriver? The ice is smooth and thick. I don't understand."

"The drift wall," shouted Fteley.

"The what?"

"The drift wall," he shouted again. "By pure coincidence, it snowed all in one place just north of Oscawana, and then the wind piled it up in a wall across the ice. It blocks the river completely, as sure as my name is Fteley, from shore to shore as high as the hills on both banks. They can't tunnel through because they fear it will collapse as it melts."

"Does it block the whole river?"

"Yes," he shouted over the wind.

"As high as the surrounding hills?"

"Yes."

"How high are they?"

"A thousand feet," he screamed back. "We'll have to climb it and slide down the other side."

223

When they rounded one of the alpine bends that made the Hudson Highlands look like a collection of looming rhinoceros horns, they saw the drift wall—which, unlike Rome, had sprung up in a day, and which had about it the smooth, thoughtless, malicious air of a modern skyscraper. The drift wall was a pile of snow that stretched from mountain to mountain across the solidified river. It was steep, a thousand feet high, and shrouded at the top by a tumbling mist that devoured itself and regenerated, blooming like time-lapsed roses.

"I can't climb that," said Mr. Fteley, "not with this luggage, certainly. I thought it was lower, and didn't know about all that stuff at the top." His head was bent in awe and fear, his eyes fixed on the long lateral summit. "Christ," he said, "you may think that I'm a chicken, but I've got to consider Mrs. Fteley and my little Felicia. Why don't you come back upriver and stay with us, free of charge, until the damn thing melts. It'd be a mistake, miss, to try to climb that."

"Mr. Fteley," said Virginia, her blood still hot from the skating and her heart still lively from the glory of resurrected colors that she had remembered in the dark icehouse, "I don't think that you're a chicken, I understand that you've got to think of Mrs. Fteley and Felicia, and I certainly wouldn't ask you to climb that because of my luggage. So why don't you go back, and send me my things whenever the iceboat can get through. Meanwhile, Martin and I will go over."

"But, miss! You'll disappear in that foam up there. And if you fall back, there's nothing to clutch on to. You'll tumble all the way down and die."

"Mr. Fteley," said Virginia, her eyes full of lights, "the way I feel now, I could leap that wall in one jump. And if I climb it, as I will, I'll go in one sure step after another, I won't be afraid, I won't fall back, and I will get to the other side."

"How can you know that? How can you be sure?"

"Simple," she said, "I've seen myself there."

"You've been over already?" he asked, somewhat confused.

"No."

224

"You've imagined then. That's different. That's a cat flying after a bird."

"No, I haven't imagined. I've seen. That's no cat flying after a bird."

"What do you mean, you've seen? You've seen the future?"

"Yes."

"You're crazy!" he said, with an aggressive, nasty lurch. "You can't see the future. You can't feel the future. People like you end up in loony bins. It just doesn't cut."

"Like hell, Mr. Fteley," answered Virginia, quite angry that she had been attacked for giving an honest answer. "It cuts. And I'll get to the other side." Then she grew even angrier, and turned on him for the way in which he was looking at her. "The world is full of leaden slugs like you, innkeeper, who are afraid of the powers of the heart. You hope that mountain climbers and acrobats fall, that daring bridges collapse, that those who can feel the future be punished. If everyone were like you, Mr. Fteley, we'd still be in hides and skins. Hides and skins. Go back to the inn. Cook up some farina. Put your spittoon on your head. You can send our luggage after the thaw, because Martin and I are going to the city."

With that, she turned away from the innkeeper and began climbing. She found that by means of a chain of small steps driven into the dense snow, she soon was high above the ground, like a worker on the face of a dam. Had she fallen backward, she and Martin would have gone through the ice like a cannonball, never to be seen again. But she didn't look back, the left foot was always forward, she breathed calmly, and she concentrated. In an hour she was nearly at the top, standing vertically in the holds she had dug in the snow, with hands and fingers stuck in as deep as she could push them and spread as wide as she could spread them to get a grip. Sleeping peacefully on her back, Martin was suspended a thousand feet above the ice. Down below, Mr. Fteley was running back and forth like an ant; amazed, afraid, and angry. Virginia slowed just five feet from the ledge that formed the top of the drift wall. Unfortunately, it leaned out. To get over it and into the curtain of mist, she would have to climb while leaning back. How? The snow was hard to hold. She imagined herself and Martin falling, and, as she did, she felt her previously strong hold loosening. Then it occurred to her that she could reverse that effect, and she tried to do so. She imagined herself sticking to the wall, proceeding with surety and grace, losing not a second of her momentum. When she had become agitated with that vision, she made her move, punching holes in the compressible snow while saying to herself, "Go! go!" and she moved up and out. She did hang outward for a few seconds, but her momentum took care of her and thrust her over the edge. Afterward, she thought she heard one long clear blast of a French horn, and realized that it was an illusion of her heart springing free. All Mr. Fteley saw was that she was swallowed up by the mist.

She found herself thrown about by gusts of wind and visible currents of whitened air that rushed at her from all directions. She didn't actually walk across the ridge, she was waltzed across by the turbulence—which occasionally picked her up and spun her upside down but always put her back again on her feet. In the end it simply spat her out on the other side, having treated her with unusual and uncharacteristic gentleness (all because of the baby on her back, for whom allowances had to be made). Straightening her hair, she walked a few steps through the thinning mist, and then was in the clear again.

There, fifty miles to the south, was the city.

It was another world—shadowy, white, and above all, silent. The city's silence, however, was only the solidification of all its countless sounds, fused by mass and distance. Against a background of viscous blue, towers rose like bone. Volumes of unheard sound lifted from among them and floated up, channeled and directed to a place unknown, where it would be received as a dense static, a hissing, a white noise, like surf. The light, too, would compress upon a distant shore. As steadily as a machine, the city signaled its existence in a spectrum of low thunder, with arms outstretched to the future, and memories of what lay ahead pulling it in omnipotent traction.

The air was as clear as that over the Lake of the Coheeries, and yet there were within it distorting lenses that magnified and reduced entire coasts, rivers, and mountain ranges—without explanation and seemingly at will, but always with pleasing effect. Virginia found that she was able to enter the scene before her wherever she wanted, approaching closely to see its every detail. What most attracted her were the ways in which things moved. Seen from afar, they seemed to fit an overall pattern of which they appeared to be (and must have been) ignorant. Ships traveling on the rivers did so with a strong counterpoint forged into their forward motion: it dogged them like magnetism, and could be felt as surely as the ship itself could be seen. The yaw and pitch of these vessels weaved invisible threads, as did the coding of the whitecaps; the passage of clouds; the very busy, mouselike galloping of traffic on distant expressways; and the hemispheric tracking of reflected light in jagged palisades of soaring glass.

Down below, the ice was clean and white, a slab of enamel that did not seem cold. She saw the enormous iceboat pinned at its dock, and a line of people stretching from the loading pier to a big Hamilton-class cutter, stacks smoking lightly, which rested on the ice, frozen in. People were streaming on board to weight the cutter and smash the ice ways upon which it unwillingly lay. It was pointed like a compass needle, its orientation an appeal for the chance to hit blue water and steam through the Tappan Zee toward open ocean. Not even a child could have been more impatient, and, even trapped in the ice, it was so lean and powerful that it looked like a cross between a steam engine and a knife.

As Virginia approached the cutter she noticed that the officers were pacing back and forth, upset that the weight of a thousand extra passengers and their baggage was not enough to break the prison of ice. She walked up a snow ramp to an open door in the hull.

"We've taken all the passengers we can, ma'am," a young officer said to her. "There's really no more room."

"But you've taken on passengers in the first place to add more weight. Isn't that so?"

"Yes, ma'am," said the officer, with an amused smile, "but one more person isn't going to make much of a difference." He indicated the great size of the ship, and he didn't seem to care that

227

Virginia and Martin would be left alone on the ice. In fact, he seemed to derive pleasure from his indifference.

"*Two* people," Virginia asserted quite severely, holding up Martin. Martin burped.

"All right," said the officer. "But you're the last."

"I can see that," Virginia said, looking about the empty ice.

She put Martin on the snowbank, and jumped onto the ship. There was a creak in the ice that made everyone look up. "Just a coincidence," the officer stated.

Martin began to kick and scream. He didn't like being the only one not on the ark. "Now, now," said his mother as she was about to pick him up and take him aboard. The officer had turned away to scold a young boy who was trying to fire a torpedo at Verplanck. As soon as Martin was lifted over the bulkhead and taken inboard, there was a sharp explosive crack and the ship settled into the river, sending up thousands of tons of green water that washed over the ice like a tidal wave and froze by the time it reached shore. The passengers cheered.

Martin was vigorously applauded by all around him. Virginia did not lose the opportunity to address the officer. She cleared her throat and said, "We want to ride on the bridge, and lunch with the captain. We would like a five-ounce filet mignon, watercress salad, a baked potato, tea, a strawberry tart, and some gently warmed milk."

"And just who the hell are you?" asked the officer, unaware of their role in the recent drama of physics.

Rather than explain, Virginia took Martin aside and fed him herself, and then had the steaming oyster pan roast and hot buttermilk bread that had been offered to the passengers. She had learned her first lesson of the city, and she was unperturbed.

Mrs. Gamely had a small book of paintings by the artists of New York and the Hudson, and when she leafed through its polished pages she felt much the same as some Lake of the Coheeries women felt when they were in church. As she looked at this holy book, she would often say things that Virginia found incomprehensible. Now, because of the ungrateful Coast Guard officer—a man whose gold regalia on a rich navy coat made him look like a painting in motion—Virginia understood, and she speculated that the city would be cold, completely of itself, unconscious, that its every move would be transcendent, and that each of its hundred million flashing scenes would strike a moral lesson.

Such a city would extend vision, intensify pity, telescope emotion, and float the heart the way the sea is gently buoyant with great ships. To do this, it would have to be a cold instrument. And, despite its beauty, it would have to be cruel.

This was deeply bound within the book of images. Only they could explain it. Out of respect and love for her mother, Virginia had learned to regard paintings as something in which time was shattered and light was understood, and to know the steadfast link between high emotions and beautiful images. She knew that the image had to be cold, because its task required silence and detachment in the presence of the intangible powers it conveyed, but she had not realized until now why it had to be cruel as well. The cruelty and coldness were almost physical forces. As they acted upon the heart, they made it rise and feel. They purified motives and tested the soul with uncompromising certainty. Images and people had to be strong enough to stand by themselves. For when they did, they had the capacity and power to be interlinked, and to serve.

Virginia stood on deck for as long as she could. The ice-choked river ebbed and flowed from and against the staid sides of the ship, and the wind was like a grindstone of ice. Though he was trim for his age and was not coated with too much blubber, Martin was as warm and flexible as an Eskimo baby, and seemed completely impervious to the cold. In the end, she had to go inside because she was cold. He didn't mind the warm cabin, and as they sailed down the river he made bicycling motions with his legs and practiced facial gestures.

Virginia peered from the porthole and saw many familiar scenes. On the mountainous banks, trees bent and swayed in the sunny wind. Houses of stone and wood stood on hillsides crossed and bound by miles of neat dry-wall. Great oaks loomed over the river. In Croton Bay, the boys were playing hockey or speeding along the ice with makeshift sails that they had filched from their mothers' linen closets. The hills of Ossining, and the streets that climbed them, seemed from the river to be sad and forgotten. Ossining was peculiar, and shoddy, too (for it had become poor), but its steep streets, slate roofs, and massive oaks were portraits of beauty and honor.

They passed Tarrytown and the Tappan Zee, where rolling jolly fields were the skirts to craggy thunderous mountains, and orchards came fearlessly to the base of cliffs. Sailing through a gap of pylons in the Tappan Zee bridge, the cutter's black steelwork came near to colliding with the high roadway but only saluted it with smoke. Half a mile south, the Palisades began, and the city itself came into view. As soon as Virginia saw the gates of the shining city, and the white clouds sweeping over, she knew that she was meant to be there. It did not draw people to it the way it did for nothing. It was God's crucible, and she was on her way into it.

Down they glided, they glided down, on the fast-flowing river that swept by the town. As they accomplished their nearly silent traverse, the setting sun made the glass palisades and gray towers a shield of gold. And as its light disappeared from all but the tips of spires which glowed like smoldering punks that children used to signal by, the city turned on its cool chemical lamps: a hundred million flashes, fires, altars, and hearths racked on mountainous towers with castled tops—the whole masterpiece bullying Virginia in the insistent and gentle fashion of a good teacher. Next to this enormous harrow of gold and green, of shining ledges and needles, the ships tied up at North River piers looked like insects running along the crack of a baseboard.

"Look, Martin," Virginia said, holding him so that he could see the whole thing, ". . . the golden city."

After ten miles of lights and towers, they pulled up at the fireboat pier on the Battery and the passengers of the cutter were discharged into the night. The officers wanted to speed them into the city so that they could take their ship beyond the Narrows for some real work amid white waves as tall as church steeples, and over a prairie of green troughs. The passengers passed through the wooden halls of the fireboat station and found themselves immediately face to face with teeming streets. Thus the country people were thrown into the city's gaping mouth.

* * *

230

Virginia and Martin began to walk aimlessly through the cold. She had neither a plan nor the slightest idea of how to make her way, and by ten o'clock she found herself, exhausted and limp, leaning against a tiled arch in Grand Central Station. Streams of people went by without noticing her, because, in her country clothes, she looked like a beggar woman. The several hours of walking in the cold had made her very hungry, and it was a fine coincidence that she was standing just outside the Oyster Bar, where rooms of happy diners deep underground ate frothy oyster stews or sizzling fish steaks while white-jacketed barmen served up clams and oysters on a production line worthy of its finer, more anarchic, deeper-underground predecessors. Virginia pressed against a window and took all this in, but only with her eyes.

Now and then, someone looked up and saw her. This was the heart of the city. In these marble corridors, beggar women roamed by the hundreds. Those who looked up would not look up for long. Virginia was about to turn away and wander, when she saw a young woman on the far side of the dining room rise and peer at her. Then the woman pointed, and asked silently, with gestures that were clear, "Is that you?" Virginia looked behind her, as she often did when people called out, thinking that they had meant someone else. But then the other woman, who was wearing a green silk dress, began to wade through the crowded restaurant.

Waiting for the green silk to duck under and then surface amid the arches, Virginia worried that, because she was tired, she must have looked terrible. But she was wrong. Even though she was slightly winter-frayed by the city, and had walked about too long without a hot drink and some moments of sitting down in a warm room, she still was painfully beautiful. And though cold and tired, she stood straight. When the woman in green emerged from the domes and tiles, Virginia saw a face that she recognized from the Lake of the Coheeries. It was Jessica Penn, a childhood friend from many summers past.

For several generations, the Penns had come to the Lake of the Coheeries each summer (the men for weekends and Augusts, the women and children for an entire season) to watch the light layer

231

itself across the lake, to sit on the porch in world-shaking thunderstorms, to sail for a day and night without coming about once, to anchor in a cove of straight rock walls that no one had ever seen or would see again, to run through blue-green forests suspended in summer's slow northern time, to come to know the faces, laughter, and eccentricities of those whose fate in life was to die and be half-remembered by children. "Yes," someone might say, fifty years later, "I think I remember Aunt Marjorie. She was the one who tied bells to the pet bear, showed us tricks with magnets, and baked ginger cookies. Or was that Aunt Helen?"

Virginia heard the sound of her oars as she rowed amid the reeds, a child in full summer. Shuddering like a crazed cymbal, the sun lighted the Lake of the Coheeries until it was as hot and as light-green as the banks of the Nile. Mrs. Gamely, a much younger woman, was calling down from the house, "Virginia . . . Virginia . . . Virginia . . . ," and the call was muted by the heat and distance. "Virginia . . . Virginia," she called, as the oars dipped in the dark water and Virginia rowed hard to return home. But, though once the oars had been dipped dreamlike into the dark water, the lake had turned to ice with the sadness of the passing years.

One winter, very early on, Theodore Gamely took Virginia with him to inspect the Penn house. Neither water nor ice, the lake was impassable, and to get to the other side they went a long distance by sleigh and on skis, and traveled at times through tunnels in the high drifts. The Penns' house was an empty ice palace of silent tortured rooms. Oriental rugs, summer furniture, *National Geographics,* fishing equipment, puzzles, and disconnected lamps huddled in the cold. Snow enveloped the house all the way up to its second-story windows and made it seem like a long-forgotten cave. As her father went from room to room checking for damage, Virginia stayed on the ground floor, trapped by the timeless stares of ancient Penns in many colorful paintings. There they remained all winter, in their old-fashioned finery, still and forgotten, trying to come out of the paintings and embrace one another. When Theodore Gamely came down the stairs, satisfied that all was well, he found that his little daughter, bundled in her furs, was crying—because, she had said, the people in the paintings were dead, and they had to stay alone and apart in this cold room under the snow. But then her father picked her up and took her to each painting, recounting as best he could its history. He showed her old Isaac, whom she had loved very much because of his sad and gentle face, and because he was almost as small as a child; he showed her Isaac Penn's wife, Abigail, their sons Jack and Harry, and their daughters Beverly and Willa. "Harry is Jessica's daddy," he said. "He's alive, isn't he?"

"Yes," said Virginia, sniffling, and not quite sure, because she was so young that she hardly remembered seeing Harry Penn a few times the previous summer.

"And here," said her father, "is Willa. Willa is alive, too. She lives in Boston."

"Who's that?" asked Virginia. They stepped forward a few paces in the gloom, and looked up at a high cold wall upon which hung a portrait of a young woman.

"That's Beverly," said Theodore Gamely. "I remember her only vaguely. One night, a long time ago, I went on a sleigh ride with Beverly. We went very fast, faster I think than I have ever gone since. We stopped at an inn, where we played Duck Thumb. I was just a little boy: almost as young as you."

"And who was that?" asked Virginia, pointing to a painting directly opposite the one of Beverly.

"That," her father answered, "is Peter Lake. He was the man who drove the sleigh. You see how they stare across the room? They loved one another, but she died when she was young—I remember the summer when they came to the lake without her—and he disappeared forever."

Virginia seemed likely to cry again, so he said, "It's true. People die. That's what happens. But think of the children. There's Jessica, her cousin John, and the Penn children from Boston. You shouldn't be worrying about these things, little girl." He brushed her hair from her forehead and kissed her. Then they left that freezing gallery, and Virginia would always remember the colorful spirits, floating about her in the half-light, as if she had known them.

But though she remembered their stories, she could not recall their faces.

Here, in another gallery, underground, was Jessica—like Virginia, a full-blown beauty, though the difference between city and country was profound and apparent.

They were somewhat taken aback by the way in which they had aged, and, at once, they knew that they could not resume the friendship they had had as young girls. Knowing this, they were restrained, though they could feel a certain new warmth between them, born of the mutual realization that they were not foolishly effusive, and had developed into dignified and intelligent presences unwilling to barter away what they had become, for a short-lived reminiscence that could not have been sustained.

Martin threw a reflexive punch at his mother's friend, who then led both of them through the Oyster Bar to a large circular table, where Virginia sat down and was introduced, round robin, to Jessica's numerous companions.

It was a journalists' dinner, and, among journalists, Praeger de Pinto (though quite young) was the most eminent. In addition to being managing editor of both *The Sun* and *The Whale* (that is, *The New York Evening Sun,* and *The New York Morning Whale*), he was engaged to Jessica Penn, and was therefore the leader of the gang—though he would have been anyway. He knew just about everything, and, due to his position, he knew that much more.

"You look like you've had a hard journey," he said.

"I have."

"Have you come from the north?" he asked, having heard of the refugees occasioned by the amazing snows and stunning cold that had gripped everything above the Hudson Highlands, and seemed to be on the way to the city itself.

She nodded.

"The far north?"

"Yes," she said.

"How?"

"Not easily," Virginia answered, and looked down, embarrassed.

"Let's get some food into you and the child," Praeger said.

234

"The maître d' has a very gentle fish porridge for babies: I've seen him prepare it, and I'd eat it myself. And, as for you, may I recommend that you have what we're having?"

"I don't know. I don't have much money."

"No no," Praeger assured her with remarkable good nature and generosity. "This is a *Sun* monthly management dinner. Everyone eats on *The Sun*. We're having some oyster pan roast, grilled haddock filets stuffed with lobster, roasted potatoes, green peas, and Dutch beer. It's coming all around, and in half a second I can order another place."

"Thank you," said Virginia, delighted at her excellent fortune.

"Don't mention it," said Praeger. "May we introduce ourselves?"

That was a rhetorical question. They were itching to introduce themselves, especially the single men, except for Courtenay Favat, who stuck his head in the air, like a turtle.

Jessica said, "I'd like you to meet my friend Virginia Gamely."

"From Lake of the Coheeries, New York," Virginia added in a voice like a bell, after which the managing editor called the roll of his subordinates according to the order in which they ringed the table.

There was Courtenay Favat, editor of the home and ladies' page, a holdover from the days in which *The Sun*'s patrons looked to it for canning and pickling hints, or advice on how to darn and crochet. Courtenay was simultaneously food, wine, fashion, and home editor, and he had half a page or less per day in which to operate. *The Sun* was devoted to hard news, literature, science, exploration, and art. Its competitor, *The New York Ghost* (a tabloid founded by the Australian newspaper magnate, Rupert Binkey, and left to his grandson, Craig) had literally thousands of employees doing Courtenay's job. They even had an editor-in-chief of vegetables, and a dry-cleaning critic. But because Harry Penn was a puritan, a spartan, a stoic, and a trojan, he brooked no full-page banner headlines about truffles or potato puffs.

Hugh Close, *The Sun*'s rewrite editor, had the boundless energy of a hound, and was always perched upright, like a Labrador waiting for a stick to be thrown into a cool lake. He had a red mustache, and red hair that was sculpted to his head like clay. He could see puns in everything, and one could not speak to him without suffering an embarrassing disinternment of double entendres. His suits were gray; his shirts had collars with bars; he could read a thousand words a minute upside down and backward (the words, that is, not him); he knew all the Romance languages (including Romanian), Hindi, Chuvash, Japanese, Arabic, Gullah, Turqwatle, and Dutch; he could speak any of these languages in the accent of the other; he generated new words at a mile a minute; was the world's foremost grammarian and a master of syntax; and he drove everyone mad. But *The Sun* was unmatched in style and linguistic precision. Words were all he knew; they possessed and overwhelmed him, as if they were a thousand white cats with whom he shared a one-room apartment. (In fact, he did not like cats, because they could not talk and would not listen.)

Then there was William Bedford, the financial editor, who lived entirely for Wall Street. Even when he hiccuped, it was said, a stock price jumped out, and he had asked in his will to be mummified in ticker tape. He looked like a British major who had just emerged from the desert, which is to say that he had a long thin face, hair of bronze, gold, and silver, and an expression that was lean, and grave, and slightly alcoholic. Both his father and grandfather had been presidents of the New York Stock Exchange, so he knew everyone and everyone knew him. His column was religion to many, and the organization of *The Sun*'s financial section was a pleasant miracle of graphs, charts, illustrations, and accurate analysis. Harry Penn always said that he wanted people who were good at what they did, even if they had ragged edges (though Bedford was an obvious smoothie compared to the various saws that headed other departments). "We're not a college," Harry Penn once declared. "We're a newspaper. I want the best people, people who live their trade, experts, fanatics, geniuses. I don't care if they're a little peculiar. Close, here, who is sort of peculiar himself, will polish out all the unbecoming oddities, and that will give us a paper which is to the newspaper trade what the Bible is to religion. Understand?"

To round it out was, appropriately, Marko Chestnut, chief artist for both *The Sun* and *The Whale*. All the time that they had been talking, he had been sketching, and he introduced himself by holding up the drawing he had done. No stranger to the powers of art, Virginia immediately knew several things about Marko Chestnut. First, as with the other senior staff of *The Sun*, he was, in terms of his skill, second to none. Over many years of rapid sketching, the demand upon a newspaper artist for speed and memorization had taught him to extract the real and essential lines of the scene before him. And Virginia was pleased that he was not content, as so many other artists might have been, to do a humorous sketch of the diners. Although she did not know it, restaurants all over the city were filled with partial caricatures that betrayed not the subjects' distortions, but the artist's lack of vision. One could, in a few lines, show the soul. One could, if one had the courage. For the world was full of feelings, and there was so much to people that even weak lines of charcoal could enlighten and amaze—not because of what they were, but because of what they showed of the truth.

In Marko Chestnut's drawing, virtues and idiosyncrasies became magically evident. Praeger de Pinto was drawn larger than the rest, and, like all people of destiny, had a look of both contentment and agitation. Bedford had shining eyes, a gray suit as pale as ash, and a smile like that of a kind wolf. Next to him perched Close, caught disarmingly in a moment of laughter. Courtenay Favat was pictured as a very small face subsumed in the floral bloom of his bow tie. And Jessica Penn, standing, was an unmistakable fusion of womanly beauty and ripening sex. In the drawing of her there was no color, but, rather, a suggestion of ivory where thighs and bosom pressured a rounded outpouring of silk. Marko Chestnut had emphasized Virginia's springy black hair, her country-straight back, and her delightful smile. Martin was given a lifted eyebrow. His skepticism was directed at Marko Chestnut himself, who was bent over, faceless, rendering the drawing in which he appeared.

When the introductions were completed, a band struck itself up in a corner under one of the many echoing arches and began to play palm waltzes. Praeger summoned a waitress to ask for two and a half more dinners, for Virginia and Martin, and for his secretary—

red-haired, green-eyed Lucia Terrapin, who had come in with some things for him to sign.

The halibut steaks sizzled, the peas glistened like medieval enamels, the potatoes sang to one another of the pleasures of their roast, and the beer was as good as if it had come from a giant cask in a Lake of the Coheeries tavern. They ate like jackals, and though they tried to discuss business, they were having too much fun. The conversation drifted while, eating ferociously and tapping their toes to the tune of Dewey's "Olives Omnikia," they attempted to find out about the long-legged northern beauty, and her baby who sang along with the music in a most unusual, unrestrained, and mysterious cacophony.

"Is your husband coming down soon?" asked Lucia Terrapin, who was young, and bound to make faux pas.

"I don't have a husband," Virginia answered without the slightest hint of discomfort, "at least not for the present. His father," she continued, turning briefly to Martin, "was overtaken with a religious fervor so extreme that he had to leave us. That's all right. We've accommodated."

Trying to smooth the ripples, Lucia said, "Is he still up there, in Lake of the Fairies?"

"Fairies?" Virginia repeated, amused. "I've never heard it called *that* before. It's Lake of the Coheeries, not Fairies."

Hugh Close was suddenly excited by the possibility of learning the derivation of a word. "What does it mean?" he asked.

"It doesn't mean anything," answered Virginia. "It's a proper name."

"Yes, but where does it come from? Which is to say . . ."

"It's etymologically uncertain," Virginia declared. "But I have my own theory. You know of course that a 'heer' is a measure of linen or woolen yarn containing two cuts, the sixth part of a hesp or hank of yarn, or the twenty-fourth part of a spyndle. Though the origin of the word is obscure, most philologists agree that it's close to the Old Norse 'herfe,' meaning skein," she said, sparkling. "But don't be fooled by Old Norse cognates!"

"Certainly not. I should say," said Favat.

"They're as deceptive as Frisian. When you start fooling around

238

with aural analogies of English and the Teutonics, especially Old High German, you're bound to make mistakes. The secret for determining the origins of upper New York State place-names lies, I believe, in morphological and orthographical distortions produced by naïve transliterations or imprecise recollections (or, of course, translingual or cross-dialectical phonological adaptation) of place-names in an unfamiliar language. What I think is that Coheeries is the American dialectical form of Grohius, who was one of the first Dutch patroons to settle west of the mountains. In encompassing most of the eastern shore of the lake, his estate may have been thought to include the lake itself. Thus, the Lake of Grohius, transforming slowly over time into the Lake of the Coheeries, just as 'Krom Moerasje,' meaning 'crooked little swamp,' in Dutch, became 'Gramercy' in English; thus your Gramercy Park. But I really don't know.'' She laughed.

Everyone who heard this, especially Close, was as stunned as a bird dog at an air show. Virginia had no idea that her little dissertation was not the normal stuff of social discourse, for, after all, she had spent her life with Mrs. Gamely, who could spit out thirty paragraphs like that as easily as she could turn a flapjack.

"Do you have a doctorate in linguistics?" asked Praeger.

"Me?" Virginia was surprised and embarrassed. "Oh no, Mr. de Pinto. I never went to school for a day in my life. There is no school in Lake of the Coheeries."

"There isn't?"

"No."

"I thought," said Marko Chestnut, "that every child in New York State had to go to school."

"Perhaps," Virginia explained. "But, you see, Lake of the Coheeries isn't really in New York State."

"It isn't?" several people asked at once.

"No," she said, anticipating difficulty. "It's not on the map, and mail never gets through unless one of us picks it up in Hudson. It's hard to explain. You can't, well, you can't just go there."

"You can't?"

"No." Now she knew she was on thin ice. "You have to be. You have to be . . .''

"What?"

"You have to be . . ."

"A resident," said Jessica.

"Yes!" Virginia exclaimed, "a resident."

Then, because Jessica brought all her influence to bear, the matter was quietly dropped. No one believed in the cloud wall anymore; no one could see it; no one understood. It was best not to pursue the subject. Anyway, recognizing Virginia's unusual perspective and apparent intelligence (not to mention her beauty), each department head proceeded to sound her out with an eye to offering her a job. Economic as usual, Bedford asked her, quite simply, what she did.

"In what circumstance?" she responded, puzzled, for in Lake of the Coheeries no one would ever think to ask such a question.

"For a living," he said, unwilling to be put off.

"Oh, all kinds of things. I help mother cultivate the grapes and corn, and tend the vegetables and the apiary. I cut ice from the lake in winter. I fish. I gather berries, weave, mend, cook, bake, sew, and take care of Martin. Sometimes, I do the calculations for the village accounts, or read to Daythril Moobcot when he has to go down underneath the dynamo to fix it. I work a lot in the library. The town has very few people, but in our library we have more than a million and a half volumes."

"That's it," Praeger said under his breath, wondering if she could write, and what she might say.

"And I tutor children and adults when they are in need, for which the village pays me a small cash sum."

Even Favat was interested in her now, imagining that she probably had some killer recipes for blueberry muffins and other rural foods (which, in fact, she did).

"Can you draw?" asked Marko Chestnut, already in love.

"No," answered Virginia, modestly looking down. She was uncomfortable now with all this attention: she had not really been aware of it at first. Jessica rescued her. They had had a difficult trip, Jessica said, and it was time for the baby to sleep.

Before they went to bed in the new Penn house (somewhere, it seemed to Virginia, inside a vast maze of overly prosperous streets), Jessica spoke to Virginia on the landing. "Praeger told me that he would like to see you, tomorrow, if possible, at *The Sun.* He thinks," she continued, with the air of an official about to award a lottery prize, "that he may want to offer you a job on *The Sun* or *The Whale,* or both, as is often the case."

"But I don't know anything about working on a newspaper," Virginia said.

"I have a feeling that you could learn. Don't you think it might be a fine idea?"

"Yes," answered Virginia. "If I'm lucky, I'll dream about it tonight, and tomorrow I'll know what to do."

On the afternoon that Virginia went down to Printing House Square to see Praeger de Pinto in the old and beautiful offices of *The Sun,* the city was ablaze in winter blue. To get there she had to pass through the Lower East Side and Chinatown, and these places full of surging color, that were the match of any Oriental city, pleased her no end. By the time she reached Praeger's office, strength had come to her from a thousand dissonant sources. She had harvested it from the city, the harbor, the ten thousand ships moving down a net of fast rivers, and the pristine geometry of the colossal bridges.

Praeger asked her questions for two hours, drinking in her soft eloquence and marveling at the way in which she thought. "Can you write the way you speak?" he asked.

"I suppose so," she said. "But I'm not sure."

Then he sent her into another room to write her first impressions of New York. She returned in an hour with a perfect essay as fresh as an apple. He read it twice, and then again. It was as pleasurable for him as kissing a beautiful woman.

"I feel," he said, "as if I've seen this city for the first time; and I thank you for it."

Virginia had written only what had seemed to her to be the truth of the way things were.

"Will you write a column for the editorial page? We'll run it in both papers, twice or three times a week. The system here is unique: it was fashioned after that of a whaling ship. Everyone is paid in shares, and—except for the size of offices and number of assistants—the benefits are equal. As an editorial page columnist, you would be well compensated because you would have a large number of shares.'' Then Praeger told her the range of the money, and even the low figure was more than she thought might have come to her in a lifetime, much less a year. The high figure was greater than the gross domestic products of Lake of the Coheeries and Bunting's Reef (the next town) put together. It scared her, but then she remembered that in traveling through the city for an hour, she had seen enough to write a thousand encyclopedias of deep praise. Surely, she thought, two or three pieces a week would be no problem considering the fact that a day's walk among the towers, bridges, and squares would send her home with her pen cocked as if it were ready to be launched from a crossbow.

''I think I'll take it,'' she said. ''But I don't know the city, and I don't know this kind of work. I fear that if I start too high, I'll have a distorted view. And, besides, Mother always said that one must be devoted to the thing itself, so I don't care for quick promotions and too much ease. Let me start from the beginning, with everyone else. I like the race rather than the winning.''

''Do you? Really?''

''Yes. I've imagined great victories, and I've imagined great races. The races are better.''

''The pay isn't the same at the bottom.''

''We're not materialists. We don't need much.''

''The custom here is to give a new employee ten days at salary, during which he can think about what's going on, and make an honorable and efficient break with whatever he has been doing. I expect you to rise rapidly. I hope that before the year is up, you'll be writing a column for us.''

Virginia walked through the spacious galleries of *The Sun,* past people whose work seemed to mesmerize them, and she skipped out the front doors and nearly floated across Printing House Square. She took half of her ten day's salary and put it in an envelope that she bought from a man who sold stationery from the inside of his coat. This she would send to her mother. She hadn't that much left, and she knew that it would be difficult. Still, she took the crowded streets and passed like a newly crowned queen through one after another of the city's exhausting districts. When she got to the Penns', she picked up little Martin and danced about.

This was only a dream. But the next day, upon her awakening, the elements of the dream fell into place exactly. Even the words spoken were the same. She had seen in her sleep the details of rooms in which she had never been, and known weather that had not yet formed, and streets upon which she had never walked. One thing was noticeably different. In Chinatown, on the way home, she bought Martin a big cherry cookie. It was sold to her by a fat Caucasian boy with slit eyes and a Chinese hat. He seemed very strange.

Now there were practical things to be accomplished. She had to find an apartment, get some new clothes, arrange for someone to take care of Martin while she worked. But these things would be easy. She believed that the city was so full of combinations, permutations, and possibilities that it permitted not only any desire to be fulfilled, but any course to be taken, any reward to be sought, any life to be lived, and any race to be run. She closed her eyes and saw the city burning before her in enticing gold. The sky, filled with great voluminous clouds, was ablaze in winter blue.

IN THE DRIFTS

THOUGH San Francisco is a
tranquil city, anesthetized in blue, when Vittorio Marratta died it
was if a clap of thunder had rolled over the hills. Had he not specif-
ically prohibited it, the line of black limousines following his
hearse would have been a mile long. He was central to several
communities at once, and when such a man dies it seems unnatural, causing even his enemies to pour out their respect. Signor Marratta was the leader of San Francisco's Italian community; a
scientist whose discoveries in astrophysics were weighty enough to
occasion the naming of not one but three galaxies after him (Marratta I, II, III) in a far-distant section of the northern sky; the
onetime president of the university across the bay, in the days before its troubles shattered the scholarly quiet in which it had been
founded; a former captain in the Navy, commander of a capital

ship in wartime; and a wealthy fleet owner whose fast container carriers graced the bay with arrivals and departures several times a day from or for Tokyo, Accra, London, Sydney, Riga, Bombay, Capetown, and Athens, and whose tugboats made all the adjustments required for the very same harbor that his ships made busy.

The obituary writers drew their incomplete sketches, touring through his life like travelers to England who do not ever see swans, sheep, bicycles, and blue eyes. They knew that he had come from Italy after the Great War, but not that he had deserted the carnage, spent a year like a thief, and finally swum into the harbor at Genoa to climb up the anchor chains of a ship, which—unbeknownst to him—was headed for San Francisco. They knew that he had married the daughter of a ship owner, but they did not know how much he had loved her before she died, or what it had done to him when she had. They knew that he had fought for the presidency of the university, but not how hard and taxing a fight it had been. They knew that he had discovered galaxies and described some fundamental truths, but they didn't know by what hand he had been guided, nor that, after many years of deep thought about what he had seen and measured, he had been rewarded by the sight of something that he was unable to reveal only because of the character of the age. And they knew that he had two sons, but they knew little about them.

When thunder clapped over the city which knows no thunder, all kinds of things happened. Relatives bustled about buying flowers and renting automobiles, only to find that they had been excluded from the procession by order of the deceased—who had wanted just his sons at his graveside, and a priest. Lawyers and accountants were put to work as hard and suddenly as Seabees who must build an airfield in half an hour. Academic buildings were renamed. The observatory flew its flag at half-staff. And everyone wondered how the sons would manage all that would be left to them. Seventy-five large ships, all the tugboats in San Francisco Bay, a department store, several office towers, enough prime real estate upon which to build another city, trusts, subdivisions, and the ownership of large blocks of stock in great corporations, were all at issue in the will. Signor Marratta had come to own a section of the economy as varied and richly colored as a long core sample from the bed of a tropical sea, and his herd of chattels was like the one on Noah's Ark. Naturally, everyone was curious about the disposition of these assets.

The will was read on a Wednesday in May, three weeks after the funeral, when the cracks of thunder had begun to fade. In May serenity, students left on sunny empty roads to see other parts of the country, and those who remained were enjoying the strong sun, and the shining clear days that were still wonderfully cool. A hundred people were gathered in the nearly ultraviolet shadows of the largest room in the Marratta house on Presidio Heights. Swaths of deep blue were visible through French doors that led to a long balcony overlooking the bay. Had it not been for the chill of the marble, as white and clean as the cliffs of Yosemite, Signor Marratta himself might have been forgotten, for, with 150 people in attendance, the reading of the will was like a cross between a private school commencement, a court-martial, and the assembly of a covert religious sect. Sitting in the first row were the two sons, Evan and Hardesty. In their early thirties, they seemed younger. And they were strong and restless in a way that suggested that they should have been not in a ballroom but out on a playing field somewhere, or in a forest where the light was dazzling on blue streams.

"I fear," said the senior of the five lawyers who directed the proceedings, "that today there will be much disappointment in this room. Signor Marratta was a complicated man, and as is often the case with complicated men, he favored simple actions.

"During nearly half a century of association with him as friend and legal adviser, I found myself in a lifelong debate about the law. Signor Marratta did not know the law, but he knew its spirit, and as often as not he insisted upon a simple approach that I rejected— only to hear from me (after much labor and research) that, indeed, he was right. I don't know how he did it, but somehow he knew what the law intended and in what places it would stand fast. I am saying this not to eulogize him or to apply on his behalf for posthumous honorary admission to the bar, but, rather, to caution you against making a quick judgment about what will undoubtedly appear to some as a rash act.

246

"Signor Marratta was the richest man I have ever known, and he left the shortest will that I have ever seen. If you expect to sit here for hours, listening to ever larger disbursements, you will be surprised, for he has provided most of everything to only one inheritor, and a small gift to another. I am afraid that many of you will be deservedly embittered."

Instead of stirring, the room was tense with silence. Expectation and fear coiled together in a stalemate as symmetrical and interdependent as the struggling snakes of a caduceus. Representatives of universities and charitable institutions, directors of hospitals, long-forgotten relatives, stray acquaintances, obscure employees, and delegates of the press strained together in suspense—all but the very last hoping beyond hope that the rash act of which the lawyer had spoken would make them wealthy beyond their most fanciful dreams.

Nonetheless, they all thought that Evan would receive the small gift, which would probably be something bitter and ironic in token of his less than exemplary character. His mother's sudden death had made him a master of calculated greed, dissolute behavior, and indiscriminate cruelty, and he lived only for what he could extract from his father, who loved him despite this.

He had bloodied Hardesty so often in vicious boyhood attacks that Hardesty was always afraid of him, even in Hardesty's late twenties after he had fought in two wars and long been a strapping athlete. The years of military service, interrupting his career at graduate school, had made the younger brother diffident and shy. He had been broken more than once in the army, and was one of those who had come back hurt and disillusioned.

The witnesses at the reading of the will assumed that everything would go to Hardesty because he was so quiet and nondescript, and they eagerly awaited the final slap that Evan would receive for all the drugs he had taken, cars he had wrecked, women he had made pregnant, and days he had wasted. They saw that even in the short space between the lawyer's announcement of the peculiar conditions of the will and the undoing of the waxen seal that had protected it, Evan was staring at Hardesty in a way that suggested intimidation, flattery, and murder.

Evan was sweating and breathing hard. His fists were tight and his eyes wide. Hardesty, on the other hand, sat sadly next to his brother, thinking, undoubtedly, of their father—not because he was pious or dull, but because his father had been his only friend, and now he was horribly lonely. He wanted the proceedings to end; he wanted to return to his rooms, where he had very little except books, plants, and the view. Evan had moved out years before to an aerie on Russian Hill, a cavernous triplex that he used for seducing women who were impressed by the vast amount of electronic equipment he had amassed against several of its walls so that it looked like a blockhouse at Cape Canaveral.

Hardesty did not even have a bed. He slept on a blue-and-gold Persian rug, wrapped in an old Abercrombie & Fitch rust-colored wool blanket. His pillow, however, was eiderdown, and he always kept a clean case on it. Apart from thousands of books, Hardesty had few material possessions. He didn't have a car, preferring to walk or take public transportation wherever he had to go. He didn't have a watch. He had one suit, and it was fifteen years old. And he had one pair of hiking shoes, and they had seen three years of daily use. In contrast to his brother's closet of eighty shaped suits, half a hundred pairs of Italian shoes, and a thousand ties, hats, canes, and coats, Hardesty's wardrobe could fit into a small knapsack. Considering his wealth, he lived rather simply.

His father had known very well that Hardesty was silent and withdrawn because he was recovering from the wars, gathering strength, learning. Signor Marratta had loved Evan the way one loves someone who suffers from a terrible disease—all in sorrow. But he had loved Hardesty out of the deepest respect and sympathy—all in hope and pride.

It was generally believed that Hardesty would be rewarded for his asceticism and discipline, and that he would emerge as a solid and engaging figure fit to control his father's wealth and manage it justly. There was much pleasant anticipation of seeing him move from his quiet world into the rush of things, where, it was presumed, his fresh and obviously keen intellect would be not only constructive, but surprising. Of all those present at the reading of the will, only Hardesty did not assume that he was due for an apotheosis in dollars, and only Hardesty sat calmly and free of expectation. The lawyer read.

" 'Herein the last will and testament of Vittorio Marratta, San Francisco, drawn the first of September, the year of our Lord nineteen hundred and ninety-five.

" 'All my worldly possessions, ownerships, receivables, shares, interests, rights, and royalties, shall go to one of my sons. The Marratta salver, which is on the long table in my study, will go to the other. Hardesty will decide, and his decision as it is first announced will be irrevocable. Neither son will be entitled to the patrimony of the other, ever, under any circumstances, the death or desires of one or the other notwithstanding. I make this declaration in sound mind and body, convinced of its justice and ultimate value.' "

At last, Hardesty was amused. Though he had a sense of humor, it was largely a private attribute. For the first time since his father's death, he smiled, and in doing so he revealed even further that he had a kind, intelligent, interesting face—unlike that of his grimacing brother. Hardesty shook his head in pleasant incredulity and then began to laugh when he saw Evan begin to quiver in anticipation of having to get a job.

No way existed for Evan to appeal the decision, and neither could he think of any means by which to befuddle his brother into taking the salver. He had always hated it, even though it was made of gold, because it was engraved with words that he did not understand, and his father had spoken about it in terms far too reverential for a tray worth no more than several thousand dollars. So what if it had been brought from Italy. It was junk, and he saw it as a pact between his father and Hardesty, a magical link between them that excluded him. The terrible irony was that he would be left with the salver (which he had often ridiculed and once even thrown out the window) and Hardesty would inherit enough to make a thousand men rich. Evan was convinced that he hadn't a chance, not because Hardesty was interested in the wealth (for he clearly was not) but because Hardesty's integrity would force him to take responsibility for managing the assets that everyone well knew Evan would mismanage. So the older brother closed his eyes and prepared to face what was for him the equivalent of a firing squad. Perhaps his father had overheard him adding up the Marratta assets (exaggerating what needn't have been exaggerated), saying the numbers to himself like a monk in a trance. Perhaps his father's soul, in ascension, had eavesdropped on his first son's spirit as it was told of the father's passing, and had been offended by the elated singing. All Evan knew was that Hardesty had the satisfied look of power.

The assembled political and communal leaders set their eyes upon Hardesty to confirm that what was obviously in his self-interest was also in the general interest, and to urge him to do the expected. Surely, they seemed to be saying, if you renounce the inheritance and it goes to Evan, you will have committed a great evil. Several of them, knowing their own children, grew quite nervous.

"I recommend," the lawyer said, "that we adjourn these proceedings until we are notified that Mr. Marratta has reached a firm decision." He wanted Hardesty's ear, so as to persuade him to do the right thing. "Is that okay with you, Hardesty?"

"No," said Hardesty. "I've decided."

The tension this engendered was, if not unbearable, at least unpleasant. On the one hand, if he had wanted time to think, it would have meant that he was not sure, and to be unsure of such an obvious choice was a dangerous sign of instability. On the other hand, a firm and quick decision could go either way, and even the right decision would have been taken too quickly. One way or another, it was frightening. If only they could get to him before he opened his mouth, to make sure that he considered these options in context.

"Such a momentous choice," began the lawyer.

"No," Hardesty said firmly. "You don't understand. My father had a way of speaking, a way of doing things indirectly so that we could learn while he slowed decisions and held them open to view. When we were young, if we asked him what time it was, he wouldn't tell us, he'd show us with his watch. Everything he did enabled others to learn. He was desirous that we 'by indirections find directions out.' And, in this instance, his wishes are very clear to me. Perhaps if I didn't know him so well—excuse me, if I hadn't known him so well—I would have a choice. But I have no choice here, not if I am to fulfill his ambitions for me, and, like him, rise out of myself and become something better than what I am.

"No. I gladly and lovingly submit to his will, and I am sure of what he wanted. The salver is mine."

A bigger stir could not have been created in San Francisco if the San Andreas fault had finally unseamed itself. Evan could hardly stand the shock. Possession of so much wealth took away his voice for an hour and a half: the sudden infusion of cash alone was like half a pound of cocaine flowing through his veins. Hardesty was forgotten by all, except for the brief moment it took to condemn him. Then, penniless and powerless, he was ignored in favor of his brother, to whom, by necessity, all eyes began to turn.

The lawyer had wanted to know why Hardesty had done what he had done. But Hardesty refused to tell. The salver had been given to Signor Marratta by his father, Hardesty said, who had received it from his father, who had received it from his father . . . etc., etc., how far back no one knew. But that was not the reason.

He thought it best to separate himself from the cacophony and gossip that he caused in San Francisco. He was no longer entitled to his room with its wood-railed balcony high above the bay (and would miss it forever), he was unsure of what he would do for a living, and possession of the salver was demanding in itself. He knew that, to satisfy what he understood to be its requirements, he had to leave.

Knowing that his brother was undoubtedly going to convert and desecrate their father's study, Hardesty would have to go there and find his way past shields and blockades of memory to claim the great and demanding gift. Then he would leave forever the city of his birth, his home, and the place where his father and mother were buried.

The study was the highest room in the house, surmounted by a small old-fashioned observatory in which Signor Marratta had spent many hours in the early days before photon-count narrow-field telescopy. Because they were on the most elevated piece of ground in Presidio Heights, the study on the top floor had a commanding view. As Hardesty climbed the stairs, he remembered what his father had taught him about views.

"See it, and it is yours," he had said in Italian to the little boy, carrying him from one window to the next, and guiding his eye over the hills, bay, and ocean. "Look there," the father had said, pointing at distant hills the color of mustard and gold, "they are like the pelt of the spotted beast. Look how they roll. Look at the muscle under their lively backs."

Outside, the fog and clouds were invading armies which swept in ragged determined lines and flying wings of devoted cavalry to surround the city and outflank the bay. They rushed past and almost buried everything with their pointed and trembling peaks, but still there was a crown of blue above the mountains, so that the light in the study was pure and deep. Light that was predominantly ultraviolet, purple, and blue washed over Hardesty's face, and over the salver, which glistened like something unearthly.

As if he were moving under water, he slowly approached the massive table where the salver had been left by his father as casually as if it had been a dish from the kitchen. The Marrattas believed that the salver was protected. It had survived wars, fires, earthquakes, and thieves, who, like Evan, seemed not to want it. Hardesty wondered how his brother could have refused such a miraculous thing, for in the cloud-buffeted sun it shone in a hundred thousand colors, all subsumed in gold and silver. Seamless rays arose from it in a solid thicket, radiating in blinding beauty from the words engraved around the rim, meeting the others above the center, and plunging downward to illuminate the primary inscription.

The light on Hardesty's face went from violet and blue to gold and silver. He felt its warmth, and saw again the inscriptions—four virtues, and one seductive and promising sentence suspended in their midst as if it were the hub of a wheel. Many times, his father had taken him to read them, insisting that they were the most important things he could have, and implying with a sharp dismissive gesture of hand and arm that wealth, fame, and worldly possessions were worthless and demeaning. "Little men," he once said, "spend their days in pursuit of such things. I know from experience that at the moment of their deaths they see their lives shattered before them like glass. I've seen them die. They fall away as if they have been pushed, and the expressions on their faces are those of the most unbelieving surprise. Not so, the man who knows the virtues and lives by them. The world goes this way and that. Ideas are in fashion or not, and those who should prevail are often defeated. But it doesn't matter. The virtues remain uncorrupted and uncorruptible. They are rewards in themselves, the bulwarks with which we can protect our vision of beauty, and the strengths by which we may stand, unperturbed, in the storm that comes when seeking God."

When Hardesty's mother had died, when he had gone to war, when he had come back, and at all other times of grief, danger, or triumph, his father had made sure that he had gone to the salver. He could almost see his father in front of him, turning the golden tray in his hands. Signor Marratta first read the silvered inscriptions in Italian, then translated. A foreign language enjoys the benefit of the doubt in much the same way that marriages between those who speak different tongues allow a gentleness and tolerance untouched by destructive wit. For example, a Japanese kitchen maid might easily mix with the stiffest of the English beau monde, for they would not be able to use her language as a handle with which to throw her out. The same with the virtues when recited in Italian. They were in no way overbearing, or the stock-in-trade of schoolmasters and ministers, so Hardesty accepted them the way he might never have accepted them in his own language.

"*La onestà*, honesty," was the first, never properly valued, Signor Marratta had said, until one must lose a great deal for its sake alone, "and then, it rises like the sun." Hardesty's favorite, even though it was the word about which his mother's death seemed to revolve, and even though he associated it with tears more than with anything else, was "*il coraggio*, courage." Next was one that he hardly understood—"*il sacrificio*, sacrifice." Why sacrifice? Was it not a defunct trait of the martyrs? Perhaps because it was so rare, it was as mystifying to him as the last virtue (which almost bumped into "*la onestà*," at the bottom of the plate), the most puzzling, the

253

one least attractive to him as a young man, "*la pazienza*, patience."

But none of these qualities, hard to understand as they might have been, and even harder to put into practice, was half as mysterious as the pronouncement inlaid in white gold on the center of the plate. It was from the *Senilia* of Benintèndi, and Signor Marratta made sure early on that Hardesty knew it and would not forget. Now, after his father's death, alone in a study that was at times high above the clouds, Hardesty picked up the gleaming salver and translated its inscription out loud: " *'For what can be imagined more beautiful than the sight of a perfectly just city rejoicing in justice alone.'* "

He repeated this to himself several times, and then put the salver into a pack that held everything he would take with him. A quick look at San Francisco from the tranquillity of the high and isolated study was all he needed to show him that this city—as stunning as it was—was not and would never be the seat of perfect justice, having no relation to it. It was a paradigm of soulless beauty—always cool, forever silent, asleep in blue—but it had nothing to do with justice, for justice was not so easy. Justice came from a fight amid complexities, and required all the virtues in the world merely to be perceived.

As he walked out of his house for the last time, he realized that any guile and sophistication that he had learned was now gone from him forever. What if he were asked where he was going? What could he say? "I'm looking for the perfectly just city?" They would think he was a lunatic.

"Where are you going, Hardesty?" Evan asked when Hardesty emerged from the house just as Evan was entering.

"I'm looking for the perfectly just city."

"Yes, but where are you going?" Evan wanted Hardesty to guide him in his new responsibilities, and had decided to offer him a very large salary if the lawyers interpreted the will as allowing him to do so.

"You wouldn't understand. You always hated the plate. I always loved it."

"For Christ's sake, what was it, anyway, some sort of a treasure hunt?"

"In a way."

Evan began to get interested. He knew Hardesty was smart, and now he suspected that the plate was the key to El Dorado. "Have you got it?"

"Right here."

"Let me see it."

"There it is," Hardesty said, taking it out of his pack. He knew exactly what Evan was thinking.

"What does it say? Can you translate?"

"It says, 'Wash me, I'm dirty.' ''

"Tell me what it says, Hardesty."

"I told you what it says, Evan."

"What are you going to do?" Evan asked, in desperation at being left.

"I may be going to Italy, but I'm not sure."

"What do you mean, you're not sure? How will you get there?"

"I think I'll walk," Hardesty said, laughing.

"Walk? You're going to walk to Italy? Is that what the tray says?"

"Yes."

"How? There's water, there's a lot of water. . . ."

"Goodbye, Evan." Hardesty began walking.

"I don't understand you, Hardesty," Evan screamed. "I never did. What does the tray say?"

"It says, 'For what can be imagined more beautiful than the sight of a perfectly just city rejoicing in justice alone,' '' Hardesty shouted back. But Evan had already gone in to claim the house.

A bridgeworker in medieval-looking gray coveralls stiff and dirty with orange paint did not understand why Hardesty, his passenger, trembled with emotion as they drove across the Bay Bridge from San Francisco to Oakland. But it was clear to Hardesty, as they tunneled through a cool bank of mist and watched ships etching white tracks across the deep water below them, that he was going from one world to another.

So great was the difference between San Francisco and its fog-horns on islands in cold waters, and dusty Oakland, that they should have been separated not by seven miles and a bridge, but by seven thousand miles of sea. The shock of traveling between San Francisco and its numbing ultraviolets and Oakland and its diz-zying sun enabled Hardesty quickly to revert to his army self. As the tollbooths disappeared behind him, he found that he was pre-pared to climb barbed-wire fences, hop freights, sleep on the ground, and cover fifty miles a day on foot. Leaving his emotions where he had shed them into the bay, he prepared to cross America and the Atlantic, with no money, a vague idea, and a golden plate. The heat on the Oakland side seemed to have started up within him sleek engines that had been silent since the war.

He didn't take long to find a good position behind some reeds on the bank of a railroad line running east. He lay there in the sun, his head on his pack, chewing a sprig of grass, until he heard the sound of traveling thunder. Squinting through the vegetation, he saw a lone engine coming down the track. Where the diesel exhaust rose above its black-and-yellow striped cabin (it looked like a huge mo-torized bee), the air wiggled like a bunch of springs, and six men in denim hung out from both sides in the fashion of circus acrobats on a horse. Everything went by with a roar, and Hardesty put his head back on the knapsack, content to wait. After falling in and out of sleep, he heard the unmistakable rumble of a multi-engined freight. Without even looking, he got himself ready: he didn't need to look, for when the eight engines came along the rails, pulling two hundred cars, the earth shook and the reeds sang.

Oil-covered water in a nearby ditch began to ripple and quiver. The first engine was as black as a gun, and had a yellow light glar-ing from the top as if it were the truth itself. Having just started out of the Oakland yards, it was beginning to pick up speed, straining to get going, and Hardesty could hear the sharp concussions of the couplers as they snapped into place to pull the hundreds of cars all the way down the line. Quite possibly there's nothing as fine as a big freight train starting across country in early summer, Hardesty thought. That's when you learn that the tragedy of plants is that they have roots. The reeds and grasses on the hot mounds and in the ditches turned green with envy and begged to go along (which is why they waved when the train went by). The train itself promised a hundred thousand hot and lovely places filled with the noise of wind in the trees, easy summer in deep valleys, brown rivers, sparkling bays, and so much prairie that alongside it infinity would look like a tick.

When Hardesty saw that a clean new gondola car was coming, he slung his pack and began to run alongside the train. The occasional stones that had rolled from the railbed onto the black loam path paralleling it dug into his feet through his shoes. Every now and then he would glance to his right to see if the gondola car was approaching. The second ladder moved into place. He put his right hand on it and felt it pulling him along. By the time his left hand had grasped hold, his legs were windmilling at a prodigious rate. Then he moved his right hand up a rung, jumped, and he was riding ahead, free. All in all, it was many times better a sensation than finding a hundred-dollar bill.

Vaulting the low bulkhead, he fell onto planks of brand-new pine that smelled like a sunny forest in the Sierra. The bulkheads were high enough to keep out most of the wind (but not all of it) and hide him from view. He might not be able to see railroad detectives standing by the side of the track, but then again, they would not be able to see him. And he would be able to see the fields, the valleys, and the mountain ranges. He could stand up without fear of being decapitated by bridges and tunnels, pace back and forth, run around in circles, whoop, dance, and leave his pack in a corner knowing that, no matter how much the train lurched, the pack would not roll off into a field, never to be seen again. He wasn't hungry, it was lovely weather, and he had the whole country before him. Not surprisingly, he began to sing, and because no one in the world could hear him, and he sang without inhibition, he sang well.

The next morning, somewhere in the mountains near Truckee, while the train was moving slowly between hills of rock studded with straight pines, Hardesty paced the length of the gondola car, still happy, though, after a night on the boards, no longer elated.

As the train labored up the grade, he realized how difficult his future was going to be.

He had often jumped freights to go into the Sierra in rainless summers, but he had always had a home to which he could return. With that no longer true, he was beginning to get some idea of what it had been like for his father to desert a unit of Italian mountain troops that had been cutting itself down to nothing in the Dolomites, and make his way (as a fugitive) to the sea and finally to America.

"For the first months," Signor Marratta had said, "it wasn't so bad. We spent most of the time building fortifications high on cliffs, and we could see the enemy only through our telescopes. But when our redoubts and theirs were finished, generals on both sides were compelled to order us to advance and fight. To me, this seemed ridiculous. We had been quite happy, up there in the mountains, until we began to get killed. I went to our *maggiore*, and said, 'Why not a stalemate, a balance? Just because they're killing each other on the plain doesn't mean that we have to do it up here.' He thought it was a splendid idea, but who was he? Rome wanted territorial gains. Our half-hearted sharpshooters began to shoot, our artillerymen stuffed the barrels of their fieldpieces and started their bombardments, and those of us unfortunate enough to have been alpinists had to trundle through the defiles and make dangerous ascents—so that we might suddenly appear two hundred feet above our unsuspecting adversaries, and shoot down at them. I left half a dozen good friends hanging lifeless on their mountaineering ropes a thousand feet high on sheer walls, because the enemy shot back. They used their cannon, in the most deadly and unpredictable flat trajectories, to burst apart the cliffs we were ascending. After a year of that, all I wanted was to live. Had I persisted in that struggle between armed chapters of the Italian and Austrian alpine clubs, you probably would not be here. Besides, you can now join either club and get reciprocal membership in the other."

But Signor Marratta had also had regrets about deserting. Both loyalty and responsibility often did justify the act of dying in place, and it was hard to rid himself of the feeling that he had made "the great refusal." Hardesty thought that perhaps he himself had shirked his responsibilities when he chose the salver. But, as usual, his father had structured the question so that either choice would have brought him doubt. The doubt, his father might have said in characteristic Marratta fashion, would propel him to seek a far more thorough, adventurous, and valuable resolution than he would seek without it. "All great discoveries," the elder Marratta had once said, "are products as much of doubt as of certainty, and the two in opposition clear the air for marvelous accidents."

At that very moment, Hardesty was thrown with irresistible force to the floor of the gondola car. In the fraction of a second before he lost consciousness, he regretted that the boards seemed to be rising toward his face; he wondered what was on his back; and he feared that the car ahead had tumbled over and was in the midst of crushing him. Then he blacked out.

When he awakened, he was lying with his face to the sky. Blood had clotted over his cheeks, he felt sore, and he discovered on the side of his head a gash as long as a caterpillar and at least as distinct. Then he noticed a creature squatting against the wall. Only by blinking, and clearing the blood from his eyes, could he see that it was a man who could not have been more than five feet tall, but who looked about two feet high because of the powerful muscle-bound way in which he was squatting. He was wearing a costume that, at first, Hardesty could not take in. Piece by piece, it was decipherable, but as a whole it was breathtaking and unbelievable. His shoes were big dollops of greasy black leather that looked like pomaded cannonballs—these Hardesty recognized as the most expensive mountaineering boots with many years of wear and a bear or two worth of grease. To fall in a river with shoes like that meant certain death. And if they were to catch fire they would burn for a month, even under water. He wore zigzagged edelweiss-design, purple-and-blue knee socks, cobalt blue knickers, rainbow suspenders, a violet shirt, and a pirate-style bandanna that was the same purple and blue as the knee socks but had a hypnotic pattern of red washed through it. His face was almost fully covered by a beard and perfectly round, rose-colored sunglasses. Two fingers were missing from his right hand, three from the left, he carried a bright blue day pack, and he wore a sling of mountain-climbing equipment that was the necklace of necklaces. It was dripping with silver carabiners, baubled with shiny climbing nuts, clanging with pitons, and festooned with two-dozen webbing runners of half a hundred fluorescent interwoven colors. Slung over his shoulder was an orange-and-black climbing rope, and he was chewing a piece of beef jerky as big as a notebook.

"Sorry about that," he said between chaws on the beef. "I jumped the train from a bridge and I didn't see you. Thanks."

"Thanks for what?" asked Hardesty.

"Cushioning my fall."

"What are you?"

"What am I? What do you mean by that?"

"What the hell are you? Am I dreaming you? You look like Rumpelstiltskin."

"Never heard of him. Does he climb in the Sierra?"

"No, he doesn't climb in the Sierra."

"I'm a climber. A professional. I'm on my way to the Wind Rivers, where I'm going to do the first solo of East Temple Spire. If I'm beartrap enough, I'll do it at night. Boy, that was some landing. I'm glad that my rack and nuts are safe."

"Yes," said Hardesty, "I, too, am glad that your rack and nuts are safe."

"That's a bad gash you've got. You oughta put some Nandiboon on that."

"What's Nandiboon?"

"Great stuff, Oil of Nandiboon. It heals anything real fast. A friend of mine brought it back from Nepal. Here. . . ." He reached into the blue pack and brought out a small flask, which he uncorked with his teeth. "I sort of feel responsible for you now."

"Wait a minute," said Hardesty as the oil was smeared over his wound.

"Don't worry, it's organic."

"What's your name?"

"Jesse Honey."

"What?"

"Jesse . . . Honey. Honey is my last name. It's not my fault. It could have been worse. I could have been a girl, and they could have named me Bunny, or Bea, or who the hell knows what. What's your name?''

"My name is Hardesty Marratta. What's in this stuff? It's beginning to sting.''

"It does sting. But it heals real fast.''

The pain from the Nandiboon Oil was on the rise, and Hardesty suspected that it would rise quite high. It did. Two or three minutes after it had been applied, the Nandiboon Oil was seething into his skin in thousands of boiling potholes. Whatever Nandiboon Oil was, it was a good imitation of sulfuric acid and hydrogen peroxide. Hardesty rolled in agony.

"I'll get some water," screamed Jesse Honey. "There's a stream crossing the switchback. I'll catch you when you come this way up ahead.'' Hardesty didn't even hear him. But ten minutes later he saw Jesse Honey's hand begging for assistance over the edge of the gondola car, and he went to help him. Jesse Honey threw a plastic jug of water into the train and grabbed Hardesty's extended arm so hard that he dislocated it. Hardesty collapsed again. Jesse Honey seized his arm (the wrong one) and proceeded to relocate it according to the principles of first aid. But, since it was already located, he, in fact, dislocated it.

"Are you trying to kill me?'' Hardesty shouted. "Because if you are, I wish you would just get it over with.''

Jesse Honey seemed not to hear, and went about relocating both of Hardesty's arms. "I learned that on Mount McKinley,'' he said with evident satisfaction. Then he washed the Nandiboon Oil off Hardesty's face, and jumped from the train once again. When he returned, he was carrying a huge pile of brushwood.

"What's that for?''

"Gotta make a fire to boil water to cook the food and have tea,'' Jesse Honey said, lighting up the kindling.

"How can you make a fire on a wooden floor?'' Hardesty asked, too late. The resinous floorboards had already caught fire, and flames were leaping in the wind. Jesse Honey tried to stamp them out, but when his greasy boots began to ignite, he withdrew.

For half an hour the wind carried the fire to front and rear.

Lubricating oil, paint, the wooden floors and interiors of boxcars, dunnage, and a thousand miscellaneous cargoes all took flame until finally the train was blazing in sheets of fire. The train crew discovered it too late to stop, and tried to make for the saddle of the mountains, where there was no wind. By the time they got there it was too hot for Jesse and Hardesty to stay on, so they jumped off and began walking east. As the sun set, they could see two red glows (the brighter being the conflagration on the train), and they heard periodic explosions marking the demise of tank cars laden with combustibles. According to Jesse Honey, it was all part of nature's way. "Trains," he said, "were never meant to be in the mountains."

For most of the night they walked along the length of cool valleys on the crest of the Sierra, where they found only starlight and the deep tranquillity of mountains in early summer. The silence of the trees and quiescence of the wind were nature's hope and disbelief that winter had passed, a time when the wild terrain holds its breath before rejoicing, for fear of calling back the bright blue northerns and the snow.

At first, Hardesty and Jesse did not speak on the chalk-white paths that blackened shafts of alpine defiles, and their eyes tracked the stars as they watched the rim of the mountains swallow them up. The air was springlike. It conveyed the same buoyant pleasure as walking into a gathering of little children, arrayed like wild flowers, in their colorful hats and scarves. As always on the first day at altitude, it was easy to walk all night, and besides, the air was so fresh and the streams so roiling, white, and numb that no living thing which knew joy or freedom could possibly have slept.

As they walked north-northeast, the moon came up as creamy as pearl, perfectly round, benevolent, a flawless bright lantern. Jesse claimed that there was an excellent freight line in the direction that he insisted they follow, just a mile or two ahead. They had covered fifteen miles by the time the moon disappeared and the east brightened, and still there was no railroad. "There's a beautiful bridge right over the track," said Jesse, "made of logs and cables. I don't know who built it, and I don't know what for, but you can drop right onto the train with the greatest of ease."

"I don't understand," said Hardesty. "Why do you have to fall from above every time you get on a freight? Why not just run alongside and catch a rung?"

Jesse looked at him with hurt and annoyance. "I can't," he stated bitterly. "I can't reach high enough."

"Oh, I see," Hardesty answered, glancing at his companion— who was breathtakingly short. "How tall are you, anyway?"

"What's the difference?"

"No difference. I'm just curious."

"Four-four and three-quarters. I was supposed to be six-three. That's what the doctor said, from the spaces in my X-rays. My grandfather was six-six, my father six-eight, and my brothers are taller than that."

"What happened to you?"

Jesse bristled. "I don't know," he said, shaking his head. "For a man who stands four feet five inches tall . . ."

"I thought you said four-four and three-quarters," interrupted Hardesty.

"Drop dead," Jesse snapped. "For a man who stands four feet five inches tall, this is a difficult world. When I read in the newspapers that they describe someone who's five-eight as being of below average height, how do you think I feel? Girls won't even look at me. Most of them don't get the chance: they see right over my head. I wasn't allowed to join the Army, though the Navy was eager to have me—as a chimney sweep. I went to college, I'm an engineer, and the Navy wanted me to sweep their goddamned chimneys. When big tall jerks strut around because they're proud of how tall they are, I just want to take a machine gun. . . . It doesn't matter. I don't care anymore. What I need is a beautiful short woman in a little cabin near a low mountain range."

"I think that there are places like that in the Black Forest," Hardesty said, "where, according to legend, at least, you might find what you're looking for."

"No trolls," said Jesse. "I was born American, and that cuts out trolls."

"No, no, no. I'm talking about pretty little blond blue-eyed women like you see on carved bottle stoppers."

"Not for me. I like California girls, slim and tall, the kind whose knees come up to my throat."

That day they covered forty miles in the full sun, talking about women, mountain climbing, freight trains, and politics. Jesse was an avid supporter of President Palmer (perhaps because he was the shortest president since Linscott Gregory), whereas Hardesty was willing to vote for him, but no more than that. They were self-consciously silent whenever they would cross the tree line, because there they would walk through vast stands of dwarf pine. Hardesty said he thought that he might have broken a bone when he cushioned Jesse's landing.

"Don't you know?" asked Jesse.

"No, I don't. I never broke anything before."

"You never broke anything before! That's crazy! I've broken nearly every bone in my body. Once, I forgot to anchor my rappel, and I broke sixteen bones at the same time. I was absentminded on the Grand, and belayed myself with a *reepschnur*. (That's like using a shoelace.) Well, I took a forty-foot leader fall on that *reepschnur*, and I think I broke everything except my word, because, after the *reepschnur* snapped at forty feet, I kept falling for another three hundred and fifty."

"I'm surprised you didn't die."

"I hit a lot of ledges."

They came to a crystal-blue lake almost as long and narrow as a river. From atop a group of boulders on the south side, they could see the railroad line about a mile across the water. Jesse said that they would have to swim, but that because the lake was geothermal it was as warm as bathwater. Hardesty put his finger in, and disagreed. "Not on the edges!" Jesse exclaimed. "Any fool would know that geothermally warmed lakes are hot only in the deeper portions. That's where all the heat exchange takes place. Several tons of refrigerated thermal currents activate an ion-intensive, BTU-rich wave transfer beginning at the upwelling parameters of the tollopsoid region of the deepest central subset. Thus, the agitated interference pattern of air-influenced temperature variations forces a haploid grid upon the dimensional flows of surface water trapped in an oscillating torroidal belt that varies only with alkaloid surfactant inversions of normal stability caused by drought-induced desiccant concentrations due to insufficient intra-aqueous leaching.''

"Still,'' said Hardesty, "we might do better to walk around.''

"Not a chance. The railroad is not even tangential to the lake. It veers down from the northwest and veers up again to the northeast, because they built it that way in the days when they needed to top off the boilers of steam engines. The lake is fifty miles long, and this is the central part of it. Besides, even if we walked to one end, we'd still have to cross a river, and crossing a river is a hell of a lot more complicated—believe me—than crossing a lake. At least the lake stands still.''

Apart from his explanation of why the lake was warmer in the middle than at its edges, what Jesse said sounded reasonable. So they set to building a raft on which to float their clothes and belongings as they swam.

"That's hardwood,'' pronounced Hardesty over a bunch of logs that Jesse was dragging toward the assembly point on the beach. (Jesse himself could hardly be seen through the thicket of gray—he looked like a porcupine with a purple skin disease.) "It won't float.''

"Hardwood? Ha! This is Montana balsam. It's what they use in the interior of dirigibles and such. Of course it will float.''

They lashed it together with spare *reepschnur* cord, and pushed it from the rocks into the water, never to see it again for it went down like heavy chain. Then they started to swim. The sun was setting, but they had decided to get wet anyway, and build a big fire on the other side, since there was plenty of Montana balsam all around. Jesse said it wouldn't burn, which assured Hardesty of a comfortable blaze by which to warm himself.

Wrapping their clothes in bundles to put on top of their knapsacks, they prepared to set out across the water, knapsacks balanced on their shoulders. In theory, only the bottom of the packs would get wet. But that theory lasted only for the ten minutes that they could swim fast. Then, at the center of the lake, they sank deeper into the water, and everything got drenched. The water there was as cold as a mountain stream at midnight on the last day of January. The colder they got, the faster Jesse talked in what sounded like a high-speed collision between a physics textbook and a politician.

"I know this may sound like an excuse," he said. "But tensor functions in higher differential topology, as exemplified by application of the Gauss-Bonnet Theorem to Todd Polynomials, indicate that cohometric axial rotation in nonadiabatic thermal upwelling can, by random inference derived from translational equilibrium aggregates, array in obverse transitional order the thermodynamic characteristics of a transactional plasma undergoing negative entropy conversions."

"Why don't you just shut up," said Hardesty.

Jesse didn't open his mouth until the frame he made to hold his clothes near their fire collapsed, and his purple knickers burned up. From that time forward, he went bare below the waist except for a New Guinea style penis shield that he fashioned from a discarded Dr. Pepper can and hung from his waist on a piece of *reepschnur*. He soon took to extolling this form of dress as if he were a Seventh Avenue designer introducing a new line. "It's very comfortable," he said. "You should try it."

Two hours after the fire burned out, a thundering mass of steel wheels and coughing diesels swung by the lakeshore, and Jesse and Hardesty found a comfortable flatcar to carry them toward Yellowstone. Hardesty got up first, and Jesse ran by the side of the tracks, flagging dangerously, until Hardesty hoisted him aboard. Hardesty was easily able to see him, because his buttocks shone in the light of the moon. Twenty-four hours later they jumped off the train rather than ride north into Montana and Canada, walked for a while, and then were stopped by what they thought was the Yellowstone River.

Hardesty looked up at the sky, which seemed to be threatening rain. "Why don't we build a shelter, and see what we can do about crossing this river tomorrow?" he said. "I think it's going to rain."

"Rain! You think that looks like rain?" Jesse asked. "Obviously, you never were in the mountains for very long. I know that it can't rain. Do you know what infallibility is? I'll tell you: it's me predicting the weather.'' He glanced at the huge cumulonimbus clouds rolling toward them from the north in a mountainlike wall that shredded up the moonlight. "That's going to pass in five minutes. Tonight will be pure velvet. Stretch out on the pine needles and sleep.''

"I don't know," Hardesty said, wary of the clouds.

"Trust me."

Half an hour after they had fallen asleep, a crack of thunder popped them up from the ground where they had been lying and turned them over like flapjacks. Lightning struck in machine-gun reports, felling trees. The river, which had already been a whipping, dashing flume, was now so fast and white that it looked like a streak of lightning itself. And the rain that came down was not ordinary rain that falls in inoffensive drops. Hardesty and Jesse tried as best they could not to drown. "Follow me," Jesse said through a mouthful of water.

"What for?"

"I know where there's shelter. I saw it on the way in."

They swam uphill for a few hundred yards until they got to the entrance of a cave.

"I don't want to go in there," Hardesty proclaimed, although he knew he would go in.

"Why not? It's perfectly safe."

"I've always hated caves. I guess it's because I'm Italian."

"Come on. I've been in this cave before, I think. If I remember correctly, a hermit used to live here, and he left a couple of nice feather beds, supplies, furniture, and lamps."

"Sure," Hardesty said, as darkness swallowed them up. "Why do we have to go in so far?"

"To get to the hermit's place."

"What about bats?"

"There aren't any bats west of the Platte."

"That's not true. I've seen bats in San Francisco."

"Or east of Fresno."

After twenty minutes of groping along dark paths in a hissing subworld of hidden streams and mocking echoes, they came to what they sensed was a great chamber, for the sounds of their footsteps fled away from them as if into the open air. They felt vast space above and to the sides, and no matter which way they walked they found no walls but only level floor of rock and earth. They crossed small well-behaved streams as warm as bathwater and saw in them glowing chains of phosphorescent creatures.

How strange it was to see these things that made their own light, blinking by the hundreds of thousands in busy silent codes. They seemed like an army of dedicated workers absorbed in preparations for an unspecified journey. Batteries of little lights that racked up billions upon billions of permutations and combinations seemed to be driving unhindered toward some mysterious goal.

For hours, or perhaps days, Hardesty and his guide wandered on the plain of lighted streams. Jesse completely forgot about the hermit's place. All they cared for was the color, the endless map of calculating rivulets, and the routes of tranquillity and silence that they followed into pitch-black emptiness. Like musical tones, the streams mixed and separated. Hardesty clutched the small pack in which he carried the salver. At one point, they stood in the middle of a glowing plain so vast that they wondered if, in fact, they were still alive.

But eventually they had to think about returning to the surface. Hardesty suggested that they walk against the flow of the largest stream. That way, they would at least be going up. Soon the other streams in the luminescent net began to drop away, the one they followed grew larger, the phosphorescence gradually disappeared, and they found themselves in a huge chamber at a distant end of which flashes of lightning were visible through an opening.

"This is perfect," Jesse said. "A nice soft floor, dry, and the exit is right over there. Let's go to sleep."

"Don't you think," Hardesty asked, "that we should light a match, to see what's in here?"

"What could be in here? There's nothing in here."

"I don't want to go to sleep without knowing what's around me."

"That's stupid," Jesse yelled. "Hey! Whatever's in here, to

hell with you! Go to hell! Kill us if you like! Arrragghh!" For a small man, he had a miraculous voice. The challenges made Hardesty's ears ring.

"Even so," Hardesty said, searching in his pack for a box of matches, "I want to take a look."

He struck a match. At first the white-and-blue spark blinded them, but then the golden flame strengthened, and they looked up.

"I see," Hardesty said quietly.

In lines as neat and well ordered as the rows of cardinals seated at an ecumenical council, were a hundred or more surprised, temporarily blinded, twelve-foot-high grizzly bears. Not knowing what to think of the two strangers who had come into their midst, they turned to each other for advice, pawed the air, and rotated their heads in confusion.

Hoping to keep away the bears, Hardesty lit as many matches as he could hold in his palpitating fingers. The augmented light enabled him to see the bats. The bats, not surprisingly, numbered in the hundreds of thousands, or in the millions. They clung to the roof of the cave in a solid mass several bats deep; they were the size of the broken umbrellas that one sees stuffed in trash cans on a windy day; and their ears and joints were hideously purple and pink. They began to move in a growing chain reaction which prompted the bears to roar, showing white teeth as sharp as a splintered hayrack.

When the matches were exhausted, the bears converged and the bats began to fly. Smothered in brown fur and silky wings, Hardesty and Jesse realized that they were not being attacked, but, rather, that they had started a panic. A torrent of bats and bears burst from the cave, like boiling mud spit from a volcano. Hardesty and Jesse were thrown out the entrance onto a pile of rocks illuminated by bolts and sheets of stroboscopic lightning.

After the animals were out, Jesse suggested that they go back into the cave to sleep.

"I suppose you don't think they'll come back, do you?"

"I would say the chances of that are only about fifty-fifty."

"You do what you want. I'm going to sleep right here on this sharp rock."

The next morning, Hardesty awakened to see Jesse trying to make a fire by rubbing two pinecones together. When that failed, he tried to get a spark by hitting a rock with a stick. Finally, Hardesty found some more matches, and they were able to build a fire that didn't burn down the forest only because everything was so wet. They still had to cross the river.

"We should walk downriver to try to find a bridge," Hardesty suggested. "Although the chances of the river getting narrower upstream are obviously greater, the altitude's going to increase, which probably means less settlement, whereas, downriver, there will likely be highways, easier terrain on the banks, and maybe a stretch that's calm enough for us to swim or shallow enough to wade."

"That shows what you know," Jesse answered with considerable indignation, since he was the professional guide, and they were in his mountains. "There isn't a bridge that we can use for two hundred miles up or down this river. If you walk against the flow you'll find yourself in a hell of rotten rock and mossy cliffs. To the south, it gets wider and stronger as tributaries join in. You'd have to go to Utah before you'd find a place still enough to wade."

"Then what do you propose?"

"Doing what I always do, what I've done a hundred times in situations like this, what anyone who really knows the mountains would do almost automatically."

"What?"

"Build a catapult."

"To throw us across?" Hardesty asked.

"That's right."

"It's a quarter of a mile wide!"

"So?"

"Let's say we could make a catapult that would do the job. All right. It throws us across. What do you think's going to happen then? I don't know what trajectory you plan, but we could be falling from very high. We'd be killed instantly."

"No we wouldn't," said Jesse.

"Why not?"

"You see how closely the trees are spaced on the opposite bank?"

270

All we have to do is ride on shock pancakes, with extended reticular netting to catch in the trees."

"Shock pancakes."

"I'll show you." Jesse then set immediately to building the catapult, the shock pancakes, reticular netting, lean-to's, and access paths. Although Hardesty didn't believe for a minute that anything would work, he was carried away by Jesse's confidence, his surety in constructing the various travesties, and the splendid, classical, intriguing idea of a machine that would enable them to fly.

For two weeks they labored without sleep, eating little except the notebook-sized pieces of jerked beef, tea, and the trout that they pulled from the river. At first, Jesse insisted on cooking the trout with body heat during the night (according to him, an old Indian method). "There are better ways," said Hardesty, who then showed his guide how to plank fish.

At the center of a new clearing, their machine rested on a foundation of earth, rock, and piles. They had felled many trees and stripped miles of vines with which to build a two-story frame supporting a one-hundred-foot tree that pivoted on a huge beam. A basket containing several tons of rock held the shorter end down until the long tree was winched close to the ground and fixed there as taut as a crossbow. Shock pancakes and reticulated nets were attached to the catapult head. They looked like wicker-weave lily pads ten feet thick and forty feet in diameter. Hardesty and Jesse were to be strapped onto them with guy wires of orange and black mountain-climbing rope. To protect themselves further, they made big balloonlike suits of soft underbark that they wrapped around themselves over alternating layers of moss and puffballs. These "cushions," as Jesse called them, were so big and unwieldy that they had to be kept on top of the shock pancakes, or Jesse and Hardesty would never have been able to climb on.

All in all, Hardesty was skeptical, and refused to commit himself to launch. But in the end he was so tired and hungry that, rather than walk to Utah, he decided to take his chances in a moss-and-puffball suit on a shock pancake thrown into the air by a giant catapult. Besides, the thing was insanely alluring.

At the appointed hour, they climbed the launching pad, put on their suits, and tied themselves in. Jesse had in hand a lanyard that would yank a wooden cotter pin from the trigger mechanism, and send them flying. "You see that clump of green over there?" he asked, indicating a soft-looking bed of young pine. "That's where we'll land. Our descent through the air will be slowed by the aerodynamically stable design of the nets and pancakes. The nets will grapple the trees, and the pancakes will take the force out of any direct impact. Needless to say, these suits are the ultimate protection.

"If you're frightened, don't be. I'm an engineer, and I've got this figured to the last decimal point. Are you ready?"

"Hold it just a second," said Hardesty. "I've got to adjust this group of puffballs here. Okay. I'm ready now. Mind you, I think you're a lunatic, and I don't know why I trust . . . t . . . ."

Jesse yanked the lanyard, and they were thrown with tremendous force, not upward into the air, but directly into the river, about fifty feet from shore.

They hit the water like an artillery shell, throwing a geyser of white foam a hundred feet high, and they, the pancakes, and the nets were quickly submerged deep in the rapids. Luckily for them, the whole package was righted in the neutral buoyancy, and when they surfaced they found themselves floating head-up. Racing downstream, tied into their suits and onto the pancakes, and unable to move, they were conscious only because the freezing water had revived them after the first shock.

Hardesty started to struggle out of his suit.

"Don't!" Jesse screamed. "You'll drown. At least this is sort of a boat."

"Go to hell!"

"Seriously!"

"Seriously?" Hardesty was frozen with accumulated anger, annoyance, disbelief, and disgust. "Seriously?"

"Take my advice or you'll be in for trouble."

"You don't think that riding at forty miles an hour down ice-cold rapids, on shock pancakes, in puffball suits, is trouble? You know what you are? I'll tell you. You're an incompetent. You don't do anything right."

"I can't help it if I was born short," Jesse screamed back over the roar of the waters. "Tall people aren't so great just because they're a few feet higher."

Hardesty exploded. "It has nothing to do with short or tall!" Then he realized that they were about to float under a bridge that could not have been more than a mile or two from the catapult. Little girls in rhubarb-colored glasses peered over the railings, fascinated by the strange boat that was passing below. "What do you call that?" Hardesty asked.

"That's a toll bridge. I don't know about you, but I don't throw good money after bad."

Too exhausted to continue shouting over the sounds of the rapids, Hardesty slumped in his puffball suit, staring with tired eyes at scenery that rushed by as if seen from a railroad train. Just as he was thinking that the situation wasn't so bad, because in a day or two they might hit calm water and be able to swim to the east bank, he saw that the river up ahead disappeared completely. The water just stopped, and a shocking picture of empty air and faraway clouds continued in its place.

"Ryerson Falls," said Jesse. "Three-quarters of a mile high. I never went over them in a puffball suit."

Hardesty was torn between wanting to strangle Jesse, and trying to gather his thoughts before death so that upon quitting the earth he could cry out something beautiful and true, and not die, as had his father, with an amused smile.

He was able to find the intensity and beauty that he wanted, in the plunge itself. Physical forces in a complicated coalition of gravity, acceleration, and temperature were powerful and intense enough to satisfy him. It made sense. Nothing was as comforting as the enduring purity of elemental forces, and returning to them could not mean defeat. But he never thought that he would die in a bark suit, strapped to a shock pancake, next to an incompetent midget. They went over a dizzying edge, and found themselves in the empty air. As they fell, they sometimes hit the water that was falling next to them and were tipped one way or another. The farther down Hardesty went, the greater his hope that, having come as far as he had, he would survive. In the last few feet, although he

273

was going very fast, his hopes skyrocketed because the water was so close.

The bottom of the falls was a blizzard of foam and bubbles in water so frothed and agitated that it was possible to breathe air a hundred feet below the surface. Their buoyant contraption was eventually hurled upward, and they popped up in the middle of the stream half a mile from the falls, greatly startling two fishermen— who weren't sure what they had seen, but knew that it was as big as a car, and seemed to be driven by two backward-facing humanoid figures in strange uniforms.

They landed in a place that was full of geysers, mud holes, and pits of boiling sulfur. Without even looking at Jesse, Hardesty got out of his puffball suit, slung his pack over his shoulder, and set out toward the east.

"It's not a good idea to go in that direction," he heard Jesse calling out from behind. "You'd do best to follow me. You have to have years of experience to walk on these crusts. Otherwise, you can go right through. It's more dangerous than walking on a minefield, and you've got no training. Look at all these sink ho—" That was the last of Jesse Honey.

After six months on a sheep ranch in Colorado, Hardesty had earned enough and been in one place for a long enough time to set out east again. The owners of the ranch, a young couple whose names were Henry and Agnes, had needed him to help bring the sheep down from high pasture, to take in the hay, and to do whatever else had to be done before the snows. But when, in November, winter came in tentative fashion, laying down snowfields that were swept away by a weakening sun, they needed him no longer. Anyway, Agnes was far too pretty for the sanity and dignity of a hired man without a wife of his own. So they took him in their ancient wooden station wagon to a railhead somewhere at the foot of the Sangre de Cristo range, from where he rode in a single diesel-powered freight and mail car, sitting on the plank floor next to the conductor, to a larger town through which passed the last of the transcontinental trains.

"In five hours," the young conductor said, "the *Polaris* will speed through here faster than a burning rabbit. If you want the stationmaster to flag it down for you, you'll have to tell him in plenty of time, because he has to climb to the top of the water tower with his lantern to do it."

Hardesty bought a new pair of pants in the town store. His jeans were so soaked with lanolin that he used them to make a fire by the side of the tracks, where he waited for the *Polaris* as it grew dark. He was used to sitting very still at the higher altitudes where Henry and Agnes kept their sheep, and he knew how to out-think the cold—with the help of a massive shearling coat that had been given to him as part of his pay. The trance he used to defy temperature robbed some senses to pay others. He felt nothing, but he could see and hear everything. And because of that he was able to detect the *Polaris* long before the stationmaster. Smothered in distance and the hills, its blinding headlight made a faintly shifting glow in the mountains far away, and its barely audible, attenuated sounds came drifting through the night air to unsettle the dogs and to alert Hardesty, who got the stationmaster to climb the water tower and light his lantern.

The swinging red lantern eye charmed from the mountains a dancing white blaze that ran across the plain, slewing its agile beam on every curve to trim the young winter wheat and catch the animals of the field by riveting in place their translucent green eyes. As it closed without losing speed, the stationmaster yelled down from the tower, "Don't be disappointed if he doesn't stop. Sometimes they just don't see my lantern. They go so damn fast, this is such a little town, and when they're on the eastern run they pass through here right after dinner. I guess it makes them a little sleepy." But he kept waving his lantern from the top of the tower, swaying his entire body, even when the train was at the outskirts of the village.

"They saw it!" the stationmaster yelled down. "Start runnin' that way. The last car will be a mile down the track before it stops." Hardesty ran alongside the squealing, decelerating train. The yellow lamps of the dining cars made the snow in front of him the color of an oilcloth slicker. Glancing up, he could see people at dinner, some lifting bottles of wine, some pressing their faces against the windows in vain efforts to see why they were stopping, some with cloth napkins held to their lips. The last car passed him very slowly. Streamlined into a teardrop, it had above the lantern on its rounded end a lighted glass nameplate that read *"Polaris,"* as if it were the title of a film on a movie marquee.

A porter pulled him in through a bullet-shaped door, and hit the go signal. By the time the door was closed, the train was clacking down the track, and had restored the smooth heartbeat of the plains.

"Where you goin'?" asked the porter.

"New York."

"Most people that get on in the middle of nowhere don't go to New York. Maybe Kansas City, and that's a big thing for them, but New York? Uh-uh. You got enough money?"

"What's the fare?"

"I can't tell from this place. It's not on my card. I'll send the conductor, and he'll calculate it. Meanwhile, you can't ride in the club car, so come with me, and wait in the vestibule."

As they walked through the club car, an old man in black stopped the porter. "Kindly leave him here, Ramsey. We'll take care of him."

"Mr. Cozad?" the porter asked, in surprise.

"We need a fourth for our game." The old man spoke in a voice colored by three-quarters of a century in west Texas. "Have a seat, young man," he said to Hardesty, pointing out the empty fourth seat at his table.

The leather was comfortable and soft. Still throbbing and red from his run in the cold, Hardesty loosened the sheepskin coat, then decided to take it off entirely, and put it and his pack near the window.

The club car was a purple and black canister dotted with incandescent lamps in red shades. The silver-haired old men who played cards were in dark suits: their hands moved about as if disconnected, and their faces were like white masks floating above an unlighted stage. The light seemed to be fueled by the rhythm of the rails, its frequency determined by the ticking of the track joints. The cards themselves glowed mysteriously, like phosphorescent bones, and the faces of the kings, queens, and jacks smiled like Cheshire cats.

"Like a gin and tonic?" asked Cozad.

"No, thank you," Hardesty replied. "I don't drink."

"Something else then?"

"Tea."

Cozad ordered tea, which was brought to Hardesty in a century-old railroad pot that was as silver as a leaping bass. "You do play cards?"

"I don't," Hardesty said. "Not as a matter of religion, but because I just don't."

They were astounded that there could be such a thing as a plains cowboy, riding in their club car, who did not play cards.

"Young man," Cozad said, "I never met anyone above the age of five who couldn't play poker. You're not trying to make it easier on yourself, are you?"

"No, sir," Hardesty said. "I never played enough to remember the rules."

"But you did play."

Hardesty shrugged his shoulders. "Mainly fish: that is to say the game of fish. I'm not describing my opponents."

"There's a game called fish?"

"Yes."

"Never heard of it. What about seven-card stud?"

Warmed and incited by the tea, Hardesty asserted, "I think I played that a little. Anyway, I could always learn, couldn't I." He smiled.

Cozad tapped the green leather table as he spoke. "I don't think you're a sharper. But if you are, you're in the right place, because we—me and Lawson here, and George—have a reputation that frightens most people away from us. What we count on is some young ram with a lot of his father's money, who thinks he can beat us. This train has proved empty of rams. You aren't one. I can tell just by lookin'. But we don't like to play without a new face. That's our invitation."

"I have only two hundred and sixty dollars," Hardesty said, "and I've got to pay my fare."

"We could put the calf in the ring, Coe," Lawson said.

"What's that?" Hardesty asked. "It doesn't sound so good to me."

"What that is, is excellent for you. We all chip in even and set you up with a stake so you can play. If you lose, you owe us nothing, and you yourself lose nothing. If you win, you pay us back and keep the rest. It's how we teach our sons to play."

After ten minutes of drill in five-card high-low draw, they bankrolled him with $10,000. Being a Marratta, he didn't bat an eyelash at that kind of money, and they were momentarily suspicious. But they knew every decent player in the country, and would have been grateful (had he been able to beat them) to have found a new one. Word would have flashed from one end of the continent to another that a young power was on the rise.

"Okay," said Cozad. "Whatever is, is, and whatever is not, is not. It's started to snow out there. Turn up the stove. This game ends at mile marker five on the west side of St. Louis: not before, not after. The Denver-St. Louis game traditionally has a limit of ninety thousand dollars. Food and beverage on the dealer. Draw for deal."

People thought that gamblers were no good because they didn't work. But anyone who thought this had obviously never stayed up all night between Denver and St. Louis staying sharp on the cards. It was sore comfort. The forward hurtling of a train through blinding snow and arctic winds was hypnosis in itself, and the warm club car, as quiet as a library, did not encourage taking risks. The snow-covered country outside was a rough place where it was possible to die just from the wind, and animals there were lowing just as if there had never been any men on earth. If a switchman someplace in Nebraska were to have overslept, the train might easily have flown off a fifty-foot bank. People didn't like gamblers, because gamblers reminded them that they were gamblers, too. So they invented the libel that gambling isn't work. It is work. It's worse than work. It's like working in a coal mine. Hardesty quickly found this out.

His throat grew sore and his muscles started to ache. His head felt as if it had been bolted to his spine by a Visigoth mechanic. But all the time that he played cards on a green leather table as the *Polaris* shot across short-grass country in the long white night, he knew that he was doing what he was supposed to be doing. It was not just that Cozad, with his patrician's beard and gentle eyes, was remarkably like his father. Nor was it that he was winning, and he was. It was, instead, that he had given himself to fortune entirely. And it had much to do with the hard beauty of the prairie outside. He couldn't see much more than the surprised coils of snow dashing against the windows like panicked sagebrush, and he sweated, because the old men (who were cold despite their angora vests) wanted the heat on as high as it could go.

He put his cards down on the table, or took them up, with graceful exaggerated motions, because the tea and the sound of the rails had gotten to him. But he was winning. He never slipped below six thousand. Then he began to build over that, steadily, without fail, in complete blind confidence.

"Which is higher, four of a kind or a flush?" he might ask, much embarrassed that the rules hadn't stuck with him. For several hours, the old men lost a lot because they thought that he knew how to bluff. But he never bluffed once, he just won—if not the high hand, then the low hand. Once, when one of the old men had a flush with the queen as top card, Hardesty had a royal flush. If one of the old men had a hand of irredeemable garbage, Hardesty would throw out worse garbage, sometimes only by a point, or not even that if it were a tie and the issue was decided by who had put out first.

"Things like this happen," said Cozad the next morning as they passed mile marker five just west of St. Louis, and the game ended. Hardesty tried to give back his winnings. They wouldn't let him.

They got off in St. Louis. "Go to the bank in the station and get a check for that sum made out to you," Cozad instructed. "People have been killed for a lot less. And another thing: it was just luck. An armadillo can play better cards than you. Be grateful."

Hardesty was saddened when Cozad left, because Cozad looked like his father, and he would never see either one of them again. He went to a bank near the station to get his check, came back, bought himself a compartment on the train, and tipped the porters the way gambling winners were supposed to.

He took a long shower, shaved, and went to bed. Winter air and daylight came in the partially open window until the compartment was blinding white and freezing cold. Hardesty peered from his warm bed at the bank check that was sticking out of his shirt pocket. It was drawn on the Harvesters and Planters Bank of St. Louis, and it was for $70,000, even. He had a few thousand in cash in the other pocket.

The ground was covered with snow outside of St. Louis and on into Illinois. He had asked the porter to awaken him only in New York. The sleep that he wanted was perhaps not deserved, but it was well paid for. Long before they reached Chicago, he was dreaming of the darkened club car, the glowing cards, and the blood-red lamps.

Early one morning in the beginning of the second winter that she had spent without Virginia, Mrs. Gamely arose and peered out the attic window. She held Jack the rooster in her arms as if he were a fat white cat. After Virginia left, she had spoiled him silly, feeding him corn until he could hardly walk, and talking to him for hours on end as if he could understand her inimitable polysyllabic Latinates and her short, strong, Anglo-Saxon phrases as fresh as new hay and as powerful as a bowman's arm. He had at least one quality which humans, especially students, might well have envied: no matter how many hours she talked, he would stare directly at her, transfixed. If there were a pause in her exposition, he would strut for a pace or two until she started up again, and then freeze in place with a look of rapture until the next silence allowed him to shift his foot or cluck to clear his throat. No chicken in her remembrance (and she could remember thousands of chickens individually) had ever had such an extraordinary attention span. Jack earned his keep. He was clever. He looked like a panorama of snow-covered hills behind which a blazing sun was just about to set (the effect of his red coxcomb). He was courteous, forbearing, bright, and sincere. And, had he been able to understand English, he would have learned a great deal. Mrs. Gamely had secrets that she had never shared even with Virginia, because she knew that all secrets worth knowing come clear in good time.

After five days, the snow finally stopped a foot short of the eaves. When Mrs. Gamely looked west she saw the village standing firm in a sea of white, its chimneys smoking busily with the breakfast fires, the inhabitants barely visible as they stood upon their roofs to survey the arctic lake. It was said that the second winter was going to be harder than the first. Predictions such as this had been nurtured into gigantism by a summer so hot that the lake water was scalding and chickens laid soft-boiled eggs. That August, houses, trees, and sometimes whole forests had burst into flame as if the sun had been beaming at them through Priestley's glass. "So the pendulum will swing," said Mrs. Gamely to Jack, as they watched the wind whipping at the snow. "And so it has swung. Forever a balance. Nature hangs on stubbornly to rhetoric and ethics, even if human populations have long abandoned them, and its grammar is strict and idiosyncratic. Lookit there, Jack. The lake has become rolling hills of snow. God is treating us to fire and ice. He must be agitated. He must have something in mind."

A sharp knock on the front door started her into a violent hiccup. She put her hand to her chest and said, "Daythril Moobcot tunneled." Racing through the cottage as fast as she could, she wondered why they had come through so early, and hoped that it was not because of any bad news. When she opened the door, there was Daythril Moobcot, standing in an ice-blue tunnel that went all the way to the village. "Daythril! When did you start this tunnel?"

"Two days ago, Mrs. Gamely."

"Why? I have plenty of provisions. You know it's unwise to tunnel in a blizzard. You're old enough to remember when Hagis Purgin and Ranulph Vonk were buried in their own tunnel and weren't found until spring. Always wait to see how much snow there'll be on top."

"I know that, Mrs. Gamely. But everyone's moving around because we heard over the telegraph that the blizzard caught the *Polaris* somewhere within the county lines. There are two hundred people on it. If they're still alive, we'll be bringing them to the village. Can you take in five or six until the plough train gets through?"

"Naturally I can. They won't be too comfortable, but so what, they'll be alive. How are they going to get from the railroad to the village? The shortest distance it could possibly be is fifteen miles. Won't it be the death of all those city people in their city clothes to come that distance in deep snow at forty-five below?"

"No, ma'am," said Daythril Moobcot, proudly. "We've been planning for two days. Fifty men left an hour ago. They're pulling twenty-five sleds loaded with food, warm clothing, and skis that we scrounged up or made. When they get to the railroad line, two scouts will be waiting, having reconnoitered the whole length of track. We sent the two fastest skiers in the village. One of them will have found the train, and will lead the others to it. They'll bring everyone back, in the dark. It'll take a long time, since most of them probably don't know how to ski."

"I'll set out the bedding," Mrs. Gamely said. "And I'd better start baking right away. They'll need some hot breads and a boiling stew, especially if they've had nothing to eat for a few days. Will they know what has happened to them, or where they are?"

"I doubt it."

"No matter. The ones with good souls will find out, and those who don't know, don't need to know." She closed the door and began to rush about, assembling the best of her provisions, lighting her bee oven, and whipping up an ambrosial batter.

During the five days of blizzard the trainmen and passengers of the *Polaris* had come to the end of their carefully rationed food and burned all the coal that had been in the hopper car. Now, huddled together in two sleeping coaches, they were wrapped in blankets, curtains, and rugs, and they faced small fires in improvised wood stoves fueled by ripped-up paneling and sacrificed baggage. The engineer had nearly frozen to death finding the telegraph line, only to discover that it was dead. Half a dozen men with pistols fitted to improvised stocks sat in the bright sunlight on top of the train, just about even with the snow, waiting for arctic hares and birds. As a result of their labor, three quail and a rabbit were boiling at length in a caldron down below. The idea was to cook the flesh out of existence, so that the watery soup could then be justly divided (infants were well fed from a special reserve of food that would remain until the last adult was unable to feed them).

Cold and hunger in concert had quickly brought forth the essential qualities of those upon whom they were visited. Two men had already been lost to their impatience after they had foolishly set out in the snow and frozen to death, unseen, in drifts only a hundred feet from the train. A woman had surrendered to madness (or perhaps had been mad to start), quite a few were deathly ill, and one man was dead from gunshot wounds he suffered while trying to steal food from the common store. Those were the casualties. The trainmen, however, faced their responsibilities selflessly. And others were equally heroic in caring for the sick, giving up rations and blankets, and working to counter the influence of people who were easily disheartened.

After the snow stopped, Hardesty spent most of his time on top of the train, scanning the sky and drifts for game. Neither he nor the other hunters talked. They were too far apart, they didn't want to scare off their quarry, and it was too cold for conversation anyway. They wondered to themselves how long it would stay so frigid that the plough train would not be able to move. The nearest town on the map was a hundred miles distant, and they knew that it was too cold for machines to fly, since all forms of lubrication had become stickier than taffy.

They sat bundled in parkas and blankets, watching their breath crystallize in front of them and remembering the five-day blizzard, when fine snow blown into perfect equilibrium by balanced and opposing winds had seemed to hesitate in midair and freeze the passage of time. They watched the sun traverse a subdued winter arc, and, occasionally, thinking that they had seen a rabbit, they fired their pistols into the snow.

In this area it sometimes remained fifty below or less for weeks at a time. They knew that even if every single one of their remaining bullets had found its mark in a fat hare, there would not have been food sufficient for a day. Most distressing was that the fittings and freight would be burned up by the next morning, and there sim-

283

ply was not enough bedding or winter clothing to keep fifty people from freezing to death, much less two hundred. Even were someone somewhere to find a piece of functional, unburied, unblocked equipment that could travel over snow, would he know to go to them? Would they be an important priority, and could the many miles between the nearest settlement and the stranded train be covered in time? It seemed to those who could reason that everyone there was soon to die.

Down below in the disheveled sleeping coaches, they didn't know how fast the train was being gutted, or how terribly cold it was outside, or that drifts forty feet high were all that anyone on the roof of the train could see. Still, they took comfort from their number. Two hundred people, together, were safe, they thought. But Hardesty knew that this was a mistake, for his father had told him of the thirty thousand Turkish soldiers on the Russian frontier, near Ararat, who had been surprised by an early mountain winter and had later been found, grouped together, frozen to death. Cold, he knew, had never been impressed by numbers.

He and the others stared at the blinding drifts, imagining at times that they were on a polar sea. Their hands and feet were long numbed, and had ceased to tingle. It was hard to believe that such freezing white light came from what they had once known as the sun. When this sun was most of the way through its short winter arc, and was so flat, cool, and tame that it looked like a metal disc trapped for show on the face of a grandfather clock, the men on the roof of the train prepared for the worst. Soon it would be dark, and the cold unbearable. Soon the fires would stutter and go out, sending up a last gray column of cooling smoke. The sun, their only hope, was quickly heading downward. They stared in its direction, trying to harvest the last of its light and warmth, but it was a cold and unfamiliar thing, and the hiss of the wind seemed like its dying exhalations.

Hypnotized and blinded, utterly still, they did not immediately see the miracle that made its way in from the west. Miles away, a line of strong winter-bred farmers moved in military formation, kicking and gliding on their long skis, dipping down into the depressions in the snow and taking them at speed to get momentum for the trip up. They came as steadily as a herd of reindeer or gazelles. Fifty men pulled twenty-five sleds. Stretched out in a wide phalanx with a sled between each pair, they looked like hills and mountains on the move, or a tide of trees. Breathing intently, they swept over the snow, heading for the stranded train—which the eastern scout had seen from a hill five miles to the northwest. He had then skied down to meet the others, who had set off on a ten-mile race with the sun at their backs.

When the train appeared to them, it seemed to be floating upon the drifts, swamped, and the thin lines of smoke rising from it seemed about to expire. In this strangely immobilized excursion craft were two hundred men, women, and children who needed to be taken to a safe place. Making for them with all their strength, the farmers thought that danger was in truth a lovely thing that had to do with air and clouds and sea.

As they closed, the men on the train began to hear their skis, their breathing, and the sound of the snow compressing as the column moved across it fifty abreast. They thought that it was the wind, risen to mark the sunset. Then they thought that it was an animal. When they finally could see through the glare, they could hardly believe their eyes. From the sheer white, from nothing, from a hundred miles of rolling drifts, an army of nearly silent skiers was closing upon them.

The men on the train cried out, but the sounds that came from their frozen throats were just gurgles and moans, so they began to fire their pistols in the air, one shot after another. Upon hearing this, the Coheeries men began to whoop and cheer as they raced along on their skis. In the cold and smoky passenger cars, whose windows were silver-gray with piled snow, everyone knew what was happening, and quite a few of them began to weep, laugh, and even pray. The cars erupted in commotion, and those who had imagined that they were lost climbed out the hatches to stand in the open air and greet their rescuers.

Who were these men in homespun and fur? There was no time to explain (they never would) if they were to get back to the settlement without too much traveling at night.

"The moon is full, and it will light up the countryside like a flare," one of the Coheeries men said to the train crew (who had never heard of Lake of the Coheeries). "But it's best to start off in the light, so that those who don't know how to ski can learn when it's warmer. We have skis for everyone, and we'll pull the sick and the children in sleds."

In an hour, everyone was fitted with skis, supplied with fur jackets and woolen anoraks, fed on dried fruit and chocolate, instructed, sledded, and eager to start out. They did not whistle across the drifts as their Coheeries rescuers had done, but, by evening, they were moving at a steady pace.

Three Coheeries men led in a vee, carrying torches for everyone to follow. The others pushed a flat track across forests and fields, migrating in starlight, following the three pitch-pine torches and their ragged orange flames. The moon came up as they were emerging from a huge stand of pine onto a flat ten-mile-wide whitened plateau. The landscape was glowing, but they kept the torches because they looked so lovely sparkling ahead, and by that time the pace had increased and everyone had grown used to chasing the three lights.

The city people, clad now in furs and wool, quickly grew accustomed to the melancholy brush of moonlight and the soft overwhelming light of the stars. They soon grew to love the cold air and the snow, and they quickly forgot why they were there. Their activity was self-justifying, far better than many things they had done before or would do in the future. They quarter-timed across the fields, with the aurora borealis faintly green and flashing off to their right.

Then, from atop a long rise, they saw the village sparkling like a group of colored candles. It was on the edge of the lake, which was crowned by the blue-and-green aurora now hanging in the sky in astounding silent ribbons. Smoke from Coheeries chimneys crept up in intertwining white garlands and tangled on the moon. Now skiers, countrymen, they raced in contentment, hissing down the slope, speeding toward the Christmas candle that danced before them by the frozen lake, and as they skied into the town they saw the people of the village standing on their roofs or in their bright windows.

When skis were stacked near the doorways, families reunited, and groups formed, they went inside to eat and rest. Having been without food for days, many were starry-eyed and entranced. They thought they were in a dream world. How pleasant it was. If they had frozen to death on the train, and this was death, then how lovely, and how much better than any life they had known, for it was something that had seemed to be flooded with light, and in it all emotions had an inexplicable buoyancy.

"No," they were told. "You're not dead. Far from it."

But they didn't know whether to believe these good people, and when they went inside they yearned to be out again under the stars, in the cold that seemed no longer capable of hurting them.

Hardesty and four others were escorted through the snow tunnel to Mrs. Gamely's. When he, a cuckoo-clock repairman from Milwaukee, a young Marine, and a married pair of Bengali tourists strained their eyes and peered into the firelit interior of Mrs. Gamely's cottage, they saw Mrs. Gamely standing by the stove, with Jack held in her arms in front of her. The way she looked (with her too-close-together eyes, and an expression of humility and mischief perfectly combined), she might have been a great snowy owl surprised in its nest. She stepped forward and bowed neatly to each of her guests—as shyly as a little girl in patent-leather shoes at her first dance in some echoing gymnasium. They reciprocated. They sensed something about Lake of the Coheeries, but didn't know what it was. So they were very cautious, and returned her bows as deferentially as explorers straining to emulate a custom of the bushmen. It occurred to Mrs. Gamely to seize upon this unusual willingness to oblige her, and she repeated the greetings. They followed suit. When she went down the line yet again, bowing gracefully each time, they had to respond in the same way. This went on for at least five minutes, until Mrs. Gamely (as bemused as she could be) noticed that one of her guests was missing.

Looking about, she saw a handsome young man sitting at the table, filling one of the new clay pipes. As he watched the bowing, he grew more and more delighted at Mrs. Gamely's sense of play. From that moment on, he understood her.

One might think that the sudden arrival of five unknown guests would prompt a flood of talk from an old woman who had been alone for more than a year, especially if she, like Mrs. Gamely, had a vocabulary of six hundred thousand words. But she had many hours each day in which to talk to Jack and to herself, and since she was the only one in the world who could understand exactly what she was saying without raping the dictionary as she spoke, she seldom unleashed her full range of words on passersby. Instead, she devoured their speech, milking them like cows for the secrets of their dialects and regional usages. She put five new words in her store from the cuckoo-clock repairman alone—escambulint, tintinex, walatonian, smerchoo, and fuck-head (all of which, save the last, were Milwaukee terms referring to the various parts of cuckoo clocks). The Bengalis were a gold mine. Their English, like waving silks and birdsong, so entranced Mrs. Gamely that she pushed them on and on until they nearly collapsed because they could hardly get anything to eat.

"What do you call that, in your country?" Mrs. Gamely would ask, pointing, for example, to a steaming loaf of Coheeries bread.

"Bread," answered the husband.

"Must be variants," Mrs. Gamely insisted.

"Well, yes," they chirped together, and the husband went on. "When a little fellow wants bread, he says, *'Ta mi balabap.'* "

"*Balabap?*"

"Yes. *Balabap.*"

"And what do you call a policeman who takes bribes?"

"A *jelby.*"

"And a broken weir upon which swans nest?"

"A *swatchit-hock.*"

So it went as she fed them milky-white Coheeries bread, venison stew, roasted Canadian bacon, and a tureen of mixed vegetables in venison broth. She apologized profusely for not having any salad. The worst thing about winter was that there was no salad, and try as they did the local people could not find a way to preserve it—by freezing or otherwise. For dessert, she had baked a batch of blueberry-walnut-chocolate cookies with cherry-brandy centers. But because there were six for dinner, she had used up all of her platters, and had nothing upon which to serve the cookies. Alert to the importance of such things to women of advancing age, Hardesty reached into his pack and pulled out the salver.

Either because it had been polished as it had moved around in the pack, or because it was somehow changing, it seemed more dazzling than it had ever been. When he held it out for them to see, they took in their breaths, for it caught the flamelight and the yellow glow of the kerosene lantern like a mythical shield, and its rays struck out in all directions, as busy and alive as the lightscape of a great city. What entranced them most was not the glimmering gold, but that here was a still thing which moved. It was molten, calculating, changing in front of their eyes.

"That is a beautiful plate," said the Bengali woman.

"Too beautiful just for cookies," Mrs. Gamely added. "I couldn't use a salver like that for serving cookies."

"Why not?" asked Hardesty. "It's not delicate. Hardly that. My brother threw it out of a seven-story window onto concrete and it wasn't even scratched. It's pure gold. It won't stain or tarnish. I wouldn't mind if you used it for serving up roast beef. Something like this, which is of the highest order, can do even the humblest tasks. That's true about words, isn't it, Mrs. Gamely? They serve peasants as well as kings."

He tossed it upon the table, where it rang for two minutes as it settled down like a spinning golden sovereign, and warmed everyone's face as if it were a coal fire.

Mrs. Gamely went to the oven and got out the cookies. As she placed them around the salver, Hardesty read and translated the virtues. When Mrs. Gamely began to lay the cookies across the plate, Hardesty read the inscription in the center.

"Does it really say that?" she asked. " 'For what can be imagined more beautiful than the sight of a perfectly just city rejoicing in justice alone'?"

"Yes," Hardesty answered.

"I see." She covered the inscription with a line of cookies, and did not mention it again.

That night, as she lay in her bed upstairs, thinking about her charges sprawled on mats and blankets in the main room the way

Virginia's friends had done in the past at their pillow parties, she wondered about things she had heard as a little girl, about certain beauties that she had once been promised would arise. And with tremendous excitement and fear, she thought that these promises might come true in her lifetime, after all. She had long given up on them for herself, and hoped only that Virginia or Martin would see them. She had once believed in miracles, shining cities, and a golden age. She had learned, however, soon enough, that such things were only illusions. But now she wasn't quite sure. A great massy wheel seemed once again to be turning. Or was it a vain and foolish misinterpretation of her past? Probably. But, no. No. The lake had frozen. And the start of the third millennium was drawing near. Perhaps it was not an illusion, for the lake had frozen early and as black as a mirror only one other time.

It was when she was a child, and the Penns had come from the city to bury Beverly Penn on their island. Tears came to her eyes as she thought of the cold night not long after the Penns had returned to New York, when she had been awakened by the pull of the stars, which hissed and crackled like an icy waterfall, and were dancing all over the sky, brighter than she had ever seen them. She was only four or five, and had to stand on tiptoe to see out the window. It was then, as she looked over the lake, that she had learned the true meaning of the word "arise."

The day that Hardesty arrived in New York was cold and dry. Nevertheless, tentative whirlwinds of snow sometimes swept the avenues, twisting about in gray light. The city had not yet been interred in its January shroud, and the fact that the streets were still bare gave December the air of fall, just as reluctant snowbanks can give the air of December even to May.

This was the first city he had ever seen that immediately spoke for itself, as if it had no people and were a system of empty canyons cutting across the desert in the west. The overwhelming mass of its architecture, in which time crossed and mixed, did not ask for attention shyly, like Paris or Copenhagen, but demanded it like a centurion barking orders. Great plumes of steam a hundred stories tall, river traffic that ran a race to silver bays, and countless thousands of intersecting streets that sometimes would break away from the grid and soar over the rivers on the flight path of a high bridge, were merely the external signs of something deeper that was straining hard to be.

Hardesty knew right off that an unseen force was breathing under all the gray, that the events and miracles of the city were simply the effect of this force as it turned in its sleep, that it saturated everything, and that it had sculpted the city before it had even opened its eyes. He felt it striving in everything he saw, and knew that the entire population, though prideful of its independence, was subject to a complete and intense orchestration the likes of which he had never imagined. They rushed about here and there, venting their passions—struggling, kicking, and shuddering like marionettes. Ten minutes after he left the station, he saw a taxi driver kill a peddler in an argument over who had the right of way on an empty street. He wanted no part of this city. It was too gray, cold, and dangerous. It was perhaps the grayest, coldest, most dangerous city in the world. He understood why young people came from all over to pit themselves against it. But he was too old for such things, and he had already been to war.

Furthermore, his intention was to look throughout Europe for a beautiful city that (momentarily, at least) might be entirely just. In such a city all forces would smoothly align, and all balances would be brought even. That would never occur in this ragged place of too much energy and too many loose ends that lashed about like taut cables which suddenly are parted. New York could never be fully at peace with itself; nor could any one vision defeat, compress, and control its crooked and varied time, for this would require the perfect and able recognition of signal beauties, and a gift of unforeseen grace. Never would New York know perfect justice, despite the greatness of its views and its well-plotted interweaving of the magnificent and the small.

For Hardesty, who was in poor spirits after a long and difficult train journey in which he had zigzagged over half of Pennsylvania and been shunted for hours into industrial towns where there were only liquor stores and snowmobile repair shops, New York was a difficult city, far too rich in the ugly, the absurd, the monstrous, the hideous, and the unbearable. Everything capable of being exaggerated or distorted, was. Normally acceptable customs and occurrences were changed into startling nightmares. The very life functions were transformed. Breathing, for example, was never taken for granted, since, half the time, thanks to the many chemical works and refineries, it was nearly impossible. Battalions of heinous voluptuaries corrupted eating into a sport of pigs. Sex was for sale as a commodity, like roasted peanuts or manganese. Even elimination, never the most regal thing, was dragged down to baser levels by snorting, grunting dilapidations who squatted mercilessly upon the sidewalk in full public view.

But then the wind changed, the light came out, and he was caught up in some sort of magic. For no apparent reason, he suddenly became king of the world, and was overflowing with the schemes and riches of mania. His heart was pumping so vigorously that he thought he was undergoing an attack. Though suddenly ecstatic, he retained enough presence of mind to try to determine why his emotions had flipped upside down. He thought it might have something to do with the city itself, since everyone he could see was either weeping at death's door or dancing with hat and cane. The city seemed to have no middle ground. Certainly the poor were poor and the rich were rich as nowhere else. But, here, wealthy women in sables and diamonds sifted through garbage cans, and paupers who slept above subway gratings strutted down the street declaiming furiously about monetary policy and the Federal Reserve. He saw great numbers of men who were women, and women who were men. And, in Madison Square Park, there were two lunatics in bedsheets, circling one another like fighting cocks, screaming that they had found a magic mirror.

Hardesty decided to deposit his check in a reputable bank and figure out later whether he would stay for a while in New York or immediately go to Italy on one of the many steamships the deep whistles of which he could hear as they started downriver and across the sea more casually than canoes on a millpond. In San Francisco, walking into a bank was like walking into a palace—which was the way it should have been. But in New York, banks were cathedrals, which was perhaps not the way it should have been. If a law had been passed to change each bank into a church and each second vice-president into a priest, New York would instantly have become the center of Christendom. Hardesty slapped down his gambling check on a waxed marble counter in the Tenth Street branch of the Hudson and Atlantic Trust.

The teller appraised it with a professional stare. "We're not taking these," he said. "We had a telex this morning instructing us to refuse any checks drawn on Harvesters and Planters in St. Louis. I imagine it's gone under. I suggest that you go to our main office on Wall Street. They might be able to clarify the order."

This complication moderated Hardesty's mania, and though he found himself on an even keel when he walked into the Hudson and Atlantic headquarters in the financial district, the only reaction appropriate for its interior was a gasp of wonder. A cream-colored marble floor stretched away like the wheat fields of Kansas. Messengers on bicycles carried documents and dispatches over it from one department to another. When a small child deliberately released a toy helium balloon, everyone watched it drift up to the ceiling, where it seemed as small as a grain of sand.

A bank officer who didn't like the way Hardesty was dressed told him, showing a newspaper to prove it, that the St. Louis bank had failed. "You have three choices," he said. "You can hang onto the check and become a creditor (or hope that someday they'll get back on their feet), you can sell it as an acceptance for about a cent and a half on the dollar, or you can tear it up."

Hardesty thought it best to rent a safe deposit box in which to store the discredited check. Perhaps in twenty years, like a locust, it would rise to fly. And, if he could lease a box wide enough, he would put the salver in it too—since he did not fancy carrying around many pounds of gold and silver in a city where, it was said, every tenth citizen was a thief.

Deep below the wheat-field floor were marble chambers and barred cages. Hardesty found himself in a little cell with an enormous metal box, in which he placed the salver and the check. He looked up. From all around came chants and tones, as if prayers were being said in the warrens of a Tibetan monastery. A score or more of middle-aged men in cells like his own were counting their coupons and their certificates in low voices imbued with the gravity of final reckoning. He leaned back in his chair, lit his pipe, and listened. The sounds of shuffling and counting were as tranquil as the lapping of a lake. The occasional shuddering metallic rattle of steel grates, and of locks set and unset, made long-lasting echoes, and the whir of combination wheels was like the purring of a cat. In the dimly lit cell, Hardesty watched his pipe smoke wind to the ceiling. He stayed there for several hours, thinking about what he had to do next.

In his pocket was a long letter in his own handwriting from Mrs. Gamely to Virginia. The letter itself was a puzzle, being beautifully yet utterly incomprehensible unless one were to have the humiliating experience of using a dictionary to understand one's own language. It read like a runic ode, but was dotted here and there with plain English gossip, quotations, recipes, and news about the condition of crops, lake, and various forms of animals identified by name and species (Grolier the Pig, Concord the Goose, etc.).

Mrs. Gamely had taken him aside and dictated it to him, making him promise to deliver it personally, because, as she said, "Coheeries mail is heteronomic and ludibund." The problem was that Virginia's mail, whether or not heteronomic and ludibund, did not get through, and her whereabouts were a mystery. But Mrs. Gamely had made Hardesty swear that he would seek her out before he left New York. Upon asking what he should do if he could not find her, Mrs. Gamely had replied, "Keep looking." Now, because the bank in St. Louis had failed, Hardesty no longer had as much time as he had thought he would have. He wondered how he would find Virginia Gamely, and he half regretted that he had agreed to do so.

But that is not to say that he was not pleased with the city, and with the prospect of searching through it.

Soon it was dark, and people were gathering for dinner or hot drinks in restaurants and cafés with slanted glass awnings that were covered with snow. But Hardesty passed by these places and did not come in from the cold until he came to the library. This was the deepest place in the city, for its hundred million isles were further subdivided into countless patterns, chapters, themes, words, and letters. The letters were merely lines derived from a series of coordinates, which the eye pieced together and united in a riverlike flow, as if all the bent and convoluted little sticks were the lights of a cityscape that was beautiful from afar. In fact, when Hardesty walked among the books that lined the high walls of the main reading room, he felt as if he were walking into a city. The plain of tables and readers flanked on four sides by tall rectangular bookcases was a parody of Central Park, especially since the reading lamps were as green as grass.

While scholars were returning to their nocturnal labors after meager dinners of bile and gravel, Hardesty began his researches. He was in his natural element, he knew what to do, and he moved fast because the walk in the cold had made him alert. First he went through every conceivable directory, looking for Virginia Gamely's name. He even went into the reception hall and called directory assistance to see if she had an unpublished number. Evidently, she didn't have a telephone—at least not in her own name. Hardesty called the police, who could not help, they said, because they were too busy chasing criminals and sleeping in patrol cars under bridges. Besides, why was it their business?

Having overturned all the easy stones, he started on the boulders. Since Mrs. Gamely hadn't the vaguest idea of where her daughter was, Hardesty decided to accomplish in the library what he had been unable to do at Mrs. Gamely's because she had been too busy to make associations. He would find out about Lake of the Coheeries, and, by discovering its characteristics, deduce enough about Virginia to help him track her down. First, the atlas. But Lake of the Coheeries was not in the index, and, in the place where he knew that he had been, the map showed a strangely empty patch of green with occasional relief and a nameless river or two. The detailed maps, the official surveys, and the historical gazetteers were similarly uninformative.

Wherever he turned, he came up with a blank. The name was unrecorded. After four and a half hours of puzzlement, he quit for the night just as the library was about to close. If there was nothing about Lake of the Coheeries in this great repository, there was likely to be nothing anywhere. While he was putting on his coat in the marble reception hall, he asked the library clicker—a man so old that he looked inside-out—if he knew of a cheap place to stay. "I have limited funds," Hardesty said, "and I'm looking for someplace that's simple, clean, and inexpensive. I don't need a bathroom in my room."

"Who has a bathroom in the room?" asked the old man, whose job was to press a clicker every time someone walked by. (It had been a long tradition at the library and could not be abandoned, and he didn't know how to do anything else.) "The bathroom's another room. It can't be in the same room unless it's right in the middle like a big box, and they don't got that."

"That's right," said Hardesty. "Good thinking. What I mean is that I don't need a private bathroom, connected to my room."

"How about sharing a room, sort of?" asked the old man.

"What do you mean, 'sort of'?"

"What I mean is that the Widow Endicott takes in boarders."

"More than one to a room?"

"Not exactly, but it's cheap. And it's clean. You look like a strong young man."

"What has that got to do with it?"

"The Widow Endicott has got certain appetites. She makes certain demands. Understand?"

"What's she like?" Hardesty asked.

"What's she like? Oh Lordy! What she is like! If only she'd been around when I was able."

"I might as well look at the place," Hardesty said. "Where is it?"

"Yeah. You might as well look at the place. You wouldn't want to disappoint a poor widow, would ya? Very kind of you. It's on Second Avenue, way downtown. I don't know what street crosses it, but it's near the old Coheeries Theater."

"The what theater?" Hardesty shouted.

"The Coheeries Theater. They don't call it that anymore, but I remember when they used to have stage plays there. Now they use it for wrestling, dance shows, and vaudeville."

"What do you know about the theater?"

"In general?"

"The Coheeries Theater."

"Just what I told you."

"Do you know why it was called that?"

"Let me see. Why was it called . . . I dunno. I never thought about it. Maybe it's a kind of clam or something, and when the curtain went up on the plays—Shakespeare—it was like a clamshell opening."

"Thanks," said Hardesty, and was off into the winter night to see what he could find out about the place from the place itself.

The marquee of the Coheeries Theater had written upon it the words "Lucha Libre," and all the stores for ten blocks around were boarded up, though diagonally across the avenue was the Widow Endicott's boardinghouse, the very sight of which made Hardesty's heart jump with fear and curiosity. Even if she turned out, in fact, to be a hag, the house itself was magnificent. Candles burned in the windows, the brass shone like gold, and the eaves and trim were kept up as if the place were a national monument.

The theater had seen much better days. Forty people sat in the front rows, eating shish kabab or hot pretzels and awaiting the wreck of vaudeville, which had been resurrected for those too poor to have a television set. After picking his way over pools of sticky litter and through drifts of spilled popcorn, Hardesty took a seat in the middle of the house. Just as he looked up, the lights dimmed and the curtain was raised. He could see that the once-elegant dome and walls were covered with murals and scrollwork. But it was too dark to make out details, and he contented himself with watching the show. For the lighting, though more than half a century old, cut out all the world except the velvety dream beyond the footlights. The darkness popped with remembered silver flashes, and the colored gels and beams were as fresh as the face of a young girl who has been out in the snow.

First came two comedians. Their jokes were in Yiddish though their audience was in Spanish; their toupees were of a material that resembled orange excelsior; and they went through their routines with closed eyes.

Then came a bicycle act during which a frightfully skinny Sicilian rode a bicycle around the stage for about five minutes. When

297

the booing became too much for him to bear, he screwed up his features in pain and determination, and tried to stand on his head on the seat. It had been enough for him just to peddle, for he was in truth not very good at riding a bicycle. But when he tried to stand on his head, he lost control of his vehicle, and he and it flew over the apron into an empty row of seats.

Next came a well-worn group called The Singing Cucumbers. How they had managed to stay out of the salad for three-quarters of a century was a mystery of considerable grandeur. In cucumber costumes, straw boaters, canes, spats, and pencil mustaches, they sang three songs—"The Mice Made a Break for Freedom," "Beethoven's Nephew," and "The Boer War Triangle."

Despite their incapacities, these touching, persistent, third-rate—seventh-rate—theatrical people strove to excel. They thought that they were artists: they said so on their tax forms and in bus stations in northeastern Delaware, and they almost had it right, for they were not artists, but art. They were in themselves like sad songs, or revealing portraits. Something about them was terribly moving. They never gave up. They never could see very clearly beyond their driven ambitions. And they had never figured out that their every move made them part of a sad tableau.

Last on the bill was a dancing act. Three odd young girls who called themselves The Spielers danced in wooden shoes and green homespun dresses. A card on a tripod identified them as Little Liza Jane, Dolly, and Bosca, the dark girl. They jumped and twirled in strange jigs, and seemed not to notice that they were onstage in a theater. They loved to dance. They danced with each other three at a time. They smiled. And in the end they gave three lovely and innocent bows.

The lights came up before the wrestling, giving Hardesty a chance to study the murals. A dozen scenes from Lake of the Coheeries were clearly depicted in shady old oils. Here was the lake in summer, spring, and fall, ice-covered in winter. Here was the village, under the stars, in the snow, or surrounded by somnolent crops. Here were iceboating, and a strange gazebo on the lake. Here were village girls, farmers, and a horse pulling a sled. But in the dome of the theater was the most unusual picture of them all. It showed an island in the lake, at night. Rising from it was a whitened column of stars, as if the Milky Way had dipped down in imitation of a rainbow.

What Hardesty next saw pushed him down in his seat and made him tremble. Engraved around the dome in letters that now were so dirty that they could hardly be seen, were the words, "For what can be imagined more beautiful than the sight of a perfectly just city rejoicing in justice alone?"

The wrestling was half over by the time Hardesty made his way out of the theater. Just before the exit was a plaque stating that the Coheeries Theater had been donated to the city by Isaac Penn. This was a lead, though undoubtedly blind, that he would have to follow. But he wanted to sleep, and the nearest place was the boardinghouse diagonally across the street.

The coincidence of inscriptions could not possibly have been more than just that. Certainly the perfectly just city would never arise on these unclean ruins, not in the lap of an industrial civilization known primarily for civilization in the breach, not in a noisy inhumane city fashioned in gray after the image of a machine, nor from amid the soot-covered spires, the ice-choked riverways, and the endless avenues of careless war-torn architecture. No. Everything he knew told him that it could never be so. It was merely a coincidence, and would not keep him from traveling on. Still, he was dazed.

And he was putty in the hands of the Widow Endicott.

She was a red-haired beauty, an Amazon, almost as big as the marble statue of Diana in the park at Winky's Hill. Ten husbands had died in her bed, so she started a boardinghouse for young men just in from the country. These she shuffled around among several rooms that adjoined her own, and among the baths, showers, and saunas in which she kept them ready at a moment's notice to pop in and copulate. She was perfect and insatiable. Each breast was a marvel. Her forest of red pubic hair was soft, fragrant, and deep. She was as white as ivory but glossed in red because of red hair and the rhythmic undercolor of her fine skin as the blood beat through it.

She liked that Hardesty was trim and strong, and she put him close by. From the way that she looked at him, he suspected that he would be making love to her soon. He went to his room, undressed, and got into bed. When he was half asleep, protesting in a borderless meditation the notion that New York might be anything but a crowded tool chest on a slag heap of materialism, the connecting doors to the widow's room flew open.

He walked carefully through a small passageway into her bedchamber, which was entirely white. Even the floor was white, and there were no windows, only a skylight. In a small fireplace a cherry basket of glowing coals rested on the bars of an iron grate, pulsing like a Pittsburgh open hearth. The Widow Endicott was redolent in her white bed in the light of the seething coals. She was undulating as she lay back, her hips propped up on a big pillow. Hardesty saw beneath the silky skin an outline of delicate ribs. She was an essay in red; her deep auburn hair, her lips just slightly apart, the tips of her breasts—as short, slight, and red as a scarlet brush stroke—and her red pubic hair gleaming like a Pacific forest. Though Hardesty wished that he were a painter, so that he might paint her, paint her is not what he did.

Hardesty's useless struggles at the library the evening before were well compensated twenty-four hours later, after he had spent most of the day recovering. Though there was not a single reference to Lake of the Coheeries, and the word Coheeries itself probably did not exist in any of the books in the library, entries for Isaac Penn filled several card drawers, and Hardesty soon found himself in the Penn archives, surrounded not only by books but by pamphlets, broadsides, photographs, letters, and manuscripts. A large number of letters and telegrams had been sent via Hudson or by hand. The Penns, a family associated with newspapers, whaling, and the arts (there was even a young collection on Jessica Penn—a Broadway actress of whom Hardesty had heard), maintained a summer house in a place that was never identified as anything but "L of C."

Enough material rested in the archives to absorb several scholars in long and productive careers, but Hardesty was drawn mainly to the photographs, of which there were thousands—all black and white—in the powerful, communicative style of the nineteenth century, when sensibilities born of painting contributed to photography what photography itself would soon help to obliterate.

These pictures were chronologically arranged in brass-hinged albums of varnished cherrywood. Each turning of a page revealed a photograph with a key in which the subjects were identified and the setting was explained. If one were to have judged the turn of the century solely by this record, one might have thought that it was a time devoted primarily to rowboats, toboggans, snow shoes, tennis racquets, oceangoing yachts, and outdoor furniture. The Penns loved to take pictures of themselves as they played sports, or sat in the summer sun looking over the sea. Although quite a few shots were of Isaac Penn at public functions or in the midst of his staff on *The Sun,* and some were of Beverly playing the piano, Jack doing an experiment with his chemistry set, or Jayga standing in an imperial pose, arms akimbo, in front of her stove, most were of the family together. They were gathered in the snow, picnicking in high meadows, racing horses, rowing in the August heat, or walking along the beach at the end of the day—sunburnt, healthy, listening to the slowly unfurling waves.

As the history of the Penns unfolded for Hardesty, welling up from the past with surprising vitality, he noticed two things especially. Two changes were unexplained among the many changes that were to be expected: after all, from his perspective in the future, Hardesty was not surprised that the infant Harry quickly grew until (in two hours) he was in command of a regiment; or by the staccato freezing and unfreezing of the lake; or when (from one wooden album to another) lovely little Willa became lean and, yet, voluptuous, in a way that reached out to Hardesty across a good part of the century. From his godlike perspective, he was able to gloss over minor inconsistencies and not worry about people who appeared and disappeared, or changes in posture, decor, and fashion. He was, after all, floating in a lake of a hundred eventful years.

But the archivists had done such a good job that when they faltered Hardesty wondered why. The inconsistencies which stayed with him were that Beverly seemed always to be in a stronger light than anyone else (some of the pictures betrayed an aura that not even the chroniclers had noticed—much less those in the scene), and that someone appeared for a short time in one of the cold and snowy years immediately preceding the Great War, and remained unidentified. He looked neither like the Penns, nor like a servant, nor like a member of the upper classes. He had a rough, solid, workingman's manner, and one could tell even from a photograph that he spoke English the way the Irish did, that he was strong, and that he was good with tools. His burly hands were not made for a pen or a piano. He might have been the foreman of *The Sun*'s mechanics, the keeper of their farms in Amagansett, or the captain of one of Isaac Penn's merchantmen—but he wasn't, because he was often dressed like a dandy, he always stood near Beverly, and, in one picture, he had put his arms around her with a tenderness that caused Hardesty to stare transfixed at the photograph for fifteen minutes. Hardesty felt that this man's affection, like Willa's coming into womanhood, was able almost to burn through the pages. It was far more than affection that moved him. It was love. And then Hardesty discovered the strangest series of images. A somber wedding, with Beverly—hardly able to stand—supported on the man's arm. A long string of photographs of an island in the lake, bare and trembling in winter, almost indistinguishable from the snow-covered ice.

In none of the photographs was the stranger identified. Underneath his silhouette in the key to each picture in which he appeared was simply a question mark. Who was he? The meticulous archivists did not know, and apologized for not being able to explain him. A note attached to the last binder said that the living members of the Penn family had refused to comment on their photographic history, or, for that matter, even to review the collection.

Hardesty studied the interloper's face. He liked it. He liked it very much, and he was moved by the half-unnamed couple who simply disappeared, and who, apparently, would be forgotten for all time.

But he did find what he was looking for, more or less. Here and there, perched on a haystack or ensconced in the upper scroll of a horse-drawn sled, were Gamelys—healthy yeomen, children, local people of the lake, who obviously knew the Penns and spent time with them. Though the Penns seemed to have left Lake of the Coheeries, disintegrated, and been frozen in place within their own dynastic archives, Hardesty decided to seek them out, in the hope that Virginia Gamely had done so, too.

As great as the city was in nearly all respects, it had one unaccountable and unforgivable failing. For the many many millions of people, there were only two major newspapers. True, one could buy ten or twelve pages of day-old news in any language of the world and in any alphabet, and hundreds of stations crowded the electronic spectrum, like the bands of a coral snake, but the population as a whole was regretfully polarized: one followed either *The Sun* or *The Ghost*.

There was a *Morning Ghost,* and an *Evening Ghost* (more correctly: *The New York Ghost,* Morning Edition; and *The New York Ghost,* Evening Edition), and there were *The New York Morning Whale,* and *The New York Evening Sun.* Their rivalry straddled both editions, dusk and dawn. Anyone native to the city knew this apposition as readily as night and day, light and dark, or fat and thin. But Hardesty did not. So when he came to a newsstand on an empty street corner, a lighthouse amid a sea of swirling blue snow, he was surprised to discover that *The Sun* was indeed still in the hands of the Penn family, and that Harry Penn—infant turned regimental commander—was its editor and publisher. He went down to Printing House Square at ten o'clock, assuming that at that hour a newspaper would be in the middle of a sprint for the deadline.

In fact, it was sprinting so hard that no one noticed Hardesty or would answer any of his questions. For two hours, he stayed in the middle of *The Sun*'s glassed-in courtyard, watching the snow brush against the transparent roof many stories above as hundreds of reporters, copy boys, messengers, worried editors, and inky printers crisscrossed around him heading him from one door to another or up and down the open stairs that led to each of the floors looking over the enclosed court. But then, at midnight, everything stopped except the presses—which began to rumble on the bottom floors, like the engines of a ship, as if they were not merely stamping out

303

impressions, but moving the building ahead in a turbulent and foggy sea. Hardesty went to the city room, on the third floor, where he stopped the first person he met. This was, in fact, Praeger de Pinto, the managing editor.

"Excuse me," Hardesty said. "I'm trying to find someone who came originally from the Lake of the Coheeries, where the Penns once had a summer house. It may have been foolish for me to have come here, but I have no other connections and no other way to locate her. I would like to ask Harry Penn if he knows where she is, or for suggestions about how to find her."

"Are you looking for Virginia Gamely?" Praeger asked.

"That's exactly who I'm looking for."

"She works here."

"Then I've found her."

"But she's not here now. We just put *The Whale* to bed, and she's on *The Sun*. She comes in at six in the morning."

"My name is Hardesty Marratta. I was on the *Polaris*. . . . I have a letter from her mother."

"I can give it to her."

"Her mother made me promise to do it myself."

Praeger introduced himself and invited Hardesty into his office on the floor above (to which they ascended via a cast-iron spiral staircase that pierced the ceiling) to talk about what Hardesty had seen in Lake of the Coheeries. Praeger had been interested in the place from the time that Virginia had first brought it up and then conspired with Jessica Penn not to mention it ever again. He was interested in Hardesty's descriptions, both for their content and because he recognized that, like Virginia, Hardesty had a gift for language. "I don't know what it is about Lake of the Coheeries," Praeger said, "or even if Lake of the Coheeries does, in fact, exist. But everyone who passes through it seems to acquire a way with words that I like very much. Maybe we'll have some seminars up there (if we can get to it), or bottle the water for our coolers."

They spoke for several hours, touching upon a dozen or more subjects and discovering that their views were remarkably similar. They were weary and relaxed; they both loved the strain of winter; they enjoyed one another's sharp conversation; and they got along extremely well, except for one thing. They disagreed about the nature of the city itself.

Hardesty was in no mood for toleration of its numerous and outstanding urban deformities, and would not forgive what he took to be the unnecessary roughness of its inhabitants and the rigid way that it was laid out, architected, built, fixed, and maintained. He hated it as if he were about to love it—unforgivingly, irrationally, sadly. Though they were beautiful and magnetic, the deep-throated whistles that shot through the snow and rattled the windows of *The Sun* made him uneasy, and the thought of the endless internal horizons incorporated into the streets, bends, alleys, and roosts made him extremely uncomfortable.

Praeger had seen this before. "You'll soon be forever in love with the things you now despise," he said.

"That's what you think," returned Hardesty. "I'm on my way to Europe. I'm not going to be here long enough to fall in love with anything at all."

"The anarchy will hold you."

"How could it? It's what I detest the most."

"You know that it isn't anarchy at all, and that, even if it is, it contains all the possibilities you seek. And you must know, as well, that the very fact the city survives and remains on its feet implies an equilibrium, which, in turn, implies the presence of a high and opposing force for each category of degradation."

"I don't see them. Do you?"

"Only rarely. But when I do, I can see that the balances are maintained. I can see traces of a perfect age, in the way that veins of the roughest ore can lead to gold."

"And what if the ugliness and the horror wear you down until you are unable to appreciate what you hope for, should it arrive."

"So much the better. I love the risk. I like it that—try as I might—the outcome is hardly up to me. The plans for the city were drawn on the same table as the plans for war. It promises nothing, and yet it can be inimitably generous. You should stay awhile and get some idea of how it works. Listen to the ship whistles. When you hear them, summer and winter, they become a song, a message. I always think that they're saying, 'Your time is a good time, and though I have to leave, you can stay. How lucky you are to be in the city just before it opens its eyes upon a golden age.' "

They parted uneasily, because Hardesty resented that Praeger had predicted a change in him, and Praeger resented having had to do it. What did Praeger care, anyway, about what Hardesty thought? But he promised to introduce Hardesty to Virginia the next day at four, just after *The Sun* was put to bed.

Hardesty walked five miles through a driving snowstorm to the Hotel Lenore, a tall tower in midtown that caught the snow against its high glass sides and sent it falling in bushels like whitewater dashing through a flume. The streets had been as empty as the prairie, and while they were white it had seemed as if the possibilities of which Praeger had spoken were indeed present in the hot and icy spaces in which the city's wars of equilibrium were waged.

The night manager gave Hardesty the highest room in the hotel. Because he had found Virginia, and could leave New York in a day or two, Hardesty felt that he could afford the astronomical price. He had left *The Sun* at one in the morning. Now it was so far in the middle of the night that the clocks had quit, and time seemed to have been obliterated by the raging storm.

When he arrived in his room on the 120th floor, he went to the window and peered into the skein of wind-snarled white ebbing and flowing against the glass. This was a frustrating, hard, unforgiving, unkind city, strong on suffering, punishment, and murderous weather. Its climate and population were a scythe that swept relentlessly until even the strong fell before it, and the weak in their great numbers vanished from the streets forever and died unremembered in the cold and dark. Standing on the 120th floor, he could see nothing—and he took that to be the signature of the city.

Nonetheless, Hardesty was cheered when he discovered that there was a sauna in the bathroom. Soon after he stepped in and closed the cedar door, the heat began to come up and a bank of sunlights blazed. After trudging across the arctic boweries, he was delighted to find himself in a dry desert, but he was so cold that it took him forty-five minutes to work up a sweat.

The next day, he would deliver the letter to Virginia Gamely, and, if he were lucky, board a liner that would charge the ice and break from the harbor. Then its whistle blasts would be in his favor, not against him. But they seemed not to be against Praeger, certainly, who thought they were like an organ in a church, commanding attention, calling forth those emotions that shook the body like a reed. Hardesty heard the deep whistles even in the desert on the 120th floor, at three, or four, or five, or whatever o'clock it was in the morning. How is it, he thought, that the whistles are shrieking now? Can ships be leaving at this time, in the teeth of the storm? And who hears them?

Ceaseless activity, even when everyone was presumed to be asleep, suggested to him that the city did have a life of its own, and that there was indeed something underneath, slowly and methodically working its way out.

Nearly faint, he emerged from the sauna and went to the window. The storm was still raging, but, staring into it, he became aware of a glow. Straight on, it, too, must have been high in the air, and it appeared to grow stronger as the wind went mad and rocked the steel cliff in which he stood.

Then, as if the snow were fog and the hotel were a ship, a space opened up as if to accommodate motion, and a lighted tower came into view suspended in the maelstrom and seemingly independent of the ground. It was the top of an old skyscraper—floodlighted in blue, white, and silver. Though the snow obscured it at times with a transparent curtain, it always managed to shine through, as bright as a halo. Toward morning, when dawn made the blizzard gray and the world was clouded over, the tower was lost.

The morning was as clear as glass. Hardesty went to the window and surveyed a forest of high towers slicing up the wind that came down from Canada herding the color blue before it like a vast number of sheep. On distant bridges, golden streams of glinting mica—cars in the morning sun—moved to and from the city. And the sisters of the ships he had heard in the storm, ships as big as cities used to be, placidly crossed the wave-etched harbor, sliding over high whitecaps like a hot iron on linen.

In the streets, people were jumping like puppets, racing around

307

at a speed that astonished even them. On those clear icy days when the full moon could not even wait for the dark, and circled the sun in the sky, they danced in what they did, they were like racehorses in the paddock, they acted like people who have discovered something great, and, in justifying the saying that New York is a city which dies and rises the way other cities go to bed at night and get up in the morning, they made the long lean island of Manhattan ring and tremble like an unsheathed sword.

Hardesty took nearly the whole day to push through these lunatics on his way to Printing House Square. They would give neither him nor anyone else an inch. Lines of traffic bolted through red lights. Bakery trucks raced on the main avenues at 125 miles per hour, assassinating bicyclists and pedestrians. Balkan pretzel vendors in two-foot-thick padded clothing and fleecy aviator caps charged each other with their flame-holding wagons, bumping like buffalos, to lay claim to a corner. With attaché cases strapped to their backs, stockbrokers in three-piece suits raced in life or death agony on cross-country skis from Riverside Drive to Wall Street. On one bustling avenue, the second story of each commercial building on both sides of the street for five miles was the home of a karate dojo. Hardesty walked past these during the lunch hour, and heard several hundred thousand combative screams, as figures in white sailed through the air, legs cocked and arms outstretched, like Russian dancers. There were fires blazing on every corner, mortal arguments on each block, robberies in commission, buildings attacked by squads of devilish wreckers, and buildings assembled by construction workers who rode single cables until they disappeared into the sky. Hardesty found it difficult to get downtown and stay the same. The city wanted fuel for its fires, and it reached out with leaping tongues of gravity and flame to pull people in, size them up, dance with them a little, sell them a suit—and then devour them.

It was late and dark by the time he reached Printing House Square, where *The Sun*'s offices faced those of *The Ghost* across the way. *The Ghost* had large electric signs on its huge headquarters, proclaiming its success and popularity, whereas *The Sun* glowed gently from inside a masterpiece of neoclassical architec-

308

ture. Hardesty bounded up the stairs to Praeger de Pinto's office. His rapidly beating heart was whipped on even faster when he found Praeger de Pinto and Virginia sitting together on Praeger's leather couch, closely and easily enough to suggest that they were perhaps more than just comfortable with one another. Intense jealousy struck him like a missile. The agony was physical. Damn this city, where there was no justice and never would be. He knew upon seeing Virginia's eyes that this was the woman for him, and he cursed the timing of it, since he could see that she and Praeger. . . . But then he thought that maybe he was just imagining it, for when Praeger stood to greet him it appeared as if the distance between Praeger and Virginia on the couch had been at least a foot. A foot and a half, he thought, full of hope, perhaps even two feet. Hardesty decided that this lovely unselfconscious woman with long black hair and supremely intelligent eyes would soon be his wife—Praeger or no Praeger. "I'll crush him like a tsetse fly," Hardesty said out loud, without knowing it.

"Who?" asked Praeger. Virginia was curious as well, and already smitten.

"Craig Binky," Hardesty blurted out, fast on his feet.

"Oh," said Praeger. "We all would like to do that. But what brought you into the fold so soon?"

"I saw today's *Ghost*. Infuriating."

Virginia smiled. From the way Hardesty had looked at her, the slight shake of his voice, and his unhappiness, she knew that he had fallen in love. This showed a certain weakness of character, yes, but it was a commitment she could not ignore. Though she tried to hang on to the steep slopes down which she felt herself sliding, after just a few minutes she gave up entirely. Still, she did not want to be rash—she had a child to consider, because she had been rash once before.

Praeger de Pinto, who had always been and would ever be in love with Jessica Penn, stepped back slowly from the awkward conversation and the not-quite-regular breathing, and watched Hardesty and Virginia discover one another while the shifts changed on the two papers and Printing House Square filled with crowds of pressmen, copy boys, and clerical workers treading down the snow.

Before Hardesty delivered Mrs. Gamely's letter, he spoke of the *Polaris* and of how, by accident, he had come to Lake of the Coheeries. As he spoke, he could feel Virginia's love for the landscape he was describing. He was glad that it was winter, when love and ambition flare in the cold. Perhaps if she had not been framed by the dark glass behind her and the snowy square dazzling with the lights of *The Ghost,* he would not have been able to talk to her in a way that almost trumpeted his intentions—that is, to everyone except Virginia, who valued them so much that she could not be sure of the obvious.

After a while, they looked up and discovered that Praeger was gone.

"How long do you think he's been out of the room?" Virginia asked with a smile.

"I don't know," Hardesty replied. "But let's have dinner."

"I have to feed the baby," she said. "Mrs. Solemnis likes to leave by six."

Hardesty's confidence left him a lot faster than it had come. Again, he felt physical pain.

Then she looked at him and said, "I'm not married."

They didn't find Praeger, but as they left the building, those of her colleagues who passed Virginia saw from Hardesty's look of unsteady triumph, and from her devilish, luminous blushing, that they had cause to give her quick knowing smiles—which only made her avert her eyes in delight.

Hardesty had laid aside his sheepskin jacket in favor of a charcoal-gray woolen greatcoat for which he had traded a good portion of his reserves. He commented on this, and on how much warmer the sheepskin jacket had been, even if it hadn't been as long. "Oh no," Virginia said, "I love that coat. I wouldn't want you to walk around in a shearling jacket. Not in the city, anyway. Wearing wilderness clothes here is as foolish as wearing city clothes in the wilderness." They walked into the ferocious north wind, letting it sweep over their faces as if they were bathing in a river. He didn't dare take her arm when they crossed congested avenues, though he very much wanted to. She said she liked his coat, and she was bringing him home for dinner. At the moment, that was enough for him.

The Chinese and Italian markets lay together back to back. Hardesty and Virginia went through the many acres of stalls, row after row, as if they were walking alone in the spring. The fruits and vegetables stacked in the cold reminded them of a garden, and the dead fish with mouths open in shock had the expressions of leaping trout. "I torment *The Ghost* sometimes," Virginia said, "by following them in their pieces and doing a better job. It drives them mad. This summer they did an article on the Chinese and Italian markets, and, as usual, all they talked about was the food. As far as *The Ghost* is concerned, if you can't put it in your mouth, it's incomprehensible."

"I know," said Hardesty. "I was rather amazed to see that page one of today's *Ghost* had a two-column headline about a new way to braise artichokes."

"Of course. They do that all the time on page one—black borders if someone's soufflé falls, banner headlines about a new kind of sauce. . . . I wrote an essay three days later, and I didn't mention food once. And yet, I think it was a better description of the market than they had, because the least of the market is the food."

"What is it then?" Hardesty asked, though he already knew.

"Buying and selling, faces, the color, the light, the stories that breed within it, its spirit. Where else would you find all these clear lights strung so high and gleaming in the cold?" she asked, indicating the chains of electric bulbs over the stalls. "Harry Penn got a telegram from Craig Binky, that said, 'How can you cover the market and not mention food?' Imagine, they send telegrams between two offices on the same square. Harry Penn cabled back, 'Eating assassinates the spirit.'"

"I like to eat," she said. "In fact, I'm hungry right now. But a rack of lamb is not the Roman Empire."

They bought a cut of steak and half a dozen kinds of vegetables, and they walked back through the acres of pearly lights, watching their breath condense in white clouds before them. "My house is that way," Virginia said, "but I don't want to go through the Five

Points; it's too dangerous. So let's walk up to Houston, and circle back."

"That'll take three times as long," Hardesty stated. "Why not walk through the Five Points? I went in there today and nothing happened."

"You were lucky. Besides, it's dark."

"Don't worry," said Hardesty. "Thieves sleep in early evening."

The Five Points had seen bandits of many races and ethnicities roost on its roosts and snake about in its alleys. Fashions in crime and demeanor had changed with the times, the languages, and the temptations. But, essentially, the thieves and brigands were the same, and their weapons were the knife, the club, and the gun. Hardesty was right, though. They rested in early evening, for they were alive only after a few hours of darkness. The streets were empty and winter had left its charm at the boundaries of the Five Points—which was like a cave without an exit. Hardesty and Virginia had the sense that they were being observed from darkened windows. The only thing they heard was the ringing of a faraway bell, and hideous laughter greeting it from within the broken tenements as if to say that its pure sound was here powerless and corruptible.

Halfway through, they began to see what they had been unable to see before. In the shadows were confused forms, bodies in pain, outstretched hands begging for mercy or release. With every step, the eyes that glowed at them grew more numerous, and the cries sharper.

"I can't explain it," said Hardesty, "but the empty streets are full." He took Virginia's arm and they walked toward a fire that burned at the edge of the district. At a fire there would be firemen and police, perhaps even the press. And the firelight would brighten their way until they broke out of the Five Points.

A row of tenements was engulfed in orange. Billows of black smoke reflected the light downward and damped the sparks. All around, for as far as the eye could see, rejoicing crowds with firelight in their eyes took pleasure. A roar went up as children fell back into the coals, and the spectators watched attentively as a

312

fight progressed from roof to roof of the burning buildings. The fighters were so taken up in their combat that they ignored the fire which silhouetted them like cast-iron figures on a lantern stage and swallowed them up one by one as they dropped in defeat.

Virginia was shaken, and Hardesty was sorry that he had insisted on going through the Five Points. "I didn't know," he said, still numb from watching the children perish, though they had fallen back without a sound and had disappeared quite neatly. "It's completely different by day. I just didn't know."

Men and women came running in from the streets, like lizards darting to catch some sun. The sidewalks were soon overflowing, and foodstands began to appear. With no fire department, no ambulances, no trucks, no spotlights to leach away the shuddering orange light, the fire blazed, the tenements crumbled, and the people died.

Through the middle of the crowd came a mutilated and disfigured draft horse pulling a wagon loaded with refuse. The driver reined in the horse and tried to go around. But horse and wagon were soon engulfed, and moved in stops and starts.

"Look at that animal," Hardesty said, not knowing whether to feel compassion or disgust. "He's the biggest dray horse I've ever seen, and he's as slim as a thoroughbred. Imagine what he must have been through."

As a gang of children beat him about the face with switches and his master beat him from behind with a heavy whip, the horse held his head down and closed his bruised eyes. Scars cut across his flanks and withers. Old craters in his hide were overlaid with the more recent burns and sores he suffered from a primitive and rudely fashioned harness; his tail and mane were clipped to a stubble; he had only one ear left intact—the other had had several pieces taken from it.

The wagon was heavy. And yet the horse, who was so badly cut up that he looked like a man who has been tortured by some unconquerable disease, pulled it easily. Despite his oppression, he was strong, and despite his enormous size, he was graceful. When the muscles moved in the difficult pace he had to hold between his master's desires and the torment inflicted by the children, they showed themselves to be as solid and lean as those of a carefully bred racehorse, but many times as massive.

When his horse and wagon cleared the crowd, the driver cracked the whip against the animal's head and made him canter in harness. This he did with surprising grace, straining against the wood and leather that cut his flesh and rubbed against his sores, as if he were free and in an open field. The curves that he described were unaffected by the load. They were perfectly elated, full, and round. He lifted his head and pushed into the darkness as if motion itself were one of the dimensions of paradise.

Winter, then in its early and clear stages, was a purifying engine that ran unhindered over city and country, alerting the stars to sparkle violently and shower their silver light into the arms of bare upreaching trees. It was a mad and beautiful thing that scoured raw the souls of animals and man, driving them before it until they loved to run. And what it did to northern forests can hardly be described, considering that it iced the branches of the sycamores on Chrystie Street and swept them back and forth until they rang like ranks of bells.

It was ferociously cold by the time Hardesty and Virginia arrived at the apartment house on Mulberry Street and climbed the dimly lighted winding stairs, their faces red with the stinging remembrance of a wind which had whipped at them and blown Virginia's scarf straight back. Now they were in the heated hallway, following the stairs, rising through the building in epicycles more appropriate to the planets. The ever-suspicious eye of Mrs. Solemnis, a Greek sponge fisherman's widow, appeared in the door periscope and bounded back and forth like a radar blip. "Who is it?" she asked.

"It's me," answered Virginia.

"Who is me?"

"Virginia."

"Virginia who?"

"Virginia Gamely. For goodness' sake, Mrs. Solemnis, I live here. I employ you."

"Oh, you." Mrs. Solemnis opened the door and thrust Martin into Hardesty's arms, saying, "You take."

Although he had not been on earth for much longer than a year, Martin was perfect, from his tiny curled fists to the long blue flannel tail (a Coheeries baby gown constructed to accommodate him as he grew) that made him look like a small, breastless mermaid. He carefully rested a cheek against the cold cloth of Hardesty's coat and closed his eyes in complete trust. Hardesty felt the slight weight in his arms, the baby's breathing, and an occasional twitch of an arm or leg. He looked down at Martin's soft sleepy face, and kissed him. "Yes," he said, bouncing him gently, "sweet baby."

Hardesty left his coat on so as not to disturb Martin, and watched Virginia move about the apartment as she straightened up. She was very neat, and Mrs. Solemnis was not. She glided through the several rooms, knocking things into place and aligning them symmetrically. In her charcoal-gray suit and ruffled shirt, she looked like a portrait from another century, the kind in which the subject stares from half-light on into time. But despite the dignity of this portrait Hardesty could not restrain his laughter, because as she walked to and fro she would stop and turn to check on him and the baby, or to smile in embarrassment for being so neat, and when she did she seemed like the mechanical bears in shooting galleries, who pause and swivel so they can be shot. The effect was exaggerated when, explaining that she wanted to change, she backed into the bedroom in little mechanical steps, closing the door after her. Wondering if it had been wise to allow him inside (she had visions of a crazed lunatic tossing Martin great distances, probably because, in his Coheeries gown, Martin was shaped like a football), she peeped out the door several times in succession.

"Do you moonlight in a shooting gallery?" Hardesty asked.

"No," she answered, reappearing in her charcoal suit because she had forgotten to change. "I'm practicing for an interview with Craig Binky. He has a notoriously short attention span. When you talk to him you have to make threatening motions and bizarre gestures. Otherwise, he doesn't understand."

"Who told you that?"

"Harry Penn. He knows that Binky can't resist any kind of flattery, so every once in a while he sends a reporter over to find out the secrets of *The Ghost*. Tomorrow it's my turn. That's how we know everything that goes on there and exactly what they intend to do in the future. But we are a mystery to them. Though we care little about secrecy, *The Sun* and *The Whale* are like the two halves of a clam. Nothing leaks, because everyone knows his job and has a share in the enterprise. As far as I know, the only tattle is some-one from the home and ladies' page. Last week, we ran the recipe for my mother's saxophone pie, and *The Ghost* had it the same day. In all the world there's only one saxophone pie (it's made with peaches, resin, blueberries, rum, and mint), and I doubt that *The Ghost* spies—who tiptoe around our building in false beards and mustaches—were able to steal it from the composing rooms."

She took the baby. Hardesty threw his coat across a chair and stood near her in a way that made them look like a crèche in a town square. He, too, was dressed in a suit that might have been from a nineteenth-century portrait—it was a little too big for him, and it made him feel as if he had just stepped from a carriage.

"Are you irrevocably divorced from his father?"

"Yes," she answered, with neither bitterness nor regret.

"Do you ever want to go back to Lake of the Coheeries?"

"Of course I do. It's my home."

"Soon?"

"When these winters end. Perhaps during the millennium. I think that, with the millennium, much will have changed; if not in the world, then in me. I hope to have seen something far better than anything I have ever seen before."

Hardesty did with his emotions what one does with one's body in sitting bolt upright. "What do you mean?" he asked.

She dodged the question, for her only answer was one of faith and intuition, and she wanted neither to burden him nor to turn him away, though she did want to tell him, and she did want to embrace him, and to be embraced.

Hardesty went to the window. Over courtyards and courtyards, a mile-long corridor of terra-cotta-colored buildings, vaulted stone windows, slate roofs, and trees that in summer were green bil-lows rising from the private gardens of the poor, were the two battleship-gray towers of the Williamsburg Bridge, alive in lights like blue diamonds.

"Not one building that you can see," she said, rocking the baby, "was built later than nineteen-fifteen. It's as quiet as a meadow. In summer, the trees hold hundreds of birds that sing in the morning. Someone has a poultry roost, and when the sun comes up and floods the yards like the tide of Fundy, the cock crows. It always sounds to me as if he's saying 'Nineteen-hundred! Nineteen-hundred! Nineteen-hundred!' "

"Do you think that in a few years he'll be saying 'Two thousand! Two thousand! Two thousand!'?"

"I think, Mr. Marratta," she answered, almost gravely, "that in a few years not only the cock will be crowing two thousand. Everyone will."

"Because it's an even number?" he asked, narrowing in on her.

"No," she said, nearly shaking, because she wanted him to narrow in, and she was afraid. "Not because it's an even number."

"Because these extraordinary winters will end?"

"Yes, because these extraordinary winters will end."

"And the city will change?"

"Yes, the city will change."

"And what if it doesn't?"

"It will."

"Why?"

"If nothing happens whatsoever, still, the relief will change everything, as will the difficult schooling in expectations. It will change. That much I know."

"How do you know?" Hardesty asked.

"You'll think I'm crazy," she replied, turning her head away as if she were hurt.

"No, I won't think you're crazy."

"I know," she said, "because these winters have not been for nothing. They are the plough. The wind and the stars are harrowing the land and battering the city. I feel it and can see it in everything. The animals know it is coming. The ships in the harbor rush about and have come alive because it is coming. I may be dead wrong, but I do believe that every act has significance, and that, in our time, all the ceaseless thunder is not for nothing.''

''I believe it too,'' Hardesty said, taking her hands. And thus, as fast as a whiplash, a marriage was made one evening in winter, in a city sure to rise.

A NEW LIFE

THERE was a lot of light on the sea, and a good-tempered wind rounded the headland in strength, pushing before it a trim outer-banks sloop with mainsail running full and a spinnaker swelling ahead. To the west was a long empty coast of fragrant green vegetation. The water flowed in currents and streams within the brine where cool rivers had broken clean of a bar and erupted into the ocean like a plume of expiring fireworks. The rigging creaked in protest, because the boat had not been made to fly at twenty-five knots. The sea was crowded with fish, and the beaches were whiter than a cut in new glass.

Although they had not spoken since they had abandoned that day's fishing and set sail to challenge the wind, Asbury Gunwillow and his brother Holman knew of one another's concern with the sunny but insistent gale. It got stronger by degrees, never slackening, until it seemed powerful enough to blow the sea off the earth and into empty space. "Can we tack against this wind, Asbury?" Holman shouted.

Asbury shook his head. "Nothing could tack against this wind," he shouted back. "I've never seen anything like it. This is the kind of gale that sinks fleets of warships. If we try to come about, we'll bust up for sure. Still, we're lucky."

"Why?"

"Because a wind like this should make sea state ten, but the sea is as flat as ice. That's because the wind is so steady. If it wasn't, it would make waves a hundred and fifty feet high. And we haven't got much of a transom," he said, looking at the water a foot below the top of the tiller post.

"Let me try at least to unset the spinnaker," Holman asked.

"No," ordered Asbury. "I'll do it. It's too dangerous for you to move. . . ." But before he could finish his sentence, young Holman, only twenty-one and rather slight, began to crawl toward the bow. Asbury called for him to come back, but he wouldn't, and he inched forward, resisting the force of the wind like a man who is trying to hold his place in a rapids.

"Just cut it loose," Asbury shouted. But though the words were snatched away and propelled forward, Holman had no chance of hearing. With one foot braced on the cowling in front of the mainmast, and the other pressed against a winch, he began to undo the spinnaker line.

"Cut it!" his brother yelled to no avail. "Cut it!"

When the line started smoking through the cleet, Holman realized that he was sitting on top of the coil. He raised himself a little to get away from it, the wind caught him, and he pitched forward into the sea.

Asbury threw a life ring to starboard and began playing out the rope. After all one hundred feet of it had shot through his hands and Holman still hadn't surfaced, he let go of the end, hoping to leave Holman something to hold onto.

But then Asbury was stunned to see that Holman was still with him, half in and half out of the water on the starboard side, hanging on to the spinnaker line. He was repeatedly dashed against the sea.

Sometimes he was lifted fifty or sixty feet into the air and thrown back against the water when the sail whipped down.

Intending to free the spinnaker and haul his brother in on it, Asbury rushed forward. But the wind blew him off his feet and knocked him against the mainmast. With his vision darkened and half his strength gone, Asbury still managed to unfold his clasp knife. He cut the spinnaker halyard. But instead of lowering the pulley the way it normally would have, it allowed the sail to flap more wildly.

While he was trying to decide what to do, Asbury looked at the end of the sail and saw that Holman had let go. Then the spinnaker flew into the air and collapsed onto the surface of the water. He peered through the blood that was thickening in his eyes, but had he been able to see he would not have seen Holman, who disappeared under the water. He determined to come about, even if it killed him.

Slipping on his own blood, Asbury went to the helm. When he reached the tiller, he slumped against it and held on. His hand stuck to it because of the blood that was over everything. "Where's it coming from?" he asked out loud, because there was blood in the wind, in hot droplets that, at first, he thought were rain. But it was his blood, spurting from an artery in his scalp. He tried to stop it with his hand, and it sprayed through his fingers.

Deciding to jibe even though it would probably snap the mast, he leaned against the tiller hard and pushed it over. But the only thing that happened was that the stern rode up in the water and bumped along like a popper lure. Because there was nothing else to do, Asbury held the tiller over until his strength left him and he fell onto the floorboards. He tried to get up, and couldn't. He pressed the wound against a rib in the hull, hoping to stanch the bleeding. The last thing he remembered was the sound of the wind.

When he awoke he was desperately cold. Though he was not far north, and it was June, it was night on the sea and he had been badly injured. He thought that his neck would be forever paralyzed in the crooked position into which it had frozen against the rib in the hull, and he couldn't open his eyes. Like someone who stays awake all night in the cold rather than get up to find an extra blanket, he remained in that uncomfortable position for a long time, many minutes, perhaps hours, until he was alert enough to understand that the smooth and varying motions of the boat signified temperate sleigh rides down shallow swells. The sound of relentless wind had vanished, leaving in its place the familiar gurgling of brine mixing itself up in the centerboard well, and the noises of rigging that ached like trees in the fall.

To get free, he threw himself over on his side. Though he felt an overwhelming pain in his head, and though his ribs collided with the anchor, he found that moving had done him a great deal of good. He moved as much as he could. After freeing his lashes of caked blood, he opened his eyes. As the circulation was restored and he grew warmer and less stiff, he looked at the stars and realized that it was early morning, probably about four o'clock.

Assuming that he had not slept through an entire cycle of nights and days, he calculated that Holman had been in the sea at least sixteen hours, and was probably three hundred miles away. Without benefit of a rogue wind such as that which had overpowered them, Asbury could not hope to get back to the approximate location where his brother had gone overboard, in less than three or four days.

Since they had been coasting, they had had no navigational instruments other than a compass. Asbury could not know where he was except by the crudest dead reckoning, and instinct, which told him to steer west-northwest for the nearest land. He put on a sweatshirt and Holman's leather jacket. He was still cold, but he knew that the sun would be coming up soon. And he finished off a roast beef sandwich and an apple that had been left from lunch the day before. In preparation for a long hard sail, he ate the core of the apple, and he considered and rejected the stem, thinking that, if it were to come to eating wood, there was plenty in the boat.

As miserable as he was for losing his brother, a steady course under the stars worked its magic. Had the night not been clear, morning would have come far more slowly, but it came fast enough, and traveling straight over a glistening sea in which he could see a raft of stars revived him.

Gliding through the oil-black sea under stars so still and dignified that they might have been decorations for the dome of a cathedral, Asbury began to realize where he was headed, and why. It was something that he could understand only with the gifts that come of early morning—one of those things, like a dream, that one cannot always piece together again to remember and feel in sunlight and day. And yet enough early risings and enough work of heart and memory will bring it, half alive, from unfamiliar depths, like a slowly panting fish, hauled on deck, with fading eyes that beg for the sea.

No one knew how old Asbury Gunwillow's grandfather was, but he claimed to be well over 175. "I've gotta be," he would say. "I've gotta be a hundred and seventy-five or a hundred and eighty. When the Civil War began, I had just bought out my partner in a dry-goods store in St. Albans, Vermont. During the war, I moved all my stock to New York and set up next to the Brooklyn Navy Yard. We supplied the yards when they built the ironclads. By the time Lincoln was shot, our warehouse covered a whole city block."

Then he would look to the ceiling, his gray eyes and delicate white hair would catch the light coming into the room, and his expression would turn to disbelief and confusion. "How could I be that old?" he would ask. "No one lives to be that old. And besides, I'm not clear on how the time went. But I remember, for example, where we lived during the war."

"Which war?" Asbury asked.

"I don't remember. Our house was in the middle of the city, on a hill that gave us views of the Atlantic, the Hudson Highlands, the Ramapos, the Palisades. . . . I could see everything from that house. I could see thousands of children playing in hundreds of parks. I could see them on the swings and slides. I could see the buttons on their coats. I saw the barges and ships on the river, and I knew where they were going, what they were carrying, and when they would arrive. I could see into every office, house, and cellar of the city, and not even a newly picked daffodil in a bottle of water on a windowsill could hide from me. I looked into every garden, over the shoulders of singing housewives, and into the committee rooms, the hospitals, and the theaters. I knew exactly what was happening at the Stock Exchange and what was going on in all the Staten Island steambaths. How could that be?" he asked, doubting himself. "I don't know. But it's true. It was like being up in a balloon on a clear summer's day, watching everything.

"On either side of our house, like doormen's epaulets, there were boxwood mazes with one-way gates. Each had miles of passages, and the leaves were so dense that you couldn't fire a bullet through them. One balcony that looked north was suspended by cables. It had an airy feeling to it, and we used to sit there after dinner and drink tea. The dog slept in the corner, in his own special dog nest under a green awning. It was very cool there in summer, that's why. Give a dog a cool place in summer and a warm place in winter, and he'll sleep for the rest of his life. The balcony faced north. Every evening, in the north light, the rivers were strikingly blue. . . . Are you my son?"

"No, Grandpa. I'm your grandson."

"Which one are you?"

"I'm Asbury."

"Where were we talking about?"

"About New York."

The old man stared vacantly ahead. "That's the point."

"What's the point?"

"You ought to go there."

"Why?"

"Catch it before it gets too late—*the engines.*"

"What engines?"

"All of 'em. They're all set up to play one sound. They're tuning, I think. It isn't right yet, but it's music. One will lead. The others will follow—and that'll be the day."

"I'm sorry, Grandpa," Asbury said, "but I don't understand exactly what you mean."

"What are we talking about?"

"The engines."

"Oh, the engines. What do you want to know about them?"

"You said that they're all set to play one sound."

"I did. They sit there as quietly as dogs, facing in all directions,

324

some abandoned in the dark, some rusting and aging, others well tended. It doesn't matter. They have souls."

Asbury looked shocked.

"Souls—every one. They move, don't they? Who do you think sets things to moving? Nothing that moves lacks a soul. I ought to know. You ever heard of a bellwether? It goes for engines too. There's one engine that'll pick up the intervals as they pass through it, and echo them just right. Then all the others will follow.

"If I was young like you, I'd go there myself," he said. Then he had a coughing fit. He turned purple very quickly, but just as rapidly cooled into blue, and finally breathed easily in white. Asbury wondered how the old man could breathe so little. He seemed to inhale and exhale only a few times each minute. Asbury must have wondered this out loud, for when his grandfather was once again in possession of himself he said, "Because I don't need oxygen. I've already come to all my conclusions. I'm just slowly gliding down. Someday I'll be as light as a feather. Promise me."

"Promise what?"

"Go to New York."

Asbury had promised. But until the day that the wind had taken him, he had forgotten what he had vowed.

Now, after a few sunny days on the sea, he was surrounded by a low-pitched rumble that he took to be the thundering heartbeat of a city, and he had no doubt what city it was.

Hardesty Marratta and Virginia had fallen in love in the obsessive and total way of two people who have seen the same truth which they cannot quite comprehend. And though the times were not as promiscuous as they had been several decades earlier, no one would have blinked had they taken up residence together (Virginia's apartment was just barely big enough for three) or maintained some sort of indecisive relationship that, like many others of its type, was half scandal and half hesitation. But they didn't. Instead, they courted almost as their parents had done. Perhaps it was that, save for when they were small children, Hardesty had not known his mother and Virginia had not known her father. They had been brought up on tender descriptions, and had heard the stories of their parents' courtships in the most glowing terms. And perhaps it was because Virginia had been unsuccessfully married, and was still wary of visions, even if they were her own; whereas Hardesty, who had been drafted into combat twice in his life, had already suffered conscription doubly. For whatever the reason, their passion unrolled in a long, easy wave, and they courted, slowly and gently, throughout the severe winter that followed their first meeting.

Hardesty lived in the attic of a house on Bank Street. The roof was peaked, and he had to bend when passing through doors, but the neighborhood was quiet and all he could hear apart from the wind and snow was the sound of bells ringing through yards and gardens as churches patiently struck the hours, their halves, and their quarters. Cats and squirrels made astounding leaps and tightroped the telephone lines in a show of hunting and escape that put the greatest circus to shame. When a cat walked in the snow, it moved like an exiled queen, the epitome of caution and pride. Once, a hawk alighted briefly in the courtyard, but only long enough to look under each of its mottled wings and then rise up. The air was often choked with snow or sweet wood smoke that darkened things and had a way with time, suspending it. And when night came early with its snowy blue light, the world looked like that quiet place depicted in paperweights filled with water and confetti.

Every afternoon, just as *The Sun* was put to bed, Hardesty called Virginia from a public phone (neither had a telephone in the house, believing it was a wasteful extravagance). They discussed the composition of dinner, and later, as they walked from different directions toward Virginia's apartment, they gathered ingredients from markets and stores on the way. Sometimes, if Virginia were working late or Hardesty had finished early, he would meet her in Printing House Square and they would go home together. Most of the time, though, Hardesty had a solitary walk at dusk down Greenwich Avenue. He thought there was no finer street in the city. Whenever he passed St. Vincent's Hospital he felt as if he were inside a great Russian novel. Its looming walls and large lighted windows spoke of things eternal; and seated next to timid interns, in local restaurants with wood fires and evergreen wreaths, were people of fashion and means who seemed in comparison to be astonishingly empty. How could they help it? The interns carried with them the truths of death and dying, and when they walked across the street in the snow they did not shed the strange melancholy of their sleepless and terrible year.

Though he felt obliged to carry out the task his father had skillfully engineered for him in San Francisco, Hardesty was held in place by powerful attractions and satisfying responsibilities. Thinking of how it would be to leave Virginia made him sadder than he could tell. The way things were set up, he would have to betray her. He truly loved her, but she was not willing to cross the Atlantic with him or anyone else, having had her sleigh ride to Canada. Thus far, she had successfully held him back. And, then, there was his job.

Praeger de Pinto had found in him not just a kindred spirit, but something better—a competitor. Praeger was never sure that Hardesty wouldn't think of what he himself was thinking, beforehand, and, despite what this implied about Praeger, Praeger considered it a magnificent talent. He had asked Virginia about Hardesty on several occasions, because he wanted to hire him. But he did not know in what capacity: he thought perhaps as a political writer, or a neighborhood reporter, since he had discovered that Hardesty knew Italian. Furthermore, he wanted Hardesty to ask for the job. One Saturday afternoon, they met by accident at a skating pond in Brooklyn.

This place was famous for a vista of New York that compressed the city unerringly, so that one could look down the rifle barrel of a long avenue and see it laid out as if in an oil painting. Sitting on crowded benches in a rectangular yellow building with roaring wood stoves, and windows that faced Manhattan, Praeger, Virginia, and Hardesty had pounded their skate blades on the floor to throw off the ice shavings and then stared in a daze through the ten-degree air. "I wonder what that strange-looking tower is," Praeger had said, almost to himself, referring to a Moorish campanile of rose-colored stone. And, to his surprise, Hardesty told him.

"That's the Clive Tower," Hardesty said, "built in 1867 by John J. Clive, in honor of his son, who died at Mobile Bay." He went on to discourse about its place in the city, its relation to the history of architecture, and the engineers and architects who built it.

Praeger asked about other buildings. Hardesty knew most of them, and soon the spots of fire that Praeger had set worked themselves into the blaze of a lecture in history, architecture, poetry, and thunder—a portrait of the city from the skating pond, that amazed Praeger, Virginia, and Hardesty himself. Only when they saw a group of local boys playing hockey by torchlight did they realize that it had grown dark.

"How the hell do you know all that?" Praeger asked.

"I've been reading and walking around a lot."

"What did you do in San Francisco?"

"I didn't do much," Hardesty confessed. "I was resting after the army. I rested for a couple of years. But when I came back the first time, I managed to get a doctorate in the history of art and architecture. That's probably what you want to know."

"It makes no difference to me," Praeger stated, "as long as you know what you're talking about, and I think you do. Why don't you write a few pieces for *The Sun* and *The Whale?* If they're as good as that little dissertation on Western civilization that just went by, you can have a regular column."

"Marko Chestnut might illustrate it," Virginia added.

"You see," Praeger began, turning toward Hardesty because he knew that Virginia already knew, "*The Ghost* has an architecture section: section thirty-nine, on Mondays and Fridays. But it's a personalities page. For example, they recently had a piece on a character—I think his name was Ambrosio D'Urbervilles—whose 'design statement' was to stuff an entire apartment from floor to ceiling with dark purple cottonballs. He called it 'Portrait of a Dead Camel Dancing on the Roof of a Steambath.'

"If we compete with them, we have to do it as if they were something other than what they are. To avoid their influence, we try to pretend that they don't exist. To counter the mirror-image effect, we fight them as if they were actually serious opponents. This takes much imagination on our part, and elevates them a great deal.

But Harry Penn would have it no other way; and, these days, neither would I."

"I understand," said Hardesty, with the sound of the stoves thundering in his ears like sunstroke. "I read the thing about the camel dancing on the roof." As the hockey players' torches flew across the night ice under the glow of lighted canyon walls, Hardesty told the editor of *The Sun* that he would try his best to portray the city.

Within a week, Hardesty and Marko Chestnut began to wander in search of those places constructed to hold and keep the spirit. These were not hard to find, because they existed literally in the hundreds of thousands, from Riverdale to South Beach, and from Riverside Drive to New Lots. On Thursdays, *The Sun* ran Hardesty's commentary across two full pages. In the center of each page was a large pen-and-ink drawing by Marko. They gave *The Sun*'s readers Brooklyn from the air: there it was, spread out before them like a pinioned eagle trying to eat the oyster of Staten Island. They gave them the chaos of Fourteenth Street, the chimneys of Astoria, silvered sections of the East Side, Gramercy Park as misty as an English garden, and Manhattan's golden spires as seen from Weehawken at sunset, when the city of glass burns like a star in space. The more they found, the more they could see to find, and they did very well by *The Sun*.

But all this only made Hardesty increasingly impatient to see the just city. He resolved to overcome all his feelings and inclinations, and get on a boat to Europe. Though he loved Virginia, loved her even more than he felt responsible to his father, there was something else apart from either of them that drove him on. Its power astounded him and made him think of those men who leave their families to go to war. And now he, too, was about to trade, to take the cold wind for the warm, because of something that was not his own, and that spoke to him from a time so distant that he had to admire it merely for its tenacity. He was wrong to leave, and he knew it. But simply to be wrong was one thing. To be wrong for the sake of a perfectly just city, was another.

He told Virginia on the first of June, and it caught her completely off guard. She cried fiercely, and then she attacked him.

329

She tried to pull his hair, and landed a punch or two. "Get out!" she screamed in rage. When he did get out, she slammed the door and bolted it, and he heard sobbing that broke his heart. After all that, he couldn't just knock at the door and step back into the house, so he bought a ticket for a ship that was soon to depart, and went back to his attic, cursing summer.

The day that Hardesty left New York he took a taxi through the city on his way to the ocean liner. It was early on a Sunday morning in the beginning of June, in perfect weather. Though it was cool, serene, and blue, no one was in the streets but the sun. Passing through Chelsea, Hardesty heard on the taxi driver's radio an aria that seemed to come from the buildings themselves, their abandoned inner courtyards, and the souls of their inhabitants. He could not have loved Virginia Gamely more, and he wondered if what he assumed lay at such a great distance were present in this very city—or even in Virginia herself, if the future were to be fair and imaginative enough to take refuge in a single soul. If that were so, then he would be doing the wrong thing. Midway through the aria, he saw a familiar figure crossing Hudson Street with an easel over his shoulder and a box of oils under his arm.

Marko Chestnut was returning from painting the Hudson early in the morning, when the light was best and gangs of hoodlums were just going to bed. The Hudson was a thousand rivers, changing with each variation of the light—mild at dawn, whitecapped in a strong autumn wind, royal blue under an empty sky, covered with white ice, green and gray in winter storms, a mist-covered mountain lake in August. But Marko Chestnut preferred summer mornings with their strong and unambivalent light.

Hardesty had the taxi pull over. He jumped out and called to his friend, who was always wary, because he was often attacked when he painted outside. Marko began to scurry away. "It's me!" Hardesty shouted.

"I thought you left already," Marko said, squinting through his glasses.

"I'm on my way now. What time is it? The boat leaves at eight."

Marko Chestnut hesitated, looked at his watch, and said, "It's seven. How come you left so early? The pier for the *Rosenwald* is only three blocks from here."

"I didn't think it was that early."

"Have you eaten yet?"

"No."

"Let's go to Petipas and have some breakfast," Marko Chestnut suggested. "We can walk from there to the boat."

They had breakfast in the garden at Petipas, watching birds in the sunlit ivy on the garden wall, and listening to ship whistles echoing off the cliffs of the Hudson. "How can you leave a woman like that? And for what? You know she was left once before, by that Canadian lunatic, what was his name, Boissy d'Anglas?"

"I know," Hardesty answered.

"It's not fair to her. It's not fair to you. It's wrong. Maybe, as a widower, I can know things that you can't. But let me tell you something—you're an idiot. You're throwing away the most precious. . . . For Christ's sake, do I have to explain this to you?"

"No."

"Then why not just stay."

"I can't," Hardesty whispered. "My father."

A ship's whistle rent the air. "Is that the *Rosenwald?*" Hardesty asked.

"It may be," Marko Chestnut replied. "But if it is, it must be heading downriver. It's already twenty after eight." He smiled.

"You son of a bitch, I'll remember this!" Hardesty said with a threatening look.

"You'll thank me," Marko Chestnut stated confidently.

They ran out of the restaurant. Struggling with his easel, Marko Chestnut overturned tables and chairs and broke a lot of china. Hardesty hailed a taxi, and sped south. Marko Chestnut followed. Their two cabs arrived at the Battery simultaneously, and the tourists did not understand what was happening as Hardesty, and Marko Chestnut (lugging easel and paints), ran to the southernmost extension of the promenade, screaming epithets at one another. As trim as an admiral in a new set of whites, the *Rosenwald* was getting up a good head of steam, and her towering stern had just cleared Liberty Island. Hardesty started to unlace his shoes.

"What's the point of swimming?" Marko Chestnut asked. "A ship like that goes twenty knots."

"That's right, and the water's freezing. I don't expect to catch it. But I'm going to try, just in case it stops. What can I lose except a little body heat?"

He dived into the harbor and began to swim. To Marko Chestnut's amazement, a minute after Hardesty jumped, the *Rosenwald* sent up a plume of black smoke and went dead in the water.

The officers of the Dutch ship *Rosenwald* were flattered that Hardesty valued their services enough to immerse himself in the outrageous pudding of filth that passed for water in New York Harbor. They took him down somewhere near the engines and pushed him into a scalding shower, after which the ship's doctor gave him ten injections, and the chief steward brought him a gallon of beef bouillon. He would have declined an invitation to dine that evening at the captain's table, had he not been wearing the captain's own sapphire-colored velvet bathrobe with Holland's royal crest in gold on the pocket. It is difficult, he reasoned, to refuse an invitation from someone in whose bathrobe one is.

When Hardesty finally managed to get on deck, he saw New York as it took the strengthening sun. It looked like a piece of flashing jewelry. Nothing of human proportion could be made out amid the blocks and towers. But an occasional dome or the graceful fall of a catenary put the glassy cliffs in scale, and reminded Hardesty that within and among them people were shouting and singing, women were stepping into the shower, and pianos were being played as dancers danced. Virginia was there, somewhere, going about in the summer sun. Not far upriver, newly awakening forests rested between greening fields and blue mountains. Here and there, early summer fires built to clear the forest alleyways of fallen limbs sent up smoke that seemed to climb as slowly and carefully as alpinists.

It was hard to leave New York in summer, by sea. Hardesty immediately began to miss the city where never-ending avenues jumped over rivers and bridges that habitually bumped the clouds, and where history and the future seemed to run side by side in shock and disorder. And he longed for Virginia. He longed for her so that he wanted to vault the railings and swim to Long Island, though the water was far too cold for him to make it. He realized as well that to do so would probably be considered eccentric, especially in light of the way in which he had come on board. Besides, he would probably get chopped up in the propellers, and his clothes were being laundered and pressed, which meant that even if he survived he would be forced to go naked on land or swim ten miles in a stolen bathrobe. His desire to leave the ship was overwhelmed by such impracticalities, until he saw what lay in the *Rosenwald*'s path.

The passengers thought it was only a fogbank. They had entrusted themselves to the Vergeetachtig Oester line and assumed that its officers and representatives would bring them through. But the officers were uncomfortable with what they saw ahead of their ship. Fogbanks do not rise to the top of the sky. Nor do they stretch across the sea for thirty miles in each direction, as straight and smooth as the platinum meter sticks at the Bureau of Postulates in Budapest. Nor do they oscillate, thundering like snare drums.

The bridge came alive while the captain decided whether to come about and watch this thing work, from a distance, or stick to his course and smash through it. Hardesty went to the bow to get a better look. These were not storm clouds, but a vast white wall that polished the sea at its base into a kind of invisibility. Its hysterical thunder sounded like a terrible argument between Klaxons and foghorns. As the *Rosenwald* drew closer, the enormity of the wall became overwhelming.

Despite all their years on the sea and all the electronic instruments they were training in on the cloud wall, they didn't know what it was. But Hardesty did, which made leaving Virginia out of the question, because it meant that he might never be able to return to her. Virginia had told him about it on several occasions, and he himself had passed through it, though he had been sound asleep on the *Polaris* as the tops of the cars were polished by a cloud of busy white emery disguised as the fury of winter. How Virginia knew was a mystery. Presumably, her mother had told her.

Hardesty was unwilling to vanish into indeterminate time. After all, if Virginia were right, the *Rosenwald* could spend an eternity there, or a second, and emerge either to stun the Iroquois or to find itself in a future it did not understand. And if the *Rosenwald* and those upon it were ever to return, no one but those who had been there would ever believe them, and they would be condemned to lives of silence or madness.

In his youth Hardesty had wondered about the feat of jumping from a moving ship. This was a complicated act that was sometimes lethal because of spinning propellers and the tendency of things floating alongside to be drawn into them. After careful thought, the young Hardesty had decided that his best chance would be to leap off the ship, fifteen degrees from its longitudinal axis, with a weight to lessen the possibility of being drawn back into the blades. His father, too, had analyzed the problem. "When you sink about twenty feet," he had cautioned, "you must compress yourself into a ball to reduce your surface area. That way, you reduce the sail effect and the likelihood of being pushed into the vacuum created by the propellers. Don't forget to let go of the weight at about forty feet. The ocean is quite deep, you know."

The captain of the *Rosenwald* decided to proceed as if the wall were an ordinary fogbank. When the vessel's narrow bow plunged into the white cliff, Hardesty sprinted down the main deck, trying to escape sternward. Resigned and expectant, showing the beatific smiles and expressions of those who have apprehended the existence of a better world, the passengers were swallowed up with the superstructure of the now half-vanished ship. As it touched Hardesty's heel, he felt rapturous pleasure spreading through his entire body, not the kind of sensuality which robs and burns the soul, but something elevated and ecstatic that he knew might take him very far. Still, everything in him told him that the city was better. He had hardly seen it, or felt its scandalous energy. Its towers, bridges, and domes, the river at midday, the life within it, were there to claim. And then, there was Virginia.

The ship's forward motion was impressive even for a Dutch liner that had a reputation for being quite speedy. Inches ahead of the wall, Hardesty grabbed a fire bucket full of sand to serve as the weight that would keep him from the propellers. The white froth surrounded one of his legs, weakening him with delight. He wrenched himself away from it, and pushed ahead. As he stood poised on the stern rail, the cloud willowed half his body into ecstasy. He might have given in, had not gravity hurled him into the waves that broke silently into the invisible space under the wall.

The *Rosenwald* disappeared. Hardesty was soon far under water, holding his breath, afraid to let go of the bucket not so much for fear of being drawn into the propellers as for fear of being swallowed by what he had just escaped. He sank deeper and deeper into a freezing green sea that was cold enough to be nearly gelatinous, and emerald to the quick.

Hardesty dropped the bucket and began to float upward. He suspected that perhaps he had imagined the voracious cloud wall, and wondered what the other passengers had thought when, in the captain's blue bathrobe, he had run down the deck, seized a fire bucket, and gone over the rail. Then he broke the surface. Neither the ship nor the cloud wall was in sight. He was alone, far from land, in a very cold sea.

That evening, as the lights were coming up in the buildings and on the bridges, Asbury Gunwillow guided his small sloop over the chestnut-colored waters of the harbor. He was amazed at the diversity of traffic plying among the many industrial islands, and in the river entrances, channels, straits, and coves. The harbor was complicated enough for Craig Binky once to have called it "octopusine," and Asbury might easily have bumbled into Jamaica Bay or tried to fight the tidal rush in the East River, were it not for the pilot he had taken on.

He had been disappointed that the figure floating in a bathrobe—somewhat like Ophelia in her buoyant skirts, but thrashing and garrulous rather than mild and distracted—was not his lost brother, Holman. And, once he had pulled Hardesty in, given him a pair of pants, a navy blue sweatshirt, and enough time to warm up and get oriented, he expected a straight answer when he asked, "How did you get out here?" They were far from land and there were no boats. Thinking to hear that Hardesty was the world's greatest cold-water swimmer, that his luxury yacht had capsized and gone under, that he had been ejected from a submarine, shot from a cannon, or thrown from an airplane, Asbury was resentful when Hardesty told him that he had ridden there on a tea tray. Hardesty had maintained this with such relieved and convincing hysteria that Asbury dared not question him further.

For a while they made polite conversation, but at the Narrows, perhaps because of the beauty of the bridge lights in soft dusk and the sudden appearance of the city across the bay, they spoke of what had brought them into one another's company. Concluding that one should not make or imply a promise and leave it unfulfilled, they wondered nonetheless about the curious net of obligations, failings, coincidences, and events that seem to tie everything together even for those who think they are free. "Apart from natural laws, from the world as we know it," Hardesty speculated, "maybe there are laws of organization which bind us to patterns that we can't see and to tasks that we don't perceive."

"I can testify to that directly," Asbury said. "I made a promise which I didn't keep, and then years later a wind came up, threw my brother out of the boat, and put me on course. The promise was to go to New York. I'm not surprised. I even picked up a pilot, for free."

"You can have my apartment, too," Hardesty said, because he planned to live with Virginia, if she would have him, forever.

Asbury accepted, thinking that, the way things were going, to look at the place before he took it would be foolish.

They glided up to the Morton Street pier, where Hardesty took off like a rabbit. When he arrived at Virginia's door, he stood outside listening to the sounds from within—water running, the baby trying to speak, a knife on a chopping board, Virginia singing to herself or talking to Martin as if he were able to understand.

Hardesty went up to the roof and lowered himself onto the adjoining roof of a police stable, where he could look into Virginia's apartment unobserved. Chinese and Italian boys from neighboring buildings often went there on the pretense of getting some fresh air, but their real purpose was to see Virginia without her clothes. Hardesty sympathized with their desires, and was appropriately severe

336

when he caught them. Now all he wanted was to see her in motion: what she was wearing did not matter. He wanted to see her, and to keep the portrait forever. One day in the future, because he loved her, he would unveil it for her pleasure. Cool night air came from the river and crossed the many rows of tenements. A huge tree, lush with new leaves, sighed and shuddered as Virginia moved about in the bright box of her apartment, every now and then darting in front of a window where Hardesty would catch a glimpse of her. She was sunburnt, and she wore a white dress with a line of violet embroidery around the neckline. Hardesty shifted position, and heard whinnies in the stable below as the horses apprehended his presence. He could now see into the kitchen, and he could hear Virginia reading to Martin as their dinner cooked.

" 'Here arrived yesterday the ship *The Arms of Amsterdam* which sailed from New Netherland out of the Mauritius River on September twenty-third,' " she read. She often read to Martin, for she did not want him just to vegetate while she sat in what he would take to be mysterious silence, staring at a paper thing with lines on it, and sometimes turning the page. He was flattered silly when his mother spoke to him as if he understood, and always tried to talk. Since she didn't want to monopolize the conversation, she would often break her narrative, put down the book, and ask, "What did you think of that, Martin?"

He usually hesitated as if weighing his thoughts, looked around, and burst out with something like "Tawiya! Tawiya!" or "Iyama! Iyama!" in a shrill infant gurgle, to which she responded by picking him up, kissing him, and saying, "Yes! Yes! That's extremely astute of you!" Now he seemed especially agitated, and she wondered why.

She continued. " 'They report that our people there are of good courage, and live peaceably. Their women, also, have borne children there, and they have bought the isle of Manhattes from the wild men for the value of sixty guilders.' "

At that, she turned and looked out the window into the summer night. He could see her straight on, though she could not see him. What a sad look she had, and how lovely was her face, framed in her black hair and the fine ring of violet tendrils embroidered on the dress. Suddenly, she bowed her head and covered her eyes with her left hand. Hardesty strained forward in the darkness. She had often told him that she merely wanted to live in the city and see what it would bring. She had often begged him not to seek, but to wait. "Churchmen," she had said, "like Boissy d'Anglas, burn themselves up in seeking, and they find nothing. If your faith is genuine, then you meet your responsibilities, fulfill your obligations, and wait until you are found. It will come. If not to you, then to your children, and if not to them, then to their children."

The lovely woman in a white dress with violet borders, in a room that gave out beautifully on gardens and the bridge, had become for Hardesty a personification of the city rising. And besides, city or no city, he loved her.

Before she cried, he would be up the ladder, onto the roof, down the stairs, and at her door. As he left the top of the stable, the horses whinnied again. Clearing the parapet, he saw the city. From this perspective its lights were like summer fires on a grassy plain.

Remember the soft air, he thought to himself as he crossed the roof. Remember the soft air and all the lights. The lights, never quite the same, always changing, were like distant spirits—those who were forever gone but not forgotten. And perhaps the distant spirits were shining in approval as Hardesty Marratta silently crossed the roof, hesitated to look back at them, and disappeared down the narrow stairway.

Virginia heard his steps. Somehow, Martin and the horses had already known. She looked up, wondering if it were he. She could hardly breathe. She tilted her head to hear better. Hardesty wondered if she would take him back. "Tawiya! Tawiya!" Martin shrieked as the knocks came on the door, and his mother rushed to open it.

HELL GATE

NEARLY every morning from the middle of September to the end of June, Christiana Friebourg emerged from her father's old hotel and stood on the porch while her eyes adjusted to the light glaring from potato fields and pastures that abutted the sea. Because hurricane waves were sometimes driven over the dunes and across the fields, the hotel was built on rock piers, and thus the porch was a full story and a half high, with a long staircase that connected it to the ground. From this height one could see past the dunes to the ocean, and, to the east, a low forest that covered the sand hills in a band of green. Christiana always stood on the porch for a few moments to look over the sea, the fields, and the forest, to listen to waves and wind, and to say good morning to the light. Then, after hoisting her schoolbag to her shoulders and hitching up her skirt, she would cobble down the stairs and start off in the direction of the northern wood. To get to school, she walked five miles over fields, past the shacks of migrant laborers, and through a forest in which lived deer, rabbits, half a hundred kinds of birds, foxes, weasels, and wild pigs that crashed through the underbrush like soldiers on maneuver.

A former Marine barracks that perched on a cliff above Gardiner's Bay, Christiana's school had half a dozen bare white rooms, into which the north light came unimpeded, glancing off the water, the islands, and a sky that sometimes could hardly be distinguished from the Atlantic itself. Winter and summer, the tops of the windows were crowned with a bright glow. And though the lessons were demanding and time passed quickly, there were intervals in which the children could listen as the whistles of ocean-going ships were bent through distance and mist until they sounded like French horns, or wonder about the composition of the wind, which always managed to push aside the shades and enter their class to speak to them of sunshine and shadow.

When Christiana was in the second or third grade, her teacher, a young woman as beautiful as Christiana herself was destined to become, asked the students one by one to describe their favorite animal. They were then to write according to their own descriptions a composition illustrative of the dog, the horse, the fish, the bird, or whatever creature they had chosen. Each child rose in turn to discourse upon the object of his affection. No one was surprised when Amy Payson spoke about rabbits, and, without realizing it, rocked one in her arms. A shy little girl who never said anything above a hoarse whisper told a tale of a dog who tried to climb a fence, entrancing her audience if only because they had to listen so closely to make out her barely audible rasp. Everyone was delighted when the fat boy of the class recited spontaneously in verse a five-minute epic about his love for a pig. "My pig it is so big,/ Its ears are like silk,/ It gives so much milk,/ With hope ahd charity it is thick,/ It takes care of us when we are sick,/ It produces much leather,/ Eats all the heather,/ Runs hither and thither,/ Wears a quiver," etc., etc. And he ended it, "Because I love him so much,/ that I thrill to his touch."

And then there was the son of a swordfisherman, who chose the swordfish, and found himself almost paralyzed by his memories of its suspended leaps, and of the courage it had as it fought, snapping its entire length above the water like a spark, giving everything it had in its struggle to stay in the sea. He concluded that the swordfish had to love its life very much to fight so hard against being taken. That in itself was enough for his essay, which, in the pure and assertive language of a child, touched upon the generative powers of memory and the definitions of courage.

The teacher was pleased with this exercise, and, as she listened to her children, she was eager for Christiana's turn. She knew that Christiana loved animals, and she knew as well that the child was unusually contemplative. Though the hotel was rarely occupied, and had been failing since Christiana was born, and though this took its toll on her as she watched her father in defeat, it was not a tragedy, for they were not greedy people, and they took their gradual impoverishment well. Christiana was a quick little girl, of deep imagination, and very pretty. But her strength was not derived from things that can be cataloged or reasonably discussed. She had an inexplicable lucidity, a power to see things for what they were. Somehow, she had come into possession of a pure standard. It was as if lightning had struck the ground in front of her and had been frozen and prolonged until she could see along its bright and transparent shaft all the way to its absolute source.

In the schoolroom with windows crowned by light, it was now Christiana's turn. She glanced out the window and saw between its pillars the quick passage of a white gull through whirling azure. Gone in a moment, it had crossed almost faster than she could see. She stood to face the teacher. She had her favorite animal, an animal she loved, and she had intended to tell about it. But she found that just the thought of it, or the saying of a few words that would lead to a vision of it in the flesh, moving slowly with wondrous unheard-of strides—just her memory of the day when she had actually seen him—brought her to the point where she had to cry.

Being practical, and not wanting to disrupt the class, she quickly decided to talk about another animal, and started to tell about a sheep that was tied up on a small patch of lawn in front of the hotel. But she couldn't. She couldn't—because for her the depth of things was always at hand, and because she had been made to think of the

341

one event in her short life which had moved her the most. She failed utterly in her restraint, and suffered the embarrassment of painful sobbing. For, try as she did, she was unable to think of anything but the white horse.

Christiana had been assigned by her mother to bring back blueberries with which to make a pie and muffins, but the real purpose of the trip was to walk among the many miles of heathered hills in June sunshine, solitary, free, and unencumbered but for a light wicker basket. At every turn or rise, she was privileged to see new views—strips of cobalt blue water held in arms of beige sand, green chevrons of forest reaching for the sea, and the sun reflecting off the Sound into flat trajectories. It seemed that each time she blinked, a new glory of landscape appeared and was celebrated by the stiff breezes that pushed in the breakers and crowned the beach with panicked bracelets of foam. In the middle of the morning, when her basket was half full, she heard a crack of thunder in a cloudless sky, and looked beyond the rim of a cake-colored dune to see that something was falling. It left a trail of mist as it plunged into the ocean, like a meteorite dipped in smoke and gold. The birds rose from the bushes, chattering, straight up, the way they do when they hear a shot. And a red fox who had been skulking in the heather froze in his tracks, listening, and held his paw in the air lest putting it down would deprive him of his senses.

She dropped the basket and rushed to the top of the dune. Shielding her eyes, she looked seaward and saw a circle of white water rocking back and forth on the waves less than a quarter of a mile out. Something surfaced in the middle of the white disc, thrashing about in confusion. It wasn't a fish (it had legs), and it telegraphed the cold and perplexed fear of someone or something that was drowning.

Walking down the silky sides of the dune, her hand still shielding her eyes, Christiana was lost in consideration of what it was and what she should do. At the water's violent edge (the surf was rough after a gale), she did what no adult would ever have done, except perhaps a strong young soldier recently returned from a war and convinced of his invulnerability. As she watched the thrashing beyond the breakers, she kicked off her shoes and unbuttoned her dress, letting it fall to the sand precariously near the lasso mark of incoming waves. In a silken camisole nearly rose-colored from age and friction, she walked into the ocean, and when the turbulent foam was at her waist and the undertow made her stance uncertain, she dived head-first into the freezing water and started swimming at the waves, sometimes going over their volu-minous crests, and sometimes diving under them into what she had always called the "salt and pepper"—because the sound was so white, and, with her eyes closed, she saw only black. She was good in the waves, having grown up in their presence. Defeating their efforts to push her back, sideways, and under, she was soon swimming in blue water that she knew was very deep.

The ocean was surging to and fro in a rhythmic fashion analagous to the movement of a violin bow. It left her in windblown blue troughs as thick with whirlpools and eddies as a lake in August is thick with lilies, and it lifted her on solid moun-tains of water that bent into lenslike plates and then collapsed to be-come a dozen little flumes. From the high points, she could see all around, as if from an observation tower, and she saw that the cur-rent was pulling her sideways. She shifted course and continued swimming, until, almost exhausted by the cold waves, she came to the edge of the foam pool. In its center, a stricken animal was thrashing in panic.

Treading water, she looked at it carefully, and saw that it was a white horse twice as big as the draft animals that pulled ploughs in the potato fields, but with the lean look of a Southampton hunt horse. Though she had never seen either a cavalry mount or a bat-tle, she knew from its motions that it thought it was in a fight. It was not drowning, but, rather, enmeshed in some sort of dream. Its front hooves left the water like leaping marlin, and smashed down into imagined opponents, cleaving the surface into angled geysers. It neighed the way horses do in a fight, in self-encouragement, and its legs never ceased flailing as it tried to trample down the brine.

If she were to approach it, she would surely be crushed, and if not, held in the vortex that it was slowly carving, and dragged un-der to drown. Even so, she swam into the ring.

The water there was far less substantial and less buoyant. Sometimes she went down in this rapids, and surfaced in a different quarter. But she kept swimming until she was literally upon him—half floating, half resting on his broad back. She put her arms around his neck as far as she could (which was not very far), and closed her eyes in anticipation of the detonation to come.

If the white horse had expected anything, it was not the sudden embrace of a young child in a silken camisole, and, unable to see what was on him, he went wild. First, he jumped out of the sea like a St. Botolph's Charger, and seemed to fly in the air. Then, four legs extended, he went under, hoping to shed his rider in the gales of water that would sweep over his back. He went as deep as he could, and rolled, and kicked in the noiseless brine, but she, lungs dying, did not let go.

When he came to the surface she was with him, and, though he continued to thrash, he seemed now to want a rider. She had to be brought to land. She was a frail child with thin arms and wet hair that streamed over her face, and despite the fact that she had come all the way out there, mounted him, and hung on, she was shaking from the cold and seemed not to have the strength to engage once more the surf and its undertow. She touched his neck, urging him toward the beach, and he began to swim the way a horse swims when it fords a river—with complete concentration and single-mindedness.

On the back of the white horse, Christiana had the impression that he might easily have headed in the other direction and been able to spend the next few months at sea, like a polar bear. He seemed to have limitless power.

As they broke through the surf he began to go faster, as if he were waking up or getting his wind back. Momentarily confused by the undertow, he took several great strides which nearly threw his rider, and was soon standing on dry land. Not realizing how far she was from the ground, Christiana slid off and hit the sand so hard that she fell backward into a sitting position. It was difficult to believe that he was so high. But she could easily walk under his belly without bending her head. She weaved in and out of his legs, passing her hand across them as if they were tree trunks. She walked through the forelegs, under his chin, and out to where he could see her. Except for his wounds—the slashes and cuts, some of which still bled—he appeared to be a public monument come alive.

He tilted his head and looked at her in parental fashion, as if she were a colt or a filly. Then he lowered his neck and nuzzled her on her stomach, and then on her head, pushing her a little one way and back again, pressing her hair enough to make salt water come dripping out of it, and yet not hurting her at all. As long as he was looking at her, she could not turn away from his perfectly round, gentle eyes.

After she had run to get her clothes, and after she and the horse were made warm and dry by the wind and the sun, she saw him glance up and search the sky. He followed gulls wheeling on thermal miles aloft, but did not seem to find what he was looking for. Then, as she watched, he galloped up and down the beach; he pranced about in a circle; and, shaking out his mane, he reared onto his hind legs. Satisfied with this, he made a single leap that, to Christiana's astonishment, took him over the high line of dunes which faced the ocean. By the time she followed, he had already taken to galloping and jumping in tremendous bounds over the duneland, the walls of scrub, and the ponds. She watched him during this exercise, wanting him to sail farther and farther at each jump—which he did. And he was not unaware of her, either, for he always stopped and looked back to see if she were still there. She was just young enough to clap each time he extended the distance of this soaring, and it made her own heart fly to see him rise into the air.

But finally he looked toward the dune where she was sitting, and raised his neck and head. Shaking them back and forth, he whinnied in the deep and beautiful way that horses can whinny when they are moved. Then he turned toward the sandflats and the Sound, and started his run. The earth shook, the beach grass trembled, he propelled himself forward, and he flew.

Stately, plump Craig Binky often sat in an exhausted daze, staring at the flickering breaker light that reflected into the living room of the illustrious East Hampton retreat which he called the "Rog and Gud Clug." His father, Lippincott "Bob" Binky, had built the club and opened it to all white gentiles of English descent. Nonetheless, the club members were not particularly fond of the founder's son. They did not like the way he pronounced things, his large entourage, the many senseless regulations that he proposed at their meetings (girls *between* the ages of nine and ten must wear waterwings *at all times*), or the blimp that he moored over the golf course. He called this blimp the *Binkopede,* and used it to cover funerals. As the deceased was being lowered into the earth, a blimp shadow would enshroud him, and the *Ghost* photographers would catch the mourners in the unusual pose of looking straight up.

Craig Binky and his friend Marcel Apand (a lecherous, candle-colored, rat-eyed real estate tycoon, whose name was pronounced "*ape hand*") believed that the job of the very wealthy, and therefore *their* job, was to find dazzling beaches and shaded groves humming with bees, to sit in a garden close as the trees swayed, and to watch the sea from well-kept summer houses as big as hotels. One afternoon, while a dozen waiters were laying out the cutlery and china of the Rod and Gun Club, Craig Binky and Marcel Apand were arguing over the former's assertion that seven plus five was thirteen. Winding through crowds of sunburned men and women, the director of the club interrupted this mathematical dispute, calling his guests' attention to the lobsters that were boiling not so far away in large steam kettles full of sea water and fresh dill, and then—anticipation of dinner having banished the argument—proceeded to ask a favor of Craig Binky.

He knew that Craig Binky's house in East Hampton had forty-five rooms, and that the double townhouse on Sutton Place had sixty, and he was aware of a great many other unused Binky habitations all over the world—a garden apartment in Kyoto, for example. He wanted to know if Craig Binky, or Marcel Apand for that matter, had an extra room to lend for a week or two. A young kitchen maid at the club needed someplace to stay in the city while she looked for a job. The club, of course, closed down promptly on the first of October. This year she had no place to live, because her father had died shortly after his old hotel—in the middle of the potato fields out toward Springs—had burned down during a terrible electrical storm. Her mother had gone back to Denmark.

"I don't know if I have room," Craig Binky blurted out, his eyes darting from place to place the way they always did when people asked him for favors. "Uh . . . the billiard room is being redone."

"Oh, that's perfectly all right," the director said, rising. "It doesn't matter."

But Marcel Apand was listening intently. "Wait a minute, Craig," he said. "Don't you want to get a look at her?"

Not long after they got a look at her, she found herself on Marcel's yacht, the *Apand Victory*. Moving through the ten thousand mothlike sails on the Sound, she felt as if she were riding on the shuttlecock of a loom that was weaving a tapestry of summer. The trip to New York by boat took two days. They stopped for the night at Marcel Apand's estate in Oyster Bay, where, in her estimation, he behaved strangely and was much too forward and direct about the kind of things that people on the tip of Long Island did not talk about in the presence of new acquaintances. But by the next day, the Fourth of July, she had generously forgiven his gracelessness, and the hot blue mist that covered the approaches to the city took up all her attention.

She had never been to New York. She had been told of its stunning size, and had made a few deductions of her own by contrasting the power and wealth of the city people with that of the islanders whom they annually overwhelmed—but she hadn't successfully guessed the half of it.

They sailed under the dozen bridges that spanned the Sound. Looking at them even from below gave her vertigo. From afar they were lovely arches and upright pillars. Like the moon and the sun, summer and winter, and all the many other things that she knew were in complementary balance, they suggested the existence of a greater and more perfect design. She could hardly believe that there were hundreds of these bridges, and their names were a delight to hear as the captain recited them for her along with the names of the rivers, channels, and bays they crossed.

At Hell Gate, when they came around the corner and saw the

darkened cliffs of Manhattan, she learned that (as fine as villages may be) the world is infatuated with its cities. The view downriver into Kips Bay was crowded with unforgettable gray canyons, and there were bridges everywhere, knitting together the islands by leaping currents that ran as fast as racehorses. Their spidery metalwork soared, and their catenaries rolled like the swells off Amagansett.

Like a rusty, bashed-up harbor tug attached to a sleek new liner, Marcel towed Christiana from one party to another. He had her by his side, turning heads, at two dozen affairs a week. When they had left the yacht on the Fourth of July and taken a taxi through a mile and a half of canyon walls of blood-red brick and mirrored glass, they had seen three or four people where normally there would have been thousands. Because no windows were open and the air was so still and hot that the trees dared not move for fear of encountering more of it than they had to, Christiana thought that she had entered a city of the dead. Had she driven in from Long Island, past the prairie full of tombs, the impression might have been strengthened. At Marcel's parties, it was confirmed.

They were the price for living in a small palace with a garden that overlooked the East River. Most of the time, Christiana had the carefully decorated reception rooms, the libraries, whirlpools, saunas, and sunny balconies to herself. Marcel was almost always at his office, but when he returned he expected her to be waiting for him, ready to go out, fully made-up, dressed in expensive silks or in gowns covered with flashing scales.

At first, she looked for work, and would have been happy to have become a salesgirl at Woolworth's or a cleaning woman in a bank. At the parties, benefits, and testimonial dinners, she was offered jobs as if they were the things that servants carried around on trays. Though these jobs paid enormous salaries, they demanded that she make herself available in the same way everyone assumed she did for Marcel.

The young men who caught her eye turned out to be either Apand employees loyal to their chief, or voracious creatures not unlike him who always managed to ask her to call them in secret.

And the men who put up the tents and hauled the food and dishes were different from the fishermen in Amagansett who did similar work in their spare time. They didn't dare look at Christiana, and she was ashamed to look at them. It saddened her to remember when she had passed out food to the Scandinavian families that came to the hotel when she was a girl, while a player piano banged out Danish songs from fifty years before, and she and the sun-burned little blond boys flushed almost to ignition at the thought of dancing or touching.

On August nights, Christiana, Marcel, and his guests would occasionally sit on a balcony that extended over the river at the garden's edge. Laden barges and intracoastal craft rode the current close to shore, passing silently and swiftly like monsters trying to sneak down the channel after having wandered by accident into the city. These poor frightened things became targets for the Apand pistols. As the barges glided by, Marcel, Christiana, and their friends pumped shots into the darkness, trying to hit the running-lights, and when they shot low they heard their bullets chime off the steel hulls and into the water.

Sometimes when Christiana found herself at a party in a very high place she would go to a darkened window and look out over the city. It smoldered in summer heat, and through the blur she could see tenements burning, perhaps ten at any one time, in the city of the poor. The many lights that shone through the misty summer air also seemed to be fires, and everything below her appeared to be alight. And yet the city was not strangled in its own smoke. It was alive, and she wanted to know it, even if it meant the risk of losing herself within it. Because there were all kinds of hell—some were black and dirty, and some were silvery and high.

In late summer the city was attacked and besieged by waves of heat which bleached and dried the marshes in New Jersey until they were as white as salt pans, scorched the pine barrens, and tried to turn the dunes of Montauk into the deserts of Mars. The city itself became a kiln—ninety-eight degrees in the shade and all through the night. The main arteries, islands, and boulevards were feathery

349

green with thirsty trees that moved like wild dancers, begging for water in the dry wind.

One airless night at the end of August, Hardesty and Virginia became crazed with desire. Possessed and hallucinating, and sweating like athletes, they struggled with everything they had to get to the other side of one another. Immersed in violent, gymnastic, wet intercourse, they felt like powerful engines, forges, furnaces, and they wondered if perhaps some great god on a journey to the outer reach had flown by the sun and passed his hot cloak over the earth. Just when it was over, they heard the steam whistle of an outbound freighter gliding downriver. They sensed the form of the ship; and its passing gravity shook their bodies and trembled through them as if the ship were not making its way down the East River, alive in the stream, but sitting across from them in their bedroom.

Not too far away, Asbury Gunwillow lay on his bed, trying as best he could to breathe. He had found work as the pilot of *The Sun*'s launch. He carried reporters and illustrators to pier fires and shipboard dedications; took them far out to sea to meet dignitaries on incoming transoceanic liners; ferried employees to and from Manhattan, Brooklyn Heights, and Sheepshead Bay; shadowed the Coast Guard, Customs Service, and Harbor Police; made it possible for the readers of *The Sun* to have fresh riverward perspectives of new buildings; accompanied Hardesty and Marko Chestnut to places like Sea Gate and Indian's Mallow; and trolled for bluefish a hundred miles off the bight. He had been pursued for a full month by a monstrous unkempt woman from Tribeca, an intellectual who did not know if it were day or night, had never seen the ocean, and thought that a goat was a male sheep. Jaundiced and liver-colored, living only through books, tobacco, and alcohol, she had the face of a bullfrog, the brain of a gnat, and the body of a raccoon. And yet she had easily lured Asbury to her loft on Vesey Street, because she had a siren's voice, and her name was Juliet Paradise. Being relatively courtly, he did not bolt at their first meeting, and she followed him thereafter like a hound. "How can I get rid of her?" he had asked Hardesty and Marko. "I look at her face, I see pizza pie.

I've tried everything. What should I do? Tell me!'' They just laughed, enjoying his distress.

Uptown, on Central Park West, Praeger and Jessica were back together again for the ninth or tenth time, knowing that they would spend the rest of their lives in convergence and reconvergence. Harry Penn, a widower, went to see his daughter when she appeared in a play, ran the finest newspaper in the Western world, and was served his at-home dinners by Boonya, an insane but cheerful Norwegian maid. Marko Chestnut, also a widower, would never fall out of love with the woman who had died, and was sustained by the grace of the children who came to his studio to be painted, the practice of his art, and the ever-changing city. Craig Binky was a bachelor who had never given a thought to love. But, then again, he hadn't ever given a thought to anything else, either. He was happy enough. He had *The Ghost,* his blimp, and various schemes to crush *The Sun.* Marcel Apand had real estate, concubines, and Christiana for show.

On the August night when Asbury had been unable to sleep and Hardesty and Virginia could not tear themselves apart, Marcel Apand, some of his closest friends, and Christiana set out in three enormous automobiles to tour the city of the poor. Marcel was not a fool: the bulletproof salons on wheels in which they rode were equipped with radios and high-voltage skins, and each automobile carried both a guard and driver armed with small submachine guns and tear-gas grenades.

They did this because they were willing to do anything for amusement, because they, too, could not sleep, and because Marcel wanted to disabuse Christiana of the notion that beyond the brownout and smoke there was a free empyrean. He wanted to show her that such things did not exist, that there was no mystery, no transfiguration, no God to save those who are thrown upon the waves.

As they rode slowly in convoy across the Williamsburg Bridge, before curtains were drawn so no one would be able to see in, they toasted each other with champagne and checked the door locks. Nervous and excited, but, most of all, curious, they spoke in barely audible whispers as they descended the Brooklyn ramp into the inferno.

"The entire city is going to burn someday," said an older man, apart from Marcel the oldest there.

"So what if it does," someone else challenged. "They probably have the right to burn it." The three cars had descended, and were moving down a long empty avenue of blackened tenements.

"I don't mean the way it burns now, the way it burns every day," said the older man. "That's controllable, acceptable. I mean a shudder of anger that will make itself heard in heaven, a fire that will leave only rubble and glass."

"We'll rebuild," said Marcel. "Let it come. We'll rebuild."

"It would be so wrong," a fashionable woman declared, "so very very wrong, to burn everything just to cleanse part of it. . . ." But then she was interrupted.

"Look!" Christiana shouted. They peered out the windows on the right side, where a group of ten or twelve skinny young men in denim jackets and tight pants were chasing a man who wore no shirt. He tripped now and then, as they did, too, because they were running across a field of jagged bricks piled three or four deep at all angles. But, still, he nearly flew, and would have kept ahead of them had not a brick thrown by someone in the front of the pack grazed his head and sent him sprawling. They closed in, beating him with steel pipes and chains. Finally, as if that were not enough, they shot him point-blank in the face eight or ten times. Then they ran.

It had all happened in less than a minute. Christiana had not been able to breathe as she watched. She begged Marcel to call the police, and wanted to get out to help the man lying on the bricks.

The glass partition between compartments went down halfway, and the guard reported that the police had been summoned. "But they won't come," he said. "Not until daylight. They're afraid. It doesn't matter: the man's dead, and he probably was expecting it." The partition closed, and they rolled on.

"Don't you own a lot of this area, Marcel?"

"I used to, Del, thirty years ago, when there was still something to own. It's all squatter's law now. And there aren't many buildings that still stand.''

"Enough to turn a profit."

"Only for the devil."

Through the tinted glass curtains came a fiery glow that made the women's faces seem rose-colored. The long avenues of flattened rubble, in which nothing stood but chimneys, were only the perimeter of a vast city of the poor that stretched to the sea. Guarded by ramparts of tenements, it appeared in the distance like an enormous pan that holds a smoky flame. The sky above it flickered and danced, and the unseen rampart walls looked like a mountain ridge shadowed against a sunset. The action of the light suggested, in red and black, the movements of a crazed barbaric army.

Though frightened into silence, they continued into the city of flame. This was no silent place, as well it might have been, punctuated only by explosions and shots. It was a hell of roaring mechanistic sounds that fought to overwhelm the senses: battalions of drums, sirens mating in the open air, engines shrieking with delight.

Hundreds of thousands of people rushed from place to place, just as in the mother city glowing coolly in the west, but these were wasted creatures with euphoric eyes. A soot-blackened man in rotted clothing bent over and pounded the sidewalk with two sticks. It appeared as if, momentarily, he would straighten his back, but he never did. Barefoot lunatics, expressions awash, staggered from street to street with their pants half down. Rows of diseased prostitutes stood at the curbs and gestured to growling automobiles that had engines powerful enough for tanks and were filled with men whose hands warmed knives and guns. There were no quiet places, no misty parks, no lakes, no trees, no clean streets. The only towers in the city of the poor were pillars of wavering smoke, and it was ruled by arrogant young men who swept through the streets. Consumed by wars among themselves, they exploited others only as an afterthought, but always well. When the cars passed by, these people pushed out their chests, gestured defiantly, and smiled. Rocks and bottles bounced off the armored automobiles like rain.

They came to a square which, though it had once been a fair-ground and a farmer's market, had become a place for the exchange of loot and drugs, for the marshaling of gangs, and for the continuous sharking and hustling that was nothing less than the city consuming itself. Off to the side, a clever entrepreneur had made the ruined foundations of a public building into an arena. A crowd was pouring in through its gates and fighting for seats on planks laid over uneven courses of dilapidated masonry. Thousands had packed themselves together to see some kind of entertainment. Marcel thought it would be all right for his party to go in as well, since everyone's attention would be directed toward what they had come to see. He sent a security man to arrange for a special box behind the lights and close to the waiting cars.

As they got out of the limousines, the women pushed back their lace veils and squinted at the carbon arc lamps that shone into the arena. The few stragglers who had gathered were silenced by the shocking differences in bearing, health, and dress that made both parties feel as if they were contemplating representatives of another species. Christiana threw back her hair and looked around. She knew that, if need be, she was able to climb or run. So often, living with Marcel, she had felt motionless, and, ironically, bodyless. Here, at least, everything was physical—the noise, the oppressive summer heat, the tumbling pink clouds which reflected the flamelight. Better to be here, she thought, where the heart pounds out of control and the hand trembles, than chatting with Marcel's friends in a drawing room or an expensive restaurant.

A man stepped into the lights. Wearing a lime-colored tuxedo and gold jewelry that seemed to be crawling all over him, he screamed in a language that Christiana could barely understand, and, as he screamed, he danced. He gestured to one entrance or another of the pit, and a fighter would appear from the shadows. Armored in shiny black metal plates that made him look more like a sea creature than a gladiator, each man carried either a sword, a long steel pike, a trident, or a mace. When the man who was being devoured by his own jewelry disappeared, a dozen strong fighters remained standing on the sand. But they did not fight each other.

Instead, a gate opened and a brown mare was pushed into the

light. At first blinded, she shied back. The roar of the crowd was a wave that struck and paralyzed her, and, as her eyes adjusted to the light, she saw the animal fighters closing in, and she knew what was going to happen. Those closest to her drove her from the wall to the center of their ring. She watched as they tightened it. There was little use in threatening with her hind quarters, since, wherever she turned, there would be a swordsman or a pikeman in front, where she was almost defenseless. Some animal fighters fought horses one to one. Not here. Even so, they moved very slowly, and the spectators were tense. The mare panicked, and reared onto her hind legs. As soon as she did, they attacked, driving their steel deep into her flesh. Pikes pierced her chest with a sound that was like a knife in a melon. She was down in an instant, swaying gently, on her knees, and they hacked at her until the sand was soaked and the pieces lay about like litter.

Christiana could barely stay upright. She had the strength neither to stand nor to cry out, and though she wanted Marcel to take her out of there, she couldn't even turn to him. She had no will, but only eyes, as in a dream.

They produced a different horse, and though Christiana begged in silence to be released, she was pinioned to the air, and she watched as another perplexed animal fell to its knees and died.

Then they brought out what the crowd had been waiting for, an enormous white stallion for whom both gates from the holding pen had to be opened. He stood calmly, neither blinded by the light nor afraid. The animal now in the ring was for Christiana the embodiment of all that she loved, all that was beautiful, and all that was good. She felt that were they to kill him they would be killing everything in the world that would someday enable it to rise. And unlike the day that she had been alone on the beach, thrown off her dress without a thought, and waded into the surf, she was now unable to go to his aid. It was a different time. Things had changed. The world was not the same as it had been when she had ridden the white horse in from the sea.

She was with him in the arc lights, and she saw through his eyes as he moved his head to survey his enemies. He stunned the crowd because he refused to be afraid. Striding forward easily, he went to the garbage that had been the mares, and put a hoof upon the bloody head of the first. It was an unmistakable gesture, and it made the horse butchers nervous. Christiana knew that he could have jumped out of the pit and left it all behind with no more difficulty than a steeplechase horse cavorting across a lawn. But he chose to stay.

He began to move about. Never before had the animal fighters faced such a large creature. During his agile dancing, muscles rose in his flesh. His legs moved fast, and the gray hooves suddenly seemed as sharp as razors. The people screamed when he reared and made the invincible fighters lower their lances and swords in fright.

A lance was thrown. The rampant stallion turned on it furiously, knocking it aside and driving it into the ground halfway the length of its shaft. The man who had thrown it tried in vain to pull it from the sand. The spectators loved this, and they would have raised the roof, had there been one, when, next, two pikes were thrown at once. The horse leapt high in the air and let one pass, and kicked the other with his rear legs, sending it up into the night air on a flight that promised to take it far beyond the smoke and clouds.

Now everyone could hear his breathing. Quick jumps took him from one side of the pit to the other, scattering the swordsmen and spear-throwers, isolating them for his attacks. They bounced off the walls, dropped their weapons, and staggered about as if they didn't know where they were. The white horse felled them one after another. He would fake to his left, and, in a split second, bound to the right, his forelegs crushing one of the horse butchers against the wall. He picked them up and shook them until they went limp, and then threw them away. He batted them with his neck and crushed them with his hooves. And in the end, he stood alone, shuddering, sweating, incensed.

Because the spectators had been worked up to a dangerous frenzy, Marcel insisted that his party leave immediately to drive back to Manhattan. When the three heavy cars took to the Great Bridge, they were raised far beyond the fiery haze of the city of the poor, and Christiana saw a full moon that had sailed over the harbor and silvered the cliffs. Away from the city of the poor there were such things as the color blue, a cool wind that had no smoke, mats of interwoven summer starlight, and the enormous pearl of the moon. The expedition, Marcel said, was a great success. Who would have known that they would see a white horse fight like an avenging angel? Marcel was credited for the discovery, and the word was spread. But other caravans would have no luck, for the white horse was soon lost deep within the city of the poor.

They returned to Manhattan quite late, or, rather, early in the morning, and they all slept soundly. That is, all except Christiana, who did not sleep at all.

She stared out over the garden to the moon-washed river. While they had been in the city of the poor, a front of cold air had come down from Canada and lifted the mist from most of Manhattan. Upriver, she imagined, it would be dark green again, rather than the diffuse jungle green of summer, in which there was no blue. Heat and haze had swallowed up the blue for weeks, but now it covered the surface of the rivers and dominated the mountainsides. The cool air shocked her into her senses.

She gathered her things together, changed into a chambray shirt and khaki pants, and went downstairs to the kitchen. There, she made half a dozen sandwiches of smoked meat, took some apples and carrots, and decided that she would steal from the petty cash jar. Marcel wouldn't miss it, and she would take only what was there. She opened it and pulled out a roll of bills that she stuffed into her pocket without looking. Outside, on Sutton Place, in the middle of the night, she felt free for the first time in months, and she almost danced down the street. She had no idea where she was headed or what she would do, but, before she turned into the depths of the city, she counted the money she had taken and was a little shocked to see that it came to $3,243. Since that was barely enough to make a small lunch for Marcel's closest friends, or to provision the yacht for a day sail, she rightly assumed that he would never know or care that it was gone. After all, this was the man who had lost $7 million at Pachinko, and said it was worth having seen the little silver balls fall past the little silver pins.

Purely by chance, she headed south to the Village. The city was empty, its only activity the blinking on and off of neon signs, an occasional plume of steam that rose from the street, or a gull that gently crossed the gap between canyons, gliding on air that was pink with dawn and equanimity. Everything seemed benevolent. But, still, she was apprehensive. Marcel had said that she would be devoured immediately by the hard city outside. "You've never lived alone," he said. "It's not easy. How will you find an apartment? Where? Do you know how difficult it is to obtain an apartment in New York? And a job: it might take months to get a job. Meanwhile, you'll starve on the street."

Early in the morning, a real estate agent showed her a tiny chamber on Bank Street, which he called an apartment. The bathtub was in the kitchen, and she could touch all four walls of the "bedroom" from one spot, but it was clean and it was quiet, and it overlooked a garden. "You'll have to share the balcony with the gentleman who lives in the adjoining residence. He works for *The Sun*, piloting their launch, so he's always out when the weather's good, and you'll have the balcony to yourself."

"But it's only a foot wide," Christiana protested.

"Two hundred dollars a month," the real estate agent answered.

She signed the lease, put down a security deposit and a month's rent, and the real estate agent left. "Bang!" said Christiana. "Just like that, and I've got a place to live!" She opened a bank account, stocked the refrigerator, and furnished the place, all before noon. Since she needed only a small table, two chairs, a white sleeping mat, some blankets, a pillow, three lamps, an old prayer rug, and a minimum of kitchen equipment for her minimum of a kitchen, she was left with more than $2,000—and some pocket money with which she bought lunch, a Danish dictionary, several Danish novels and geography books, a notebook, and some pens. She was going to teach herself the language that she had first known and that still lay dormant within her needing only to be awakened. By three o'clock that afternoon, she had found a job.

At the service entrance of a beautiful house in Chelsea, a most astonishing-looking ageless woman named Boonya took her inside and began to explain the duties of an occasional maid.

"But I said *full-time*," Christiana protested.

"Mr. Penn pays you for full-time, dear," said Boonya, who was as round as a medicine ball, "but you only work part-time. In the interbules, you're supposed to go to liberries and concerps. If you go to college, he'll pay your tuition. Me, I prefer to work around the house, to cook and do the washtub and stuff. But each is different. Bosca, the dark girl, who was here until she left, was studying in the theater. Do you see what I mean?"

"Yes. Extraordinary."

"If that's how you want to put it. All right, can you cook?"

"I used to cook in my parents' hotel."

"Good," said Boonya, as she led Christiana to the kitchen. "But you may not be familiar with the foods that Harry Penn holds dear to his heart. He and his daughter have favorites, which I'll teach you how to make."

"Like what?"

"Oh, durbo cheese stuffed with trefoil, camminog, meat of the vibola, roast bandribrolog seeds, satcha oil hotcakes, young Dollit chicken in Sauce Donald, giant broom berries, crème de la berkish tollick, serbine of vellit, pickled teetingle, chocolate wall hermans, trail lemons, Rhinebeck hot pots with fresh armando, parrifoo of aminule, vanilla lens arrows, fertile beaties, archbestial bloodwurst, Turkish calendar cake, fried berlac chippings, cocktail of ballroom pig, vellum cream cake, undercurrents, crisp of tough boxer lamb, sugared action terries, merry rubint nuts, and rasta blood-chicken with sauce Arnold."

For each of these products of Boonya's crazed imagination, she had a recipe. Christiana looked on in wonder as Boonya pantomimed the preparation of fresh teetingle, or the proper way to cut vanilla lens arrows. "Always flour the marble before you put down an uncooked lens arrow. Sprinkle the vanilla. Cut it fast!" she screamed, her fat sausagelike arms flailing about the medicine ball. "Otherwise, it sticks. Sticky little bastards, lens arrows. Did your mother ever teach you how to properly bone a good serbine of vellit?"

Boonya took her through the house, which was filled with books, paintings, and nautical relics, all of which required regular dusting. There was an illuminated painting of Harry Penn as a regimental commander in the Great War. "That was years ago," Boonya explained, "ages and ages ago. He's a young man there, but not now. Now he's old. He spends a lot of time at *The Sun,* but when he's here, he's always reading. He says books stop time. I myself think he's crazy. (I put a book right next to my alarm clock, and the clock kept on going.) Don't tell anyone, but when he reads something that he likes he gets real happy, turns on the music, and dances by himself, or with a broom sometimes. Mum's the word."

"I suppose it's because his wife's dead," said Christiana, "that he dances with a broom."

"I don't think so," said Boonya. "He dances with a mop, too."

"Maybe he had a mistress."

"He did, but she had short hairs. I also got short-haired mops. They're for precision cleaning, like those small wheels they got in racing cars. In them European formula P's, the wheel's the size of a silver dollar. That's why they have midget racers, who can grab it in their tiny hands." She looked around in conspiratorial fashion and beckoned Christiana toward her. Whispering softly, she said, "Their little bodies fit between the struts. My cousin Louis tried to be one. He's small enough, Lord knows. But Louis always pretends to be a shadow turkey, so they threw him out."

"What's a shadow turkey?"

"That's one of those things that boomatooqs use to wash windows with, but they're illegal in New York and New Jersey, so Connecticut boomatooqs have to smuggle them through to get to Pennsylvania. Get my drift? Louis wasn't all there. One day, the Lord was cracking nuts, and Louis was taking a nap in the nut pile. Get it?"

Christiana smiled, but, when Boonya looked away for an instant, duplicitously rolled her eyes.

"Shh!" hissed Boonya, holding her finger up in the air. "Do you hear castanets?"

"No," Christiana answered.

"I think I hear them passing on a funeral wagon. Maybe the Spanish ambassador kicked the bucket." And then, with drops of sweat dripping from the unified eyebrow that marched across her forehead like a centipede, Boonya gradually stoked the fire of her madness until she intoned like a druid, singing to Christiana what she said were her ten favorite Egyptian Christmas carols, delivering a long and intense dissertation on Eskimo sexual utensils, and talking about the coconut, which she maintained was exclusively the symbol of military preparedness. She would stop to quiz Christiana.

"What's the symbol of military preparedness?"

"The coconut."

"Exclusively?"

"So it is said."

But all in all, Boonya was a good maid and (in her work, at least) as stable as the Rock of Gibraltar. And she looked like it too, or, rather, like a sphere with three melons on it—two enormous breasts that swayed with gravity, and a head upon which were coils of thin blond hair wound in basket-weave. She was Norwegian, and thought she was superior to the slim and beautiful Christiana, who was Danish, because Norway was above Denmark.

They got along in a fashion. Going to work became for Christiana an extraordinary entertainment, for Boonya's declarations and pronouncements were never-ending, she could clean like a demon, she sang songs in languages that no one knew, and she had recipes for a thousand foods that did not exist.

Not until winter, when during a prolonged blizzard *The Sun*'s launch was idle, did Christiana discover the inhabitant of the apartment on the other side of the wall. A steady northwest wind drove the snow in hypnotic trajectories as the blizzard rushed through the garden, turning it into an alpine cirque. Asbury and Christiana sat facing one another for hours, though between them were two fires and several thicknesses of brick.

She was deep in Thorgard's *Winter Seas,* speeding along at two pages an hour in the original Danish. Asbury was at a little table before the fire, struggling with *Dutton's Problems in Advanced Navigation,* over which he soon had to triumph if he were to continue his progress toward a master's certificate. For six months, they had lived in adjoining rooms, and been completely unaware of

361

one another's presence, though they slept literally less than a foot apart.

Were the forces of nature less concerned with the mounting of stupendous blizzards and the greening of mountain ranges than with maneuvering together a good man and a good woman, the bricks that separated them would have crumbled long before. But the forces of nature did not seem to care, and it was not until Asbury got up to get his fire going that he and his neighbor were finally enabled to meet. He rocked the logs with a poker, watching the red coals chip off into devil's candy. When he was satisfied with the activity he had promoted in the crucible before him, he banged the poker against the back wall of the fireplace three times, to rid it of a few glowing embers that had lodged in its hook.

Christiana put down her book and stared at the inner wall of the fireplace. Then she got up, seized a poker, and knocked back three times. It was answered. Soon the telegraphy moved from the firewall to the wall above the mantel, and then to the wall between their beds. There, discovering that voices could carry through, they introduced themselves, but then cut off their conversation quite rapidly thereafter, out of embarrassment. "What place is this in your apartment?" she had asked.

"My bed," he had answered. "What about you?"

"The same," she had said, realizing that they slept only inches apart.

"Are you going to move it now?" Asbury asked.

"No."

Sometimes they spent hours lying next to the wall, saying anything that came to mind, telling their histories, what they had thought, and what they had dreamed. In this way, they became so intimate that it was as if they were having a blistering love affair without anything like a wall between them. In the summer, he told her, they could travel by their narrow balconies to a valley between the peaks of the roof. "From there you can see the river," he told her.

She said that she would like to go there. But was it dangerous to climb up? "No," he answered. They would meet during the summer. But not until then.

"What do you look like?" Asbury asked one night, months later, because he knew that, since it was already the beginning of May, he would soon see her.

"I'm not pretty. I'm not pretty at all," she said.

"I think you're beautiful," he shot back through the wall.

"No," Christiana insisted. "It's not true. You'll see."

"I don't care," he answered. "I love you."

When he heard her crying, he thought that perhaps he had gotten himself in deeper than he should have. But he did love her, and he didn't care if, as she steadily maintained, she was homely. This he made clear to her on a number of occasions during the late spring. Finally, he asked her to marry him.

Everyone, including Hardesty, thought that Asbury had made a terrible mistake. "I understand," Hardesty said, "how people, especially lonely people, might fall in love through a wall. But if she is, as she claims, physically repulsive, you'll need that wall between you for the rest of your lives."

"I know," Asbury said. "If she's really hideous, you might be right. But she says that she's just overly plain, whatever that means. I still can't see how she could fail to appear to me to be the most beautiful woman in the world."

Hardesty offered to go look, and received a resounding lecture on trust, after which Asbury affirmed that he was going to take the risk. Her voice was beautiful, and he knew that he loved her—that was enough.

She agreed to marry him, and they decided to meet in the roof valley on the first fine day. Naturally, it rained throughout most of the spring.

But one day early in June, in the morning, before the sun was too hot, Asbury went out on the roof. At first he climbed to the peak of his own side and stayed there, looking at the river, trying not to tremble too much, because it was the perfectly blue day for which he had been waiting. Hell, he thought, let's just do it. He went into the valley and up again, and spoke through a chimney.

"Christiana," he shouted. "Are you up? I hope I have the right chimney."

"I'm up," she yelled into her fireplace, her heart racing.

"Come to the roof. It's time we met." He tried not to be nervous. "After we get over the shock of this, one way or another, we can go sailing. Maybe all the way to Amagansett."

"Coming," she said, in motion, in a voice that had reverted to nearly pure Scandinavian, though the word was hardly audible as she sprang away from the hearth.

Asbury went down to where the two roofs met, and stood with a foot on each one, facing the direction from which she would appear.

First, her hand came over the edge while she climbed up on the balcony rail. Then she rose in one quick movement, and stood before the lover that she had never seen. She was more than pleased. And he was stunned.

"I knew it," he said, in triumph, struggling to take her in all at once. "I knew that you would be the most beautiful woman in the world. And goddammit," he said, stepping back a pace so as not to be overwhelmed, "you are."

·III·

THE SUN ...
AND
THE GHOST

NOTHING IS RANDOM

NOTHING is random, nor will anything ever be, whether a long string of perfectly blue days that begin and end in golden dimness, the most seemingly chaotic political acts, the rise of a great city, the crystalline structure of a gem that has never seen the light, the distributions of fortune, what time the milkman gets up, the position of the electron, or the occurrence of one astonishingly frigid winter after another. Even electrons, supposedly the paragons of unpredictability, are tame and obsequious little creatures that rush around at the speed of light, going precisely where they are supposed to go. They make faint whistling sounds that when apprehended in varying combinations are as pleasant as the wind flying through a forest, and they do exactly as they are told. Of this, one can be certain.

And yet there is a wonderful anarchy, in that the milkman

chooses when to arise, the rat picks the tunnel into which he will dive when the subway comes rushing down the track from Borough Hall, and the snowflake will fall as it will. How can this be? If nothing is random, and everything is predetermined, how can there be free will? The answer to that is simple. Nothing is predetermined; it is determined, or was determined, or will be determined. No matter, it all happened at once, in less than an instant, and time was invented because we cannot comprehend in one glance the enormous and detailed canvas that we have been given—so we track it, in linear fashion, piece by piece. Time, however, can be easily overcome; not by chasing the light, but by standing back far enough to see it all at once. The universe is still and complete. Everything that ever was, is; everything that ever will be, is—and so on, in all possible combinations. Though in perceiving it we imagine that it is in motion, and unfinished, it is quite finished and quite astonishingly beautiful. In the end, or, rather, as things really are, any event, no matter how small, is intimately and sensibly tied to all others. All rivers run full to the sea; those who are apart are brought together; the lost ones are redeemed; the dead come back to life; the perfectly blue days that have begun and ended in golden dimness continue, immobile and accessible; and, when all is perceived in such a way as to obviate time, justice becomes apparent not as something that will be, but as something that is.

PETER LAKE RETURNS

$\mathbf{F}$OR several years or more, the
run of severe winters had been broken by a series of sunny
counterfeits that were called winter only by Hawaiians. The
worker-devils who tore up the streets in mid-Manhattan as traffic
swirled about them like floodwaters around a caisson, did so in the
middle of January with their shirts off. At Christmastime, women
were seen on high terraces, sunning themselves. There was no
snow; the garment industry was convulsed; the news weeklies had
a series of identical covers about the weather. (*Newsweek*—"No
more winters?"; *Time*—"Where are the snows of yesteryear?";
The Ghost News Magazine—"It's Hot.") Then, just at the peak of
complacency, when it was assumed that the climate of the world
had changed forever, when the conductor of the philharmonic
played Vivaldi's *Four Seasons* and left out an entire movement,

and when to children of a young age stories of winter were told as if they were fairy tales, New York was hit by a cataclysmic freeze, and, once again, people huddled together to talk fearfully of the millennium.

Snow filled the parks in volumes that would have impressed the inhabitants of the Coheeries, overwhelming half the trees and hills. It soon became the custom to ski from place to place, passing silently over dead and buried cars. The air was so clear that people said, "Shake it and it will shatter," and day after day, week after week, month after month, a dense freezing wind descended from the north, pushing snow and ice before it like a calving glacier. Winter abounded and exploded. Always the season of testing and extremes, it made some people euphoric and others suicidal; it split granite boulders, tree trunks, and marriages; it tripled the rate of winter romances; brought back sleds and skis, and chapbooks about Christmas in New England; and it froze the Hudson into a solid highway. It even froze half the harbor.

Though it was said that winters like this one had come before, hardly anyone was old enough to remember them. The last one of such severity that it threatened not only the physical world, but beliefs and institutions, had been not too long after the turn of the century. Only the great wars had obliterated it from people's memories. During that winter, it was as if time itself had been alive, had a will of its own, and wanted it to be forgotten. Much about those years remained unexplained, as if they had been preparing a coup, and, shortly before they might have been discovered, had retreated to await a more propitious moment. The expressions of the men and women of that era, surviving in photographs, seemed all-knowing, and the subjects of the portraitists seemed to peer through time and know the innermost thoughts of those who studied their images decades after they had died. Such faces and eyes, constructed of light and truth, did not anymore exist.

A plain of ice encircled Manhattan. Its southern limit was about a mile and a half past the Statue of Liberty (to which one could now walk), and icebreakers continually ploughed across it to keep a channel open for the Staten Island ferry. Even after the ferry moved into open water, however, it had to pass gingerly between enormous blocks of ice that had broken from the shelf and were floating toward the sea.

One January evening at dusk, in a blinding downpour of driven snow, the ferry was halfway to Staten Island when it smashed its rear shafts and propellers against a submerged reef of ice, and went dead in the water. The captain chose to steam on the front blades and go back to Manhattan rather than to turn among the icebergs. The ferry was drifting slowly in the snow, about to shift power. This was a routine task, but it had to be accomplished quickly, because the boat drifted at a different rate than the ice, and was bound therefore to suffer collisions with it.

On the bridge, officers and crew were properly calm—alert professionals enjoying the tension of the moment and the silent precision that it elicited from them. Suddenly, a passenger burst in. The public was not allowed on the bridge for any reason, and this gesticulating lunatic had not only interrupted the satisfying drama of the propeller transfer, he had also brought into a dim and elegant silence some of the cacophony of the city from which the ferry was usually able to keep a comfortable distance. He hardly spoke English, and none of the pilots spoke Spanish. Throwing himself around in a sort of epileptic dance, he seemed like the more dangerous type of escapee.

"What do you want?" the captain screamed, enraged.

The man took a deep breath, tried not to shake, and pointed out the window. When they looked through the falling snow, they saw an object in the water, about fifty feet away. It was moving in barely visible spasms. It was a man.

As soon as they could hack the ice off the davits, they lowered a lifeboat, and pulled him in. He was so badly wounded and stunned that they didn't expect him to talk. They would not have been surprised had he rattled over and died.

Propped up in the crew's shower, he faced the steaming water in apparent gratitude. Several minutes more in the chill harbor would have frozen him brittle.

A Spanish speaker was found to interpret the account of the discoverer, now inflated with pride. He had been gazing absentmindedly into the snow, when he heard a whistle in the air like that of an approaching artillery shell. Before him appeared a bright streak of light, and the water under it exploded as if someone had set off a dynamite charge to break apart the ice. Surprised by the intense white flash, he was further amazed when a body was elevated on the mushrooming foam. Then he had run to the bridge.

"Are you sure you didn't push him during a fight?" asked the captain of the *Cornelius G. Koff*—an ancient boat that was still in service. "I'm told he's wounded."

The man who could hardly speak English stormed off the bridge. His countenance was enough to prove his innocence.

"Call an ambulance to the slip," the captain told his mate. "If the overboard wants to press charges against anyone, inform the police. If not, forget it. We have enough to do."

Several decks below, the overboard in the shower heard the engines start, and felt the boat lurch ahead. Someone beyond the shower curtain asked if he wanted to press charges.

"Press charges against who?" inquired the wounded man, from within the hot water stream, startled by his own Irish accent.

"Are you sure?"

"Sure I'm sure," said Peter Lake, staring in amazement at his wounds, which, from their appearance, had to have been received recently.

"But you're all cut up."

"I see that," answered Peter Lake. "I think I got some bullets in me, too."

"How did it happen?"

The mate heard the shower dashing off Peter Lake's pale skin. "I don't know," Peter Lake answered.

"What's your name?" There was no reply. "It's not important, though they might want to know at the hospital. If you don't want to say anything, that's your business."

Feeling so weak that the foghorns speaking to each other across the winter harbor seemed like the music of a dream, Peter Lake struggled to put on a pair of torn pants, a work shirt, and a wool sweater that was dotted with specks of white paint. He was also given a pair of old shoes which, by some accident, fit perfectly. Leaning over to tie them made his heart race, and spots appeared before his eyes, but this was almost as pleasant as getting into a warm bed on a cold night. He was told that his own clothes—nothing more than soft shreds—had peeled off him and disintegrated when he had been hauled into the lifeboat.

As the ferry was docking, he stepped before a small broken mirror on the bulkhead.

"There's an ambulance at the pier," the mate said. "You're bleeding like hell, but we had to put you in the shower. You would have froze to death. Besides, the harbor's not exactly lily-white."

Peter Lake put his hands against the wall to steady himself. He was faint from loss of blood, and he felt and moved like a drunk. Staring at his image in the mirror, he shuddered. "Funny," he said. "I don't know who that is."

Then he saw two ambulance attendants coming down the stairs, carrying a stretcher between them. They caught him just as he was about to hit the floor.

He awoke at dawn in one of the very old ward rooms of St. Vincent's Hospital, looking out on Tenth Street. It was snowing, and because the light was diffuse, all the shadows in the room were gray. He remembered the cold water, the ferry, the shower, and little else. Certainly, he would snap to at any moment. Sometimes you forget your name, he thought. Like hell you do. Maybe he was drunk. Perhaps he was dreaming.

Written on a plastic band around his wrist were the day and month that he was admitted, a four-digit number, and "No Name." Never before had he seen plastic. He felt how smooth it was, not knowing why he was amazed, because, although he knew it was not familiar, he couldn't imagine that he had never come across it. There were certain things that he simply could not recollect, and this he found unbearably annoying. Who was he? How old? What month was it (the bracelet said "2/18")? Still, he believed that everything was near at hand, at the tip of his tongue.

A group of doctors and medical students entered the ward and began their rounds. By the time they got to Peter Lake, attendants were serving breakfast to the patients who had been examined, most of the white curtains were drawn back, and the silvery light—

within which the snow wound and unwound in the manic convulsions of a spinning jenny—had a bright daylike sheen.

As a dozen medical students and nurses gathered around Peter Lake's bed, the senior physician snatched a clipboard from the bedstead, glanced at it, and addressed the patient. "Good morning," he said. "How are we feeling this morning?"

A shot of hostility welled up in Peter Lake. Although he didn't like the doctor and he didn't know why, he trusted himself, perhaps because he had nothing else.

"I don't know," he snapped back, eying them one by one. "You should know how you feel."

"I see," the doctor said. "If that's how you want it, that's how you'll get it."

"Just don't saw off my legs," Peter Lake responded.

"Then let's start with your name. You were unconscious when you were admitted. You had no identification. . . ."

"What's identification?"

"A driver's license, for example."

"For what, a locomotive?"

"No. For a *car.*"

"When you say 'car' do you mean an automobile?" Peter Lake asked. The students nodded their heads. "You don't need a *license* to drive an automobile."

"Look," the senior physician said, "you had three bullet wounds. We had to take your fingerprints and give them to the police. They'll have your name, so you might as well tell us."

At the mention of the police, Peter Lake lunged forward, and discovered that he was handcuffed to the bed. The medical students started at the rattle of the chains. "What are fingerprints?" he asked. But they had lost their patience. Rather than an answer, he got a needle in the arm, and he watched them depart.

Breathing slowly, Peter Lake stared at the ceiling. He had no strength, and could not move. His eyes were wide open, and a million thoughts crowded his head, like snowflakes in a blizzard. And yet, despite manacles, wounds, and drugs, he felt as if he had some fight left in him. He didn't know from where it came any more than he knew who he was. But he did know that deep inside the immobile body handcuffed to a hospital bed, there was still a lot of fire. And when he fell asleep, he was smiling.

Five days later, Peter Lake awakened to a springlike evening. The ward was quiet, and he had been corralled within a screen of frilly snow-white cloth. Opening his eyes, he saw a dark violet sky through the upper corner of a window, and strange white lights in the ceiling, which he took to be some sort of adaptation of a cathode ray tube. When he turned his head to the side, he saw that there was a young girl in the cubicle with him.

She was sitting on a chair at his bedside, staring with a youthful optimism that seemed to flow from every atom in her body. She looked no more than fourteen or fifteen, had astonishing green eyes, and red hair that was piled up in beautiful waves and falling tresses. She was freckled, as someone of her coloring might be, and she was slightly chubby. Peter Lake noticed (and then felt properly ashamed for making such an observation about so young a girl) that she had a most attractive bosom, moving visibly and seductively under her white blouse. This he attributed to early development and healthy plumpness.

The girl, in fact, was twenty-seven years old, and looked young for her age. She was a former resident of Baltimore, a hardworking, good-natured young woman—his attending physician. But, of course, he didn't know that, and he smiled at her with a slight elongation of the strange smile that he had during his five days of sleep. "Hello, missy," he said.

"Hi," she answered, responding to the warmth of his greeting.

"How long have I been asleep; do you know?"

She shook her head to indicate that she did. "Five days."

"Jesus Christ."

"You got a lot better in that time. Sleep did wonders for your wounds."

"It did?"

"Yes. You should be up and about in less than a week."

"Is that what they said?"

"Who?"

"The doctors."

"No, it's what *I* say."

"That's nice, but what do *they* say?"

"They generally agree," she stated, after thinking for a moment. "If the matter isn't too complicated. These things are pretty straightforward."

"No handcuffs," Peter Lake said, looking at his wrists. "When did they take them off?"

"I took them off when it became clear that you were going to sleep awhile. Then the police report came: you're not under suspicion of anything, and they didn't have your fingerprints. They would like to know how you were shot and slashed, but they're not going to press."

"Where's the women's ward?" Peter Lake asked, wondering if perhaps this little girl were some kind of loony, because she seemed to think that she was in charge, and, besides, she was probably not allowed to be with him.

"It's on the floor above," she answered, pointing up. As her lovely eyes swept upward, she looked like some sort of mystical icon. "Why do you ask?"

"Don't you think you better get back, dear, before they catch you?" In fact, he wanted her to stay—perhaps because she elicited from him both paternal goodwill and a slightly nagging sexual interest. She laughed at his question, and her amusement convinced him that she was an escaped lunatic who had broken out of her chains.

"This is my ward," she volunteered, thinking that he assumed a female doctor would not be allowed on a male ward. She didn't suspect that he was ignorant of her position, for her tunic, her paging unit, and the stethoscope sticking out of her breast pocket were obvious signs of her profession.

But Peter Lake had never seen that style of doctor's tunic, had never seen or heard of a female doctor, had never seen a paging unit, was just nearsighted enough that he could not read the small print of her security badge, and thought that the flesh-colored rubber tubes coming out of her pocket were part of a slingshot. "Why would they put you in a men's ward, missy, when you're obviously, delightfully, and undeniably a woman?"

After a short silence, she spoke up. "Don't you know that I'm your doctor?'' she asked. ''I'm the physician in charge of this ward. This is my second year as a resident. Is that what's confusing you?''

Certain that she was mentally ill (though a pure delight), since no adolescent girl—especially one who carried a slingshot—could possibly be chief of a men's ward in a hospital, Peter Lake decided to go along with her. ''Oh, now I see,'' he said. ''Yes! That was what was confusing me.'' He smiled. She smiled. ''But it's all clear now''—he hesitated, to give emphasis to the next word—''Doctor.''

''Good,'' she said, pleased that she had gained the confidence and cooperation of a patient she had been told would be difficult and, perhaps, violent (a burly orderly sat on a cart on the other side of the curtain). As Peter Lake took her sweet, rather chunky little hand, and squeezed it, she said, ''I'll be around tomorrow. We have a lot to talk about. I'm going to try my best to see that you can leave here as quickly as possible.''

''Thank you, Doctor.''

''It's my job,'' she said. ''Meanwhile, believe it or not, you need to sleep some more. So I'm going to give you an injection.'' She pulled out a needle the size of a meat skewer, and began to top it off in the fiendish way that needles are topped off.

''Now wait a minute!'' Peter Lake screamed. He hadn't bargained on actual treatment, and didn't know what was in the syringe, or where she wanted to stick him. ''Let's not. . . .'' It was too late.

With an expert thrust, she got him in the arm, and he dared not move for fear of breaking the needle in his flesh.

''What's in it?'' he asked, as the fluid entered his veins.

''Trioxymetasalicylate, dimethylethyloxitan, and Vipparin.''

''Ohhhh . . .'' cried Peter Lake, perhaps one of the most confused beings that had ever been on earth. ''I hope you know what you're doing.''

She smiled her reply as he drifted off to sleep.

Awakening several hours earlier than the young doctor had thought he would, Peter Lake stretched out his arms. At first he had no idea of where he was or what had happened. Then he grew anxious, for he was able to remember that, in fact, he could not remember. He turned his head. The only thing he could see was the white cloth screen, and in that quiet moment he finally understood that he was alone. If there had once been those whom he had loved, who had loved him, he was now separated from them. Even were they suddenly to appear, he reasoned, he might not know them. Though the way in which he was lost was the most serious way in which a man can be lost, still, he hoped that it would pass, and that his confusion would dissipate like fog as it burns off the bay on a hot morning in July.

The silence was suddenly broken. Peter Lake rose onto his shoulder to free his ears from the pillow so that he could hear better the sound of horses on the street. This was something he knew, something at last familiar. There was a whole detachment of them, fifty or more, and he could tell from the way they were shod, the way their bits clinked, and the way they were packed close together that they were police mounts changing shift. It must be four o'clock, he thought. They're on their way downtown, and right now the night horses are stomping as the black boys curry them, and mounted policemen are filing in from all over to begin the rides that end at midnight.

The horses soon passed, and he was left with the discomfort of the many things around him that were not familiar. A box that was bracketed to the wall, at a tilt, stared at him with a blank glass face. It couldn't have been a cabinet, because it was too high to reach, and, besides, everything in it would have been all jumbled up. He couldn't imagine what it was. And then, the way things were shaped, and the materials of which they were made, seemed almost otherworldly. "There isn't any iron in this place," he said to himself, "or any wood." Everything seemed to have grown smooth, to have lost its texture.

What, in God's name, were the panels above his head, that seemed to glow in red and green. He thought at first that they were stove doors, but the light was green as well as scarlet, and he knew that neither coal nor wood burned green. He propped himself up and got close enough to them to see that they were tiny lights jumping around like fleas. Astonishingly, they made their little pulses and flickered on and off in sympathy with his breathing and his heartbeat, or so it seemed, for when he strained to get near them they went mad with activity, and when he recovered, they did, too. He wondered if he were dreaming.

It was still broad daylight when the girl doctor appeared. Her patient was sitting up in bed, freshly awakened, pensive, and obviously much improved. When they are absorbed in thought, certain people become so paralyzed by the play (or circus) that takes place invisibly before their eyes or in their hearts, that they command a silence that others give them without resentment. Peter Lake had not always been like this, but now he was, perhaps because he needed so badly to solve the riddle into which he had awakened. Even his physician was silent out of respect for his reverie.

"Oh," he said when he saw her. "You are a doctor, aren't you?"

"Yes. I am," she answered.

"I never heard of a girl doctor."

"I'm twenty-seven."

"You don't look it. You look at best fifteen—forgive me—and, still, I didn't know that they made women doctors. Then again, that doesn't mean very much, does it, seeing that I don't even know who I am."

"While I was gone," she said, "I checked to be absolutely sure that there were female doctors in Ireland. There are."

"I'm not from Ireland," he said. "I'm from New York."

"You speak with an Irish accent."

"That's true, and it's a mystery to me. But I'm from the city. I know that."

"You were found in the harbor. You could have been a sailor or a passenger on a ship. Knocked on the head and all that."

"No," Peter Lake asserted. "I wouldn't be so certain except for the police horses. That was about twenty minutes ago. They must have been on their way downtown to break the shift. Where are we now?"

"St. Vincent's Hospital."

"That's on Sixth Avenue and Eleventh Street."

"Yes."

"It would take about ten minutes for them to get from here to the stables, and ten minutes to get in. Therefore, it must be about four o'clock."

Just then, as if to confirm that here was a man of precision, who would and could find his way out of the confusion that had temporarily overcome him, a church bell chimed. He counted silently, moving his lips, "One . . . two . . . three . . . four." The doctor looked at her watch. (He didn't understand that she was touching it to cue it, and he thought she was petting it the way a railway man does with his chronometer, or a baseball pitcher does with his hat.) It was exactly four.

"That's an unusual way to tell time," she told him. "By horses! It certainly shows that there's a good chance for you to find out who you are, if only by deduction."

"I don't need a watch," Peter Lake volunteered. "I can tell the quarter-hours by the bells, and (here, he wanted to orient himself and to impress her at the same time) I know that trains will pass by on the El approximately once every . . ."

"What El?" she interrupted.

"The El."

"What El?"

"The Sixth Avenue El."

A shiver went up her spine.

"The elevated train," he said, his voice rising. "I couldn't be more positive."

She shook her head. "There's no elevated train on Sixth Avenue, or anywhere else that I know of. Oh, maybe in the Bronx, or Brooklyn somewhere. But not in downtown Manhattan."

"Don't be ridiculous," said Peter Lake, sure of himself, yet not sure at all. "They're all over the place. You can't miss 'em. They're everywhere."

"No," she stated emphatically. "They're nowhere. There aren't any."

"Let me take a look out the window."

"You're tied into an IV and monitors, and besides, we're on the side street."

"I've got to see."

380

"Trust me. There hasn't been an El for half a century."

"That's why I've got to see," he said, starting to move. "I've got to see the city. It's the only thing by which to really measure the time."

"How about your horses?" she asked, sympathetically.

"Horses aren't enough. They're too small. You understand? I need the whole city."

"When you recover."

"I am recovered."

"Not quite yet."

"I *am*," he echoed. He pulled the hospital gown from his shoulders. She went to stop him, but when she saw where his wounds had been, she saw only scars. The man was sound, and in trim as well. He had no business in a needed hospital bed.

She put her hands to her mouth. It was not possible. She herself had dressed the wounds, and she knew his condition exactly. She tried to think of ways in which she could have been fooled. Perhaps it was an elaborate practical joke. No, he was well. Inexplicably, he was well.

"What year is this?" he demanded.

She told him, but he was not ready to believe her until he himself had seen the city, fine and irrefutable clock that it was.

"Show me to the roof," he said.

She helped him disconnect the tubes and sensors, and he got into the clothes that he had been given on the ferry. They walked quietly through the ward and went to the elevator. It would be dark out, but what did that matter in New York?

From the way that he stared at the stainless steel, the thermal call buttons, and the lights, she knew that he had never seen such things before in his life. She observed, as a physician would, that he was trembling, that his lips were slightly quivering, that his complexion alternated between flush and pallor. And then, as perhaps a physician would not, she observed that she, too, was trembling. "If this is a joke, I'll kill you," she said, wondering how she could believe what she believed and think what she had thought.

They came to the top floor, which was empty and white. The old building had been redone, but it was familiar enough to make Peter

Lake think that he was about to see the city that he knew. The El would be there, as would everything else. Ferries with rows of black smokestacks as tall as top hats would drift across the bay, spitting out sparks as big as oranges. He would see distant girderwork against the sky, but, overall, the city would be the same—the nineteenth century opening its eyes, casting off its veils of steel and ebony. The dream would end. It would all fall quietly into place.

They came to the roof door. "It's funny," Peter Lake stated. "I don't think that this notion I have could be so, but I'm afraid to open the door."

"Just push it," she said.

He did.

THE SUN

$\mathbf{O}$N the fifteenth of May, *The Sun* celebrated its 125th anniversary, and several thousand people embarked upon the Staten Island ferry as it rested in the harbor in a cool fog that drifted across the surface of the water. Harry Penn had decided to celebrate the longevity of his newspapers by taking his employees and their spouses on a spring cruise "up the Hudson and under the Palisades," as it was originally billed, although the phrase "under the Palisades" made Hugh Close, the rewrite editor, protest sarcastically that they weren't going to do any tunneling in rock. The cruise was then to take place "beneath the Palisades," after "in the shadow of the Palisades" was rejected because, as Close pointed out, there would be no moon that night, and, therefore, the Jersey cliffs would cast no shadows.

The brightly lighted ferry was as orange and gold as a bowl of fruit in the sun. Thousands of bottles of champagne and tons of hors d'oeuvres and desserts filled linen-covered tables that ran like ribbons through the long cabins. An orchestra on each deck played at full steam as the celebrants came on board. They were elated and optimistic, because they had put *The Sun* to bed early that afternoon and received surprise 125th anniversary grants equivalent to a full year's salary, and letters of praise and thanks from Harry Penn, singling out their heroic, constructive, or generous acts, assuring them of the paper's fiscal health, and inviting them to stay on and share in its future.

For Hardesty and Virginia, the 125th anniversary grant was quite a windfall, since it meant that their household would receive that year four fully adequate salaries. In addition, the Harvesters and Planters Bank of St. Louis, after five years, had recovered, recapitalized, and sent Hardesty a letter promising to honor his long-dormant check. Altogether, they felt very comfortable. Virginia had had her second child, a girl whom they named Abby. Mrs. Gamely had gotten a letter through, inviting them to visit as soon as they could, and reporting that, in these years just before the millennium Lake of the Coheeries had had hard winters—yes—but also extraordinary summers which had made the village overflow with natural wealth, "in the agrarian and lexicographical senses of the word. There is so much food, everywhere," her friend had written for her, "and so many new and wonderful words being generated, that the storehouses and closets are overflowing. We are tub-flooded with neologisms, smoked fish, and fruit pies." She had even enclosed in the letter itself a very thin and very delicious cherry pie.

Hardesty and Virginia began to dance to the concert waltzes even before the ferry pulled out into the harbor, and were among the happiest of the happy couples. Their children were at home, safe, sleepy, and content; they were solvent and advancing; they were in perfect health; and they had just finished a hard day's work. This, plus the few glasses of champagne (which was so dry that, if spilled, it vanished) made them waltz in perfect ellipses and dips. At times they orbited Asbury and Christiana, who were especially striking in their youth and vitality, and just as happy. With extraordinary ease, they danced across the ferry's transformed deck, moving like the planets. They passed Praeger de Pinto, who danced with Jessica Penn. They interwove with workers and staff—the pressmen and the truckers, the mechanics with their long noble faces and carefully clipped turn-of-the-century mustaches, lovely young secretaries who had never been to such an elegant affair save for the very sedate and civilized Christmas and July parties held in *The Sun*'s roof garden, the cubs who had just joined the paper and who were as awkward and overly grave as adolescents, the ancient librarians, the cooks, the guards (in their absence, the police were watching the empty *Sun* building), and Harry Penn himself: wizened, dapper, sagacious, spry, and as thin as a lightning rod. When everyone was on board, the ferry moved out onto the Upper Bay and turned north into the Hudson, which was as smooth as oil. They glided past the deep inner-glowing buildings, and except for the muted orchestras and engines, the ferry was silent. From Manhattan's streets and highways a singing sound arose. Mist obscured stars and sky, and as they approached the George Washington Bridge, the mist descended to curtain both banks of the river, though not the bridge itself, or its catenary, which sparkled with blue and white diamonds and looked wide enough and broad enough to cradle the world in its curve.

Manhattan's glass walls, running in a smooth green glow down the Hudson to the Battery, were as nothing compared to the white curtain that marked the conflict of the seasons. Its chill and purity upon the glassy river put the ferry on a stage. Soon the celebrants were no longer celebrating. Cathedral walls had been raised about them, and their quiet drifting was like a journey to the world of the dead—all of which suggested that, perhaps, beyond the whitened curtains of mist, was something far more momentous than New Jersey. And it was suddenly quite cold—a message from far beyond the chain of lights that marked the Hudson's northern turn.

The orchestras stopped the concert waltzes and the engines were stepped down, until the gliding ferry silently held its breath. Then the bow orchestra began to play an apocalyptically beautiful canon, one of those pieces in which, surely, the composer simply transcribed what was given, and trembled in awe of the hand that was guiding him. The orchestra in the stern soon followed, and the canon swelled throughout the decks and across the water until the ferry seemed like a musical instrument, a thing of delicate glass that shone from within and floated upon the same mirror as the city itself.

As the music drifted into the ether, they stood at the rails and on the upper decks, staring outward, away from themselves, transfixed. They had come aboard the ferry without a care, to dance and laugh. Then a white sash had been drawn around them, and they had realized how quick and insubstantial were their lives, how, in a second, in the blink of an eye, all is lost. This brought them far from their worries and ambitions, and, caring only for the music and the laws of which it was part, they stood upon the ferry's open decks and were deeply moved. Whatever would come, would come. Whatever they would see, they would see. And they would be thankful to have seen it.

How brave they are, thought Harry Penn, who had known such moments at the height of war, on the sea, and in looking into children's eyes. How brave they are to see straight through to their own deaths, and how well they will be rewarded.

Visiting from the summer that was on its way, sheets and chains of silent heat-lightning struck the billowing mist, and the shattering of its tributaries was mirrored in the river. This sight stopped the orchestras and silenced the music as the ferry and its passengers glided under the soundless flashes that were battling above. And then, just below the sparkling bridge, the ferry made a silent breathless turn and started for home.

Isaac Penn had left Hudson, New York, on a whaling ship when he was eleven years old and as skinny as a thread. Never having seen the sea, he was quite astonished when, as they tacked downriver, they came upon the open miles of Haverstraw Bay, and then the broad expanse of the Tappan Zee. As they sailed past Manhattan and the Palisades, the rows of buildings, the distraught wharves, and the thicket of masts tighter and webbier than raspberry bushes near the Lake of the Coheeries impressed him deeply and forever. He took it all in as best he could, and vowed to return to Manhattan someday to participate in the rise of a city that even he, an eleven-year-old whaler boy, could easily see was on an unshakable northward march up the island. His vow was set into steel when he perceived what was beyond the Narrows. Here were no rolling green hills spotted with mobile-jawed, gaudy-colored cows; no reedy bays choked with white herons and swans; no blue mountains in the distance; and no cool and windy evergreen forests along the ridges, but just the sea, and nothing else, in a great circle of water and sky. The whalers then put him to work washing pots—for three years.

He went to sea again and again. Each time, they tacked down the Hudson and passed Manhattan, and, each time, Manhattan had bounded north by several leaps. Isaac Penn was just as steady. He went from galley boy to cabin boy, to apprentice seaman, to able-bodied seaman, to third, second, and first mate, to captain, to ship-owner, to owner of a fleet. Just before whaling collapsed, he withdrew his fortune and put it into merchant vessels, manufacturing, land, and a newspaper of his own design.

He knew how to run a tight ship, the best way to treat a crew, the means to navigate through darkness and storms, how to find elusive and valuable whales, and the trick of writing in the log all the news of the day both clearly and economically. He knew how to keep perfect accounts, how to arrange efficiently the plan of the decks, and when to sell his oil. He had placed correspondents in foreign ports to send back news of other fleets, to prepare him for the fluctuations of the market. He had patience—he could pursue good fortune relentlessly, or wait for it to come within reach—and he himself had driven not a few well-placed harpoons.

Thus he was able to design The Sun to be, if not a perfect instrument, then something rather close. On Printing House Square in lower Manhattan, at the quadripartite junction of Dark Willow, Breasted, Tillinghast, and Pine streets, it had been placed near the center of government, for the political news; the wharves, for the collection of foreign dispatches; the Five Points, for crime; the Bowery, for theater and music; and Brooklyn (via the ferry, until they finished the bridge), for human interest. "In those days," Harry Penn was fond of saying, "they thought that the only human

387

interest was in Brooklyn. 'We need a human interest story,' someone would say. 'Get a kid and send him to Brooklyn.' I used to
point out that there were human beings in Manhattan, too. They
didn't really believe me. Off I would go to Brooklyn, searching
desperately for a human interest story, which, more often than not,
would be about a cow.''

Though the downtown location became slightly disadvanta-
geous in view of all that later occurred in midtown, it permitted
many of the staff to live on Staten Island and in Brooklyn Heights,
and it encouraged a sense of history and activity, because it was the
center of a great old hive.

Even from afar, one could distinguish *The Sun* from those buildings that surrounded, and, over time, nearly overwhelmed it. *The
Sun* was always recognizable because of its flags. These were not
like the chorus lines of national underwear hung out to dry
in front of the United Nations or around the skating rink in
Rockefeller Plaza, but, rather, individual beacons of flamelike
color. Five enormous flags played on the wind. In the four corners
were the banners of New York the city, New York the state, *The
Sun,* and *The Whale,* and in the center was the American flag. *The
Sun*'s flag was a brassy gold sun with a corona of sharp triangles,
set on a white satiny field. *The Whale*'s flag was half light blue and
half navy, scalloped by waves to divide the sea from the sky, with a
huge whale resting motionless above the water and flipping his tail
in articulated strokes of blue, white, and gray. In the rare case of a
demonstrably just and unjust war, in which one side was purely the
aggressor and the other merely a victim, the victim's standard
would fly underneath the national flag. Banners decorated the inner
courtyard and were hung like tapestries in the city room because
Harry Penn held that these were to a building what a tie and a scarf
are to a man and a woman. ''A good tie can make an old gray bastard like me look like the king of Polynesia,'' he would say. ''I
love to wear a nice tie, and so does the building.''

The building itself was an iron-framed, stone-faced, French, neoclassical rectangle by the nineteenth-century architect Oiseau. It
was light on its feet and spacious, and yet it was substantial. It had
been completely refurbished 110 years after its completion, and

now the huge window frames were filled with rimless smoke-colored glass that looked like large flat gemstones in classical foils. At the heart of the building was a large courtyard with gardens and a fountain. On the four walls of the courtyard, lighted stairways were hung over the open space. A conservatory shell of glass and steel covered this atrium, and in the warmer seasons was cranked open like a cargo hatch and folded conveniently out of the way.

The interior was eggshell white, though some walls were shaded in quiet colors or draped with tapestries; and here and there were enormous paintings of active whaling scenes. Looking into them was to be on the sea; the white water seemed so real that one shied away lest one's face be slapped by the gleaming tail fin of a fighting whale. The ceilings were three times as high as in the modern idiom, and rimmed with moldings skillfully executed by craftsmen who had gone to their rest many generations before. Throughout the building were Oriental carpets, warm woods, brass trim, and subtle recessed lighting that was sometimes focused in to make bright pools, and sometimes drawn back for a palatial wash. The flooring was of oak, the staircases of mahogany. The elevator cages were of brass, teak, and real crystal: they were lifted silently in elevator halls filled with palms and bright spotlights that caught them on the rise and made them sparkle like diamonds.

In the basement were the power plants; one for the generation of electricity, and one solely for the presses. These were ancient and elaborate constructs of iron, brass, and steel that took up half an acre in a collection of puffing samovars, madly racing wheels, sesquipedalian drive rods in frantic intercourse with capacious cylinders, boilers big enough to cook the entire apricot crop of the Imperial Valley, and a forest of catwalks and ladders to allow access to the valves, levers, tickle pumps, gauges, and dials that made some passersby, who saw the whole apparatus through greenhouselike windows set in a moat of air, think that they were looking at a clock factory or a distillery. When both plants were humming, with their lights shining on the cheerful puffs and tiny plumes of escaping steam, they seemed to be the heart of the world. Busloads of schoolchildren were brought from as far away as Ohio just to stare down at *The Sun*'s power machinery and the aged mechanics who ran and maintained it. The mechanics alone knew the secrets of the old technology. And even they, who had learned the works from their fathers, did not know the names of half the parts, or what whole inactive appendices were for. Much of the machinery sat in place without being used, and yet all the gears, wheels, and pistons had to be kept polished and oiled.

Also in the basement were a vault, five squash courts, a seventy-five-foot swimming pool, a gym, saunas, steambaths, and rows of showers.

The first floor held paper-storage facilities, the presses, truck bays, and a reception hall. The second floor was taken up entirely by linotype and computer composing rooms, and the classified department. Advertising, layout, accounting, personnel, and payroll were on the third floor. The fourth floor was the city room. Instead of horrible metal desks jammed together in an overlit airplane hangar, *The Sun*'s center of operations was contained in four spacious rectangular rooms arranged around the courtyard, with rows of tables running along their lengths. Affixed to the tables were green glass lamps, and underneath were cabinets, drawers, and the electronic cables that connected each reporter's desk with the library, the morgue, the composing rooms, and the data banks. In the four corners were pulpitlike rewrite desks from which the various departments received their assignments, and to which a reporter advanced humbly with story in hand, or, if he had a hot potato, like Caesar crossing the Rubicon. The divisions, each with its own electronic status board, specialized library, data terminals, and director, were as follows: City, National, Washington, Latin America, Western Europe, Eastern Europe & the U.S.S.R., the Middle East, South Asia, East Asia, Africa, Science, Arts, Finance, and Editorial. One entire division was simply designated *ad hoc,* and was used to pick up the pieces or take up the slack. Unlike most city rooms, *The Sun*'s was tranquil and well ordered. On one side was a quiet courtyard, and on the other a long view of the city.

Spiral staircases punched up through the ceiling to the fifth floor offices of department heads, columnists, editors, and the publisher. Harry Penn's office, which once had belonged to Isaac, took up half of one of the building's long sides. It was probably the

390

world's only indoor harpoon range. Racks of the finest harpoons lined the walls. When someone wanted to practice, he took up one of the lances and stepped into a box that simulated the prow of a rocking whaleboat. Ahead, at thirty feet, wooden representations of whales were towed across the room.

The sixth floor was the site of the communications, computer, facsimile, meeting, and board rooms. The seventh floor was comprised of common rooms and a restaurant. The eighth and ninth floors housed the library. It had several million volumes in open stacks, all the major newspapers and periodicals either bound or on computer, and a map section. Expert librarians maneuvered a seemingly limitless budget to keep it well maintained and up-to-date. The reference collections were wonders of the world.

On the roof were a conservatory, a greenhouse, a sundeck, a promenade, and an outdoor café from which one could see the harbor, the bridges, a magnificent cityscape, and sections of open sky bluer than the sky above Montmartre. Here, the flags flew, and here, on summer afternoons and evenings when the paper was working with vigor and grace, a string quartet sometimes played.

The Sun building was so perfect in execution and so full of energy that, upon looking at it from a distance, one could easily imagine that it was on the verge of coming alive. Just like Isaac Penn's ships, which gathered in riches from across the seas, *The Sun*'s writers and reporters had packed it with memories of all the wonders they had seen and assessed. Though the lights were never off, because either *The Sun* or *The Whale* was always in the works, it was said that were they to be extinguished there would still be more than enough light by which to see, for 125 years of clarity were impounded in the timbers and arches.

No less ingenious than the physical quarters of *The Sun* was its social and economic organization. Perhaps owing to Isaac's hard days washing pots, the Penns had always believed in a high minimum wage. Their editorial columns persistently inveighed against the idea of welfare for the ablebodied, and government social programs that were little more than elaborate patronage schemes. For this, they were repeatedly condemned in liberal circles. On the other hand, they were just as persistent in advocating what was considered to be a sky-high minimum wage. (They believed that hard and good work deserved its reward, and responded to arguments from conservatives that such a wage would create unemployment and dampen entrepreneurial drive, with the counterargument that the latter could be sustained and would flourish with the concomitant business-tax reductions made possible by greater income equality and a smaller welfare burden.)

The Penns were not a hundredth as rich as the Binkys, and, whereas the Binkys had accumulated their wealth by grinding people into the ground, the Penns had done nothing of the sort. First, everyone on *The Sun*, from a kitchen helper who had been there for an hour, to Harry Penn himself, received exactly the same wage and benefit package—*exactly*. And it was a good one, too, good enough to make any job on the paper a great prize. Every *Sun* employee enjoyed equal privileges in regard to pension, health care, access to the athletic facilities in the basement, and admission to the café and restaurant. Anyone could take advantage of the generous educational benefits, and throw in music lessons on the side. And yet, there was every reason to work hard and advance within the organization.

The Sun was patterned after a whaling enterprise. After all expenses were paid out and everyone had his living, the profits were divided according to an elaborate system of shares. No one other than an employee of the paper was entitled to shares, and they were neither inheritable nor transferable. Each employee received five shares upon joining. Thereafter, for every advance he made he received another five, and one share for each year he had worked. There were twenty levels of advancement, and there was seniority. For example, after his first year, a kitchen helper would normally own six shares. After several years on the staff, Hardesty Marratta (who had come in on level eight) had worked his way to level twelve. Thus, with his five original shares, sixty for his work level, and five for the years he had put in, he would have had seventy shares. But he actually had eighty, because he had won two merit awards of five shares apiece. Harry Penn had been with the paper (starting at age ten as a copy boy) for eighty-five years. He was, naturally, at level twenty. He had five original shares, and, when he was younger and could win awards (for which the editor-in-chief and the publisher were not eligible), he had won ten of them. This left him with 240 shares, quite a lot more than his kitchen helper's six, but not that many more than Hardesty's eighty. Were the kitchen helper to stay (as indeed he probably would, for the wages and benefits alone) for ten years, advance two levels to kitchen supervisor, and win an award for his salad, his lentil soup, or, let us say, pulling a baby from the path of Craig Binky's speeding limousine, he would have a total of thirty shares.

This system tickled not only ambition, but productivity as well. Since the number of shares was not fixed, and since whatever profit accrued each year was finite (the notion of infinite profit haunted only Craig Binky, who hired economists and sorcerers to see if it was possible), it was to everyone's advantage to work hard—not only to produce a higher profit, but to hold down the number of jobs and, thus, the number of shares.

The Sun's employees wanted to serve it as best they could, not only because doing so was in their interests, but because *The Sun* was fair—and they could feel this in the same way that they could feel beauty in a landscape. How delightful, too, to know that not only could they feel it, but it could be demonstrated by several systems of logic, and by the way people looked when they came in, morning and evening.

And *The Sun*'s remarkably equitable and effective social system originated not in the barrel of a gun, nor in any cruelty, nor in the French Communes, nor with revolutionary violence, nor in the imagination of a reader in the library of the British Museum, but in the nineteenth-century American whaling ship.

That *The Sun* was not a dull instrument was probably due in large part to its lively and unusual competitor.

Rupert Binky had once issued a famous challenge to Harry Penn. Boasting on his editorial page and to his friends at the Alabaster Club that *The Ghost* would extinguish *The Sun* by the millennium, he claimed that, if it did not, he would attach weighted chains to his body and jump off New York's highest bridge. "Will Harry Penn attach weighted chains to *his* body and do the same, if we have succeeded, as we will have by the millennium, in burying *The Sun*?'' he asked in print.

''No,'' Harry Penn had written back on his own editorial page. ''And I absolve Rupert Binky of the responsibility to carry out his vow, if only for the sake of the maritime traffic on our rivers. For if Mr. Binky jumps headfirst, we may witness an unwitting demonstration of the wisdom of Billy Mitchell.''

Soon after, Rupert Binky was killed by an enraged swan on the river Isis in Oxford. A group of Magdalen College oarsmen, weary from a bump race, had heard his last words, which were, ''Crush *The Sun*.'' Far from being the mystical and elevated utterance that they thought it was, this was a specific instruction immediately grasped by his grandson, Craig Binky, who then took it upon himself to avenge his grandfather as if the swan had been a trained assassin in the pay of Harry Penn.

The means at his disposal were most impressive. To begin with, he had the Binky zillions and *The Ghost* circulation base. But with just those, an attack upon *The Sun* would have been no more effective than an assault upon its natural counterpart. Though Craig Binky thought that his stratagems were the cause of *The Sun*'s occasional misfortunes, he was, in fact, assisted by a mammoth presence invisible to him and to many others—the times themselves. Many skills and arts had atrophied, the public was not what it had once been, and most of the population sat immobile for a third or more of its waking hours, absorbing without reaction or resistance whatever they saw on their televisions. Morals and mores had become so rational and progressive that criminals and prostitutes resurrected from another age would have faced neither barriers nor censure. In fact, a criminal such as Peter Lake would have been greatly offended by the dishonesty and corruption of the norm, and disoriented by the general refusal to distinguish between right and wrong. The city had rotted, until the anarchy was such that islands of reconstitution were allowed to thrive within it. These islands steadily grew. Amid waters that were anything but pure, they were like a rising reef, and though they were rising slowly, when the force that carried them finally broke the surface, it would break it all at once.

The Sun was such an island, threatened by the swollen seas in which Craig Binky swam like a fish—and always with the current. While Harry Penn stood as firm as a rock in the rapids, Craig Binky had a marvelous, easy time flipping about in the foam. He could find ten thousand times more readers for a *Ghost* article about the newest wet-look roller-dancing costume than Harry Penn could find readers for a *Sun* essay on colonizing the moon, and *The Ghost*'s investigation of the aphrodisiacal qualities of crème de caramel created more revenue than the entire *Sun* series on the brilliant new practitioners of electronic music.

And yet *The Sun* thrived. Still, Harry Penn was not content to share *The Sun* with only its minority of careful and intelligent readers, for he wanted it not just to survive, but to triumph. This had little to do with *The Ghost,* though admittedly *The Ghost* was a dreadful irritant: it had to do with his sense of order and his vision of the world. Harry Penn wanted *The Sun* to fight *The Ghost* and all it stood for, if never on its own terms, then at least on its own ground. So he marshaled his troops and sent them to fight Craig Binky. Because they would not use *Ghost* methods or cater to broken tastes, they fought at a continual disadvantage. But the disparity fired their imaginations.

Although *The Sun* was the model of accuracy and formality in its news pages, its editorial section covered a wider spectrum, and was divided up like a parliament into warring factions. Editorial I was a page devoted to sober, dignified, and eclectic assessments not unlike those of editorial pages in other great newspapers around the world, except that you were less likely to know what *The Sun* would say, because its politics were so fluid, practical, and idiosyncratic. In Editorial II, the Right was allowed a full page to present, often admirably and brilliantly, its completely predictable line. So with Editorial III, a full page for the Left. Editorial IV, however, was controversial, for in it *The Sun* columnists and guests were encouraged to write without regard to libel or any other consequences, though by some sort of unwritten code abusiveness and sensationalism were filtered from articles that might otherwise have been vitriolic or provocatory. In writing for Editorial IV, in fact, Virginia Gamely, now Marratta, began to push her luck.

She started out gently, but was soon caught up in a compulsion the origins of which she did not understand. This was not a surprising pattern, for in Lake of the Coheeries the biggest blizzards, the ones that covered the houses and made the countryside like a rolling white sea, always started with small tentative flurries that were nearly invisible. At first, Virginia's columns went largely unnoticed, for they were appreciations of a city that loomed so fiercely in the eyes of its inhabitants that they were seldom able to apprehend it as a whole. The irony of its beauty was that they, who made it, could not see it. They were too busy rushing and fighting, lost within it like mites.

Virginia often accompanied Hardesty and Marko Chestnut on their long walks in search of forgotten architecture and revelatory views. When they found a subject, she would wander off to the side, to a scrub-covered lot or a flight of stone stairs, and watch them work. While they sketched and made notes, she would fix her gaze upon a scene, either the one they had chosen or one close by. For example, she might watch the afternoon light against a carved façade of reddish stone, and see that the light and the stone were in love, and that they moved back and forth in sympathy like two sea fans in the same transparent current. She could hear in the traffic a white sound that threw veils across the present and allowed her to hold the scene to her the way that she held her own children—fighting time, conquered by it, ravished by it. For she believed that only through love can one feel the terrible pain of time, and then make it completely still. She followed the sway of reeds in windy, broken, summer lots, until they swayed no more and she saw them motionless and within a stopped frame. And then she would walk back to *The Sun* and write essays that drove Craig Binky and his readers crazy, because Virginia saw the world not as a system of material blocks in which one thing was connected to another, but, rather, as a magnificent illusion of the spirit. In one essay she wrote about the dome of the old police headquarters and how it managed to "watch the city *by means of its shape,* for," she wrote, "apart from the inexplicable magic of color, images are transmitted and received in terms of shape. The receptors themselves are of a recognizable, constant form that is derived from the attributes of light.

After all, what we see of the eye is itself a dome." In these specu-lations, she explained the quality of the air in the morning light. And she went on from there, in a vein that was simultaneously met-aphysical and sensual, to talk about ultimate purpose, symmetry, beauty, God, the devil, balance, justice, and time. This was a Co-heeries trait. They were always very serious up there, and in mat-ters of nature and religion they could talk wallpaper off the wall, with the patience and intensity of nineteenth-century German phi-losophers.

When Harry Penn read the first of these essays, he called Vir-ginia into his office.

"Do you realize," he asked right off the bat, "that because of these essays *The Sun* will be viciously attacked?"

Virginia was so surprised that she couldn't reply.

"Do you?"

"No," she answered. "Attacked? For what reason? Who?"

He closed his eyes for a moment, and nodded in confirmation of his own suspicions. "Sit down," he said, and proceeded to explain to her in fatherly fashion about the savagery of intellectual dispute in a city where many held the intellect above nature. "Most peo-ple," he told her, "arrive at tortured conclusions via blind and painful routes. They don't like it when someone like you shows up in a balloon. You can't expect anyone to trust revelation if he hasn't experienced it himself. Those who haven't, know only rea-son. And since revelation is a thing apart, and cannot be accounted for reasonably, they will never believe you. This is the great divi-sion of the world, and always has been. When reason and revela-tion run together, why, then you have something, a great age. But, in the city, now, reason is predominant. To argue from any other point of view or by any other means, as you do, is subversive. You will be attacked. Perhaps if we run your pieces in the religion de-partment, alongside the sermon summaries, they won't create so much controversy . . ."

"What controversy?" she interrupted. "There hasn't been any controversy."

"There will be."

She found this hard to believe.

"Where are you from, young lady?" he inquired.

"From Lake of the Coheeries. When I arrived in New York, I stayed with Jessica at your house. You were in Japan."

"*You* are little Virginia Gamely?"

"Not anymore," she said with a smile, because she towered over him.

"I hadn't realized," said Harry Penn, looking directly at her. "I'll be interested to see your columns as they appear."

"I don't really remember you," she said.

"The last time I saw you," Harry Penn replied, "you were a very young child. You wouldn't have remembered."

What Harry Penn had predicted came to pass. Virginia was attacked from several quarters, and treated as if she had suggested that the city's children be forced to drink hemlock. *The Ghost* hit her on its front page, ignoring the news of the world to castigate her and *The Sun* for "religious reactionism. There are court rulings against this sort of thing," they wrote, "and it should be suppressed in the name of modernity and good sense." Not that Craig Binky held that opinion (he generally didn't know what opinions he held), but this seemed to him to be the way people were thinking. Other publications, too, rammed her broadside, but in a less than energetic, condescending fashion. This was because they thought that since she was new it would not take much to sink her. Such mistakes are often made in wartime.

Virginia had seen Mrs. Gamely pick up her shotgun and pump away at marauders in the night, and in many respects she was just like her mother, which is not to say that the course she chose was wise or correct—it was neither—but, rather, that it was spirited. Abandoning caution, she took out after her enemies.

A *Ghost* editorial questioned the propriety of the complex essays on esthetics that were regularly appearing in *The Sun*: "Does the man on the street, in his millions, be he Hincky, Lester, Jocko, Alphonse, or John, have any understanding whatsoever of the mystico-religious obsession that has seized *The Sun*?" Soon after, Harry Penn looked up over his ancient leather-covered desk to see Praeger de Pinto and Hugh Close standing opposite. His editor-in-chief and his chief-of-rewrite were involved in a dispute about the wisdom of running Virginia's answer to *The Ghost*.

"Mr. Penn," implored Hugh Close, "we simply cannot print this article anywhere, except, perhaps, in Editorial IV. No, not even there." He held up a copy sheet that was titled, "Oh *Ghost*, where is thy sting?"

All the while, Praeger de Pinto was silent.

"Please look at it, sir," Close pleaded. "Let me call your attention to lines such as these: 'I would rather be torn to pieces by the poison-clawed cat, than suffer one instant of acceptance by the resident intellectuals of *The Ghost*. . . . Men like Myron Holiday, Wormies Bindabu, and Irv Lightningcow don't know their asses from their elbows, much less how to see the truth. Just yesterday, for example, Myron Holiday wrote in his column that Oliver Cromwell was a famous bullfighter, and that strategic bombing was introduced in the War of 1812. . . . The rationalists of *The Ghost* are mechanistic beasts who thrive in darkness and wither in the light of the sun. If they pass within twenty feet of a bottle of milk, it sours. They live at cocktail parties full of unkempt women who are always smoking cigarettes, they don't know how to swim, they frighten children, and they masturbate in bookstores.'

"We can't print things like that. Her brush is far too broad."

"However," said Harry Penn, holding up his index finger in a patriarchal gesture, "what she says is true. Put it on the front page."

"But, Mr. Penn," Close begged. He was the paragon of exactitude, and such a careless, all-encompassing attack was contrary to his nature. "It makes us so goddamned *vulnerable!*"

Praeger de Pinto turned toward the window to hide his smile. He knew Harry Penn better than anyone alive.

"Close, our indiscretions sometimes serve us well," Harry Penn wheezed. "For a divinity shapes our ends. The Lord is my shepherd. I shall not want. He maketh me to lie down in green pastures. Runneth it on page one."

"Page one?" Realizing that he was not going to win, Close tried to trim his losses.

"Page one."

"Page one?"

"What are you?" Harry Penn asked. "A parrot?"

Virginia was pacing back and forth in the roof garden. *The Sun* did fire people, and she had gone too far. Defiance and remorse alternated in such strong waves that she felt as if she were in the crow's nest of a ship with a fifty-degree roll. When Praeger approached her with a grave and frozen look set upon his face, she thought the worst.

He stared at her for a moment, watching her begin to fall apart. Then he launched her to the moon by telling her that he and Harry Penn were going to print her polemics on the front page. But he told her as well that it had been a close call, and that if she wanted to live dangerously she could make a lot more money driving nitroglycerine trucks. Nonetheless, she walked across the roof garden with a May stride. When she went down to the city room to tell Hardesty, he, too, cautioned her to be careful.

She was, for an entire day. After that, she reverted to her old ways. She was afraid, but she pushed ahead unmindful of the hazards. Perhaps it was because the Coheeries people were descended from the audacious raiders of the French and Indian Wars. Perhaps it was because she felt that she was caught in a deep and clear backwater of time, or because she was a daring believer well versed in the omnipotence of God and nature. Or perhaps it was because she was just a little bit out of her mind.

Virginia's conflict with *The Ghost*'s intellectuals and their followers was soon stalemated, as both sides exhausted themselves heaving into one another's camps huge unsupportable generalities that were more taxing to deliver than to sustain.

Each article brought pressures for her removal, both from within and from without *The Sun*. At every juncture, however, Harry Penn intervened to protect her. No one understood why, especially in light of the fact that even his own daughter, Jessica, sometimes received scathing reviews in double salvos from *Sun* and *Whale*.

After the first reprieve, Virginia had felt the near miss reverberating through her in the same way that a knife-thrower's assistant feels the vibrations of the board against which her back is motionlessly pressed. The second time, she had swung gaily in a ham-

400

mock supported by the twin posts of relief and gratitude. The third time, it had seemed rather humorous. The fourth time, after a column entitled "The Mayor Looks Like an Egg. Period," she had expected it. And the fifth time, after "Craig Binky and the Question of Mental Nudity," she would have been surprised had the reprieve not come.

No one on *The Sun* had ever been treated with such deference. She was free to do anything she wanted to do, and took risks enough in a week to last a lifetime. Those of good will suspected that Harry Penn's advanced age had led him to experiment in folly. According to loose tongues, she had become his mistress. But Harry Penn remained alert and dapper. Always in tweed, he sported a gold-handled ebony cane with which he poked dogs who were fouling a footpath, and though he was still able, every now and then, to toss a harpoon, he clearly was well past the age for having a mistress, or even trying. His solicitude for Virginia Gamely remained a mystery.

. . . *AND* THE GHOST

Look, there is no sane orga-
nized way to describe *The Ghost,* and no place to start. *The Ghost*
was circular and rotund in time, and it was laid out in complete
chaos. It crawled with absolutely serious people demanding an infinite variety of insane things. For example, at one time, a major
crisis occurred when the newspaper divided into two factions—
those who said that white wine came from fish and those who
maintained that it didn't, although they either would not or could
not say where it did come from. They shunned each other like Hu-
guenots and Walloons and for eight or nine months, *The Ghost* appeared with many blank spaces, missing pictures, and upside down
or sideways articles, because the factions would not cooperate.
Craig Binky conferred with his advisers, and then did exactly what
he had wanted to do anyway. Calling the board back together,

he announced: "Gentlemen, you remember the story of the Accordion Knot. Pepin the Short, when presented with the Accordion Knot, couldn't untie it. So he set it on fire—just like the Russians and their Pumpkin Villages. I plan to follow the same strategy, with adaptations for this, a more euphonious age." He then proceeded to fire every single one of *The Ghost*'s eleven thousand employees. The next day, *The Ghost* was completely empty, even of rats, and this might have knocked some sense into the feuding employees, had Craig Binky not given each of them three years' severance pay. For five or six weeks, *The Ghost* and its subsidiary enterprises were as dark as a moonless night in a cave, while an army of professional skip tracers roamed the French and Italian Rivieras.

The lesson of Craig Binky was quite simple. As Virginia wrote to sum up her interview with the editor and publisher of *The Ghost*: "Too much power makes for the ridiculous. It is as true for politics, in which the powerful are often brought down by their own pomposity, as it is in religion, in which the man who sees angels returns most times with a tale of harlequins; as it is in newspaper publishing, in which being a mirror to the world makes fools of those who would say what it is and what it is not. Of course, someone always has to risk saying what is and what is not. Those who do so in ignorance of their place in nature, however, bring down upon themselves things such as Craig Binky's carefully rendered judgment that 'white wine does not, in fact, come from fish, or from any other mammal. It is made by pressing the juice of the immature zucchini.' "

But *The Ghost*'s board of directors were irreversibly intimidated by the Binky zillions, and dared not contradict their chief. Although at times they would beg him not to do this or that, it was always in the tones of garden mice. His power over them was nearly absolute. For example, he made them change their names to the guide words on the bindings of *The Encyclopaedia Britannica*. This was so that he could remember better who they were, since he spent a lot of time staring at his encyclopaedia. Reluctantly, they became Bibai Coleman, Hermoup Lally, Lalo Montpar, Montpel Piranesi, Scurlock Tirah, Arizona Bolivar, Bolivia Cervantes (the only female member), Ceylon Congreve, Geraniales Hume, Newman Peisistratus, Rubens Somalia, and Tirane Zywny, who, to his everlasting shame, shared his appellation with the rat-catching Zywny, a type of dog.

Flanked by his two blind bodyguards, Alertu and Scroutu, Craig Binky marched into a monthly board meeting. As usual, he had a sheaf of new proposals and projects (which he called "projectiles"), all of which the board was obliged to approve.

"First of all," he said, "I want to let me thank you for the compliment of calling you here. What I mean is to say that, frankly, how nice I am to meet you. Well! How the day is! The sun shines in blarts and twines, and everything sustantiates. So, you see, what a pleasure it is to address you, from me, your friend and chairman—always concerned, never happy, and quite willing to talk it over, yesterday, today, or tomorrow." Then he swiveled in his chair and stared out the window for five minutes. It bothered him not at all that his board members were sitting rigidly at attention behind him. Sometimes he left them that way for an hour. What did he care? He paid them each $200,000 a year to applaud politely when he came in, to nod and widen their eyes at his suggestions and proposals, to call each other by the names he had made them adopt, to discuss the things he said, in big words that he didn't understand, and then confirm that it was a brilliant idea, for example, to grow mushrooms in unused safe deposit boxes. He swung back around.

"Lalo, Hermoup, Bolivia, Bibai, Montpel, Newman, Tirane, Ceylon, Geraniales, Arizona, Scurlock. I'm glad you're all here, glad you're all mortal. Listen to this.

"What would happen if we took everything that exists in the universe, and divided it by one? I'll tell you. It would remain the same. So, therefore, how do we know that someone isn't doing that right now, at this very instant? It makes me shudder to think of it. We might be constantly divided by one, or multiplied by one for that matter, and we wouldn't even know it!"

Everyone feigned a look of wonder, turned to his neighbor, and sat erect again, waiting for what was next.

"Let me enumerate today's points, if I will, beginning with number A.

"Number two. I've thought about it, and I don't like it. As far as I'm concerned, it's out the window, finished, *caveat.*"

"Good idea," said Scurlock Tirah (whose real name was Finny Pealock).

"Number L. We're somewhat behind the times in corporate organization. Marcel Apand was telling me about a little electronics company he set up in India. He got a business school to design it from the floor up, and I really like the way they did it. So, as of next Monday, *The Ghost* parent corporation will be recast into clusters, macroclusters, microclusters, pods, micropods, minipods, macropods, macronuggets, supernuggets, bulbo-aggregates, and pings. Some departments will tie into other clusters, pods, nuggets, bulbo-aggregates, and pings, and some will remain essentially stable. For example, a secretary in what is now the secretarial pool of the real estate section of the classified department, will henceforth be referred to as a ping in the secretarial cluster of the real estate pod in the classified macronugget. This, of course, is in turn a bulbo-aggregate of the revenue-generating supernugget."

The board sat with nervous smiles on their faces, feet tapping, fingers drumming, eyes darting from side to side.

For the next two and a half hours, during which he was served a seven-course lunch as everyone else looked on, empty-stomached and salivating, Craig Binky held forth, and ideas flowed from him in manic density. He firmly believed that he was the center of the universe, that, a thousand years in the future, people would refer to the late twentieth century as "The Age of Craig Binky," to its music and art as "Binkian," or "Binkyesque," or "Binkotic." He had even flirted with the idea of "Binkonian," "Binkese" (which, in fact, did exist), and "Binkritude."

The Ghost itself was a puzzling document. Unlike *The Sun* and most other newspapers, it was run by headline writers. Over the years, the success of their sensational declarations had transformed them into a caste of elevated mandarins, and they discovered that their headings did not need to have any bearing whatsoever on the copy below. A story entitled "Mercy Killing in Manila," for example, might well be about the Norwegian building boom, or about a department store in Hartford, Connecticut. "Queen Goes Nude in London," was about a new form of insect repellent developed at the University of Iowa. And below "African Playboy Kills Self," was the Nobel Prize acceptance speech of a Harvard biochemist. The front page of *The Ghost*, as might be expected in a tabloid, was all headline, and as often as not, in red. Unlike the other tabloids that it had long before knocked out of the picture, however, *The Ghost* had headlines unaccompanied by any story. It didn't seem to make any difference. Millions bought the paper no matter what. Harry Penn's favorite example of a *Ghost* banner headline with no further explanation was framed in his office. In huge block type, it read: "Dead Model Sues Race Horse."

Still, *The Ghost* grew, and so did the billions. It was as if Craig Binky was protected by an angel.

And if one were to believe *The Ghost*'s editor and publisher, there was an angel. Once, Craig Binky had stormed into Harry Penn's office, demanding that *The Sun* close down immediately. When asked to explain his audacity, he replied that an angel had come to him, thrown plastic nets over his body, imprisoned his will, and told him to make this exact demand. Harry Penn was eating a piece of hard candy, something which always made him seem even cooler and more ironic than he actually was. As he thought, the candy went from side to side in his mouth, like a die in a dice cup. Finally, he held it still. "Craig," he asked, "did the angel give you a receipt?" Silence ensued, during which Craig Binky's apparent inability to overcome this hurdle flooded the room as if it had been hundreds of silver dollars that had burst through his pockets, fallen like a waterfall inside his pant legs, paid out over his feet, and rolled everywhere. "Because, Craig," Harry Penn insisted, "if you don't have a receipt, we can't accept the claim as valid."

But little else could deter Craig Binky, for he believed that everything about him was destined to be triumphal. Harry Penn was certain that in his nearly one hundred years he had never encountered a soul more intensely marinated in self-satisfaction. Craig Binky's pomposity was often relieved, for others, by what

Harry Penn generously termed "Mr. Binky's somewhat inexact intelligence."

Partly to crowd out other opinions, and partly to make his views become known, he craftily filled the letters page of *The Ghost* with anonymous communications which he signed "Craig B." Even if that hadn't given him away, most people would have been able to guess who had written the letters, because his style and syntax were unmistakable: "Craig Binky says that there are too many water fountains on the third floor. Craig Binky says take some away." His sentences frequently included a subject that was its own predicate: *"The Ghost, New York's most beloved newspaper, published and edited by Craig Binky, is The Ghost."*

He was proud that he knew so many influential people, drank expensive wines (and water imported from a frozen spring in Sakhalin), and went to restaurants where a piece of toast (Toast Almondine, Toast en gelée, Toast Safand) was priced at the equivalent of fourteen hours of the minimum wage. He seemed to himself to be genuinely superior. Perhaps for that reason he regularly arranged testimonial dinners in his own honor. Still, Craig Binky and *The Ghost* were the necessary counterbalance for Harry Penn and *The Sun*. There could not have been one without the other, somewhere, in some form. As it happened, they faced one another across Printing House Square.

If all the months and all their days could be like June weather in New York, there would be paradise on earth. Often, in early June, momentous decisions are made, power waxes strong, quick wars are fought, and love affairs are begun or ended. This was apparent even to Craig Binky.

On a day so fine that the pressmen sat lazily in the sun, watching bees, when tranquil opera music welled up in peaceful, darkened streets, and when trees took the early summer breezes through new jewel-like leaves, a messenger sped in from the airport in a *Ghost* helicopter. Before it landed on *The Ghost* roof, the messenger jumped onto the helipad, injuring his leg John Wilkes Booth style, and ran toward Craig Binky's office.

He broke past the receptionist and dashed into Craig Binky's inner sanctum. Alertu and Scroutu locked arms and stood to, barring the door through which Craig Binky was visible addressing a board meeting. Betty Wasky, his secretary, arose from her station and implored the stranger to be patient. "These guys are blind," the messenger said, sizing up Alertu and Scroutu. "I don't want to hurt them." Such strong talk impressed Betty Wasky, who went to fetch her chief. Craig Binky took the messenger into his private office, and emerged five minutes later shouting orders.

He dismissed the board and ordered up the fleet of corporate planes. "Wind them up!" he shouted. A phone call to the airport readied all of *The Ghost*'s small air force. The aircraft honored to receive Craig Binky would take off in the lead, with the rest following in an armada of gleaming titanium and screaming engines. When Craig Binky flew, a hundred planes took wing, like the doves that were released to greet a Roman general returning in triumph. In the largest plane of the fleet, a giant commercial craft, he had installed an elevated seat that enabled him to look out from a plastic bubble on the roof of the fuselage. A familiar sight at the New York airports, this aircraft would start out for the far-flung reaches of the *Ghost* empire, with Craig Binky's head visible in the bubble.

That day, the airport was gripped with excitement as a hundred planes rose into the air one after another as if on a bombing raid. They threw the controllers into chaos, for their hastily filed flight plans said they were going to Brownsville, Texas, but they all veered eastward, out to sea.

"Where the hell is he going?" one controller asked as the armada dipped low and disappeared from the radar screens. He received no answer, because no one knew, except Craig Binky. And Craig Binky wasn't telling.

AN EARLY SUMMER DINNER
AT PETIPAS

O N the same day that Craig
Binky took off for Brownsville and then veered mysteriously out to
sea, a group of journalists and managers from *The Sun* met for an
early summer dinner at Petipas. As they sat in the garden, blinded
by the white and gold flare of the setting sun, they heard a fleet of
airplanes racing across the sky in the distance, and they wondered
what it was.

They had just finished their last task of the day, which was to
transfer material to *The Whale* for reprinting. After an early dinner,
a quiet walk, and a good sleep, they would be at *The Sun* by 6:00
A.M. to start work on the edition that had to be put to bed by 2:30
the following afternoon. After transferring their stories, checking

the plates, and organizing the next day's work, they would usually be through at about 7:00 P.M.

They liked to meet at Petipas, because it was quiet and airy, and yet they could see river traffic heading down from the north, and hear lonely trucks driving across the cobbles of the deserted market. The sound of the wheels on the cobbles was inexplicably comforting. Best of all were the surprised emotional cries of the tugs and the ferries—the *New Weehawken,* the *Staten Island,* the *Upper River,* the *New Fulton*—as they echoed around the harbor and off the cliffs of the financial district. Plaintive, foggy, and full of the afternoon, the whistle blasts were unmistakably altered by their multiple courses through the shady canyons. In the east, a thousand golden fires reflected from the windows of loft buildings and brick warehouses the color of oxblood, and illuminated the cake-white municipal towers that had statues, colonnades, and extraordinary nests of detail so far above the street and beyond human view that the stuff must have been intended for birds. Across the river was an eighteenth-century knoll with trees standing upon it like peasant women with arms akimbo, and the spotlight of the sun firing their green tops, while black shadows below suggested a grove of infinite proportions. Harry Penn stared at the dark anchoring of this grove, and saw in the velvet tunneling exactly where he was soon to go. He sensed in the darkness sheathed by brilliant light the compressive presence of the future and the past running together united, finally come alive.

He turned from the hypnotic blackness of the trees to his daughter and the others. In their youth, their passions, and their enthusiasms, they were like a group of singers onstage, whose mobile laughter and expressive limbs were dreamlike under strong light. With age, their energies would transform into the powers of contemplation and memory. And the dreams that would bring back to them the people they had loved and the landscapes of thirty thousand days would be more than a match for the decades of youth in which they ran about dodging brewery trucks and trying to make a living. If in another three-quarters of a century they would be like the old man, in the garden at Petipas, who was so delighted by their grace and animation, they would be lucky. For Harry Penn was a happy man, content to remember.

This dinner was for fifteen. Hardesty Marratta, Virginia, and Marko Chestnut sat at the end of a long table, opposite Harry Penn. Asbury and Christiana were in the middle. (Asbury had caught the halibut that was fragrantly grilling over charcoal.) Courtenay Favat had left his chair to make notes in the kitchen, and Lucia Terrapin blushed every time a burly pressman named Clemmys Guttata looked her way. Acquainted with the Penn tradition, Hugh Close was working intently at table, caught up in a gin and tonic, and a dispatch he was rewriting with the enthusiasm of a symphony conductor. Delighted with a stock market that had closed like Halley's comet on its upward swing, Bedford looked dreamily at the maroon-and-white tugboats skating slowly over the silver Hudson. Awaiting Praeger de Pinto, Jessica Penn was bent over the menu, studying it as if it were the Rosetta Stone. She was notoriously tight with money. Praeger himself was due to arrive any minute with Martin and Abby Marratta, whom he was to have picked up in Yorkville after interviewing the bedridden mayor. In early June, various pollens always did the mayor in. A waiter put down two enormous platters of smoked salmon, black bread, and lemon. There were the general oohs and ahs.

Then Praeger de Pinto came in carrying Abby, with Martin bird-dogging him all over the place, since Martin was of the age during which a child cannot sit still. Praeger handed Abby to Virginia, like a package. Abby, who was not yet three, looked with great disapproval at the adults, wiggled out of Virginia's arms, and went in a postnap ill-temper to stare at the charcoal glowing under slabs of gently sizzling fish. Martin soon joined her, to demonstrate how leaves of grass burned on the grill.

"Did you hear?" Praeger asked. "This afternoon Craig Binky got a bee in his bonnet, rushed to the airport, and took off in all one hundred of his planes without saying where he was going."

"He doesn't usually do that," Harry Penn commented. "What's on the wires?"

"Nothing, absolutely nothing, a lot of repetitions and human interest stories. You know. A woman in St. Petersburg was bitten by a rhesus monkey.''

"Maybe,'' Hardesty speculated, ''that's the story Craig Binky wants to get.''

"Craig Binky doesn't sacrifice a June weekend in East Hampton for anything,'' Bedford asserted.

"Are you sure there's nothing on the wires?'' Harry Penn asked again. ''Phone the office and check. If there's some real news, I don't want to have to find out about it in *The Ghost*. Something must be going on. Virginia, would you call the air traffic controllers? Hardesty, please call *The Ghost* and ask them point-blank—maybe they'll tell you.''

As the calls were being placed from the restaurant's lobby, Harry Penn jumped up to pace the narrow row of flagstones between the table and the grills. Hands behind his back, head bent, swinging at the turns like a tiger who always brushes against the exact same spot on the bars of his cage, he caught Abby's fancy, and she began to follow him, mimicking his pace and posture. And when he spoke, she mimicked his words but since she was unused to speaking in long sentences, her version of what he said was incomprehensible.

Harry Penn turned to look at her in delighted amazement. "You're a brave little lass, aren't you?'' he asked. Then he swung around and they both resumed the pacing.

"What's on the wires?'' Harry Penn asked Praeger as he came onto the terrace.

"Nothing.''

"Still nothing?''

"I checked and rechecked.''

Hardesty returned. ''*The Ghost* says, and I quote, 'Mr. Binky is away for the weekend, researching an article on political pleurisy.' ''

"The FAA claims that Craig Binky filed a flight plan for Brownsville, Texas, but that his planes veered out to sea and ducked below the radar. They're furious, but they're always furious,'' Virginia added as she came in from the lobby.

Just then, the very last piece of sun disappeared behind the dark hill, and all the pleasant and enticing tunnels under the trees turned into a single threatening mass unrelieved by any light. Deep in thought, Harry Penn didn't even look. They all began to eat the smoked salmon and black bread (Martin grilled his), and to speculate, in evening shadow, about the news that they suspected they were missing.

"Patience," said Harry Penn. "Binky might have heard that the President lost a golf ball in the rough. And if it is a real story, he's likely to misinterpret or ignore it. I remember, a long time ago, when Tito died, and *The Ghost* headline read, 'Pope Finally Hits the Road.' And I'll never forget the front page of *The Ghost* when a Brazilian mental patient assassinated the President of Ecuador: 'Brazil Nut Zips Ecuador Biggie.' Besides, there's nothing more that we can do."

They ate silently, and the dusk came in from the east like an ocean tide. Dozens of thick halibut filets, basted with soy and retsina until they burst into flame, were lifted off the grills and delivered to the table. The vegetables steaming in seawater had a way of filling the air. And the smell of fresh fish sizzling over hickory was spread throughout the darkening neighborhood on clouds of white flashing smoke.

After the children had been instructed in what they were eating and how to eat it, and after candles had been lit, Christiana looked up, and was suddenly startled. She dropped her fork on her plate, and it rang like a bell. They followed her gaze to the wrought-iron garden fence. A derelict was leaning against it, looking at them with a strange, powerful, slightly irritated expression. One and all, they stopped eating.

His was not the imploring stare of someone who wants something (although it was likely that he was hungry and had been drawn there by the aromatic smoke). Nor was there any hostility in it. Nor did he act like one of the many men of the street who were caught up in hopeless lunacy. To the contrary, raggedly dressed, sun- and windburned, both gaunt and strong, he looked at them without a blink, in the chilling fashion of a man who is trying to place familiar and haunting faces that he knows he cannot identify. Rising and falling in intensity like pulsating stars, his eyes fixed precisely on Jessica Penn, and seemed to be sweeping over her like harrows. She, who had been onstage a thousand times in the high pressure of strong lights and unforgiving stares, who was used to crowds on the street turning almost in unison as she went by, was reduced almost to breathlessness by the intensity of Peter Lake's searing examination.

They were so stunned by him that they couldn't move. He looked at Virginia for a moment, but then returned immediately to Jessica, who thought she might faint. Though frail with age, Harry Penn stood to meet the derelict's gaze, and managed to return it. But for the differences in age, weather-beatenness, and fortune, they looked almost like mirror images. Harry Penn methodically scanned every detail of the man opposite him, and this seemed to dampen the strange fire in the interloper's face. The smoke wound through the wrought iron that he gripped in his fists, and wrapped about him. Harry Penn felt a terrible sadness, and was sorry that he had taken it upon himself to rise. He felt as if he were being dragged back through time to a moment in childhood when he had had no learning or wisdom, when there was only the future, and his own vulnerability.

No one knew how to break the stalemate. They thought that the impasse would hold them forever.

While they were transfixed by the sight of Peter Lake straining to make sense of what he saw, Abby wandered to the fence and stepped right through it. She slipped easily between the bars of a forged gate that would have contained a dozen of the world's strongest men even had their lives depended upon breaking it. When her parents saw that she was on the other side, they called to her. But she didn't hear, and they were reduced once again to racking passivity. Now the tables were turned. Theirs was the world of silence; they were the lost ones looking in; Abby had crossed over, and was with Peter Lake.

In slow strides that lifted her from the ground ever so lightly and allowed her to sail toward him in slow motion, she skipped to Peter Lake as if she had known him for an eternity. And then she seemed to fly through the air (though perhaps it was a trick of the light), her arms outspread, until she rose into his arms. He embraced her, and when she was settled, she put her hands on his shoulders, rested her head against his chest, and quickly fell asleep.

Hardesty approached the fence, and looked into Peter Lake's eyes. There was nothing to fear. The man's distress and dereliction were of little meaning in a world in which other worlds were always looking in. And as Peter Lake handed the sleeping child through the bars to her father, Hardesty felt a strong desire to see what Peter Lake had seen, to go where he had gone. Hardesty Marratta, a prosperous family man, a man with all the proper joys and privileges, was nearly about to pledge himself to a lost derelict. It made no sense, unless one were to consider an eternity of things that fly in the face of the proper joys and privileges. Though Peter Lake was of the world of shadows, and Hardesty was of the solid world, they were in need of one another. The child had brought them together for an instant, but then Peter Lake stepped back into the darkness, and disappeared, as if he had never really been there.

They let the food get cold. Virginia held Abby on her lap, and Hardesty vacantly tapped a knife against the table. When ten minutes passed during which no one said anything, Harry Penn took the responsibility for breaking the silence. "All right," he said, as if reassuring not only them but himself as well, "things like that happen sometimes, and the world remains the same after all."

They looked about. Ordinary and familiar sights were a great comfort. "The world remains the same after all," repeated Harry Penn. "It isn't yet due for any miraculous changes. I imagine that the man we just met was ahead of his time, as are, perhaps, all men like that."

Marko Chestnut smiled. Though they had hardly known it, the tension had been immense. Now they found relief in the fire's white smoke and glowing coals, the dark cliffs beyond the river now silvery blue, the ramparts of high buildings that had become translucent with evening and seemed to be releasing pent-up inner light, and even in the expression of Tommy the waiter, who, because no one was eating or talking, feared that the chef was drunk again and had put something awful in the food. These things told them that the world was the same after all.

But they were not to finish the broiled halibut, steamed vegetables, and retsina, and that night they were to remain hungry, although they would hardly notice—because the world, in fact, was not the same.

Sitting calmly and thinking that she had recovered, Virginia saw it first. The hair on her neck stood up, and she shuddered. "Oh God," she said. They raised their heads and saw what she had apprehended.

Half in light and half in shadow, the land across the river had the look of farmland, fields, and orchards. Because a power plant in New Jersey had failed, they could see neither buildings nor lights on the riverbank opposite them. Though most of New Jersey had had to watch the sunset from pastoral darkness, the power failure was merely a coincidental backdrop to what they witnessed from the garden at Petipas. For the illusion of fields and orchards across the water, and the light western sky itself, were slowly and steadily obliterated by a wall that traveled sideways, the prow of a ship that moved slowly up the Hudson, a massive guillotine, the lid of the world, closing from south to north.

They were a quarter of a mile away from it, or more, and they had to bend their necks and lean back in their chairs to see the top deck. It was centered in the channel, as well it had to be, for it took up the whole thing, and was so big that it seemed like a part of the landscape itself.

This ship, which glided up from the south and seemed to emerge from a garden wall that cut off the southern view, was among the largest structures they had ever seen, rivaling the new giant towers that recently had been built to overshadow the old skyscrapers—and only its prow had cleared the wall: the rest was yet to come. The ship moved on, curling great volumes of water gently before it, shaping them into slow whitened coils that unwound in exhaustion. Then the superstructure came in sight. Ten thousand pure lights rode parallel to the long lean city they resembled, and lit the blackened water into an icy glare. Slanting towers and castled walls rose twice as high as the prow. *The Sun* staff at Petipas leaned farther and farther back, in awe of the marvelous conspiracies of size and complexity which are the elements of cities themselves, and which lead the spirit in a chase that the eye can seldom follow.

The midsection kept on coming, rolling out from behind the wall in a surprise that was sustained by unprecedented mass and height, leaving the onlookers speechless. Just as they thought that the stern would appear to make a proper end of the fine and long proportions, the ship burst into yet another fanfare of sparkling towers and terraced white decks, as if whoever built it had wanted it to be so lean and sleek that its staggering height would seem entirely reasonable.

Then, at last, after several thousand feet of it had paraded before them, the superstructure and the hull ended abruptly, not in a flowing curve, but in a steel cliff that dropped straight to the water. Closely following, connected in a dozen places by struts so large that trucks could have been driven over them, was an enormous rectangular barge the same height as the main deck of the ship itself. This glided after the mother ship, and was followed by two identical siblings.

The ship reduced speed and slowly came to a halt. Now that the sky was dark and the city lights had come into their own, it was possible to see that its hull and the barges were light blue. And, like most great things, it had attracted swarms of lesser attendants. Helicopters and private planes circled like gnats and dragonflies, turning circles and figure-eights in astonishing tours between the great masts and pylons. A fireboat from the Fire Department's maritime headquarters on the Battery had belatedly rushed upriver, and was shooting plumes of whitewater into the night as its crew pulled on their pants and wondered why no one had informed them that this . . . whatever it was . . . was going to arrive. The great ship itself lowered yacht-sized launches that prowled about it jealously, and those of its crew who could be seen at all were seen only momentarily—like soldiers who rise for an instant above a parapet but dare not linger.

Everyone at Petipas had come to his feet, electrified. It was as if they had won a great victory merely in seeing a wonderful thing. They were so excited that they hardly knew what to do, and they were content for a while just to share their amazement.

To a city dweller high on a hill, amid the trees, or on a busy street, ships always seemed to creep into a harbor with unnecessary hesitation. But to a sailor who had been racing for weeks or months between spacious horizons, his ship's speed was dizzying in view of the insanely narrow confines into which it had to come, and he was happy only when it reached a full stop. When a great ship entered New York Harbor, it realigned the city's notion of itself, its place, and its purpose: the ship proclaimed that there was a wide world beyond the Narrows. "I have been there," it said. "I have seen it. Now do your best to imagine the wonderful things that lie beyond, for I will not tell you exactly."

Harry Penn climbed onto a chair and began, as usual, to direct his staff. "Craig Binky probably missed it," he said. "Who knows, he might have turned north and flown to Canada. I wouldn't put it past him to scout for a ship on land.

"All right. Asbury, get the launch ready so we can have a good look when we want to, close up. We have time, if we can get some information, to have a special edition of *The Whale*. Praeger, there has never been a ship like this. I think it may be bringing us a great gift."

"Which is . . . ?"

"The future."

They left the restaurant almost at a run. Even Harry Penn raced up the cobblestone streets that led to Printing House Square, tapping now and then with his cane to remind himself that he was not young anymore.

That night no one on *The Sun* got any sleep, and although it did not know it, the city began to come alive.

THE MACHINE AGE

SPRING in New York is often
rough and dirty, when enticing stretches of near-summer weather
are followed by ten-day sleet storms. For derelicts it is by far the
most difficult season, if only for its frequent showers and rebel-
lious winds. After the desperate battles of winter, when one can die
in less than an hour if one is in the wrong place, the prospect of
slow death in April, while the plants are greening, is like the prospect of dying on the last day of a war. Much the same as those who
are in school, the men of the street graduate in June, and then the
summer takes good care of them.

Not until June was Peter Lake able to reflect upon his dilemma.
After his release from the hospital, he had to struggle just to stay
alive during the winter. For several months he lived in subway tunnels, sleeping near heat pipes, burrowing in next to people with

whom he never exchanged a word. Most of them were mad, and all were scared—that a train would cut them in half, that dog-sized rats would attack, or that they would run afoul of some lunatic with an easily inflammable grudge. Eating was neither difficult nor pleasant, since restaurant garbage cans always held enough to feed more than just cats and dogs. Sometimes, on subzero days when he couldn't get a meal either by washing dishes or by experiencing sudden rushes of piety in front of religious institutions with soup kitchens, Peter Lake turned to this source. He quickly discovered that kitchen workers, and truck loaders at commercial bakeries, were always willing to give him a carrot or a roll, if he would take his intense and disturbing presence somewhere else. Pigeons were not healthful to eat, but they could be roasted over a fire in a trash barrel, and there were charitable trusts here and there which sometimes offered a shower, a turkey dinner, and a bed for the night.

Holding a job would have been possible, but he hadn't the time. He was extremely busy doing absolutely nothing, and had he been comfortable for just an instant, he would immediately have been captured by his obsession and defeated. He neither liked nor felt at ease with the idea of work, and decided that he would not take a job until he had some idea of who he was, or until some passion seized him and he did not even need to know.

No longer desperate, at the end of May and in early June he began to walk the city, to see what he might remember, and to note the changes. It was almost all glass and steel. The buildings seemed to him more like coffins than buildings. The windows didn't open. Some of the buildings had no windows. And their graceless and exaggerated height made the streets into wispy little threads strung together in a dark labyrinth. Only at night did they redeem themselves, and only at a distance—when their secretiveness, their inaccessibility, and their arrogance disappeared, and they bathed the city in light and shone like stained-glass cathedrals turned inside out. Oppressed by the size and power of the city's architecture, he found for himself a string of holy places (only one of which was a church) to which he could and did return time after time. He sensed there what seemed to him to be the remnants of the truth, and he returned to certain rooftops and alleys the way that lightning repeatedly strikes high steel towers in an argument between tenacity and speed.

The first of these places was the Maritime Cathedral, which had endless fields of stained glass as blue as the sea. He could see into the light itself that made the illusion of waves and water, and into the light of the eyes and faces of the people depicted riding in the ships and boats. The power of the spectrum increased dangerously when it was woven into images of the broken and the redeemed, of those who were stubborn, of those who fought, of those who were unshakable, and of those who had seen a great thing. The rays of these delicate lights and pictures combined to splay upon the wide cathedral floor to make a representation of the sea under a line of miniature ships in glass cases. The ship models often drew Peter Lake into the cathedral, though he had no idea why. They seemed infinitely touching and full of meaning, as if the real life of ships had been concentrated and trapped to oscillate within the glass, waiting to be freed. Though the artful windows and little ships of the Maritime Cathedral were motionless, to Peter Lake they seemed always to move. The ships traveled across the glass, the whales rose into the air, the hearts of the sailors were beating and their brows were wet with spray.

The second was the alley outside Petipas, where the child had run into his arms. He appeared there often in the days that followed, hoping to encounter the same group of people. But the courtyard was either empty or filled with another party: usually they were raucous, they drank a lot, and they didn't notice him. The wrought-iron fence became something sacred to kiss or touch. To hold it made him feel better, and the first time he returned when the courtyard was empty he closed his eyes and hoped that everything was a dream, and that, when he awoke, he would find himself not looking in from the outside, but in their midst, slightly inebriated, tired, at dinner on a summer evening trapped somewhere in the amber of time. How nice it would have been to have discovered that he was, say, the owner of a clothing store, a railroad dispatcher, a lawyer, or an insurance man, and that he was at Petipas—a century back—with his wife and family. If only he could have returned to that, to a house of dark wood, with friendly fires and a city garden, to the sad wails of the ferryboats, and the sense that the future was going to be quiet, infinite, and green, rather than a pent-up thing of suffocating glass and steel. He would keep the dream in mind, and reform whatever bad habits had plunged him into it. Remembering how it had been to be lost in time, he would do good works and be forever grateful for his return. When he gripped the iron and shut his eyes, he hoped that he was going to cross over. Of course, he didn't.

There were small shrines and forgotten places that were for Peter Lake like the roadside altars of the Alps—an old doorway lost in shadow and peeling paint, a cemetery tucked between monstrous buildings (though a hundred thousand people might pass in a day, very likely not one turned his head to look in, or hesitated to read an inscription or a name), hidden gardens, house fronts, meaningful views down strangely crooked streets, places that seemed to harbor an invisible presence.

The last and best of these was an old-law tenement still standing in the Five Points. It was the kind of place the inside of which no decent, educated, perceptive member of the middle classes has ever seen and been able to describe. For no decent, educated, perceptive member of the middle classes has ever gone into such a place and come out alive. The people who lived there envied the rats in their tunnels. There was no light, heat, or water, and the hallway never lacked an angry man with a knife in his hand.

One day Peter Lake just walked into this place, climbed the stairs, and threw open the rickety door to the roof. He would come back a dozen times, and never know why. He went up the ramp that formed the roof of the stairwell, and inspected the chimneys. The round pipes that had once been oil flues had been out of use for a decade or more. Then what of the chimney, the real chimney? It had been sealed up for three-quarters of a century, and the mortar between the bricks was as loose as windblown sand. Looking into the abandoned shaft, he saw nothing. But he was almost overcome by the upwelling smell of sweet pine. As it rose from the hollow beam of darkness, the fragrant air carried the sense and stories of many winters long forgotten. This shaft with its cool unlikely air was a vault of memory. It comforted Peter Lake to know that the fires of the moment have blue and ghostly echoes that long outlast them to rise in another time. And it took him back so well that he had to embrace the disintegrating chimney so as not to lose himself and tumble off the roof. There were fewer buildings then, and much more forest and field. Morningside Heights was a farm, and Central Park really a part of upstate that had been inserted into Manhattan like a drawer in a bureau. The buildings often had high echoing halls reminiscent of great open distances nearby and on the frontiers. Because they were constructions of space, wood, and stone, they were portraits and parodies of the wilderness. It had been good to be alive then. You could leave your door unlocked. (Peter Lake had no way of knowing that he had been a thief, and no way of knowing that he had been, nevertheless, impeccably honest.) You could always smell a pine fire in winter, and the snow stayed white.

It wasn't all easy, however, and this he understood when he realized that half of the reason he clung to the chimney was that just to look at the roof was inexplicably painful. Perhaps if he had read a history of the old-law tenements, he would have come across an offhand reference to the legions of consumptives that took refuge on the roofs, making a separate, higher city, and then he might have begun to know who he was. But perhaps not, for he had a long way to go.

His existence was not without its compensations, and he had moments of elation and discovery that few of the settled ones he envied would ever know. Desperation is the lower half of something, which, in order to plunge, must climb. The streets of New York and some wards of its venerable institutions were packed with people who, despite being entirely forsaken, had episodes of glory that made the career of Alexander the Great seem like a day in the life of a file clerk. Peter Lake was always coming alight, firecracker-style, with golden enthusiasms which made him dance in the street. No one noticed. No one cared. Bums were always dancing in the street, singing, proclaiming, shouting that they had found the truth. And never, ever, had one spoken anything other than the incoherent sonnets of the insane. "Chester Mackintosh! Chester Mackintosh! Chester Mackintosh bedid with flowers what

423

Hilda did to the moon! Come ahead in the hive, and do with me what the crook who crawled slimmering into the cat neck did. Who?'' one of these people might declaim—to a mailbox. The arguments and counterproclamations stimulated by posters were legendary, and the poster was always addressed as "you." Often the men of the street were lordly or threatening in regard to parking meters, treating them like indentured servants or boys in the lowest form. Sometimes, though, at the height of these mad ignitions, they struck gold. It happened to Peter Lake.

Not long after he had served as the apparition of Petipas, he was walking in a splendid evening, as fast and bright as a Roman candle, master of the world in shreds and tatters, elated, benevolent, even operatic. He came to the greenhouselike panels above which schoolchildren often stood on an off-sidewalk parapet to see the ancient machinery of *The Sun* shimmer and tingle in its chores. He leaned royally on the empty rail and looked inside. The sight of the humming self-contained machinery was nothing less than a booster rocket for his already flaring mania. But it was more than that, because it had turned his gratuitous euphoria into something real. At once he knew that his optimism had been illusory, and that now—by chance—it had been substantiated. There, right in front of him, were the machines, spitting and coughing like babies, agitating like a hundred boiling kettles, turning and shuttling with devoted concentration. There, at last, was something he knew and was sure of.

Two harried and depressed mechanics walked through the gallery below, carrying a freshly oiled steel shaft between them and talking in frustrated grunts and curses that could be heard even above the noise of their engines. They approached a three-quarters disassembled contraption that stood between two other machines that wound up cables and then hissed and whistled as the cables unwound and spun several sets of Newtonian governors. Though their hands were covered with oil, they scratched their heads. That's a bad sign, thought Peter Lake. They probably don't know the workings of the double mutterer. They may not even know what it's for.

He rapped on the glass. They looked at him, and then turned away. He rapped again. "What do you want?" they asked.

"I would like to explain the intricacies of the double mutterer," he screamed. They couldn't make out what he was saying.

"Go away," they said. But he wouldn't, and kept on pounding the glass, until one of them came over and opened a transom. "What do you want?" Peter Lake was asked again.

Composing his words as carefully as a man who stands before a judge, Peter Lake answered. "I saw that you two fellas are working on that double mutterer there. You seemed puzzled. I'd be glad to help."

The mechanic looked at him with a skepticism tempered by the fact that Peter Lake, like the mechanic himself, was Irish. "Double mutterer?" he repeated. "Who said it was called a double mutterer? We don't even know what it's for. We were just trying to see if we could get it going and then find out."

"It's called a double mutterer," Peter Lake said, "and it's an important adjunct to the power train. If you haven't been using it, chances are that you've been getting power-train breakdowns about once every week."

"That's right," the mechanic said. "But how the hell do you know?"

Peter Lake smiled. "I can take apart and put back together a double mutterer, or anything else you've got in there, with my eyes closed."

"That I'd like to see!" exclaimed the mechanic, who for years had been laboring on these machines that had outlived all others of their kind, and who was obsessed with the dozens of puzzles that were implicit in their mechanisms. Though he had spent half his life there, and had been taught by his own father, he was unable to understand most of what he tended, and incapable of taking a great deal of it apart—much less of putting it back together again.

"I'd be happy to show you," responded Peter Lake, knowing that his challenge would be irresistible.

The mechanic went to his friend and spoke to him, looking around every now and then to make sure that Peter Lake hadn't vanished. Then both of them got a ladder, and put it up against the transom. "Come right in this way," the other mechanic said.

Peter Lake climbed down into paradise.

Walking through that place, he felt like Mohammed in Bismillah. Everything was shiny, sparkling, alert, and familiar. The machines seemed to greet him with the same ingenuous affection as a class of kindergarten children receiving the mayor. And as they puffed and revolved and did their mad angular dances, Peter Lake realized that he was a mechanic. In each section of the half-acre of machinery, years of knowledge charged out from the interior darkness and stood at attention like brigades and brigades of soldiers on parade. The realization was locked in place as if with strikes and bolts. At last, a victory.

They came to the double mutterer. The two mechanics leaned against a piece of long-inactive machinery and eyed Peter Lake with a powerful Irish skepticism that trembled and boiled and was as hot and smoky as a burning hearth. "Now. You, sir," said one of them, cruelly, "will show us how to bring to life this—what you call a—double mutterer, or we, sir, will show you back to the Bowery."

Peter Lake was aware that he was unshaven, badly sunburnt, filthy, and sapphire-eyed. "What's a double mutterer?" he asked. "I thought maybe you two gentlemen would like to purchase a ticket to the garbage-man's ball."

The mechanics were confused—until Peter Lake fixed his mad gaze on the machine, and began to work.

"Now look here," he said, after removing a large panel. "You see this oscillating slotted bar that's rubbing up too close to the powl and ratchet of this here elliptic trammel? That, my friends, distorts the impact load on the second hobbing, up there, which is applied to that helical gear. But the trouble is, it isn't. Without that little helical gear, the antiparallel linkage on the friction drive won't disengage, and this wormwheeled pantograph can't come into play. Clear so far?" They nodded.

"And it's not only that, but you've got a jammed friction brake. See? It has to be lubricated with the finest spermacetti. And two cams on the periflex coupling are on backward.

426

"If one of you fellas will mill me a buttress-threaded lug nut with a fifty-five-degree flank angle, I'll put the oscillating slotted bar back where it's supposed to be. Meanwhile, we'll rearrange the cams, and unfreeze the friction brake. Well? What are you waiting for?"

In less than half an hour the double mutterer was muttering like crazy, and the power train had begun to run as smoothly and quietly as an owl's swoop, whereas, before, its belts had flapped about like the flesh of a sprinting fat man, making concussive leather slaps against the cast-iron flywheels that it struggled to embrace.

"These belts will now last for six months to a year," Peter Lake informed his awed hosts. "And the horsepower drain will be much less, as the slack in the power train is moderated by the double mutterer. It'll save you a lot of fuel. It's like a trumpet."

Though they didn't understand the part about the trumpet, they didn't care, and were eager to take Peter Lake on a tour of the many dormant machines that had puzzled them all their lives.

"What the hell is this?" they asked him of a bell-like dome that sat on top of a working steam engine. "We've been trying to figure it out since we were kids. Every once in a while, it rattles like crazy—as if there's a loose bolt inside—but only now and then. We've tried to open it, but, no matter what we do, it doesn't move. You wouldn't happen to know what it's all about, would you?"

"Of course I would," Peter Lake replied, offended. "You take your average stray dog out in Canarsie, and he could tell you. In fact, it's so simple that I think I'll explain it in Filipino."

"Oh no! Please don't!" they begged. "You don't understand what torture it's been all these years. Suddenly it begins to jingle in the middle of the night, just like a baby calling for its ma, and we don't know what it wants."

"Right," said the other. "And we try and try to take it apart, but it won't budge. You can't even make a dent in it. Look, I'll put it in as honest a fashion as I can. If you don't tell me what that goddamn thing is, I'm going to commit suicide by striking myself on the head with a clock mallet."

"Me too," offered his friend.

They were frozen with expectation.

"This," Peter Lake said, patting the much abused bell-like piece of metal, "is a perfection tattle."

Their mouths hung open. What in hell was a perfection tattle?

"Look at this engine," he said, staring enthusiastically at the huge and graceful piece of machinery under the perfection tattle. "She's gorgeous, isn't she, like a young girl come back from a June day at Coney Island. This is called a comely engine. When she approaches a hundred percent efficiency, superheated steam turns inward, and becomes so volatile that it pushes apart two rather heavy tandy pieces (the kind with calabrian underglides) and rises through a secret flue into this chamber here, where it pushes around an eighteen-eighty-three silver dollar at near-musical speeds. I'm ashamed to say that I don't know why it has to be an eighteen-eighty-three dollar, but that, as I recall, is the custom."

The two mechanics were speechless. Peter Lake took it for disbelief.

"I'll prove it if you'd like," he said, guiding them into a far corner to a set of handles that seemed locked onto the floor.

"We've never known what these are, either," they admitted.

"These? These are the tattle release notchets. Look," he instructed, turning the handles. "You set the tapered ends at this angle. Oh, I see, it's eighty-three degrees. That's why the silver dollar is an eighteen eighty-three—it's a memory device. And it frees the perfection tattles."

"Tattles?"

"Sure, there are probably two dozen of them spread about, from the looks of the place. It's like that with machinery of this sort. You always have to go across the room to find the release for the part you're working on. When they designed it, they had more in mind than just power in and power out. The whole business is like a giant puzzle. It's sort of an equation. The pieces are interrelated, as if they were the instruments of an orchestra. To be the conductor," Peter Lake said with a grin, "you have to know every instrument. And you have to know the music."

He took them back to the perfection tattle, which he lifted quite easily from its position atop the comely engine. A silver dollar fell out and rolled across the floor with a ringing sound. One of the mechanics ran after it and slammed it down with his foot. He picked it up, examined it, and stared at his friend, goggle-eyed. "Eighteen eighty-three," he said.

Ordinarily, if *The Sun* had hired a new chief mechanic, he would have had dinner with Harry Penn either at home or at Petipas. That June, however, *The Sun* was in turmoil as it devoted most of its resources to the seemingly insoluble mystery of the great ship that had anchored in the Hudson and stayed in place ever since, unfathomed by either the general public or the press. Try as they might, none of *The Sun*'s people could find out anything. A large portion of the staff had been reassigned to this story—to wait at dockside twenty-four hours a day, to hammer at the mayor (who had gone in the middle of the night to visit the ship, and stepped back on the dock doing a little dance), to take aerial photographs, to make infrared profiles, and to attempt to break the stalemate with information from serendipitous sources all around the world. In their frustration at discovering so little, they neglected everyday matters at the paper itself, including the customary welcoming of new employees.

By the time an overworked and exhausted Praeger de Pinto quickly interviewed Peter Lake, Peter Lake had transformed himself into what a good mechanic was supposed to look like, which was very close, in fact, to his appearance in the days he could not quite remember when he divided his time between various oyster houses, workshops, and burglaries. He rehandledbarred his mustache, got a haircut, and took half a dozen showers and baths. Then he bought himself a new linen suit which had an old-fashioned cut that was both pleasing to him and not out of place at *The Sun*, where Harry Penn and a large number of other geezers dressed in styles with more than a hint of the nineteenth century. When Peter Lake had been on the bum, the scars on his face had been covered with soot and grease. Now they emerged, although some of the finer lines were already beginning to disappear. If Praeger had looked deep into his eyes, he might have seen that Peter Lake's soul was caught up in the storms of another place and time. But he didn't, and Peter Lake's face telegraphed only that he was a work-ingman who would always try to do his best. He looked neither like an intellectual, nor an artist, nor a lawyer, nor a banker. He looked, instead, like a man who lays down rails, builds buildings, and tends fires, forges, and machinery. He had strong arms, thick hands, a nonaquiline nose, and a deep voice. Praeger de Pinto liked him at first sight. He had no inkling of his complexity, didn't rec-ognize him as the apparition of Petipas (nor did Peter Lake remem-ber Praeger), and quickly forgot about him, although he was happy that his mechanics had promised far fewer breakdowns and delays now that this expert had been taken on, at their urging, as their chief—even though he took only apprentice's shares, because Trumbull, the former chief, was willing to follow Peter Lake but not willing to retire.

Most of the time, Peter Lake stayed with the machinery, for there he was genuinely happy. He spent his free hours in a little rented room that looked upon an endless valley of empty roofs and wooden water tanks, and he quickly became like so many people in New York; that is, comfortable, forgotten, and alone.

Though at the beginning of that summer the perfect June weather always reasserted itself, it was shattered many times by dramatic thunderstorms that swept in from the west. Gray clouds that did not know if they were mountains or snake nests of lightning would suddenly appear and ride over the city on a cushion of rain, wind, and hail. Lightning that coiled and tangled in plum-colored clouds loved to aim for Manhattan's high spires, loved to strike them with precision, and loved the magnification of the thunder as it rolled down the avenues from Washington Heights to the Battery. Its flashes and booms made every living being into a tenpin, and propelled otherwise imperturbable crowds into doorways and ar-cades to wait out the storm, necks bent and hearts stopping now and then when a big stroke decided to punish something nearby.

Peter Lake always stopped whatever he was doing to watch a thunderstorm. Sometimes he looked up through the glass plates over *The Sun*'s machinery hall and watched the rain drumming and the lightning cracking the sky, and sometimes he witnessed the ar-tillery strike from his room, as the wooden tanks in the water tower valley thundered in sympathy. He always felt like a fifth columnist for the wind and rain, hoping that they would be strong enough to flatten the structure of time and make him free. Everyone, he supposed, had his own particular view of the lightning.

Stalking about their suddenly darkened apartment thirty floors above the East River, Martin and Abby weathered one of these storms in primal fright. This was the first time either had seen such a performance and been old enough to appreciate it. Martin remembered a few small thunderstorms, but there is all the difference in the world between a storm ten miles away and one right overhead. Hardesty and Virginia were at work, and Mrs. Solemnis was taking a typically unshakable nap. When the two children couldn't wake her, they thought that she had been killed by the storm, and they went into the kitchen to peep out the window toward Hell Gate.

After Martin told her that he was sure their parents were dead, Abby cried. In fact, now that Mrs. Solemnis was dead, they might be the only people left in the world. Though they were heartened when they saw a towboat charging through Hell Gate, it then disappeared, and the thunder grew so intense that it nearly broke the windows. "Don't worry, Abby. I'll take care of you," Martin told her as she began to whimper. He then went over in his mind the various steps in cooking eggs. He had just been taught how to light the stove and make breakfast, and that, he reasoned, was a great stroke of luck now that he would have to feed himself and Abby. He was beginning to wrestle with the problem of what to do with Mrs. Solemnis' body (throw it off the terrace? put it in the refrigerator?) when the storm vanished, the sun came out, and Virginia called to ask how they were.

Time for them was much as it was for Peter Lake. He and they were not as sure of its workings as were those who had been deceived by clocks. Though people readily understood that a line was imaginary, and a point, too, they were true believers in seconds. Abby and Martin rested easily in the lateral infinities of timelessness, and lived in the Marrattas' apartment high over Yorkville like two young birds in a aerie.

Their capabilities were frequently surprising. For example, Har-

431

desty and Virginia were delighted that their children apparently had a rich fantasy life. They had hundreds of invisible friends with names like "Fat Woman and Baldy," "The Dog People," "Lonely Dorian," "Snake Lady," "Underwear Man," "The High Plant People," "The Low Plant People," "The Smoke People," "Alfonse and Hoola," "Screecher and Tiptoes," "Crazy Ellen," "The Boxer," "Romeo," "The Garlic Boys," etc. The list was long, leading their parents to worry that (despite the fact that neither child had ever seen a television) their imaginations were overly fragmented, until, one night at dinner they overheard a peculiar conversation:

"Catwoman from the moon was crying today," Martin told Abby, matter-of-factly. "The cat Bonomo was turning backward somersaults. I think it doesn't feel well."

"Who?" asked Abby, frazzled after a nap that had gone on too long and taken her further than usual into the land of Morpheus and Belinda—any Marratta arising from a nap was truly wicked.

"Catwoman from the moon," said Martin, annoyed that he had to repeat himself.

"Who?"

"Catwoman from the moon! Catwoman from the moon!" Martin screamed in five-year-old arrogance, freezing Hardesty's fork between plate and mouth. "You know, fourteen down and seven over."

Only then did Hardesty and Virginia realize that the invisible companions were real, the inhabitants of a huge high-rise visible from the children's room, whom they had named according to observed idiosyncrasies and possessions. They had pegged almost a thousand people and animals, and were familiar with them on almost a day-to-day basis. Virginia was not surprised, for she had learned early on, ten or twenty thousand of Mrs. Gamely's more common words so that she might know what was happening if Mrs. Gamely were to say, for example: "Marry! Le Blonde and his men are here, asking the village to divvy its piscaries among diglots holus-bolus." Virginia had been able to read the clouds so as to predict the weather days in advance, like a farmer, having grown up with land and sky her constant companions. In Yorkville there were just as many signs to read, though they seemed far less graceful than the raw and unspoiled nature of the Coheeries.

But her children's skills were as real as hers had been. And her children were daring, too. She remembered with a chill how close she had come on many occasions to a horrible death—taunting an enraged timber rattler; or feeding an itinerant black bear that was ten times her weight, putting berries in its mouth as if it were a raccoon, scolding it, and leading it around like a dog for half an hour or more in a meadow where, Mrs. Gamely had assumed, nothing could hurt her; climbing to the summit of the ice blocks in the icehouse; and playing with the shotgun while her mother was out delivering pies. Her children were safe from such things. Or so she thought, until one day when Abby appeared on the balcony wall, walking in time to a waltz that was playing on the phonograph, unmoved by the three-hundred-foot drop.

Many mothers might have screamed and dashed out to snatch the child from the railing, but Virginia remained cool. The first thing that occurred to her was that living where they did her children were like cliff dwellers, and having known no other life, they were probably gifted, in much the same way as squirrels or mountain goats, with abilities unhindered by fear. She determined to suppress her own fear in favor of Abby's fearlessness, to put her arms around her gently, and to waltz her off the wall. She did, and she remained forever an admirer of her daughter's instinctual grace.

Walking on the balcony rails was an exceptional episode in the children's otherwise tranquil lives. Their powerlessness, innocence, and imagination fused to enable them to turn time inside out, travel on the wind, and enter the souls of animals. That they thought the city was the whole of the universe and its center, put them, in compensatory fashion, close to the borders of the infinite and the unexplained, since whatever was beyond the known realms of existence was therefore no farther than Fort Lee, New Jersey, or Yonkers. They had a better grasp of cosmology than the fast-talking physicists, because the physicists and their predecessors had been forced to see the universe with the tools at hand, and so devise models that were like thimbles tasked to hold the open sky, whereas the children had skipped over the obstructions of doubt and fear, and gone directly to the heart of the matter. They were still close enough to having been born to remember in their deep dreams the perfect stillness of all things. They did not doubt that, by believing, they could rise and travel through the air, leaving at their feet a blurry trail of light like a long white gown.

They accepted from Virginia, as she had accepted from Mrs. Gamely long before, an explanation of the white curtain that sometimes walled in the city.

"It is nothing and everything," she had said to them during one of the storms, as they lay in their beds listening to it howl. "There is no time in it, but only islands of time. It moves within itself in currents and contradictions, and if you get too close, it will take you, like a huge wave that sweeps someone off a rock. It swirls around the city in uneven cusps, sometimes dropping down like a tornado to spirit people away or deposit them here, sometimes opening white roads from the city, and sometimes resting out at sea while connections are made with other places. It is a benevolent storm, a place of refuge, the neutral flow in which we float. We wonder if there is anything beyond it, and we think that perhaps there is."

"Why?" Martin asked from within the covers.

"Because," said Virginia, "in those rare times when all things coalesce to serve beauty, symmetry, and justice, it becomes the color of gold—warm and smiling, as if God were reminded of the perfection and complexity of what He had long ago set to spinning, and long ago forgotten."

They were the keenest of observers. Because they stayed home all day in an apartment building that was like a vast beehive, they grew sensitive to many things that most people overlooked. For example, the building in its entirety became a musical instrument as unattended telephones rang through various parts in many tones and muted intensities (variations depended upon distance from the hearer, how many walls were in between, the wind, whether a window was open or not, the original pitch, etc.). They listened as if to the birdsong that penetrates the dark voluminous mass of a forest. The plumbing—rushing water in impenetrable caverns—spoke to them as authoritatively as if it had been the underground rivers of

Hades. From their high perch they saw at eye level the freer movements of flight, and could sense the harmony between the birds and the blue air, something that did not exist close to the ground in the shallows and straits. They made the telephone "sing to itself" (via a feedback and interference loop) as if it were a farmyard pet. From their mountainlike redoubt they observed the subtleties of sound and light in thunderstorms, dusk, and dawn. They could tell time by the half-mile shadows of nearby buildings, and by the clouds of scented air (sweeter and heavier than half the perfumes of Arabia) which upwelled along the walls and over the terraces when professional ladies showered and bathed by the hundreds as if to sanctify the space between eight and eight-thirty in the morning.

Marko Chestnut said that they were as attentive to nature as they would have been had they grown up on a farm or in the mountains. "It is true," he said, "that they live in a machine—the city itself. But if the machine can emerge from nature, then, surely, nature can emerge from the machine."

Every Saturday, he painted portraits of children—either singly or in groups. His studio was downtown, near *The Sun,* overlooking the approach to the Manhattan Bridge. One rainy day in spring, Abby and Martin came to him in their yellow slickers. This pleased him a great deal, because the real oilskin in the Coheeries slickers was dappled with light brown, and the deep yellow was subdued by gray light from a busy sky full of rain and wind. The colors of the children's flushed faces, their young eyes and hair, and the slate-colored rain-light were just what he wanted. Not knowing exactly what was expected of them, they were embarrassed and terrified, and thought of Marko Chestnut as a kind of medical personality. It was almost impossible to get them talking, and when they did speak, they spoke in whispers. He fed them cranberry juice and chocolate-chip cookies, and gave them little paint sets, magnets, matchbox trucks, and museum catalogs.

They stayed in his studio for several hours, watching the rain and the lashings of the wind as intently as he watched them. All they could hear was the rain—washing the gutters and the sides of buildings, dashing off the roofs, and flowing in the streets. Abby walked over to the canvas, grasped Marko Chestnut's brush, and said that it sounded like the rain. It did, and Marko Chestnut thought that, indeed, nature was in the beams, girders, and engines of the city; in all things and their arrangements; in a still life illuminated by an electric bulb as much as in a wheat-colored field in pure sunlight. The laws were the same, and ever-present.

Whereas in his wildest imaginings Marko Chestnut had dared to think that the city and its orphaned machines might find their origins and come awake, the children already had greater things in mind—flight and rising, the whole world rising to the perfection beyond the ragged edges of the ragged machine in which they lived.

Somewhere in the city of the poor, the white horse, Athansor, was imprisoned in a mill, turning a creaking central shaft by walking a circle under a heavy beam to which he was harnessed. He rested only when the dilapidated machinery he powered broke down, or when the materials it processed were in short supply. Otherwise, he worked continuously. He could eat as much oats and hay and have as much water as he wanted, taking them on the run when he passed a recess in the wall into which the fodder and water were fed by gravity. The wood and metal around the recess had been polished by countless horses swooping in and rubbing against it as they ate or drank.

Here, horses were run down in a month or two, and died from exhaustion often before the keepers could shoot them for stopping. The practice of working an animal until he died meant that the mill had to come by about ten horses a year, whereas, if they had kept three on alternating shifts, they could have worked them for the whole of the horses' natural lives. But the city of the poor had its own economics, and in the end the owners of the mill found themselves in the black, because they got their horses for next to nothing—from carts that the horses could no longer pull, from lots where they had strayed, and from the horrible stables in burnt-out tenements to which thieves transported them from the countryside in the dead of night.

After they were worked to death, they were cut up for meat and hide. The viscera went for rendering, the hooves and bones for glue. There was profit for the workers who worked the margins, for the devilish, the greedy, and the shortsighted, and their little industry consumed horses at a terrible rate.

But not Athansor. They had taken him from the arena thinking that he could go for many more rounds than those of his innocent cousins apprehended at night in mountain pastures and trucked into the bowels of the city. Once, a prize Virginia Percheron had run the mill for five months, never stopping, with a determination that astonished even his hardened captors. They pegged the white horse for no more than that, since he was about the same weight but was built almost like a thoroughbred. And they reckoned that he would go under sooner than the Percheron, because he was a fighting horse and the Percheron had been a worker.

They did not know, however, that Athansor had no intention of going under, whether in the sea, drawing a junk cart, or hooked to a perpetual mill. How could they have known that he consumed perpetuity the way that the mill had consumed horses, and fed upon it much as he fed upon the oats and water that they provided? The origins of his strength were, for them, a mystery, but they saw quite clearly that the more he was driven, the stronger he got. He carried the beam in fever and sweat, in lightness and elation, in sorrow, when his heart felt as if it had stopped, through blindness and dawn, trembling with weakness, or dancing with strength. But he carried it forward, and he never missed a step.

During the first few weeks of August, it was very hot, and in the afternoon, or even at night, he would sometimes be covered with froth, and his sores and wounds would open and fester. When fall came and the air cleared, he knew what was intended for him, so he raised his head, shook his clotted mane, and looked forward. For he was the engine that pushes the seasons, and the mill that grinds the salt in the sea. In winter, half the circle that he worked was covered with snow and ice, and it was hard to get traction. But he found enough traction to take him into and through spring. And then there was that perfect June when he knew that he was in the clear, and when every step he took was another victory. Early that summer, when beautiful weather alternated with quick and stupendous lightning storms that boomed out thundercracks in a war upon the canyons, he was sustained and buoyed by many things, not the least of which was the wonder of his tormentors when they saw that he was still alive.

From a third of the circle, he was able to see westward over the plains of brick and rubble, the ridges of charred houses, and the river, to the skyline. That he could see this marvelous, shining thing, no doubt sustained him as well.

A bell tolled. It tolled for the mayor as he rode on a city launch down the East River from Gracie Mansion to City Hall. And it did not stop tolling until he walked into his office, put on his ceremonial robes, and called on the chief marshal to announce that the mayor was "in his office at the pleasure of the people, ready to govern for the greater good, and pleased that the sun is risen over the intact and thriving city." This was an ancient ceremony that many took for granted. But every day it provided the mayor with an egalitarian perspective, a reminder of his task, and a sense of continuity.

The council of elders (on which Harry Penn and Craig Binky managed to coexist) met before the inauguration of each mayor solely to choose an appellation for him. Though the name was purely symbolic and would neither unseat him nor guarantee his reelection, it weighed heavily with the electorate and in the conscience of the man himself—if he had one. For he would be known in perpetuity by the name that would smother out his given name entirely and fuse his history to that of the city. Thus, mayors had resigned or committed suicide when the council of elders had called them the Ash Mayor, the Bone Mayor, the Rag Mayor, and similar names. Others had swallowed hard and continued on, despite being called the Fox Mayor, the Egg Mayor, or the Bird Mayor (since, in politics, gentle ridicule and gentle reprimands could always be borne). There were those who suffered neither ridicule nor condemnation, whose administrations were favored either by their own talents and luck, or by the felicity of the age. They had been given splendid names with which to spend the rest of history. They were the Ivory Mayor, the Water Mayor, the River Mayor, and (once, at the turn of the century, when the council of elders had decided to call attention to the approaching millennium) the Silver Mayor. How the council knew in advance the character of the mayor and his term was a mystery even to him. Certainly Craig Binky didn't know. And even Harry Penn was amazed by the strong and absolute sense of the future that permeated their meetings.

The present officeholder would finish his term either when the first ice was seen on the river (usually in late January) or when the first flower bloomed in Prospect Park (late March), and would be up for election the previous November. Considering that his predecessor had been the Sulfur Mayor, he had done rather well in winning the title of Ermine Mayor. In the complex symbology of the titles, this signified a pleasant harmony, because the robes of office were ermine, and the council of elders seemed to be suggesting that man and office were properly suited. It pleased him very much, did not go to his head, and boded well for his reelection. True, he looked like a hardboiled egg and had a high-pitched voice, but he was a skilled politician and a fair man who had fulfilled the responsibilities of office with balance and humor. And, lest it be forgotten, he was supported by the most awesome and omnipotent political machine that ever was—a virtual parallel government that worked every kind of magic, from Christmas baskets, of which literally millions were distributed, to computer recognition. Hooked up to a powerful mainframe, the mayor knew the name, nickname, and favorite food of everyone with whom he shook hands. Though his campaign conversation grew tiresome ("Hey, Jackie, how's the lasagna been treating you lately?" or, "Good to see you, Nick. Boy, do I love eggrolls!"), the technique seemed to get votes.

The Ermine Mayor had three offices, each at a different level and each for a different purpose. The City Hall office, closest to the ground, was the place for ceremony and tradition. In the Old City Hall, string quartets often played for the public, and there were many fine paintings. Each mayor could go to the gallery of his predecessors and see in their ancient portraits the smiles and eyes of men like himself looking forward from the past to offer reassurance and courage, as if to say that when one was finished one could view the struggles of one's life and term with equanimity.

439

The high offices were half a mile up, at the top of one of the tallest towers. The city spread out below them, and clouds drifted under the windows. From these offices the city was so remote that it seemed to be only blocks and cells of color that took the sun and softly glittered. Here it was easy to make decisions that would benefit the future, for here it was not possible to see faces, or to listen to the cries of those overcome by the waves of history.

The third office was fifteen floors up, in a building on the Battery. Its wide windows gave out on the harbor, the sea, the fields of Governor's Island, the rust-colored brick of Brooklyn Heights, and the green swards of Brooklyn's parks and cemeteries. From this office, the mayor was afforded a middle view. He could see far, and yet he was able to make out the moving forms of men below. The ships which cut wolflike up Buttermilk Channel were far more arresting than the little toys on blue glass that they seemed to be when he was in the high office. When he had the middle perspective, these ships could speak to him of the ocean. Their bow waves were visible, rolling over, bridal veils in the wind, and with binoculars one could see the pilots' hand calls as the ships made their perilous runs through the tidal shallows.

In the middle offices, with mild light coming in through the wide windows, the Ermine Mayor accomplished most of the city's business. Because they were neither as moving nor as worn as his chambers in City Hall, nor as ethereal as the higher ones, they were the best place in which to deal with the paradoxical questions that are the heart of politics. He was good when he was in the middle, in Purgatory, as he referred to it, and here he received most of his callers, including Praeger de Pinto.

The editor-in-chief of *The Sun* had been in this office many times, and he slumped down in a comfortable leather chair as if it belonged to him. "What's going on?" he asked the Ermine Mayor.

"I don't know. What's going on?" the Ermine Mayor replied.

"I believe you do know."

"What are you talking about, Praeger? What's the matter with you? Have you caught Binky-itis or something?"

"All right, I'll be specific. Last week, you went aboard the ship

440

in the Hudson. Our reporters wrote that you looked worried and miserable, and on television you had the air of a prisoner walking his last mile.

"Two hours later, the launch pulls up to the dock and the Ermine Mayor jumps out as if his legs are made of steel springs. He's smiling as if someone has put a baton between his cheeks, and—in front of the entire city—you, the Mayor, do a little dance on the pier."

The mayor threw his head back and laughed, probably recalling whatever it was that had made him dance.

"In the week that's followed, you haven't seen the press once."

"I've been busy."

"The city is going mad trying to figure out what's on that ship and to whom you talked. *The Ghost*, your ally, has compared your dance to Hitler's victory jig in Paris. Do you want that? Do you realize the pressure that's building up for us to unravel this whole thing, and the damage that could be done to you if the public perceives that you are in league against its curiosity?"

"My job," said the mayor, "isn't to do your work for you. If you don't know who's on that ship, it's not my problem. Why don't you go out there and ask? You know, hire a boat."

"We have our own boat. We were out there half an hour after the ship dropped anchor. I'm sure you're aware that they don't let anyone on board, that they won't even speak over the rails. But we're working on it. There are lots of ways to skin recalcitrant cats. However, since you know, you ought to give us an indication. . . ."

"Or *The Sun* won't support me this fall."

"Politics is the art of equation. We very well might not support you."

"Just for that?"

"In our view, it's not a minor matter. The mayor has what the city wants and he won't put out. Why should the city put out for him?"

"What if it were in the city's best interests that I keep quiet?"

"How is anyone to judge?"

"There is no way. It's best if I keep my counsel."

"Why don't you let the people decide what's best?"

"Because, in this case, they can't."

"I don't understand what you're doing," Praeger said. "Television is going to hammer you to death."

"I realize that."

"How do you expect to be reelected?"

The Ermine Mayor smiled. "Who's running against me?"

"No one, yet."

"That's right. And by the time anyone does, it'll be too late. This is the middle of June. Who's going to match my two hundred ward captains, and twenty thousand precinct workers, in three and a half months?"

"They're not an infallible guarantee."

"I'll have to take it nonetheless."

"Why?" Praeger asked, wanting not to believe the Ermine Mayor's inexplicable transformation from a statesmanlike leader to a bunker politician.

"Look," said the mayor. "If you were to run against me, win, and then find out yourself about this question, you would then do exactly as I'm doing."

"That's what you think."

"That's what I know. A great opportunity awaits this city, and I'm going to deliver it. I care about history: I'm quite willing to sacrifice my career. Anyway, who the hell *will* run against me?"

"Maybe I will," said Praeger.

The Ermine Mayor hesitated. "That's not even a joke. This city never elects tall, clean-cut, literate men—unless their heads are full of cotton, or they're deeply corrupt. You're too smart and too honest even to get the nomination of an idealistic fringe party. And how would you deal with the machine?"

"Maybe I'd bypass it entirely," answered Praeger, who had no idea whatsoever of running for office, and was merely following the Ermine Mayor's lead.

"Can't be done, though, I admit, it's the dream of every young man. I suppose it starts with children. They want to be President, they make wonderful speeches in the shower, they are lifted by the divine political afflatus, and they never make it. Nor should they.

442

This is a world of savage equalities. The city has to be run by a hard man, not by someone who makes magic with a pen. And the city knows it.''

"What about the Silver Mayor?"

"He wrote it all down after he did it, not before."

"I haven't written anything down," Praeger said. "And I may be a bit rougher than you think."

The Ermine Mayor looked at Praeger and, for the first time, did not like what he saw. Before him was a rangy six-footer with a fighter's gleam in his eyes, and a face that was held combatively tense—the way some hard cases get when they're mad, squinting as if in preparation for taking punishment.

"Where were you born?" the mayor asked, positive that Praeger did not have the streets in his blood, and could never call the city his own, could never assert in front of a crowd the special pride and sureness that comes from being born in the place. He had all the marks of an immigrant from the suburbs.

"I was born on Havemeyer Street, your honor," Praeger said, "almost directly beneath the Brooklyn ramp of the Williamsburg Bridge. How do you like that apple?"

"I couldn't care less," answered the Ermine Mayor, returning to his papers as a signal for Praeger to leave. "You're not running for anything."

By the middle of July, much of the ardor in the matter of the colossal platform that floated in the Hudson had disappeared. The mayor was as quiet as a slab of granite, no one came from or went to the ship, and uniformed men appeared on its decks only when someone attempted to board it. At first galvanized by the challenge, the press employed every kind of stratagem to figure out what the ship held. A dozen journalist-parachutists had drifted down onto its massive two-acre hatches, only to be apprehended on each occasion and escorted to shore by mute guards. Frogmen swam about the hull and climbed the side with magnets and suction cups, and were met at the railings by the same humorless guards. Helicopters, seaplanes, balloons, floating duck blinds—everything that could move across water or air was attracted to the ship during its first weeks in New York. It was scanned by infraredometers, magnetometers, and subatomic particles, but for deducing its contents the only valid calculation was one which, in comparing the ship's volume and displacement, determined its exact average density, including whatever was in it. This revealed nothing, since no one knew how tightly the holds were packed. The fires of the press soon died down, and were just as quickly rekindled in response to other events. Television had chopped the world into tiny bits, and what had once been the gaping maw of popular interest had evolved into a hair-thin pipette through which the ship in the Hudson was simply too big to pass.

After returning from a frenetic search of most of the Finger Lakes, Craig Binky made sure that he outdid his rivals in trying to unravel the mystery. He, Binky, a child of the Enlightenment, commissioned most of the advanced scientific studies, going so far as to have a particle accelerator built in the west Village, and its target apparatus installed across the river, so that what he called "bideo beams" could pass through the ship and draw a picture of its innards. But it didn't work—the bulkheads were impenetrable even to gamma rays—and Craig Binky, ever aware of the public's thrashing insomnias, pointed *The Ghost* in other directions. He himself was swept up by the poetry vogue of the second week of July. (Those lucky poets whose books were published that weekend became millionaires.)

It took Harry Penn much longer than Craig Binky to drop the story, but he did. *The Sun* staff was surprised, for it seemed out of character, but he told them to accept defeat, temporarily, and await a turn in events. Banner headlines soon devolved into tiny paragraphs on the back page. The ship vanished from the editorials and did not even appear in "Shipping and Mails," since it was not tied to a pier.

So forgotten, it became a part of the landscape, a third palisade, the kind of thing that people look at and do not see—which is to say that it became a part of the city. Peter Lake took time off from his machinery to view it, but it meant no more to him than to anyone else.

Only Praeger, Hardesty, and Virginia refused to let the matter drop, because Harry Penn had not merely advised them to wait for a turn of events, he had ordered them to discontinue work on the story. It was the first time he had ever restrained Virginia, and Praeger would have resigned had he not loved the old man as much as he did.

After many nights in the library trying to discover where the ship had been constructed (there seemed to be no building ways in the world big enough to accommodate it), Hardesty was so exhausted that he fell asleep at a reference table and dreamed that he was in San Francisco, in his father's house, looking over the bay. When he was a boy, he had liked to watch the brick-red tugboats, compressed in the clean bright ring of his telescope, as they pushed a carpet of rolling white water before them. On the stacks were a gilt figure of the rampant lion of San Marco, and the name *Marratta*. It always sent a chill down his spine to see these boats charging across the bay, with his name written on them in the color of a golden lion—not so much because he was proud, but because they reminded him of his father's steadfastness and strength.

When he awoke, he saw Virginia bent over a thick maritime register. "We're not going to find anything here," he said as Praeger emerged from the darkness loaded down with half a dozen shipping tomes. "Why don't we just watch the ship. Asbury can take us over to the Jersey side, and pick us up before dawn. Now that they're off the front page, they may loosen up a little and give something away."

Every evening after dark, for the next ten days, they went over to the Palisades, where they found a broad ledge halfway up a cliff, and kept the ship under surveillance all through the night—taking turns sleeping and watching. Asbury picked them up just before dawn. They saw nothing. Though Hardesty had suggested that they follow this course, he was the first to want to abandon it. But Praeger wouldn't let him. Long after Hardesty and Virginia had lost any hope of seeing anything, Praeger had bright eyes for the deserted decks, and when he was awakened for his shift he always looked like a hunter anticipating a kill. They kept at it into August, when the river was like a warm bath and mists and steam circled all about the ship.

And one day, not surprisingly, it was Praeger who electrified them with a call to awake. The mist had vanished, and they opened their eyes to see Manhattan outlined against the pure colors of a clear dawn. On the opposite shore, in the shadows of the canyons, a signal light was flashing. Had they been ten feet to the left or right of where they were, they would not have been able to see its blinkered sparking. But they were directly opposite the ship's bridge, and the message had overshot its target. With binoculars, Praeger could see that two figures stood by a long black car on a pier across the river. One operated the light, while the other paced about. The pacer was short and fat; the signaler was in some sort of uniform.

"Let me see," Hardesty demanded.

"No. Wait a minute," said Praeger. "Asbury's coming up along this bank of the river. If we're fast enough, we might be able to catch them in whatever they're about to do."

They scrambled in the half-light and reached the base of the cliff as Asbury pulled in. He was surprised, since he usually had to climb to their post. According to him, their situation was difficult. If a boat were to emerge from one of the ship's water-level bays and strike out for the pier, they would get to the other side too late to follow whoever emerged from it. On the other hand, running the river in anticipation of this would scare off their quarry.

They were lucky, however, because a small tanker was heading upriver from the open harbor. They let it come up even, and then moved along with it, hidden from view. Half a mile north, the tanker followed the channel to the east side of the river, and as it did they pulled forward of it and were sheltered on the starboard all the way to a long pier behind which they vanished completely out of sight of either ship or the pier on which the limousine was still waiting.

After they climbed a mass of rotten pilings, they ran toward the street to search for a taxi. Hardesty was in the middle of thinking that they would never find a taxi at dawn on Twelfth Avenue, when he looked into the pier shed alongside which Virginia and Praeger were still running, and saw five hundred taxis starting their engines. He didn't even have to say anything, and several empty dozen of them arrived in a gleaming phalanx.

Heading downtown toward the pier where the light had been flashing, they passed the limousine, going in the opposite direction.

"Turn around unobtrusively," Praeger instructed their driver.

"What does that mean?" the driver asked, veering a hundred and eighty degrees in a blaze of burning rubber.

"Nothing," Praeger replied. "Just follow that limousine without him knowing."

The limousine cut a devious trail, going in circles, passing the same place three or four times, careering through the park, and insinuating itself as often as it could in whatever traffic it encountered at that early hour. After its tour of Manhattan, it stopped in front of the Metropolitan Museum of Art, and three men got out. They entered the museum via a little-used door embedded in the base of a huge plinth.

As Praeger and the Marrattas sped by in the taxi, they saw the three men from the limousine quite clearly. One was extremely tall, another was the fat figure who had been pacing, and the other was the signaler. The fat one was an adolescent. Even from a distance, in a moving taxi, trying to look askance with nonchalance, they were able to see that his face was so fat it made his eyes into squinting, smiling slits. At first they had thought that, since the signaler had been in a uniform of some type, he was dressed in livery and had been driving. However, as he vanished into the museum they saw that he was not a chauffeur, but, rather, a man of the cloth.

Had Peter Lake seen these people all together he probably would have lit up like an electric eel, because they were Jackson Mead, the Very Reverend Mootfowl, and Cecil Mature—who had long ago changed his name to Mr. Cecil Wooley, and who had come in advance of the other two, posing as a street vendor who worked the area near the Brooklyn Bridge.

Hardesty, Virginia, and Praeger paid the taxi a small fortune, and repaired to the sidewalk café across the street from the museum to sit on its unoccupied veranda and wait for the three odd people who had gone in, to come out. While they were waiting, well concealed, another limousine pulled up, and out jumped the Ermine Mayor, known for his bald head and springy step.

"Mighta known," said Praeger.

Then another limousine pulled up.

"There are an awful lot of limousines around here," Hardesty said. "You'd think this was the Upper East Side."

Its door opened slowly. A cane poked out, then a foot—obviously an old foot. Then a pant leg of houndstooth. Then all the rest of the diminutive, aged, and spry—Harry Penn.

A long time before, Harry Penn had been embarrassed and shamed almost to death, and had rolled in agony across the accommodating expanse of Isaac Penn's capacious dinner table, when his carefully hidden pictures of husky seminude maidens of the evening had broken through the ceiling and drifted down into the dining room like overdue mail. Nearly a century later, he still turned a bright color in recollection of the moment when the postcards had fallen onto the serving platters, and his father had actually caught some in midair. If there were such a thing as archeologists of the soul, they might reconstruct all that has gone before from shame and love, two everlasting columns that rise into time though everything else is worn away. For Harry Penn, the sting of that moment was still dreadfully hot, despite the fact that over the years it had been joined by a dozen others—fewer and fewer, it is true, as he grew older and more adept. Yet, now another was added to the pack, suddenly to envelop him when he least expected it. As he came out of the museum, at a little after eight in the morning, he found Praeger de Pinto, Hardesty Marratta, and Virginia Gamely (who was still known by her maiden name) standing between the limousines. He had misled and lied to them, and excluded them from important things. Hardly able to look at these people that he knew so well, he entered his car like a slope-shouldered dog. He was not used to feeling that way.

Jackson Mead glared in their direction with the not inconsequential power of his very steely, very blue eyes. He seemed to be eight feet tall (he nearly was), and almost to glow—as if everything

448

about him were pure, and he were not a man. In stark contrast was the semifunereal Mootfowl, who looked like a nineteenth-century missionary trying his best not to enjoy the South Seas. Though he was Lincolnesque and grave, it was easy to think that any hand that touched him would forever remain tainted with the supernatural. Complementing the white glow and the dark streak was a fat ball—Cecil Mature. Whereas Jackson Mead was angry, and Mootfowl looked amused and wise, Cecil Mature (or Mr. Cecil Wooley, as he insisted) was a one-man mob of unrestrained affection. Virginia felt like kissing his big smiling face, and Hardesty and Praeger were tempted to embrace him with one arm and smile back as if for a photograph.

These three were so strange that Praeger, normally the model of self-possession, spread his arms with outwardly facing palms and asked, in amazement, "Who *are* you? And where do you come from?"

Jackson Mead seemed to think that this was a reasonable question, and he answered it. "From St. Louis, and beyond, and other places," he said.

Then the mayor came out, and all the cars started their engines and drove off, leaving Jackson Mead's answer to hang in the air like a cloud of diesel exhaust: "From St. Louis, and beyond, and other places." Even though he was no longer saying it, they kept hearing it.

"Who is it?" screamed Boonya, from beyond the heavy door.

"Praeger de Pinto."

"Who is it?"

"Praeger de Pinto."

"Who? Praeger de who?"

"Praeger . . . de . . . Pinto!"

"No."

"What do you mean, 'no'?"

"We don't want none."

"None of what?"

"Whatever."

"This is Praeger de Pinto!"

"Who?"

"Open the door, Boonya. You know who it is."

"Let a minute pass. Cool off." Five minutes later, she opened the door. "May I help you?" she asked.

"I would like to see Mr. Penn."

"He ain't here."

"Yes he is."

"No he ain't."

"Yes he is."

"No he ain't."

"I know he is."

"All right. He is. But he's in the bath. You can't see him."

"Why? Does he become invisible in water?"

"Huh?"

"Why can't I see him—hello, Christiana," he said, as Christiana came down the backstairs, carrying a tray of sugar cookies with jam blobs. "I'm a man. He's a man."

"He never sees anyone in his bath. It is outrageous."

"That's okay," Praeger said, heading for the stairs. "I am outrageous."

Harry Penn was sitting under a fall of sun-heated water that cascaded over his shoulders into a ten-by-ten, eight-foot-deep, slate bathtub. It was hard for him to speak over the noise of the water, so he adjusted a droplet-covered brass lever, and then invited Praeger to enter the room. He hadn't known for sure that it had been Praeger knocking at the door, but he suspected as much, because indignant people always rap on doors, like woodpeckers in their prime. "I thought you might be coming," he said. "I suppose that I retreated to the bath almost to hide."

"I imagine that's possible," said Praeger, humbled by the frail and naked body that he had never seen except in tweedy suits. The shock of seeing how thin and slight a man becomes in his late nineties reminded Praeger that, no matter what happened, he would have to be respectful.

"Sit down, Praeger," Harry Penn instructed, pointing at a towel-covered cedar bench. "I was intending to tell you all this

450

when the time was right. I still can't say much, but I'll explain as best I can. I owe that to you.

"When you get to be as old as I am, Praeger, you have long finished with ambition—that is, for yourself. Oh, I admit, there is a species of beast that punches and kicks until the coffin's nailed, but you take the average man as he approaches a hundred, and you'll see that he's pretty calm, interested mainly in memory, his children and grandchildren, small pleasures and graces, and very abstract things like the public weal, kindness, or courage—things that, from a perspective of serenity, are as visible and real as anything else.

"I knew in my late teens that all my life would be never-ending revisions and revisions yet again, of that which many times over I thought I knew, and did not, and still don't. But the light grows deeper. And you rise higher and higher, until, close to death, you view the history of your life as if an angel is describing it to you from an elevated platform on a cloud.

"It would be hard for you to understand, because you are so young, the abiding love and affection that I have for young people and their passions. I suppose one learns this, or begins to learn it, in bringing up children, and it is one of life's great surprises— looking back to see those who have come after you struggling through what you have nearly finished.

"Normally I would sacrifice a great deal rather than put obstructions in the way of a young man like you. I never have, have I?"

Praeger shook his head to confirm that Harry Penn hadn't.

"No. It was quite deliberate. I try to do my best for you all. So, then, why suddenly have I become secretive and misleading? Why has the horse in the pasture begun to run with the foxes? I'll tell you." He laughed. "I can't tell you!"

Praeger began to pace back and forth on the slippery ledge at the side of the pool. "For several weeks this June I wrote editorials condemning the mayor for his secrecy in this matter," he said, "calling in behalf of *The Sun* for public disclosure. And all the time that I was doing this, you knew."

"No, I didn't. I met Mead for the first time today."

Praeger froze like a hunting dog who catches a scent. "Mead? Who's that, the big one?"

"Yes. I shouldn't have told you. But it hardly matters. His name is Jackson Mead. The cleric is called Mootfowl."

"Mootfowl!"

"Yes, Mootfowl, and the little fat one is Mr. Cecil Wooley. However, their names won't do you any good."

"I'll go through every archive that exists."

"They're not in archives."

"You don't travel around in a mile-long ship without someone, somewhere, writing it down."

"You can," said Harry Penn, interrupting himself to move the lever and shut off the water. A silence followed. "There are men who move through history without leaving a trace of themselves, even though they may change the world. Jackson Mead has been here before, several times before, but you won't find it written down. He arranges it so that the traces disappear."

"Is he going to make arrangements this time, too?"

"I'm afraid so."

"Meaning *The Sun* will ignore him?"

"Yes."

"Meaning that, even though I have enough to fill a column, there will be no such column?"

"Yes."

"I'll have to resign. I don't want to, but you're forcing me."

"I know." Harry Penn's expression was almost joyous.

"I thought I knew you," Praeger said.

"I knew you *didn't*," Harry Penn answered. "No one really does. But hold through. It's a pity. I don't want to see you go. Why don't you meet with Jackson Mead himself?"

"Don't tell me that to do so I'll have to saw off my right arm," Praeger said. "Because I will."

"I'll see what I can do, although I don't know if you'll profit by it, or simply be overcome. He has a powerful presence."

"Mr. Penn, before I met Jessica I was engaged to a young woman whose parents insisted that prior to our marriage we speak with a Jesuit. They wanted to convert me, and had in mind putting me under the fire of a large gun. The engagement was broken off

452

later, for other reasons, but we did manage to see the Jesuit. We had lengthy discussions and disputations. He became a rabbi!"

"So you think you can make Jackson Mead a rabbi!"

"I might just do that."

"Take Hardesty and Virginia with you."

"Why?"

"He'll have Mootfowl and Mr. Wooley. Do you want to be outnumbered?"

They were met at the small door in the plinth. It opened and closed in an instant, after which they found themselves shaking hands with a beaming Cecil Mature, who introduced himself as Mr. Cecil Wooley, and was full of laughter that gurgled from his nose and throat like water going down a stuffed drain. He was wearing a medieval boy's tunic and a Chinese hat. It was a miracle that he could see, and they imagined that he looked out through his eyes like a sentry peering through firing slits. He was his usual good-natured self, and he waddled along with notable rapidity.

It was four-thirty in the morning, and the museum was empty even of guards. As they passed through its palatial chambers and long halls, they became aware of music, and the music swelled until it filled the corridors and made their hearts race. On a balcony overlooking a dim atrium, they were hit by the full flood of it, for a dozen musicians were playing below.

Then they found themselves in the New Great Hall, under a sky of gray and white opaque glass that suggested a perpetual March afternoon. Jackson Mead was working at a long desk in the middle of the room, seemingly half a mile away, surrounded by half a dozen paintings on three-legged easels. Mootfowl, who also wore a Chinese hat, was on his knees in prayer before a large canvas depicting St. Stephen's Ascension. St. Stephen arose, his limp legs and downward-pointing feet trailing after him as if he were being pulled through water, or as if they were the swaddlings of a baby held high above its father. His clothing appeared to have been molded into the shape of the air. As light flooded down upon him, he stared beyond the upper edge of the painting, while in the background golden splays of birds were aflutter in the wind. Distant mountains, purple and white, looked almost as if they were rearing like frightened horses. Rivers leapt from their channels and leapt back in again, leaving dry bends of riverbed in which fish were straining to swim and breathe in water that was not there. Underneath St. Stephen was a ring of golden light. The skillfully rendered grasses on the little prairie from which he is said to have been assumed were beginning to kindle where they met the circle of light.

When he finished praying, Mootfowl got up and pulled a cloth across the papers on Jackson Mead's desk. Cecil Mature showed the three visitors to their chairs, and they sat down opposite Jackson Mead, after which Cecil began to pace back and forth, laughing to himself now and then, calculating on his fingers, and muttering "Oh my, oh my."

The music stopped. Praeger was about to speak, but Jackson Mead held up his hand and warned that the piece was not yet finished. "I'm wedded to the last movement," he said. "Do you know what it is?"

"The allegro of the 'Third Brandenburg,' " Hardesty answered.

"Yes," said Jackson Mead. "The 'Third' is the only one without wind instruments. I never liked them in the other concerti, because they tend to clutter things up. They remind me of a bunch of monks running down a corridor, breaking wind. So many years in those monasteries, all through the Dark Ages. It was horrible.

"Here it is. Listen!" he commanded. "This part. It sounds like a good machine, a perfectly balanced rocker arm, something well-oiled and precise. Notice the progressions, the hypnotic repetitions. These are the tunnel rhythms, derived from the same timed intervals which are the irreducible base for planetary and galactic ratios of speed and distance, small particle oscillations, the heartbeat, tides, a pleasing curve, and a good engine. You cannot help but see such rhythms in the proportions of every good painting, and hear them in the language of the heart. They are what make us fond of grandfather clocks, the surf, and well-proportioned gardens. When you die, you know, you hear the insistent pounding that defines all things, whether of matter or energy, since there is nothing in the universe, really, but proportion. It sounds somewhat like an engine that became available at the beginning of the century, and was used in pumps and boats and that sort of thing. I thought for sure that people would realize what it was, but they didn't. What a shame. Nonetheless, there is always music like this, which, in its way, comes just as close—as if the composer had actually been there, and returned."

When the music stopped, Jackson Mead turned to Cecil Mature. "Mr. Wooley, please tell the musicians that they won't be needed until five-thirty. Thank you." Cecil Mature waddled out, flailing his sausagelike arms and legs. Mootfowl took his place by the side of Jackson Mead, looking maddeningly like an eighteenth-century Connecticut undertaker.

"The Reverend Doctor Mootfowl and I would be delighted to answer your questions—up to a point. We do have our privacy. If all things were one, there would be no privacy. But, since we are in a state of multiplicity, there are shades and differences, and privacy must be maintained—if only as a complement of and testament to physics."

"We're grateful that you're seeing us," Praeger said. "And we have no intention of violating your privacy. However, we didn't come to talk about the unified field theory, or the aesthetics of architecture."

Hardesty seemed slightly offended. Registering this, Jackson Mead imagined a path between Hardesty and Praeger, down which he intended to walk quite easily.

"Though, evidently, our newspaper won't be making your answers public, we are, by habit, compelled to inquire of you in the manner of reporters. We feel that we are justified in this because of your private dealings with our elected officials, the general public curiosity about your arrival, and the unprecedented size of your ship."

"Makes sense," Jackson Mead answered.

"I'm glad you agree. Who are you, where do you come from, what are you planning to do, why have you kept your activities secret, what does the ship hold, where and how was it built, and when will you begin whatever it is that is to be begun? These are

455

the things that we must know to satisfy the public's curiosity and our own.''

"That's a rather arrogant approach," stated Jackson Mead.

"How so?" Praeger returned, undisturbed.

"Why must you insert yourself in my business?"

"I told you, sir, and you said that it sounded reasonable."

"What sounded reasonable to me, Mr. de Pinto, was your curiosity, not any idea that I'm obligated to satisfy it. You are sitting there and asking me brazen questions."

"People buy *The Sun* to learn things they wouldn't normally know. Normally, they wouldn't insert themselves into your business or ask brazen questions, which is why I must."

"I see," replied Jackson Mead. "But apart from the fact that, as you yourself have guaranteed, the results of this interview will not appear in *The Sun,* tell me, for the sake of discussion, why people have a right to know my plans. You justify your right of inquiry by referring to theirs. What is theirs? Is it, despite their greater numbers, any more legitimate than yours, which you seem to have forsworn defending? What gives *them* the right?"

"It pertains to them, Mr. Mead. They don't always see everything—which is no reason to fault them, since they have to get on with their lives. Sometimes ships pass down the Hudson at night, big oceangoing ships, and no one, literally no one, sees them. I'm the watchman, here to make sure that the people know what is on their horizon, what ships pass down the river at dawn or, in your case, come upriver in the evening."

"Mr. de Pinto, the dog who protects sheep quickly learns how to direct them, and it becomes a habit. The people have been trained by their watchmen to jump, and to trample what the watchmen want trampled.

"I have found, in many cities and in some places that were not yet cities, that those who would guard the people are their governors. The government admits that it is a government. The press pretends that it is not. But what a pretense! You orchestrate entire populations. They get all worked up, like children, running here and running there. It is certainly no coincidence that advertisers use your pages to influence the public. What do you think your editorials, your selection and emphasis, your criticisms, even your use of quotations do? And who elected you? No one. You are self-appointed, you speak for no one, and therefore you have no right to question me as if you represent the common good. When I'm ready to let the public know my purposes, I will. Until then, I will continue to make ready, so that I can weather popular opposition."

"You know they'll oppose you?" Virginia broke in.

"They always do. And they should."

"Why?" she asked, mystified. "If you think they're right to oppose you, why don't you just refrain from whatever it is you're planning? Wouldn't that be the simplest way?"

"Of course it would, if I wanted to be loved. I would simply cut and run. But my purpose here is not to be loved."

"What is your purpose, then?" Hardesty asked.

Because Jackson Mead thought he saw in Hardesty's face that Hardesty wanted, above all, to understand, he confided in him. "My purpose," he said, suddenly soft and benevolent, "is to tag this world with wider and wider rainbows, until the last is so perfect and eternal that it will catch the eye of the One who has abandoned us, and bring Him to right all the broken symmetries and make life once again a still and timeless dream. My purpose, Mr. Marratta, is to stop time, to bring back the dead. My purpose, in one word, is justice."

Hardesty blinked. This peculiar man who talked about machines, time, and eternal rainbows, had dealt him the same hand that he had put down when he decided to stay in New York. "When?" he asked, and was truly stunned when Jackson Mead looked at him with a slight smile, and said:

"Patience."

Though Jackson Mead had worked some kind of magic on Hardesty, Praeger pressed on, determined not to be taken up by the siren song that he could not, anyway, hear.

"With all due respect, Mr. Mead," he said, "I don't have the vaguest idea of what you're talking about. If I were to publish in my paper the full quotation of what you've just said, in context, the state hospitals would be clawing each other for a chance to receive you."

"Do you think he doesn't know that!" snorted Cecil Mature, who had returned to the room.

"Thank you, Mr. Wooley," snapped Jackson Mead. "I can speak for myself."

"And furthermore," Praeger said, "if you've been at this for a while, tagging the world with rainbows and such, pursuing the extraordinary goals of which you speak, then obviously you've failed. Meanwhile, you do whatever you do. If it's disruptive, well then, maybe people ought to know about it, so they can stop you."

"You see this painting?" Jackson Mead asked, gesturing toward *The Ascension of St. Stephen*.

"Yes. Of course," Praeger answered.

"Do you believe that St. Stephen rose, actually?"

"No."

"Then why did the artist paint it, and why do people venerate it and St. Stephen himself, if they did not and do not think that he rose? After all, if he didn't rise, then who the hell was he?"

"They do think he rose," said Praeger. "That's why they venerate the painting, and St. Stephen himself, however mistakenly."

"No," Jackson Mead insisted. "They don't think anything of the kind. Oh, maybe some do, the ones who believe in spells and amulets. But the painter, and I, and most people who have come to venerate St. Stephen, do not think that he actually rose, as if he were attached by wires to stage machinery." This encouraged Praeger, until he heard more. "Absolutely not. They think, to the contrary, that he is rising, that he rises. The act is not complete. Even the painting freezes him in midair. It is, rather, in progress. To debate its actuality is useless, as it will not be confirmed—until we are able to see everything at once."

"I beg your pardon," said Praeger, somewhat indignantly.

"What I am saying is that, until the canvas is set, actualities are no more than intentions, and intentions are as much as actualities. You see, it has all happened before, and it has not happened yet. And, whereas it is true that I have failed, and failed miserably, I have also succeeded—gloriously. The memory of that glory, in what you would call the future, is what I am intent upon retrieving, just as St. Stephen knew that he would rise, and was rising, though he was not. It has to do with time, you see. There is no such thing: only the suggestion of it, only a series of actions that we, because of our imperfection, must run together to comprehend. Look at the painting. You do see motion in it, don't you? And yet, no one moves. How is that?

"I will tell you. The painting is close to the true state of things. Just as, in a film, there are only stills arranged in an illusion of motion, so in life and time. It is all locked hard within a matrix, and breathtakingly complicated, as if an infinite number of miniaturists had been employed forever in its startling depictions. But I assure you, there is no anarchy, everything happened/happens at once, and it does not move."

"And yet, it moves!" said Praeger.

"Not from sufficiently afar."

"Now how would you know?" Praeger asked. "Have you been there? And another thing: you said that when one dies one hears a pounding like that of an engine that was produced at the beginning of the century. How do you know?"

"Oh," said Jackson Mead, modestly. "I've died many times. Let's see," he continued, and began to count on his fingers. "At least six. Maybe more. It's hard to keep track. After a while, you tend to forget the exact number."

"I see," said Praeger, his eyes as wide as eggs.

"These assertions are enough to spin the dead in their graves," Hardesty volunteered. "To debate them is useless. In the end, they must be judged in the heart."

"Not so," held Praeger. "The intelligence is the best instrument for weighing mad speculations like these."

"Indeed not, Mr. de Pinto," held Jackson Mead. "The spirit is far more intelligent than the intellect. But though the spirit often moves less cautiously, it is far slower than the intellect to grasp a point, which is why I need time, and why I will not tell you the exact nature of my intentions."

"That's perfectly all right," Praeger answered. "I'll find out anyway. I'll defeat you with practicalities."

"And how do you propose to do that, if you have no access to *The Sun*? That doesn't seem very practical to me. Does it to you?"

"Unlike you, Mr. Mead, I have something solid in mind, with which I will sweep away the cobwebs that you scatter, as if with iron."

"Interesting that you should say that," said Jackson Mead. "I mean about the cobwebs." Suddenly, he was enjoying himself immensely, as if he had seen the very instrument of victory that Praeger did not think he had. "Wait till you see my cobwebs, Mr. de Pinto, just wait." He rose to his full height and leaned over his desk to peer at his inquisitors. "Compared to them, iron is nothing."

The interview was over.

·IV·

A GOLDEN AGE

A VERY SHORT HISTORY
OF THE CLOUDS

Long before even the first millennium, when there were no people whatsoever on the islands and bays that were to become the city, the cloud wall had once blown in from the sea and tried to lift meadows, forests, and hills. An exceptionally beautiful fall was cause for this premature agitation, for the leaves were so perfectly gold and red, and the light reflecting off the water or from purple-bellied storm clouds was so pure, that the white wall had moved without discretion to capture the autumnal clarity. But because the time wasn't right, because physics alone would not suffice, and since beauty was not the only issue, the meadows, forests, and hills were not lifted.

No longer susceptible to mistakes of infancy, and primed with the knowledge that justice sufficient to forge the opening into a new age would have to be derived from matters of the human heart, the cloud wall had run in one August to a harbor crowded with masts and sails. Amid the wharves and streets, there had been some saintly doings, and justice had been well served. But the machines were too young, and were not yet properly in place. They were still mounted on wooden bases, and their rough-hewn iron could not cleave the sky.

Once, in the jazz age, when steam and steel might have fulfilled iron's promises of power, the wall had rolled in like an angry lion, on a winter morning when they were dumping snow in the harbor and the mist was rising in anticipation of the signal plumes and clouds. But circumstances had been a trifle uncertain, many elements had been out of place, and the city had remained firmly rooted, as if it would never rise.

Only at the beginning of the third millennium, when arduous winters had returned just as in the little ice age that had caught the hunters in the snow, did the wall open and rise, and the bays and rivers turn bright gold. It was a masterwork of precision. The choir of machines had been tuned to shout back and forth across the ages. The means by which justice was proffered were strikingly humble, and yet cardinal to the principles that bind this world. And at the beginning of the third millennium, in those years of unrelenting winters, the just man finally emerged.

BATTERY BRIDGE

FROM either madness, truth, or charm, Peter Lake, listening hard, thought that he could hear the coming of the future in his machines. Cockeyed and still, directing all his attention to their sermons, he stood before them like a climber who has made some glorious peak. Their hoots, screams, and singing, like the static of the nebulae, enticed him deep into a confusing jungle of dimensionless sound and light. From the darkness, jaguars' eyes without jaguars glowed and circled in symmetrical orbits as red as rubies. On infinite meadows in the black, creatures made of misty light tossed their manes in motionless eternal swings that passed through the stars like wind sweeping through wildflowers.

He was abducted from the everyday world by contemplating for a second or two a whirling flywheel, or by listening to the symmetrical clicking of an escapement. When he had to fix a machine that only he could fix, someone had to be with him all the time, or, faster than he could stop himself, he would be drawn into a motionless trance at the foot of a crackling gearbox. These trances rendered him as stiff as a statue. It was almost as if he himself were a piece of reluctant machinery that now and then needed to be kicked. At first, in the company of another mechanic, he talked volubly and appeared to be in thorough control of himself. "Get me a number six metric spanner with a ratchet head," he might say to his escort. The escort would disappear into the hive of machinery on his way to the airfieldlike rows of red toolboxes that were kept in the long open ways between the machines, and return to find his mentor frozen solid, staring ahead into an open mechanical gut.

Master mechanics were as eccentric and idiosyncratic as Episcopal priests, and over the centuries they had learned to operate freely in each other's presence, respecting differences and allowing for peculiarities. But Peter Lake remained an outcast even among them, though, in his more lucid moments, he tried to make friends and to be like everyone else. These attempts were odd in themselves, since he could no more hide the fact that he was chosen than a rhinoceros could pass himself off as a calloused dairy cow. For example, at the end of the day, Peter Lake's co-workers often congregated around a makeshift table upon which was a huge glass pitcher of beer. In a show of good fellowship, he would join them, feigning relaxation and joviality. "You know," he might start off, in amazingly thick Irish, "this place is strange. I've been working on the master belt governor for the past day or two, and . . . and . . . and . . ." And he would be frozen block-solid in remembrance of the master belt governor's tapping code that ordered all things into a central symmetry. The other machinists would look at each other and snort, for they had been expecting this kind of thing, and they would never kick him awake until they were ready to go home.

In the beginning they called him "You," even when he wasn't there, because he refused to be called by any name, in the hope that he would discover his true identity. His paychecks were made out to "Bearer," which was how he appeared on *The Sun*'s payroll register—"Master Mechanic, Mr. Bearer." He was surrounded by many a mystery that the other mechanics wished to penetrate, especially because they never quite got over their awe at his extraordinary knowledge of the machines to which they were pledged. They wanted to know, for example, what he did on his days off. He was so odd at work that they assumed his free time would put the Arabian Nights to shame. So they sent one of the long-haired, adolescent apprentices to follow him into the depths of the city.

"He did all kinds of strange things," the apprentice reported upon his return two days later.

"Like what?" they inquired.

"I dunno . . . all kinds of weird stuff. It's hard to explain."

"Be specific," they urged, readying themselves for a feast of gossip.

"What does that mean?" the apprentice asked.

"Just tell us some things that he did!" they screamed.

"He peered at a lot of things."

"Peered? No one peers at anything except in books."

"Well, You peered at a lot of things, I can tell you that."

"Who, me?" asked a senior mechanic.

"No, *You.*"

"Oh."

"He peered at walls, stones, and gates. He ran his hands over the sides of buildings and stared at rooftops. He had conversations with fenceposts and fire escapes."

"What did he say?"

"I don't know. I couldn't get close enough. He went into the Five Points. I almost lost him then because I had to buy grape gum to black out my teeth. He can go there because he's gotten to look pretty funny again. I had to black out my teeth, take off one of my socks and put it over my head like a hat, rip my shirt, open my fly, and limp—then they thought I was one of them. He went straight for a tenement that stood alone on a brick lot. In the hallway there was a gang that would have killed me for the tallow man. But they thought I was with him, so they kept off.

"You went up to the roof. He put his arms around an old chim-

467

ney, like it was someone he knew, and started crying. He was talking to it, sort of begging or something.''

"What did he say?'' they interrupted.

"I couldn't hear. . . .''

"Because you weren't close enough?''

"No. I was close enough. There was too much, like, static.''

"What static?''

"You know, like on a police radio. I was in an airplane once: they have powerful radios, like a ham. It was like that—a ham.''

"From where?''

"I dunno.. It rained down. I couldn't hear anything. It was like when you're in the ocean and a big wave catches you and pulls you under and along with it. You hear the foam. It says something to you. I don't know what, but it does. That's what I heard.''

"Well what was it, foam or a ham? Make up your mind.''

"It was like both,'' said the apprentice, getting all worked up, "like a foamy ham. You know! Wait!''

"What, what!'' they asked.

"My brother's girlfriend is a Greek.''

"So what.''

"She's an Orthodox. Once I went to church with her, and they got this choir there—guys singing in tones, real low. It sounded like that.''

The mechanics asked no further questions, for they had stoked up their apprentice and he was going full-steam.

"And it was like an airplane in the distance, an antique one with propellers, and bowstrings quivering, and women going 'Ah! Ah! Ah!' and an orchestra playing all kinds of different things, and the way a dog growls when it's really mad, and metal—hot metal—plunged into a tub of cool water, and a teletype machine, and a harp . . .''

"All right,'' they said. "What did he do then?''

"He walked around.''

"Where?''

"Everywhere. Whenever he'd come to something that was a bright color, he'd stare at it for hours. He sniffed it. There was a house in Brooklyn Heights that had just been painted red. You caught it right in the sunset: he didn't move for an hour and a half."

"Where does he live?"

"No place that I could see. He didn't sleep. He just walked around, walked around. He didn't eat, either."

"He eats when he's here."

"He didn't eat out there, not for two days. Oh yeah, I forgot to tell you. Sometimes he would get so happy he would dance. And sometimes he would go into a broken-down factory or an old pier shed, when he thought no one was there. That's when the sound came back again. It was like people singing in one of those choirs, but not together.

"It got really loud on Pier Eleven. Nobody ever goes there, 'cause it's too dangerous. You was on his knees. It sounded like the whole world was shaking the roof. Beams fell down, and parts of the ceiling blew away. The sunlight pushed through, and lit up the dust. It was the weirdest thing I ever saw. I thought the building was going to fall down. It got so light I could hardly see, and the dust was all over the place. Even the pilings were vibrating back and forth in the water. That's when I decided to get out of there, and that's when I lost him."

The apprentice leaned forward and beckoned to his hearers. "I think," he said, in a whisper, "that what we're dealing with here is not your ordinary type of guy."

After *The Ghost* aerofleet had swept in manic arcs over the Finger Lakes, turning up absolutely nothing, Craig Binky was at a loss for something new. In the wake of the poetry craze, one of his lieutenants had suggested asparagus: "It has that style, that swing, that unaccountable fascination. . . ." Yet another was partial to a Hapsburg Empire revival: "Every fashionable woman in New York will be dressed in mouton lamb and bandoliers. Places to do the waltz will spring up. And our Sacher torte bakery might not have to shut down." Someone else suggested photographs of leather fruit: "It's sweeping San Francisco right now," he insisted. "It's tasteful, biogenic, relaxing, and capacious. Soon, and

469

you can mark my words, every house in Peoria will have pictures of leather fruit above the fireplace."

Nonetheless, Craig Binky was unsatisfied. He rejected their proposals, and went into seclusion. A full nine minutes later, he emerged. "The idea bulb has lit in Craig Binky's head," he announced. "Bring me Bindabu!"

Wormies Bindabu was the dean of *The Ghost*'s book reviewers, a group of half a dozen men who sat in a windowless basement next to the hottest boiler and underneath the noisiest web press. They looked and dressed exactly alike—five foot two inches tall, 108 pounds, brushy mustache, stomach-length beard, long bony hands, gray hair parted down the middle, black wire-rimmed glasses, undertakers' suits, stringy ties, and crossed eyes. They sat next to each other in a ramrod-straight row and read twenty books a day (apiece), smoked Balkan Sobranies, ate hardboiled eggs and pickles, and listened repeatedly to one particular atonal concerto for bassoon and ocarina. Their names were Myron Holiday, Russell Serene, Ross Burmahog, Stanley Tartwig, Jessel Peacock, and Wormies Bindabu.

Craig Binky harbored special affection for Bindabu, because Bindabu was one of the very few people in the world who made Craig Binky look bright. Though he would quote (without having read) Spinoza and Marx faster than a waterbug could cross a cup of coffee, he did not know what an apple was, and he had never swum in a lake. Though he had never read Melville, he knew by heart the work of most anti-American Bolivian poets. Though he railed against puritanism in his dyspeptic reviews, he could neither sing, dance, nor wave his arms.

"Get the mayor," Craig Binky said.

"Did he write a book?"

"Of course not. But he won't tell me about that ship."

"What does that have to do with me?"

"Attack!"

"I resent that, Mr. Binky. I'm not an assassin, a guard dog, a thug, a hatchet man. . . ."

"Of course you are. You're the best. What I love about you,

470

Bindabu, is that you conceal it so well in all the big words you use.''

"But Mr. Binky, the mayor is your ally. Are your sure you want me to go after him?''

"Run him down, beat his brains out, bite his ass!''

The next day, *The Ghost* published a shocking attack on the mayor, in which he was called, among other things, a lout, a pimp, a crocodile, a Nazi, a populist, a Fascist, a pederast, a porcupine, and a glowworm.

The Sun rushed to his defense, putting the two papers on opposite sides of a question in what appeared to be reverse order. Both *The Sun* and *The Ghost* began to lose readers. Since those who could read one could not read the other, because of difficulty in one case and revulsion in the next, many switched reluctantly to *The Dime,* a reckless new tabloid that cost a dollar. *The Sun* and *The Ghost* were once again at war. But no one on *The Sun* understood or sympathized with Harry Penn's support of the mayor. There were resignations and defections. Some thought it was the powerful effect of the approaching millennium. Two thousand years—of course, they said, things are bound to be confused as we head through the rapids toward that glittering fall only months away.

Even in September, cold winds arrived from Canada and shut people in by their fires, making them think of the city of old. Winter, it was said, was the season in which time was superconductive—the season when a brittle world might shatter in the face of astonishing events, later to reform in a new body as solid and smooth as young transparent ice.

Hardesty Marratta and Praeger de Pinto rode their bicycles down the riverway, propelled by the pressure of traffic behind them, which, as the lights tracked the length of the avenue, surged forward like a cross between a tidal wave and the charge of the Light Brigade. The silver bicycle wheels sang through the indolent autumn blue. That fall the colors were the brightest in memory. Despite their immersion in a lake of cold clear air, they seemed hot, Caribbean, and metallic. Dark shadows passed over the landscape quietly enough to make a ringing in the ears, and after months of being lost in the summer mist the skyline had suddenly jumped back into sharp focus.

Praeger had secretly designated a dozen reporters and researchers to the matter of Jackson Mead. They were hard at work in archives, libraries, computer centers, and on the street. Five of them continued the surveillance. Hardesty, Praeger, Virginia, Asbury, and Christiana devoted a great deal of time to the question. Christiana spied on Harry Penn (without being directly intrusive, she was, nonetheless, all eyes and ears), and the others followed leads in any way they could. Everything they got was fed into a computer, which shuffled and reshuffled the data in search of hidden correlations. Because all this was accomplished without Harry Penn's knowledge or approval, Praeger thought he was quite a fox. Little did he know that Asbury, who he thought was working for him sub rosa, was really using most of the time to search the city for engines, and that Christiana was concerned far less about Jackson Mead than she was about finding a certain white horse.

Praeger and Hardesty were on their way to the Erie Lackawanna freight yards, because of a rumor that train after train had pulled in from the west and disgorged heavy construction equipment. As they sped south, Praeger told Hardesty of a major disruption in the metals futures markets. Bedford had reported that two dozen new companies were buying up enormous amounts of strategic metals. They paid in advance, in cash, and had already parted with close to a billion dollars. The metals were stockpiled all over the country, but were slated to move toward New York.

"What about the government," Hardesty asked. "Don't they suspect the meddling of a foreign power? Aren't they investigating?"

"According to Bedford," Praeger answered, "the government claims that everything is all right. They say they're familiar with the companies, that the dislocations are only temporary, and not to worry. But Bedford went to see the head of the Commodities Control Commission, and he said the man seemed as if he'd been drugged or hypnotized."

"You think it's Mead," Hardesty said, pedaling against a wind that nearly lifted them into flight.

"I have a feeling that it is, yes."

"A billion dollars is a large amount of money for one man to spend on raw titanium."

"I think he could manage that from his change pocket. We're dealing here with something different than we're used to. Things of the world seem to be no obstacle for him, and his problems no doubt lie elsewhere. If he's struggling, as he appears to be, it may be in a way we can't even imagine. The Reverend Doctor Mootfowl and Mr. Cecil Wooley are not the typical billionaire's assistants."

"What makes you say that?" Hardesty asked sarcastically.

"I can't put it out of my mind that both the fat one and the thin one wore Chinese hats and pointy silk slippers. And according to the half-dozen art experts to whom I've spoken, the painting of St. Stephen ascending—supposedly by Buonciardi—was never painted."

"Who painted it, then?"

"They don't know. But that's nothing. One of the researchers was looking for records of other instances in which unknown ships have come into the harbor. He was working through the files of the Quarantine Commission, since they, probably more than Customs, would be interested in the origins of a ship. For a while the Quarantine Commission had charge of the potter's fields. Just out of curiosity, he started to look through their records (which are alphabetical), and was promptly thunderstruck. At the turn of the century, a Reverend Dr. Mootfowl was given over to the potter's field gravediggers by a Reverend Overweary. In the ledger, under Mootfowl's name, Reverend Overweary had written, 'Murdered by an Irish boy named Peter Lake, and his fat slit-eyed friend, Cecil Mature.'

"Isn't Mr. *Cecil* Wooley the fattest, slittiest-eyed thing you've ever seen? And don't you suppose that being called Reverend Doctor Mootfowl is not a common phenomenon, and never has been?"

"Yes, but the one supposedly murdered the other a hundred years ago. Mr. Cecil Wooley is no more than twenty, and Mootfowl is certainly less than fifty. What, exactly, are you saying?"

"I'm saying that it sends a chill up my spine."

"Was the murder reported?"

"Neither the papers nor the police have any record of it. The city was in the midst of gang wars, and individual murders didn't get much play."

"When did they ever?" asked Hardesty.

They locked their bicycles to a fence, and crossed through the tubes to the New Jersey side of the Hudson, where railyards moribund for half a century were suddenly springing to life. Though it was Saturday, automated machinery, robots, and a thousand construction workers flooded the yard, and yellow hardhats were as much in abundance as the dandelions that grew between the ties. For as far as the eye could see, ranks of freight trains were drawn into orderly rows. Long flatcars held bulldozers, cranes, and parts of disassembled construction machines that were bigger than a house.

"What's the purpose of all this?" Praeger asked a bearded workman. "These yards have been abandoned for years."

"Two new lines coming in," the worker said above the din of track-laying machines and pile drivers. ". . . be finished in about a week."

"Railway lines?" Praeger asked incredulously, since no railways had been built for decades.

"Railway lines—one from the northwest, Pennsylvania. And one from the west, from who the hell knows where."

"What's that?" Hardesty asked, pointing to a fenced area in which half a dozen ruined buildings leaned, one against another.

"I don't know," the workman answered, looking from behind sunglasses that reflected the dazzling autumn light. "It's supposed to be a loading dock, but a lot of these guys," he said, meaning the other workers, "won't touch it. So it looks like it's never going to be a loading dock, even though the plans call for a concrete platform right in the middle."

"Why won't they touch it?" Praeger asked.

"They're nuts, that's why. They say it's a holy place. You always get guys like that on a construction site. Construction is special. I can't explain it, and I have to get back to work. But, believe me. It happens."

Hardesty and Praeger stood aside to watch the work. The yards had long been dead, but now it seemed as if they had merely been biding their time. Rusted and disheveled track, rotten ties stacked like corpses, flapping tin-skinned buildings, and splintered piers that smelled of pitch were rapidly becoming forests of gleaming rails, new platforms, solid towers, and switches and signals that covered the plain of cinders as if they had grown there like crops.

Because Hardesty and Praeger were hungry, they decided to walk to the Broth House. To do this they had to climb over fifty fences and a dozen parked freight trains. Soot and dirt from the fences and boxcar ladders covered their hands, and when they wiped the sweat off their faces, the soot ran down their temples. They were chased by fierce watchdogs running loose in the freight yards, and at one point Praeger was trapped on a signal tower by a wolflike dog who seemed to be barking "Vengeance is mine."

When they arrived at the Broth House their cheeks were red with cold and exercise, their clothes were filthy and torn, they were pleasantly tired, and they fit right in with the laborers and sailors who were there, milling in tough, crazy, senseless circles, threatening everyone around them with their eyes, staying upright and untouched in a play of evasion and maneuver that was as close as one could get, without getting wet, to swimming in high surf. "Praeger," Hardesty declared, "these are the same people who drive their cars into guard rails. You know, the ones who rob a jewelry store, make a clean getaway, and then pass a state trooper at eighty-five miles an hour over the limit. During the chase, they take curves as if there were no such thing as physics, and then they hit the guardrail. Guardrails are their destiny."

"Shut up," Praeger commanded. "That guy's listening, he looks real mean, and he's offended."

Hardesty burned his fingers on the scalding clam broth, which flowed free of charge from a copper kettle on the bar. They ordered ten grilled prawns, and ate them with bread, hot sauce, and a beer or two, or three—and soon they were limp in the waves of music and noise, brothers to the guardrail men. The entire Broth House seemed to be swaying pleasantly in the wind, like one of the sailing ships that, long before, had tied up at the nearby wharves. They felt that they were on the sea, and the smoke swirling in the center of the room became clouds, sails, and gulls.

Hardesty quickly forgot all his problems and narrowed in with guileless desire on the brave waitress who, with trays balanced in her hands, repeatedly negotiated the dangerous rapids of the Broth House and its lecherous patrons. To keep the trays level and move through the ravenous crowd, she had to do something like a dance. She was small, but she was lean, strong, and sexy enough to drive everyone in the Broth House crazy. She was deeply tanned from free days in the sun, her legs were trim (undoubtedly from running), and her long graceful arms were lightly muscled in a way that made Hardesty unable to turn away from her or drop his gaze. She wore a white shirt that was open enough to show that the top of her chest was smooth and dark. Her hair was jet black and bouncy, and cut with an upward twirl like that of a popular singer who was the latest rage. Hardesty began to go mad. He, truckers in cowboy hats, local Hobokians, ex-sailors, strangers from Manhattan, and the guardrail crew were mesmerized by her. As she passed Hardesty, she had to turn to face him the way one must do when moving through a crowded corridor on a European train. For Hardesty, breathless and astounded, it was as if a clock had struck midnight on its chimes forty times over, for as she passed him, God bless America, she slowed down, the crowd compressed, and she was pushed up against him as if they were both in a duck press. When he felt her small breasts and nipples sweep slowly across his chest; when he looked into her sunburned face; when he smelled her heated perfume; when her black eyes smashed into him like a lance and ran him over from top to toe with deep extractive pleasure; when, during the friction-laden passage of her thighs and breasts, she smiled and he saw a bright moonlike flash of large, perfect, glistening white teeth; and when as either a joke, an invitation, an involuntary movement, or a commemoration, she briefly pushed her lower body into his, Hardesty's legs refused to hold him and he went down in excruciating pleasure, dropping to the floor with a strange cry of both frustration and satisfaction that turned Praeger's head in search of his friend.

"Where are you?" Praeger asked. "Where'd you go?"

Hardesty was crawling and lunging forward on the floor in pursuit of her ankles as they receded into a lugubrious forest of pant legs. The patrons of the bar did not like a wave under their feet. It unsettled them, and when Hardesty started knocking people down, Praeger knew that the hornet's nest had been bumped too hard.

They began to fight, each man against the other, as if the flood were coming and only one place was left on the ark. There was some poetry in it, in that men were thrown in lovely swanlike parabolas and they produced deep cries of anguish. Mainly, however, it was the kind of nocturnal anarchy that September sees so often, and Hardesty was lucky that his single-minded friend was able to drag him through the smash-up and throw him out the door.

"Where is she?" Hardesty begged as Praeger pulled him to the old Erie Lackawanna terminus. This was a federal wedding cake, as elegant as a stubborn old dame, made of cream-colored stone and painted iron, and completely deserted. They stumbled through its dark hallways to a ramp of the long-deceased Barclay Street ferry, from the end of which they dangled their feet and hung over the water like lanterns.

Across the river, Manhattan shimmered in the moonlight—miles of white buildings sparkling like a forest of fireflies. Hardesty was still thinking of the waitress, but Praeger sat and stared over the water like a mad dog. Manhattan, a cage of white ribs and a mass of glowing crystal, seemed nearly alive. The beauty in it lifted them far above their enemies and their troubles in the world, as if they were looking at life from the vantage point of the dead. Suddenly overcome with affection for the people they loved, they saw before them the city of sunshine and shadow, now covered in moonlight, and they loved it so much that they wanted to hold it in their arms.

As they watched, a huge front of clouds began to close in from the northwest. Whiter than ice and sparkling as softly as a Swiss mountain village, the city seemed totally unaware of the huge black-and-purple wall that was approaching it. Hardesty thought of the medieval cities that fell to the Mongols or the Turks, and, had it done any good, he would have shouted a warning. The pale buildings looked as vulnerable as spun sugar, and the clouds came forward, their huge rounded fonts like the buttocks of war-horses or the shoulder plates of armor. And their retinue of snakes, the silver and white lightning bolts, struck the ground ahead of the horsemen.

The first wave broke over New York as the wind came up and made the Hudson into an impassable strait. The cable-hung ramps upon which Hardesty and Praeger sat began to buckle and sway, but they held tightly to the rails, unable to take their eyes off the city. Ten thousand bolts of lightning struck the high towers, plaiting them with white gold and filling the air with thundercrack after thundercrack that made all fixed objects rattle. It flushed rats from their burrows and sent them, in rare panic, squealing through the rain-filled streets. It set a hundred fires in the city of the poor, but the rain was so hard that they were extinguished as quickly as they started—which made them look like the slowly disintegrating spheres of airborne fireworks. When the storm was at its height, it seemed as if waves were breaking upon the city from a sea that floated and raged above. But the city neither flinched, nor blinked, nor bent its back for a moment. It stood fully upright like a range of great mountains, and harvested in the bolts. All the time that the storm was pounding, New York remained serene with its lights aglow, for its ranks of steady towers were built on bedrock. And in the end, when the sky was blue and white and slow rivers of lightning made only melodic apologies of rolling thunder, it was still shining, innocent, and intent.

Hardesty thought for a moment that he had seen something of the perfectly just city. When the storm was almost over, he had turned to see Praeger, elated and resolute, staring through the thunderous captions and the thick gray rain.

"I went to see Binky," Praeger said. "I sold my soul, and I'm going to be mayor. I'm going to be mayor—of that," he declared, looking across the water. "And I'm going to do it the way it's never been done. All the mayors before have stirred, and patched, and maneuvered, and run. We measure them by how well they put off battles. Because they've been putting off battles for a hundred years, they've divided and armed the city so that if there is a confrontation it will rival Armageddon. I don't want that. No one

478

does. No one ever did. But should there be a reckoning, I'm going to lead the city as it falls . . . *so that I may lead it as it rises.*"

Although he was moved by the verity and magic of Praeger's resolution, Hardesty still called upon reason, and asked, "How do you know?"

If human faces are an incentive to clairvoyance, then Praeger, at that moment, was the touchstone of the future. He looked over at Hardesty, and smiled. Hardesty saw in the cold blue eyes, the carefully cut blond hair, the slightly chipped front teeth, and an expression that told of great strength, long-suffering, and everlasting humor, that Praeger had been taken up by the same thing that he himself was seeking. Though he did not know why, he believed him, and he was saddened to see that Praeger's face told of a future battle as certainly as if it had been a memorial frieze.

To be mad is to feel with excruciating intensity the sadness and joy of a time which has not arrived or has already been. And to protect their delicate vision of that other time, madmen will justify their condition with touching loyalty, and surround it with a thousand distractive schemes. These schemes, in turn, drive them deeper and deeper into the darkness and light (which is their mortification and their reward), and confront them with a choice. They may either slacken and fall back, accepting the relief of a rational view and the approval of others, or they may push on, and, by falling, arise. When and if by their unforgivable stubbornness they finally burst through to worlds upon worlds of motionless light, they are no longer called afflicted or insane. They are called saints.

The last thing that Peter Lake would have called himself was a saint. And he was right, since he was not a saint, and never would be. However, he was certainly becoming more and more unhinged with each passing day, and he knew that the way things were he would not be able to take refuge in reason even were he to desire it. A terrible agony possessed him, made him giddy, and caused him to walk about and chatter hysterically. Everything was either exquisitely light or irredeemably black. Though his only middle ground lay in the machines, even they led him into the uncontrollable reveries of which his fellow workers had taken cautious note. They had learned to live with him, for his madness had not turned to cruelty or greed. But, as they suspected, when he was with them, he was restrained. On the outside, it was quite different.

"Gimme some Spanish mountain-climbing eggs," he demanded cheerfully in his Madison Square Irish. "Three over easy, two very sqwunchy and wet, like newborn wildebeests wrapped up in the amnioc, and one lone hardboiled—*the Aztec god of the sun*. Ya folla? Whatsa matter? Cat got your tongue! You know what a cat is? I'll tell you . . . but soft-ly. A cat is an excuse for a lonely woman to talk to herself. That's what a cat is. Tugboat.

"But, coming back around to breakfast, I like bananas. I demand them with my meals. I demand them! Bring me some. No! Wait! I'll have a footcake instead. Tugboat.

"I am poor, it is true. I am one of those about whom nothing was ever known—but the city is mine. Then why is it, tell me, that I look around, and there I am, way up there, the master of nothing I see? Is it possible that, on this continent of earth, there are those primitive creatures who never wear a hat, those gandy dancers and girls who jump out of cakes, those saps, tools, berks, and ocuses who do not actually exist no more than I will or not, and accept that which well-nigh cannot be? Impossible. It's impossible! No more likely, say, than a Baptist church without a school bus. You say what you will, my healthy-faced friend, standing there as jovial as Humpty Dumpty. I like your patience. However, there's something intensely frustrating about talking to you, and I'd rather sail through the gilded mist. Tugboat.

"All right. I relent. Change my order. Bring me Wildensteen's monkey bread, hot liverwurst, coconuts, and sea foam. That's a good breakfast. You see what I'm driving at? I desire . . . I desire. I'm confused, you see. But I try! I try! And I've got this strength which pushes me there, *pushes* me. It hurts, but I'm going, I'm going. Tugboat."

He went on like this for hours, overflooding with words that broke and popped in strangely ordered disorder, and fell from his lips like the foam that he thought he liked for breakfast. The faster he talked, the faster he talked, until he was white-hot, talking in tongues, demanding this, demanding that, slamming his fist down, screaming about order in the world, balance, rewards, justice, and veracity. There was no justice, he said. Oh yes there was. But it was very high and very complex, and to understand it you had to understand beauty, because beauty was justice without equation. "Tugboat."

No one objected, no one was inconvenienced, and no one was frightened. This was undoubtedly because Peter Lake was not in a restaurant, and he was not addressing a waiter or a cook. He was, rather, at the edge of an empty parking lot, talking to a mailbox. If anyone came to mail a letter, Peter Lake would become silent, lean against the object of his diatribe, and smile as the stranger pushed paper down its throat. Then Peter Lake would say to the mailbox, "Who was that? Did you know him? I mean is he a regular around here or what?" He was jealous.

When night fell, he was often hungry and thirsty and would go to Times Square to get some papaya juice, which he loved because, when he drank it, it made him feel just like anyone else, just like a businessman or a registered nurse. Perhaps because it made him feel this way, he had thrown before the act of obtaining it an almost impossible obstacle. On his way through the streets, he practiced ordering in a full mellifluous voice that the best professional announcer would have envied. Needless to say, speaking in full voice as he moved through the crowds of evening did no more for his reputation than did declaiming to mailboxes, gas cylinders, and motorcycle sidecars. But in New York no one had a reputation anyway.

"I'll have a large papaya, to go," he said. "I'll have a large papaya, to go. I'll have a large papaya, to go. I'll have a large papaya, to go."

He said it a thousand times. But when he finally approached the dazed, juice-stained man at the papaya counter, he went completely blank.

"What do you want?" the ragged papaya man asked Peter Lake.

Instead of answering, Peter Lake began to giggle, laugh, and snort. He exploded into half-suppressed shrieks, clenched his eyes

481

in hysteria, and swayed back and forth until his laughter was a series of wild squeals and bellows and he could hardly stand up. This was the affliction that kept him from papaya juice.

Finally, he took control of himself. He had to stop laughing, because his chest and stomach were sore, and he opened his eyes and cleared his throat. But when he saw the suspicious one-eyed squint of the papaya man he burst into a breathless shriek that took possession of his entire body.

In painful hysteria, laughing all the way, he returned to the city of the poor, where he entered an abandoned tenement, descended to the basement, and stretched out, sobbing, on a sack of coal. He didn't cry for long. Exhaustion spared him that, and kicked him deep into oblivion.

Sometime during the night, when the streets had fallen silent and the October moon was about to descend into the Pennsylvania forests, Peter Lake was suddenly awakened. He felt his heart jump as it started in panic to deal with whatever it was that had grabbed him from behind. As soon as he was awake enough to think, he assumed that three or four attackers, all of enormous strength, had surprised him as he slept on the coal sack. He expected the exquisite tortures that people who go to abandoned tenement basements at four in the morning mete out to the people who are already there. His only hope was to frighten his assailants with his insanity. However, he felt regretfully sane. In fact, he was so lucid, rational, and calm, that he might just as well have been a diplomat at work on his memoirs in front of a crackling hickory fire in the hunt country north of Boston.

"Gentlemen!" he blurted out as he was powerfully lifted into the air, but could think of no further appeal.

Amazed by the absolute steadiness with which he was raised, he imagined that the thugs who had him were Olympic weight lifters. He turned his head a few degrees in each direction, but was unable to see their feet. Nor could he hear their breathing. Nor could he feel their hands.

Though it was not entirely beyond the range of the local criminals to approach their craft with such refinement, it was not likely, either. Peter Lake tried to look over his shoulder, but he was held as firmly as if he were a kitten grasped by the scruff of its neck. He cleared his throat, and was about to address his tormentors once again, when he saw that he had begun to move very rapidly across the room. The acceleration was such that he felt the wind whistling in his ears, and he was pointed at the far wall. It came at him so fast that he hadn't even time to blink (much less protest) before his head smashed right into it.

But, rather than being killed, he went right through, with a gust of air that blew his hair back against his skull. Then he was in another cellar, still accelerating, heading for another wall. Expecting the worst, he closed his eyes. But again he went right through, and was still picking up speed. Soon he learned to keep his eyes open and bless the pace. Wall after wall appeared, and was passed as if it were mere air. He was traveling so fast that he saw the basement rooms go by as if they were frames in a motion picture—until the walls were no longer evident.

He flew underground as fast as a jet, whistling through earth, stone, and innumerable cellars, cisterns, tunnels, wells, and, finally, graves. For, as effortlessly as if he had been flying through clear air, he was taken on a tour of all the graves of the world. Though they flickered by with such rapidity that they became no more than a beam of sullen light, he was able to examine each one separately, as if every flash of his journey were a full-scale inquest. He saw the faces and clothing of the newly buried, and he registered their expressions without emotion.

Peter Lake's eyes were the only vital part of his face as they took in the quickening images that hurtled past, and they moved with machinelike, supernatural speed, fastening precisely upon every detail, catching a glimpse and more of each of the billions that he was assigned to see. The velocity and rhythm of these many lives combined into a pure and otherworldly whistle, like that of a loon in the deep forests on a still, clear night. They lay in all positions. Some were merely dust, others the ivory bones that children fear, spookishly luminescent. In unending scenes and drolleries, they clutched amulets, tools, and coins. They were buried with icons, photographs, newspaper clippings, books, and flowers. Some were in tattered shrouds and others wrapped in tape. Some had cradles of silk and wood, and many many more lay without any accoutrement in the soft or stony ground. Some he found in steel chambers, smothered under the sea, and some in great masses, thrown one atop the other like kindling. Chains, ropes, and iron collars were as much in evidence around the neck as were pearls and gold. They were all ages—infants, warriors with swords still stuck in their thighs, scholars who had died peaceable deaths, and Renaissance servants in red caps. As they shot past, they hesitated for an immeasurable instant to greet him. He flew over their great legions in the darkness of the ground, and his eyes kept working to take in the bearded ones, the toothless, the laughing and the insane, the worried women and the smiling, those who were profound and those who had never known more than a fish knows, the ones who had lived their lives on the ice and were still there, perfectly preserved in smooth white vaults, and the ones who had been washed down hot rivers and had lost everything but the tiny sparkle in the mud that betrayed their final positions.

His mouth fell open, but, still, his eyes worked. Something within him refused not to honor each one, and as if he had been born for the task, he saw and remembered each fleshless head, each whitened hand, each cavelike eye.

The graves of the world went by him with the hypnotic speed of the counterrhythms that dash from the spokes of a rushing wheel. He was unmoved, and he did not feel compassion, for he was far too busy and his eyes too darting and quick. There was much to be done. He had to know them all. And, in his mad and breathless flight, he did not miss a single one, but worked as if he had been created to be their registrar—the mechanical mole, the faithful observer, the gleaner of souls, the good workman.

Late in the afternoon, one day in the middle of October, the light on West Fifty-seventh Street created those perfect conditions that medieval churchmen had used to elaborate upon the idea of heaven. Virginia was returning from a North River pier where she had been sent to interview a noted political exile—who never arrived, because he had been secretly taken off his ship at sea and flown to Washington. She had several hours before she had to be

484

home to wake the children from their nap, and had decided to do some shopping on Fifth Avenue. Abby hadn't been feeling well, probably because of the change of seasons. Mrs. Solemnis said that she was sleeping comfortably and had no fever.

Virginia needed a winter coat. Because she was tall, even for a Gamely, she took large sizes. This, combined with her deeply ingrained thriftiness, meant that she would probably have to look hard to find something decently styled, and warm enough for the Lake of the Coheeries. It had been years since she had seen her mother. Both Virginia and Hardesty knew that they would have great difficulty getting to the Coheeries, and that they might not be able to return. Hardesty was willing, in that case, to become a farmer by the lake, and pass his winters on skis, in iceboats, and skating many miles from village to village and inn to inn. They planned to go in December or January, if conditions were right. They would bundle the children in wool, down, and fur, and take the train early one morning when the smoke from the few chimneys that still existed stood skinny and straight in the cold air, like undertakers waiting outside a church. These, at least, were their plans. But since they had planned in this fashion for many winters and had never been able to leave, the plans seemed like dreams. Every winter, they were going to go back to the Coheeries, but something had always occurred to force them to put off their move for yet another year.

Passing Carnegie Hall, Virginia noticed a crowd filing in for a concert, and saw on several billboards that the famous orchestra of Canadians P. (his full name) was going to play the *Amphibological Whimsey Dances* of Mozart. Because it was rather hard to tell what was what on the mixed bill, it might have been the *Divertimento in C Minor* of Mozart, and the *Amphibological Whimsey Dances* of Minoscrams Sampson. That seemed more reasonable. She was about to continue walking, when, right in front of her, as fast and round as a ball of quicksilver, the fat slit-eyed thing that they called Mr. Cecil Wooley bounced up the steps of Carnegie Hall. Undoubtedly, she thought, Jackson Mead's quintet did not include in its repertory such things as the *Amphibological Whimsey Dances*, and young Mr. Wooley, soft for lighter forms, had weaseled away to attend this concert. There was no mistaking his truant stride. He had the air of one of those schoolboys whose eyes bounce back and forth in rhapsodic perjury as he tries to pretend that he has walked into a women's steambath because he neglected to read the sign.

She dashed into the lobby. He had just bought his ticket, and was heading for the balconies. She approached the ticket seller. "You see that fat thing?" she asked, pointing to Cecil Mature as he was just barely swallowed up into a doorway. "Give me a seat right behind him."

"But miss," the ticket man protested. "I'd have to give you seat forty-six in balcony Q. That's the worst seat in the house. Unless your mother was an owl and your father was a hawk, you wouldn't be able to hear or see a thing."

"What was that?" Virginia asked. "Speak up!"

"Oh," the man in the box office said, and issued her the ticket.

She raced up the carpeted stairs, with Cecil panting several flights in the lead. At the top, Virginia paused to let Cecil take his seat. Then she went up and around, and took her own seat behind him, unnoticed. Were it not for half a dozen sound-asleep policemen, Virginia and Cecil would have had the upper balcony entirely to themselves. She looked down, and put her hand over her chest in fright. From where she was sitting, the stage was nothing more than a little fan-shaped cookie crawling with black and white ants.

The lights dimmed, and Cecil Mature popped up and down in joyous anticipation. After he opened a little white carton that he had taken from his coat pocket, Virginia was overcome with the aroma of lobster Cantonese. As the concert began, and the bassoons, piccolos, and snare drums started to play (to the cheers of the Mozart and Minoscrams Sampson devotees—and the police, who clapped automatically in their sleep), Cecil Mature began to eat the lobster Cantonese, using his fingers to shovel it into his mouth, and his teeth to crack the shells.

Virginia was soon swept up in the sad amphibological harmonies. This music was like riding gentle waves, or motoring through the Cotswolds. It lifted and raised its hearers as gently as if they had been the wounded coming from war. It was very strange stuff, and Cecil Mature loved it. He must have been devoted to it, Virginia thought, the way her mother was to the works of A. P. Clarissa. Except that Cecil was young and somewhat rowdy, and every once in a while he would toss his arm into the air and say, "Play that music! Play it! Yeah!"

As the concert was ending, Virginia went into the hallway so that she might run across Cecil accidentally. When the lights came on, Cecil flashed around the corner. "Mr. Cecil Wooley!" she exclaimed, just as if she were surprised, and had known him all her life.

He went dead in his tracks, shut his squinty eyes, and clenched his teeth. "How do you do," he said in evident pain.

Virginia went on. "What a surprise that you like Minoscrams Sampson. He's certainly my favorite composer. You know, he lived not far from where I grew up, in a big windmill on the shore of the lake, and every day. . . ."

Before Cecil knew what was happening, she had captured him and was towing him along East Fifty-seventh Street. He could not protest that he had to get home (or wherever he had to go), because she was chattering away about this and that, and wouldn't let go of his arm. In truth, he was very proud to be seen with such a tall beauty, and she could have taken him anywhere she wanted. He blushed and blinked in pride and embarrassment. It was as if he and she *were on a date*. All the executives walking home in the dusk would see them, and since Fifty-seventh Street was the street on which to be seen, what could be better? Thinking that they might take him and Virginia for husband and wife, he felt a thrill of pleasure.

Virginia snapped her fingers. "I know!" she said, in response to a question that had not been posed. "Let's have an ice cream soda in the bar of the Hotel Lenore. They make a special ginger chocolate cream that my children love. You might want to try it."

Cecil stopped where he was, and shook his head from side to side.

"What's the matter, Mr. Wooley?"

"I can't," he said, gravely.

"You can't what?"

"I can't. We're not allowed to go to a bar, to have ice cream sodas, to eat chocolate, to talk with strangers, or to be alone at night away from the ship."

"Who said?"

"Jackson Mead said."

"Does he have to know?" Virginia asked.

"I couldn't."

The Hotel Lenore had an overelegant bar where those who didn't know any better went to feel important, but they made the best ice cream sodas anywhere.

"Look at that beautiful dame with that fat slit-eyed thing," one of the bartenders said to another. "What does a knockout like her want with a ball of India rubber like him?"

"I dunno," answered the other bartender. "Some dames like a crazy salad with their meat, if you know what I mean."

Since, perched on a bar stool, Cecil looked like a memorial sphere atop a victory column, which was architecturally correct, he had a measure of confidence that he would not otherwise have enjoyed. Nonetheless, he was dreadfully ill-at-ease.

"Two chocolate ginger cream sodas," Virginia said, "and go very, very, very heavy on the special ingredient." The special ingredient was rum.

A $65 ice cream soda should be served without delay, and they were, the two of them, all $130 worth, as big as buckets, in Baccarat vats with platinum spoons and gold straws. Cecil was beside himself. He thanked Virginia, and grabbed the straw, but after half a draw he turned to her and said, "It tastes good, real good, but there's something in it that reminds me of tetrahydrozaline."

"That's the ginger," Virginia said, and touched her lovely lips to the gold straw.

At first Cecil hesitated, but then he set to work. Whereas Virginia took little dainty bee-wisps of the iced chocolate, Cecil would have been useful when Mussolini drained the Pontine marshes.

Like a first-class rotary pump, he hummed with the pleasure of the work, and, even though the Baccarat vats in which the Lenore served sodas had special sumps to prevent the final "Aarchh . . . Roooch!" when the bottom was reached, Cecil's velocity rendered their design moot, and the "Aarchh . . . Roooch!" sounded like a volcanic pumice shower. He leaned back a little and swung his glazed eyes at Virginia. He had drained a gallon in five minutes, but it was the quart of rum that had glazed his eyes. Now Virginia had him.

The little bee-wisps of rum had given to Virginia a beneficent fuzzy glare. She was just enough out of phase with the rest of the world to be able to look Cecil in the eye and elicit from him all that he wanted to say, though she didn't really look him in the eye, since it was harder to see his eyes than it would have been to see what the soldiers of an enemy machine-gun squad were reading inside their pillbox.

"There was some stuff in that soda, wasn't there," he asked, accusingly.

"A quart of rum," she answered.

"A quart and a half," said the bartender, in passing.

"God!" said Cecil, angry for a moment. "Why'd you have to do that?" He pounded his fist against the air. "It doesn't matter. No bye, no goodbyes."

"What does that mean?" Virginia asked.

"I dunno. Sometimes I used to have a glass of wine, or a glass of beer, with dinner. I found that it helped me appreciate the food, cleared the palate, aided digestion, and made me drunk. But this! I dunno what I'm going to do. How long does it take for a quart and a half of rum to go away?"

"Half an hour."

"Oh, that's not so bad. But the thing is, I feel so vulnerable. What if Pearly came in? Peter Lake's not here to protect me." His eyes went all misty and his mouth cranked up into an abysmal expression of primal sadness.

"Who was Peter Lake?" Virginia wanted to know. The name sounded vaguely familiar to her.

Tears now ran down Cecil's cheeks, and he regained control

only after a few minutes. "I remember those days," he said. "We used to live in water tanks and on the rooftops. Sometimes, we would hire ourselves out under false names and work in a forge or a machine shop. They couldn't begin to touch us for quality work. Mootfowl knows more about that stuff than anyone in the world, and he taught us. We worked whenever we wanted. Sometimes I'd do small tattoo jobs, and we carried everything we had in little stonemason's bags. The weather was great. Always clear skies. And, if it did rain, we'd go see one of Peter Lake's girlfriends. We went to Minnie's a lot. I would always sleep in the other room and listen to the springs squeak when Peter Lake and Minnie were in the bed. It was all right. If I got too jealous, I'd go to the market. By the time I got back and started cooking, they'd be finished anyway, and we'd all sit around and eat squash. I used to cook squash good.

"As far as I was concerned, we coulda just had squash, all the time. But Peter Lake wanted roast beef, duck, and beer, so we used to go to places to eat. That's where the trouble started, when Pearly threw the apple at him."

Listening to this was very confusing for Virginia. It didn't sound contemporary. And though Cecil was only an adolescent, it did sound true. She wanted to find out more. But as she was about to question him further, the doors of the Lenore were flung open by costumed lackeys, and in came Craig Binky with a huge party of hangers-on and sycophants.

They made their entrance as if they had been following operatic stage directions: "From stage left, enter Craig Binky and a group of young aristocratic rogues who have returned from the hunt, flushed with good cheer." Surrounding Virginia and Cecil, they filled up all the nearby stools and banquettes, and began to order, in French, each and every $250 dish and $150 drink.

"I said to the Prime Minister," Craig Binky declaimed to no one in particular, "what your country needs is the Binky touch. With more than half a billion people, no natural resources, and a per capita income of thirty-five dollars per annum, you might just wake up one morning to discover that you're in deep trouble.

490

"There I was, me, Craig Binky, talking to the leader of all those millions! And do you know what he wanted to know? I'll tell you. He was most interested in hearing from me how to open a numbered account in Zurich. Can you beat that! The man was a saint. With all his country's domestic problems, he wanted to aid tiny little Switzerland!"

Virginia tugged at Cecil until she maneuvered him out of the Lenore. This was not easy, and he continued to speak even though she was unable to hear him. Only when she got him on the sidewalk did she again pick up the thread of his confession.

". . . and since it was that way, I had to leave. Then he disappeared. It was a surprise to us all, since Jackson Mead thought that this one was going to be the eternal rainbow, the real one that had no end. And then he and the horse just vanished. I told them that Peter Lake knew the city better than anyone. If he wanted to lay low, he could do it for as long as he liked.

"And it's useless now, without him. . . . It just isn't time yet, I guess.

"I loved him," said Cecil, not with tears, but with certainty. "He was like a brother to me. He protected me. And he never knew who he was."

Hardesty watched the fog blow in on a whistling wind that tugged it into white streamers and pushed apart the silent masses from which they were drawn. Because San Francisco is surrounded by a cold sea, when the ocean winds decide to put the city to bed and reclaim it for the North Pacific, they do so without challenge, and hurl it into an oblivion of blue sky, white fog, and wind lines etched in silence across the bay.

From a fiftieth-floor hotel room, he looked over the city of his birth almost in its entirety. He could see his house on Presidio Heights, the highest thing around, as white as a glacier, the study tower easily visible against the green Presidio forests behind it. As the fog captured it whole, left it high and dry, or floated it upon the white tide so that it looked like a house in the air, Hardesty wondered if the gentle clouds that partitioned space and time were compassionate as well, and would let him look in to see his father and

491

himself seated at the long wood table, turning the pages of an old book while his father explained its intricacies. Those events which have passed, and which are the foundations of our lives, must be somewhere, he thought. They must be recapturable, even if only in a perfect world. How just it would be if for our final reward we were to be made the masters of time, and if those we love could come alive again not just in memory, but in truth. A light went on in the tower and shone momentarily through the dark before the fog swallowed up the Marratta house for the night. Hardesty felt longing and pain, because he suspected that in the light that had winked across the fog there had been a living presence free of the constraints of time.

When Jackson Mead had spoken of the ''eternal rainbow,'' Hardesty had been transported into the past, and could think only of the Pacific and the forests above it drenched in fog. He felt that the answer to Jackson Mead's riddle was somewhere in the pines of the Presidio, where he had spent half of his boyhood as if he had lived not in a city but in a range of isolated mountains. He had booked a flight and a room so that he might call upon his past. Except for a brief visit to his father's grave (where Evan certainly would not be), he was in San Francisco solely to go back to the Presidio, to see if by doing so he could decipher two of Jackson Mead's words.

The next day, he crossed the city, walking north in the clear sunshine until, in the forests he knew so well, the sun disappeared and fog rushed through the trees like an army of white-haired sorcerers. The fog hissed and sang like jangled and discordant harps. Shadows and mists closed off the world behind, and Hardesty found himself in a seemingly endless grove of delicate trees. He followed the fog contrary to its course until he lost sight of the trees and the ground. After crossing a patch of soft heather, he realized that he was standing at the edge of a cliff high over the sea. The wind was white, and, though he knew where he was from the sound and spray, he could see nothing. The sea grew so loud that he had to drop to his knees so as not to lose his balance. The shrieking of the wind pushed him to the ground as if he were being beaten by the waves. Because the flat ground seemed to be turning circles in the air, he held fast to the greenery and pressed himself against the sand and heather. It seemed like a safe place, and, covered over by the fog, he fought his dizziness and exhaustion with sleep.

Hardesty Marratta had been to heaven in his dreams often enough, for they were like all the paintings that Brueghel had ever painted, combined, in searing unearthly colors that moved 360 degrees 'round. But these dreams, no amateurish work to be sure, were now eclipsed as he rose quietly upward. For a while he could not see, but then the fog vanished and the air became as clear as ether. He found himself in a house of wood and glass, high over a blue lake. At first he didn't know where to go or what to do, but he was soon approached by a woman who glided to him—flew to him, really—a woman whose hair was graceful and elastic in the wind, as if it were made for air and motion. She stretched out her hands and led him through the golden light, sidestepping (though she did not touch the floor), to a high terrace overlooking the blue lake— which was not so much a lake as a condition of the light. It seemed to enclose them in a dome of weightless azure that extended to the horizon and was filled with light of a different sort than its own, light that was full of gold and silver, airy, hot, and blinding. He held her hands as she floated before him, smiling, and he tried to recognize her, and to memorize her features, but she would not let him. She undid his vision with her eyes. Unlike anything that he had ever seen, they were a liquid, electric, bright, uncompromising blue, and she held him transfixed while they burned into him like rays, searing and cooling at the same time.

He awoke at dusk in the darkening Presidio, lying in a cold drizzle. The fog had been shredded by the rain, and the sea was now visible below, its breakers gray, dark, and dirty. Exhausted and sore, he felt like a pair of eyes carried by bones.

Dripping wet, he passed under the Golden Gate Bridge on his way back to the city. The toll plaza was choked with northbound traffic, the bridge itself a gently rising curve of glowing red eyes. It was as dark, wet, and bleary as Manhattan on an early winter evening after a day of sleet and rain.

Hardesty found a neglected little park just east of the tolls. In the center of a flagstone floor was a bronze head mounted on a plinth. He was so worn out that he leaned against it. He thought this was a bad place for a statue, since the park and its memorial were practically inaccessible to the public, and he went around to the front of it to see who was memorialized. Though it was already dark, Hardesty was able to make out an inscription.

1870   JOSEPH B. STRAUSS   *1938*

He skipped a paragraph of smaller letters in favor of the single line beneath it:

CHIEF ENGINEER OF THE GOLDEN GATE BRIDGE
1929–1937

He then returned to the paragraph of smaller letters, and read a bronze inscription that had been there, patient and immobile, for most of the century. His guess had been right. He had seen it before. And now, even in the half-darkness, the dull bronze seemed as bright as the sun.

> *Here at the Golden Gate is the*
> *eternal rainbow that he conceived*
> *and set to form. A promise indeed*
> *that the race of man shall*
> *endure into the ages.*

Like a parachutist about to make a jump, Hardesty briefly closed his eyes. Then he opened them, and with a restrained and ironic smile he lifted his gaze to meet that of Jackson Mead, who had been there in the fog and the mist all the time, staring toward San Francisco for more than sixty years. Hardesty was sure that in other places there were other statues with other names, but the same far-reaching stare.

In one of the halls of the museum, where Hardesty had gone early in the morning to see Jackson Mead, was a huge painting that depicted scientists at work in the court of Frederick the Great—who stood in the midst of several men and a complicated laboratory apparatus, posing heroically in a black-and-gray coat.

When told by an assistant that he could go in to see Mead, Hardesty walked down a long corridor with a floor and walls of the soft-polished beige stone that so often finds its way into museums. Cocksure for days, he suddenly felt as if he were on his way to an audience with Frederick the Great, and was somewhat taken aback to realize that, indeed, it might have been so. Neither Mootfowl nor Mr. Cecil Wooley was present, and the easels and paintings had been removed. Jackson Mead was sitting away from his desk, on a simple wood and reed chair. Under the artificial March light, smoking a pipe of cherry tobacco, he looked pensive and kind. He motioned for Hardesty to sit down. When Hardesty was comfortably settled on a couch of gray crushed velvet, he took out his own pipe, filled it, lit it, and began to puff in silence.

After a while, Jackson Mead looked down at the floor and said, "I get so discouraged sometimes." Then he resumed puffing on his pipe as if he hadn't said a thing.

"You do?" Hardesty asked.

"Oh yes. Deeply discouraged. It's not easy to architect these big projects: it's like holding together an empire. Without a perfect balance of art, passion, and luck, all the elements tend to fly their own ways. And then there's the opposition. I always seem to be dogged by some mistakenly high-minded elitist who has taken it upon himself to protect from me and my work the people he is sure that he will permanently have underneath him, or by cliques of self-proclaimed intellectuals who have ruminated for decades upon a Marxist hairball that has turned their thinking to bile.

"For example, your friend Praeger de Pinto, a very long shot for mayor, seems to be focusing his campaign on me. Why doesn't he just leave me alone? I'm not going to do anything to hurt his sheep."

"Praeger's not one of the elitists of whom you speak," Hardesty asserted. "He's the most egalitarian man I've ever known."

"Then he's a Marxist."

"Of course he's not. Marxists are people whose insides are torn up day after day because they want to rule the world and no one will even publish their letter to the editor. Praeger *is* the editor. Besides, he grew up in the city of the poor. You know as well as I do that in this country Marxism is a religious passion of the middle class.''

''Then why is he so intent on hounding me? Which of his principles demands that he poke around in my affairs? Neither a city nor a civilization can be run by its critics. Critics can neither build nor explore. All they do, really, is say yes or no—and complicate it. (Not book critics, of course. They are second only to the angels.)''

''He's not hounding you because of any principles. He's after you because he's curious, that's all.''

Jackson Mead sighed. ''Eventually, I will satisfy his curiosity, but I need time to get things into place. It's my only chance.''

''I know,'' Hardesty said. ''The railroad lines from the steel-making regions have to be completed. The reception docks and piers have to be put in place. The stockpiles of tools and alloys have to be assembled and moved.''

Jackson Mead took the pipe from his mouth. He wondered if that was all Hardesty knew, and imagined that it was. But Hardesty went on. He was slumped back on the velvet couch, and his hair shone in the simulated daylight.

''You've got to get condemnations, and move God knows how many people. You've got to clear away factories, houses, and commercial buildings. Then you can begin to lay the foundations. Everything will have to be right before you build this bridge, Mr. Mead, for this eternal rainbow is going to anger the city, since what you have in mind is so much greater than anything that has come before, and you know very well that people don't like to feel small, to be left behind as the hinge to the future is put in place by someone like you. In the old days, they burned the mills and put their natural philosophers on the rack. These days they think it's their duty to tie down the builders and humiliate them with the smell of the ground, and they love it, to boot.''

''I hate them!'' Jackson Mead screamed, rising to his full height, and pacing.

''They don't understand that we have a mandate. I can't just re-

496

fuse to build these things: it's my responsibility. All the engines, bridges, and cities that we put in place are nothing in themselves. They're only markers in what we think of as time—like the separations of notes in music. Why do people resist them so? They are symbols and products of the imagination, which is the force that ensures justice and historical momentum in an imperfect world, because without imagination we would not have the wherewithal to challenge certainty, and we could never rise above ourselves. But look! We have already set the wheels spinning. Their progress impels us forward in like proportion and, when they rise, we too will rise. Such a rising, Mr. Marratta, will mark the end of history as we have known it, and the beginning of the age that imagination has known all along. Machines challenge certainty so well. They should not be able to move. But they do. They turn, and move, and never cease—there is always an engine going, somewhere—like generations of silver hearts that keep the faith of the world and stoke imagination in its continued and splendid rebellion."

"But what about the real hearts," Hardesty asked, "of those who get in your way? There is nothing greater than what can occur in those lowly hearts, the least noble of which is capable of putting a thousand bridges across a thousand harbors."

"In their hearts rests the potential to throw a thousand bridges. In my heart rests the actuality of one. Who is more deserving?"

"The world needs both, equally."

"I won't deny it. Their course is perhaps more just than ours. Ultimately, I am their servant. But to be so, I must first be their master. Besides, I have no choice in the matter, do I? It has all happened before. They and I will fight like dogs, though, finally, I will prevail. The harder course prevails, because the bones of the world are made of rock and steel." He stopped pacing, and stood in front of Hardesty. Their pipes produced even columns of white smoke. "How did you know?"

"A dozen of us spent four months on this, but, in the end, we were enlightened accidentally. I found the statue of Joseph Strauss, the chief engineer of the Golden Gate Bridge, and when I looked into his eyes, you were looking back at me."

"A coincidence. I knew Strauss. We did look alike, though not so much then, when I was younger, as perhaps we do now."

"Be that as it may," Hardesty replied, "I was able to find out what you meant by an eternal rainbow."

"Do the others know?"

"No."

"And where do you stand? Are you with Praeger de Pinto, or are you with me?"

"I don't know. At the moment, things seem to be in balance, and my inclination is to let them stay that way. I'd like to know what's in that ship you've got riding at anchor out there."

"The tools and materials for building the bridge."

"I don't suppose they're conventional."

"You're right."

"What are you going to call it?"

"The name isn't important, but we're going to call it Battery Bridge."

WHITE HORSE AND
DARK HORSE

WHILE Hardesty Marratta and
Jackson Mead were debating the future, the city kept to its silent
track. Nearly immune to the changing of the seasons, and forgotten
by history, the people of the city of the poor struggled within a
timeless empire that stretched from Manhattan to the sea, over
fields of brick upon which factories stood like walled towns and
flew snakelike pennants of blackened smoke from their chimneys. Talk as Hardesty Marratta and Jackson Mead might in the
perpetual March light of the museum gallery, the city of the
poor was always the same, and always would be. It was a
weapon ready-cocked, a shotgun in the mouth of those who did
not think they had to get down on their knees to get to heaven,

but imagined that they would ride there upright in something with wheels.

The white horse had lasted under the beam for more than fourteen months, during which he outlived several masters and ignored many chances of escape. While marching ahead in trancelike circles, he had lost his sense of time and come to believe that he was winding up an eternal spring, to which others from the starry meadows had been apprenticed long and often. Like the mill that ground the salt of the sea, the beam had to be kept going. He thought that he was almost done, and he wanted to see his combat with infinity through. Working the beam to crush himself, so that he might return to the place from which he had come, he kept turning it, and he refused to die.

Sometimes, at the oddest hours, because the city of the poor had long been disjointed from the clock of day and night, heads popped up over the board fence which hid Athansor from an alley that he could not see. Children stared at him. Drunks seemed to be amazed that he had the temerity to be a horse. Criminals on the run, or those who had just stripped a purse, smiled as if implying that he was one of them. The heads might suddenly arise at four in the morning or at noon, and they frequently talked to him. Perhaps because they assumed that he was lower than they were, they were at their worst—cruel, vulgar, and vulnerable, all at once. And the most bedeviling thing about these marionettes was that what they said and did was so inconsequential. He half wished that a head would pop up from behind the fence and give him something to worry about.

Though it had been only half a wish, it was granted. October was extraordinarily cold, and everyone knew that the coming winter would be apocalyptic. One night, as the north wind made the water in rain barrels ice, Athansor was, as always, moving forward at the beam. Passing the fence, he felt that someone was looking at him. Then he came around again. Though the white horse had not paused once in fourteen months, the man staring at him from behind the boards made him stop dead. His nostrils flared and his eyes moved back in their sockets.

Still tied to the beam, he broke both the lashings and the beam

500

itself as he reared to his full height, and bellowed like a war-horse. But though his hooves flew, his eyes flashed, and the ground shook, he did not frighten the man resting his elbows on the fence.

The intruder smiled, and his eyes went electric, digging into Athansor's flesh like augers. Sparks flew, and the wind brought thunder. "You don't know how long I've been looking for you, horse," he said. He held up his left hand, fingers spread, thumb on the palm. "And now that I've found you, I hope that you're properly surprised."

Athansor broke from the remaining tatters of his harness and smashed through the boards, knocking aside not only Pearly Soames, but a large ill-attired contingent behind him. "That's right, you marble bastard," Pearly said as Athansor galloped off into the windy brick lots and the forests of dead and splintered trees. "You find him for me. Take me right to him."

It snowed on the twentieth of October, not a raging blizzard, but not a light dusting of the pumpkins, either. The ground was covered with almost a foot and a half of fresh white powder, which did not melt, as it usually would have so early in the fall, but stayed fearlessly in place while a paralyzing dream of absolute zero floated down from Canada and made the winter sky into a brittle blue arch. The street-cleaning equipment was trapped unoiled in its garages, and the streets went unploughed as the Ermine Mayor decreed that no salt or sand be spread on the roads and sidewalks. "Hell," he said, in a magnificent preelection gesture, "if nature thinks we're the Yukon, let's roll with the punch. The snow will be left undisturbed, all schools will be closed for the duration, and city employees other than those in essential services need not report for work."

Only partly to satirize the Ermine Mayor's decree, Praeger de Pinto issued a statement promising that if he were elected mayor the city would enjoy the most beautiful winters it had ever experienced, that white snow and blue skies would be its share for months on end, that sleighs and skis would become the conventional means of transportation, that horses would return to the streets, that every house would have a fireplace, that black nights

501

would blaze with stars, that skaters would have their run of the rivers, bonfires shine in the parks, children's cheeks be redder than cranberries, and snow fall almost incessantly in dizzying dances and waltzes of winter that would make the population giddy with happiness.

Stunned at first, then hostile, people gradually began to believe him. They called him "The Apostle of Winter," "The Snow King," and "Daddy Christmas."

Praeger was anything but greedy. He wanted to win the election, but he wasn't willing to tie himself in knots to do so. Thus, his campaign became unorthodox, even for the darkest of dark horses. Though Craig Binky was supporting him, the populace was in one of its periodic fits of pique regarding this celebrated publisher, and it mattered little that Praeger's smiling face was plastered all over *The Ghost,* or that Craig Binky appeared on the television news programs to declare sanctimoniously, "Just vote your conscience. Vote de Pinto." Praeger started the campaign with six percent of the vote, the independent candidate Crawford Bees IV had thirteen percent, and the Ermine Mayor polled eighty-one percent.

Far from discouraging Praeger, this state of affairs ignited him, and he proceeded, in turn, to ignite the voters. Where most politicians, including the Ermine Mayor, were quick to promise things they would never deliver, such as clean streets or the absence of crime, Praeger's approach was different, and he left the others far behind in his wake. The Ermine Mayor might address a street gathering and say that in his next term he would put 30 percent more police on the streets, step up garbage collection, and lower taxes. Of course, everyone knew that in the next mayoral term, no matter who was in office, thirty percent fewer police would be on the street, the garbage piles would get higher and bigger, and taxes would go up. But they applauded anyway.

Then Crawford Bees IV would give them another set of figures, and they would applaud politely for him, too.

But then Praeger de Pinto would rise. He never talked about garbage, electricity, or police. He only talked about winter, horses, and the countryside. He spoke almost hypnotically about love, loyalty, and esthetics. And just as they thought he was beginning to sound slightly effete, he would get very tough, in his Havemeyer Street way, and lacerate the mayor for conspiring with Jackson Mead. He would throw low punches, where it hurt. He would be terribly cruel (they loved that), and then he would surface again into his world of light to make the crowds sway and daven with longing for the purity of winter. He promised them love affairs and sleigh races, cross-country skiing on the main thoroughfares, and the transfixing blizzards that howled outside and made the heart dance.

They thought, or so it was generally stated at the time, that if they were going to be lied to, they might as well pick the liar who did it best. Since in describing the world he wanted Praeger could leave them with their mouths open and their hearts beating, he advanced slowly in the polls. The Ermine Mayor panicked and declaimed ferociously about garbage and taxes. Praeger held his ground and raved with unexcelled charm, dizzying the electorate with visions of justice and paradise.

"We can't go to the Coheeries, at least not today. The north roads are blocked, and the railroads shut down because the plough trains are still being overhauled," Hardesty reported upon his return to Yorkville one wintry Saturday in October, after he had skied from place to place to get information.

"Who cares about trains?" Virginia said disparagingly. "Or whether the roads are blocked?"

"How do you propose to get there?" he asked.

She looked at him as if he were an idiot, and said, "By sleigh."

"Sleigh?"

"Yes. Just because they don't work in San Francisco doesn't mean that they don't work here."

"You've been listening too hard to Praeger's campaign speeches. I'll bet you're even going to vote for him."

"Of course I am," she returned. "And so are you. Go out and get a sleigh. I'll get the children ready."

"What sleigh? Where am I going to get a sleigh?" he asked.

"That's your problem, but don't forget to get a horse to pull it, and hay, oats, and a blanket for the horse. We may be on the road for several days before we get to Fteley's.''

"Fteley's?''

"Hurry!'' she commanded.

He returned at dusk in a beautiful sleigh with a supple new harness and gleaming silvery runners. Hitched to it was an elegant mare as black as obsidian.

"We can't leave now,'' he told Virginia. "It'll be dark in a few hours.''

"That's the way you do it,'' she said. "At night, when there's a full moon, and the world is white.''

Abby had been listening to this conversation, and she decided that she was not going to have any part of either Lake of the Coheeries or nocturnal sleigh rides. She went to the kitchen, took five rolls and half a pound of baking chocolate from a cupboard, and retreated to the top shelf of the linen closet, where she planned to stay until she had to go to college.

"Where's Abby?'' Hardesty asked Martin.

"I don't know,'' Martin replied. Though he knew exactly where she was, he didn't want to compromise the hideout, since he had invented it.

For two hours they looked frantically for Abby. They thought that she had fallen from the balcony, but, of course, she hadn't. They went to the neighboring apartments, to the local stores, and they even looked in the linen closet, but she had burrowed toward the back of the top shelf, behind a rampart of pillows, and didn't answer when Martin called her—though she knew that he realized where she was.

Eventually she was starved out, and they caught her waddling from the kitchen with a fresh loaf of dough in her hands. The minute she saw them, she broke and ran, screaming, "I don't want to go!''

"Is that why we couldn't find you?'' Hardesty shouted. "You were hiding?''

"I don't want to go!'' she screamed back, and took refuge under the kitchen table, where she was able to stand without bending her head.

"I'm sorry, but you're going to have to," her father said, crouching. "Now come out of there, because we have to get you in your snowsuit and leave before it gets too late."

"No."

"Abby. Come *here!*" he said, snapping his fingers. She was terrified, but she refused to move.

"I'll just come in and get you," he threatened, feigning anger this time, because the expression on her face, her little bell-like yellow dress, and the soft intense blue eyes, focused in defiance, moved him a great deal. Nonetheless, he went on his knees and reached under the table. She threw the dough at him, and missed. It slid across the kitchen floor. Then he grabbed her. In two minutes she was in her snowsuit, clutching Teddy—her stuffed gray rabbit with red button eyes and a gingham dress, a present from Harry Penn.

They packed the sleigh with provisions and presents for Mrs. Gamely, and climbed into the front seat. Hardesty drove; Virginia sat next to him, with Abby on her lap; and Martin sat on the outside, with a buggy whip in his hand and instructions never to hit the horse, but just to touch her on the hindquarters when Hardesty told him to. Abby was bundled up into a melon-sized cocoon of fur and down; her little face showed through a silver-colored ruff like an Eskimo's, and her eyes darted back and forth in trusting anticipation. Looking like the child of nomads, Martin was dressed in seal leather and coyote furs. His mother was in her sable, and Hardesty was once again in the sheepskin jacket that he had earned in the Rockies. Thick green plaid woolen blankets covered them up to their waists.

"Have we got everything?" Hardesty asked.

"Yup," Martin replied.

Virginia nodded.

"All right," Hardesty said. "To the Lake of the Coheeries."

He snapped the reins, and the sleigh moved off. The horse was strong and well rested, and she seemed to crave a night journey, especially since, being a horse, she knew how bright the moon was going to be.

They went through the park, their sleigh bells ringing, and were

505

soon on Riverside Drive, heading north as the last piece of sun vanished behind the Palisades like a melting ingot, fiery hot. The river was choked with blocks and shards of ice. Lights flashed on and fires were lit in apartments along Riverside Drive as the Marrattas passed by in their sleigh, almost silently were it not for the muffled hoofbeats of the horse and the soft wild sound of the bells. After running through the deserted tolls, they crossed the Henry Hudson Bridge and made their way entirely along roads that were empty and white.

In a diminutive Westchester valley between two low hills, they saw a glow in the sky. The horse picked up her pace instinctively, and when they came out from between the hills into a little prairie of snowbound gardens and small fields, they saw the moon hiding in an orchard, ready to climb through a tangle of limbs until its mild pearl color would turn fiercely white. When the cool globe finally rested atop the delicate black branches, it seemed so close that Abby held out her arms and tried to touch it.

Then it climbed smoothly to its customary place among the stars, and the Marrattas sped northward through the dark shadows of its white light.

Somewhere in Dutchess, when the moon had reached its apogee, and the children were asleep, they found themselves running through hollows and pitch-black places where snowy owls and eagles perched on ramparts of rock and dead trees like the pickets of some lawless mountain stronghold. The way was proving too difficult and steep for an elegant carriage-puller born and raised at Belmont.

"Go left at that fork," Virginia directed.

"Do you know this place?" Hardesty asked.

"I know the terrain. It's just like the mountains that lead to the Coheeries. A road like this has got to descend to the river. The horse is tired because she's city-bred and her legs are far too thin for running all night in the hills. Our horses, with their thick frames, can go for a week without stopping, just like the polar bears that swim in the sea for a month at a time, or the seals that migrate from Alaska to Japan. If she's going to make it through the

506

night, this mare needs some running on the flat. We'll take her to the river, which will be frozen solid."

"Hee-ya!" Hardesty screamed in a manner not exactly characteristic of local horsemanship. With the snap of oiled leather, he flicked the reins, and the Belmont mare veered left.

It was even darker by the river, the true abode of owls and eagles, a place that was haunted by mysterious loonlike hoots, and the black horse sped through almost on tiptoe, cursing the bells that gave away their position to the leering pumpkin-headed ghosts who lived in the crags. The only way to follow the road was to follow the ribbon of slightly luminous sky between the trees. The sleigh passengers and the horse lifted their heads to see the pale and dusty track above. Had there been a brick wall across the path they would have smashed right into it, but the road was unobstructed, and they were able to navigate successfully its numerous descending switchbacks solely by reference to trees and sky.

When they came to the riverbank they saw a white highway on the snow-covered ice. Knowing that the ice could hold her, the mare went right onto it, making the slightly airborne transition in a way that bumped the sled and woke the children. Hardesty whistled, and she veered north. Soon she was satisfied and calm, and she found a gait that swallowed the miles. Snow blanketed most of the river, but where the wind had blown it clear, dazzling lakes of silver ice reflected the clockwork motion of the moon. The mountains on the western side stretched into the distance in white ranks that, as the moon sank, seemed to rise to it like a staircase.

"Look," Hardesty said to the children, and when Abby didn't see, "Abby, look there. Those mountains are the stairs that lead to the moon. Would you like to go? All we have to do is turn left before it sinks down beneath the last step. . . ."

As they considered their father's offer, the children's faces were bathed in the light of the moon. Sitting at the top landing of the mountain staircase, it was so voluminous, pearly, and entrancing that they nodded their heads. Yes, they wanted to go. They would give up the earth, which they hardly knew at all, for a round eternal place where everything glowed in cream and silver. They would gladly take the mountain staircase to another world, and were sad when the opportunity vanished, as the moon, ever faithful to its obligations, disappeared behind glacial balustrades that darkened as it left.

After an hour in which the temperature dropped to the crystalline realms and the river unwound into a long straightaway that promised to deliver the northern lights (if only they would follow it), they were contentedly listening to the hissing of the runners over ice and snow, thinking that all that remained was to find the turnoff, sail past Fteley's, and hope that they might penetrate the invisible geographical cask that held the Lake of the Coheeries. But no one had ever come easily to the Lake of the Coheeries.

They approached one of the tributaries of the Hudson that came from so high in the mountains and fell so fast that it never froze. They could hear it from miles away, and as they drew close they saw it tumbling down in a long angry string of white water. They could hardly take their eyes from it, and did not see that its upwelling had made open lakes in the ice. Unsuspecting, they galloped at full speed right into one of these narrow straits.

The horse broke the water into two white wedges that fled from her, and the sleigh followed with a percussive thump. Both horse and sleigh stayed upright and buoyant. Her forward momentum and her inbred sense enabled her to get her forelegs up on the ice. She pushed with everything she had, rising onto the shelf in front of her, and it held.

But she didn't have the strength to pull the sleigh across the ledge, though she strained to do so. As the sleigh began to take on water, Hardesty was about to throw everyone out onto the ice and then try to unharness the mare before she was pulled by the waterlogged sleigh back into, and under, the river, when he heard the ice thundering behind him. Before he had time to turn, something huge sailed over his head, and landed next to the struggling mare.

An enormous white horse had come from nowhere, and pulled the mare forward with him as if she were entrapped in a magnetic field. The sleigh hopped onto the ice before Hardesty even knew what was happening, and then they started a wild race. Running in tandem with the stallion, the mare was able to pull the sleigh like a rocket. The Marrattas bent forward into the cold wind as the two horses, almost an illusion of white and black, attained unnatural speed. The steel runners glowed with heat and watered the track underneath. The horses were going so fast that they seemed close to shattering the sleigh, which vibrated and rattled until Abby was frightened out of her wits.

Then, without a signal, they turned left into the mountains, roaring past Fteley's and blowing the doors off their hinges as they went by, traveling up the high road as if they were hurtling down it, leaving great rooster tails and washes of loose snow as they rounded the high desolate corners of the mountain track.

They crested the highest divide, and flew down onto the endless plain of the Coheeries. Virginia was overjoyed to see in the distance a lighted string of tiny pearls—the villages along the lake, their fires and lamps burning in the very early morning just before the sun came up.

Their horses took to the plain and bounded ahead on the straight road. Surely, they thought, the white horse was an illusion of the cold and the swirling stars, because, when he parted from the mare, he banked up and to the left in a blaze of white. Even after he was gone, the mare kept up the race until sunrise, when she gently led the Marrattas across the rolling ocean of snowfields that bordered the lakeshore of the Coheeries.

They entered the village the way travelers from the outside often did—shaken, exhausted, elated. Just before turning off for Mrs. Gamely's house, they passed Daythril Moobcot, who was pulling a sled piled high with cordwood.

"Daythril! How's my mother?"

"She's fine," Daythril shouted back. "I hope you brought your dictionary."

New York had always been a city destined for the rule of dandies, thieves, and men who resembled hardboiled eggs. Those who made its politics were the people who poured gasoline on fires, rubbed salt into wounds, and carried coals to Newcastle. And its government was an absurdity, a concoction of lunacies, a dying man obliged to race up stairs. The reason for this condition was complex rather than accidental, for miracles are not smoothly calculated. Instead, they are the subjugation of apparent anarchy to a coherent design. Just as music must be like a hive of bees, with each note that strains to go its own way gently held to a thriving plan, a great empire depends for its driving force upon the elements that will eventually tear it apart. So with a city, which if it is to make its mark must be spirited, slippery, and ungovernable. A tranquil city of good laws, fine architecture, and clean streets is like a classroom of obedient dullards, or a field of gelded bulls— whereas a city of anarchy is a city of promise.

Of this, Praeger de Pinto was convinced. He believed as well that human institutions often show the greatest inner brilliance at a moment when their outward decay is furthest advanced. Thus, he was not overcome by the anarchy or the madness of a city that could not even live up to its seemingly highest aspiration, which was to imitate hell, and so he was determined to plunge into the corruption of city politics like hot steel into water, and to boil it dry. The more the campaign matured, the less he cared about either his original purposes for running or Jackson Mead. Now he saw that the city was headed for a storm, and when, at the millennium, laws would confront laws and rights would confront rights, he wanted to guide the city through its tumultuous passage to the slow water that lay beyond.

If his suppositions were correct, and the coming clash would by indirections find directions out, he had to do the same. This was the logic behind his abandonment of traditional methods and his use of winter as a campaign theme. It would have been quite devious, he reasoned, to win the office by conventional means, and then embark upon an unconventional term such as he envisioned. Instead, he would risk alienating the electorate by telling the abject truth in all its madness.

"Campaign buttons?" he asked his chief of staff. "A waste of money. Here, take this down for the press. 'This is my position regarding campaign buttons. No de Pinto buttons will be fabricated for this or any other election. Anyone who consents to using his body (without pay) as a walking billboard is a fool who hopes to participate in the disgusting phenomena of mass suggestion and coercion, and I want no part of it. People who wear these buttons are as emptyheaded as those women who make capital of their breasts. I don't want their vote, either of them.' ''

"And what shall we say, Mr. de Pinto, about Gracie Mansion?" The Ermine Mayor had almost lost the last election to Councilman Magiostra, after the councilman pledged to live in his hovel in the Bronx instead of in the mansion.

"I don't plan to live there."

The chief of staff sighed in relief, because the Ermine Mayor was already moving out his possessions and had rented a prestigious little hovel on Mother Cabrini Boulevard.

"We'll use Gracie Mansion as a conference center," Praeger said. "It'll be nice to have conferences up there, overlooking the Bird S. Coler hospital and that beautiful wicker-basket factory. But I don't want to *live* next to any goddamned wicker-basket factory."

"That's good. We'll shoot that horse right out from under the Ermine Mayor."

"Right. There's a lot of tax money in this city. The mayor of the greatest city in the world should have a proper place to live, a place that has something to do with the overriding theme of the city's architecture. We'll take some of this tax money, about a billion or so, and build a mayoral palace. We can buy the top floors and air rights of four or five skyscrapers, put box girders between them, and then use the platform we've created for the base and gardens of a small, aerial, Versailles-type structure. But what am I talking about? We don't have to buy the skyscrapers, we can use eminent domain, and simply appropriate them."

"But the real estate trusts! They've given us most of the campaign money."

"To hell with them," said Praeger. "Give it back. If we've spent it already, give promissory notes. These real estate guys are just a bunch of pompous billionaires—especially Marcel Apand. I get so sick of seeing that flag of his, with the gorilla fist, flying from every other building in the city. It's time someone told the truth about them, Apand in particular. They're corrupt and venal. Schedule a news conference."

"But the bankers. We can't back our promissory notes. You've already condemned the bankers."

"And well they deserve it," Praeger said. "Those calculating bloodsuckers. I'll condemn them again."

"At least that will be populist. The people love politicians who hit the bankers. As long as you don't get too specific, you may be able to carry it off."

"Populist? I think that the greedy little horseflies who sell their souls to get wall-to-wall carpeting and color TV's deserve every bit of exploitation that can be visited upon them. They and the bankers were made for each other."

The chief of staff was much perturbed, and drummed his fingers against his hip flask. "Does this mean that when you condemn the billionaires you're going to include Mr. Binky, too?"

"Isn't it time that someone called a spade a spade?"

"Craig Binky is your chief supporter."

"Don't overvalue him."

"Mr. de Pinto, no one's going to vote for you."

"Yes they will. They'll vote for me because I tell the truth."

"But you don't always tell the truth. Sometimes you lie like a dog."

"And they'll vote for me because I'm the best liar, because I do it honestly, with a certain finesse. They know that lies and truth are very close, and that something beautiful rests in between. When I lie to them the way I do, I'm confiding in them simultaneously my understanding and grief for their condition, my hope for them, and my contempt for the monkey on their back. This makes me one of them. After all, I *am* one of them. You'll see for whom they vote."

"All right, all right," said the chief of staff. "You know I can't get philosophical with you. There is, however, a practical matter that I wanted to discuss."

"What's that?"

"Your next rally."

"What about it?"

"Who the hell's going to show up for a dawn rally at The Cloisters? The purpose of a political rally is to gather together a mass of

512

people so the TV cameras can show them as you speak. I doubt very much that many people will go to The Cloisters, at dawn, in ten-degree weather, to hear you denounce them. Why not make it lunch hour in Grand Central Station, or in Foibles Park?''

"Look," Praeger said, leaning forward, "you can't engineer these things. The chips have to fall where they may.''

"But this is one of only three rallies that you've scheduled. What a waste to. . . . At least let me arrange a few more!''

"No. I hate rallies. If there's anything I can't stand, it's crowds.''

After his chief of staff left in incipient tears, Praeger leaned back on the wooden stool that was the only piece of furniture at his headquarters (he was still undecided about whether or not to install a telephone). He was filled with a profound and deep certainty that he was headed for victory. Had he been running in Chicago, Miami, or Boston, it probably wouldn't have been so. But New York was like a runaway horse that had been stung by a bee. The only way to catch that horse, Praeger reasoned, was to follow it along its bee-stung course, and better its speed—which is precisely what he intended to do with the improbable city that he wanted to lead because he loved it so improbably well.

The mass rally at The Cloisters was held at dawn on a cold, clear day. Praeger stood for half an hour watching the river come alive in blue and white as the morning sun struck its ice floes and the open water. Attendance was low—as no one had shown up, not even one of his aides or workers, much less any reporters or spectators. In fact, because it was so cold and the sun had yet to war against the lingering shadows among the trees, game-rich Fort Tryon Park had not produced a single squirrel, pigeon, or politicized vole to sit on a wall and listen to the candidate, or to peck through the snow in what Craig Binky would then have reported as a "glorious fund-raising breakfast attended by supporters clad in luxurious furs.''

Praeger was entirely alone. Undaunted, he started in on a fine political speech that was not merely rolling and mellifluous, but brilliant in its analysis of a wide range of political problems. This was the speech in which his qualities as technician, statesman, and historian of the present were best observed. Anyone hearing it

513

would have been convinced that a vote for de Pinto would ensure a precise, benevolent, careful, and responsible stewardship of the city's affairs. The bankers and real estate tycoons would have loved it. It had all the beauties of stability and none of its drawbacks. Here, at last, was the correct synthesis. He spoke neither of winter nor of Armageddon. On that cold and sunny morning, his skills and common sense combined in the kind of political appeal that is both invincible and technically flawless.

When he finished, he was shocked to hear applause. A balding man with an old-fashioned mustache was standing in the snow not too far away. He looked like a yeoman mechanic, which was, of course, exactly what he was. Praeger assumed that he had come to the park to walk his dog.

"I don't have a dog," said Peter Lake. "And if I did I wouldn't take him all the way up here on such a cold morning. I came to see you."

"You did?" Praeger asked in astonishment.

"That's right. You made a good speech, as far as I can tell. I've liked what you've said about winter. I don't know whether to believe it or not, but it doesn't seem important whether it's true, if you know what I mean. Is music true? You can't say that it is or that it isn't, and yet we put our faith in it. I do—at least I used to, although I don't remember when.

"But, lately," he confessed, "my mind's been clearing, and I remember certain things—such as, for instance, refrains on a piano. But I can't remember where I heard them. You know what I mean?"

"No, I don't."

"It's as if they're coming from the past, as if the past is a light coming up in darkness. I feel it strongly, but I can't see it, I can't remember. But there's a piano playing there for sure.

"I'm glad that I caught you alone, sir," he continued. "You see, what I'm trying to say is very difficult. But things have been clearing rapidly for about a week, and I was wondering if . . . perhaps . . . well . . . let me say it right out. Are you one of us? I mean, are we the same?"

"A Freemason?" Praeger asked, puzzled. "I'm not a Freemason, if that's what you mean."

"No, no, I don't mean that," Peter Lake said, shaking his head, and giving it another try. "It's more personal and more important than that."

"Am I gay? I certainly am not."

"No, sir. I'm not inquiring about your disposition."

"Then, what?"

"Where do you come from?" Peter Lake asked, looking right at him.

"I was born in Brooklyn."

"In what age?"

"In this age."

"Are you sure? Because, you see, I think I wasn't. And the way you talk about winters leads me to believe that you weren't either, because what you describe as the future was once the past. I know. I've been there."

"I. . . ."

Peter Lake held his hand up. "Don't worry," he said. "It's all right. I'll be sure to vote for you, although I don't think I'm registered. I'll register in the Five Points, that's what I'll do, and vote for you a dozen times. I'm very grateful, because after you began to talk about the winters I began to hear the piano—and to see that the past is brightening all around us. I thought that maybe you could help me more, but you've helped a great deal already."

"What is the piano playing?"

"Oh, I wouldn't know even if I could hear it clear."

"Who's playing it?"

"I'm afraid, sir, that I don't have the slightest idea. Whoever it is, though, she's playin' it real nice."

Lonely people have enthusiasms which cannot always be explained. When something strikes them as funny, the intensity and length of their laughter mirrors the depth of their loneliness, and they are capable of laughing like hyenas. When something touches their emotions, it runs through them like Paul Revere, awakening feelings that gather into great armies. Poor Mrs. Gamely had been by herself for years. When suddenly she was confronted by her daughter and a new, full-blown family that was now her own, she could hardly take the shock of it, and she cried thunderstorms.

Virginia embraced her mother, and she cried too. Then the children began to wail like young cats, although they didn't know why. Even Hardesty, touched by the love between mother and daughter, remembered his own parents, and had to hold back the tears.

But the wailing continued long after Hardesty's eyes were dry, and as the clock struck the quarter-hour (even the clock bells pushed the weeping women and children into further squalls of tears), he paced back and forth impatiently, waiting for them to finish. "What is this?" he asked. "What is this, a waterworks?" And then, seeing Virginia's charcoal-gray suit within the folds of her coat, he was taken so by the versatility of the city journalist in a well-tailored skirt and jacket, and the Coheeries daughter thoroughly at ease in the countryside, that he put his arms around her, stroked her hair back from her tear-reddened face, and kissed her with such affection that Mrs. Gamely's heart rose like a weather balloon.

That night the children could hardly sleep. Their anticipation of awakening to see the Lake of the Coheeries in full daylight was stronger than their anticipation of a Christmas, and as they expected, they were soon lost in the beauty of the lake's wintry blue days and cold nights that knew no beginning and no end. A good sailor, Hardesty was quick to learn iceboating. They often took the *Katerina*, the biggest and slowest of the boats, filled it with provisions and quilts, and set off at dawn into the limitlessness of the lake. The children would sleep on the women's laps until the sun was strong, and when they awoke they would be amazed to see nothing but blue sky and mirror-smooth ice across which was blowing a nearly invisible sandstorm of snow. The high velocity of the wind had shorn the snowflakes of their ornament, and they shot by like bits of shining glass, in a mist that seemed like a fallen banner.

On these expeditions they glided across the ice for hours, until they were so isolated from any point of land or any boat that they might well have been the only people in the world. At noon they would let down the sail and dig in the double ice brakes. With the *Katerina* between them and the north wind, and the sun in their reddened faces, they would make a fire in a box full of sand and cook up a caldron of boiling stew. This they would eat with hot buttered rolls and Algonquian steam tea. They might skate for a time (Hardesty and Martin played an informal game of hockey and discovered that Virginia could easily take the puck away from both of them and keep it in her possession as long as she wanted), or drill through the ice so that in ten minutes they could pull up as much salmon, bass, and trout as they wanted, to be stacked perfectly frozen in a bin on the *Katerina*'s outrigger. Or they might simply sail into infinity, perfectly content to travel hundreds of miles into a seductive world of ice and sun that was theirs for the taking. Usually, on the day following their departure, having spent the night wrapped up in the softest quilts and blankets, they would make their way home after dark—drifting aimlessly across the starry ice. The Milky Way was so bright that Mrs. Gamely warned them not to stare at it for too long. "Daythril Moobcot's grandfather," she asserted, "old Barrow Moobcot, went blind that way. And tonight, if the moon comes up, we'll need smoked glasses."

They gave themselves up to the stars the way swimmers can surrender to the waves, and the stars took them without resistance. The days and nights on the ice changed the children forever. Lake of the Coheeries Town would rise over the ice horizon as a chain of lights embedded in white hills that lay next to the lake like a stallion prone on the hay. Then Hardesty would point the *Katerina* to the brightest light, and race for it. Though the children loved the race home, they wanted to stay on the lake forever.

As time rolled forward and took up golden day and silver night to weave them in a braid, they skied and sledded into the hill forests of spruce and pine, they went to the inn to dance the Grapesy Dandy and the Birdwalla Shuffle, they made traditional Coheeries maple candy in the shape of a crescent moon, and they sat for many hours as the real moon, the planets, and the stars set the time, and wood burned brightly in the stove. Mrs. Gamely's rooster, Jack,

517

came very close to learning how to play checkers with Martin, but he was never able to understand the idea of making a king.

One evening it grew unusually cold. An arctic wind descended from the north and placed the village in a vise of frost. As Mrs. Gamely's house accommodated to the sixty degrees below zero that controlled the outside world, it creaked as if it were a ship at sea. The house was well caulked, but a pinhole-sized river of air was enough to chill an entire room. They stoked the stove until it flared like the firebox of a racing locomotive.

Abby and Martin were building a house of dried corncobs. Dressed in robes and down booties, they sat in the middle of the floor between the stove and the fireplace. Mrs. Gamely rocked back and forth, watching her grandchildren. Virginia, wrapped in a shawl, was reading the old 1978 edition of the *Britannica*. Hardesty was at the window, ostensibly because the thermometer was there. That it kept dropping steadily, and was well below minus sixty, was for someone of his temperament an irresistible attraction. But really he was at the window to look at the stars. In the cold, away from city lights, they burned like white phosphorous.

There was a great deal of motion in the stars that night, and the comings and goings made it seem as if the space between stars and earth were a busy harbor crowded with launches. Flashing lines that might have been meteorites ended in fading white bursts that cascaded softly, the way the ice flies from the brake of an iceboat. These little showers of light bloomed and then were gone. Hardesty remembered how the white horse had parted from them on the plain, climbing into the predawn sky in a curved needle of white light that had dissolved with a faint hiss.

He was about to call Virginia over to view the little flashes on the horizon. They were unlike anything he had ever seen, except for the trail of the white horse. But when he turned he saw Virginia and Mrs. Gamely bent over Abby, who was lying on the floor, thumb in mouth, breathing heavily. "What's the matter?" he asked.

"Abby's got a terrible fever," Mrs. Gamely answered. "She's burning up."

"She must have caught a chill on the lake today," Virginia said as she lifted the child and began to carry her to the children's loft. Then she hesitated. "It's too cold up there. We'll have to make a bed for her here."

Hardesty put his hand on Abby's forehead. He winced. "It came so suddenly," he said.

"She was building the corncobs just a minute ago," Martin whimpered.

"It's all right, Martin. She's going to get better," Virginia said in a voice that was a little too shaky to be reassuring.

After putting Abby to bed, they took her temperature. It was 104 degrees. "That's not so high, for an infant," Hardesty said. They moved about the bed, arranging things, in silence.

"Where does the doctor live, Mrs. Gamely?" Hardesty asked.

"Why don't I prepare a poultice?" Mrs. Gamely asked back.

"To hell with the poultice," Hardesty said. "Where does the doctor live?"

"In the house at the end of the lane between the inn and the lake."

Hardesty pulled on his boots, gloves, and parka, and was out the door in an instant. The insanely cold air hit him like a hammer and almost knocked him down. He ran toward the town, his way brightly lit by the seething stars.

When he arrived he saw men running up the street, inland. They, too, were pulling on their parkas, and doors were slamming all over the village. But he hadn't time to be curious, and went straight for the doctor's house. The doctor's wife appeared at the door in response to Hardesty's agitated knocking (which she knew from experience to be that of the father of a sick child). "He's not in now," she reported. "He'll be back in an hour or two. I'll tell him to get right over there when he returns. Meanwhile, why don't you go home and put a poultice on the little girl."

"Don't talk to me about poultices," Hardesty commanded. "Where'd he go?"

The doctor's wife cleared her throat. "He went with all the others to the Moobcots' sheep barn, about two miles up the road."

"Why?"

"I don't know why. A lot of men carrying shotguns came to the

519

door. The doctor grabbed his kit and ran out. He didn't tell me what it was all about. He never gets. . . ."

Hardesty didn't stay to listen. Instead, he ran along the snow-covered road that led to the high fields. He was in no condition to overtake the Coheeries men, who, when they closed on the stranded train, had seemed as fit as alpine troops. Alone on the open road, he found that the stars on all sides and above made him feel dizzy and out of control.

A huge sheep barn was visible on a hillock in the fields. The door was open a crack, and bright light spilled out on the snow.

Hardesty went in. The sheep were all packed together in a corner, the Coheeries men were in a tight semicircle facing the far wall, and the barn lights burned above their heads. Hardesty could see from the way that the butts of their guns were aligned in a fanlike arc that the barrels were trained in one general direction. Several men were arguing. One said, "These are different from him. They're obviously not the same."

The other answered. "They came at the same time, and in the same way. I don't like the way they look. I just don't like it. They're trying to appear harmless, but do you believe it?"

"What do you want to do, Walter, kill them?" asked a voice from the far side. Hardesty tried to see over their shoulders.

"Yes," was the answer, followed by a buzz of disapproval.

Hardesty stood on a bucket and looked over their heads. Sitting on a bunch of hay bales, tapping their feet, smiling, and chewing sprigs of straw, were fifty or sixty of the oddest-looking men he had ever seen.

Their faces were either pinched and squashed, or as long and sharp as saws. Snub noses, overly bushy eyebrows, huge boxing-glove chins, and wickedly bowed legs were among their conspicuous features. But each and every one had in his eyes an emptiness that was terribly threatening, even if one could not say exactly why. They were dressed like vaudevillians, in derbies, and seemed to think nothing of it. They were further decked out in Edwardian three-piece suits, watch chains, and canes, all ratty and inelegant. They flashed the ingratiating smiles of those who do not have to conceal an evil and violent nature. But what proof was this of what assertion? And from where had they come?

"They were just suddenly all over the place," was the answer to the question that Hardesty had spoken aloud, "rummaging in people's barns, trying to hitch up sleds, stealing horses. We caught about twenty of them that way. And then, when we thought we had them all, we ran into another fifty in a field near the mill. Who knows? Maybe there's more out there."

"As long as we've got *him*," someone said.

"Who?" Hardesty asked.

A dozen men pointed past the doorway of another room, to the doctor and several other men. The doctor's kit was slung over his shoulder, and his shotgun was aimed at whatever he was observing. On his way over, Hardesty kicked a pile of something that jangled. "We took it all off these muskrats here," he was told. He bent to examine the pile, and saw silver- and gold-plated pistols, including ones with pearl handles, a set or two of derringers small enough for a dollhouse, brass knuckles with projecting stilettos, spiked beaver tails, blackjacks, a miniature shotgun, and ivory-handled garrotes. There were no rifles though. No skis, snowshoes, or heavy clothing. Whoever they were, they were poorly equipped for the Lake of the Coheeries.

Hardesty put his hand on the doctor's shoulder and gently pushed him to the side so that he could see. When he did see, he shrank back, trying to catch his breath and stay upright.

"Who in God's name is that?" he asked, still off balance.

"I could say, but I don't want to," the doctor replied.

Hardesty then moved between the men with the guns and looked into the little room where they kept the prisoner, who was bigger than the runts in the derbies, but not all that big, and quite thin. He had a dreadful face, and his limbs twitched almost as much as his darting tongue—which seemed to have a life of its own, and was obviously beyond his control. His eyes, too, moved on their own, like angry rats trying to get out of a cage. Hardesty had the distinct impression that this man was a construct. Neither the eyes nor the bony fingers ceased moving for a second. Now and then, electricity seemed to spark from him, and, clearly, imprisoned within him was a destructive agony entirely inappropriate to the peace of the Coheeries.

"Who is he?" Hardesty asked.

"Ask him," was the reply.

"Me?" Hardesty said.

The doctor looked at Hardesty askance. "Yes, you."

"Who are you?" Hardesty begged in a barely audible voice. Then he took hold of himself, stepped closer to the prisoner, and repeated the question with admirable firmness and authority.

Pearly Soames bristled. His hot electric palsies filled the air as if he were a hundred rattlesnakes dangling from a chandelier. Hardesty suspected that this strange man and his companions were not actually captive but, rather, just resting in a warm barn to which the farmers had been courteous enough to bring them. This notion was fairly well confirmed by whatever it was that shook the barn walls when Pearly was displeased.

But as far as Hardesty knew, this had nothing to do with Abby's sickness, and he stole the doctor away from the Coheeries men, depriving them of the doctor's learned opinions as they deliberated on what to do with the outlandish creatures that they had discovered in their fields and barns.

The next night, under a sliver of silver moon, Hardesty drove the sleigh out of Lake of the Coheeries Town at an astounding pace. He cracked the whip over the mare's head until she devoured the road in front of her like a hungry dog. Though she was on fire with the race, it still wasn't enough for him, and while he scanned the landscape in every direction, he shouted for her to pull even faster. An automatic shotgun lay by his side. Virginia held another on her lap. And Mrs. Gamely, inside a tentlike structure in the back seat with Martin and Abby, had her double-barreled twelve-gauge Ithaca right next to her.

The odd gentlemen had been escorted from town onto the high road. Now the Marrattas and Mrs. Gamely had to pass through their ranks on the way out, because the doctor had said that he was unable to treat Abby. She was to be taken to a hospital without delay. Now they could no longer consider the luxury of being trapped in the safety and stillness of the Coheeries. Now they needed the city as much as they had needed before to get away from it, in fact much more. The doctor had been unwilling to educate them in the particulars of the disease. "That will come later," he said. "You'll want to know everything there is to know about it, and you will. It won't make much difference." They were stunned, and they didn't believe him—what would a country doctor know?—but they left immediately.

They had set out armed to the teeth, because they expected that the prisoners who had just been released would want the sleigh and the horse. There was only one road, and the snow was too deep for travel across the open terrain. Hardesty calculated that he would intercept the strange lot of men before the climb from the plain to the mountains. In that case, the sooner the better, since the horse would have more speed on the flat than in the hills. He drove her as hard as he did not only because they needed to get Abby out quickly, but because he wanted to be halfway through the brigands before they knew that he had overtaken them.

The horse seemed to understand. But whether she did or not, she bulled them at a delirious pace, locomotive style, along the snow-packed road.

When they had crossed most of the plain they came to a rise from which it was possible to look down the road that led into the mountains. Here they paused to search the steppes in front of them.

Apart from the mare's breathing and the gentle luffing of the sleigh blankets in the night breeze, there were no sounds. Though the temperature was less than zero, the breeze seemed balmy. Only after Hardesty and Virginia had looked carefully about them to make sure that no one was close by, did they again look up to see the faint bloomings of the night sky. Against the stars and ether, red plumes as squat and symmetrical as mushrooms, as graceful as parachutes, and as quick to fade as shooting stars, flowered and disappeared, floating downward. Every few seconds one of these would flare and vanish, though sometimes several would appear at one time or in rapid succession.

"Parachutists," Hardesty said. "And they keep on coming.

Who knows, maybe it's been that way all night. Maybe it'll continue. And it's not the Eighty-Second Airborne, either.''

Then they looked downward, and as their eyes adjusted to the change in light, they saw that the plain was filled with scattered forms—gray individuals and dark formations struggling through the snow to converge on the road, where they made a ragged column that stretched for miles. These night soldiers moved silently and deliberately, without signals or lights. There was a thud in the snow nearby, and Hardesty and Virginia saw a doubled form unfold and run down the hill like a rat. It had been a man, clutching his hat to make sure that the breeze coming up the hillside did not roll it off his head.

"Can we go around?" Virginia asked.

"The horse would be chest deep. She could never pull the sleigh."

"Is there another road?"

"You know better than I do that there isn't," Hardesty answered. "Undo the safety," he said, readying his own gun, "and brace yourself with your feet. Mrs. Gamely?"

"Yes, dear?" came the answer from the tentlike enclosure in the back of the sleigh.

"How fast can you load that thing?"

"Fast enough to keep a pie plate in the air. Before Virginia was born," Mrs. Gamely said, "Theodore and I had to drive now and then to Bucklenburg in the hills. The wolves there were as big as ponies and as hungry as stecthaws. That's where I learned."

"Are Abby and Martin sleeping?" Virginia asked.

"Tucked away, sort of behind me," Mrs. Gamely answered. "Jack is in the hatbox. So is Teddy."

"All right," Hardesty said, "let's get to the forest." He snapped the reins and the mare moved forward, picking up speed as she went down the hill. Her hoofbeats were muffled in the snow, and the bells had been removed.

As their runners hissed along the smooth road, they passed stragglers who hardly had time to get out of the way, but soon the sled began to break into formations of ten or fifteen men, scattering them against the snowbanks like mailsacks tossed from a train. Pistol shots were fired, alerting those ahead, who still were not aware of exactly what was coming at them from the dark. The horse began to thud against the ones who tried to stand their ground. This slowed her down. Muzzle flashes appeared from the front and the sides, the children awoke and began to scream, and dozens of the marchers were hanging on to the sled or trying to jump into it.

Hardesty, Virginia, and Mrs. Gamely opened up with their shotguns, and the deafening noise was amplified by the shouting of the men on the road. The mass of the marchers seemed likely to stop them, and they soon slowed down to a trot. The horse was wounded. Her nostrils flared and her teeth showed. She was no Athansor, no war-horse, and as she bled, she cried out for him. Because she was bound by the traces of the sleigh, she could use only her forelegs, and only directly in front of her. This she did, knocking down her attackers and then pulling the knifelike runners over their limbs and bodies. But there were so many of them that eventually she found herself standing still.

Though they reloaded very fast, Hardesty, Virginia, and Mrs. Gamely could not reload fast enough. "Don't stop firing," Hardesty called out as they were gradually overwhelmed by ranks of squat, insistent fighters who grunted and groaned, and held onto the sleigh with fleshy podlike hands. The more it seemed that the Marrattas were about to go under, the harder they fought. There were hundreds and hundreds of little men in a black knot around the sled.

No one saw the white trail in the sky ahead, far brighter than when it had been a thin lashlike bend to the southeast. Now it appeared like a comet, dripping a million diamond embers that flared briefly and left the sky full of white smoke. It passed over them, a weaving shuttlecock, and then descended to the battle, lighting the white horse at the end of its blazing beam.

First he froze the Short Tails in astonishment, and then he cleared a path through them for the sleigh. When he was rampant, his forelegs were a wheel of white knives, opening a bloody cut in the snow. When he kicked, the unfortunates who took the blow were propelled into the air like artillery shells. And when Athansor

525

used his head and neck and teeth, he moved so fast that there seemed to be several of him.

Then, a miracle of sharp and deadly grace, he began to move forward, wading through them, gaining speed, until he was fighting and running at the same time. The mare followed. Hardesty stopped firing and drove. They were galloping now, past the thinning ranks of the Short Tails. With the white horse a length and a half ahead, they broke into the clear and ran toward the mountains.

He took them effortlessly to the top, from which they could see the Coheeries stretching away into the night. It seemed like a place that was too close to the stars to be cold, one of those tranquil high overlooks where there are no senses, but only the spirit. The white horse stretched his long neck down to the snow and then raised himself. He took a few turns around the sleigh and approached the mare. He was twice as big as she was. He bent his huge head and touched the side of her face. She backed a pace or two. Then he turned his attention to her wounds. He licked them, one by one; and, one by one, they were healed. Then he walked a few paces ahead, looked up, and broke into his long strides.

The next thing the Marrattas knew, they were alone, and a white band that had stretched across the sky was beginning to fade. They heard a faint whistling.

Now it was almost morning, the moon was down, and the stars were tired. Hardesty flicked the reins, and the mare led them into the mountain forests.

Old aldermen with beards on their jowls, monomaniacal ward captains, party officials, ex-mayors, and precinct hacks insisted as one that the preelection debates embrace a topic or two other than the holiness of winter and the theory of balance and grace. Skilled even in his thumbs at political maneuver, and used to telling audiences exactly what they wanted to hear, the Ermine Mayor finally forced Praeger to participate in a series of debates co-sponsored by *The Sun* and *The Ghost*, neither of which backed Praeger, since Craig Binky had deserted Praeger after Praeger had denounced him in public as (among many other things) "the slow dim-witted boob

526

who runs *The Ghost,*" "our most beloved moron," and "the *jerk de résistance* who floats around in a blimp that he calls a *Binkopede.*"

Seasoned old rhinoceros that he was, the Ermine Mayor was sure that in the debates he would trample the clean-shaven young idealist, who was an assimilated patrician of sorts, and who had opened himself up to attack with the lunacy of all his talk about winter. At first it had been successful, but the voters were now hungry for the hard stuff, and the Ermine Mayor looked forward to his frontal assault on the newcomer, eager to crush him in the triple millstones of the mayor's experience, age, and incumbency.

The first debate had to be held in Central Park because Praeger refused to be on television. He hated it, and attacked it whenever he could. Since a substantial plank in Praeger's platform called for the abolition of television, it was not surprising that the station owners threw their support to the Ermine Mayor and ran his political ads for free. They refused to cover Praeger at all, but Praeger would not allow television cameras to come anywhere near him anyway. He hit hard at what he called electronic slavery, and implored his listeners to reassert the primacy and sacredness of the printed page. It was the first time in half a century that anyone had attempted to be elected to public office without the use of captive electrons. In the debate only the Ermine Mayor was televised, and it appeared that he was debating a phantom. After ten minutes, Central Park began to fill with people who had abandoned their electronic hearthsides to see the first man in history with the courage to defy what had become the most powerful instrument of persuasion ever developed. Praeger had wisely insisted on the park. Though the evening was frigid, he eventually faced several million people and implored them to smash their televisions. For many, this was shocking and almost inconceivable. They stayed for hours in the cold, stomping from one foot to another, while vendors of hot drinks did a brisk trade among them.

"Who is this character who talks about winter and tells you to throw out your hard-earned television sets?" the mayor asked in a mocking tone.

But Asbury Gunwillow was in the crowd, and he answered,

"Praeger de Pinto! Praeger de Pinto!" until the chant spread among the millions, and the mayor was forced to change his tack.

"Well, actually," he said, "I seldom watch television myself—only the good programs. You know, the culture stuff."

"What's the difference what you watch?" Praeger shot back. "When that stream of hypnotic electrons starts winging into your brain, you're finished, good-as-gone, condemned to hell. No matter what it is, if you don't move your eyes and set the pace yourself, your intellect is sentenced to death. The mind, you see, is like a muscle. For it to remain agile and strong, it must work. Television rules that out. And besides, Minnie"—which is what he sometimes called the Ermine Mayor—"you just watch all those dramatizations of literature because you've forgotten how to read."

"You're not just talking about me, sir," said the Ermine Mayor. "You're referring to and insulting the entire electorate!"

"The number of disabled and electronically pickled brains is not at issue, Mr. Mayor," Praeger stated. "The issue is that the slaves may want to be free."

"You call our citizens slaves?"

"Yes. They are slaves of the winking eyes that tie them down and tell them what to think, what to buy, and how many blankets to put on their beds each night."

Forced onto the defensive, the Mayor blurted out, "Television is the common ground, the agora of democracy, the great communicator."

"That's correct, but it only communicates in one direction," Praeger answered. "It subjects everyone to its decrees, and will not discuss a single one. It takes away not only the right, but the ability to speak. Besides, I don't want to communicate with pickles." The crowd was enormously pleased. They could not have been more grateful if he had contrived to pass out several million pints of hot buttered rum. "Look at 'em all out there," he continued. "They have legs. They have muscles. They can breathe, and go outside at night. They can even walk in the cold. In fact, I'll bet they can even hunt, ski, chop wood, weave, whittle, and fix huge machines.

"Give me a night by the fire, with a book in my hand, not that flickering rectangular son of a bitch that sits screaming in every living room in the land."

"That's retrogressive," the Ermine Mayor declared.

"I rest my case," Praeger answered.

Then the moderator introduced the question of whether or not to abolish the garbage man's training academy on Randall's Island, since most of the cadets had recently been unable to pass the noisemaking course.

"I won't talk about that," Praeger said, after the Ermine Mayor delivered a long treatise on how to rattle a trash can. "I only want to talk about important things—a decent wage for hard work as well as for skilled work, getting the criminals off the street, banning automobiles from Manhattan. I want to talk about great things, about history and the city, about where we're going, about the minor tyrannies and the major tyrannies that must be overturned, about my love for this place where I was born, and where I grew up.

"I don't care about garbage cans. I care about the bridges, the rivers, and the maze of streets. I believe that they're alive unto themselves. . . .

"Look," he said, "sometimes I want to quit, to withdraw from the race and leave the city. It's a hard place—too big for most, and nearly always incomprehensible. But at those times, I stop, throw aside my ambitions, and view the city as a whole, and in so doing I am immeasurably encouraged. For, then, the city's fire burns away the mists that frequently obscure it. Then, it looks like an animal perched upon the shore of the river. Then, it seems like a single work of art shrouded in changing galleries of climate, a sculpture of unfathomable detail standing on the floor of an orrery that is filled with bright lights and golden suns.

"If you're born here, or if you come here from some distant place, or if you see the city rising over fields and forests from a home not far away, then you know. Rich or poor, you know that the heart of the city was set to beating when the first axe rang out against the first tree to be felled. And it has never ceased, for the city is a living thing far greater than just its smoke and light and stone.

"The city," he said with emotion that moved even his opponent and held him in the rhythm of the rolling words, "is no less an object of divine affection than life itself or the exact perfections of the light-paced universe. It *is* alive, and with patience one can see that despite the anarchy, the ugliness, and the fire, it is ultimately just and ultimately kind.

"God, I love it. I do love it. Forgive me," he said, covering his eyes and bowing his head.

The mayor dared not break the silence of the crowd that stretched from the Sheep Meadow to Eighty-sixth Street, on a great cold night, bathed in the silver glare of floodlights. The open-mouthed incumbent feared that his challenger, who stood before him plainly overcome, was going to take the election for having seen the soul of the city and fallen deeply in love. He feared that the city was going to answer Praeger's unusual appeal. And indeed it did. Not only were its citizens enthralled, but, when Praeger looked up, the city made itself very clear. For it was all around him, and it was sparkling like a diamond.

THE WHITE DOG OF AFGHANISTAN

PETER Lake thought the healing powers of time had finally overcome his madness, and that he was learning to live in harmony with other men. In fact, when the man for whom he had cast his twelve votes in the Five Points was elected by a landslide, Peter Lake began to feel rather like a power broker. On election eve he was intensely self-satisfied. It was easy to reinforce this budding pomposity by obtaining from Fippo's, the city's best men's clothing store, an outfit that was not only respectable but handsome as well. With a haircut, a shave, and a careful trim of the mustache, his face emerged from the raggle of white beard's nest and shiny eggish cock-eyes that had been his madman's trumpet, and he was surprised to see that he did indeed look like a power broker, or, if not that, a stockbroker, or, at the very least, a ship broker.

His face had been aged and tutored until he looked like the kind of war veteran who didn't talk about war, a family man, a good citizen, a senatorial businessman whose ambitions had long cooled—paternal, understanding, a lover of good music and poetry who held some great secret in his soul, the way all such men do, never to be fathomed.

The greatest shock was to see that his face was kind. Where, he wondered, did he ever have the time or opportunity to become kind? He did not associate kindness with the recent past in which he had been powered through cellar walls like an artillery shell. And rather than puzzle about it, he set out to milk for all it was worth the new mildness that had found its way into his heart.

He took decent lodgings. His salary at *The Sun* had accumulated, and he had more than enough to make him comfortable. He chose a small room in an old building in Chelsea. It was in such a backwater that returning home to it every evening was like coming back to a farm. And the woodwork and moldings around the fireplace and near the ceiling, having had the tranquillity and patience to remain unflinchingly in the same place for 150 years, were a great comfort.

At night, Peter Lake made a fire in the grate and rocked back and forth, listening to the clock ticking in the hallway. Like all old clocks, it said, "North Dakota, South Dakota. North Dakota, South Dakota. North Dakota, South Dakota." Although he did not know why, he was moved to tears whenever he heard the hoofbeats of a horse passing by outside. Even as he lay in bed in the early morning and listened to the clomping sound of women in high-heeled shoes as they rushed to work, he thought he was hearing milk horses. Perhaps, he hoped, this would be enough—the clock that said North Dakota, South Dakota, the quiet old room, the fireplace, the shadows, an occasional horse that passed by, the slightly Edwardian cut of his suit. Perhaps he would be forgiven for not remembering what he could not really remember. Perhaps that time was truly lost, and he, like others who had been hurled ahead or

532

backward, would succumb and adapt, and become a quiet citizen with faint and inexplicable memories.

This path was easy. The small pleasures were intensely satisfying—not only the eloquent clock, but the fine sound of the piano, which he pretended was welling up through the floors from the apartment of a young musician (but which he knew, in fact, to be coming from within). No matter, the music was beautiful, and he did not question it. He had to rest, to survive. What a delight, then, was survival. Forgoing meals at *The Sun* (since he preferred to be alone), he ate in a restaurant called the French Mill, where the waiters brought over a slate that had some ten things written on it. He said what he wanted, and it was delivered without fanfare. The food was always extremely good, cheap, and accompanied by a glass of fruity alpine wine.

Every night after dinner he went to the public baths. First a barber gave him a shave and a day's trim. Then he put his clothes in a locker and took a high-pressure shower in one of a hundred marble cubicles. After that came a series of alternating steambaths, ice dips, saunas, whirlpools, and showers, until he staggered out, as clean as a baby pearl (even his insides felt whitewashed and scrubbed), all set to rock for an hour or two by the fire and then go to sleep on clean sheets under a vast down comforter.

He had no difficulty falling asleep. Not only did he walk ten miles every day on his way to and from *The Sun,* but he was not the kind of master mechanic who farmed off the heavy work onto his skinny apprentices. When a web skirt, a piston, or a roller had to be moved, Peter Lake strained as hard as anyone else, and five hours in a health club could not have done him better.

Now the exercise, the good air on his long walks, the fresh vegetables and lean meats at the French Mill, the daily small glass of wine, the restorative baths, the clean linen on the bed every night, and his heavy reliance on the Swedish Hand (a local laundry) to provide him with starched shirts and clean socks each day, were excellent prods to health and vigor. But his body would have remained the wreck that it had been, were it not for the magical recuperation of his mind.

And this, in his opinion, was due to the meadowlike calm of his old room, the ticking of the clock, the soft talk of the fire, the many many hours of solitude, and the rest that had come to him after his unspeakable dream of hurtling through all the graves of the world. He tried to put it out of his mind, for nothing was more contrary to the new serenity and equanimity of his life in Chelsea than the frightening truth of the matter—which was that he, Peter Lake, the master mechanic, the citizen who imagined that he had at last settled in and found peace, was indeed the living registrar of the dead, and was capable of recounting them, in their multitudes, each and every one, all of them, one by one.

One evening, Peter Lake was sitting by himself at the French Mill, awaiting a small steak, shoestring potatoes, a salad, and a glass of Brennero mountain wine. As it somehow always manages to be before the winter solstice, but never after, the early darkness was cheerful and promising, even for those who had nothing. For Peter Lake, who had at least half of something, the lights up and down the length of Hudson Street were like those of a Christmas tree.

He leaned against a wall and watched as people hurried through the unusually frigid November wind. Bombarded by ice crystals that were the emissaries of a blizzard, a subway motorman clutching his hat raced for the warmth underground. An expensively dressed woman, who, to judge by her appearance, looked as if she seldom ventured outside the Upper East Side, went by with a pained expression. How impudent of the cold to sneak under her furs. Her pearls gave Peter Lake a painful start. He took note, for it had happened before.

He had to consider women for the first time since he had awakened to see the young red-haired doctor at his bedside. It did not occur to him that part of his reason for going on the bum may have been to avoid women. And he had no memory of any former loyalties, except that he was unable even to look at a woman with blue eyes, at least not directly; and young girls with a certain kind of face had the same effect; and, now, the pearls.

The main door of the French Mill opened, let in some glassy snow, and shut. At first, Peter Lake thought that the wind had done this, but then he looked down and saw two small men walking to a table on the opposite side of the room. Not only were they no more than five feet tall, but they both wore bowler hats, and ragged jackets that, before they were trimmed in the back, had once been tails. Their eyes were sunken, their faces had a leathery look, and they had bony cheeks and mouths that would have been large and toothy on men twice their size. Their hands were fat little balls of flesh with flat infantile thumbs, as delicate and strange as the paws of a tree frog. Their voices matched the rest of them in that they were small and sounded like the supplicating chirp of men who are married to female lumberjacks or prison matrons.

Feeling neither antipathy, nor sympathy, nor curiosity, Peter Lake was, nonetheless, unable to take his eyes from them. They weren't conversing: they were conspiring. They seemed to hate one another ferociously, and yet they were apparently close. They quickly began to argue, and the more impassioned they grew the more they bounced up and down in their seats. Their peculiar voices kept on rising as they grew agitated and angry.

Peter Lake's food was brought to him by a waiter who motioned in the direction of the screaming midgets in bowlers and cut-off tails, and then rolled his eyes up to the ceiling and back as if to say, *"La Madonna!"* (All the waiters at the French Mill were, naturally, Italians from the Brenta.)

Peter Lake started to eat, trying as best he could to ignore the two little men. But try as he might there was no way he could avoid hearing those words that were emphasized in their argument. He had wanted to enjoy his steak, but at one point he almost choked on it.

Their conversation had gone like this: "Something something, something something, something something something . . . *the White Dog of Afghanistan* . . . something something something, something, something, something else, something entirely unintelligible."

"The White Dog of Afghanistan." These words stuck in Peter Lake like a fishhook.

The next thing he knew, he was walking briskly against the north wind. He overshot Chelsea and was aimed toward midtown.

535

Whatever the "White Dog of Afghanistan" meant, it had a powerful effect on him, and he feared that it might smash his newfound equilibrium. "Fuck!" he said, impelled forward by legs that were hardly under his control. "Damn!" He didn't even know why he was walking, but he felt that if he had returned to his room everything would have been spoiled.

"Save the clock, save the clock, save the clock that goes tick tock," he found himself chanting, as in the old days of his dereliction. And when he neared the bright and crowded shopping districts he discovered that despite his cleanliness and fine clothes people on the street were once again giving him a wide berth.

"No!" he cried out, unwittingly providing himself the luxury of an empty path. "Stop it! Stop it! Stop it. Stop it. . . ." And then, very softly, "Stop it." He restrained his maniacal strides. "I'll buy a dog," he said to himself. "I'll buy a white dog, and take him to my room. He'll be a good companion. I've always loved dogs. Actually, I don't know if that's true, but I'll buy one anyway, a white dog, a white dog of Afghanistan. That must be it. I must be yearning for a dog." He cleared his throat. "Aaarrch! That's it—a dog, a white dog." He walked toward the great stores.

Kublai Khan could not have decreed a better shopping district. Anywhere anyone looked, anyone could buy anything, because everything was everywhere, in department stores that were half a mile square, a hundred stories high, and lined up along the avenues like dominoes. The people of the city of the poor could see these temples of materialism across the distant river, flashing their electrical signs in the night or gleaming like fixed bayonets in the daytime sunshine. They wondered what they were.

Peter Lake found a dog store, where he asked for a white dog.

"Would you like a nice Shar Mein?" the salesman inquired.

"I already ate," Peter Lake replied.

"A Shar Mein, sir, is a very fine white dog."

"Oh. All right, let's have a look."

The salesman disappeared, and returned with a dog under his arm.

"For Christ's sake," said Peter Lake, looking at the dog. "I don't want a mop. Where are its eyes? That's for an old lady who doesn't even know what a dog is. Don't bring me anything that can't jump over a sawhorse."

"What about Ariadne, then," the salesman said, pointing to a beautiful snow-white Saint Bernard.

"Now, that's a nice dog," Peter Lake responded. He went over to Ariadne and patted her fat head. "Good dog, good dog," he said.

"None finer," the salesman added.

"She is lovely," Peter Lake said, "but I'm afraid she's not big enough."

"Not big enough?"

"No. I had in mind . . . a rather large white dog," he answered. "An heroic-sized dog."

"You'll have to go to Ponmoy's," the salesman advised. "They specialize in huge dogs."

Ponmoy's was not far, and was easier to find than the Third Circle. Huge dogs were everywhere, pulling against thick stainless-steel chains, bellowing like the insane on a night of the full moon, and drooling by the bucketful from floppy jowls that hung like the curtains at the Roxy. Attendants threw them twenty-pound buffalo steaks and clipped their fur with hedge trimmers.

"I'm looking for a big white dog," Peter Lake said to Mr. Ponmoy himself.

"Big?" Ponmoy asked. "Right here."

He showed his customer a five-foot-high snowy-colored mastiff. Peter Lake did a few turns around the beast, and shook his head.

"Actually, I had in mind a dog of a larger size."

"A larger size? This is the biggest dog in the shop. He weighs two hundred and fifty pounds. They don't make dogs any bigger than this."

"Are you sure? For some reason, I feel as if I want a really big white dog, a *really* big white dog."

"You don't want a dog," Ponmoy said. "You want a horse!"

Peter Lake stopped still for a moment, the model of placidity, happiness, fulfillment, and contentment. "Yes . . ." he said. "I couldn't keep him in my room, but there's a stable not far away. I could ride him in the park. A horse. . . ."

* * *

Soon the bookcase in Peter Lake's room, in which he had previously kept examples of well-machined gears or bearings that were worthy of study, became the home for a hundred volumes on horses. There were the classics, of course, such as *Care and Feeding of the Horse* by Robert S. Kahn, *Equine Anatomy* by Burchfield, and Turner's *Dressage*. But he had combed the bookstores almost as thoroughly as he had toured the graves, and come up with a good collection of secondary, tertiary, and trenta-septesimal works as well, books that, like most lives, would know only the faintest glory, and that of the Last Judgment. There were Moffet Southgate's *Memoirs of a Military Groom* (all his long life he had been a stableboy at a naval air station), *Catalog of Albama Curry Combs, 1760–1823* by Georgia Fatwood, *The Afro-California Jumping Style* by Sierra Leon, *Ride Like Hell, You Son of a Bitch!* by Fulgura Frango, and a coffee-table book that weighed forty pounds, was printed on vellum, bound in silk, engraved in gold, and priced at one week of Peter Lake's wages, *Pictures of Big White Horses*.

This last one kept Peter Lake up on many a night, leafing through it with searing concentration that tried to extort from the tip of his tongue, as it were, a connection with one of the animals, or the reason he needed to seek them out. He stared for hours at the white beauties rampant on the Camargue or dressed in scarlet and silver on an English parade ground, and gained a mysterious satisfaction from doing so. Less satisfied, to be sure, were Peter Lake's neighbors, who were awakened at odd hours when this otherwise respectable gentleman galloped around his tiny quarters and neighed—not because he thought he was a horse, but because he was trying to understand what it was about horses that drew him on so strongly. He held his arms out in front of him in imitation of a running horse's forelegs fro zen in a photograph, but there were no means by which he could match the grace of a perfectly balanced white-maned racer. He had a picture of a fire horse running so hard in the traces that all its legs were airborne at once and its head was elevated as if it had just turned a sharp corner and felt the weight of a trailing engine. This photograph obsessed Peter Lake, who in examining it tried to look into the horse's eyes, turned the book sideways and upside down, and used a magnifying glass that he had brought from the tool room at work. There was something about how the horse seemed to be sailing above the ground. All Peter Lake had to do was close his eyes, and he too was flying. The difference between being on the ground and being several feet above it was not to be minimized. The few inches that separated a man's limp and relaxed feet and the surface from which they had risen and over which they could effortlessly float, were equal to a voyage of a longer distance than anyone had ever imagined. Peter Lake wondered if, after so long a time in pure suspension, angels remembered how to stand, and if one could tell those artists who worked for a higher purpose from those who didn't—not only by the depth of the angels' eyes, but also by the ease of the limbs. He himself had seen this kind of suspension, at Petipas, when the child had risen into his arms, passing over the stones of the courtyard far more smoothly and slowly than physics allowed.

But that might have been one of those things that he had imagined, one of the many things that, like this terrifying knowledge of the dead, weighed upon him heavily nonetheless. He would never be able to explain such illusions when he hadn't even the slightest idea of who he was. The horses, however, were of both the inexplicable mystery that drew him to one thing or another, and the reality of flesh and blood. He seized upon them for the very sensible reason that even if their appeal to him was otherworldly, still, they could be seen pulling junk wagons or transporting tourists around the park. And it was easy, of course, to love horses, since they were exceedingly beautiful and exceedingly gentle. So Peter Lake stared at pictures of white horses without understanding why, and his love for a white horse that he didn't know he had ever seen filled him with unexplained emotions.

After a while, there was not a stable in the city that did not know his face. If horses were auctioned or shown, Peter Lake was there. He often sat on a rock above the most heavily traveled bridle path in Central Park. Had he been stuck in the madness of his bagman's thatch, he never would have understood any of this. But now he was at peace, and he began to catch on. In a very short time, he was able to realize, more from the pattern of his behavior than from any understanding of his desires, that he was searching for a particular horse. He despaired of finding the very one he sought, since he knew neither why he was looking nor exactly what he was looking for, and there were a lot of big white horses around.

But the deeper he drove, the sharper he became. As he healed and strengthened, his faculties served him better. Were it not for that, he never would have noticed Christiana.

She was not hard to notice. She was the kind of woman who. . . . Well, we know what she looked like. Strangely enough, Peter Lake was as comfortable in her presence as other men were not, perhaps because she had none of the very specific attributes that held sway over him, such as blue eyes, the habit of wearing pearls, and the certain kind of face that he could not encounter without deep pain and longing. He noticed Christiana early on, after having passed her several times as he was coming out of or going into a stable. He saw her watching the cart horses at their dawn muster in Red Hook (most of these were small Shetlands who drew flower carts and worked birthday parties, but occasionally there was a full-sized white, or even a white stallion). He bowed slightly in recognition when he encountered her at horse shows. And he noticed at the auctions that she and he were the only people who consistently did not bid.

When finally they spoke, they were amazed to find that they had in common not only their interest in horses (neither dared inform the other of what they did not know was a mutual obsession), but *The Sun*. Peter Lake told her that he was the chief mechanic there, and she said, "You must be Mr. Bearer."

"How do you know that?" he asked.

She knew because her husband had told her. And who was he? He was the man who ran *The Sun*'s launch. In fact, her connection with *The Sun* and therefore, by extension, with Peter Lake was even stronger, since she was a maid at the Penn house, and had often read to Harry Penn when Jessica was either on the road or when she had been making appearances on behalf of Praeger de Pinto, when he was running for mayor.

"I met him," Peter Lake said. "I voted for him twelve times,

540

and I know your husband. Sometimes he gives me fish. I took one of his bluefish to the French Mill, and they broiled it with herb butter. The mechanics always look forward to Asbury's visits, whether or not he brings along a fish, because there's no one with greater patience for listening to us explain our machines. He wants to know about every single one of them."

"He doesn't have much to do these days," Christiana reported. "The harbor's iced over, and he's put the launch in overhaul because he's having terrible trouble with the engine. It's an old model, and he doesn't really know how to fix it."

"Why didn't he ask me?"

"He probably didn't want to trouble you."

"Trouble? I love engines. Tell me when he'll be at the slip."

"All the time, these days."

"I'll go there tomorrow and see what I can do."

Peter Lake parted from Christiana in a daze, because he seemed to have made a friend. A friend implied happiness, and too much happiness might lead him to give up his struggle. But why not fix Asbury's engine? Certainly it could do no harm. It did belong to *The Sun,* after all, and, as far as he could tell, taking care of *The Sun*'s engines was his reason for being.

ABYSMILLARD REDUX

ONE week in November, the fad among corporate giants was church buying. Craig Binky didn't want to be left out, so he bought half a dozen Baptist churches on the Upper West Side. He was depressed because, by the rules of the game, this was a pretty poor showing. After all, Marcel Apand had three midtown Episcopals and a Greek Orthodox in Astoria, and Crawford Bees had gotten hold of sixty synagogues.

He had been terribly hurt when Praeger de Pinto turned against him during the campaign, and frustrated when Praeger had gone on to win the election. He felt that, at the very least, he was owed some information about the ship that lay at anchor in the Hudson, but the mayor-elect refused to tell him anything, stating that he was going to announce the project himself, in December, and that Craig Binky could find out then along with everyone else.

"But I'm a newspaper!" Craig Binky sputtered. "I'll lose my momento if I don't know these things. I supported you, and now you're asking me to water-ski without a rope."

Craig Binky was back in his office before he realized that he had discovered nothing. "I'm the only one in this city," he said to Alertu and Scroutu, "who knows no thing." He frequently said "no thing" instead of "nothing." "I'll remedy *that.*"

He turned to the underworld, paying $100,000 to learn that the central figure was Jackson Mead, and $50,000 apiece for the names of Reverend Mootfowl and Mr. Cecil Wooley. At one of the many fall publishing banquets, Harry Penn, who had heard rumors of the buy and that Craig Binky thought he knew more now than anyone, was assured in one glance that the rumors were accurate. Craig Binky was puffed up like a Cornish rock game hen (as he would say), so happy with himself that, even though he was sitting down, he was strutting. After Craig Binky's speech (which was supposed to have been in praise of the columnist E. Owen Lemur, but went like this: "He always liked me. He thought I was great. He said that someday I would. . . ."), Craig Binky could not resist standing again to say, "I know the names of the people on the ship in the Hudson. Ahem!" Then he sat down.

Harry Penn leaned over to whisper in his ear, "You mean Jackson Mead, the Reverend Mootfowl, and Mr. Cecil Wooley? Craig, your newsboys know that, and they didn't have to pay Sol Fappiano two hundred thousand dollars to find out, either."

"How *did* they find out?" asked Craig Binky, whiter than confectioner's sugar.

"They read it in *The Sun,*" Harry Penn lied. "They always read *The Sun.* I thought you knew."

Craig Binky decided that to salvage his position he would bear any burden and pay any price, and find out exactly what was going on. He had to redeem his honor. He decided to ask a computer.

He put snow tires on one of his touring cars and drove deep into Connecticut, where, perched upon a limestone cliff, a huge warlike building looked over a peaceful valley. This was one terminal of the National Computer in Washington. Most of the time, the silicon behemoth in the capital was busy with things that no one understood, but it occasionally worked a few minutes for the general public.

"Is that it?" Craig Binky asked the facility's director, as he was brought into a room the size of two hundred large barns, filled to its high ceiling with banks of electronic tombstones.

"That?" the director asked back. "Of course not. This installation is only the terminal. Here we convert the user languages into a specific algorithm that the big computer in Washington can understand."

"You mean the computer in Washington is bigger than this?"

"Actually, no. It's only about the size of a house, but its heart is always kept at absolute zero. One of its random access memories the size of a grain of sand has the capabilities of a room-sized model from, say, nineteen ninety. It's like a brain, and the terminals are like the senses distributed throughout the body. Make the analogy with your own brain, which, despite being the size of a . . ."

"Basketball," said Alertu and Scroutu.

"All right, a basketball. It's still a lot smaller than your body, but it's a lot smarter."

"Let's get to it," Craig Binky said, impatiently.

"Did you bring your chips?"

"What chips? I just want to ask it a question."

"Only one question?"

"Why not?"

"The threshold charge is a million dollars."

"It's worth it to me."

"Very well. It's your decision. What's the question?"

"Who is Jackson Mead?"

"It'll cost you a million dollars just to access the Washington mainframe."

"Just ask it for Christ's sake!"

An operator approached a terminal, and typed a series of codes and orders. Then he typed, "Who is Jackson Mead?"

A moment later, these words flashed across a red rubidium screen: "I don't know."

"What do you mean, I don't know?" Craig Binky screamed. "Let me talk to it!"

"A voice hookup can be arranged."

"Let me talk to the goddamned thing."

"I don't really recommend it."

"Put that son of a bitch on the line!" Craig Binky screamed.

"Okay, go ahead."

"Look, you stupid son of a bitch," Craig Binky began. "I paid a million dollars just to ask you a simple question, and you say you don't know the answer."

"So?" the computer wrote.

"You're supposed to know everything."

"Like hell I am."

"You're a fake. I ought to come down to Washington and beat the lights out of you."

"Are you threatening me?" the computer asked.

"Yeah," said Craig Binky, hopping from foot to foot, fists raised. "I'm threatening you. 'Cause you're a chicken."

The computer took its time, and then wrote, "You suck."

"Just try collecting your bill," Craig Binky shouted as he stormed out.

The computer summoned the registration numbers of every single financial instrument in Craig Binky's substantial portfolio, and before he was out the door a legal brief had been filed and answered, a judgment rendered, his accounts attached, the appropriate fees and penalties confiscated, and news of the case flashed to every newspaper in the country—except *The Ghost*.

"That goddamned automatron!" Craig Binky said in the car to Alertu and Scroutu. "The lousy automon!" Still, he knew no thing of Jackson Mead, and everyone else did. Day by day, details were being revealed in the press, and elsewhere, in preparation for Praeger de Pinto's announcement on the first of December. For Craig Binky, it was most frustrating. Although he did not know, even Abysmillard knew.

Abysmillard? Yes, Abysmillard.

Of all the creatures made by God, the most abysmal was Abysmillard. Even as a baby he had been dank and unpleasant, and then, as he grew older, his hidden abysmillarities flowered. The

Baymen had kept him on (the only one they had ever thrown out was Peter Lake, because he was not truly one of them) but had always hoped secretly, and sometimes not so secretly, that something quick and effective would do him in—an Indian raid, a bad clam, a sudden storm that would catch him far from land in his moss canoe.

He had frightened his mother to death in childbirth. Since no Baywoman would suckle him, he was put in a thatched quonset with a blind goat. He never learned to speak beyond grunts and burps, and yet he was as long-winded as a state senator who has had too much to drink. When the Baymen grieved, Abysmillard was usually taken up in joyous mania, and when they rejoiced, he sulked. One eye looked stage right, and the other leftward and to the ceiling. To fasten upon something he wished to observe, he had to swing his leathern and shaggy head. In so doing he had knocked down many an old person and child, rendered unconscious the strongest men, and thrown a great number of oyster stews into the dirt.

The Baymen were not famous for bathing, and, in not bathing, Abysmillard was their champion by far. He had to have his own hut on his own acre, and this for the sake of people who liked to eat live eels. Nonetheless, he had a wickedly strong lust for the girls, and caused much trouble with his stunning and monstrous flirtations.

His teeth were like the signposts that appear in the remoter camps of expeditionary armies to point the way to the world's brighter and more congenial locations. They thrust in all directions. Sores marched around his body and were visible through all his matted and well-manured hair—as were the occasional living things that sometimes poked from within. He was by far the loneliest of men: even he could not tolerate his own presence, and was often seen galloping across the shallows—flailing his arms, screaming, trying to shed the horrible husk that surrounded and tortured him.

It was assumed that his crookedness, massive size, and unwholesome agitated way of living would quickly send him to the grave, and the Baymen were puzzled that he lived on while the rest died off. They thought he had nothing to live for, but they were wrong. He loved butterflies, and secretly believed that he, like the caterpillar, would lose his monstrous self to become a bright and graceful creature that everyone loved. As the years passed, he waited for his own molting, infused with a single purpose and strengthened by a single expectation. He was so invigorated by this belief, in fact, that he lived far beyond his time, until he was terrifyingly old even among a people of noted longevity. By the winter months just before the third millennium, he was the only one left on the marsh, and had been alone for several decades. It was fortunate, in a way, that the Baymen were no longer there to see what had happened to their world, and that the one who remained had been trained all his life to weather every kind of misery and see only into the far and hopeful future.

Hard times, prosperity, and war—in short, history—had brought about the development of the harbor and the decline of the marsh upon which the Baymen depended completely. In boom times, factories and the port expanded over the reeds and mud, changing living ground into something no more productive than rock. In depressions, public-works crews came to fill in the margins between land and water: since it was impossible either to walk there or go there in a boat, these areas were perceived as enemies of the body politic. In war, the land was taken for shipyards, freight terminals, and matériel depots. New roads, beginning with the Pulaski Skyway, were driven like arrows and spears through the heart of the marsh, and airboats and helicopters took from it its depth and serenity. The waters were poisoned and littered with greases and filth. Half a hundred refineries and chemical works made breathing a valiant deed. The cloud wall receded to a different locale. Though now and then it would sweep in and throw down some confused soul, or pull one after it as it fled, it seemed to prefer the open sea.

Some of the Baymen had been shot by police at the edges of the marsh, some crushed by huge ships in the expanded roads, and some caught under rushing cabin cruisers that sped down the channels with music blaring and oiled sunbathers splayed across their decks. As the century progressed and the refineries increased their output, the children began to be born in fantastic shapes, but, unlike Abysmillard, most of them had no talent for survival. Eventually, only Humpstone John, Abysmillard, and a younger man named Boojian were left. Humpstone John died of the ague. Boojian ventured too far toward the edge of the ice and was swept into the winter sea.

Abysmillard tried to live on in what was left of his house, but duck hunters and trappers were drawn to it in hopes of using it as a blind or a storage place, and if they encountered its owner inside their response was invariably one of such fear and loathing that they would shoot as a form of therapy, to exorcise the creature that lay in the darkness and stared at them with the impossible hollow eyes of the past. Though they missed him when they shot, they made a lot of holes in the thattle and waub. Fearing that they would someday hit their target, he moved into a soft damp hole in the earth, a muskrat burrow that he claimed after the muskrats had fled because the water in its vicinity had become too oily. This was a kind of grave, but it had an exit.

Every few days, he went out in the darkness to forage. He lived on reed shoots, snails, little darters that he caught in the nets that he could still weave, and a clam or two when he was able to find them. If he were fortunate, he might land a salmon or a shad that had come into the rainbow slicks by accident, or catch a migrating bird that had had the temerity to land. Everything he ate tasted as if it had been raised in a garage, but he didn't eat much, and was saved.

For most of his life he had been huge—seven feet tall and three hundred pounds. Just before the beginning of the third millennium, he was only five feet tall and he weighed about a third of what he had weighed before. For twenty years or more as he lay in his burrow, breathing slowly, staring blankly ahead like a man with a fever, he had been changing. It was so slow that he never knew, but his flesh was rearranging.

The teeth had gradually aligned until they no longer pointed hither and thither, but only hither, and his eyes had become syncopated. What a great relief not to have to stare in two directions at once! And now that he could perceive depth he felt that he was more of the world, rather than an observer of flat pictures. As his body fed upon itself, it showed admirable discipline in partaking of the worst first. The boils, sores, goiters, and fungal constructions disappeared. His hair, no longer matted after he had nearly drowned in a sump hole filled with turpentine and kerosene (this killed all the bugs, too), was now white and flowing. Thoroughly dry-cleaned for the first time, his clothes became as soft and fluffy as they were the day the Baywomen made them from the wool of beach sheep and peccaries.

Abysmillard was aware only that he was slowly starving to death, that the seasons passed, and that he was still alive. Like the animals, he was capable of staying still for periods that seemed like an eternity. He did little more than look at the light and listen to the wind. In winter he could see snowflakes landing just beyond the exit of his burrow, and the sun would come down low enough to shine like a hunter's flashlight and blind him as it reached to warm the underground. Blizzards sometimes raged above, entertaining him with their wailings and concussions. If a low-flying plane roared over the marsh, he thought that an angel was coming to take him.

This slow diminution could have continued until he was as thin as a thread, at which point he might have been eaten by the air or taken up by the wind and blown as far away as Polynesia. But he was forced from his resting place.

In the ancient fire dreams of the Baymen, the last days, though difficult, were not to be feared. According to the Thirteenth Song, a sure sign that the last days had arrived was "when a solid rainbow springs from the ice to leap the white curtain, and on its arc of beating lights are a thousand smiling steps." As workers stayed through the night to build them all around the marsh, Abysmillard was able to see the piers and foundations of this rainbow. Though the sites were cluttered with huge scaffoldings and shrouds, they often lit up and glowed, and light in many colors practically burned through the flapping tarpaulins. Because he knew the Thirteenth Song, Abysmillard suspected that these piers would generate beams to be joined into a single magnificent arc.

He would have been content to wait for this quietly, but the ice was so thick that he could no longer get food. He tried to chop through it with his wooden adze, and even with his sword (the sword was seldom disgraced with such a task). Never had he seen such a perfect mirror. And the last time he had tried to make a hole in it, he had seen when the leads were connected in the scattered foundations that the light on the surface was as nothing compared to the multicolored streets and avenues which shot through the frozen world below. The woven beams ignited like flash powder and remained in front of Abysmillard's eyes for half an hour as he groped about, blinded, trying to find his tools.

His only hope was to get to the edge of the ice where it met the sea, where he could fish right off the shelf or bore a hole in it because it was not as thick as the more stable inland ice. A long time before, when the harbor had frozen over and the Baymen were still on the marsh by the thousands, in dozens of villages, they had gone to the sea and had lost many men. Sometimes, he remembered, eight-foot waves had leapt over the ice like a great tongue, and pulled the fishermen into the frigid ocean. Men vanished among the undulating shards of razor-sharp ice, and were cut up in so many pieces that by the time their friends reached the spot where they had disappeared, the only thing to see would be a bright red patch blooming smoothly against the underside of the transparent floor upon which they stood.

To go there alone at night was most dangerous, since it would be hard for him to make his way over the fractured ridges, the wind was high, and the ocean sent tides slithering for miles along the frozen surface. In the dark he would have little chance of seeing or avoiding them. It was not likely, however, that he would ever reach the sea, since a fifteen-mile walk in subzero winds was not an easy matter for someone of his frailty. Like all Baymen, he was drawn to danger, and he set out one night when the moon lit the way and the cold was an angel with a sword of ice.

Though he was only partially aware of it, he had finally come into his own. He moved with grace, his eyes had become kind and intelligent, his long white hair flowed like that of a patriarch, and he was now ready to enter the thriving communities from which he had been excluded all his life. But there was no one left! Though he had come through to the end, he had come through without ever having been embraced. He supposed that there were others like him, perhaps whole legions. And he imagined that it would not be just for so many people to have lived through such loneliness and not come to a final reward. This gave him courage for his last walk on the ice.

People were thrilled by the sudden onset of so great and (they thought) so unprecedented a winter. Even those who feared and hated cold weather and snow were quickly seduced by the silvery polar nights, and joined in a medieval pageant of sledding, gatherings about the fire, and evenings under the stars. It was as if the occasional joyful paralysis that winter sometimes lays at the foot of Christmas had come for good. Layers of clothing made the flesh more mysterious and enticing than it had been in many a year, a certain courtliness was restored, and the struggle against the elements reduced everyone in scale just enough for people to realize that one of the fundamental qualities of humanity was and would always be its delicacy. The entranced citizens did not go to so many places or work as hard as they usually did, but they lived far better than they had ever lived.

A favorite pastime was to skate down the rivers to the harbor. High winds kept the surface of the ice clear of snow and piled it up against the banks of the Hudson, the East River, and the shores of the bay, in many-storied ramparts through which had been driven—on the model of the Roman catacombs—a hundred thousand passages and tunnels leading to the snow rooms that served as impromptu restaurants, hotels, shops, and inns. The informality and variety of these nameless places proved far more attractive than the conventional stores in the city, and New Yorkers did everything they could to escape the squares and rectangles into which Manhattan had been scored, and get to the serpentine snow cities. Crescents, circles, dim galleries with partially inclined paths, and rooms that led to chambers that led to chains of halls, caverns, and secret places, did a lot to free and delight those who had been brought up on the right angle. Skaters glided from place to place, losing track of time and disappearing for days into the cities of the snowbanks. Whole families went there to sleep in the snow rooms, eat roasted meats on tiny skewers, and take part in the ice races—only to realize that they had been gone for days at a time, and that all their appointments had been violently broken. But often those with whom they were supposed to have met had forgotten as well, and were themselves to be found on the ice. The snowbanks and the long frozen rivers were, however, just the means to get to the harbor, which, by day, was now like a plain that held assembled armies, and by night a festival and observatory of the stars.

Thousands of tents were pitched on the ice, rivaling the snow palaces. If one did not cheat and move between rows, one could easily be lost in a maze of alleys and avenues that were filled with skaters, merchants, and teams of colorfully clad hockey players, racers, or curlers traveling to tournaments in the great squares that were placed at random throughout the tent city. Above innumerable fireboxes, caldrons steamed and boiled, lobsters tumbled, and many grosses of eggs jiggled in the hysterical dances of the legless bald. Roasted meats, hot drinks, and fragrant fruit pies that were baked in brick ovens which had been built on the ice, were everywhere and cheap. Trick skaters, jugglers, acrobats, music students, and dancing pigs performed at the busier junctions. Children zipped about on their skates like supersonic mites, passing through crowds and under tables laden with merchandise or food. The nine-year-old boys seemed to be the fastest and most daring. They were as skinny as elastic bands, knew no danger, and stopped only long enough to shovel fruit pastries into their mouths. Then they were off at a hundred miles an hour, dodging, darting, and continually raving in squeaky voices for everyone to move out of their way. As speedy as pions, muons, and charmed quarks, they were all places at once, the possessors of pure and boundless energy.

At night the fires burned until nine, and then were damped down and put under grates so as not to interfere with the astronomical observations. A strange residue of warmth lingered until well after midnight, permitting intense scrutiny of the heavens. Entrepreneurs rented out thick pads and quilts for people to use as they lay on their backs absorbed by the celestial sphere. Though the inhabitants of New York had hardly been aware of the stars for a hundred years, they now were highly enamored of them.

Not only astronomers, but various astrologers, charlatans, and quacks in pointy hats and sequined boots discoursed for a fee upon the Pleiades, Sextans, Rigel, Kent, Pavo, Gacrux, Argo Navis, Betelgeuse, Bellatrix, and Atria. Little books about the stars stuck out of many back pockets, telescopes and tripods proliferated into a forest of three-legged trees, and the populace became aware for the first time in a long while that something existed that all could love and never lack. Had it continued, this might have taken the city very far. But every night the wonder was balanced by the scourge of winds so fierce and cold that the tents came down, and the ice was abandoned so completely that in the morning all that was left were the boxy ovens—and even they were moved by the wind, colliding like curling stones. As the days grew shorter and real winter piled its severities upon those of the winter that was charmed, the ice became less and less hospitable, and the hours of astronomical observation were steadily reduced.

Early one morning, Peter Lake went down to *The Sun*'s slip at Whitehall to help Asbury fix the engine of the launch.

Though the sun had just risen and was putting things in a fresh and vigorous light, the air was still very cold, and they could hardly speak. They built a fire in an oildrum, and every five or ten minutes they climbed down from the launch to warm their hands. Since they were working with steel and had to touch it often, their fingers quickly got numb. As Peter Lake and Asbury crouched by the fire, they stared across the deserted plain of ice that had formed over the once busy harbor.

A hundred thousand people had been there the night before, but that morning there was not a single soul. All the tents had been packed up, everyone had retreated either to the snow city or to the city itself, and the ice was clear except for a few brick ovens which looked like mileposts, or pegs stuck in the ground. When the sun cleared the tops of the houses in Brooklyn Heights, the harbor turned blue and white, and a tremendous wind was generated as the sunlight woke the cold air over the ice. Their fire blazed up, and

553

they bent their heads to protect their eyes from the wind. Pieces of paper flew past them in the air, and bits of litter (cans, tiny chunks of wood, sticks, tent stakes) shot across the ice like hockey pucks, and lodged in the walls of the snow cities. This was the wind that swept the ice clear of anything except the ponderous brick ovens, which moved as slowly as sick elephants.

"What's that?" Asbury asked, pointing to a sacklike thing that was skidding along the ice. Judging from the way it moved, they thought it was fairly heavy. Sometimes it would stay put on a dent in the ice until the wind turned it. Then it would start off again, slowly, and build up momentum. And when it stopped, it stopped as gradually as it had started. Unlike the smaller projectiles that shot by, it appeared to be moving with graceful deliberation.

Only when they saw the arms flailing listlessly in slow motion did they realize that it was a man. Undoubtedly he was frozen solid, but constant movement had kept the shoulders supple, and his arms tumbled alongside his body as delicately as petals falling off a rose.

They ran out on the ice, where they caught him and turned him over. Grimacing and immobile, coated with hoarfrost and snow, a St. Nicholas face greeted them from a mass of homespun rags, wool, and pelts.

For a moment, Peter Lake hesitated. He nearly let the opportunity pass. But, kneeling on one knee, he lifted the body halfway off the ice, and held it in his arms. "Abysmillard," he whispered, suddenly pulled back a full century by a strong recollection of the harbor when the Baymen were its masters. Though Abysmillard's face was coated with rime, it spoke to Peter Lake only of summer.

Now he remembered poling a canoe through infinite shallows and jumping out to drag it across sandbars the color of butter. The city itself was far away, obscured by mist and waves of heat. As a boy, he had never really had to look at it, but he had always known that it was there. He saw in memory a shabbily clothed child lost and contented in the world of the marsh, where it seemed to be summer all the time, and the strength and accuracy of his recollection suggested that although he had left that time behind, it was still replaying itself.

"You know him?" Asbury asked. "Where did he come from?" Especially in his frozen and gnarled condition, Abysmillard did not look much like a modern man.

"Over there," Peter Lake answered, looking toward what had once been the Bayonne Marsh. "People used to live there, like Indians. They had clams, oysters, scallops, lobsters, fish, wildfowl, saltwater boar, berries, peat, and driftwood. But that was a long time ago, and things have changed. Now the marshes are hell."

"He must have been the last one," Asbury said, unnerved by the savage and unfamiliar face of Abysmillard.

"No," said Peter Lake. "I am."

EX MACHINA

PERHAPS instinctual knowledge
of the Last Judgment is widespread because a life that leads to
death is a perfect emblem for a history that at some time will be
judged: both are stopped, stripped, and illuminated by the same
powerful light. Or perhaps it is because, in living, one muddles
through the years for the sake of those one or two moments which
are indisputably great. Though such moments can occur on the bat-
tlefield, in a cathedral, at the summit of a mountain, or during
storms at sea, they are experienced more frequently at a bedside,
on the beach, in moldy courts of law, or while driving down sun-
warmed macadam roads on inauspicious summer afternoons: for
the castles of the modern age are divided into very small rooms.
These rooms, nonetheless, are often crowded with large numbers
of people, because history favors mass, and proffers greatness

most readily when all the soldiers of an army have gathered on one field, when a cathedral is packed to the rafters, or when the mist lifts and the ships of an invasion fleet discover that, far from being alone, they are a breathtaking armada.

Many a time when walking through the city's magnetic and reverberatory streets, Praeger de Pinto had been overcome by too much light let loose, by a whiplash of energy that thundered through the gray canyons like a snapping cable. And sometimes when the city was so much itself that it shuddered and quaked, his spirit was lifted into the timeless corridors that ran invisibly above and through the streets, close to the blinding frictions that bind together all form. For him, the ferry's low whistle, that elementary growl, opened corridors and corridors not only through the lacy and enticing fog.

These events were excellent preparations for his inauguration, in which he got what he wanted and lost himself at the same time. The ceremony was much like an execution, though he was not killed. He was, however, removed from normal life and permanently set apart. In other, friendlier eras, the mayor had been just one of the boys. Now he was cloistered by grave responsibility, and his youth flew from him—like the pigeons that, choosing to ignore the traditional proceedings, rose into the blue and carefully threaded their way among the ice-covered twigs that cracked the morning sky into dazzling cells.

The Ermine Mayor came out, dressed in the ermine-clad robes and ruffs, with the ermine cap, the ermine stole, and the ermine muffs. He peered from the mass of purple, white, and black fur, and, looking like an effeminate shell-shocked woodchuck, moved onto the platform to stand sadly next to the mayor-elect.

Turning to greet the mayor, Praeger saw beyond the furry thing that glided up to him a line of bosses sitting on the dais. Behind them was another line of bosses, and so it went all the way back to the cream-colored walls of City Hall, where the reviewing stand came to a halt. Why were all political bosses, with hardly an exception, six feet two inches tall, 225 pounds, with red noses and red cheeks on fleshy faces crowned by fluffy white and silver hair? They were either that or they were short skinny beings with pencil mustaches, hoarse voices, and sunglasses permanently attached to their faces. The big fat red ones had no necks, and the little thin ones always limped slightly. Surely, Praeger thought, this was part of a divine plan.

He was the first mayor ever to be elected without the bosses, and now they and every notable in the city were gathered to hear his speech. They did not know what to expect from him. He might speak about winter's charm, excoriate the evils of television, or wonder out loud about the city's destiny. With exactly a month to go before the millennium, he chose in his inauguration address to discourse upon the metaphysical balance that informed all events and was so characteristic of the city as almost to be its hallmark.

"I see a lot of puzzled faces," he said. "Why? Don't you understand that this city is a hotbed of the mechanism which keeps things in trim?

"Ah, I know. You have mistakenly called it contrast, looked upon its social lessons, and then turned away. But do you think, really, that the patrician clothed in ermine is more elect than the derelict who sits in a winter doorway slowly dying?

"My mother used to tell me, when I was small, that if I studied jujitsu with the local barber who taught in the loft over his shop, I would be able to throw a big man with only one finger.

" 'How many big men have only one finger, Mother?' I asked, being literal to the quick. But when I understood what she meant I was not surprised, since I had realized even earlier than that, that adversity has its compensations, that in falling, and in failing, we rise. It is as if there is a hand behind us that sets to right all imbalances. Why do you think the saints seldom had the temporal power that we mistakenly identify with the fruits of justice? Do you think they needed it, or cared?"

The bosses began to sweat in the cold. Not only was this new mayor talking like a man of the cloth, he also made the same churchified gestures. They had always known that the only real threat to their power was theocracy, and not only did they sweat in the cold, but their sweat itself was icy. Conversely, the prelates who were assembled like multicolored cockatoos in the back rows of the reviewing stand grew terribly excited. Could it be, they wondered, that their long-abandoned dreams would be realized by this man who had taken City Hall in a frontal assault through the back door? They itched to know his religion, so as to claim him. With a name like de Pinto, he could have been a Catholic, a Sephardic Jew, even Greek Orthodox. Who knew?

"Do not mistake my views of temporal power and material wealth as a device to protect the current social order. I see the Marxists in row thirty twisting in their seats. Stop twitching. Redistribute wealth, if that's what makes you happy. I agree, somewhat, with your notions of equalization, though not enough to accept the tyranny that people like you, who have no eyes for grace, would unleash if you were allowed to govern solely according to your mechanical precepts. Since I believe that the curmudgeon in his club chair is just as likely to see beyond the realm of the world as is the derelict of whom I have spoken, I have no objection to maneuvering the derelict in from the cold and letting him have beef Wellington, too. In fact it's only fair, but it is, in itself, a theology of a very low order.

"Far beyond that, though, is an artful, ever-present, recurring balance. One can see it in nature and its laws, in the seasons, in terrain, in music, and, most magnificently, in the perfection of the celestial sphere. But it is illustrated here as well, in the city.

"At every turn, the city presents scenes of triumph and scenes of dejection. It is a kaleidoscope of sunshine and shadow that represents our condition far better than the wheel of fortune, for the wheel of fortune, though correctly polar, does not allow the proper fragmentation of time and events. The perfect simplicity of salvation is broken up upon these rocks that we have built, and scattered for us to ponder and piece together in a test that tries our patience and understanding. We learn that justice may not always follow a just act, that justice can sleep for years and awaken when it is least expected, that a miracle is nothing more than dormant justice from another time arriving to compensate those it has cruelly abandoned. Whoever knows this is willing to suffer, for he knows that nothing is in vain.

"Now, let me tell you about the bridge that Jackson Mead is going to build."

Craig Binky was seated in a prominent place, and none of what follows was missed by a single soul. He clutched his chest and brow like a man suffering a heart attack and a stroke simultaneously, and then proceeded to grimace through a range of rapid-fire facial expressions that would have put Pantaloon to shame. And as Praeger continued, Craig Binky sank to his knees like a penitent, his spastic movements signifying greed and chagrin rather than newfound enlightenment or contrition.

"He showed me the plans," Praeger said. "In the sketches and elevations that I saw first, the curve of the great catenary seemed able to hold the entire globe in its jeweled and sparkling slope. Imagine my surprise when he told me that this was only a minor approach to the main structure. He then unfolded several dozen blueprints of astonishing bridges, unlike anything we have ever seen, and explained that these would radiate like spokes from the central span.

"Of the central span, there is no rendering. It is to be made of light. He speaks authoritatively of using the sea and the ice as a lens for beams which will be generated by several stations already under construction. Light of all frequencies will be shuffled, husbanded, harbored, held in reserve, magnified, reflected, reverberated, refracted, tuned, arranged, and focused so that it builds on its own strength. The key to achieving a beam of infinite power, I am told, is not the magnitude of generation, but the subtlety of control. Light under flawless tutelage knows no limits, and Jackson Mead proposes to train and tame a flurry of separate rays, escorting them through a complicated maze of development and augmentation, until they combine into a cool and solid beam upon which it will be possible to travel.

"Though one foot of the arc will rest upon the Battery, he would not say where this bridge will lead, preferring to leave that to my imagination—as I will leave it to yours."

There was an immediate protest from the crowd. Neighborhoods would be destroyed, expressways rerouted, and the city's vital resources channeled into a rainbow bridge that had no end. It would have been easier to get the pimps in Times Square to rebuild Chartres than to get the practical citizens assembled for the inauguration to agree to expend their powers in such fashion. Indignation choked them like thick wads of cotton. Had not Praeger de Pinto's initial campaigning, before he fooled them into the winter madness, been in opposition to Jackson Mead?

Anticipating this question, the new mayor answered it by stating that he had merely been against the secrecy. "Now, I have ended the secrecy," he said.

The bosses were enraged, which was, after all, how they earned their salaries. When they got mad, they lit up like flashing signs to signify to their constituents that they were working hard to represent them. The boss gallery was like a row of slot machines that had all hit the jackpot at once, because each boss wanted the people of his precinct to witness the luxury of his indignation. Even the clerics began to wonder if this bridge were not likely to denude their cathedrals after everyone had walked up it and disappeared into the clouds. "The city of the poor won't take this lightly," someone said. "They'll imagine that the bridge is yet another enemy in a world of enemies. It will take a while for them to move, but when they do, they'll move with a vengeance."

All that remained of the inauguration was for the council of elders to announce the new mayoral appellation. Praeger was apprehensive, believing that, after devaluing their currency in recent years, they would now have to be stringent. He feared that he was going to be called Pork Mayor, or Tin Mayor, and would have settled for a compromise, such as Bird Mayor. For as long as anyone could remember, there had been bone mayors, egg mayors, water mayors, and wood mayors. After the last bone mayor, the council had embarked upon an inexplicable and exciting trend, naming a Tree Mayor, a Green Mayor and then an Ermine Mayor. Praeger thought that it couldn't last.

As the clock struck noon and the ice-covered trees rattled like belled tambourines, the Ermine Mayor shed his robes (which were then folded by his deputy), knelt, and presented Praeger with the scepter of office. There were no cheers, for the crowd was angry and confused. Then the council of elders (including Harry Penn) marched in line to the podium. Craig Binky had been summoned, but, having missed the meeting, did not have the courage to appear. The head of the council cautioned the populace to refrain from needless speculation. "What we say here is not necessarily the future. We are not that wise. But we, like you, can dream." Then he announced that Praeger de Pinto was to be called the Gold Mayor.

The crowd gasped, and the bosses, too. Their machine, it seemed, was breaking apart. They feared not only for their livelihoods, but for their lives, since they knew that a machine coming apart as it runs is like a war unto itself. What, in their great wisdom, did they do? They scurried off the reviewing stand like a routed army and hurried home through the snow-packed streets to lay in stocks of food, firewood, and whiskey.

It didn't seem fair that Abby Marratta should be confined with dying old men, or that she should pass them in the corridors as she was wheeled from place to place on a long bed over which hung bags of blood and saline. Even the old men, who were adept at making their own misery their guard of honor, forgot about themselves entirely when she passed by. They were terribly moved to see that the bed was largely unused, and that the child lay on only a small part of it in the center.

At first she was taken from one place to another by orderlies who arrived at all times, even in the middle of the night, as if her survival depended on how many rooms she visited and how many different people she encountered. These long and frequent journeys down hallways as clean as bone angered Hardesty and Virginia, until the journeys stopped, which angered them even more. She was now confined to her room, abandoned by most of the specialists and technicians, alone except for her parents, one or two nurses, and a young red-haired doctor, who cared for her, in shifts, twenty-four hours a day. Abby would often wake up, and when she did they had the difficult task of lifting her halfway into their arms and holding her as if the forest of plastic tubing that tangled around them were not there.

Then there were the specialists, half a dozen of them—no, a dozen. They came highly recommended, and the names of physicians to trust flew about like parchments in a prayer wheel. Hardesty had so many slips of paper with the telephone numbers of doctors written on them that the long list he typed out to keep them in order took up an entire page. Each of the listed specialists was supposed to have been "the very very best."

After only a week of being worn down by changing faces and guarded opinions, Hardesty guessed the worst. No one offered any hope. They simply referred him on, until the last man he consulted took pity on him and told him the truth.

There was no greater authority, for he was the chief of the chiefs of the most prestigious medical institution in the city. Friends of his had forwarded the records, he had studied them carefully, and visited Abby not once, but twice. He invited Hardesty to his office overlooking the East River because he knew that the majesty of the place, the painting of Lavoisier, the heavy furniture, the quiet, and the snow-covered gardens outside would make it easier for Hardesty to believe what he was going to be told.

"The best thing in the world," the doctor said, "is the truth. You find it out anyway, in the end, or sooner."

Of course, he needn't have said anything else. Hardesty fought back tears.

"Make your daughter as comfortable as possible, save her from pain, and don't let her know what is going to happen. You do have other children, don't you?"

"Yes," Hardesty answered.

The doctor nodded, and stared at him, smiling just slightly.

Hardesty blinked his eyes, breathed in, and went to the window. First he saw the gardens, covered in snow. Then, beyond them, the river. The wind blew across the ice, bringing with it the bellows and whistles of ferries and tugs trapped at their docks like hounds confined by deep snows. Though afternoon had not ended, lights came on along the riverside, and in Queens the thin skeins of smoke issuing from many chimneys betrayed many early fires. Perhaps nothing is as sad as dying light in a quiet city.

"My mother died when I was a child, and when my father died," Hardesty said, staring at a light and persistent snow that descended past the window of Abby's room, "I was too young to

563

take care of him, even though I was a man. It wasn't my place. I suppose I could have taken charge and made him rest more, or eat differently, or do whatever he had to do to prolong his years, but the months he might have gained would have been all wrong. He was my father, and I had no right to father him.

"I didn't know what to do as I saw him getting weaker and weaker. I was paralyzed. But he took that as a good sign. He said, 'You save your strength to care for your own children. That's the best you can do for me. Only a fool would waste his energy on a man as old as I am, and I'm glad to see that you know enough to conserve your courage for when it's really needed.' He left me with the sense that I hadn't failed him, and he taught me how to die properly.

"But, you see," Hardesty said, in controlled rage, his face tightening with determination, "I can't let this happen to Abby. It's not supposed to be this way. It's wrong. I don't just mean that it's unpleasant, or that I don't want it. I mean that it's wrong. It isn't her time yet. She's too young."

When Virginia asked, "What can we do?" it was not entirely in rhetorical fashion. She was willing to believe that something could be done, and that it was their responsibility to do it. Everyone had cautioned them against this, saying that, afterward, they would never forgive themselves for imagining that intervention was in their power when it was not.

"But who says it isn't?" Hardesty asked, remembering their words. "Surely, more miraculous things have occurred. We hear about entire armies that are resurrected, or saved by a closing sea. Pillars of fire arise in the desert, thunder and lightning rage, and hills skip like rams to protect those who believe from fierce and vicious enemies."

"Do you believe," Virginia asked, "that a pillar of fire actually rose in the desert?"

"No," Hardesty answered. "I don't believe that. I believe that the account of the pillar of fire was merely a metaphor, but for something so much greater and more powerful than just a pillar of fire, that the image, for all its beauty, doesn't even begin to do it justice."

"Isn't it vain to imagine that we can tap that same source by an act of will?"

"I don't think so," Hardesty said. He seemed to be piecing something together. "I think it would be vain to imagine that we could be favored without effort. As I understand it, miracles come to those who risk defeat in seeking them. They come to those who have exhausted themselves completely in a struggle to accomplish the impossible.

"I held back when my father died. He said it was my duty, and that I was right. His last wish was that I save myself for a battle I would not understand. Do you know what he said? He said, 'The greatest fight is when you are fighting in the smoke and cannot see with your eyes.' "

Peter Lake wanted to go to the marsh to see what he could remember. Because the harbor was frozen, he didn't need a boat. Instead he bought a pair of skates and laced them on tight. Then he tied his shoes together and threw them over his shoulder. He set off across the ice early in the morning, with his hands in his pockets, as a strong east wind pressured by the rising sun poured down the darkened streets of Brooklyn and sped over the harbor. Peter Lake found that he didn't have to skate, but could lean back on the wind and let it push him toward the marsh. As he sailed effortlessly over many miles, he saw again the familiar outline of the Bayonne peninsula, and the way it once had been began to come back to him even though it was now covered with factories, wharves, and huge construction sites. In the cold dawn, men labored by the thousands under floodlamps and rows of sparkling bulbs that made the caissons and steel girderwork look like naval ships in liberty lights. Shooters Island came into view. The Baymen had called it Fontarney Gat, and there had been fresh water and fruit trees on it.

As he sped into the Kill van Kull, which the Baymen had called Siltin Allandrimore, he turned to look at the city. It gave him a shock, for it was so familiar from that perspective, and his recollection of it so strong that he thought he had lost touch with both worlds. Still, he found pleasure in seeing the cliffs of the city lighted in the dawn, as he had seen them so many times before.

Though its glass palisades blazed, and the light that passed through them covered the Jersey shore in refracted rainbows, enough older buildings were left to give Manhattan the air of an island of rock cliffs, and to make the Battery seem like a very tough chin.

He was about to head up the Kill van Kull to explore the bays, reed-covered bars, and salt-water channels, when he noticed a group of barely perceptible black dots above the ice, several miles behind him. He wouldn't have known for sure that they were after him were it not for the graceful ebb and flow of their movements as they rushed forward at high speed, changing course at different times but keeping to the same general line. Knowing that in physical mechanics the appearance of such smoothness meant either unearthly precision or high speed at a distance, Peter Lake wondered not why the skaters would be out at dawn, but why they would be so determined and fast.

Instead of vanishing into the Kill, he skated east against the wind, and watched the intoxicatingly beautiful sway of the forms, much larger now, as they realigned themselves according to his position. They were headed beyond him, on an intercept. Then he turned and raced west. Sure enough, they wheeled gracefully to the right, keeping him, as it were, in their sights.

Peter Lake came to a sudden stop, shredding the ice into a cascade that fell upon its smooth surface and broke into crystals that were scattered by the wind. He stared at the approaching skaters. How steadily they moved, with none of the lurching of those not lucky enough to have the wind at their backs. They came on straight. And they were coming for him.

Despite the apparent peril, Peter Lake was glad to find himself in what seemed like a familiar situation, and he felt a rush of strength and elation which seemed inappropriate for a man of his age—as if the strange forces which had battered him and beaten him down while he was on the street, and the powers that had worked against him and punished him with lightning flashes and thundercracks, were now in him.

The sun caught his pursuers. There were at least a dozen, and the steady and determined way they moved was threatening. Peter Lake headed for the island. They had the wind, and there was no way he could escape to the left or right of them, since, if he tried that, all they needed to do was to change course slightly and intercept him. Nor would it have made sense to continue west. The marshes had changed, and he was not so sure of his knowledge of them anyway. The best strategy was to round the island and go to the middle of the far side. When he saw them coming around on one side or another, he would set out again to the northeast, with a slight lead, and the wind would be against everyone.

He got to the far side and stood there only long enough to realize that, if they were smart, they would break into two groups and put him in a pincer.

After a high-speed leap across the cattails, he flew onto the beach, and dug his skates into snow and sand as he raced awkwardly across the island. At its highest point, he saw that they had indeed divided into two groups, and were coming around in a set of slowly spreading phalanxes that would have trapped him had he followed his original strategy.

He was already on his way down to the free ice. But these skaters in black coats were not to be written off lightly. They had left two of their number as pickets several hundred yards offshore. The only thing he could do was to head straight for them, and he did.

They saw him shortly after he moved onto the ice. They put about a hundred yards between them, and fired two shots in the air to call back the others. He went right up the middle. As he gathered speed against the wind they braced themselves and fired at him. He heard the bullets in the air and was grateful, for bullets in the air seemed to be his calling.

As they shot at him methodically and accurately, but missed because he was bobbing wildly and going too fast, he caught a glimpse of them. They wore black coats of an old-fashioned cut, much like the coats he had seen on the two short men in the restaurant. He still didn't know who they were. Their tactics had been masterful, and it was only by luck that he had been able to remain unscathed.

But they were not as smart as they could have been. This he discovered as he flew between them. They had been training their pistols at him, waiting for the moment at which he would be closest—which was, obviously, when he intersected the line that went from one to the other. They pivoted mechanically, taking good aim. When he crossed the line, they fired with an exactitude that identified them as creatures of geometry. Anticipating this, Peter Lake sank down in the kind of compressed crouch from which barrel leapers spring, bent his head, and listened to the doubled Doppler effects of the converging bullets as they passed just above him. It was an unusually long sound, spindle-shaped. Rising to skate, Peter Lake was delighted to see that his two attackers had slaughtered one another with enviable precision, and lay sprawled on the ice, motionless.

"My sincerest apologies," he said out loud as he pushed forward without a pause, not wanting to waste even a second to look back at the others, who he knew would be building up speed. He went straight for the populated ice under the East River bridges. There, he could vanish among the newly rising tents and in the snow walls and burrows along the banks.

He skated effortlessly, taking hard forward strides that made his skates quiver and threatened to crack the steel blades. Then, crossing toward Manhattan, he remembered that the last time he had returned to the city across the ice he had been on a white horse. Such fragments of memory falling into place were common now, and though they were at present more enticing than edifying, he was certain that if things continued apace he would know everything.

The ice city that lay under the Brooklyn and Manhattan bridges, and its sister cities to the north, were the intermediary ground between Manhattan and the city of the poor. Although, unlike their rich cousins, the poor did not fear for their physical safety in neighborhoods other than their own, they were intensely uncomfortable in the sparkling enclaves that they saw day and night from their own drab city. Walking down a well-kept street as doormen watched and matrons looked on disapprovingly was an experience to be avoided. The two cities had long been polarized, and though the lines were not physical they did exist, as the invisible boundary of the Five Points could easily attest. When the rivers froze, however, new territory was opened and neutral ground was established.

Though the contact between the rich and the poor might have brought about a positive exchange, it was the grosser appetites of each that sent them to the city on the ice. While most people and their children were on the bay looking at the galaxies, a cynical transaction was occurring under the bridges. The wealthy came to abandon just those virtues that they might have contributed, and to indulge in a licentious parody of what they imagined were the morals of the poor, and the poor came in turn like sharks to prey upon them. One group wanted to buy slaves and sycophants, and the other wanted cash, watches, and jewelry.

It made for a place of raw nerves and much ugliness, completely unlike the other ice cities on the other banks, for, as is almost always the case, the architecture followed the plan of the inhabitants' souls. Peter Lake sailed in on his skates at breakfast time, making zigzags through the warrens of ice and snow until he was lost in them. After one last turn, he found himself in the courtyard of an inn. Snow walls had been raised against the wind, and a fire burned in a brick oven that had been stolen on the open ice to the south. At a large wooden table, a group of revelers sat awaiting their food, which was a crisp corn gruel and a milky cereal mixed together into a yellow paste. What faces they had, rich and poor, men and women, even the dogs who were curled up next to the oven: the greedy eyes, the chins and noses that flowed together into an undisciplined snout, the loose intoxicated smiles that came far too easily, the oyster-sack bellies that hung by threads, and the horseshoe-shaped rows of teeth that stuck out in aggressive unpearly necklaces from mouths that were continually barking.

Peter Lake took a place at table and was given a wooden bowl of gruel. The food was carried to the diners on a stretcher made of thick boards and logs. To transport eleven little plates of porridge, two men had to carry a 250-pound sledge. It wasn't bad stuff, and all except Peter Lake ate like a pig, surrendering to their appetites and to the food. Peter Lake's eyes darted about to take in the scene. Prostitutes in upper-floor windows were stuck in public kisses that were not so much kisses as the draining of swamps. And the bogs from which they sucked were slovenly boil-covered creatures with hairy backs and meat-red lips. Before he was halfway through his gruel, Peter Lake saw two pockets being picked, and then he saw someone picking a pickpocket's pocket.

For a moment, Peter Lake forgot where he was and lost himself in trying to remember a rhyme of his boyhood in the Five Points that had to do with pucks and woodchucks, and what one might do to the other. But, glancing through pillars of the snow courtyard, he saw a huge delegation of black-coated skaters passing by like the centurions of a Roman city.

Peter Lake quickly found himself under the table, staring at fatty calves and trench foot. He noticed that, as they were eating, half of these people had their hands either on their own genitals or on someone else's. In fact, he shared his place of refuge with a poor anonymous woman who knelt on the ice, rendering service between the legs to both sexes in return for a coin held out in the hand of someone who never even saw her. The black coats came in and questioned the diners, who hadn't noticed Peter Lake, and could not provide any information. They were so drunk that they couldn't answer anything straight anyway. Peter Lake peeped out from a thicket of varicose veins and saw the bottom halves of his pursuers. They wore coats that looked like abruptly shorn tails.

"That . . . those are. Oh Jesus, Short Tails!" he said, bumping his head against the table.

The Short Tails heard it, and toppled the diners onto the ice. Peter Lake bounded, knocking the table into the next enclosure. With the Short Tails in pursuit, he ran for the inn and raced up the stairs. Although the walls were white, it was almost pitch-dark inside. At the third story, Peter Lake stopped short and nearly reeled backward. A child who probably belonged to one of the prostitutes and was more than likely involved in the activities at hand, staggered from one of the rooms onto the landing. She was only four or five years old, but she wore a loose dirty gown, and she moved like an aged drunk. Peter Lake was so stunned by this sight that he nearly let the Short Tails catch him. But then he took hold of himself, and continued.

The top of the stairs was a dead end. Everywhere he looked there was a snow wall, and in back of him the Short Tails were crunching and burbling up the steps. Peter Lake took a leaf from his time as a derelict, and rammed the wall head first.

After bursting into an adjoining bordello where thirty people were moaning in a bath of thickened coconut milk, he excused himself, ran down the stairs, and skated back to the city.

In the real, solid city, the Short Tails now were everywhere, like cinch bugs in flour. Though not all of them recognized him, those who did gave chase. He obliged them with leaps through windows, theatrical bounces on snow awnings, and plough runs through unsuspecting crowds, in which people were bumped about like billiard balls and parcels flew into the air in ballistic arcs.

As difficult as this was, he loved it, and could not imagine a better sport than to be chased from place to place and have to climb up the sides of buildings, hide in drains, and leap from roof to roof. It kept him so busy and was so pleasurable that he forgot everything except the city itself, and this was of tremendous value when he had to decide where to go or how to hide, since the whole of the city seemed to be in his blood, and he was able to rush forward at great speed and never miss a step. It seemed to him a fine destiny, and he would have been disappointed had they not tracked him everywhere he went. Sometimes he would pull himself up onto a fire escape and drop down on a couple of Short Tails as they ran underneath, knocking their heads together savagely. Once, he cornered one of them in a deserted building. The terrified Short Tail had long, greasy black hair, which he nervously twisted into tiny little pigtails with his left hand, while, gun in the other hand, he paced about the rubble looking for Peter Lake, who was hiding in a closet. When the Short Tail opened the closet door, Peter Lake screamed "Boo Hoo Hoo!" so ferociously that the Short Tail began to dance and jiggle, firing his pistol into the floor at uncontrollable rhythmic intervals. When all the chambers were empty, Peter Lake said, "That's a nice dance you've got there. You ought to get up an act and take it to the Rainbow Room." The man's teeth were knocking together like an automatic stapler. Some were dislodged, and fell on the ground. "When you get through with yourself," Peter Lake told him calmly, "you're going to need a good dentist. I was going to knock you out, but this is better. Still, I have to be

571

going. When you finish, would you be so kind as to turn out the lights and tear down the building?''

Then Peter Lake vanished into the darkness, the snow, the vast sea of lights, and the plumes of steam that on a winter night are feathers in the city's cap.

He dared not go back to his room, for, whoever they were, they had found him out. He knew that they were called Short Tails, and that their job was to chase him, but he didn't know why, and he still knew precious little about himself. "As far as I'm concerned," he proclaimed out loud, to no one in particular, striding down Fifth Avenue on a night bustling with shoppers, "this is a dream, and they can chase me until kingdom come."

But he had to sleep. What a delight, then, to be able to remember yet another piece of what he now realized must have been an extraordinarily rich past. He went straight to Grand Central.

Commuters and passers-through crossed the prairielike floor much as they had always done, in a silence that invited the eye to rise and view the vaulted sky above. It was as if the building itself had been skillfully constructed to mirror life on earth and its ultimate consequences, and to reflect the way in which men went about their business mostly without looking up, unaware that they were gliding about on the bottom of a vast sea. From the shadows of the gallery above Vanderbilt Avenue, Peter Lake looked above him and saw the sky and constellations majestically portrayed against the huge barreled vault that floated overhead. It was one of the few places in the world where the darkness and the light floated like clouds and clashed under a ceiling.

They hadn't tended the lights of the stars for decades, and the unlit sky was stormy and somber. Perhaps no one remembered how it was done, or even that the stars were there to be lighted. He went straight to the little hidden door, where he found a familiar lock. "I know how to pick this lock," he said, taking out his wallet of fine tools, and not realizing that he himself had set the lock in place almost a hundred years before. "It's an old brass McCauley six." He opened the padlock with such finesse that it finally occurred to him that he might once have been a burglar. But, since he had no memory of it, he dismissed the thought.

Once inside, in back of the sky, he threw a familiar switch, and all the stars lit up. Not a single bulb was burnt out or missing. It was just that no one had ever been there to throw the switch. In the forest of steel pillars above the warm vault, Peter Lake heard the distractive sound of low faraway engines, something that he had once taken to be the rhythmic blizzard of the approaching future. He went to his bed, which, after nearly a hundred years, was dusty but intact. Cans of food now probably deadlier than nerve gas were neatly stacked between the pillars. Stacks of *Police Gazettes* and old yellowed newspapers lay by the bed. He looked at all this in wonder.

Peter Lake lay back contentedly on the bed. It was winter, the stars were on, and he was safely in back of the sky. Down below, on the cream-colored marble floor, people still glided silently by without ever looking up. But had they done so they now would have seen stars shining brightly in a sea-green sky.

Hardesty hit the streets in an hypnotic fury that barely distinguished him from the thousands already there. Of all the places in the world, New York was the one where it was easiest to get your blood up. All you had to do was step out on the street, and immediately you were ready to pit two short human legs against the Belmont ponies. Hardesty knew that on the avenues and thoroughfares the surf was always in a gale. His plan was to agitate himself until he discovered some random secret by which he could then save the life of his daughter. Though there was neither much time nor much chance, he sought voraciously that which Peter Lake had never been able to avoid. He was willing to risk everything, and he didn't even know exactly what he was looking for.

His first desire was to fight, and there was plenty of opportunity for that, as the streets were filled with armed and desperate men who had been trained since childhood to rob and kill. That they, too, had no fear, and sought violence the way bees crave pollen, did not bother him.

"What are you out for?" he was asked by two men who blocked his way late that night on Eighty-seventh Street.

"I beg your pardon?" Hardesty asked in return, smiling in what they took to be appeasement. It was, rather, pleasure.

"I mean, what are you doing in this neighborhood? Answer it straight!" one of them said, stepping forward aggressively.

"I live here," Hardesty said with perfect calm.

"Where!" they screamed, one after another, in a manner calculated to terrorize him.

"On Eighty-fourth."

"That's not this neighborhood, man. I asked you what you're doing *here*," the bigger one demanded, pointing a finger at the ground as he worked himself up into a rage.

"You don't think very big, do you," Hardesty asked rhetorically. They were amazed. "That's because you're pinheads. But I have a friendly feeling for pinheads, and I'm going to tell you exactly what I'm doing here. I'm here because it's gambling time, pinheads. I went home to get some cash, which I have in my left coat pocket. There's so much of it that I have to keep it in one of those thick document envelopes. It won't go into my wallet. The wad's too fat. Now, just to make sure you two pinheads understand what I'm talking about, I'm talking about money, thirty thousand dollars, and an extra five or ten thousand in the wallet." Hardesty actually had less than eight dollars on him, and he didn't move an inch.

His assailants blinked, and started to back away. "Just leave us alone," they said, but Hardesty came after them, his eyes narrowed with fight.

"What's the matter? Aren't you going to rob me? Are you afraid?" he screamed. They began to run, and he ran after them. He chased them for ten blocks, screaming at the top of his lungs. When they jumped over the wall into the park, he followed, racing across the moonlit snow.

The beads of sweat on their faces made them look as if they were studded with tiny dazzling moons. They turned to fire their pistols, but this made him run faster, still screaming. Then they threw their guns on the ground and ran for their lives, finally managing to disappear in the thick underbrush near the north pump house. In a mad double time, Hardesty walked out of the park and into the West

Side. It was one o'clock in the morning. The city was just waking up. He figured that he would start on Broadway and rake its spine.

His first stop was a pool hall in the Eighties, a place where everyone's every gesture was calculated to convey the smoothness and certainty demanded by the game. The idea was to make others think that you were a great pool player who was trying to hide it. The real sharps had no need for any kind of pose, because those from whom they extracted their living were too busy cultivating an image to notice anything else, or, for that matter, to shoot good pool. It was de rigueur for each player to have something to wiggle in his teeth—a cigar, cigarette, pipe, or toothpick—to accompany his use of the pool cue the way a dagger complements a sword. The studied motions of the pool players, who walked about the tables making decisions of angle and force, were appropriately geometric.

Hardesty, who arrived with not much more than wild eyes, threw off his coat, paid a five-dollar entry fee, and asked for the best man in the house. This quieted the players en masse, and they stood motionless as Hardesty was led through a grid of brightly lit tables to the corner of the room where the top shooter held court. Usually, such professionals were very fat or physically unimposing. They tended to look like burnt-out cases from West Bend who were obsessed with truck-stop waitresses. They tiptoed around the table like mushrooms on wheels, and were seldom flamboyant. The flamboyant players were the fakes who wanted to scare off big bets because they didn't dare take them.

The top player here, however, was not only flamboyant, he was a huge rail-splitter type at least six and a half feet tall, dressed in a tuxedo and a fancy shirt with small diamond studs. His was the kind of face which, when attached to a large frame, made even a man like Hardesty (who was no midget himself) feel like something the size of a navy bean. This fellow had vast waves of swept-back blond hair which, along with his forward-looking bone structure and wildly confident expression, made him look like a wing walker straining into a three-hundred-mile-an-hour wind. He and his entourage were delighted to see Hardesty.

Hardesty's tortoise-shell glasses and Brooks Brothers suit (he could not afford Fippo's) indicated to them that he was a man of some responsibility, honesty, and means. They didn't know if he could shoot pool, and they didn't care. "I don't care how good you are, and how good you're not," said Wing Walker. "I have ten thousand dollars, and I'll play for any sum up to that and over a thousand."

"Make it ten."

"Have you got it with you?"

"No, I have only two dollars and change. But I'll give you identification and a marker."

"Would you like to play eight-ball, tortoise, or planetarium?"

"Tortoise sounds fine," Hardesty answered. "But you'll have to explain the rules."

"Now wait a minute," Wing Walker said, sensing trouble.

"Don't worry," Hardesty assured him. "If I lose, I'll pay." Then, almost under his breath, he said, "I intend to win."

"Then how come I have to explain the game?"

"Look," Hardesty said as he chalked his cue, "I don't play pool. The last time I did was in college, and that was a long time ago. I wasn't very good then, and I haven't played since." He looked up. "I'm going to beat you."

"How do you propose to do that?" Wing Walker asked. "I never fall for a bluff. So you better not have a bluff in mind."

"I never bluff," Hardesty declared. "Let's play."

Wing Walker smiled. "I know you," he said. "I've met guys like you before. You're in love with the impossible."

"For the moment, yes."

"What for?" Wing Walker asked, with some sympathy, as he took off his jacket and prepared to beat Hardesty and take his $10,000.

What Hardesty said made Wing Walker slightly nervous: "To bring back the dead." But Hardesty was not interested in the effect, only in the shining green felt of the newest table in the house.

After Wing Walker explained the rules of tortoise, they shot to see who would break. The professional's ball returned to within an inch of the cushion. Hardesty prepared to shoot, and this is how he did it.

First, he remembered what he was doing and why he was doing it. It was for Abby. It was to learn the feel of the impossible, so that he might know what to do when the time came when no one ever knows what to do. It was an act of defiance, dangerous not because of the money at stake but, rather, because it was a rebellion against omnipotence. But love moved him, and he trusted that he would do well in his attempt to travel through a succession of gates that seldom had been opened. To do so, he had to concentrate.

And concentrate he did. He drove from his mind the way angels were flung from heaven all thoughts or desires unrelated to the table in front of him. He did not see or hear the spectators, his opponent, or anything living or dead beyond the green felt. He did not think of winning, or losing, of Wing Walker's flowing hair and diamond-studded shirt, of the time of night, or where he was, or the nature of his gamble. He thought only of one thing—the geometries before him. Here was God speaking in His simple absolute language, according to the same grammar that He had used to start the planets on their smooth and silken dance. With purity and concentration, Hardesty would force his imperfect eye to make the proper movements, and sense the truth of distances. He would will that each cell and each fiber of every muscle do as it was bid, to impart to the cue the necessary force and correct guidance to impact upon the cue ball an impulse that would allow it, in turn, to serve a higher will without subsequent degradation.

They watched him prepare, and felt heat coming from him as if there were a fire in the middle of the room. They saw that he was tense as steel, and they knew that Wing Walker was in for a hard time. A hundred and fifty spectators had crowded around to see this, many of them doing the unheard-of in a pool hall—standing on the tables. But Hardesty was aware of nothing save absolute physics. The bright lamps above the table shone like double suns, and blackness reigned everywhere but on the green floor of the universe.

He mastered his sweating hands and positioned the cue. With a deep infatuation for the true and exact force that would bring the ball close to the cushion, he struck. His eyes followed it as it rolled smoothly to the end of the table. Its crash against the far side was as shocking as the collision of two express trains. Then it rolled back, with a telltale smooth deceleration that elevated the murmuring of the spectators. Slowly, slowly, it rolled past Wing Walker's ball, nudged itself silently against the cushion, and stopped. Cheers went up. They loved it. But Hardesty didn't hear, for he was preparing to break. Neither did he see Wing Walker, whose expression indicated that he, too, was conjuring up all he had. The game was being played for $10,000, but there was something far more valuable at stake—the idea of certainty itself.

Two hundred spectators were now ringed around the corner table, and their money was changing hands so fast that it made them look like an academy of lettuce handlers. As he studied the rack of pool balls, Hardesty felt himself slightly derailing, but he was calm enough to note that the bettors standing on tables and chairs were like the spectators at a cockfight. This in turn led him to see the triangle of multicolored balls as a formation of freshly painted Easter eggs. Further associations would endanger his concentration, so instead of following or denying them he bent them into a curved needle which he then aimed at the heart of the matter. Here were the planets, suddenly disordered, herded together on a single orbital plane under two suns. It was his task to set things aright, to clear the savannah of the perfect spheres. But how was he going to do this? It was one thing to return the cue ball close to the cushion, but the variables here were overwhelming. Wing Walker's lifetime of experience and his wide-apart angle-judging eyes were not to be duplicated merely by intense resolution. Hardesty again felt himself derailing, and his hands were sweating so much that every few seconds he had to dry them on his thighs.

The more nervous he appeared, the more the betting went against him. While Wing Walker began to breathe easy, Hardesty trembled and felt incipient tears. To hide them, he stared at the bright suns over the table. Their rays diffracted in the water of his eyes, and made rainbows, roads, and square beams of light that guillotined the room like a thistle of crystalline broadswords. This diamond-shattering, thundering light took him back to the cathedral in North Beach, where a line from Dante inscribed across its front had always served him well in times of difficulty. Often, he had stood in the park, facing the cathedral, and read it with great satisfaction:

La gloria di colui, che tutto muove,
per l'universo penetra e risplende

He had always believed that ultimate justice would be brought about by the light (though he had not considered that the reverse might, in fact, be more likely and more splendid).

"Shut up!" he commanded the rowdy onlookers, for what he had to do demanded primeval silence. He was going to remember what his father had taught him, and apply the laws of celestial mechanics to set straight the dazzling but disordered model of the solar system that was in front of him. It was not an easy task. He had to calculate all possible effects of velocity, acceleration, momentum, force, reaction, static equilibrium, angular momentum, friction, elasticity, orbital stability, centrifugal force, conservation of energy, and vectoring as they would apply to the sixteen spheres, the waiting pockets, the mechanical qualities of the cushion, the coefficient of drag of the felt, and the exact force and import of the big bang from the cue. This he had to do without the benefit of precise measurement, and in a relatively short time. He consoled himself by thinking that since all forms of measurement were relatively inaccurate, and never as perfect as the theory that had spawned them, he would be able to get by with eyes and instinct. He worked at the calculations, doing the mathematics in a way that made the spectators rather nervous. He had to contrive so many sets of figures and then abandon them for later recall that, even in his heightened state, it was difficult to work the numbers and remember them at the same time. He solved this problem by changing the spectators into an abacus for his memory. By associating their faces and dress with his vectors and coefficients and the figures by which they were expressed, he was able to store a prodigious amount of information. He broke up each man into anatomical shelves, assigning various sums and angles to kneecaps, feet, head, neck, etc. This made categorical comparisons far easier.

But to do this successfully he had to prevent them from moving.

Had they changed positions, his equations would all have gone to hell. "Don't move!" he commanded. They and Wing Walker thought this was strange. But it was nothing compared to what he then did, which was to walk about and stare at the onlookers, talking to himself under his breath at high speed, pointing, lifting invisible burdens (his numbers) with his fingers and moving them from one man to another. And if they did not heed his commands he barked at them ferociously, calling them by the function he had made them represent. "Shut up, Sigma!" he yelled at a little fat man in a Hawaiian shirt. "Cosine! Damn it! Stay put!" he screamed, pointing at a tall black in a leather jacket. Dripping sweat from all the rapid-fire thinking, he found that he was going faster than his lips could move, so he began to sing the calculations in a strange, unearthly song. After five minutes, he was finished, and he was nearly dead from exhaustion. He had calculated the exact aiming point on the rack, the point of departure for the cue ball, the aiming point for the cue, its coordinates of approach, and the force necessary to do the job.

"All right," he said, waving his hand at those who, with open mouths, had been unwittingly holding his numbers for him, "erase." He had it now. There were only a few things to remember, and he had fixed most of them visually.

"I'm going to break," he announced. "The one ball goes to the left side pocket; I'll put the three, five, and fourteen balls in the far left corner pocket; the two, four, sixteen, and seven balls in the near right corner; the six and ten balls in the right side pocket; the nine, eleven, and twelve balls in the near left corner pocket; the thirteen and fifteen balls in the near right pocket; and then, lastly, the eight in the far right corner.

"That is," he added, clearing his throat, "if all goes according to plan." He nervously chalked his cue.

"Aren't you going to give me a chance to shoot?" Wing Walker asked sarcastically.

"No," Hardesty answered, and took his stance.

He had to impart a great deal of force to the cue ball, for not only had all the numbered balls to find their pockets, but some had to do a lot of bouncing and traveling around before they actually fell in, while others were slated to give encouraging bumps to their more reluctant confreres. And yet the force could not be greater than that which would make the balls jump the sides of the table. Needless to say, Hardesty placed the cue ball very carefully. He lined himself up, got his cue into position, drew his arm back, and shot.

As the rack exploded, Hardesty turned to Wing Walker and said, "This is going to take some time." He was perfectly relaxed, and looked on approvingly as the balls began to leap into the pockets. About four or five dived in immediately. The others, however, seemed intent on presenting a tattoo, and they careered about the table, missing one another, sometimes colliding, and sometimes even stopping. But, certainly enough, when they stopped, they would receive a glancing blow from a speedy cousin, and slink off in shame to the mouth of a nearby cave. As Hardesty had predicted, it took some time, until, finally, the eight ball, after a long drive in the country, rolled in at a businesslike pace and slapped itself into the right corner pocket.

No one dared move or speak—except Wing Walker, who, with a packet of bills in his hand, bravely approached Hardesty. Wing Walker's big face was half twitching in puzzlement and shyness.

"I don't want the money," Hardesty said, already lost in consideration of his next task. "I didn't do it for the money." He walked out.

They would have followed him, had they not been rooted in place. Eventually, they began to tremble and shake. And then they screamed and wailed like Holy Rollers to whom an angel has appeared. These men were very tough and very big, but their shrieks were shrill and squeaky. They didn't know what was happening to them, and people passing on the street looked up in wonder, imagining that they had stumbled on the climax of some great urban voodoo.

Hardesty was already half a mile south.

Early one morning, after several hungry days of terrible encounters and unspeakable physical tests, all of which brought nothing, Hardesty awoke in what appeared to be a Byzantine cathedral that had been converted into a gymnasium. With no memory of how he had come to be there, he knew only that he had exited from a cold and uncomfortable sleep, and found himself lying on an exercise mat. He went through a long hallway to a deserted lobby where he discovered that he was in a health club on Wall Street. He had it all to himself. From investigation of the time clock, he determined that the first employee punched in at ten.

Just as the clock struck six, the heat began to come up. Little whistles and plumes and the strange briny smell of radiator steam vied for attention with the knocking pipes. In the big room where he had awakened, the light from the rising sun hit a high bank of frosted windows and exploded in fumes of white and yellow that colored the ropes and balance beams, warming the hemp and the wood. Hardesty watched the sun track its course. Nearly drained, he could think of nothing, and had so little strength that he ignored the beckoning gymnastic equipment.

Had it been a few days earlier, he would have tried to make an iron cross on the rings, or fly gravityless on the high bar, to see what he could see about such things. But now it was difficult for him even to raise his head to look at the sun in the windows at the top of the Byzantine dome.

The clear morning light had been bent by the circle of windows until it made a perfectly round golden platform that dazzlingly plugged the dome. Hardesty rose to his feet. The climbing rope which fell from the center of the cupola now seemed to lead to the first platform of heaven. Even the rope itself sparkled like a thick golden braid.

A hundred feet above, the golden disc had thickened. It seemed solid, and he wanted to get to it. But he could hardly stand, much less climb, and there were cuts on his hands, as if he had been hauling steel cables. From the way the sun was moving, pumping gold into the platform until it seemed that the dome would no longer be able to hold the weight, he could see that, as it had been given, it would be taken away. He began to climb.

In climbing, he found the compound mortal agonies that he had sought, and as he moved higher on the golden rope he really did rise. The rope itself ran scarlet as his blood poured from him like

582

hot water escaping from a breached pipe. Though the braid below him was now as red as it was gold, he pulled himself upward without cease, thinking only that if he could reach the platform he would need neither blood nor strength. His palms were rubbed away, and the grip on the rope became so slick that he had to clamp it with his bones. In agony and delirium, he saw whitened hands and dry bones leading him up and pulling him on. Halfway up, his hands became mechanical things with a life of their own. As he rose, he seemed to be hauling more and more weight. What fish, he wondered, are in this net that it seems so massive and unyielding?

Almost at the top, the rope burst into gentle flames that wound around it in a soft helix. He moved his left hand into its base. It was hot, but it didn't burn, and as he climbed into the flames, the blood on his clothes vanished and his hands began to heal.

The platform just above was almost too bright to be seen. Beyond, the windows were ablaze in white and silver frost. He saw engraved upon them an infinity of precisely etched forms. Winglike chevrons seemed to be moving into the sun like flights of black angels. Deep inside the thicket of feathery etchings were gleaming landscapes, and in every pane of glass the engraved rime led to worlds within worlds. The deeper they went, in long tunnels to the vanishing point, the wider they opened up and the more they seemed to hold eternal battles, fields that burned as aerial forces fought above them, and round suns that bled in pinpoint gilding dashed about in waves of blue. The sun tractored across the forest of lines in the glass, cutting them into bundles that flowed like handfuls of broken wheat.

Hardesty Marratta tried to poke his head through the golden disc. He was immediately pushed back. He grabbed the rope and viciously hiked himself up, but was slapped down with equal ferocity. Finally, he tried for all he was worth, rising like a high-powered shell, to attempt to get through the impenetrable mat above his head. He was swatted like a fly.

He fell backward, arms spread, fingers outstretched, through a hundred feet of empty air below him. It would have done no good even had he been able to turn, like a cat, and land the way he wanted. A hundred feet were a hundred feet, best taken however they would be delivered. But as he fell, he realized that he was coursing from left to right, swaying in pendulum arcs, and dropping only slowly. The air around him beat with a thousand unseen wings which damped his fall and set him down so gently that, for a moment or two, he hovered above the mat.

Hardesty opened his eyes. Several men in gymnasium clothes had him by the arms.

"Are you one of us?" they asked.

"What are you?" Hardesty returned. Then he looked at their expressions. "You must be bankers and brokers."

"Are you a member here?"

"It's all in your numbers," Hardesty said, "if only you would read them in the right way."

"He must have come in from the street," one of the men said. "I thought for a moment he was a member who had had an accident."

"I floated like a butterfly," Hardesty declared as they picked him up and carried him out in a sort of invisible sedan chair. "When I rose into the flame and fell back, I thought I was going to hit the floor. But I floated like a butterfly."

As he was carried past the clock in the lobby, he saw that it said eleven. With the mixed reverence and disdain that people have for lunatics, they set him down on the street.

"One more thing," he said.

"What's that," one of them answered as they were going up the steps.

"Your gymnasium was packed with angels."

They didn't hear.

In the December cold, without a cent in his pockets, and not having eaten for days, Hardesty began to walk the length of Manhattan. He had failed Abby, and, in failing her, he had also failed his father. The pride that had allowed him to think that he would have the strength for a raid on heaven now filled him with nausea and fear.

As he passed people rushing by the scores of thousands on the streets, he saw the glory of their faces. He saw in the way their eyes were set—in their reddened cheeks, and in their expressions of hope, determination, or anger—whatever it was that made them more than skeletons and flesh, for the life in their faces far transcended the material into which it had strayed. And yet if he were to grasp for it, all he would have would be the lapels of a coat and a startled and fearful pedestrian inside. Though the light he sought was shining all around, he could not capture it.

He might think of the small coffin (like a salesman's sample) in which his daughter would have to be buried. But then the life of the streets and the glory of people's faces would rush into his blood, and he would believe once more that he would be able to keep her alive, if only he could understand the force behind the city's many vital scenes: the harried expression of a hooded boy pushing a garment rack through snow-filled streets; a tailor in the fur district bent over his machine, stitching forward into the eternity of tailors; a squad of street breakers machine-gunning the concrete with the concentration of working infantry—something there was that knitted all these scenes together and pushed them on a forward course. The empty corridors and rising shapes held the secret, which rested invisibly upon the city, like a column of clear air. And yet when he clenched his fist around it and wanted to wrestle it down, it wasn't there. Thoroughly beaten, he was swept up in the crowds. He was weak and dizzy, and the human tides on the streets just before Christmas proved impossible to resist.

Like a chip in a flume, he ebbed back and forth on the avenues. He was carried into huge department stores and drained out. He fell with the stream down the steps of the subway, and rode a stop or two before he was lifted once again onto the street. And he found himself stuck in an intersection as if it were a whirlpool. Crossing and recrossing a hundred times, limp, feverish, and defeated, he was taken completely at random by millions of people who were galloping about as if their lives depended upon it.

When the offices let out at five, a torrent of gabardine and wool flooded the streets in blue and gray. Everyone was running. In some places, the waves of clerks and typists were three or four layers deep. It sounded like water, or a grass fire pushed by the wind, and at five-fifteen the streets of midtown Manhattan were like the aisles of a burning theater.

Finally, in a convergence that looked like the Niagara River pouring into Horseshoe Falls, a stupendous mass of frenzied overcoats and taut faces fell into Grand Central Terminal, drawing Hardesty with it. He was lucky to be on the edge of the flow, and he managed to maneuver himself to safety on a balcony overlooking the main floor. Here, primarily because of an overwhelming dread of traveling to Hartsdale on the five-twenty, he held fast to a marble balustrade. Clamping himself to the rail, he rested for an hour, until the tide receded and he was warm.

Except for a stream of commuters still moving between the doors and the staircase that led down to the main floor, the Vanderbilt Avenue balcony was nearly deserted, and the vast concourse began to show bald spots of caramel-colored marble where empty islets had formed in a carpet loomed with the thread of all the comings and goings since 1912. No one ever looked up. The ceiling had been dark and cloudy for so long that it had been forgotten. Though for most people the barrel vault was too high to bother with, Hardesty slowly tilted his head until, as he leaned back, he was able to see it in its entirety.

The stars were on. They shone in incandescent yellow from deep in the green. Since when? They were supposed to have been extinguished forever. It was believed that they had burnt out one by one and would never light again, and that they had been placed too high to be reached or changed. No one tried, and eventually the stars were forgotten and denied. But now they were lit. And not one was missing.

"Look," Hardesty commanded a young woman in the uniform of a dental assistant, "the stars are lit."

"What stars?" she asked, without looking up at them, and ran toward the tunnels to catch her habitual train.

"Those stars," Hardesty said to himself, staring at the green sky.

As his eyes traversed the high vault, he saw something move in the center. It seemed as if, in an earthquake of the heavens, a piece

586

of the sky had been jolted out of place. He thought it had to be an optical illusion. But a crack appeared. Then it vanished, but it appeared for a second time, and oscillated, as if someone were struggling with a heavy door. Suddenly a patch of green sky was pulled back, and a dark square appeared in the ceiling. Hardesty found it difficult to breathe. The door could not have opened by itself.

Though no one was visible, Hardesty waited patiently for someone to appear, and his patience was rewarded when, high above, a face emerged from the shadows to stare down at the rushing armies clothed in gabardine and wool.

FOR THE SOLDIERS AND SAILORS OF CHELSEA

IN old age, moments of great energy and lucidity are like wet islands in a dry sea, and in powerful rages and sudden joys an old man with a cane may discover that his many years have added nothing to his innocence but proof and explanation, and that, as much as he may have learned in his long life, he cannot see as far as he could see when he was seven. Harry Penn was often subject to such moments, during which he was electrified to find that he was learning what he had at one time known before he paid the price of finding out.

He had grown up with the millennium in his eyes, and now he wanted Jackson Mead's bridge to go as far and high as could be imagined, and beyond, speeding like a lance through the cloud wall. For this to happen, he knew, conditions on the ground had to be improbably perfect. No human agency could see to the many alignments, lock up the unraveled stitches, or bring about the complete and resounding justice that would be required: and yet everything had to be in place and everyone would have to move briskly on the lighted stage exactly according to his part. Harry Penn believed that he had not yet completed the task of his life, and this saddened him. It wasn't enough just to grow old. He wanted miracles. He wanted life where there was no life, the negation of time, and the gliding of the universe—if only for one truly wonderful moment. He wanted to see the huge whitened plumes, like those ceremonial plumes on carriage horses, which his father had promised him would rise above the city in announcement of the golden age.

So he romanced his books and encyclopedias, to no avail, remembered as much as he could of what he had seen, and kept alert to the architecture of the spirit as it suffered its periodic and allegorical devastations and restorations. He often filled the huge slate tub with water and jumped in just to let his thoughts float free, but they never floated free enough to prepare him for the millennium that was fast approaching.

One evening, Jessica's performance was canceled because of unusually bitter cold. From all over Manhattan, as materials contracted in the low temperatures, came the sound of snapping cables and cracking masonry—local whippings that were winter's answers to the lightning. As the small thundercracks reverberated, Jessica rode in a sleigh from the theater to her father's house, where she cooked some lamb and peas, and they had dinner in front of the fire. Though Praeger was expected later on, they were alone. Christiana was with Asbury, and Boonya had gone to see her sister who lived in Malto Downs.

After Jessica had cleared the table and washed the dishes, she came back with two mugs of black tea and a tin of shortbread cookies upon which was a picture of a Highland Fusilier in a Black Watch kilt. Strong tea was good for Harry Penn's imagination. As the fire burned, its resinous pine and bone-dry hickory became a

Waterloo of advancing red lines and tiny gunshots. Harry Penn was still bedeviled. The tea and the fire stoked him up.

"What happens," he asked Jessica, "when you forget your lines?"

"I don't."

"Never?"

"Very rarely. Almost never. Because, you see, in portraying the character I play, I learn the lines to become the character, not the other way around. Once I become her, I can't forget the lines. It's unthinkable."

"Do you mean that learning lines for the stage has very little to do with memory?"

"Exactly. Only bad actors memorize lines. Good actors are perpetually writing them as they act."

"Even though the playwright has already written them."

She nodded her head.

"Isn't that presumption?"

"The playwright understands."

"You go into sort of a trance, then."

"Yes."

"The play has been put down, but it is still new to you. When you say the lines, you are saying them for the first time. They are as much yours as they are his. How can you explain that?"

"I can't, but I *can* tell you that this is the quality that distinguishes the good actors from the bad."

"Now, let's say," Harry Penn said, staring at the top of the tin box, "that you were out of sorts, and at the end of a long and complicated play you did forget your lines. What would you do?"

"I probably wouldn't have time to think it out, and I would say whatever occurred to me. The other lines would have been a gift, and I'd take the lines I'd improvise as a gift, too, though perhaps a gift from a different source."

There was a loud rapping on the door. "That's Praeger," announced Harry Penn.

"The mayor," Jessica said proudly.

"It doesn't make the slightest bit of difference," Harry Penn declared. "He's a fine fellow. Open the door for him before he freezes to death. Some years before I was born, you know, the Cranberry Mayor froze to death in Newtown Creek.''

When Jessica brought Praeger into her father's study, they saw Harry Penn standing in front of the fireplace, the lid of the cookie tin in his hand. He was crying.

"What is it?" Jessica asked.

"The Highland Fusilier," he said. "These boxes have been around for years, and I've never looked closely at his face. Now I see."

"See what?" Praeger asked.

"Do you remember the derelict at Petipas?"

"Yes."

"This was his face, more or less, if he had been shaven and clean."

Praeger looked at the box. "It's not clear to me," he said. "I don't remember well enough."

"That's because you hadn't ever seen him before."

"You had?"

"Yes."

"When?"

"When I was a boy." He put the Fusilier on the mantle, and stepped back. Turning to Praeger, the mayor of the city, Harry Penn commanded him to go to the stable and hitch the three best horses to the fastest sleigh. "I want you to drive me north."

"To the Coheeries?" Jessica asked.

"Yes," her father said, smiling. "I have, at long last, found my place in this world."

Praeger went outside. As the stable light flicked on across the courtyard, Harry Penn turned to his daughter and told her that a miracle had happened, and just in time.

"What miracle?" she asked.

"Peter Lake," was the answer.

Harry Penn was the only man in New York who could command the mayor to hitch up his sleigh, but he didn't think twice about it, since Praeger had worked for him and been his virtual son-in-law for more than ten years. Apart from that, a sound man of a hundred is entitled to the highest conventions of protocol, and need not defer to presidents or kings, because presidents and kings have come so high that, if they have any stuff, they think only of history, and a hundred-year-old man *is* history.

The three horses that Praeger harnessed to the racing sleigh were aching to run, and almost before they knew it they were on Riverside Drive, flying to the north.

"Go down and get onto the river at One Hundred and Twenty-fifth Street," Harry Penn directed the mayor.

"Will it be entirely frozen at Spuyten Duyvil?" Praeger asked apprehensively. "The whirlpools themselves never freeze, and then there's the navigation channel."

"Sure it'll be frozen. In a winter like this," Harry Penn stated, looking ahead, "there's always a strong ice bridge in between Spuyten Duyvil and the channel. It curves slightly to the west and then bends east again, and it rises a little, almost like a section of prairie. After that, there'll be empty ice all the way to the turn-off. We can go like hell."

Praeger gave the reins an enormous snap, and the troika turned left and descended toward the river. "How do you know that?"

"I've been making this trip for nearly a hundred years. If you know only a dozen winters, it looks completely chaotic. But after a hundred you begin to see where certain patterns surface and intersect. I always know the weather. That's easy. And I know the ice. That's easy, too."

"What about human relations?"

"Do you have a problem?"

"No, just curious."

There was a silence. "Not so easy, but possible."

"What about history?"

"History is very difficult. A nearly infinite number of waves interact within an infinite number of conjunctions. As you might suspect, there has been of late a tendency for strong alignment, and many different waves are running together, in phase. I don't see, however, that they can be aligned by the year two thousand, which is only two weeks away, unless by some catastrophic event."

"And then what?" asked Praeger, for he, too, had his ideas

592

about these things, and had imagined the city spinning head over heels in a heart-filling, noiseless, fall without end.

"Then we will see," Harry Penn replied.

The sleigh hit the ice hard enough to crack it for half a mile. With clear running after Spuyten Duyvil, the troika sailed north so fast that watchmen in the towns along the river noted in their logs that something dark had passed along the ice and disappeared before it could be identified. Praeger didn't know that the towns of the hills, like lanterns on the cliffs, were in a different time. And Harry Penn didn't tell him, because, when the immediate future promised to be so decisive, he didn't want Praeger to be seduced by the wonder of a living past. They passed the towns and left the golden lantern light behind, rising north into the mountains that led to the Lake of the Coheeries.

They arrived at the lake on the evening of the next day. They were exhausted, and their throats were sore. Unlike the villages on the banks of the Hudson, those on the shores of the lake, including Lake of the Coheeries Town, were dark. Harry Penn stood up in the sleigh, looking up and down the shoreline. "They've never been dark," he said. "Something's wrong."

The road across the plateau that led to Lake of the Coheeries Town had not been traveled since the last snow. The village itself appeared in silhouette, totally dark, against the huge curtain of sky and stars behind it. They went in slowly, bumping over what they thought was a log in the middle of the street. But it wasn't a log, it was Daythril Moobcot.

Bodies were all over. They were splayed from doorways, and they were bent and frozen over fences, like game drying in the sun. Rifles and shotguns lay next to the dead. There seemed to have been a terrible battle, and the streets were full of furniture and small objects that were evidence of the evisceration and looting of the buildings. The open doors of the houses swung back and forth in terror on the ebb and flow of the wind, or banged shut like pistol shots.

"I almost knew," Harry Penn told Praeger. "But I didn't think it would really happen." Praeger was speechless. "But if it had to happen, then so be it. They're dead. It's over now. And it means that a hundred epochs have finally come to their end. Drive that way."

They went past the gazebo and onto the lake, not so slowly now, heading for the Penn house on an island lost amid the islands and promontories of the opposite shore. "A bit left," Harry Penn would say, his voice shaking, or, "A degree right," to guide them. Maneuvering around pine-rich rocky islands in places that had long ago been left to the loons, they came upon a huge house looming suddenly at the end of a smooth white turn. It was intact.

"At least this place was hidden," Praeger said.

"That hardly matters, as you'll see. They wouldn't have taken the one important thing, and as for damage, well, damage will soon be of little moment."

First they went to the barn, where Harry Penn spilled a whole sack of oats onto the floor in front of the horses. He was extremely agitated, almost as if the battle in the town, long over, was still taking place. "Bring those," he ordered Praeger, pointing to two or three brooms that had been discarded because their straw was clotted with pitch.

After struggling through thigh-deep snow on the island, they reached the porch, a huge gallery more than a hundred feet long and twenty-five feet deep. The front door was its usual solid self.

"How would you get in?" Harry Penn asked, nodding at the door.

"With a key," Praeger answered.

Harry Penn laughed. "Look at the keyhole. It's solid, just a trompe l'oeil. My father was obsessed with burglars, and he played games with them. In those days, burglary was a more respectable profession than it is today. It was sort of like chess. My father spent a lot of time and money outwitting thieves. I suppose a modern burglar would just smash in one of the windows, but, then, there was a certain etiquette. Look." He put both hands on the doorknob and moved it like a gearshift, in a ten-part code, at the end of which the door was pulled open automatically by counterweights.

Praeger was delighted. "Do you like it?" Harry Penn asked. "I'm glad you saw it, because this is the last time that this particular piece of machinery will ever be worked.'' He disappeared into the dark house, and Praeger followed.

Harry Penn took out a cigar lighter and passed its pencil-shaped flame across the broomheads. They erupted into huge yellow fires. Praeger commented that it was lucky that the ceilings were so high. Otherwise, he added, they would be likely to ignite. Harry Penn said nothing, and led the mayor of New York through the enormous ice-cold rooms.

With torches blazing, they stopped here and there, and lifted the fire into the air to illuminate paintings that stared down at them from the walls in immeasurable sadness. Though the portraits had been mostly of happy or contented faces, years and years of silence and stillness had given those who were portrayed the hurt expressions of abandoned ghosts. They seemed to resent that they had been forgotten, and were perhaps horrified that the wizened old man now walking among them with a torch had been at one time a young child in whom they had placed their hope. Emerging from the darkness for a second or two, the portraits seemed bitter and angry that they had been condemned to stillness forever and ever, and that, despite their sacrifice and concern for future generations, their house had been abandoned to the wind and night.

''These are the Penns,'' the old man said. ''I could tell you the name of each one, and a lot more than that, too, because they were people I loved. They're all gone now. But even they may be surprised—when they awaken.''

''Awaken?''

''Yes. I believe there is a distinct possibility of that, and I'll tell you why. There is an island in the middle of the lake where we are all buried, or will be. My sister, who died before the first great war, was put there. But she's not there now. She left rather quickly, it seems. And the explanation was that her grave was destroyed by a meteorite. Meteorite! No one seemed to care for the fact that meteors fall *to* earth, not *from* it.

''That the grave was completely obliterated, gone, fit her epitaph, which was: 'Gone into the world of light.' I can't explain it, but I do believe that she did what she said she was going to do.''

He stopped at an entrance to the cavernous living room, and

turned to Praeger. "She gave me instructions from her deathbed. I didn't understand them at the time. I thought she was delirious. She said to carry them out when I next saw Peter Lake, who was there with us. He left right after she died, and though we expected him to return at any moment, he never did, and I never saw him again—until Petipas."

"How can you be sure?"

"I can't."

"Who was he anyway?"

"I'll show you." Harry Penn then led him into the room. The shadows had a rhythm as they rose and fell, and Praeger could smell the slight dampness of the carpets and the covered furniture. The air began to fill with pitch smoke which obscured the ceiling and made it seem as if they were in a roofless cave or under a November sky. Harry Penn walked a few steps to the hearth, and held up his torch until two paintings, one above the fireplace, and another facing it, were brightly illuminated. "Beverly," he said. "My sister. And that was Peter Lake."

Though frail and weak, she was smiling and beautiful. He seemed puzzled and out of place. "Even by the time these portraits were painted," Harry Penn told Praeger, "he felt ill-at-ease with us. He thought that Beverly was too good for him, and that we didn't like him because of his origins, and because of what he did for a living."

"What did he do for a living?"

"He was a burglar," Harry Penn said. "And a good one, evidently. He had been a master mechanic, and had gotten himself into some kind of trouble. I was never told how or why.

"And now, a century later, he's somewhere in the city, and he hasn't aged a day. Look at the background: comets and stars. Look at their faces. These people are not dead. . . . I'm sure of it. Please take down the paintings for me."

As Praeger stepped back and lowered the paintings to the floor, he turned, and saw Harry Penn torching the curtains and the furniture.

"What are you doing?" Praeger screamed.

596

"Her instructions," Harry Penn answered, his voice itself ablaze.

"What about the paintings?"

"They would have burned too, but I need them. Come on. Carry them with you."

They walked quickly through the halls and the galleries, and Harry Penn brushed the walls and furnishings with his torch. By the time they reached the front door, the house was brighter than a clear summer afternoon. Flames roared on the inside, remaking the rooms into hollow orange chambers and blinding fireballs. Sawtoothed jets of flame roared up the stairs like a huge serpent that had come from the lake to search for the children. The house seemed to dance and turn, as if the fire were a fast play of all the events that had ever occurred inside, as if a hundred summers were burning under one lens, and a hundred winters were frozen stiff and brittle, and all the fires and dances and kisses and dreams that had once been within were liberated to turn about in pale hot whirl-winds and ignite the frail wood with their sudden rebellion. As if it were a rocket, the fire screamed upward and broke through the roof.

They put the paintings on the back of the sleigh. Praeger held the fretting horses while Harry Penn torched the barn. The entire green cove was gleaming as if in daylight. They made a turn around the house, and the horses started out in panic for the village across the lake. The wind stretched the flames of the torches like hair swept back from the brow, and sparks disappeared into the darkness. The horses whinnied as they rushed over the ice, because they didn't like the fire in such proximity, drawn closely after them on the sleigh, inescapable.

Both Harry Penn and Praeger burned the village. The houses caught quickly, and soon the streets were a grid of flame. "They're all dead," Harry Penn said as they left the town. "I wonder if the past can be sealed off as Beverly wanted, or if her expectations will be confounded."

They reached the top of the hill and turned the sleigh so they could look over the town and the lake. Across the ice, the Penn house was still burning steadily, and the village was alight like something that had been soaked in paraffin.

There was little to say. Now the moon had risen and was very bright. Harry Penn threw the torches down on the snow, and Praeger turned the horses away from the Lake of the Coheeries and toward the mountains.

Hardesty ran up the first flights of steps that led to the glass-enclosed galleries that led in turn, he presumed, to the back of the sky. As he rounded the landing at the beginning of the fourth flight, he was stopped suddenly by a blue plug of six policemen and a sergeant who completely blocked the way. They were drinking coffee from paper cups, and they dripped with guns and clubs. "Where are you going?" the sergeant asked belligerently.

"The six-twenty to Cos Cob!" Hardesty screamed, to put them off his scent, since their job was to keep people out of the galleries.

"That way," they said, and pointed. He ran down.

Back on the Vanderbilt balcony, he glanced up at the open space in the sky and saw that the same face continued to stare down tranquilly. He had to see who it was. If necessary, he would attack the police. If he could take them by surprise, he might kill or wound four of them immediately. He could overcome the two who remained with the application of his superior knowledge of assault tactics, and his willingness to take wounds. But to do this he would need at least two pistols, which meant that he would have to overcome at least two other policemen. It seemed unreasonable that eight men would have to die just so he could walk up some stairs. Perhaps he could bribe them. But where would he get the money? Even were he to rob fifty people, the chances were not very good that he could raise the several thousand dollars that he would need. But he had to get up there.

· The trapdoor closed, sealing the heavens.

"Damn it," he said to himself. Then he decided to go around the police. He went over the balcony rail, and started to climb on the marble wall that intersected with the glass curtain in front of the catwalks. Long before, patient artisans had carved wreaths, eggs, and dentils into this corner. The ledges and holds that they provided were just big enough for Hardesty's fingers. For contrary pressure, he had to push against the glass.

Daring to climb up, but not to look down, he moved rapidly and with no security, managing to cling to the wall primarily because of his upward momentum. Had he stopped, he would have fallen after a terrifying second or two of clawing at the marble like a cat. Nothing here carried him effortlessly, as on the golden rope. There were, however, contradictions and paradoxes in the physics, and although he himself hadn't time to consider them, his fingers, muscles, and heart knew them perfectly well. If he hadn't the force to stay on the wall without moving, how could he have the force to move up? Was the balance so delicate that the original power of his first step from the ground could be carried with him as high as he could go, as long as his attachment was equal to the force that pulled him down? In that case, why could he not cling to the eggs, wreaths, and dentils in a purely neutral stance? There was at least a tiny bit of magic in reckless faithful climbing, which abrogated the laws of conservation, perhaps eventually to restore them. But now, with the blessing, amnesty, and encouragement that good climbers requisition from the thin air, he ascended a nearly sheer column in the interior of Grand Central Terminal.

When at last he reached a sooty ledge far above the floor, he put his right hand over it and breathed in relief. Though hanging at many times a killing height (four fingers kept him safe enough for his thumb to be unengaged), he felt as secure from falling as if he had been strapped prone to the ground. After a short rest, he pulled himself onto the ledge.

The police were many stories below, and probably could not have imagined that someone had passed them by and was now almost as free as the swallows that were the masters of the airy upper levels. And even had the commuters looked up to see the stars (which they did not), they probably would not have seen the man running along a high unprotected ledge.

One of the lower panes of an arched window had been knocked out. Perhaps a bird had crashed into it, or it had been hit by a stray bullet. Hardesty crawled through the space and found himself in a dimly lit hall. The floor was covered with thick dust which showed a single set of tracks leading to a set of spiral stairs at the far end of the corridor. Seven turns on the iron stairs, and he was in a little vaulted room that looked like a chapel, facing a small metal door that had been locked from the other side.

Hardesty, who knew pitifully little about breaking and entering, began to throw himself against it. It gradually started to loosen.

Peter Lake had been reclining on his bed in the iron beams, reading a *Police Gazette* of November 1910. He was by now used to a good many strange things, and he had greeted not with wonder but with pleasure the images of sullen vandals and meditative crooks, all of whom he didn't know that he had known. As he turned the pages, he met again the likes of James Casey, Charles Mason, Dr. Long, and Joseph Lewis. Although they seemed familiar, he was not sure where he himself fit in. Why was he so moved by an old photograph of William Johnson, pickpocket? Was it because of his bowler hat and Edwardian suit, both of which (now vaporized, as, undoubtedly, was their owner) reminded him of a time in which neither nature nor man held sway, but had reached an accommodation allowing even the coarsest of men, by means of his culture and surroundings, to reflect upon his circumstances with remarkable results? How else could he explain their sad and knowing eyes? William Johnson (an alias, of course, one of a dozen), a pickpocket, showed in the sparkle of his eyes that he had seen through time and understood those who would come after him. When the dross of time had lifted, the pickpockets, confidence men, and thieves sometimes turned out to be the possessors of the gifted and magical faces that painters of the Renaissance used in portraying saints and angels.

Strangely moved by William Johnson's trusting and fatherly glance, Peter Lake was about to turn the page onto a large photograph . . . of himself, but was jolted from his comfortable bed by Hardesty Marratta ramming against the metal door. The *Police Gazette* flew out of his hands like a tossed chicken, and landed with the portrait of Peter Lake facedown in the dust. By pure coincidence, the expression of the burglar in the Rogues' Gallery and that of the steadily unperplexing master mechanic in the beams above the sky, were exactly the same.

He had been pulled in without a charge, just before a hit at Delmonico's, for which he had had to dress to the nines and twenties, and they had roughed him up because they knew that they would have to let him go. When they were ready to flash the pan, after he had adjusted his torn formal collar and remnants of bow tie and was posed and ready, he heard the screams of someone in a death agony coming from beyond the wall. Though Peter Lake had often been exposed to such things, he had never been completely hardened, and the photograph revealed a compassionate expression appropriate for a man trying to see through a wall on the other side of which one of his own was being murdered. He was alert, apprehensive, and yet sardonically cool, as if he were saying, "Well, if I'm next, I'm next. But don't count on it." This was exactly what he looked like while Hardesty Marratta, crazed and incorrigible, ran against the door again and again, like a goat who had lapped up a quart of strong tea.

Because Peter Lake had forgotten about the door that led outside to the roof, he thought there was no place to go. He froze at first, but then he threw the switch that controlled the stars. They stayed lit, because now they were on for good. Deprived of darkness, he still had the advantage of surprise. Perhaps, he thought, if I open the door as he charges, he'll knock himself out on that iron pillar. No, that won't work: whoever he is, he has a hard head. I'll let him wear himself down a little, and then play it by ear.

Peter Lake climbed up into the beams and lay partially hidden in shadow for half an hour while Hardesty continued to hammer at the door. Both Hardesty and the door were suffering greatly in a war of attrition in which the door would have won, had not its opponent been convinced that if he found his way to the other side he might begin to get to the root of things. The intervals between his charges grew larger and larger, the charges grew slower and weaker, and the door became more and more like a loose tooth pleasurably near the brink.

Finally, he burst through, ran a few feet inside, twirled, staggered, and collapsed. Peter Lake waited for others to follow. When none did, he dropped down, closed the door, and dragged Hardesty to the bed. Hardesty was badly bruised, and breathing in gasps.

Thinking to help him, Peter Lake took a tin that ninety years before had held a meal of New Zealand lamb stew, filled it with warm water, and splashed Hardesty's face.

Hardesty made drowning motions and opened his eyes.

"Why did you break in here?" Peter Lake asked.

"I saw you looking through the trapdoor. I wanted to find out who you were and how you got here."

"What caused you to look up? No one else ever does."

"I don't know. When I saw that the stars were on, I couldn't take my eyes from them."

"Didn't you have to catch a train?"

"No."

"How did you come up?" Peter Lake asked suspiciously. "Are you friends with the cops?"

"I climbed up the sides, along the wreathed eggs and the lousy little dentils."

Peter Lake looked skeptical. "That's hard to believe. What are you, a mountaineer?"

"In fact, yes," Hardesty answered. "I used to be. . . ."

He stopped himself in midsentence, drew back his throbbing face, and peered at Peter Lake. Peter Lake did the same (except that his face wasn't throbbing). They had recognized one another from Petipas. Their throats tightened, and they shuddered the way one does when one discovers or reconfirms higher and purposeful forces brazenly and unconvincingly masquerading as coincidence.

"Who are you?" Peter Lake asked.

Hardesty shook his head. "That doesn't matter," he said. "Who are *you?*"

Jackson Mead unleashed all the forces that he had been preparing and conserving, in a mad bone-shaking spectacle that would last for a full ten days until the beginning of the millennium, and would not cease even though the city would be consumed by fire and civil disorder occasioned by the rainbow bridge itself.

After centuries and centuries of building, he had learned exactly how it all had to be done. He believed in a law of equalities which ordained a perfect balance. For everything that was raised, something had to fall, and there was no free form, since all form had shadow and counterpart. Hence his opposition. He respected them and had no desire to win them over, for that would have implied that he believed they were fighting without reason. Their actions, too, were just, and he might well have been on their side. But he wasn't, for his task was to move things forward, and to do this he had to fight them. He was fond of saying that there had never been a builder who had not understood war.

He had prepared for nearly a century the actions that would take its last ten days by storm, with Cecil Mature and the Reverend Mootfowl his unlikely generals. Despite their personal oddities, they were perfectly suited for their responsibilities, and had been with him for countless years, ageless and unaging, possessed of extraordinary knowledge that they guilelessly concealed—not so as to deceive, but to satisfy their own temperaments.

The winter solstice brought to Sandy Hook an armada of huge ships whose mass alone calmed the seas. From their decks began an unprecedented transfer of machines and materials. Hundreds of heavy-lift helicopters, covered along their hundred-foot lengths with rows of flashing lights and penetrating blue beacons, roared through the sky, carrying beneath their crooked mantis-like bodies things of many times their weight and size.

The humming of these helicopters could be heard from miles away. As they got closer, they shook the ground and froze all living creatures with the paralyzing frequencies that bloomed from their mysterious engines. Their flashing lights and the wavelengths of their beacons were perfectly synchronized with the rhythmic sounds, in exceedingly complicated harmonies and counterpoints. They could turn on any axis, and hold any position. They were as delicate as butterflies and as big as the largest jets. Crossing paths in constant motion above the harbor and yet never colliding, they shuttled between the ships and the construction sites.

Enormous doors opened in the sides of Jackson Mead's ship in the Hudson. From the shore or on the ice, one could see that the vast interior was comprised of many levels that were lighted in different shades. Inside the ship were roads stacked ten or fifteen high, over which traveled speedy little vehicles rushing in several directions (at the head of multiple trailers or alone), coursing along the arteries, under urgently flashing lights. At intervals that were staggering in their precision and frequency, lifters emerged from this huge hangar and exited at great speed, turning in the air with a gust of wind that polished the ice and formed loose crystals and remnants of snow into expanding clouds half as high as skyscrapers.

Transparent towers twenty stories tall telescoped from the ship. Day and night, operations were directed from within them, in a subdued bronze-colored light that suggested yet another kind of perpetual daylight—not of March, but of August. The construction sites themselves threw off their shieldings, revealing half a hundred fortresslike redoubts of smooth concrete that rooted deep into the ground. Upon their upper surfaces were emplaced the many types of machinery lifted from the ships and from railroad trains that never reached the harbor, but were unloaded from the air, and then were themselves lifted off the track car by car and discarded so that other trains could follow and discharge their cargoes without cease.

Emplaced upon the foundations were blocklike substructures, big boxes, and the graceful girderworks that held their weight. The sky was filled with helicopters towing multi-colored engines, huge constructs of glassy silicon, round aggregations of fire trucked about like little suns, ancient and arcane contraptions resembling Priestley's giant burning glass or Herschel's telescope more than any modern thing, pulsing spirals of crystal that were the icy twins of the little suns, and limp networks of wire and circuitry that made the lifters look like jellyfish drifting through the air above the harbor.

As soon as the stunned populace thought it had regained its breath, some unheard-of exquisite assemblage would suddenly be lifted from one of the ships, the traffic would double, or the net of sounds would thicken. Jackson Mead's strategy was to make each hour more intense than the hour that had preceded it. The idea was to hold them off balance, shock them, disorient them, wade into their sensibilities, blind them with flashing lights, and hit harder and harder, so that the opposition might be incapacitated, and the bridge might take. For ultimately, despite the force and the planning, it was a delicate and fragile construction that depended upon circumstances for which Jackson Mead could only pray.

Virginia sat at the edge of Abby's bed, watching the fading light in a thick and gentle snowfall. The hour when the turning on of lights gave the evening hope and energy passed in serenity and silence. Since Abby was fed intravenously, no one at her bedside was able to anticipate even the ambivalent cheer of the hospital meals that came on ungainly platters that looked like huge nickels.

Hardesty had been away for more than a week. It was unlikely that in a thousand years of deliberate searching and suffering he could redeem his dying child, much less in a few days. Nothing he saw or imagined would save Abby. Children did die. At one time, not so long before, they had known death far more frequently than their elders. Though she could not explain it, Virginia was sure that she remembered a potter's field in which half a hundred tiny coffins lay in the falling snow, waiting to be interred, while the grave-diggers hurried to finish before nightfall. Since she had never seen such a sight, or anything vaguely like it, she wondered how it could have been so vividly emplaced in her memory, and she thought that perhaps in difficult times the past and the future were better able to emerge from the shadows. In the fixed gallery of infinite scenes, all events were always accessible. Nothing was lost, ever. The gravediggers in potter's field, hurrying to beat the dark, would hurry to beat the dark for eternity.

She dreamed an evening dream. A sudden thunderclap found her ankle-deep in freshly fallen snow as a dark carriage pulled by a dark horse flew by, its wheels four perfect studies in hypnosis. Not knowing where she was, she turned to see what was in back of her, and though ironwork, trees, and streetlamps were gray with snow, she slowly drifted into a summer scene in which she saw herself pushing a baby carriage by the side of a lake. It was in a park, and there were benches and a paved promenade next to the water. Trees across the lake were reflected on its surface, misty and indefinite: the city was full of dark forests. She bent over the rim of the carriage to see the baby, but the carriage was empty because the baby had been taken by the lake, and was somewhere under the water.

Then the summer afternoon turned to darkness, and she found herself in a dim hallway. Badly scuffed wainscoting gleamed in the half-light. The floor was covered with rubble. As her eyes adjusted to the dimness, she saw a child in an old-fashioned gown standing near the banister. Her hair had fallen out, her hand was in her mouth, and she shook with a kind of palsy. She was dying, she was entirely alone, and she was standing up. Virginia stretched out her arms to embrace her, but couldn't move because she was tied to the banister. She spoke in a choked voice, but the child didn't hear, and continued to sway back and forth as if she didn't know that one of the things allowed to the sick and dying is the right to lie down. Virginia strained against her bonds, weeping because she could not move.

"Wake up, wake up," Mrs. Gamely said, shaking her daughter. "You're in a dream. Wake up." Virginia sat bolt upright as Mrs. Gamely turned on the light. "How is she?" the grandmother asked.

Looking at Abby, entangled in the tubes and electric leads, Virginia answered that she was just the same.

Mrs. Gamely said, "When the doctor comes tonight, I think we should go for a walk and get some air. You haven't been out for a week."

"Where have *you* been?" Virginia asked, because her mother's cheeks were redder than the most scarlet Coheeries apple.

"I went to a lecture, dear. Now don't be upset. It was given by that man who irritates you so, Mr. Binky. I rather liked him, though his vocabulary needs a great deal of work. He spoke movingly about his great-great-grandfather, Lucky Binky, the one who went down with the *Titanic*. I was quite touched when Mr. Binky kept on referring to the *Titanic* as the 'Gigantic.' "

Mrs. Gamely did not know that Craig Binky had fixed his gaze on her throughout his discourse, and afterward had commanded Alertu and Scroutu to find her. They then began to tap their way through the city in search of a stolidly built, dumplingesque, white-haired woman whom Craig Binky had described only as "That Seraphina, that lovely one, that white rose!"

Virginia looked at her mother with disbelief. How could she

606

have left Abby's bedside to attend a lecture by, of all people, Craig Binky? But Mrs. Gamely thought it perfectly appropriate, because, unlike her daughter, the doctors, and other experts, she felt that though the child was gravely afflicted all that was needed to help her recover was to apply a certain poultice. Just to be safe, she always carried it in her bag. But every time she suggested the poultice they yelled at her as if she were an idiot. This had discouraged her a great deal, and in her view it was a shame for the child to suffer because the doctors put so much faith in strange machines and foolish drugs that did not work. She considered overruling them. This she might be able to do because, among the bric-a-brac and other things that she carried around in her carpetbag (such as, for example, a live though somnolent rooster) was a most persuasive instrument that she called a shotgun. But she was not as sure of herself as she had once been. This was not the Coheeries. She let them have their way, and though she kept the poultice, she dared not apply it. What if it made the child even sicker?

The doctor was late that night, but after she had made her examinations Mrs. Gamely and Virginia went outside into the snow while a nurse stood watch. "Where do you want to walk?" Virginia asked.

"Any which way," her mother replied. "Look at you. You're quivering. You need to walk, and get some strength."

They walked for hours, in circles and long bending curves, treading silently amid stark and dreary loft buildings that the snow had dusted like sugarcakes. Virginia began to tell Mrs. Gamely her dream.

"Did the baby rise from the lake and clap its hands?" Mrs. Gamely interrupted with surprising urgency.

"No. The baby never rose from the lake. But I saw her later, when she was older, in the hallway of a tenement," Virginia said, and then related the rest of the dream. "I think it's obvious," she stated at the end.

"You think that the child in the dream was Abby, and that you dreamed because of your anxiety."

"What else would it signify?"

"It might signify nothing, and be valuable solely in itself. A

607

dream is not a tool for this world, but a gateway to the next. Take it for what it is."

"What am I supposed to do with it?"

"Nothing. It's like something beautiful. You don't have to do anything with it."

"Oh, Mother," Virginia said, nearly in tears. "Abby is going to die, and all you and Hardesty do is walk around the city, talking like mystics and bagmen. Half the time, I don't know what you're saying. I don't know what the hell it means, and it's not going to make a bit of difference to Abby."

"Virginia," Mrs. Gamely said, wanting to embrace her daughter.

"No!" Virginia said.

The old woman took her daughter's arm, and they began to walk through the snow back to the hospital. They traveled in silence, except for the wind and the church bells that struck the hour and its quarters. Despite the misty cold, they felt dry and hot inside.

In a little square in Chelsea they saw a statue of a soldier of the first great war. He was covered with snow and nearly lost to the white clouds of mist and snow that howled through the streets and made whirlwinds in the squares. The two women stopped to read an inscription on the pedestal, which said, *For the Soldiers and Sailors of Chelsea.*

"Do you remember this statue?" Mrs. Gamely asked.

"No," Virginia answered, somewhat apologetically.

"When you were a little girl, Virginia, we came to the city to meet your father when the war was over. Don't you remember?"

"No, I don't remember that at all."

"It was very difficult to get here, but we did get here, and we waited for several months while the troopships were arriving. Many men had been killed, but their families had received telegrams. Though we hadn't heard from him, we assumed that Theodore was all right, because we hadn't heard any bad news either.

"During the time that we were waiting, we lived on the West Side, at the edge of Chelsea, near the river. Sometimes we would come to this park. You told the other children that this was your daddy. Your daddy never came back. He had been killed months before, and the notification had never reached us.''

''How did you find out?'' Virginia asked.

''When his division returned, we went to Black Tom, where they were debarking. You were very excited. I had dressed you up, and you had a little bunch of flowers that you carried all day, even after you found out. You wouldn't let go of them. I took them from your hands only when you had fallen asleep that night. Harry Penn was the one who told us.''

''Harry Penn?''

''He was in command of your father's regiment. All the men of the Coheeries were together. You made him cry. Don't you remember?''

''Of course not,'' Virginia said, shaking her head.

''He never brought it up? You've known him now for years.''

''There was nothing I could do to make him fire me. I guess that that's the way he brought it up.''

''You moved him so, Virginia. You were excited and happy, and he had to tell you that your father was dead. It broke his heart.

''It was in early summer. You got sick that day and ran a fever until winter came. You were trying to join your father. I would have done that, too, but I had to take care of you.''

''If that's why Harry Penn never lifted his hand against me, what good did it do?'' Virginia asked.

''If during all this time you didn't even know his motive, then why do you assume that you would know its effects? A benevolent act is like a locust: it sleeps until it is called.

''No one ever said that you would live to see the repercussions of everything you do, or that you have guarantees, or that you are not obliged to wander in the dark, or that everything will be proved to you and neatly verified like something in science. Nothing is: at least nothing that is worthwhile. I didn't bring you up only to move across sure ground. I didn't teach you to think that everything must be within our control or understanding. Did I? For, if I did, I was wrong. If you won't take a chance, then the powers you refuse because you cannot explain them, will, as they say, make a monkey out of you.''

609

"They already have."

"All right, Virginia," Mrs. Gamely said. "You've failed a bit. But you're still alive. You may not find a way to save your child. But you have to try. You owe it to her, and you owe it in general."

The snow came down ferociously now, hissing softly the way it does when it falls in earnest, and the mother and daughter embraced.

THE CITY ALIGHT

$\mathbf{A}$T first not even the fire department or the police knew that anything was wrong. Visitors to the observation decks of mile-high towers could see pillars of fire in the limitless distance. However, like all visitors to high places, they assumed that everything on the ground was under control.

But the pillars of fire that rose over the city of the poor went unnoticed by officials who were apoplectically fixed on the remarkable activities of Jackson Mead. Fires were not unheard of in the city of the poor, either. Summer and winter, it smoldered on, consuming itself in self-made arson. This time, though, the flames were higher and in many more places than usual. While the rest of New York hid from the cold and stayed indoors in comfortable houses where children played and winter-weary dogs slept by the hearth, an army hit the streets in the city of the poor.

Two days after Christmas, young men and women were dancing at the Plaza, the lifters were roaring over the harbor, the bridges to Brooklyn and Queens were alight with evening traffic, and the factories had resumed their rhythmic work. Lawyers who never slept took in bushels of facts and regulations, and spat out arguments twenty-four hours a day. Deep underground, repairmen were at war with pipes and cables to keep the city above them illuminated and warm. They moved with the tireless determination of tankmen in an armored battle, straining to turn huge ten-foot wrenches, facing explosions and fire, digging like mad, rushing squads and battalions through the dark tunnels, their miner's lights bobbing over dirty and timeless faces. Police fought through mortal encounters in separate incidents all over the city, foreign-exchange traders held six phones in each hand, scholars in the same room at the library were, nonetheless, in a thousand different places as each bent over his book in one of the thousand clear pools of steady lamplight. And they danced at the Plaza—women in white or salmon-pink dresses, and men in black and white and cummerbunds. Balding violinists with pencil mustaches and amazingly dissolute faces filled the marble-columned court with music. Hanging thickly from the columns and the ceiling were streamers and bunting in pink and gold that gave the dancers a summer glow. The backs of the chairs were draped with beaver, mink, and other furs which, as if they could remember the cold, were cool to the touch. Outside, carriages were trotted by, and warring winds from the north shook the icicle-covered trees like crystal bells. The finery and fine movement, the health and dancing, the joy itself, were soon to come undone.

Somewhere in the city of the poor, where the roads and streets had eroded away and what was left was a tea-colored meadow strewn with pits and shacks, were an old man and his wife who had made their living over the years by keeping a little store. Their wooden shelves were almost bare, but now and then they managed to stock a few bags of rice and sugar, some soft-drink bottles full of kerosene, some secondhand housewares, and a few shrunken and mutilated vegetables. The one room was lit by a lamp which burned beef tallow and waste oil. When it got very cold that winter, the old man and old woman put on all the clothes they had and took refuge in the back of the store, behind a home-sewn burlap curtain. Sometimes the old man went out to find scraps of wood, which he then burned in a coffee can. They were too cold to tremble, their lips were blue, and they stayed still so as not to offend the chill, hoping that it would let them live. Though the cold spell didn't break, and would not break until long after they had died, they didn't die of the cold. They died of heat.

At about the time when the dancing at the Plaza had reached its apogee and the bare-shouldered women were waltzing in sensual unison, the old man and old woman heard the beginnings of something that sounded half like surf and half like fire.

They heard the wind, and people running in long strides the way animals race from forest fires, in huge heart-pounding leaps. And then came the stragglers. Someone pounded on the door of the shop. The old man swallowed, too frightened to move. His wife looked at him, and cried. The tears ran down her face regularly, one at a time. Before they could come to rest on her dress, the front door was pushed down and it slapped the floor explosively. In the blink of an eye, fifty people were inside. Everything on the shelves disappeared immediately. Then the shelves themselves were ripped down. Anything that stood about was kicked and thrown. Crates and boxes hit the ceiling and ricocheted off the walls, lighted torches brushed against the wood, and as the hovel was beginning to burn and the crowd was already on its way out, someone ripped down the burlap curtain. Half a dozen men seemed to take offense that the storekeepers had dared to remain still on the other side, and they torched them.

Their clothes burned away, and then they themselves burned like tallow. As everything went up in flame, the drab interior became a furnace of white and silver. Under the buckling roof beams, a bubble of gold fire arched up like the roof of a cavern. From a distance, this appeared to be a small twirling pillar rising through the roof, dancing for a few seconds above a bed of sparks.

Across the darkened landscape that told of its poverty in showing no light, little pillars flickered and grew, sometimes combining, until small firestorms whirled like waterspouts, feeling out each contour of the land, sweeping to and fro, seeking wood, dead trees, and oil-soaked earth on the banks of stagnant creeks and foul canals.

Jackson Mead sat in total silence in an unlit room that looked out over the harbor. He had chosen the thirtieth floor of a medium-sized building as his final observation post, though he might have put himself many stories higher. But it made little difference, in view of what he hoped to witness, whether he was thirty stories off the ground, or ten miles. And this perspective—neither too high nor too low—suited him best, because he had always said, rather cryptically: "All ages pass most swiftly through the median doors." Not even Mootfowl or Mr. Cecil Wooley knew exactly what he meant, but they did know that everything he did echoed his central purpose, and that when he chose the median floors it was a decision that had evolved over many thousands of years, and that had its origins in one great event, when something huge, broken, and laced with flame had tumbled through the air after being hurled from a place so bright that compared to it the sun straight on seemed as black as pitch.

The machine he had established no longer needed his control, but just his looking on while breathtaking hierarchies flowered below him. A thousand directors faced a thousand powerful screens. They, in turn, were controlled by supracontrollers who had in turn their captains and captains of captains. In a score of great underground rooms and in crystal towers on the ships, the work proceeded at maximum speed. The ground had been prepared most thoroughly.

In the tranquillity of his carefully guarded refuge, Jackson Mead saw his plan unfold. Cecil Mature and Mootfowl sometimes approached him quietly and spoke a few words. But most of the time he watched his lifters and his ships as they warred to build, rapid-fire, on the ice over the harbor.

Mootfowl approached Jackson Mead, who was staring through the slightly smoke-colored walls of glass at the lights weaving to and fro outside. "The city is beginning to burn," Mootfowl said quietly. "There's a general rising."

"Where?" he was asked, in complete calm.

"In the remoter sections of the city of the poor, fifty miles out. Probably as I speak the fifty-mile line has been breached."

"Are there firestorms?"

"Yes, little ones, scattered about. From the top of the highest towers, the outer belts look like burning stubble, like a slow-moving grass fire."

"In a few days," Jackson Mead said, "there will be pillars of fire outside these windows, as high as the clouds, and the sky, black with smoke, will be as heavy as a vaulted ceiling."

"Do you want me to inform the new mayor?"

"Doesn't he know?"

"As far as we can tell, he doesn't."

"No. Let him find out himself."

"If we warn him now, he might be able to stop it."

Slowly shaking his head, Jackson Mead turned to his subordinate. "Doctor Mootfowl," he said, "we have always failed before, though we have come close, not because we lacked the science, but, rather, because we lacked the circumstances."

"Sir?"

"It is true that the prayers you generate so splendidly for grace, Reverend, accumulate, but they have yet to trigger the event that will allow our undertaking to succeed. Our bridge is now ready to spring. But unless something draws us closer to the opposite shore, we haven't a chance in hell."

"The burning then?"

"Not the burning itself, but what will occur within it. The high energy and dissociation, the abstractions of light and fire, and the extremes to which they drive the human soul put our mechanisms—as beautiful as they are—to shame. The city is going to burn because its time is over. Everything in the world, Mootfowl, comes down to love or a fight, which, when they are hot enough to be flame, rise and combine. Should the fires push a human soul to the highest state of grace, at that moment we will throw our bridge.

"No matter how skillful you are, my friend, you cannot rope a horse in an open meadow unless you draw him in close."

"I understand," said Mootfowl.

Cecil Mature emerged from the shadows. "The fires have crossed the thirty-mile ring," he reported. "There's no accounting for their sudden speed."

"What about Peter Lake?" Jackson Mead asked, taking his eyes off the panorama for the first time.

Cecil shook his head and closed his narrow eyes. He snorted, and then sneezed. "Not a trace," he answered.

Abby had been still for so long that her own mother knew she was dead only when the monitor held to a straight line and set off alarms that brought nurses and doctors running. Despite everything they did, and despite the machines that they wheeled in on silently rolling carts, Abby Marratta would not be revived. She had probably had enough of machines, after being attached to one for so long.

The electronic whine from the monitor of vital signs seemed to Virginia to be the music that announces the end of the world. Even after it was switched off, the machines were withdrawn, and the bedsheet was pulled up to cover her daughter, she continued to hear it.

Mrs. Gamely bowed her head and cried. She had been unwilling to believe that a little child with only a few years of life would die before she would. It did not seem proper according to her vision of a future that, she had been sure, belonged to her granddaughter.

Virginia found it very hard to breathe. She could not imagine that she would ever have another moment free of grief and terror. She stared at the cloth over Abby, trying to make some sense out of the simple pattern woven into it, but it would tell her nothing. Seconds passed, and then long minutes and long hours in motionless silence during which nothing happened and there was no redemption, no rising, no miracle.

And then an intense and brilliant picture came before her eyes. She was ashamed to harbor such a lively image when the world should have been irredeemably gray. It was like laughing in chapel during a deep and ponderous sermon. She saw a beautiful and giddy thing, in a waking dream that drew her into another time.

It was blatant, gorgeous summer. The mist was so thick and hot on the harbor that it turned everything to sepia and black. But that which was white, by contrast, glowed with unusual strength and seemed to float lightly in the sun-spoiled daze. A ferry with a tall dark stack materialized from the mist and drew closer and closer to its whitewashed pile moorings just off the Battery. Virginia watched in disbelief. This was no dream. It was stronger than anything she had ever felt in life. From the position of the sun, and the heat, she knew that it had to have been July—ninety or a hundred years before, to judge from the sheen and integrity of the ferry and passing lighters which seemed different altogether from the battered museum pieces that now limped and begged on the water when the harbor was not frozen over. The ferry's passengers stood forward on the decks, waiting to disembark into a July morning long passed, and silently observing the convergence of boat and dock, as if they were at the wheel themselves. Dozens of scalloped white parasols as light as floating dandelions twirled in impatience and gently fanned the air. Men without jackets glowed like white lanterns in their carefully pressed cotton and linen shirts. They looked with disdain from pier to wheelhouse to protest a less than perfect docking. But then the ferry drew into the slip and bumped up against the land. Engines disengaged, and waterfalls shot from bilge pipes as if the ferry were sighing with relief. The shaving-mirror gates were collapsed into tight metal plates, and everyone streamed forth past Virginia, whose eyes were guided to the back of the crowd, to a young woman whom she did not know or recognize. Nonetheless, she followed this frail and pretty girl, who could not have been more than fifteen or sixteen, up the ramp and through the terminal.

Just her presence moved Virginia very deeply and made her happy. Then the young girl walked between a set of iron gates through which Virginia was not allowed to pass, and vanished in the dark and lofty canyons that buzzed with summer as if the light itself were a swarm of never-contented gnats. As she disappeared, Virginia wanted to drop to her knees and cry, for, as long as the girl remained in view, until her white blouse was a dancing speck that didn't seem real, Virginia was overcome with a feeling of benevolence and gratitude.

But the sight of the small form under the shroud made her horribly bitter. She could not bear the contrast between the powerful, reassuring image that she had so clearly in mind, and the fact that Abby lay dead. She needed Hardesty. Where, in God's name, she wondered, was Hardesty?

"You know," Hardesty said in between breaths of dank air as he and Peter Lake ran through a darkened subway tunnel, "when you buy that little token, it entitles you to more than just the right to use the tunnel."

"I know that," Peter Lake responded, running effortlessly, while, behind him, Hardesty strained to keep up.

"Then what are we doing this for?"

"Didn't you see them?"

"Who?"

"The ones in the black coats!"

Hardesty panted. It was hard to keep up a conversation with this mechanic who must have doubled as an Olympic runner, for he sailed down the ties apparently without effort, restraining himself only for the sake of his companion. "The short ones?" Hardesty asked.

"Yes, the ones who kill, rob, and set fires. They're right behind us."

They stopped. After a few heavy breaths, Hardesty was able to listen, and he heard what sounded like hundreds of ratlike padded feet. Then he saw a wavy, jiggling motion as the Short Tails' alternating strides pushed them up and down and they blocked the dim lights in the tunnel.

618

"They're always everywhere," Peter Lake said, "though, at times, they do seem to disappear. I'm glad they exist. When they chase me, they make me do things I never thought I could do."

"I saw them at the Coheeries," Hardesty said. "I didn't know they were here, but I should have figured it out, because they seemed to be heading someplace with a vengeance, and people usually take their vengeances to New York."

"The Coheeries," Peter Lake echoed. "That sounds familiar, but I couldn't tell you why."

"The Penns have a summer house there."

Peter Lake didn't respond.

"Harry Penn," Hardesty said, "our employer."

"Never met him," Peter Lake answered, with a surliness that surprised him.

When they came to the Thirty-third Street Station they vaulted onto the platform, amazing waiting subway riders who were then much further stunned as a hundred or more Short Tails, with bird-like gurgling cries and high-pitched speech, vaulted after them in a river of cheap nineteenth-century formal clothes that had been altered and savaged by tailors, friction, and time. The Short Tails carried brass-knuckled knives inlaid with mother-of-pearl, and pistols that were engraved with the kind of reclining nudes one might expect to see above a bar.

Hardesty and Peter Lake ran directly through Gramercy Park—without opening the gate, which seemed to disappear as they went through and reappear only when the Short Tails were inside the park, trapped like a flock of sweatered weasels, cursing a lock they could not pick from the inside, hanging by their suspenders after they had tried to scale the posts and slipped. But enough of them squeezed through, or under, to continue the chase, which then led swiftly through Madison Square, now gaudy with gentrified restoration and new corporate headquarters. They raced under the old copper skywalks with whitened sides that glowed in the mercury vapor like sheet-metal moons, and they passed the huge old clocks decked out with incandescent berries which told the time in red and white. Now Hardesty was warmed up, and he followed Peter

Lake's long weightless strides with some weightless strides of his own.

They thought to get the Short Tails off their track by taking a circuitous route through the Village. But wherever they turned they saw Short Tails, as ubiquitous as the thin and acrid smoke that tainted the air and darkened the longer views up and down the avenues. The Short Tails' sentinels would summon the others, and the fox hunt would resume: not with hunting horns and red riding coats, but with ululations and glottal gurgles, helium screams, witches' shrieks, and midgets' sighs.

Peter Lake came up with a proposal. "Look," he said, "they're everywhere and every place, and they always will be. And I admit that they can be terrifying. But whenever I've fought them, I've won, and I always seem to get better and better at it. Now, there are about fifty on our tail at the moment. Though I haven't dealt with fifty at a time, while I was in back of the sky I seemed to feel that I could do something with my hands, something unconnected to physical laws, something amazing.

"I'm a mechanic, and I work by the universal ratios and indestructible laws. But strange things have happened lately, and I suspect now that, although the laws remain the same and cannot be abridged, we may have little idea as yet of the variety of their applications. In other words, I'm speaking of abilities that, by all logic . . ."

"Say it plain!" Hardesty urged.

"All right. Why don't we choose a nice dead-end alley into which we'll draw these devils and test out this new stuff that I think I can do?"

"Why not," Hardesty answered.

"If I can't do it, they'll kill us, the little snub-nosed bastards."

"Let's try your magic in Verplanck Mews," Hardesty said. "It's wide, and it's a dead end."

"It doesn't have anything to do with magic," Peter Lake stated as they turned into the closed alley. "What I'm talking about is, shall we say, concentrated and unexpected redistribution."

"Whatever it is," Hardesty said, his voice cracking with excitement, "you've got your chance right now."

The Short Tails appeared at the end of the mews like a flock of sheep arriving at the open end of a canyon: they formed a line that slowly lengthened until it blocked the entrance completely. Then they advanced in the same slow and methodical fashion. At the far end of the mews, Hardesty and Peter Lake heard what sounded like the operations of a huge casino spinning its wheels and paying out, with metal dashing against metal, as the Short Tails cocked their weapons, opened their spring-loaded knives, and limbered up garrotes and razor-studded chains.

"Okay," Peter Lake said, beginning what promised to be a calm exposition. "This is what I thought of when I was up behind the sky . . ."

"Just do it!" Hardesty screamed. "Don't get professorial! They're right here!"

"Don't worry about them," Peter Lake reprimanded. "Watch."

He rolled up his right sleeve, shut his left eye, and held out his hand, sighting into the Short Tails as if his arm were a rifle. Then he closed his fist slowly around the air.

One of the Short Tails suddenly dropped his weapons and seemed to compress upon himself. He looked like a man undergoing a rare and untreatable fit. His arms were plastered against his body, and he turned purple from lack of air. The Short Tails were impressed.

Stiff-armed, Peter Lake raised his fist in front of him. The constricted little Short Tail rose into the air. "Ah!" exclaimed Hardesty, nearly fainting in delight.

"Okay," said Peter Lake, with the same detached air he had had before, rather like a high-school science teacher, "let's see if it works."

"Of course it works!" Hardesty shouted.

"No," Peter Lake said. "This." He dropped his fist, smashing the Short Tail against the ground, and then drew it up as fast as he could, opening his hand at the apogee.

The Short Tail was launched like a rocket. Even from a distance, one could see his bulbous cheeks and fleshy nose as the G-force padded them down into Buddhaesque folds. Off he went in a white streak, whining like a bullet into the thickening smoke above the city.

"It does work," Peter Lake affirmed. "Now I want to try a lariat trick that I figured out."

"Please do," said Hardesty. "I'd be very interested to see it."

By the same technique, Peter Lake seized a Short Tail and elevated him above the rooftops. Swinging his closed fist around his head, he made the Short Tail circle at phenomenal speed, ten feet above the gables and chimneys of the mews. The Short Tail went faster and faster, and his colleagues spun their heads like a group of dogs following an energetic bee, until he began to leave a trail of smoke, and suddenly burst into flame. A shower of cool sparks, all that was left of him, rained down upon the alley. Because the Short Tails did not have Pearly to mold their courage for them, they turned and ran.

Peter Lake grabbed one from afar, turned him upside down, and shook him until the coins and weapons fell from his pockets and jangled onto the ground. Then he turned him right side up again and let him go.

"The way I remember it," Peter Lake offered as they walked peaceably and undisturbed through the Village, "these black-coated ones, who are called Short Tails, chased me once before, and the same sort of thing happened. I always get better and better at fighting them, but they increase in number."

Two blocks from St. Vincent's Hospital, as Hardesty and Peter Lake were walking through the thick miasma that had gradually taken hold of the city, a lone Short Tail came running at them from a side street, as fast as his little legs could carry him. They braced for an attack, but just before he reached them he threw himself on the snow, belly-flopping like a seal and sliding on his stomach to Peter Lake's feet, which he then proceeded to flood with kisses.

"I beg you! I beg you!" he implored, accidentally taking in a mouthful of snow, and choking. "Master! Spare me!"

"I'm not chasing you," Peter Lake said, pulling the Short Tail up. "I won't harm you, if you'll be civil."

The Short Tail brushed the snow from his coat and houndstooth-check pants. His derby was a repulsive, fly-colored, liver-green. "P-P-Pittsburgh!" he shouted, still spitting out snow. "P-Pittsburgh!"

"What about it?" Peter Lake asked.

"What about what?" the Short Tail, whose nose curved like an English saddle, replied with apparent sincerity.

"Pittsburgh."

"Oh, Pittsburgh," he answered, rather mechanically, suddenly afraid. "I was born in Pittsburgh. They kidnapped me and killed my parents. Or, rather, they killed my parents and kidnapped me. They made me go to their school—ape school, all kinds of flying things, horrible insects, death. They made me go to their school, and, uh, learn terrible things, and, uh, I don't want to be with them no more. I want to be on your side."

"I don't have a side," Peter Lake told him.

The Short Tail looked at him blankly. "You mean there's just you and him?"

"You might say so."

"What about the horse?"

Peter Lake was catapulted into melancholy thought. He looked as if he were on the verge of something, indeed, as if the dawn were coming up in his eyes.

"You mean you don't got the horse?"

"No . . . no . . . I . . . I think I. . . ."

"We're not afraid of *you*," the Short Tail said, almost in triumph, "if you don't got that fuckin' horse!"

With a single swift motion that reminded Hardesty of a magician retrieving something from behind his cape, the Short Tail pulled a knife from his coat and stuck it into Peter Lake's abdomen.

Peter Lake's silence was compounded and his breath was stopped by this blow. He reached for the knife, and pulled it out. Blood flowed in a streaming bright red arc. Staggering slightly, he stepped forward, and covered the wound with his left hand.

The Short Tail seethed with self-satisfied laughter, but was too terrified to move.

"You laugh," said Peter Lake, with great difficulty, "in spite of what I'm going to do to you."

"You're a dope! You're a dope!" the Short Tail yelled, in growing terror. "I'm not from Pittsburgh. I'm one of them from way back. You trusted me!" Peter Lake grabbed the air, and crushed the little man's arms to his side. "My own grandmother, if I hada had one, woun'ta trusted me!" the Short Tail screamed. He grimaced as he was lifted into the air.

Clutching his wound, Peter Lake moved his arm back like a javelin thrower, and pitched the Short Tail forward as hard as he could, hurling him up Sixth Avenue in a blur that whizzed away with a high-pitched sound, caught fire, flew above the sleighs and taxis like a blazing comet, and then disappeared in a puff of sour gray smoke.

Praeger de Pinto was studying a huge leather-bound book of reckonings and accounts, trying to discover in the history of the previous century a metaphysical solution to the city's tragic and intractable financial problems. The clock had struck nine. He had noticed that he could not see the stars through the window of his office in City Hall, but assumed that this was attributable to thick clouds that soon would bring snow.

Suddenly, one of his newly appointed aides burst into the room without knocking. Tears were running down his face.

"What is it?" Praeger asked. The hysterical young man tried to talk, but an atonal sob burst from his lungs, and more tears came.

"What is this!" Praeger screamed, more frightened than he was angry.

Then the fire commissioner, Eustis P. Galloway, an enormous man of great authority and dignity, appeared behind the young aide. He put an arm around the boy's shoulders, and made an electrifying statement.

"The city is burning," he said.

"Where?"

"Everywhere."

"What do you mean, 'everywhere'?" Praeger asked, looking out the window. Though the nearby buildings were intact, the sky behind them was a fiery orange color as in the apocalyptic paintings that had always hung unheeded in the basements of historical societies. Even from a great distance, it was a superb and extraordinary sight. Galloway, huge strong Galloway, the Rock of Gibraltar, had had a slight quivering in his voice.

Now Praeger the man vanished, and Praeger de Pinto the holder of office appeared. This immediate and magical separation and elevation was something appropriate to ancient chieftains and leaders of empires and clans. The office enfolded him in its powerful shroud, investing him with a hardness and a coolness of nerve that would have made it easy for him to give his own life or, for that matter, the lives of his family, because he was no longer himself. He had become the mayor, and the responsibility of office threw him into a selfless trance that heightened his powers, deepened his judgment, and banished fear from him forever.

The mayor turned to his commissioner. "What have you done so far?"

"Each company is covering its own section as best it can, with an eye to shoring up natural firebreaks. But the fire is spreading faster than if it were traveling on its own. It's as if there are ten thousand arsonists out there. That's because there *are* ten thousand arsonists out there."

"What about reserves, and other cities?"

"We've just put out a general call to every city within three hundred miles. We no longer have any reserves. They're all on the street."

"Good," Praeger said. By this time, his office was filling up with aides and commissioners. He organized them, and dictated instructions.

"First: get a truck, and move the radio-telephone and radio-teletype equipment to the observation floor of the Fifth Grand Tower. Get everybody out of there and set up a command post.

"Second: tell the police commissioner to join me up there, with emergency links to all his precincts.

625

"Then call the governor. Tell him that I'll be speaking to him as soon as possible, but that meanwhile I'm requesting that he mobilize the entire militia. Tell him to get as many troops from whatever source he can and send them toward the city. I'll designate marshaling areas before they arrive. If he balks, tell him that we've got general insurrection, and that the whole city is burning.

"Send all the commissioners up there.

"And get a supply operation going to send cots, blankets, food, chairs, and desks to the tower."

A dozen sheets of paper were ripped off a dozen pads as his subordinates started to move.

Praeger and the fire commissioner left for the observation deck. The fire commissioner spoke into his radio as they walked hurriedly across the little park in front of City Hall, which, because it was surrounded by tall towers in an unbroken ring, had always reminded Praeger of the bottom of a deep well.

The Fifth Grand Tower was the highest building in the city. It took five minutes by express elevator to reach the top, and when they got there the last tourists were being herded into glass cabins for the windy trip down. An observatory guard handed Praeger and Eustis Galloway each a pair of high-powered binoculars, and told them that he had opened all the coin telescopes.

When Eustis Galloway and the mayor strode onto the wide glass-enclosed deck, they looked first to the north. Praeger had intended to berate his commissioner for letting things get so far out of hand, but when he saw how fast the fire was spreading he realized that he couldn't. Arsonists were surely at work, for the dark areas were the scene of sudden sparks which quickly became fires that then combined into cyclical tornadoes and firestorms. It was as if the world had begun the self-consumption that myth had always promised with the turning of the millennia, but in which, long before, most everyone had ceased to believe.

The city was trapped within a dome of orange smoke that seemed as solid and smooth as alabaster. Not a star was to be seen: not even directly on high, where an upside-down maelstrom that

626

was twisted into a cowlick rotated upward at great speed. Across the horizon, clouds of different densities, some glaring flame off their bellies, some broken into flak, circled clockwise, speeding up as they climbed toward the tumultuous vent where they were then braided out.

"Look," Praeger said, as a glass tower on the Palisades suddenly erupted. In less than a minute, flames shot from it in flaring wings and stable coronas that made the seasoned fireman draw in his breath. Before the building collapsed, they saw that its steel skeleton was darker and redder than the sheets of white and gold flame which, for a moment, signified its rooms.

As tank farms exploded, spewing gasoline and oil, streams of fire ran onto the rivers and bays, cutting canyons of flame into ice several hundred feet thick. The fires that burned in these trenches sent aloft clouds of white steam and black oil smoke, and branched out laterally into hollow caverns. A section of the harbor half a mile in diameter had become a delicate crystal roof over a cave hewn from the ice underneath it. As the fire raged inside, the ice lit up and glowed like a titanic lamp. Water and steam surged through the crust, making geysers that were a thousand feet high.

After the communications net was in place, a technician told Praeger that the governor was on the line, and that he need only speak: everything would be amplified, including his own voice.

"What are you going to do with all those troops down there," the governor boomed out from nowhere, his words echoing through the observation deck.

"To begin with," Praeger said, "we've got ten thousand arsonists running around."

"Troops are not trained for that kind of police work," said the governor's voice.

"What police work?" Praeger bellowed in return, looking about to see from which part of the air the voices came. "They're not going to do police work, they're going to shoot arsonists and looters."

"To what end?" the governor asked.

627

"The whole goddamned city is burning," Praeger asserted. "The more arsonists and looters we shoot, the less arson and looting there will be. Isn't that self-evident?"

"But at what price?"

"Price? There's not going to be anything left!"

"Then why bother?" the governor asked, in such a way as to confirm his long-standing hostility toward a city in which he seldom dared to set foot.

"I'll tell you why, Governor," Praeger returned, his words rising all over the place. "The city's not going to burn forever. We're going to rebuild it. By summer, you'll see, it will have become something that you've never dreamed of. Do you know what else? If this fire stops at night, we'll begin to rebuild on the next morning. If it stops in the morning, we'll begin to rebuild in the afternoon. When that happens, I want all the arsonists to be dead, and I want anyone who even entertains the idea of lighting a match to be able to remember what happened to the people who started this fire."

"I'll believe what you say about rebuilding," the governor said, "when I see it."

"You'll see it. We're the quickest rebuilders in the world—we don't talk as fast as we do for nothing. As much as the fire takes from us, we'll take from it. We'll pretend it's a tourist."

The governor relented. The militia would soon begin to move toward the city.

"Eustis," Praeger said, still amplified, "pull all your trucks in. I want to create safe islands where, if necessary, we'll protect each and every building individually."

The fire commissioner shook his head, as if to say what Praeger wanted was hopeless.

"Do it now," Praeger said. "Choose the islands, and protect them. Fire anyone who doesn't move fast. I'm sorry," he added. "I suppose that wasn't the proper word." Then he turned to look over the city.

"As yet there are no fires in all of Manhattan," an aide reported. "Shall we try to hold the whole borough?"

"No," Praeger answered. "It's too big. It would never work. Make islands. Make islands, and keep them safe."

On Abby's floor at St. Vincent's, a row of tall windows gave out upon a northward view. "Look," Peter Lake said, when he saw the color of the sky.

"What *is* that?" Hardesty asked, stepping close to the window. The entire sky was red. But unlike a sunset or a dawn, it pulsed and flickered. Outsized snowflakes that had formed around particles of ash fell leadenly and straight.

"It must be a fire," Peter Lake said, "which explains the pall in the air. The flames are probably a thousand feet high."

When she heard someone at the door, Virginia thought that the mortuary attendants had arrived. Anything but eager to receive them, she recoiled, and stared blankly ahead. But then she got up and slowly walked across the room. When she opened the door, she was crying.

Upon seeing Hardesty, she bowed her head. He didn't want to believe that the sheet was drawn up over Abby.

"She's dead," Virginia told him.

"I know you!" Mrs. Gamely said to Peter Lake, almost accusingly. "You drove the sleigh. You haven't aged, not a day. How can that be? Why are you here now?"

"Stop babbling, old woman," Peter Lake commanded. She was hysterical, and although he had a vague idea of what she was saying, he was tired of inexplicable memories.

"Don't you know what I'm talking about," she asked. "It was a long time ago, in Lake of the Coheeries. Beverly. . . ."

Peter Lake shuddered. "Shut up, old woman!" he screamed. "Shut up, or I'll throw you halfway around the world!"

Mrs. Gamely shrank back. Martin sprang to her side as if to protect her from Peter Lake.

With the air of a master locksmith called to open a vault, Peter Lake walked to the bed and drew back the shroud. Staring at the dead child, he touched her forehead with two fingers of his left hand, and looked into her eyes. Hardesty thought that perhaps this man—derelict, mechanic, or whatever he was—was about to bring her back to life. But it soon became clear that he did not intend even to try.

Peter Lake's face softened momentarily into a barely perceptible smile. "This is the child . . ." he said. "This is the child that flew to me. And this is the child in the hallway. That was a long, long time ago.

"As I remember, I thought it was a boy. No matter. She was dying and blind, but she remained standing. She didn't know that it was her privilege to lie down."

Virginia tried her best to speak, but no words came. A man was standing in front of her, talking about her dream as if it were not a dream but something that had actually happened in another time.

Then the lights were extinguished. The whole city went dark. Even distant towers, where the lights had never dimmed, now looked like smooth black slabs. Patients screamed, and orderlies ran through the halls, knocking each other flat. Without the lights, the fire seemed many times brighter than it had been. It was strong enough to illuminate the room. Clouds of smoke miles away reflected the firelight, which flashed onto walls and faces as if it were a lighthouse beacon. The steep reflective clouds had climbed so high that they dwarfed the city.

"I have to tend the machines at *The Sun*," Peter Lake announced. "Even though there isn't any power now, those old engines can still work, and someone has to make sure that they do. The generators have to generate, and the turbines have to fly at full speed. I must keep them running. I have no choice."

Confused as much by his power as by his powerlessness, Peter Lake walked through blackened streets underneath a sky pulsing with firelight. By holding a hand against his wound, he was able to halt most of the bleeding. Still, it hurt a great deal, and he feared that his heart would stop, or that he might yet bleed to death.

Every time he saw a Short Tail, he threw him mercilessly into the air to light up the street ahead of him. He seemed nearly invulnerable to them now, though what use, he thought, was invulnerability, if he could not protect a suffering child? As he turned west on Houston Street, half a dozen Short Tails rushed at him from a vacant lot. He picked them up and made them into comets so quickly that they didn't know what hit them. As he crossed Chambers Street, he noticed another group of Short Tails several blocks away. The last of them had run half a mile up Broadway before Peter Lake seized them with his left hand and aimed them so that there would be fireworks over the Manhattan Bridge.

He was surprised to see that *The Sun* was as dark as *The Ghost* across Printing House Square. Candles burned as *The Sun*'s reporters worked to meet their deadlines. In the lobby, Peter Lake was astonished by the many reporters, printers, and copy boys who came and went with candlesticks.

"What is this!" he cried out, "a monastery?" But they climbed the stairs and crossed the courtyard without answering.

"There's no power in the city, Mr. Bearer," a guard informed him.

"I know that," Peter Lake said indignantly. "What about our machines?"

"They can't get them to work," he was told.

The pain of his wound grew fierce as he took the stairs down to the mechanical floors, where the mechanics and the apprentices were hard at work by candlelight. When they saw him, they rushed up with oil-blackened faces, and told of their efforts, over days, to start the machines. "The whole thing's jammed up!" Trumbull, the former chief mechanic shouted. "I doubt if even you can fix it. Every single machine seems as if it's been welded into one goddamned piece!"

"Put the cover back on the tribuckle," Peter Lake commanded the apprentice who had once followed him.

"But, Mr. Bearer," the apprentice protested from a garden of gears and shafts that he had painstakingly removed from the tribuckle's interior, "I've got to reassemble it."

"Then stay still," Peter Lake ordered. The boy looked at him in wonder as all the metal pieces flew like a torrent of autumn leaves, and replaced themselves inside the tribuckle.

Shafts banged into place, gears clicked together, plates were slammed down with a satisfying thump, and each screw whirled like a dervish into its hole. If a piece did not quite fit, it jiggled wildly until it was able to force itself in smoothly. And in their race across the floor, metal pieces of lethal weight carefully detoured around the trembling legs of the bug-eyed apprentice.

"What else didya strip?" Peter Lake asked.

After they listed the machines that they had disassembled, they heard the rush of the pieces, as if a thousand nimble mechanics were working in perfect coordination. It sounded like a tin coin bank turning over and over, or an attacking army clad in chain mail and spurs. The outside covers slapped themselves on, and the screws raced for their holes.

Peter Lake staggered down the aisles of machinery, touching each machine as if he were patting a cow. Each cow thus signaled responded with a deep, powerful, well-oiled whirl, and ran from then on as if it had learned the secret of perpetual motion.

When Peter Lake passed one of the generators, the lights of the machine decks blazed on, and the spent mechanics cheered. Then the big steam engines slowly fired and hissed, sending out plumes and exhalations. Their huge arms and ellipsoidal wheels set the light in order and organized the magnetic fields into obedient bustles and hoops.

As Peter Lake struggled down the rows, different areas of *The Sun* burst into clear light one by one, and the workers cheered just as the mechanics had done. When the presses began to roll, the pressmen felt a surge of emotion, for they loved their charges as much as Peter Lake loved his.

After he had started every machine, Peter Lake sank down near an elephantine walker beam. Upon seeing the blood running from his wound, the other mechanics wanted to help, but he dismissed them. Thinking that nothing could happen to Peter Lake that he would not allow, they backed off to find their own places amid the perfectly running engines.

Peter Lake now felt the full power of the machines among which he lay. And had it not been for their counterbalancing motions, he surely would have been torn apart by the forces that swept through him. Coursing magnetic fields as sinuous as the northern lights lifted him on swanlike waves. As heavy flywheels spun without a tremble, the smooth rotation of mass pounded him like jackhammers. Though it might be rushing in a blur, he had absolute sympathy for each wheel as it turned, and each strike of each bolt hit him as if he were a drum. But far more influential than the magnetism or the variations of mass, was the light. It streamed from the old-fashioned clear bulbs in conical lamps hanging like fruit above the machines. Peter Lake watched it move. Slow and capturable rivers showered the surfaces of oiled steel, and made rainbows, jewels, and sparkling thistles with open arms.

On an errand for *The Sun,* Asbury and Christiana had been driving toward Manhattan along an expressway that skirted the city of the poor, when they noticed the pall and the hellish sky. A few minutes later, they were stopped in halting traffic after a mob had toppled a sign bridge onto the road. From half a mile back, they watched the crowd begin to attack the stationary automobiles.

Afraid to leave their cars and venture into the city of the poor, especially since pillars of fire were now twisting amid the rubble, most people locked themselves in, petrified with fear, as thousands of marauders streamed onto the highway. Cars were rocked, windows smashed, and lighted pieces of wood dropped into gas tanks. Families were pulled from their cars and dragged separately into the darkness. The shoulders of the road became a slaughterhouse in which trembling victims and shining blades met to produce rivers of blood. As the mob moved down the line and the cars began to rock, the passengers closed their eyes and said their last prayers.

The first troop-carrying helicopters passed overhead in ten minutes of thunder, but the murder below was concealed in smoke.

Asbury and Christiana left their car and jumped over the guardrail onto the plain of bricks.

"How far does it go?" Christiana asked about the vast prairie of brick.

"For miles."

"At least no one's here. If we stay in the bricks, maybe we'll be safe," she said, remembering what she had once seen, and knowing that there were some men who could run across the brick as fast as gazelles, and who, like a specialized order of predatory animal, preyed upon those who strayed onto that angular and difficult ground.

"Maybe," Asbury answered, "but we'll be visible in the daylight, so we've got to get to the river by dawn."

They set out, using the darkened mass of tall buildings in Manhattan as their guide. There were at least five miles between them and the river, half of which was over the brick and the other half of which passed through the unknown hollows that had long been forgotten by all but their inhabitants, who knew nothing else. They got off the brick several hours before dawn, and moved through the hollows as fast as they could.

They had planned to walk across the East River, but the center channel was now a swiftly running canal cradled in a bed of melting ice, cutting deeper and deeper, and covered with a slick of burning oil that made flames a hundred feet high. "The only thing we can do is get to the harbor and go around," Asbury said. "But we'll have to wait until dark."

Thinking to hide all day in the rubble, they backtracked to the quietest hollow, hopping from one burnt-out building to another, and moving only when no one was around.

As they were hurrying from a ruined tenement covered with rusted fire escapes that wrapped around it like dead ivy, they were accosted by an old man who jumped up from a pit in the ground. He motioned for them to come over to him, and they did.

In a dialect that they could hardly understand, he told them to follow him to the church.

"What church?" Asbury asked, and was informed, in the same obscure dialect, that the people of the hollow had always been able to hide safely in the courtyard of a church.

Because of the way the rubble had fallen, the churchyard was invisible from the street. Long disused cloisters ran around its sides. At the far end, a thousand people were gathered, so frightened that even the children were still. The old man was proud to have rescued the strangers and to show them how cleverly he had hidden so many people. He was about to leave, to save others, but Asbury asked that he stay. "If you keep on going out and coming back in," Asbury said, "you'll be sure to give us away."

"Ta feerst woones asay tha than," the old man replied. "In'now saf be thay." He smiled toothlessly, and slapped his thigh. "Tauntin uld Flinner gut mir chik fas thin rabbitin. Goone ameed feers com chik fas rabbitin!" he said, and he went to bring more people to safety.

Asbury and Christiana were surrounded by men, women, and children with sunken eyes and distended bellies, whose bones showed through their sallow skin. These people lived for a very short time, and were buried without markers. They were the people of the hollows, who thought that the inhabitants of the city of the poor were well-off, and that the once-shining towers across the river were a place of the gods. They were afraid even to look at Asbury and Christiana, who towered above them.

"Can you defend yourselves," Asbury asked, "if we should be discovered?" There was no answer.

"We'll just have to wait until dark," Christiana said, "and then leave them to what they know."

The old man brought back dazed survivors, who leaned against the brownstone columns and watched as clouds of smoke and ash were rammed across the sky by the edges of hot cyclones. It was hard to tell whether it was night or day, and the sounds of firestorms, explosions, and artillery came from every direction.

In the middle of the afternoon, Asbury and Christiana looked up and saw the old man proudly leading into the hiding place three little men in black coats.

"Those are them!" Asbury screamed. "You've brought them in."

The Short Tails pushed the old man to the ground, and stepped back. Asbury pleaded with the men among the huddled survivors to help him prevent the Short Tails from leaving, but as the Short Tails walked backward toward the exit, brandishing their weapons, no one moved.

Finally, when the Short Tails were halfway across the courtyard, Asbury ran toward them, and Christiana followed.

He tackled one and slammed a fist into his chest. The Short Tail said something in a voice full of air, and quickly expired. But the other two began to beat Asbury with chains. He was unable to separate himself from the one he had killed, and was choked by the body as if he were drowning in it.

After a confusing struggle with the remaining Short Tails, Asbury killed one of them, and the other escaped. They tried to get the people in the churchyard to scatter, but it was no use. Led by the one who had escaped, the Short Tails had already arrived. Some blocked the exit, and others ran up the stairs to the roof, where they took up positions once occupied by the gargoyles that had been there to guard the monks. They flooded into the end of the courtyard, urged on by one of their number who stepped to the front and beat his chest as if he were a baboon. Asbury raised a chain, and the baboon skittered behind his comrades. Asbury and Christiana stood near the two bodies, wondering what would happen when the Short Tails found the courage to close. Even the gargoyles, who were archers, were afraid to fire, and contented themselves with arrows casually loosed into the trembling crowd. The sounds of the arrows finding their marks—like a sharp axe penetrating deep into dead wood—finally emboldened the Short Tails, and they moved forward.

But Athansor came from out of the whining ash-wind, and made four stunning passes that knocked over the living gargoyles and hurled them from the walls and towers. When the Short Tails looked up, they saw him descending slowly toward them as if he were coming down a beam of light. Christiana believed that she was imagining him, but down he came, stamping his feet on the air, sidling, bending his muscular white neck, and flaring his just and terrible eyes.

As the Short Tails scattered, Athansor galloped around the courtyard, springing off the walls so hard that they collapsed, and catching little men in his teeth. He trampled them, knocked them over, and butted them murderously into stone columns. A few

636

stood to fight, and for these he went up on his hind legs—twenty-five feet in the air—and then fell upon them with his hooves.

As the white horse fought, what was left of the cloisters reverberated as if in an earthquake. When he finished, he came to within a few yards of Asbury and Christiana and whinnied.

He knelt, and Christiana mounted him. "Come," she said, and Asbury followed. In one silent bound, they left the smoky cloister and climbed over the river. A million fires flickered at them, and they looked down upon a landscape that was trembling and dark. Because of the ash-wind, night had come early. As they flew through clouds of smoke, they had to close their eyes and lean forward, pressing their faces against the soft white coat of the horse's astonishingly broad and spacious back. Asbury thought that they were dreaming, but Christiana knew that they were not.

On the last day of the last year of the second millennium, Hardesty and Virginia put the body of their child in a small wooden coffin, and walked south through the city. Hardesty insisted that she be buried before the turn of the millennium that night. To leave her behind in the set of a thousand years into which she had been born, while they crossed into the next, seemed appropriate and decent. They wanted not to tease her with even an hour or a day of the new time that she would never know.

It was a strange procession—Hardesty in front, with the coffin on his shoulder; Virginia following, her eyes downcast; Mrs. Gamely behind her, with Martin walking by her side and holding her hand. Late that afternoon, the canyons were dark because of the ash-wind and the early setting of the sun. The city of glass windows, which had once been illuminated by a billion scattered fractions of the sun, was now as black as ink. They navigated through the narrow canyons, and their compass points were the low buildings outlined against the throbbing orange of the firelit sky. Eventually they reached the Battery, where they heard midtown's glass towers igniting like Roman candles in the flames that swept down from the north.

They stepped onto the uncertain burning ice below the Battery's old stone wall, and started toward the Isle of the Dead, a mile and a half across the harbor. Usually a small ferry plied back and forth several times a day. During the freeze, people had simply walked behind the sleds that carried the coffins. But now tremendous crevasses had shattered the solid and beefy hunk of glass that had once locked up all the islands and touched the harbor floor. From dozens of wide fissures, flames would sometimes rise several hundred feet above the burning rivers of oil that had carved out the canyons. Walls of black smoke and white steam floated upward, gradually becoming rose-colored in the firelight. Geysers from caverns stuffed with roiling green water and flaming oil would suddenly burst from amid a lake of clear ice and throw heavy knife-edged shards for miles. The surface began to melt because of the heat that radiated from the cloud-filled sky, and the ten- or twenty-foot-deep ponds that appeared were sometimes instantly drained by a new crack through which the water vanished into an anarchic network of tunnels, caves, and underground rivers.

They crossed a lake of warm water, sinking to their waists. Emerging from this, they looked back and saw that the lake had disappeared. They next had to go a mile out of their way to round a crevasse that held a million tons of burning oil. There were fast streams to ford over beds of wet ice, and pitch-black coils of smoke through which they had to charge, emerging on the other side to see that the maze had many more walls.

Suddenly appearing overhead and vanishing in a roar were the thousands of lifters, flying low through the billowing steam and smoke, their lights flashing along their hundred-foot lengths as they dashed from place to place. Their rotors and jets parted and stirred up the clouds so that small bolts of lightning and trailing thunderclaps followed them across the ice, dragging along like a veil. These would crisscross in strange garlands across the Marrattas and Mrs. Gamely, who soon learned not to flinch as they passed. Hardesty wondered what was going to come of Jackson Mead's plan now that the great ice lens was irreparably broken, and guessed that the master-builder had gone much deeper than the ice.

They searched to find a gravedigger on the Isle of the Dead. These were the descendants of Baymen and escapees from what the

Baymen had called "hospitals for the congealed." And they looked it. Because of their skins, their wild beards, their thooid and mangy rawhide lacings, and their expression of jilted, wall-eyed confusion, they seemed to be fit heirs for their peculiar forebears.

Hardesty found one burrowing under a huge leaning tree.

"Bury her," he commanded, indicating the coffin.

The gravedigger protested that it was night.

"You'll have night for the rest of time, if you don't start digging," Hardesty threatened.

"Pay me."

Hardesty dropped coins into the man's cupped hands.

There was a grave already waiting. They went to it, and lowered the coffin.

The grave was filled in well in advance of midnight. They knew they had to hurry, but before they started across the ice, now covered with hot green lakes and soon to be subsumed, they stood for a while, unbelieving. The whole world seemed to be dying. Virginia cried. "Goodbye, Abby," she said.

A GOLDEN AGE

Iɴ the first hours of the new millennium, Peter Lake lay asleep among the machines at *The Sun*. The mechanics took him at his word. Now that they had seen what he could do, they held him in awe and dared not disturb him. Had he had other followers, supporters, or, for that matter, friends, they might have awakened him just before the stroke of midnight, in expectation of a miracle. But extraordinary events seldom keep appointments with precision, and Peter Lake, entirely alone, slept through the moment when the clock struck twelve and the year 2000 arrived. His right hand covered the wound on his left side, and his mouth was slightly open as he lay half sitting up against a machine that he himself had kicked awake several hours before. There were no clocks in sight, but the clocks of *The Sun* ticked off their seconds exactly as if nothing had happened. Plants remained in their pots and tubs, and did not become animate or walk about; doors still squeaked when they were opened; and a janitor was spreading some sort of green stuff to catch the dust as he swept.

The Sun and *The Whale* were preparing a joint edition, as was the custom when the news warranted, and double the usual number of people were at work. The place had come alive in the dead of night as reporters with shocked expressions came in from all the boroughs to write of what they had seen as their city was destroyed. Because there were so many stories to tell of how the old era had died, the paper the next day was going to be almost as thick as a typical *Ghost* (*The Ghost,* however, had been shut down by the power failure). For example, the animals in the zoos and the riding horses in the West Side stables had put up such a racket that they had been freed. Panicked by the fires, they galloped in herds, running up and down the avenues between ranks of burning buildings. When they turned a corner, *The Sun* reporter wrote, the blurred sight of their smooth pelts and muscular backs suggested a river in flood.

Compared to people, however, the animals were a study in rectitude and self-control. The streets were filled with racing automobiles. Drivers seeking routes out of the city found them blocked with traffic, people, or debris, and sped as fast as they could to other exits. But there were no exits, and the result was that everyone tried one and then tore off toward the next. Every two-way street or boulevard had automobiles running at ninety and a hundred miles an hour in both directions. When there were crashes, and there were crashes, those who survived simply continued on. Each minute, on any block, a car could be seen hurtling out of control into a storefront or the terrified mobs on the sidewalks. The tension was not alleviated by the fact that every fire engine and police car in the city was rushing to and fro, sirens blaring, and the tanks and helicopters of the militia were using up gasoline in trying to find the islands that Praeger de Pinto had told them to guard.

The bridges were crowded with uncountable thousands of refugees who streamed across their darkened roadways unaware that the belts of subcities ringing Manhattan had become a single wall of fire. They walked in stunned silence, children on their backs, briefcases and bundles in their hands. The streets became a huge rag-and-bone shop as people carried off an infinite assortment of objects that they wanted to save. Thousands upon thousands fled with books, paintings, candelabras, vases, violins, old clocks, electronic appliances, sacks of silverplate, jewelry boxes, and— wonder of wonders—television sets. The more practical-minded headed north on Riverside Drive, laden with backpacks full of food, tools, and warm clothing. But what real chance, in the dead of winter, in a world turned upside down, did a man with a chainsaw strapped across his back really have?

Not tens of thousands, but hundreds of thousands of looters swelled into the commercial districts. Because the more ambitious among them contrived to ram bulldozers against bank walls, explosions were heard as cache after cache of dynamite blew open vault after vault. But one boom was impossible to distinguish from another as stores of combustibles were ignited by the fires and the militia blasted out firebreaks around the islands. Overjoyed and overloaded looters moved as slowly as snails, pushing or pulling refrigerators, obese furniture, racks of clothing, and sacks of money. The money sacks were the saddest of orphans, for no sooner had they found a new parent than he was shot and killed and they were adopted by someone else. This was repeated without cease, so that if the money bags had been tracked, the plot would have shown them oscillating like bouncing balls, exquisitely juggled by the powers of insensate greed. All the things abandoned on the street made even the most expensive districts seem like gutted, ruined slums, and it was hard to tell where those with stolen objects in tow thought they were going. Mainly, they moved in circles, wild with happiness that they now had a new this or a new that. Because there were no places left in which to live, those who had stolen furniture would probably never sit or lie on it, but would, instead, spend weeks or months carrying it around on their backs.

Looters of a different sort joined in intoxicated gangs seeking libertine pleasures in the rubble. The furniture abandoned by those who found it too heavy to carry served as stations for copulation between people of all sexes and all ages. The combinations thus effected of groups and individuals, the willing and the unwilling, were terrible and sad.

The police did not know whom to shoot or what to defend, since everything appeared to be at odds with everything else, thunder and fire were everywhere, criminals vanished easily into the dark ashwind, and the streets had filled with lunatics carrying bundles.

The Sun's reporters were also able to report on families that held together and defended themselves against the chaos, on acts of selfless charity, and on the brave and the mad who had tried to stop the dissolution. These acts were rare, isolated incidents which did not turn back the tide—not through any fault of their own, but because they were neither auspiciously timed nor placed.

Witnessing the unraveling of the city, those of Harry Penn's reporters who were not killed (as many of them were) returned to *The Sun* to write about it. They sensed that this was the proper thing to do, even if everything else had gone to hell, because they knew enough to know that whenever the world ends it always manages to begin again, and they had no intention of being left out.

While the city burned under skies crawling with dense electrical storms, and his machines worked flawlessly to light *The Sun*, Peter Lake slept.

.

Praeger de Pinto had hardly turned to greet Harry Penn. Standing in the center of the north deck, peering out the window through a pair of night-vision binoculars mounted on a tripod, the mayor was busy. "Who's watching Island Six?" he asked over the amplification system, almost like a god.

"I am," replied a normal human voice from a rank of men to his left: deputy commissioners, staff assistants, and a patrolman or two brought in to shore-up missing spaces, all equipped with night-vision optics just as the mayor was.

"Do you see the gap in the southwest side?" Praeger asked.

"I can't see it now, sir," was the reply. "The ash is too thick. But I saw it before, and reported it."

"Did they acknowledge?"

"No."

"Island Six went off the communications net," a technician announced.

"When?" Praeger inquired.

"Five minutes ago."

"Try to get it back on. Eustis, send a man on foot to the command post there, to tell them about that gap. And give him a radio. Island Six is in Chelsea. If he runs, he should make it in twenty minutes."

While the city burned below, exchanges like this transpired in utter calm and tranquillity as Praeger and the others worked to maintain their defenses and save as much as they could save. After several hours, they had grown used to a city of flames and smoke. For Praeger de Pinto and his generation, the notion that their future would be spent in quiet command posts and apocalyptic battles was one with which they had been comfortable almost from birth. Most of the men on the high deck were cool and unmoved. This was their task, something they had always expected. The logic of the preceding decades, the wars against dreams and illusions, the life of expectations in themselves, not surprisingly, had led to this. In fact, rising to meet the challenge of its inevitability, they had, at times, actually wanted it.

But Harry Penn was an old man, who had had different expectations, and he grieved as he watched the tens of thousands of flames flickering in the darkness, seeking out whatever was left to burn. He was deeply hurt by the triumphant clouds of smoke and steam, reflecting orange light as they soared above the city, turning over and unfolding like dough in a baker's hands. They seemed to be laughing at the ruined burnt-out blocks which they had so cowardly abandoned.

Unlike the others, Harry Penn remembered the city when it was young. In general, the people had been kinder and more capable than their descendants, and the city itself had been different, innocent. The curve of the carriage roads, long since obliterated; the billow of sails, long since gone; the flanks and manes of horses working on the streets, long gone too; and the shape even of people's dress, soft and gentle as it was—were, in themselves, a prayer that found continual favor. God and nature had been pleased by the immortal and correct curves, by the horses, by the tentativeness of expression, by the city's remarkable ability to understand its place in the world, and the city had been rewarded with clear north winds and a dome of blue sky. The city that Harry Penn had known and loved had been young and new.

In a lull, Praeger turned to Harry Penn, and saw that the old man's face, faintly illuminated by the harsh firelight, was full of pain. "What is it?" he asked.

"Let's just say," Harry Penn answered, "that a lovely child I once knew has grown old and hard, and is now dying an ugly death."

"It isn't so," said Praeger. "It isn't dying. This is going to clear the way."

"I'm too old," Harry Penn told him, "too attached to one time, I suppose, ever to lose faith in it."

"Look," Praeger said. "Out there, in the blackness, I see a new city rising, already."

Harry Penn looked out, and saw only the past of which he so often dreamed.

"Of all people," Praeger continued, "I would have thought that you would see this for what it is. I thought you knew. *The Sun* is publishing, isn't it?"

"We've never missed a day."

"Right now," Praeger said, *"The Sun* is the only lighted building in this city—like a beacon."

"That's not so," Harry Penn replied. *"The Sun* is dark. The machinery froze, and the mechanics say it will take them six months to fix it. When I left a couple of hours ago everyone was working by candlelight, and we were going to run the joint edition by hand, on the treadle press."

"Then you must come with me," Praeger said as he put his arm around Harry Penn's shoulders and led him toward the east gallery. He deeply loved the old man.

At first they saw nothing except a gray cloud sweeping by, filthy with ash and cinders. But then, as if it were being cranked up, the cloud slowly and awkwardly lifted, and a light shone through the last of its dirty skirts.

Alone in the darkness of Printing House Square, *The Sun* was lit like a faceted jewel. Astonishingly angular and precisely aligned beams of light radiated from its windows. The floor of the square reflected back a diffuse glow, over which lay the swordlike projections as if they were the branches of a thistle, or the hard metal representations of light in the cross of St. Stephen.

"There," Praeger said. "One of the rewards of virtue."

But Harry Penn knew better. "Even a thousand years of virtue," he replied, "are not strong enough to shape the light. Something far greater than virtue . . . must be very close."

Then Harry Penn left to go back to *The Sun*, and Praeger resumed his direction of the difficult battle that was unfolding silently below, and for which he had probably been born.

While Harry Penn walked across Printing House Square, he was so taken by *The Sun*'s light cutting the ash-wind like a surgeon's scalpel that he didn't notice that three men were following him. Half hidden by the miasma surging in and out like a tide of polluted water, they were on a course that would cut across his path two hundred feet from the doors of *The Sun*. They had been able to tell from his gait that he was a very old and wealthy man. The majestic, endearing, and surprising way in which he walked did not only express the optimism of another age, but seemed to telegraph quite clearly that he was carrying a fair amount of money, a gold pocket watch, and, probably, cuff links, a tie bar, or a stickpin. And old upright codgers like Harry Penn didn't hear too well, their reflexes were shot, and they went down with one quick blow. So the three men who stalked him on the square were not careful of their approach. Had they been Short Tails (which they were not) they would have been very careful. In the Short Tails' day, hundred-year-old men were, even if greatly at risk because of their age, veterans of the frontier, the Civil War, and other action much rougher than the Short Tails had ever known.

The three men were sure that they were going to have an easy time. And they almost did, because, some way before *The Sun*,

Harry Penn stopped for breath. But one of Jackson Mead's huge lifters was flying perilously low among the high towers. Harry Penn turned at its roar and, as it parted the smoke, he saw them. They kept coming. At first he wasn't sure that he was in danger. Then he saw their knives and blackjacks. His slow and indignant look of surprise both amused and enraged them.

Having lived for a hundred years, Harry Penn was absolutely fearless. He didn't shake, he didn't breathe hard, and he didn't blink. He considered himself a representative of the era of Theodore Roosevelt, Admiral Dewey, the great soldiers of the Union, the Indian fighters, and (as Craig Binky would say) Wild Bill Buffalo.

Because his reflexes were really quite slow, he stared at his three assailants for much too long as they came toward him. He was able, however, to summon the past, and the past emerged to protect him. His eyes sparkled. He smiled. (And he reached into his pocket and pulled out a four-barreled pepperbox handgun.)

This little machine looked ridiculous and ineffectual. It had the same harmless air as a blunderbuss. They were about to tell him so when he fired the first barrel and knocked down the man closest to him, with a bullet in the solar plexus. The other two were startled, and stopped for a fatal instant in which he shot them, also.

He stood for a moment, looking at the three bodies over which the fog and smoke arched as they blew past. In all his long life, he had never killed anyone, not even in several wars. He trembled a bit, but then he thought that he was too old to bother. He already knew all the terrible lessons that a younger man might have had to learn after doing such a thing, so he turned around, put the old-fashioned pistol back in his pocket, and walked toward the office.

The Sun had become a paradigm of light and activity. Isolated by the natural firebreak of Printing House Square, with armed guards in position behind sandbags at the entrances and on the roof (these men had heard Harry Penn's three shots, but had been unable to see very far into the smoke), with their own source of power, and with their families sheltered in the courtyard and throughout the vast interior of the building, the employees of *The Sun* worked as they had never worked before.

As he took the several flights of stairs, Harry Penn was stopped a hundred times by excited young men and women who wanted to show him that they were doing their job and were full of hope. They asked him unnecessary questions, and he answered carefully, so as to encourage them. He knew that to reconcile the festive air at *The Sun* with what was going on outside, he had only to consider the youth of his reporters.

At the top of the stairs, he ran into Bedford. "How'd you get the lights on?" he asked.

Bedford shrugged his shoulders. "They just came on. I guess the mechanics were able to fix the machines."

Bedford went downstairs to interview the mechanics.

When, later, Bedford reported to Harry Penn's office, Harry Penn was sitting on a couch, smoking a cigar and staring at the paintings of Peter Lake and Beverly.

"The mechanics say that the machinery was hopelessly frozen and jammed," Bedford told Harry Penn, whose eyes never left the paintings. "They had half of it eviscerated and out on the floor, and were prepared for six months of work, when the chief mechanic returned and fixed it in . . . well, they say a minute."

"What! Trumbull? I don't believe that Trumbull could fix anything in a minute. He takes a year to sharpen my Swiss Army knife. Something's not right."

"Trumbull was the one to whom I spoke."

"That liar."

"Mr. Penn, he's no longer the chief mechanic."

"He isn't? Since when? Where was I?"

"For quite a while now, the mechanics have had a new chief, whom they themselves have elevated to the position."

"Damnation, Bedford," Harry Penn said furiously. "Nobody elevates anyone around here except me. No one designates shares except me."

Bedford shook his head. "He takes apprentice's shares. They made him chief because, they say, he was so good they couldn't wait."

"What is he, one of those computer kids? Get the son of a bitch up here. I want to talk to him."

"I can't do that."

"Goddammit," Harry Penn said, glancing at the ceiling in exasperation. "Who runs this newspaper?"

Bedford tried to answer, but no words came. At first Harry Penn was livid, but then he was simply amazed.

"What's his name?"

"They call him Mr. Bearer."

"Mr. Bearer," he echoed.

"That's correct."

Harry Penn was not sure whether to reload his pepperbox or lapse into hysteria. "Why can't you get him up here?" he asked.

"He's taking a nap."

"He's taking a nap?"

"Yes, sir. They won't let him be disturbed. They stand in awe of him. They seem to think that he's the king of mechanics."

"Look here," Harry Penn said, fierce-eyed, rising from the couch. "I don't care if he's the king of the gypsies. I'm going to wake this 'Mr. Bearer' up, I'm going to fire him, and I'm going to kick his ass. And *then* I'll rehire him as chief mechanic, and get down on my knees in front of him because I'm so grateful that the son of a bitch was able to keep the light burning."

As Harry Penn took the stairs, rhythmically, one by one, he felt at first a chill, and then his hair stood on end, and then he could neither feel the steps under his feet nor hear his own footsteps or the sound of the machines on the machine deck. It couldn't be, he thought to himself just before he confronted the mechanics. But— the best mechanic in the world, who fixed all the machines in one move, who was elevated by the other mechanics and still takes an apprentice's shares—it could *only* be.

Numb with fear and anticipation, Harry Penn questioned the mechanics. "Where is Mr. Bearer? Is he here?"

"Yes, he's here," one of them answered.

"Show me."

"He shouldn't be disturbed," Trumbull declared. "He's sleeping now."

"Oh no," Harry Penn said, falling into Trumbull's reverential tone. "I just want to *look* at him."

"He's down there," Trumbull said, pointing. "Two rows, and then turn in by the compressor. You'll see a little alley of generators. . . ."

Harry Penn was already on his way. He passed two rows, turned in by the compressor, and followed the little alley of generators until he came to a man who was sleeping up against a busy, smoothly running machine.

At first Harry Penn could not see his face. He knelt down, trembling, and shielded his eyes from the bright light of a lamp in a conical tin shade. And, then, he saw. He saw what no man has the right to expect to see even in a life of a hundred years. He saw the past arise. He saw the past victorious. He saw time and death beaten. He saw Peter Lake.

To see Peter Lake unchanged after eighty-five years was not only to see that time could be beaten, but that those whom one has loved do not simply disappear forever. Harry Penn might have died contentedly on the spot as Peter Lake slept before him. But privileges come in droves, this was not the last great thing that Harry Penn was to see, and he did not choose that moment to expire.

He grabbed Peter Lake's wrist and tugged at it to wake him up. Still asleep, Peter Lake pulled back his arm, and said, "That's not what I asked you."

"Wake up! Wake up!" Harry Penn shouted in delight, but no matter how much Harry Penn shook him, Peter Lake still slept. So, Harry Penn resorted to an old and effective reveille that he had used in the wars. Leaning over to within several inches of Peter Lake's right ear, he shouted, as hard as he could, "Hand grenade!"

Peter Lake's body coalesced into a bolt of lightning that took to the air, where he somehow managed to remain until he had scanned every inch of the floor. When he descended, he saw a very old man with a wide smile. "What did you do that for?" Peter Lake asked.

"You wouldn't get up. It's good. . . . What do I mean it's good? It's not just good, it's magnificent, a glory, the happiest thing in my life, to see you again."

Peter Lake eyed him with some apprehension. "Have we met?"

Harry Penn threw back his head and laughed with maniacal satisfaction. "I'm Harry Penn!" he said.

"You're the publisher of *The Sun*. You're my boss. But we never met."

"Oh yes we did," Harry Penn affirmed, gleefully bouncing up and down on his bent haunches. "More than eighty-five years ago! I wasn't even fifteen. Of course, you wouldn't recognize me now, but I know you. You haven't aged a day. Ha!"

Peter Lake looked carefully at the old man, waiting for some more of the story. He tried to envision what Harry Penn had looked like as a boy, and found that it was too difficult to do.

But Harry Penn, still enraptured (as he would be until the day he died), slapped his thigh, and gathered up his thoughts. "You know," he said, happily, "this reminds me of a time when I was just a small kid, and we were up in the mountains, on the way to the Coheeries. I was about four, I think.

"It was a beautiful June morning, and at the inn where we stayed the night, my father was sending a telegram, or waiting to receive one—I don't know. I was itching to get to the Coheeries, but I was told that we wouldn't be leaving until the afternoon. I went up to a high place that seemed to overlook all the world and take in half its sunshine, and there I found a field of blueberries. Soon I was lost in the grazing, and would have stayed there, eating, until my father called me—were it not for the approach of a train winding up the mountainside. The tracks were just a short distance from where I was, and I knew it was going to go past me.

"As I watched it draw close, I was greatly agitated. I wanted to stop it, because I realized that if it were going to come to me, it would have to leave me, too. And because I grieved in advance for its leaving, I decided to stop it, even if it meant that I had to destroy it. Do you know how I contrived to do that?"

Peter Lake shook his head to show that he didn't.

"I was going to throw a blueberry at it," Harry Penn said in a hoarse whisper.

"I got the biggest blueberry I could find, and went to wait by the side of the rails, stricken with guilt that I was going to slay a fine train, merely for my love of it. I remember that as it came closer and began to bear down on me I was trembling with remorse. At the very moment that the seventy-ton locomotive pulled up even with me, I forsook the world, and threw my blueberry at it.

"The next thing I knew, I saw the caboose rushing away into the meadows where I had been afraid to go because there were too many bees in the wildflowers, and the train continued on, disappearing into the bright snowfields at the top of the ridge.

"Never in my life have I been so relieved. With that terrible weight off my chest, I skipped down to the hotel, and resolved not to throw blueberries at locomotives.

"I thought that when you saw me you would be as amazed as I am to see you. But you don't have the slightest idea of who I am, do you?"

"No, sir, not really."

"It was as vain of me to think that you would know me, or that I would matter, as it was for me to think that I could derail a seventy-ton locomotive with a little berry. You hardly knew me even then. But, don't you recall my sister?"

"I can't say that I do. You see, I know that you're right when you talk about a hundred years ago. I remember it in flashes. But it's never clear."

"Then you don't know who you are, do you?"

"No."

"I do."

"I would be most relieved if you would let me in on it. It's been at the tip of my tongue ever since they pulled me from the harbor."

"You don't even know your own name?"

"No, sir, not even that."

"Then come," said Harry Penn. "Come upstairs with me, and I will show you who you are, not in words, but in beautiful images that could not ever be counterfeited or forged. And you will know

652

exactly who you are, forever, by knowing what it is that you love."

As he and Harry Penn ascended the hanging staircases at *The Sun*, Peter Lake clutched his side. Each step was a greater agony, for the wound had not healed. But, still, he almost floated up the stairs, and when they reached the last floor, Peter Lake continued to rise beyond the landing, and had to pull himself down so as not to strike the ceiling. A young copy boy who witnessed this dropped both his lower jaw and a large sheaf of papers that he had in his arms, and the breeze carried the papers down the hall with the same graceful, free, weightlessness that had been the mark of Peter Lake ascending the stairs.

Only with ironclad discipline and concentration was Peter Lake able to move through the long halls one step at a time. He knew that if he lost himself for even a moment he would accelerate through the walls and into the open air—hurtling toward something that pulled him forward with mounting and limitless velocity. He wondered what it was that was pouring into him the power to float, and run, and rise.

All that had been raging within him subsided in the gold and blue aura of the paintings that stood upon a long table in Harry Penn's office, leaning at a slight angle that made Peter Lake and Beverly seem to look into the distance.

A crown of color emanated from the life-sized portraits, in rose, yellows, and blues that boiled in the air, perpetually unfurling, like the sunlit spray of a wave that hangs in the light. To Peter Lake and Harry Penn, it appeared that the two figures were actually alive. The dark background with its slight radiance (as if a strong beam of light were passing through invisibly except for a few telltale glimmers of the dust) was in no way flat, and even though it was merely a few millimeters of paint, it led the eye far and deep. Beverly seemed perpetually to be reaching a smile. She had not only the look of grace and forgiveness common to those who stare from the past, but she seemed to be brimming over with the knowledge of something excellent and good. In his portrait, Peter Lake seemed unsure, uncomfortable, and not as well initiated in the brilliant mystery that surrounded Beverly with such force and confidence—despite the tentative way her left hand touched the folds of blue silk that billowed from her shoulder and were tied by a silver clasp. But he was, obviously, soon to learn. In her right hand, she held a folded fan against the pearly gray of her dress. Though it was not apparent in the portraits, they had been standing almost together when the artist had painted them, and her left hand was reaching to touch Peter Lake. Though their hands were not together, one would, if one were to know the circumstances of the sitting, see them on their way.

They were alive. To say so is not just a figure of speech, a device, or a metaphor. They were alive, and, what is more, she had seen everything.

"Your name is Peter Lake. And that was my sister—Beverly," Harry Penn offered.

Peter Lake held out his hand as if to say, "Shhh! I know. Of course I know." And he knew, as well, exactly what he had to do, though he didn't know how he was going to do it.

With a last look into Beverly's eyes, for courage, he turned from the portrait and left the room, with Harry Penn hard on his heels.

Harry Penn could only just keep up with him, and Peter Lake didn't turn when he spoke. "We sat for that portrait on a very beautiful day," he said. "I wanted to be outside, but she made me stand beside her from morning until night. Sometimes when I got tired of standing, I knelt on a little stool in back of her. I didn't see the sun once that day, but only a perfectly blue sky through the upper part of a north window.

"Later, at night, I was quite surprised to find that my muscles were pleasantly sore, and that my face and arms were sunburned.

"She said it was my reward, and that it was only a part of what was to come. I didn't know then what she meant, but now I do know."

Harry Penn stopped, and looked after Peter Lake as he disappeared down the stairs. The old man had done his part, and he returned to his office to direct *The Sun*.

* * *

654

Fat, gentle, slit-eyed Cecil Mature was in a rage. "Do this! Do that! Do this! Do that!" he said furiously to a desk littered with bushels of request slips, materials orders, looseleaf papers, queries, demands, and several dozen bright red and blue memos from Jackson Mead that had all arrived at the same time bearing the following inscription: "Most urgent, absolute, top, 1,000% priority—if I were a king in ancient times, I would lop off your head were you not to deal with this immediately."

He clenched his fist until it resembled a small stack of bagels, and slammed it hard against his huge desk, causing half a dozen cathode-ray screens to flicker in effeminate protest. Seething with an anger that threatened to compromise his extraordinarily sweet disposition, he tried to lose his temper the way other people did, and to become mean. Edging himself on, as it were, against an edgeless nature, he found himself in a struggle between a hard external voice and an inaudible but omnipotent inner gentleness.

"He just sits there, and doesn't even move," Cecil said, trying to work himself up. "Just commands, commands, commands. His lips hardly part when he talks, all for conservation of energy. 'Mr. Wooley, send twenty thousand freight cars to the iron fields of Minnesota. Mr. Wooley, convert the supertankers we are building in Sasebo into carriers of liquid hydrogen. Mr. Wooley, draw up the plans for a titanium smelter in Botswana. Mr. Wooley, do this. Mr. Wooley, do that.' I can't!"

Mootfowl glided up from nowhere. "He wants you to find out about the progress of the fire. It's coming down from the north at a fast pace, and he says you ought to get close to it, scout around, and try to pick up some information about the Short Tails."

"What about all this stuff?" Cecil asked, referring to the stack of "urgent" memos. "What about the charge fluctuations at Black Tom, the polarity reversal at Diamond Shoals, the switches that have to be changed in South Bay? How's that going to get done?"

"He says not to worry."

"Not to worry? After all those years? You mean he's not worried himself?"

"He isn't."

Cecil was astonished. "What about you? Aren't you a little tense? God knows, I am. The city's burning; we're pressed from all sides; the harbor's so turbulent I don't see how in the world the lenses will remain stable, and they've got to be completely immobile for the beams to concentrate perfectly, since the ice lenses are gone, and. . . ."

"I wouldn't lose too much sleep over that, Cecil," Mootfowl said. *"I'm* not going to."

Cecil couldn't believe his ears. "How can that be?" he asked. "You? You, the most nervous, jumpy, stiff, keyed-up divine that ever lived? We're so close!"

"Cecil, do you understand what happens if we throw that bridge, and it takes?"

"Eternal salvation, heaven on earth, the sight of God's face, the golden age—everyone slim and trim," Cecil answered in a sort of reverberatory awe.

"That's right," Mootfowl confirmed. "And what's left for us?"

"Wha?" said Cecil, nearly rolling off his chair.

"We'd be out of a job. If everything were bliss, there'd be no need for us, would there?"

"Don't you want it that way?"

"Quite frankly, I don't. I've changed my mind. And he's having second thoughts, too. We like it the way it is. We're enjoying the oscillating balances, the ongoing war between good and evil, the wonderful small triumphs of the soul. Perhaps it's too soon to end all that. Perhaps we need some more time to think things out."

"Another hundred years?" Cecil inquired.

"We were thinking about the excellent times that we've had, and we decided on maybe another thousand . . . or two."

"What about Peter Lake?"

"Must his triumph be absolute? None of the others had that, not Beverly Penn, nor any of the ones before, though when it's his time to act he may far outshine the others, and take the matter out of our hands."

"They don't do that."

"They haven't done it as yet. Who's to say that he won't? By the way, it's all working out very well with him, as far as we can tell."

"You've found him!"

"At about two o'clock this morning," Mootfowl said, "sleeping against a bank of machinery. *I* trained him to that."

"Like hell you did," Cecil snapped. "Don't you remember where you grabbed him?"

"Well, yes. But I sharpened his sense of the machine's nature. You do recall, don't you, that he thought they were animals?"

"Where is he?"

"You were always loyal to him, much more than to any of the others."

"He's been through a lot."

"They've all been," Mootfowl said. "The last I heard, he was at *The Sun*. Don't be too long. We're going to throw the bridge in a few hours, and if it takes, if it takes . . . I imagine you'll want to be around."

Printing House Square was crowded with dazed survivors looking for the people they loved. For fear of creating too great a contrast with those who were lost and alone, families whose members found one another suppressed their joy, which made it all the stronger. The Marrattas met Asbury, Christiana, and Jessica Penn just inside the doors of *The Sun*. They sat down together by a bank of palms illuminated by a number of spotlights in the ceiling. *The Sun*'s steam engines beat and hissed in a muscular rhythm to provide power for the presses and the light. But across Printing House Square, *The Ghost* was as black as pitch. Its employees stared at its triumphant rival, and their faces, illuminated alternately by flamelight and by the light of *The Sun* itself, were sad, moonlike, sallow, and held in hands that had nothing to do.

When Peter Lake reached the bottom of the stairs, he saw the Marrattas across the lobby, and went toward them. Just before he reached the bank of palms, he clutched his side in response to a sudden pain that nearly toppled him, and stood quietly, hoping for it to pass. They were talking. Hardesty and Asbury were speaking about the vault where Hardesty had left the salver. With the salver's several pounds of gold, the huge and powerful horse, the launch, and the many skills and strengths that the Gunwillows, the Marrattas, and Mrs. Gamely possessed, they could make a new beginning in the city, whatever its shape, when the fires died down and the morning came.

Peter Lake emerged from the palms. Just as he did, Cecil Mature scurried into the lobby of *The Sun,* breathless after pushing his way through the crowds. When he saw Peter Lake, his hardly visible eyes filled with tears. Peter Lake, too, felt a surge of brotherly affection for Cecil, and when he spoke his voice broke with emotion. "Have you got the tools to blow a vault?" he asked.

Cecil nearly collapsed with happiness at the sudden and perfect resumption of their old ways. "I can get them," he answered, overjoyed.

"We've got braces and hammers at *The Sun,*" Peter Lake said, "but the metal in these machines is soft. What I'll need from you are diamond bits of all sizes, nitro, variable chucks, and safe-cracker's probes. I'll bring the rest."

"I can get 'em easy!" Cecil yelled as he left. "Wait here."

Peter Lake turned to Asbury. "Tell me about the horse that you were talking about. Is he really huge, so that you almost need a ladder to get up on him? Is he as white as snow, and more beautiful than any equestrian statue? Does he fight as you wouldn't think a horse could ever fight, with his forelegs twirling and his head swinging back and forth like a mace? And does he have a tendency to take extremely long strides, which, if he has his way, become flight? I don't mean retreat. I mean *flying.*"

"Yes, it's all true," Christiana answered.

"You have my horse," Peter Lake said in such a way that Christiana lowered her eyes for having lost him once again. But Peter Lake then turned to Virginia. "Where's your little girl?" he asked.

"She's dead," Virginia answered. "You saw yourself."

"But where is she now?"

"We buried her on the Isle of the Dead," Hardesty said.

Peter Lake closed his eyes and thought. Then, shaking his head in the affirmative, as if he had just convinced himself of something, he opened his eyes, and he said, "Dig her up."

"What are you saying?" Hardesty replied, suddenly angry.

"What am I saying? I'm saying that you should go to the Isle of the Dead, and dig her up. Disinter her, if that's what you want to call it. Remove her from the grave."

"But why?" Hardesty asked, not knowing what to think.

"Because she's going to live," Peter Lake said quietly. "And that I know because of Beverly." He held up his hand. "Just do as I say. I'll take the horse, since he's mine anyway, but I'll open the vault and retrieve the salver for you in return."

"You spoke to Beverly," Hardesty said to Peter Lake. "Do you mean Beverly Penn?"

"Yes," Peter Lake answered, "Beverly Penn."

"Then I know who you are, from the pictures in the archives. You're the man who stood next to her in all the photographs, and was never identified. How is it that in all this time you haven't aged?"

"I'd like to know that myself," Peter Lake said. "It's been perplexing me for quite a while. But now Cecil Mature is back. If you'll tell me the location of the vault and the number of the box, we'll go get the salver, and leave it in place of the horse. Where is the horse?"

"Mr. Cecil Wooley," Cecil corrected, even though he was breathless from hauling a heavy leather sack full of diamond bits and titanium probes. "Remember?"

"I do remember," Peter Lake replied. "Mr. Wooley, would you like to crack one last vault?" Cecil beamed, and bashfully swung his right foot to and fro as he stared down at the ground.

Hardesty told Peter Lake the number of the box and the location of the vault. "I know that one," Peter Lake said, "from back then, when it was the ne plus ultra of vaults. With modern tools and techniques, it shouldn't be that difficult."

"Do you want the combination of the box, and a key for a padlock that holds down the lid?" Hardesty asked, pulling out his key ring, and then, realizing that he had insulted Peter Lake, putting it back in his pocket.

Christiana told Peter Lake where to find the white horse—in a courtyard on Bank Street. He could see that she didn't want to part with him. "I'm not going to keep him either," he said. "He's going home."

During these exchanges, Mrs. Gamely had been sulking unnoticed on a bench. Peter Lake approached her. "Sarah," he said. "I'm deeply sorry for having been so rude to you a little while ago. I didn't really remember. Will you forgive me?"

"Oh yes," she answered. "You're Peter Lake, aren't you."

He nodded his head.

He and Mr. Cecil Wooley, as Cecil preferred to be called (since he thought that, unlike the heavy-set syllables of "Mature," "Wooley" sounded very thin and graceful) left to crack the vault.

After they leaned through the transoms and had the mechanics pass them the other tools they needed, they left *The Sun* for the bank that Hardesty had chosen years before because it had looked noble, responsible, and burglarproof.

If by will, imagination, and desire, one can cross from one time to another, Peter Lake and Cecil Mature did so on their half-mile walk. They existed in the present only with a great deal of sufferance anyway, and they suspected that they were soon to rise and actually fly out of it. Hanging on to the modern age by only a thread, they could almost hear the choirs of voices, the tremulous sounds that would shake the ground, and the tones that would come from beyond the swirling smoke. They sensed very strongly the imminent marriage of chaos and order which seemed to be on its way to the turbulent city surrounded by calm blue bays.

They saw images projected from afar into the billowing eruptive smoke, and Peter Lake quickly surmised that the record of all things, though rushing away into uncharted infinity, could still throw back a strong and indelible reflection. They saw, briefly unfolding, the flowering of the city they had once known—the horses straining at their wagons, the snow dumpers hard at work, the firemen and their urnlike engines, the ice-hung maze of telephone wires, the old silks and diamond lapels, innocent and fleeting expressions born to light an unknowing face for the rest of time. They heard hoofbeats, the mourning whistles of many-stacked ferries, the clatter of harness, peddlers' calls, and wooden wheels on the cobbles. And Peter Lake knew that these things were nothing in themselves but the means by which to remember those he had loved, and to remind him that the power of the love he had known was repeated a million times a million times over, from one soul to another—all worthy, all holy, none ever lost. He glided through the illusions that flashed bravely on the smoke, and he was touched very deeply by the will of things to live in the light.

The bank was a looming old stone building. Every window and door was covered with Spanish ironwork that looked as delicate as lace. But the bars, far from being frilly tendrils, were hardened steel as thick as Craig Binky's head.

"Now there's a bank to be admired," said Peter Lake, pointing to the motto engraved in four-foot letters across the architrave: "Neither a borrower nor a lender be."

"We never did a job like this, not even close," Cecil said apprehensively.

"I did," he was answered. "Quite close. Some of the private vaults I opened were probably almost as big as the one that's in here. All you need are the right tools, patience, and a little practice. It's only metal."

"How are we going to get in? The front door?"

"We could use the front door, since there aren't any cops around, and it's dark. But banks always concentrate their strengths in the places that the public sees. We'll save fifteen minutes if we go through a second-story window in the back."

They went around the corner and climbed to a wide ledge which formed the sill of a window that was itself behind thick iron bars. "In the old days," Peter Lake said, "we'd have had to cut or blow these bars, or use a jackscrew as big as a telephone pole. But now, thanks to diligent metallurgists, we've got these wonderful little creatures." He reached into his bag and pulled out two silver jacks, each about the size of a loaf of bread. They were comprised of a gearbox in the center, and something that looked like a combination of a threaded shaft and a ratchet post. Peter Lake fixed them between a set of bars, and then attached folding cranks which he and Cecil Mature began to turn. After a minute of furious circling, hardly any change was visible.

He explained that hundreds of wafer-thin alloy gears were packed in so densely as to give a mechanical advantage of two thousand. Though it would take a lot of turning, it would work, he said, and pointed to little cracks where the bars met the stone. There were even battery-powered models, he informed his partner, but what was the point? What could you do while the thing was working, sit on the ledge and eat your lunch, or read *Field and Stream?* The idea was to work *with* the machine.

Soon the bars began to sing like old Irishwomen who tend sheep in the fog. Ten minutes later they had spread far enough apart for Peter Lake to reverse the jacks, pull them out, and step through. However, Cecil became wedged firmly between them, and was only able to get inside after Peter Lake plastered him with graphite and pulled at him. The exertion reopened Peter Lake's wound, and he bent double with pain.

"I'm all right," he declared. "Let's move on."

Now they were on familiar ground, working together with the old tools on an old-fashioned break-tape window alarm. They drilled a dozen tiny holes through the tape, and connected them together with copper probes and wires. Then, knowing that the current would not be interrupted, they carefully cut a hole through the glass, and pulled it out with a double suction cup, placing it neatly between the window and the bars. They were careful about the alarms not because they feared the police (who had their hands full), but rather as a matter of pride. They anchored a block and tackle to the bars, maneuvered themselves and their tools through the opening in the glass, stood in the stirrups of their tackle, and slowly lowered themselves to the floor thirty feet below.

When they touched down, they touched lightly and without a sound. Peter Lake looked into the turbulent darkness high above him. "Shhh!" he whispered to Cecil, who thought the police were nearby. "Do you hear it?"

"What?" Cecil whispered back.

"The music."

"What music?"

"Piano music, a very soft and beautiful piano. Listen."

Cecil closed his eyes, held his breath, and concentrated deeply. But he could hear nothing. Peter Lake said, "Ah . . . beautiful! How tranquil."

Cecil took another breath, and tried again. "I like music," he said a minute later, after he had exhaled. "But I didn't hear anything."

"It's very faint. It's circling up there, near the top of the dome, like a little cloud."

They slid across a little prairie of madly waxed marble, their way dimly lit by the red glare of the fires, and went down some wide stairs that led to the sepulcher in which the vault had been set. A ceremonial gate of bronze-colored steel bars proved easy enough to pass simply by punching in the lock with a hardened awl and a sledgehammer. Once they were beyond the gate, they switched on their headlamps and approached the vault.

The door was ten feet in diameter, with hinge pins twice as thick as a fire hydrant. The stainless-steel wheels and rods that were scattered over its front made it look like the interior of a submarine. But Peter Lake was not discouraged, and immediately lapsed into an analytical monologue the beguiling likes of which Cecil had often heard from Mootfowl as he felt his way through something difficult and unknown. "These wheels, here," Peter Lake said, touching half the capstans as he spoke, "are just to impress the safe deposit customers. They're stuck on to make the thing look like it's impossible to move. They turn, see? But they have nothing to do with the problem.

"These two—" he patted two spoked steel thistles each a yard in diameter—"they turn the four bolts. That's it. If we could rotate these, the bolts would crawl from the strikes like woodchucks backing out of their holes. Each bolt is as thick as a small log with roughly the diameter of a dinner plate, in solid vanadium steel.

"In the old days, you could manipulate the locks, even the time locks. You'd have to drill to get to the workings, but you could do it. Now the mechanisms have been retrofitted so that they're controlled by those little silicon things, tea biscuits that are smarter than we are. If you want to outwit them, you've go to be able to deal with individual electrons. Maybe Mootfowl can do that, but it's not my style.

"So we've got to bypass the control, get to the four bolts, and destroy them. That means drilling three holes for each bolt, and blasting the bolt itself into the vault, since the back of the door is covered only with quarter-inch-sheet steel that's easy to buckle. The holes have to be placed just right."

He removed a bushel of calipers and rules from the leather bag, and began to etch a Euclidean diagram on the conveniently smooth surface of the burnished steel. He sang while he worked, which delighted Cecil (even though Cecil could not hear the distant piano that Peter Lake was accompanying), for the sound of it was druidic, tantalizing, and vaguely Oriental, and it reminded Cecil of his years as a tattooist. In about an hour, everything was marked out in precise diamond-etched targets. After they drilled anchor holes for tripods that would hold the bits at the proper slope, they set up the bits and braces, and began to drill.

They used the ultrahigh-speed water-cooled electric drills that Peter Lake had appropriated from dental science and adapted to his needs at *The Sun*. When the shafts had been opened in practically no time, they poured in nitroglycerine from a dozen glass bottles, sealed the holes with gutta-percha, pushed long copper spark probes through the soft sealant, connected these to an octopuslike distributor, gathered their tools, and ran a wire out of the vault and across the cavernous banking floor.

As he connected the leads to a blasting box, Peter Lake said, "I hate to blow vaults with nitro, but speed is of the essence here, and these tea biscuits just ask for it. The bolts are going to be propelled into the back of the vault like armor-piercing shells. I hope they don't hit the plate." He turned to Cecil. "Do you remember Mootfowl's nitro prayer?" Cecil nodded. "Then say it, and I'll push the plunger."

Cecil mumbled something about a ball of fire, Peter Lake put his palm on the plunger, clutched his side yet again, and shoved the rod into the piston.

The bank shook as if there were an earthquake. Above them, a giant chandelier was suddenly lit, and its several tons of surprised and protesting crystals were swinging back and forth.

"That's it. It even turned on the lights. Batteries, all banks have battery circuits, just for people like us. Let's go." They ran down into the sepulcher, which was now brightly lit. "Turn the wheels," Peter Lake commanded. "I can't. My side hurts too much." Cecil turned the wheels to remove the remnants of the bolts from the strikes. Then they pulled at the enormous door, which was perfectly balanced on its fire-hydrant hinges, and the vault was open.

"What's the number of the box?" Cecil wanted to know.

"Fourteen ninety-eight," Peter Lake answered. He was in considerable pain, because he had not been able to resist helping Cecil pull open the door.

The box was at waist level, on the right side of the chamber. Peter Lake approached it, sank to his knees, and began to work the combination. He watched himself in the floor-to-ceiling mirror on one wall of the vault, looked in his own eyes, and glanced at Cecil's rotund form alongside, bobbing up and down with anticipation. He saw a pool of blood forming on the marble tiles beneath him. Despite the pain, he seemed to be getting more and more alert, and more and more powerful.

"Finished," he said, moving the bolt lever. The little door swung open, and Cecil pulled out the box. They clipped off the small padlock, lifted the lid, and spread apart the folds of cloth that wrapped the salver.

Peter Lake held it up before them.

This was not a still thing. Like a good painting, it moved. And like light, it moved. In the forever lively interaction of the pure and untarnished metals from which it had been fashioned, it glowed in a thousand colors, glinting in whites, blues, silvers, and gold. It seemed to be on fire, and it lighted their faces.

"It's alive," Peter Lake said. "No one's ever going to melt it down. No one ever could."

* * *

Chelsea had become a dark and quiet island surrounded by lines of nervous militiamen armed with rifles and fixed bayonets. Because Cecil was short and squat, he superficially resembled a Short Tail, though he did not have either the stubby curled nose or the paddle chin. The militiamen, mainly farmboys from upstate, were not too sure of what a Short Tail looked like close-up, and they weren't partial to the leather bags full of burglar's tools, either. But the salver dazzled them, and they let Peter Lake and Cecil pass through their lines.

Though the fires had liberated enormous amounts of energy, and numerous inversions had trapped warm air close to the ground (making some areas as hot as summer and most of the city comfortably springlike), it was still winter, and cold breezes much like cold streams in an otherwise tepid river wound through the mild inversions like smooth serpents of ice—refreezing pools of melt water, slicking down the sidewalks, and contracting whole neighborhoods of air in strange ebullient booms. Chelsea was warm. The trees were in leaf. The bushes had thickened up, and stood in stable plumes pressed against iron fences or congregated in the square. Flowers repossessed flower boxes, as self-assured as cats who sleep outside on a summer night.

"A florist must have been here," Cecil offered, his mouth slightly open as he tried to take in more air than usual, so that he might smell the flowers.

"A florist indeed," Peter Lake answered. "These are some of the plumes. Some will be a mile high, others no bigger than a leaf."

They turned into a narrow passage that led to a garden courtyard. An iron gate secured with a bicycle lock barred their way. It could not have been opened with its key as fast as it was picked by the chief mechanic of *The Sun*. At the end of the passageway was an enclosed garden that ran from east to west for two blocks. The residents of the buildings looking over it had torn down the fences that separated their plots, to make the narrow close a private park.

Peter Lake realized that he would best reclaim Athansor alone. He stopped, and turned to his friend, who knew that yet another very short time was now over. Cecil was not about to press himself on Peter Lake the way he had done at the beginning of the century, begging to be his squash cook, promising to make money with tattoo jobs on the side, sticking to him wherever he went even though it was hard to keep up.

Often when someone dies those left behind think to themselves, if only I could have one more day: I would use it so well—an hour, perhaps even a minute. Cecil Mature had been given his time with Peter Lake, and it was now over. Tears would have tumbled down his cheeks had not Jackson Mead and Mootfowl taught him not to cry. "It's not good for the digestive system," Mootfowl had said, as severe as the Connecticut undertaker he had once been.

"It's all changed now," Peter Lake said. "For us, it's come to an end. But, you'll see, when you sleep it'll well up so strongly that you won't know which is the dream. And when, finally, there is nothing left of you, you'll be overpowered by the strength of another time that will—mark my words—reclaim you. It will snap you up and pull you under like a trout taking a bug—all suddenness, all surprise, something silver rising from the depths. And then you may find that it starts all over again, because it has never ended."

"I understand that. It doesn't make it any easier."

"Now you've got to turn your back on me and go."

"I can't."

"Yes you can. You'll have to do it sometime, so you might as well do it now."

Cecil thought that it would be impossible to turn from Peter Lake. But Peter Lake was smiling, and perhaps because of the promise that he sensed in the smile, Cecil was able to turn and leave.

Now Peter Lake was alone in the garden. He moved slowly among the trees until, halfway through, he found himself on a slight rise, from which he could see the other end. Standing there in perfect calm, looking straight at him, was his white horse.

The minute he saw the white horse, all the powers that had brought him to that very moment left him forever, and he became just a man with a wound in his side. The horse, too, seemed no longer like the great balloon-limbed statue that he had been. He seemed to be smaller, perhaps not as good a fighter, and there was something about him which suggested . . . a milk horse. He followed Peter Lake with his eyes, and bent his neck way over to one side when Peter Lake went around a clump of bushes. When Peter Lake emerged, Athansor's ears were pointing back, his face was strained forward, and his right legs were touching the ground only tentatively, which was the way he used to lean sometimes when he was drawing milk wagons in summer, and would stop under a curbside horse-shower of the Horses' Aid Society.

Peter Lake looked into Athansor's eyes. Though the horse seemed more diminutive now, and his wounds and scars were anything but beautiful to see, and though he would not have seemed out of place harnessed in the traces of a wagon, he still had his round and perfect eyes.

After leaving the salver against the new branches that had stubbornly sprung from the foreshortened stump of a tree, Peter Lake made a quick mount, and they started for the tunnel at the other end of the close. Green leaves rushed by them as if it were spring or summer, and when Peter Lake looked up, he knew that dawn was not too far away. "Come on," he said, as he guided the white horse through the dark foliage. "Hurry now. You're going home."

Though the fires had died down, they had burned nearly everything, and the beams of gutted buildings glowed with heat. Apart from these dark red bars that made the city a luminescent blueprint of what it once had been, very little was left intact. The protected islands stood amid fields of destruction that once again reflected natural features of the underlying terrain, and open distance had returned to Manhattan after many hundreds of years. Smoke and steam drifted upward from the rivers, in white, gray, and silver. The streets were deserted. The city had been conquered and destroyed, and it looked much smaller.

Just before dawn, Peter Lake cantered Athansor up and down

the long avenues. Athansor's strides, matchless in their grace, carried them from one end of the island to the other, and back, as if they were using a razor strop or looming a sheet of cloth. They sailed to and fro so smoothly that it was as if they were gliding on ice, and as they passed by, time was compressed in the ruins, enabling them to see the city as it was and as it would be, all at once. No richer tapestry had ever been devised, for here all time was at issue. They were able to see it not because they were gifted and high, but, rather, because they had been humbled, and because the world had been pushed back as quiescent images had rebelled and surged forward in disorder and victory. Though the city lay in ruins, nothing about it seemed dead, and it continued as if its spirit had never needed the material frame that now was gone.

They saw a black thunderstorm race in on a summer day and scatter children through the park, their hair blowing in the sudden wind, hoops rolling free, the forked ribbons of the little girls' gondoliers' hats luffing as violently as the wings of a bird trapped inside a house. They saw an airplane rising alone at night, its powerful white light coming for them in the empty air as if God had sent an angel. They saw ships and barges rush from north to south and south to north as if supplying far-flung endangered regiments, cutting the clear blue band of the Hudson with silver wakes that flashed like swords. They saw wrestlers straining on the mat, their struggling limbs unknowingly symmetrical, parodies of bridges, beams, and rock formations. They saw a poor child kissing a doll. They saw a pile driver six stories high hypnotizing a lunchtime crowd in the garment district with the otherworldly strikes of metal upon metal and the crazy exhalations of steam that lifted its heavy weight over and over, again and again—very much like the garment workers themselves, who sewed and stitched through the hours and days of their lives. They saw a family walking by a pool, and they knew from the houses and the wooden walls that the ducks in the pond had never heard any language but Dutch. They saw courageous little boats rushing through Hell Gate, waltzing in a white current between walls of rock. They saw a young actress who, bathed in rose light, was playing her part, and mastering her fear. They saw the steel-gray bridges, in the sunshine and in snowstorms, standing about the city like giant bedsteads.

These things unfurled before them like flags rolling out on the wind, and seemed to be an important part of the truth if only because they presented again and again the same curves, the same colors, the same flowing symmetries, the same feelings, operations, and acts, all of which, over time, spoke and sang in one language and one song of one central beauty.

Peter Lake rode past dance halls and symphonies ten deep in the same space, and discovered that their sounds combined in a single perfect tone. Part of the overlay of flawless images seemed to be that Athansor was leading a phalanx of fifty horses, or more—mares and stallions, colts and fillies, grays, chestnuts, blacks, and spotted ponies, red Shetlands, Percherons with manes above their hooves like African dancers, Arabians, war-horses, thoroughbreds, and dray horses. But when Peter Lake looked carefully, he saw that they were real. More than just images, they were flesh and blood, and they had gathered to Athansor as he shuttled along the streets. Pulled from their hiding places in rubble-filled lots, they had banded together, and now all were cantering with the same smooth stride, the milk horse in the lead.

As it grew light enough to make out individual forms in the distance, Peter Lake saw astonished Short Tails, their mouths hanging open as he thundered by at the head of the procession. This suited his purpose well enough. They would soon discover the pattern he was making, and get the news to Pearly, who would probably also hear that Athansor had now turned himself into fifty synchronized horses.

On their last pass over the north of the island, they sent the fifty horses into the river, and watched them ford to Kingsbridge and escape along the river's edge. Now Manhattan was cleared of its horses but for one. Because they saw that the sun was about to rise, Peter Lake and Athansor galloped this time, and they stopped somewhere south of the park. There were hardly any landmarks left, and it was hard for them to know exactly where they were.

The rider dismounted. One cannot properly embrace a horse—they're too big. So Peter Lake was content to look in Athansor's eyes. "I suppose," he said, "that you know where you're going." The horse sneezed. "Do you think they'll let you in up there with a cold?" Peter Lake asked. "In those pastures, they probably don't worry about that sort of thing. But who knows, maybe they've got a quarantine. Maybe that's what kept me out.

"Now it's time for you to do what you've been able to do and haven't done, on my account, for God knows how long. Go ahead. I won't be with you. You have to do it by yourself."

The horse didn't move until Peter Lake clicked his tongue and waved his hand.

Then Athansor whinnied, and began to walk. The very fact of his motion took hold of him, and he started to gallop, faster and faster, until the ground rumbled beneath him and he was far away from Peter Lake, who was deeply saddened. He would never see the white horse again, but he was confident that the horse would find his right and proper place, where he had started, home.

Athansor vaulted from the ground as if to rise. Though he came down after sailing only ten or fifteen feet, he was little discouraged. He tried once more, in much the same spirit of a man who, awakened from a dream of flying, goes back to sleep confident that he will fly again. He found a long rubble-free avenue, and began to run. At first, he cantered, holding himself back. Then he started to gallop. The air whistled past his bent-back ears. His hooves seemed to touch the ground as lightly and infrequently as the hand that seems effortlessly to power the potter's wheel. Now, certainly, with the speed he possessed, he had only to draw up his front legs, tighten his neck, and turn his face to the sky—the way he had always done—and he would soar into the air in a strong ascending curve. He threw himself forward and up, and courageously refused to expect anything but flight.

And then, despite his courage, he came crashing down on the pavement, lost his balance, rolled several times in uncontrolled somersaults, and smashed into a line of garbage cans that had

671

formed a barrier on either side of which was absolutely nothing. The tremendous clatter shocked him, but not half as much as his simple earthboundedness.

After the shock and humiliation of skidding along the street and bowling over the garbage cans, he retreated to the park. Alone in an empty field, he bent way down and pushed his head between his forelegs until he was rolled up in a compact package that resembled an equestrian statue done by a cubist, or, as Craig Binky would have said, a cuban.

The purpose of this was inspection. From various stables and from the street, he had many times witnessed the churchly and unassailable process wherein an auto mechanic elevated a car in the presence of its silent and intimidated owner, and examined its entrails from underneath. So, he did it himself. He was no mechanic, however, nor a veterinarian, an anatomist, or (more to the point) an aeronautical engineer. Everything seemed perfectly fine—his hooves were glistening, black, and hard; his muscles were taut; the tendons underneath his hide were as strong as steel cables; and his belly was firm and streamlined.

Encouraged because nothing seemed to be amiss, he decided to try again. He would gain speed in a mad rush up the walkway to the Belvedere, and then sail out over the lake and past the high rubble on Fifth Avenue, to make a breathtaking orbital curve to the south.

Going up the trails was as easy as if there were no grade. Even the steps and curves of the walkway were no hindrance. When he flew outward in the turns, he checked his inertia with four hooves against the vegetation on the side of the path, bounding ahead as if he were rushing down a mountain. Reaching the top, he dashed across a surface of flat rock and pushed himself into the air with the power of his briefly coiled and compressed rear quarters. Up he went, enthralled. Remembering what it was to fly, he experienced the lovely weightless updraft that the angels feel. And then he began to fall.

This was by no means the controlled glide that he had habitually used to descend, a fall in which every moment of apprehension had brought a cease-fire with gravity, until he and it signed a treaty on the ground. Not at all: it was a flailing, tumbling, sinking rout. He turned in the air, his nostrils flared, his eyes opened wide, and he fell into the lake a hundred feet below the Belvedere, sending up plumes of foaming white water that looked for a moment like wings sprouting from his sides, though, fortunately for him, he was unaware of that irony.

Despite the way in which he had taken to the water, he swam beautifully, and climbed up on the bank as nobly as ever a horse emerged from river or lake. Perhaps because he was dripping wet he seemed crazed or panicky. But he was not to be deterred, and he started for one of the long and straight avenues, where he hoped to gallop for however many miles it might take before he flew.

Though at first they could not see its color in the strange light that came between the darkness and the dawn, after the fires had died and the moon had poked between tremendous Himalayan clouds of vapor and ash, the surface of the harbor was as green and smooth as emerald. Asbury guided the launch through the repentant waters, steering between upturned chunks of ice that looked in the blinking moonlight less like icebergs than the harmless polar bears in paintings, that are forever immobile and only three or four inches high.

On the Isle of the Dead, the gravedigger had disappeared. He had fled when he heard the launch, leaving his hat and his shovels. Hardesty threw aside the hat, took one of the shovels, and began to dig. He wouldn't let Asbury help him, and he wished that before his shovel struck wood he would die and awaken in another world. He lifted shovelfuls of the soft earth, and the others watched.

It did not take long to get the little coffin above ground. "Now what," he asked, afraid and unwilling to open it.

"Take her out. It hasn't been long, and the ground is cold," Virginia said. Hardesty clenched his teeth, and thrust the shovel under the lid of the coffin. He pried it up, took it in his hands, and threw it violently to the side. Abby lay within, much the same as she had been when they had last seen her. From a distance, someone might have thought that she was asleep.

Hardesty bent to pull her close to him, listening for life. But she was completely still. He carried her as he had so often done when bringing her home in the evening, when she had fallen asleep in his arms.

Asbury held the launch against the dock while Hardesty stepped down, took Abby from his shoulder, and laid her on the hatch cover. Virginia and Mrs. Gamely lifted Martin in and climbed aboard, and Christiana pushed off, nimbly jumping onto the stern.

The rumbling of the old engine beneath the hatch cover cleared Abby's hair from her face. Only Martin noticed, for he alone dared look at her, since he alone truly believed that she would awaken. He knelt beside her, waiting for her eyes to open. Mrs. Gamely nervously fingered the poultice that she carried in her bag, but she knew it was for curing the sick, not for bringing back the dead. The rest of them looked everywhere but at Abby, though Virginia kept her right hand on the little girl's shoulder. They set off across the harbor, among the melting cakes of ice, with a gentle wave from their bows, and hardly a wake.

It was beginning to get bright.

Indeed it was. The sun was just about to come up on the first day of the third millennium, to view the destruction of the city and see with what pleasure, determination, and nerve its inhabitants would face this, the newest of their days. As always before the dawn, there was a certain sense of urgency.

The messages and messengers that had been coming to Jackson Mead in a steadily swelling flood in the previous hours suddenly broke off. No one arrived to break the silence, and even Cecil Mature sat quietly in his place, gazing sadly through the large windows that gave out on the green harbor. Tranquil now for the first time in too long a time to recount. Mootfowl was perched on a sort of dunce chair behind and to the side of Jackson Mead. He had prayed silently for at least an hour, though for what, exactly, no one knew.

In the quiet, Jackson Mead reflected upon what he was about to do, and doubted that he would succeed. He had never succeeded before, when the elements were simpler, the air was purer, and the horizon trembled with the immediate presence of the cloud wall. But now hardly anyone knew the cloud wall for what it was even when it swept through the city and scoured their souls white. And though the machines were ready, Jackson Mead doubted that conditions had properly coalesced. He doubted the coming of the high shimmering gold that would commend an instance of perfect, balanced justice, for he doubted that anyone remembered or cared for justice either natural or divine. They had all defined it according to their own lights, which meant that it always had to be quick and uncomplicated.

It had taken ages for him to realize that he had to make a bridge of light without a discernible end. Before that, he had built wonders of lovely proportion and airy grace, silvery catenaries that sang in the breeze high above windblown straits all over the world, connecting one heather-covered cliff to another, or marrying the two sides of a choked and impoverished city. It had been right and good to fashion those vast curves which were in themselves an ideal synthesis of rising and falling, aspiration and despair, rebellion and submission, pride and humility. In imitation of universal waves, they were the strongest things ever constructed, and probably the most religious of structures except perhaps for the church steeples, that pointed up into the far distance.

Now he had the thick and precisely aligned bundles of light, perfectly parallel, perfectly pure, to aim in a curve so gradual that by all known means of measurement it would appear to be absolutely straight. It was to take root in the Battery and pierce the air with its smooth particolored girderwork, straight as an arrow, at forty-five degrees.

Jackson Mead walked over to a twelve-foot-high tinted window, and kicked it out. "I want to see this in its true colors," he said as the glass shattered and the pieces flew outward to glide and tumble on the wind.

The breeze pushed against their faces and swept back their hair, and they had to lean into it as they surveyed what was before them.

The sky was crowded with plumes of steam and smoke. High and white, slowly turning, slowly rising, their tops already in the sun, they looked like a range of golden mountains that were far away not on the horizon, but on high. Jackson Mead tilted his head and squinted at this sight, and then turned to Mootfowl. "There are the plumes of smoke and ash. We can't wait any longer."

In an arresting gesture of hand and eye, he signaled for the bridge to be thrown.

In the launch, they thought that they had been struck by lightning. The blinding spectral flash and its ensuing concussion pushed them down into the bilge. The only one who was not thrown was Abby.

Just east of the park, staring down a seemingly endless avenue and trying to summon his courage, the white horse had his breath knocked out of him by the sudden burst of light and crack of thunder that rolled over the city and brought even the ruins to attention.

From the Battery rose a beautiful angled beam of light in every color. Each section was as tall as a man, a yard wide, and how long no one could tell. The warmer colors—the reds, greens, violets, and grays—were the core, and the more ethereal and metallic colors the sheath. Solid beams mitered the air, rose through the plumes, and disappeared beyond sight. The blue, white, silver, and gold beams that comprised the sheath were transparent, blinding, and jewel-like, and a halation that appeared substantial enough to walk upon followed and echoed the main structure in a diffuse, spangling, silvery road.

As the minutes passed, Jackson Mead watched. "How much time?" he asked, second by second, for he knew that even at the speed of light, or faster (because of the curve), it would be neither seconds nor minutes, but hours before they would know if the bridge had taken. They would know if the long arch had found a resting place when a back wave would return through it and shake the earth. And if it failed, it would simply go out, as if someone had blown out a candle.

They were not the only ones in the city who were transfixed by what they had made. No one anywhere moved, for fear of breaking the spell. Especially for those who were not aware of the test that was yet to come, it seemed as if it were working. The plumes kept rising. The sun was now so close to the eastern horizon that, to watch it, one would think that all Europe was burning. And the bridge appeared to be on its way.

But Mootfowl, the expert mechanic, suddenly stepped forward, for he had seen amidst the light what no one else, not even Jackson Mead, was capable of seeing. Cecil Mature turned away from the bridge for the first time, and looked at Mootfowl. And then Jackson Mead saw what it was that Mootfowl had discovered.

The interior had begun to vibrate, a sure sign that it would not take. Hardly perceptible at first, it was soon oscillating in a regular rhythm. The whole bridge began to shake. Then it buckled, and, as suddenly as it had been thrown, it disappeared, leaving only a fine and confusing afterimage to those who now found themselves in the morning light, aching in memory of its beauty.

Now the sun was up. It appeared to sit on a blackened line of rooftops in Brooklyn and drip gold into the streets. As it rose higher, it poured molten metal down the hills and into the harbor, making a thousand dark alleys into a thousand golden sluices.

In the ruins of the Maritime Cathedral, Peter Lake watched the light run in from behind columns and buttresses, steadily driving away shadows and reflecting off whatever glass was left in the windows that still had a shape. He imagined that when the cathedral had been surrounded by fire it must have been blacker than ink, and that red light had danced in scalloped patterns on the high ceilings. And perhaps a bright flare, a gas line igniting, or the sudden kindling of a wooden house had sent straight rays glinting through the whale's white eye, or made the sails appear to billow in the delicate glass ships. Now, charred beams lay across the floor, and as the sunlight streamed in, Peter Lake could see that in a very short time weeds would begin to grow over the stone.

Not exactly sure of what to expect, Peter Lake was startled by a noise that sounded like a gloved fist hitting metal. He shielded his eyes and looked toward the door, where, backlighted, someone

677

was staggering about, his hands clutching his head. "That has to be you, Pearly," Peter Lake shouted, even though he couldn't see clearly because of the sun in his eyes. "Only Pearly Soames would knock his head coming through a door that's forty feet wide." Moving to the center of the cathedral, Peter Lake felt his blood running hard. He had not intended to be full of fight, but, as if from nowhere, the fight had returned.

After smashing his head quite hard against a pipe that had fallen diagonally across the doorway, Pearly was hopping about in pain.

"Or maybe it's not Pearly Soames," Peter Lake taunted. "The way it's hopping around, it looks like some bastard jackrabbit that stepped on a nail." Pearly stopped still, his anger greater than the pain.

"Now, Pearly Soames, he's a dumb evil bastard too. He falls downstairs twice a day, and he mistakenly shoots his own men. He mixes up words because his tongue is a snake fighting for its independence. And he has dreadful, disgusting fits, after which he comes to and finds that his hands are full of blood because his long filthy nails have raked his flanks and attacked his face. But the bastard—and I mean, literally, *bastard*—hasn't yet been known to hop like a jackrabbit. So, who is it, now? Is it Pearly, or is it a rabbit?"

"It's Pearly, and you know it," replied a deep scratchy voice in barely controllable anger. Pearly Soames walked slowly up the center aisle between two forests of pews that had been crushed by falling masonry.

He was tremendous. Peter Lake had not remembered that Pearly had been so big, but now he seemed to be ten feet tall. There again were the eyes that made Rasputin's seem as soft as a lamb's. Even Peter Lake, in whom there had resided nearly every kind of power, was impressed by the mobility of Pearly's eyes. They were shallow, self-consuming whirlpools that terrorized not because of what they threatened, but because of their emptiness. They took note of the wound in Peter Lake's side.

"I see that little Gwathmi did stick you," Pearly said, warming to the possibility that, as Peter Lake had rustled through time, his invulnerability had been scraped off. "His brother Sylvane told me

678

about it, hoping for a reward. I didn't believe him, so I killed him."

"Let's see," Peter Lake interrupted, mockingly. "With which one of your ivory-handled doodads did you kill him? Was it with pimp's knuckles? An ebony beaver tail?"

"With my hands. Sylvane was very small, smaller even than Gwathmi. I reached out and grabbed his neck in my right fist," Pearly said, clenching his teeth together as he imitated what he had done, "and squeezed until it snapped. He went for his weapons, but he didn't have time. He should have known."

"You can't do that to me, can you?" Peter Lake asked, staring without fear into Pearly's eyes. "You never could touch me, remember?"

"Oh no, not *you*," Pearly answered. "No, not you. A *woman* protects you, Peter Lake, a girl. I've tried, haven't I, but you do have a shield. Or, you had a shield. She must be getting tired of the job, since she let Gwathmi through. Nothing lasts forever, Peter Lake, nothing, not even her love for you."

"Love passes from soul to soul, Pearly. It does last forever. But you wouldn't know about that."

"I might, in fact. You'd be surprised at what I've come to know. I grant you that it passes from soul to soul, but you must grant me that it is a finite commodity, and that, as it is traded, it leaves some souls unprotected and abandoned."

"I don't think so," Peter Lake offered. "I think that nothing is lost in the giving."

"That's a bloody myth," Pearly screamed, "and violates all laws! The world is held in perfect balance. When you give, you lose. When you take, you gain. There's nothing more to it."

"No," said Peter Lake. "The laws that you think are absolute have on occasion been abridged. Anyway, they are vastly complicated, and what is apparent is not always what is true."

"Are you sure of that?" Pearly asked.

Peter Lake hesitated before he answered. "No," he said, "I'm not sure."

"Of course you're not, because your protection is gone," Pearly insisted. "You're abandoned now, Peter Lake. I knew that if I hung on long enough, I would find you when you'd be worn down.''

"My protection may have disappeared,'' Peter Lake asserted. "But you've still got me to fight.'' Then he did something that no one had ever dared to do. He raised himself up, and he spat in Pearly's eyes.

Pearly's short sword was out instantly and on its way down, but Peter Lake jumped to the side. Only then did Peter Lake see that Short Tails were perched on the walls, hidden in the broken pews, and standing in packed ranks near the altar.

As Pearly bellowed, and swung his sword from left to right, Peter Lake threw himself back and landed perfectly on the base of a broken column. "What makes you think that I can't dispatch you just like *that?*'' he said, slamming his fist through the empty air. "What makes you think that I can't take all the little men who are standing here and hurl them to Canarsie faster than the speed of sound?'' Sparkling with anger, Peter Lake had momentarily forgotten what he was intending to do.

Pearly rushed him with the sword, trying to cut through his ankles. This time, instead of dodging, Peter Lake lifted his left foot and trapped the sword against the stone. Try as he might, Pearly couldn't move it.

"Why are you so sure that things have changed?'' Peter Lake asked, his foot firmly against the sword.

Pearly smiled.

"Why?'' Peter Lake asked again.

"Because we butchered the horse.''

"You couldn't have,'' Peter Lake said, his eyes beginning to swim.

"Ah, we did, not even ten minutes ago.''

"I don't believe you.''

"You don't have to believe me,'' Pearly said. "You can see for yourself.'' He turned to the men drawn up behind him. There was a stir in their ranks, and a passage opened in them, through which came a dozen men, all of whom were soaked with blood and carrying the limbs, quarters, and head of a horse. They looked like the men in the meat markets who hoist

680

whole lambs or sides of beef onto their shoulders. But the hide was still on the pieces that they carried, and though it was covered with blood, it was white.

Thus, Peter Lake was broken. He stepped off the column, and let the sword clatter onto the ground, where Pearly picked it up.

"Here, you see," Pearly said, indicating the pile of horse flesh, "is your invulnerability. Here are the results of your beliefs. Here is what your sentiments have brought, and here is the end that you must endure."

Peter Lake dropped to his knees.

Pearly raised the sword in both hands, and rested the tip between Peter Lake's collarbone and the base of his neck.

"Do you know what will happen now?" Pearly asked.

Peter Lake remained silent.

"You'll rot on the floor until the dogs stream back into the city. They'll fight over what's left of you and the horse, and take the pieces to their dens under the piers—that is, if the rats don't come first. And as for Beverly Penn, you saw her for the last time at the beginning of the century, and will never see her again. You have come to the common and inevitable end, though you struggled hard to get to it. In a moment, you will be forever mute and forgotten. There will be no one to remember you. Nothing. It was all in vain."

Peter Lake looked up into the morning sky and saw the great plumes. Perfectly shaped, pure white, many miles high, they stood immobile in the cold blue air.

"Just clouds of steam and ash," Pearly insisted. "It happens sometimes, after a fire."

"In my understanding," Peter Lake said, "they were to have been more than that. . . ." But suddenly he became still, and his eyes vainly sought what he could hardly hear.

As Pearly, too, strained to listen, the tip of the sword left Peter Lake's shoulder, and hung in the air. From the north came a sound like rolling thunder that grew louder and louder as it approached. It was steady and electrifying. Then it swept by them—hoofbeats drumming the ground. The whole island was shaking.

Peter Lake turned to Pearly once again. "I thought we had seen all the horses on the island ford to Kingsbridge," he said. "But it seems," he continued, nodding at the carcass piled near him, "that at least one unfortunate animal didn't cross the river.

"*That's* the white horse," Peter Lake declared, his outstretched right arm pointing toward the thunder. "And the way he's running, he's going to make it."

Pearly hadn't changed his stance. Peter Lake took the tip of the sword and replaced it above his collarbone. "And so am I, Pearly, so am I, although in a way that will never be clear to you. You see, it works. The balances are exact. The world is a perfect place, so perfect that even if there is nothing afterward, all this will have been enough. Now I see, now I'm sure of what I must do. And it must be done quickly."

He moved the sword until it began to cut into him. Then he looked up, far past Pearly. "Only love . . ." he said. "Drive hard."

The sword was driven into him until its hilt came to rest on his shoulder and he was dead.

From the sound and speed of his galloping, the milk horse had appeared to those who saw or heard him, and to Peter Lake, to have been taken up by thunder. But to him it was a smooth and easy transit in which earth and air faded into a silken dream, enabling him to fly. As he gathered speed, the ground and sky blurred into lines of viscous color, and he soon began to leave the ground in buoyant leaps that left only the sound of wind whistling past his ears and the edges of his hooves. Then he would touch the ground again, and recall what it had been like to be enmeshed in the machinery of the world and to know first-hand its frictions, complications, and love. But he found that in his weightless acceleration a smooth and perfect silence pulled him on—the sure sign of pastures where the wildflowers were stars, and where enormous horses lived in a perpetual stillness, and yet never ceased to move.

Though whenever he touched the ground his love for those who were still full in the world held him back, the clear ether pulled him from his long dream, and he rose high into the air. He saw the white wall closing in over the bays and inlets. As he flew into the clouds, he saw that they were as he remembered them. And once more, Athansor, the white horse, many times beaten, passed far beyond the cloud wall—never to fall back again.

In the courtyard where Christiana had kept the white horse, the salver lay in shadow, but light hit the wall just above it, and, as the sun rose, the clear and perfect line between sunshine and shadow descended. At first, the salver was illuminated only along a thin upper strip that burned like a hot wire. And then, as the light dropped in a golden curtain, the tray caught fire. Almost as strong as the sun itself, it lit the dark side of the garden with rich light that emanated from the untarnished metal in blinding colors. As the inscription took the fire of the sun, the courtyard began to fill with gold light.

The Sun's launch motored across the cold currents that now made the harbor green, gold, and white, and its engines sang in a deep and perplexing sound as the boat pushed gently through the unbroken swells. The passengers turned to the south, where a vertical white wall had transformed the harbor into an infinite sea. Even as the wall kneaded and tumbled, buckling out and pulling in, it rose straight up, beyond the limits of vision. Hardesty said that it had swelled with the ruined city's smoke and dust, and that such a thing could be very beautiful if it were caught in the morning sun.

The only one not looking at the cloud wall or speculating on things to come was Martin, who, almost as a matter of faith, had not taken his eyes from Abby.

The reverberations of the engine, which was just below the hatch cover on which she lay, had long before cleared her hair from her face. They made her seem as if she were moving of her own accord, although she was not, and sometimes her hands would roll slightly in response to the motions of the boat. When her left index finger stretched out, and then receded, Martin held his breath. He thought he saw her lips purse, just slightly. Then he thought he saw her breathe. When they told him to look at the white wall, he could not tear himself away from Abby. Because she was moving. It had to be the vibrations from the engine, and nothing else. But now her fingers were stretching. And now she was breathing. And now, in a sudden and decisive moment, her eyes opened in shock.

After Martin found his strength, he told them. She had already looked at him and smiled. When Asbury saw that the child had opened her eyes, he gripped the tiller very tightly, because now that he had found what he was looking for so close at hand, it was difficult to keep the boat pointed to the Battery. Mrs. Gamely tossed the crumpled poultice into the harbor, and cried. Virginia, with supreme self-restraint, approached her daughter as if the child had just awakened from a nap. Though Virginia was trembling and blinded by tears, she did nothing extreme or abrupt, and simply took Abby onto her lap.

Hardesty, as was his wont, was putting things together. He knew that, in the eyes of God, all things are interlinked; he knew that justice does indeed spring in great surprise from the acts and consequences of ages long forgotten; and he knew that love is not broken by time. But he wondered how, without proof, his father could have known, and how he had found the strength to believe. Hardesty's thought then turned to Peter Lake. But he was interrupted by a marvelous thing.

For then, in an overwhelming confusion, he saw before him all the many rich hours of every age and those to come, an infinitely light and deep universe, his child's innocent eyes, and the broken city of a hundred million lines which, when seen from on high, were as smooth and beautiful as a much-loved painting. All time was compressed, and he and the others were shaken like reeds when they realized fully what had come about, and why. And then they were taken by a wind which arose suddenly and carried them up in full and triumphant faith. As they ascended, in mounting cascades, they saw that the great city about them was infinitely complex, holy, and alive.

Rising above it, slowly and in silence, they saw that all its parts were of one piece, a painting of risen gold and animate clouds the long plumes of which climbed gently upward, billowing to heaven. The fine bays and rivers that surrounded the city had been moved to come alight, and for a hundred miles the bays and the rivers and the sea itself were a pale shimmering gold.

EPILOGUE

*T*HEY *rose far enough to see that the swirling gold was real, and that it covered all the oceans, and rolled through all things with a promise of final benevolence that was certain to be kept. And then they were gently set down, in the heart of a new city that was all spring and sun.*

We, on the other hand, must continue up into the islands and seas of rushing cloud, to leave them in their reborn place, which is now visible to us only as a lake in the clouds opens to reveal its thriving color and its new breathing. But, as we part, there are certain things that we can know.

Because Jackson Mead's bridge was not able to penetrate the empyrean, he, Cecil Mature, and Mootfowl disappeared with no trace, and were soon forgotten. But Jackson Mead was convinced, as always, that the next time, a new means at his disposal would allow him to return to the high place from which he had been cast. And he knew that if he could not return, he was now perfectly willing to bide his time. When he would come back once again, no one would know him, and he would have the great privilege of starting over.

That very morning, they began to rebuild the city. Barges appeared in long chains, taking rubble out to sea, and the sound of the pile drivers, the muffled explosions under iron nets, the optimistic banshee shrieks of saws, and the puffing and the whistles of The Sun's *machinery itself, was music.*

Though Harry Penn lived to see some of the new building, he died soon after it began. He died in full faith, and later Jessica Penn bore Praeger de Pinto's child, who was a Penn through and through and would himself guide The Sun *into an age that we cannot even imagine.*

Pearly was left in the streets. He had his place even in a new city that was so young and innocent that it could not know evil. He recovered after a fashion, and awaited developments. Without him, after all, everything would be milk and roses, which is not enough to turn the world gold.

It is all white now. . . . We have left the city. It is on its own. But there are a few more things to tell.

So much was changed and renewed that some circumstances might puzzle us. Nonetheless, the fact was that Mrs. Gamely wed Craig Binky in what turned out to be a marriage made in heaven, and the lion lay down with the lamb.

Do you remember the children who came to Marko Chestnut's studio and were speechless and terrified while he painted their portraits and the rain dashed off the slate roof and cascaded down the skylight? Most of them became painters themselves. They remembered. And Abby Marratta would see it all. Her future, and the one great demand made upon her in the end, would also be something that we cannot imagine, though perhaps we can if we look at the good faith of her predecessors.

Now there are no more lakes in the clouds. The city is deep within its new dream. What of Peter Lake, you may ask? Was the past fully reopened to him? Was he able to stop time? Did he rejoin the woman that he loved? Or was the price of the totally just city his irrevocable fall?

At least until there are new lakes in the clouds that open upon living cities as yet unknown, and perhaps forever, that is a question which you must answer within your own heart.